P9-CFF-432

PRAISE FOR
Whence Came a Prince

"Not only do I feel I've lived the story of Leana, Rose, and Jamie, but enjoyed a lovely journey across Scotland as well. A wonderful read!"
— FRANCINE RIVERS, best-selling author of *Redeeming Love*

"*Whence Came a Prince* is the incredibly compelling conclusion to Liz Curtis Higgs's remarkable Scottish trilogy. Liz has taken what could have been a triple threat—biblical history, Scottish history, and the difficulty of not overwhelming the reader with either one—and has created a story that is sure to last the ages. I highly recommend this book—this series!"
— TRACIE PETERSON, best-selling author of Heirs of Montana series

"A triumphant conclusion to Liz Curtis Higgs's remarkable trilogy. Liz's impeccable research, sense of history, and love of her subject bring her characters' struggles and victories to life in a story you'll never forget."
— DONNA FLETCHER CROW, author of *Glastonbury*

"I savored every wonderful word and rich detail of *Whence Came a Prince*. Romantic, heartbreaking, joyful, and full of hope, *Prince* met all my expectations and more. I was eager to discover how the story of Leana, Rose, and Jamie would end, but I'm oh so sorry to bid these characters good-bye after turning the last page. Magical!"
— ROBIN LEE HATCHER, best-selling author of *Beyond the Shadows*

"Liz Curtis Higgs's depiction of life in eighteenth-century Scotland immersed me in a world I was reluctant to leave. I could hear the Scottish brogue, smell the heather, and taste the baked salmon and scones. But my greatest delight was in her finely drawn characters. Jamie, Rose, and Leana are real, imperfect people whom I grew to know and love. *Whence Came a Prince* is an unforgettable conclusion to an unforgettable series."
— LYNN N. AUSTIN, author of The Refiner's Fire series

"In *Whence Came a Prince*, Liz Curtis Higgs has created a masterpiece, a literary gift that I will long cherish. As with *Thorn in My Heart* and

Fair Is the Rose, this novel is richly complex and beautifully captures the depth of the human spirit in Leana, Rose, and Jamie. This truly is Liz Curtis Higgs's most powerful book yet!"

—DIANE NOBLE, author of *The Last Storyteller*

"Liz Curtis Higgs keeps getting better and better. In *Whence Came a Prince,* the story of a man loved by two women, the inner battle is universal. I saw myself in each of these finely drawn characters and ached for their very human struggles. This trilogy is indeed a keeper."

—LAURAINE SNELLING, author of *The Way of Women*

PRAISE FOR
Fair Is the Rose

"With excellent writing and a keen understanding of human nature, Liz Curtis Higgs delivers a first-rate, fascinating historical saga."

—B. J. HOFF, author of *An Emerald Ballad*

"Admirably, Higgs keeps her protagonists multifaceted and readers' allegiances shifting as the story unfolds…and historical details create a vivid backdrop."

—*Publishers Weekly*

PRAISE FOR
Thorn in My Heart

"A luminous sense of hope shines through this truly wrenching story of characters who are both larger than life and all too human. This unforgettable saga is as multilayered, mysterious, and joyous as love and faith can be."

—SUSAN WIGGS, *New York Times* best-selling author

"Higgs's fine writing…incorporates many lovely historical details, and her strong storytelling skills stand her in good stead here."

—*Publishers Weekly*

Whence Came a Prince

LIZ CURTIS HIGGS

WATERBROOK
PRESS

To the many faithful readers
who embraced both Thorn *and* Rose...
Your Prince *has come.*

WHENCE CAME A PRINCE

PUBLISHED BY WATERBROOK PRESS

2375 Telstar Drive, Suite 160

Colorado Springs, Colorado 80920

A division of Random House, Inc.

All Scripture quotations are taken from the *King James Version* of the Bible.

ISBN 1-57856-128-0

ISBN 0-7394-5249-5

Printed in the United States of America

And Jacob, how they lingering
love to dwell
On portions of thy strangely-varied tale,
Thy patient toil, thy faith that did excel,
Thy strength with th' angel
wrestling to prevail,
Whence came, a prince with God,
thy new name Israel.

JOHN STRUTHERS

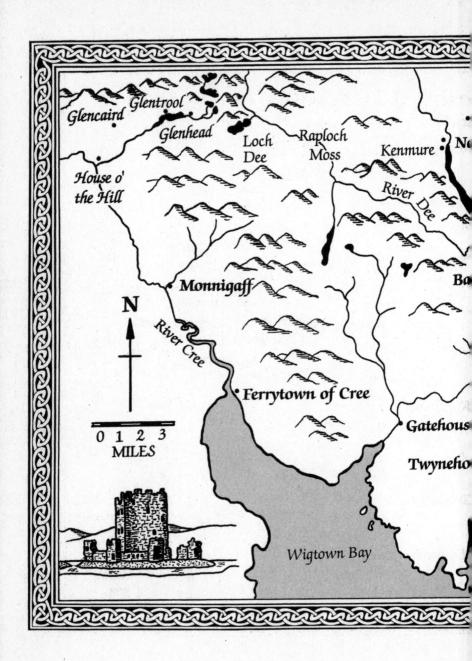

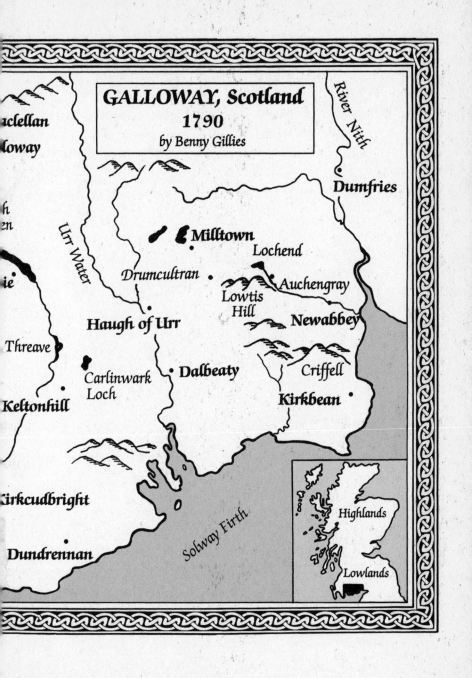

GALLOWAY, Scotland
1790
by Benny Gillies

River Nith

Dumfries

aclellan

oway

Milltown

Lochend

Drumcultran

Auchengray

Lowtis
Hill

Newabbey

Haugh of Urr

Urr Water

Threave

Carlinwark
Loch

Dalbeaty

Criffell

Keltonhill

Kirkbean

Kirkcudbright

Solway Firth

Highlands

Dundrennan

Lowlands

One

The heart that is soonest awake to the flowers
Is always the first to be touch'd by the thorns.

THOMAS MOORE

Burnside Cottage
Whitsuntide 1790

I will never leave you.

Leana McBride sat up in bed, disoriented, grasping at the threads of her dream. She'd been sitting under the yew tree on the edge of Auchengray's garden, cradling her infant son to her breast, brushing her fingers through his silky hair, singing softly as he nursed.

Baloo, baloo, my wee, wee thing.

Ian's warm scent seemed to permeate the air of her aunt's tiny cottage in Twyneholm. The recalled softness of his cheek felt more real than the linen nightgown beneath her fingertips, the memory of his small, hungry mouth more tangible than the rough sheets against her bare skin.

She gripped the edges of the bed as grief pierced her heart anew. Aunt Meg had insisted the pain would ease with time. Leana glanced over her shoulder at the older woman, still fast asleep. Her aunt meant well, but two months had not diminished the potent memories of her son that haunted her dreams and clouded her thoughts.

By the hour she'd contemplated going home to Auchengray. Only two dozen miles, yet "a world away," as Aunt Meg had once said. Leana had pictured herself running up the stair to the nursery, gathering Ian in her arms, and holding him for days on end. She would have done it. She *would* have. If somehow she could have seen Ian yet not seen Jamie.

Oh, my dear Jamie.

Aye, she missed him as well, desperately so. In a different way, yet the same. *Bone of my bones, and flesh of my flesh.* The smooth planes of his face, the dark slash of his brows, his generous mouth and strong chin rose before her like a portrait painted by a master artist. She had loved Jamie McKie from the first moment he walked across Auchengray's lawn one bright October afternoon. Though it was more than a year before he returned that love, when he did, Jamie had given her his whole heart.

But now that heart belonged to her sister. To Rose.

Leana turned her head on the pillow, imagining Jamie beside her. Did he love her still, as she loved him? Did he think of her at all? Did he suffer as she did? She was ashamed of her thoughts, but they would not be silenced.

This much she knew: No letter had arrived begging her to return. No carriage or mount had come clattering up to Burnside's door, prepared to carry her home. She had left Auchengray of her own free will on the day of Rose's wedding, intending to stay at Aunt Meg's long enough to mend her shattered heart. And long enough for Rose to mend Jamie's, as much as it grieved Leana to think of it.

It was nearly June. With the spring lambing ended at Auchengray, surely they'd left for Jamie's ancestral home in the glen of Loch Trool, taking her precious Ian with them. "We will wipe the dust of Auchengray off our feet come May," Jamie had promised her in February. Instead, it was Rose who'd traveled to Glentrool.

Would her sister write once they settled in? Describe how Ian was growing? Declare he looked more like his father every day? Though such news might wound her, Leana preferred it to no word at all. Not a single post bearing Rose's *kenspeckle* script had arrived at Burnside Cottage. Nor was there one from her father. But thoughtful Neda Hastings, Auchengray's housekeeper, had sent a long letter last month, brimming with details of Ian's progress.

There was no mention of Jamie. The man who was once her husband. The man who'd blessed her womb with Ian. The man now married to her sister.

"Be thou my strong rock," Leana whispered into the darkness. Drawing the Almighty's comforting presence round her like a thick plaid, she rose from the *hurlie* bed. Meg had trundled it out from beneath her own bed the March night her niece had arrived. Low to the floor and narrow, it was much like the one Leana had slept in at home in the nursery. With Ian.

Her gaze fell on the small nightgown draped over her sewing bag. She'd pieced it together from remnants of soft cotton, intending to embroider the sleeves and hem with purple thistles. By the time she completed it, Ian would be nine months old and in need of a new sleeping gown. If she could not see him, she could at least sew for him. Holding the fabric in her hands brought him closer to her. Imagining her stitches brushing against his tender skin gave her a small measure of comfort.

While her aunt snored soundly, Leana bathed her hands and face in a warm bowl by the hearth. She slipped on her plain green gown, then swung a kettle over the coal grate to boil water for their tea, ever aware that her days in Twyneholm were numbered. Her aunt could ill afford a houseguest much longer. And Leana missed home.

She lit one of the beeswax candles made from Meg's own hives, then collected the tools for her baking—a wooden *spurtle* for stirring, a notched rolling pin, and a heart-shaped iron spade to move the oatcakes about—recalling the many times she and Neda had worked side by side in Auchengray's spacious kitchen.

A handful of meal, a pinch of soda, a dash of salt, a spoonful of goose fat from last night's supper, and the first oatcake took shape beneath her hands. She sprinkled the board with meal as she went, added hot water sparingly, and kneaded the small lump of dough with her knuckles. Neda's voice echoed in her head. *Spread it oot evenly. Keep yer hands movin'.* Leana rolled the dough as thin as she could and pinched the edges with her fingers before the first oatcake went onto the *girdle* over the fire, and the process started all over again.

A faint light spread across the room as she worked. Soon a cock's crow from a neighboring farm announced the break of day.

"I've ne'er seen a finer pair of hands at a baking board."

She looked up to find Margaret Halliday beaming at her from across the room, a threadbare wrapper tied round her waist. Leana managed a wan smile in return. "Good morning, Auntie."

"You'll spoil me yet, lass. Preparing my breakfast for me. Weeding my kitchen garden. Filling my coal pail."

"'Tis the least I can do." Leana kept an eye on the oatcakes. When the edges curled up, they were done. "My hands are full of meal, or I'd pour your tea."

"*Och*. I'll see to that."

The women moved round to accommodate each other in the small cooking space and soon were seated at table, their breakfast on a crockery plate. Leana nibbled a piece of oatcake but put it down half-eaten, her appetite vanished.

Aunt Meg reached across the table and turned Leana's chin toward the window, eying her. "You've grown thinner since you came. This morn in particular, you've a *dwiny* look about you."

"My stomach does feel a bit queasy." Leana swallowed the disagreeable taste in her mouth, then pressed a hand to her forehead. "But my skin is cool."

"We've not had an epidemic in the parish for nigh to thirty years. Ague, it was. Terrible fevers and chills." Aunt Meg peered at her more closely. "Did my roasted goose not sit well on your stomach? I thought it a pleasant change from mutton and fish."

"I ate too much of it, I fear. I'll go for a walk shortly, which should help." She stared down at her teacup as if the dark liquid contained the strength she needed to say what must be said. "Auntie, it's time I went home to Auchengray."

"Oh, my dear niece." The disappointment in Meg's voice was obvious.

Leana looked up and touched her aunt's wrinkled cheek. "I've stayed far too long already. Nearly two months."

Meg's eyes watered. "When you came to my door that rainy Sabbath eve, I was happy to make room for you. And I'd gladly share Burnside Cottage with you for all of my days, if you wouldn't mind an *auld* woman's company."

"You are far from old, and I cherish your company." Leana tenderly brushed away Meg's tears. "But you cannot afford to feed and clothe me.

And I have duties to attend to at home. With Rose gone, Auchengray has no mistress. The gardens will suffer, and the wool won't be spun." She squeezed Meg's bony hands. "Do forgive me, dearie. You knew this time would come."

"Aye, though I hoped it might not." Her aunt regarded her at length, compassion shining in her blue gray eyes. "Will you write Willie and ask him to bring the chaise?"

"Nae," Leana said firmly. She could not involve Willie, Auchengray's *orraman,* without her father's permission. Not again. "This must be my own doing. My own silver. A hired chaise."

Her aunt's mouth fell open. "But you have no silver."

"A predicament I shall remedy shortly." Leana tried to sound confident, though she had yet to think of a means of securing such a sum. "Mr. Crosbie at the tollgate said a chaise and driver would cost me fifteen shillings." A fortune for a woman with mere pennies in her purse.

Meg propped her chin on her hand. "Would that I had the silver to give you."

"You've done more than enough, Auntie. Suppose I go for that walk and see if some clever notion doesn't present itself." Leana stood, feeling lightheaded for a moment, then slipped on her cloak and prayed the brisk morning air would calm her stomach. One of her aunt's two collies bounded through the doorway ahead of her and shook itself awake from ears to tail, then turned round, waiting for her to follow.

Leana pulled Burnside's red wooden door closed, then absently scratched the dog's silky head. Twyneholm was not a proper village, merely a cluster of two-room cottages—some with thatched roofs, like Meg's, others with slate—built along the military road. Reverend Scott, the parish minister, insisted that a great and ancient battle, fought nigh to the kirk, had left a king slain and his vanquished men staggering home in a winding direction—hence the name *tae wyne hame.* Aunt Meg scoffed at his romantic notion. " 'Tis a low patch of land, or holm, that lies 'tween the Tarff Water and the Corraford Burn."

Leana only knew that Twyneholm had served her well. A quiet refuge for a heart torn in two. In a handful of days, when the month of

June arrived, she would look to the north, to Auchengray, and pray for the means—and the strength—to return home.

She no longer had a child to mother or a husband to love. But she did have faith in the One who had not forsaken her. *I will never leave you.* Words the Almighty had spoken to Jamie in a dream. Words she had whispered to Jamie when their future was certain. Words Leana still held close to her heart.

Two

Of all the spirits abroad at this hour in the world,
insincerity is the most dangerous.

JAMES ANTHONY FROUDE

Patience, lass." Jamie McKie gazed into his young wife's face, her dark eyes alight with expectation. In his hands he held a post from his mother, delivered to Newabbey village, then carried to Auchengray's door. His future with Rose hinged on the letter's contents.

Late afternoon sunlight cast a warm glow across their bedroom. Rose stood on tiptoe, her hands clasped before her, as if she were prepared to fly down the stair. "Now that word from Glentrool has finally come, we are free to make our announcement, aye?" She pressed her palms below her waist, spreading her fingers across her blue linen gown. "I fear if we don't inform the household, our *bairn* will soon do so for us."

Jamie acknowledged her words with a slight nod. Though Rose's figure had yet to change, there were more subtle indicators. An ever-present blush on her soft cheek. An untouched cup of porridge each morning. A nap each afternoon. He knew the signs well. Last summer he'd watched her sister blossom with child: Leana, the woman he'd loved too late. This summer it was Rose's turn to bloom: Rose, the woman he'd married too soon.

The twittering song of a linnet distracted Jamie for a moment, drawing his gaze to the open bedroom window. Summer was nigh upon them, and still they'd not departed for Glentrool as he'd planned. Every delay only sharpened his desire to return home and claim his inheritance. No matter what news the post might bring, their future lay to the west.

"Please, Jamie." Rose captured his attention once more. "Open the letter, for I cannot bear another minute."

Jamie unfolded his mother's post, the creamy paper stiff beneath his thumbs, and put aside the stack of guinea notes she'd enclosed. Funds for their journey, no doubt. Her elaborate handwriting and the word *Glentrool* inked across the top of the page stirred his memories of home. The distant hills and glens would be at their greenest, a lush pasture for his father's flocks. "Haste ye back," Alec McKie would say. Surely the time had come.

Rose hovered beside him, a hint of meadowsweet on her breath. "Written a week ago, I see. Read it to me, Jamie," she asked, and so he obliged her.

> To James Lachlan McKie
> Monday, 17 May 1790
>
> My dearest son,
>
> I pray this letter finds you enjoying good health and fair weather. Though our ewes did not all bear twins, as yours did, we had a fine lambing season. Henry Stewart is eager to see what you will do with our flocks for the autumn breeding.

Jamie's chest swelled at the thought of a seasoned shepherd like Stew welcoming his help come October. He read on, certain good news would follow.

> I know you have waited patiently for your father's invitation to return home. When we sent you east to Auchengray to seek a wife two autumns ago, neither of us imagined so lengthy a visit. Now we must ask that you tarry at Auchengray a bit longer…

Rose groaned even before he'd finished the words. "Whatever is the matter this time? Will Evan ne'er make his way to Wigtownshire?"

Jamie shook his head, too frustrated to speak. Throughout the winter months his mother's letters had assured him that Evan, his hotheaded twin brother, would move south come spring, paving the way for a safe return. Now another delay loomed before them. As usual his mother offered little explanation.

"Wait until Lammas." He jabbed at the words as if to banish them from sight. Lammas, a Quarter Day, fell on the first of August. "Another *two months* hence!" He strode toward the window, tossing the letter onto the bedside table. How dare the woman ask him to wait any longer?

Rowena McKie had once dared to ask a great deal more. *Just do what I say, Jamie.* At his mother's bidding, he'd done an unspeakably foul deed, then had run for his life. Her letter was curiously silent on that subject. Had his father not truly forgiven him? Or was Evan sharpening his dirk, still threatening revenge?

Rose trailed after him, her skirts whispering across the wooden floor. "Can naught be done to change her mind?"

Jamie stared at the farm steading below, his eyes unfocused and his temper barely in check. "You do not *ken* my mother."

"Not as you do." She touched his coat sleeve. "But I know my father, and so do you. You must not let him take advantage of this delay, Jamie, for given half a chance he will."

"Nae!" He ground out the word like oats on a provender stone. "Lachlan McBride will ne'er *swick* me again." After twenty long months beneath his uncle's roof, Jamie had learned to hold his tongue and hide his coin purse when Lachlan was present. "If I must live at Auchengray through the summer, I'll labor under my own terms, not his."

Rose's hand on his sleeve tightened. "What terms have you in mind?"

"Suppose I tell your father that waiting until Lammas is *my* idea." Already Jamie liked the sound of it. Not his mother's plan, but his. "By the first of August the lambs will be sold and my duties here ended. Naught will remain but to claim my share of the earnings." He turned abruptly, nearly knocking her off balance. " 'Tis better to wait, or we risk losing everything. Will you trust me in this, Rose?"

She looked up at him, a half smile decorating her bonny face, a twinkle in her eye. "The first of August will do nicely." Since he'd taken Rose to wife, Jamie had cataloged her many expressions; this one bore the mark of mischief. She wanted to outwit Lachlan McBride almost as badly as he did.

Rose swept her thick braid over her shoulder, then brushed his cheek with a kiss. "We shall celebrate my seventeenth year and quit Auchengray on the same day." Sliding her hand inside the crook of his elbow, she tugged him toward the door. "As to our glad tidings, I suggest you tell Father at once. You know how he loathes *saicrets*."

"Indeed he does." Jamie tucked the guineas from Glentrool in a drawer, then escorted his wife into the upper corridor. "Unless the secrets are his."

The aroma of meat roasting on the kitchen hearth wafted up the stone stairwell, calling them to table as clearly as the laird's clanging brass bell. When they entered the dining room, Lachlan greeted them with a curt nod, fingers drumming as he awaited the midday meal. His dark suit of clothes marked him as no ordinary farmer but a bonnet laird, who held the deed to the land he worked and straddled the great chasm between highborn society and the peasantry. Lachlan cared nothing for either class; he resented the rich and ignored the poor, claiming neither understood the value of hard-earned silver.

Jamie and Rose were the only ones welcomed to the low-beamed dining room at mealtime, where the final course was always a fancy pudding, at Lachlan's insistence. The household servants would take their dinner later—without pudding—at a well-scrubbed pine table in the kitchen, while the farmworkers and shepherds ate their meager rations out of doors.

"Uncle Lachlan." Jamie made an effort to keep his tone pleasant. "Isn't the weather fine?"

They spoke of trifling matters while Neda directed her staff in serving the meal. "Gentlemen," the housekeeper said with a broad smile that belied her years, "ye'll fancy this plump hen, I'll wager." A stuffed pullet was presented to the laird for his approval, then quickly sliced and served. Jamie ate prodigious quantities, gathering strength for the confrontation to follow. Rose poked at her food; little traveled from fork to mouth. When the citron pudding appeared, stained pale green with spinach juice, Rose blanched and made a hasty exit.

"*Whatsomever* has happened to my daughter's appetite?" Lachlan plunged a spoon into his pudding. His ebony hair, pulled into a taut knot, was streaked with silver—more each year, Jamie thought. Lachlan's piercing gaze met his. "Is your wife ill?"

"Nae, not ill." Jamie pushed aside his dish without tasting it. "Perhaps you've already *jaloused* the nature of her discomfort."

Lachlan lowered his spoon, even as his brows lifted. "Is she…with child?"

"Aye." Jamie watched the man attempt to mask his elation. "Rose tells me 'twill be January before the babe arrives, though one can never be certain. The Lord alone kens the hour."

"Indeed he does." Lachlan folded his hands over his stomach. "Are you thinking this child of yours should be born at Glentrool?"

Jamie seized the opportunity to present his case. " 'Tis high time I headed for home." His heart quickening, he pressed further. "And once the lambs are sold, 'tis time you paid me my wages, Uncle. My growing family must be provided for. Even you cannot deny the work I've done for you."

"Impatience doesn't become you, Jamie." His uncle wagged a finger at him, as though reprimanding a child. "The laird of Glentrool may be auld, but Alec McKie has yet to lay *doon* in his grave."

Jamie winced at the image. Please God, many years would pass before he saw a headstone raised over his father. "I meant only that my sire has need of me, for his flocks have grown in number just as yours have. I have served you long enough, Uncle. My wife and I will leave at Lammas."

"Ah, Lammas. When all of Scotland celebrates the bountiful harvest." Lachlan was practically beaming. "The *verra* date I'd chosen. 'Tis a sign."

A sign? Jamie knew Lachlan was a superstitious sort, despite the man's allegiance to the kirk. Lachlan insisted Neda cut every loaf of bread into three *farles* for luck, took care not to wear red and green together lest he suffer misfortune, and slept with his head to the east in the belief it would bring him riches. After waiting for an explanation, Jamie prompted him. "A sign of what, Uncle?"

"Providence." Lachlan's gray eyes were clear. Guileless. "I've come to realize the Almighty has blessed my lands because of you, Nephew."

Jamie's mouth fell open. Never in all their dealings had the older man spoken so generously.

With a look of satisfaction, Lachlan splayed his blunt fingers and set to counting. "Since coming to Auchengray, you worked a full month without asking for a shilling, then labored for Rose's hand in marriage seven weeks, then seven months, aye? After that you served as husband to the ewes, choosing the *tups* and seeing the woolly lasses both bred and delivered of twins. Even Reverend Gordon sang your praises from the pulpit. Yet here you sit without *twa* coins to rub together." Lachlan reached across the corner of the table and clapped his hand on Jamie's shoulder, squeezing hard. "The hand of God is on you, James."

Jamie was so taken aback, his tongue felt glued to his teeth. "Sir, I…I am blessed…blessed to hear you say…"

"And you've blessed me." Lachlan released his grip on Jamie with a final squeeze, then stood. "I intend to sell the lambs at the Lammas Fair in Lockerbie, where they'll fetch a fine price."

Jamie watched Lachlan glance toward the spence, the room that served as his uncle's study and bedroom and contained all the man held dear—in particular, his wooden *thrifite* full of coins and bank notes. Lachlan's eyes then focused on Jamie, gleaming like the contents of his money box. "When you leave for Glentrool in August, I'll see your pockets full of silver."

Jamie stared at him, incredulous. Lachlan had accepted his departure plans so readily. Could the man's words be sincere? "I have worked hard for you, Uncle," he said slowly. "The proof is spread across your hills and glens."

"Then what shall I give you, lad? Name your price, and I will pay it."

All at once Jamie realized the truth: He did not want the coins his lambs would earn at Lockerbie; he wanted the lambs themselves. A seed of an idea that Duncan Hastings, the overseer of Auchengray, had once planted in his mind suddenly took root. *A plan tae see ye get half o' the lambs, seein' as they're all twins.* Just the thought of it made Jamie's pulse race. He would herd his share of the lambs to Glentrool and breed them with his father's hardy flocks. If the lambs were indeed blessed of God, only a fool would let them out of his sight.

"Do not give me silver." Jamie surprised himself and his uncle more so. "Instead, let me have the smaller of the twin lambs. I'll mark each runt as mine so you need not fear I've claimed one amiss." He took a deep breath, letting his latest scheme settle in his mind, so quickly had he concocted it. "If you are in agreement, I will tend your flocks 'til Lammas, then take my family and my lambs west."

Lachlan said nothing for a moment, studying Jamie as if weighing his resolve. " 'Twill be no easy task, for sheep are not easily driven across rough land. They cannot be shod, nor will they ford moving water. You'll cross the Urr, the Dee, the Fleet, and many a burn afore you see Loch Trool."

Despite the wisdom of his uncle's counsel, Jamie refused to be dissuaded. "I'll haste to Dumfries for the *feeing* fair and hire enough *herds* to see the lambs safely home when the time comes." He stood, infused with confidence, and stuck out his hand. "Are we agreed then?"

Lachlan offered his hand for a brief shake, then slid it inside his coat pocket. "I'll see you get what you deserve."

Three

The rose is fairest when 'tis budding new,
And hope is brightest when it dawns from fears.

Mistress McKie? Are ye *unweel*?"

Rose struggled to sit up, one hand pressed against her mouth. Had her sister, Leana, felt this ill when she carried Ian? How embarrassing to be found collapsed upon the lawn in a graceless heap! "Bless you for asking, Willie." She eyed the elderly servant, who stood a safe distance away as if what ailed her might be catching. " 'Tis not the croup this time."

"Guid." His cap bobbed up and down as he ventured closer. Even on a day as warm as this one, Willie kept his tattered wool bonnet firmly stationed on his balding head. "Neda said ye tore oot o' the *hoose* in a hurry."

"Dinner did not agree with me," she explained. Once Jamie informed Father of her condition, the whole of Auchengray would know why their mistress had fled from his table.

Rose gathered her skirts, then held out her hand for Willie's assistance. His gnarled fingers gripped hers and pulled her to her feet.

"God be *wi'* ye, *mem.*" Willie touched the brim of his plaid bonnet, then shuffled off toward the stables. Duncan Hastings found plenty for the orraman to do. Willie drove the chaise when needed; groomed Walloch, Bess, and the other horses; journeyed to Newabbey village on errands for the family; and performed whatever odd jobs he could still manage.

Rose watched his tottering gait with fond affection. One wintry week he'd escorted her to Aunt Meg's cottage in Twyneholm. Willie had driven Leana there as well on the night of Rose's wedding. But Leana had not returned home. Nor would she, Jamie said.

Standing amid her sister's gardens, Rose imagined Leana with her golden circle of braids bending over the pink gillyflowers, drinking in their fragrance sweet as cloves. An ache swelled inside Rose, like an old wound in rainy weather. *I miss you, dearie.*

Five years older and decades wiser, Leana had taken her little sister under her wing when Agness McBride died giving birth to Rose. Though the two were utterly different in temperament, their sisterly love had held fast, season after season. Until their cousin Jamie McKie had arrived two Octobers past and turned their lives *tapsalteerie.*

The tender way Jamie spoke her sister's name still gave Rose pause. He softened all the vowels, as any Lowlander would. Almost singing it, like a lullaby. *Leh-ah-nah.* Rose pronounced it that way too. But when Jamie said her sister's name, Rose detected a faint note of longing in his voice.

Och! She shook off the blades of grass that clung to her skirts. *She* was the woman carrying his child, was she not? His *son,* if intuition and custom could be trusted. That morning she had dangled a needle and thread over her womb. Back and forth it went, not round in a circle. A brother for Ian, then. Another son for her husband.

As if summoned by her thoughts, Jamie appeared at the back door. "There you are, lass." Her husband reached her side in a half-dozen strides, his long legs sheathed in doeskin breeches, his old boots freshly polished. The ewes would not see their master in the sheepfolds this afternoon; Jamie was dressed for business. "I'm headed to Dumfries for the last hours of the Whitsun Monday feeing fair," he explained, clasping her hand. "We'll need more herds come Lammas. Best to make arrangements now."

"More shepherds, you say?" Whatever had she missed?

"I've much to tell you, Rose. All of it good." The excitement in his voice was palpable. "Your father has agreed to let me take half the lambs with us at Lammas."

She let the unexpected news sink in, the silence between them punctuated by the bleating of sheep in the pastures surrounding the mains. "Lambs instead of silver?" A shiver of apprehension crawled up her spine. "Are you certain that's wise?"

Jamie laughed and drew her closer. "Listen to me, dear wife." His moss green eyes glowed with a fervor she'd not seen in many months. "Your father declared it a blessing to have me here. A *blessing*. That's what he said, Rose. 'The Almighty has blessed my lands because of you.' Have you e'er heard the likes of it?"

Nae, she had not. Nor did she believe her father meant a single word. Dared she tell her husband and dash his hopes to the ground?

"Jamie…" She looked up into his smiling face. "What if my father's praise is naught but a ruse? What if he's hiding something, hoping you'll miss the truth amid all his compliments?" When Jamie's smile began to fade, she rushed to add, "If Duncan were here, he'd tell you, 'Guid *wirds* cost nothing.'"

"Duncan is busy in Dumfries," he countered, the hurt evident in his voice. "He's feeing farmworkers for the harvest. It's time I joined him."

When he stepped back as if to leave, she did not release him but moved forward, her hands still resting on his forearms. "Please, Jamie. Tell me more about your agreement with Father. Your future is also mine, aye?"

Rose dutifully listened while her husband described his plans, praying her instincts were wrong, yet fearing the worst. *Jamie, dear Jamie, do not be fooled!* Though Lachlan McBride credited Jamie with Auchengray's increase, the man's wooden money box told a different story. She'd once spied a knotted gold cord stretched across her father's bounty of coins. Some folk might call it a harmless superstition meant to ensure wealth, but Rose knew better: A talisman from a *wutch* like Lillias Brown called upon darker powers.

"Come now, Rose." Jamie's tone softened. "What say you to my uncle's change of heart?"

"*Yours* is the heart I treasure." She looked down at the toes of her leather slippers, giving him time to respond in kind. When he said nothing, Rose swallowed her disappointment and lifted her head to meet his gaze. "I am glad you shall have your lambs."

The warmth in his eyes seemed genuine; so did the tenderness in his voice. "Rose, the lamb you carry matters most of all."

Oh, Jamie. Had his own heart changed? Might he return her affections at last? He had not confessed his love for her, not since Ian's birth October last. On the March day she had married Jamie, Rose had claimed her sister's husband and her son. No wonder Leana had fled from Auchengray. *And from me.*

"You're too quiet," Jamie chided her. "I ken where your thoughts have strayed. To a second-floor nursery where your stepson sleeps."

Afraid of what Jamie might read in her countenance, Rose donned a smile like one might a scarf, covering what she could. "I was indeed thinking of Ian. The lad will be waking soon." Rose released her hold on Jamie, knowing he must depart for Dumfries. "You'll be home before dark?"

"I will." He started toward the stables, inclining his head toward the kitchen door in passing "Do tell the household our news, for I ken how the waiting has tried your patience."

She watched him leave, even as the fragrant warmth of the kitchen pulled her into the house like a shepherd's crook. A copper-bottomed pot simmered on the hearth—barley broth, by the smell of it. In the adjacent scullery, steam rose from a great tub of sudsy water into which red-haired Annabel was dutifully plunging their greasy dinner plates. Lachlan did not approve of idle servants and forced them to work above and below their station. Annabel served as lady's maid to Rose when she wasn't chopping vegetables for Neda or gathering soiled garments for Mary, the laundress from Newabbey village. Across the brick-floored kitchen stood Leana's maid, Eliza, her arms full of table linens, a sandy curl poking out from beneath her white cap.

"Guid day tae ye, Mistress McKie," Eliza said brightly. "*Whan* yer lad *waukens,* I'll see tae his supper." Though her former mistress was gone, Eliza had continued caring for Ian, much to Rose's relief. Ian's naps grew shorter as the Lowland days grew longer. In another week the sun would rise even earlier than the servants did and would not disappear below the horizon until many had taken to their beds. "I'll find a proper spot for these," the maid said, "then head up the stair."

Rose sent Eliza on her way, knowing Ian would be glad to see the cheerful girl who kept a sweetie in her apron pocket just for him. Though Rose loved the boy to distraction, she was still unsure of herself as a mother. A fortnight ago she'd carelessly tumbled down Auchengray Hill at nightfall with Ian clutched in her arms, frightening them both. By some miracle he'd escaped with only bruises and she with no more than a badly sprained knee. In seven months the Almighty would bless her with a bairn of her own. Rose prayed the household would share her joy and not cast wary gazes toward Twyneholm.

"*Leuk wha* has come tae see me." Neda emerged from the larder, a pot of marmalade in one hand, a fistful of almonds in the other. One glance at Rose and a smile creased Neda's ruddy face. "Methinks ye're not searchin' for victuals." She emptied her hands, then waved Rose over to a quieter corner, lowering her voice. "Are ye here *aboot* yer guid news?"

Rose laughed softly. "I cannot pull the wool over Neda Hastings's eyes."

"Ye canna," the older woman agreed with a wink, "since I dinna wear a periwig. Am I not the *mither* of grown *dochters*? And a *granmither*? Ye'll hardly be keepin' *sic* blithe tidings from yer auld Neda." She aimed a pointed glance at Rose's waist. "I ken the signs."

"I am not far along," Rose cautioned her. "There might still be… complications. My mother…"

"*Wheesht.*" Neda hushed her in the kindest of tones. "Dinna *fash* yerself. Ye're a healthy, *green* lass wi' naught tae fear. And growin' *mair* quickly than *mony* women do." She took Rose's hands in hers and squeezed tight. "Have ye written Leana?"

"Not yet," she confessed. "I shall send a letter before the week is out." Rose dreaded the prospect, for whatever would she say? *Forgive me, Leana.* Except there was no need to apologize, not for this. She was Jamie's true wife, however awkward the circumstances of their wedding. She had a perfect right to bear his child.

Still, the need for forgiveness lingered, despite her sister's generous vow. *Though you cannot forgive me, Rose, I forgive you.* Was that possible, when the truth Rose had once spoken cost her sister everything?

"She'll be happy for ye, Rose." Neda's unlined face reflected the sincerity of her words. "But ye best write Leana *suin,* afore she hears it from *anither.*"

Later that evening Rose sat propped up in the curtained shadows of their box bed, waiting for Jamie to return from Dumfries. Built into the wall, the wooden bed was enclosed on three sides, leaving one long side open to the room. In winter Rose thought it cozy; in the summer, confining. Yet, in any season, her box bed was more comfortable than Aunt Meg's hurlie bed at Burnside Cottage.

With her writing desk perched on her lap and a cluster of candles on the bedside table, Rose had started a letter to Leana half a dozen times, to no avail. *I have good news… Jamie and I have learned…Ian will have a brother or sister next January…* The words dried up each time, as if they were lodged inside the nub of her ink pen, needing only to be shaken out.

Forgive me, Leana. It always circled back to that.

After crumpling yet another sheet of expensive paper and tossing it to the floor, Rose reached for the letter from Jamie's mother on the table, glad for any excuse to delay her task. Jamie had read aloud every word of Aunt Rowena's post; he would not mind his wife's perusing it again. Rose felt guilty nonetheless as she unfolded it with care lest she wrinkle the paper. Leaning nearer the flickering candlelight, she squinted at the elaborate hand that decorated the page with swirls and flourishes.

One thing became apparent with a second reading: Jamie's *birsie* brother, born with red hair and a temper to match, was not the problem, or his mother would have stated so. Instead, the scandal at Auchengray had cooled his parents' welcome; Rose was certain of it. The gossips of Monnigaff parish would *blether* for years about the heir of Glentrool and his two wives—first the older cousin, then the younger one—just as folk in Newabbey jabbered about it without ceasing.

She read her aunt's words again. *Wait until Lammas.* Rowena's meaning was unmistakable: *Stay away for now.*

Dropping the folded letter onto the table with a weary sigh, Rose resigned herself to spending the better part of the summer at Auchengray. The endless days ahead would have been much cooler in the remote glen of Loch Trool, where northern winds blow down from the Merrick range, and the rushing waters of the Gairland Burn refresh the herds. When Jamie described the steep green hills, the granite crags, the blue depths of the loch, Rose saw them clearly in her mind's eye.

Two months seemed a long time to wait.

Remaining in her own parish offered one advantage: All of New-abbey would soon discover she was as fertile as Leana. Rose tucked her bedcovers round her, thinking how swiftly her news would travel from farm to village. "Have ye heard? Rose McKie is wi' child. She didna waste time catchin' up wi' her sister."

Her conscience did not let her gloat for long. Heat crawled up her neck, and contrition filled her soul. She did not wish to triumph over Leana. Not the sister who'd loved her from the day she was born. All Rose wanted was a house full of children tugging at her skirts.

Thanks be to God, Dr. Gilchrist's dire prediction last winter had proven false. The croup had not rendered her barren; instead, the Almighty had answered her prayers. *He maketh the barren woman to keep house, and to be a joyful mother of children.*

"Two children." Rose pictured dark-haired Ian in the nursery next door as she smoothed a hand across her stomach. "Leana's. And mine."

Four

A mother is a mother still,
The holiest thing alive.
SAMUEL TAYLOR COLERIDGE

Leana took a steadying breath and began to walk, grateful for the sanctuary of the quiet countryside on a lovely morning. She'd not slept well and had awakened feeling queasy again and wishing her physic garden were at hand. In lieu of chamomile and ginger, a short walk round Twyneholm seemed the best remedy.

Before her the horizon glowed a vibrant pink, and gold bands of sunlit clouds streaked across the sky. A *freshening* breeze lifted the wisps of hair round her face. All was still, save for the low murmur of moving water behind her. A deep burn full of brown trout flowed through the center of Twyneholm, passing her aunt's cottage before it slipped beneath a stone bridge.

Leana felt every bit of loose gravel beneath her calfskin shoes, the soles thin from constant wearing. She had left most of her possessions behind at Auchengray, bringing only a small trunk of necessities and two gowns—the simple green one she was wearing and her favorite, the embroidered claret gown she'd worn on her wedding day. 'Twas just as well she'd packed sparingly; the tiny cottage could hold no more.

Twyneholm had cracked its doors a handbreadth to welcome her, but nothing eased the pain of missing Ian. From the hour of his birth, the lad's gaze had shone with the promise of a clever mind. Would Jamie engage a teacher to reside at Glentrool and tutor him? Leana's thoughts flew across Galloway and her hopes as well. *I would come, Jamie. I would teach our son.*

Her conscience mocked her. *Teach him what?* Reading and writing? Simple bookkeeping? She had no mastery of Latin or Greek, no training in logic or rhetoric. Jamie went to university, not she. Even Rose in her short time at Carlyle School for Young Ladies had learned a smattering of French. Leana could confidently handle a busy household and tally its ledgers; she could love a husband and raise his children. None of those skills was required of her now.

Distraught, she started up the hill leading to the crossroads. A sudden clenching in her stomach sent her scurrying back to the burn instead. Bending over the steep banks, she deposited her breakfast in its rushing waters, taking care not to tumble in after it.

"Heavens!" Leana straightened, shaking all over. Whatever was the matter? She'd seen what ague could do. And croup. And pneumonia. Best she remain withindoors, at least until her stomach settled. A weak saucer of tea and another hour's sleep might help.

Her aunt greeted her when she came through the door, a look of concern stretched across her parchment-thin skin. "Back so soon? Come sit by the hearth. You'll be wanting tea with a spoonful of honey from my hives, aye?"

Leana merely nodded, her insides still churning.

Meg pulled a chair close to her and patted her hand. "Might it be your courses starting? Many a lass feels unweel on the first day."

Leana sipped her tea and mulled over the last two months, a jumble of days that all ran together, colorless and undefined. When *were* her courses due? They'd waxed and waned without any certain pattern after Ian's birth. Since Jamie was no longer her husband, such things hardly mattered, did they? Still, to appease her aunt, Leana began counting silently on her fingers.

Was it two weeks ago or three? Perhaps four. Six weeks, then. Nae, ten.

Leana's eyes widened. "'Tis not my courses."

'Tis a child.

Unthinkable. Yet undeniable. The weariness, the nausea, the tenderness. *Yestermorn* she'd cringed when she laced her bodice. Leana had dismissed such symptoms, convinced that weaning Ian had taken its toll on her body, nothing more.

Nae. Much more.

She swallowed hard. *Oh, my dear Jamie!* Memories of their last nights together assailed her. Before they met with the kirk session. Before the terrible truth was spoken. Before her world fell apart.

Aunt Meg smiled at her, eyes wreathed with tiny lines, her gaze alight with curiosity. "'Twould appear something has stolen your appetite and your tongue as well. Will you not speak, or must I guess?"

Leana put down her tea saucer with trembling hands, her emotions scattered to the four winds. However could she tell her maiden aunt, a *stayed lass* who had ne'er shared a man's bed, that she was carrying Jamie McKie's child?

She slipped her hand beneath the table's edge to examine her waist. Though she'd lost weight, she sensed a slight rounding there. Why had she not noticed it before? The answer was simple: Aunt Meg did not have a looking glass. And without Jamie in her life, Leana had paid scant attention to her figure. Had her wise relative seen what she had missed?

She studied her aunt's pale features, the broad cheeks and full mouth so like her mother's, so like her own. "Aunt Meg…," she began, her voice fading along with her courage. Having a babe outside the bonds of wedlock was no small thing. The neighboring cottagers knew nothing of the scandal that had sent Leana running to Twyneholm. Woe to Margaret Halliday if folk learned the whole of it.

"Auntie," she began again, "you know that Jamie and I were…well, we *thought* we were rightfully wed for more than a year. Until the kirk session decreed otherwise, Jamie and I continued living as husband and wife by habit and repute according to Scottish law. And…we…"

Meg arched her silvery eyebrows. "Aye?" was all she said, though her expression spoke a great deal more.

Leana clutched the dress fabric beneath her hands as though her unborn babe might provide the strength she needed. "Aunt Meg, I believe I am with child."

The older woman's features stilled for a moment, then softened. "I thought as much. Two women cannot share the same cottage and not mark the pull of the moon." She reached out and grasped Leana's hands. "What's to be done, dear niece?"

"What *can* I do but raise the child myself since Jamie is married to Rose?"

"But he loves *you.*"

The gentle reminder soothed Leana's heart like a balm. Jamie's last words, spoken in Auchengray's garden, whispered to her afresh. *I will ne'er repent of loving you. Do you hear me, Leana? I will always love you.* But her own words written to him that next morning came to mind as well.

Leana met her aunt's troubled gaze. "You'll recall I sent Willie home with a letter for Jamie."

Meg glanced at the finely polished writing desk, one of the few items brought from Auchengray. A gift from Jamie. "You ne'er told me what you wrote, lass."

"I wrote—" Leana's voice caught on the words. "I wrote, 'Love my sister. Seek your future together in Glentrool.'"

Her brow wrinkled. "Has he done those things, do you suppose?"

Have you, Jamie? If only she could be certain. "He has ne'er written back to tell me. Nor should he," Leana quickly added, masking the regret in her voice. "'Tis not proper for a married man to do so."

"Och!" Meg was on her feet, her arms folded across her bosom. "If your dotty session clerk had done what was proper, if he'd made the necessary entries in the session records, you'd still be married to Jamie."

Leana held up her hands, too exhausted to wrestle with the past. "What is done cannot be undone. With Jamie's child growing inside me, 'tis even more urgent that I return home. For if I stay, I'll put you in a dangerous way with the kirk and with your neighbors."

The woman jerked her chin, though Leana saw the slight tremor in it. "I can manage being snubbed at market in Kirkcudbright."

"'Twould be more serious than that, Auntie. An unmarried woman with an unborn babe? I'd be sentenced to the repentance stool for weeks and would drag you into the muck with me. For your sake, I cannot remain in Twyneholm."

"But…" Meg hesitated. "I hate to even mention it, but…what will your own parish say?"

Leana's stomach, already unsettled, drew into a knot. What *would* Reverend Gordon say when he learned the news? Since the kirk session had demanded she give up Ian, might they do the same when this child was born? *Please God, it cannot be!* The minister's voice rang through her heart like a *deid* bell on a funeral morn. *It is our wish to see Ian McKie reared in a devout and pious home, free from improper influences.*

Nae! Leana pressed her hand to her mouth. She would not allow it. Not again. Not if she had to live alone in the woods like Lillias Brown, shunned by decent society. Not if she had to board a ship for the Americas with her bairn beneath her wings. Not this child. Not this time.

Leana answered Meg at last. "I don't know what they might say. I only know what *I* will say: My sins have been atoned for. And this child was conceived while all in the parish considered us married. Including the kirk." She was glad to confess the words aloud, if only to remind herself of those truths.

Her aunt reclaimed her seat and clasped Leana's hands in hers. "Remember this, dearie: No child is a surprise to the Almighty."

The knot inside her eased. "How right you are, Meg." Her child would have a heavenly Father if not an earthly one. When the child was born at Auchengray, she would send news to Jamie at Glentrool and see if he might willingly give the child his name.

Not his fortune nor his *heirship*. Only the name *McKie*.

Five

Look! how he laughs and stretches out his arms,
And opens wide his blue eyes upon thine,
To hail his father.

GEORGE GORDON, LORD BYRON

Come, little one. Let me mark you as mine."
Jamie wrapped his arm firmly round the lamb and dabbed its
neck with paint. Thinned with linseed oil, the scarlet *keel* mark would
eventually wash out, leaving the wool white once more. Although the
meat of the blackface, rather than the coarse wool, made the animals
valuable, he would see their lightweight fleece put to good use as well.
The blood-colored mark identifying the smaller lambs as his needed to
last only until he herded his flock to Glentrool. "Two months from
today," he promised, nudging the bleating animal toward its mother.

He stood and stretched his cramped legs. The blackface breed flour-
ished in cool, damp conditions; a shepherd's joints and muscles did not.
Last night while he'd slept, the month of June had made a showery
entrance, drenching the countryside in a fine rain that had lasted all
morning. Good for the gardens, especially the rose bed, but not the best
weather for rounding up skittish lambs. Still, choosing which ones to
mark was a task he dared not entrust to others, especially not the new
shepherds who'd worked at Auchengray but a few days.

He'd arrived at the Whitsun feeing fair in Dumfries last Monday
afternoon only to learn the most experienced herds of the parish had
already been hired for the next term. When he'd happened upon
Duncan near the Midsteeple shaking hands with a black-haired plowman to seal their agreement, Jamie pulled the overseer aside and told
him of his bargain with Lachlan.

"*Weel* done," Duncan had said, a smile decorating his weathered
face. "Ye'll be *sairlie* missed at Auchengray, but ye deserve tae have yer

ain flocks and live in yer ain hoose." He'd tipped his head and eyed Jamie with obvious amusement. "Is *thar* anither reason why ye're anxious tae *flit* tae Glentrool? *Mebbe* a certain wife wha carries yer bairn?"

Few circumstances in life slipped by Duncan Hastings.

Jamie was standing there in the forenoon rain, still chuckling at the memory, when that same gruff voice came floating o'er the *braes.* "Will ye leuk at the *ill-faured* spots ye're puttin' on yer *puir* lambs this wet Tuesday?"

"My keel marks are not ugly," Jamie protested, grinning all the while. "And my lambs will make me wealthy someday, not poor."

Duncan made his way down the hillock. " 'Tis a *blissin* yer uncle will let ye take that mony lambs tae Glentrool." He surveyed the flocks, slowly nodding as he did. "I'll see ye have the help ye need come August, Jamie. Rab Murray and Davie Tait will be pleased tae join ye on yer *raik* west, and *ithers* as weel. A fortnight later they'll a' be hame again, nae *warse* for wear. Ye'll be generous wi' them, aye?"

"You ken I will." Jamie would make certain Alec McKie pressed a fair amount of silver into the itinerant shepherds' hands before they were sent east again. Fifteen shillings each would be a fair stipend. "You're bound for Kingsgrange, I'm told."

"Aye, tae visit me youngest dochter, Mary. Anither bairn has come tae her hoose. I promised tae finish buildin' her a cradle." Duncan shrugged. "Her man could do it just as weel, but she wants her *faither* tae make it, she says." After another long pause he added, "I'll be hame in the morn should ye need me."

Jamie dropped his paintbrush into the pail at his feet, determined to hear whatever Duncan seemed reluctant to say. "What brings you out on the hills looking for me when you should be riding to Urr parish?"

Duncan shifted his gaze to the watering trough. " 'Tis yer uncle, Jamie. He's been studyin' his ledgers mair than usual, makin' marks I canna follow. Sendin' posts tae Embrough and Edingham Farm as weel."

"He's marrying a widow with a sizable estate come July," Jamie reminded him. "Correspondence with the courts in Edinburgh is to be expected. And letters to his future bride too."

"'A' I'm sayin' is, be mindful, Jamie. Yer uncle is not above a bit o' *swickerie.* I willna stand by and see ye lose a' ye've worked for." With a tip of his checked wool bonnet, Duncan bid him farewell, then trotted down the hill toward Bess, a seasoned mare waiting patiently for her rider.

Jamie watched him go with misgivings. Duncan seldom spoke so candidly about his master. Was the man seeing deception where there was none? Or were Duncan's fears well grounded?

The bleating ewes drew his thoughts back to the task at hand. Two months old now, the lambs were ready to be weaned from their mothers, a slow process of increasing the oats for the lambs and decreasing it for the ewes. The mothers bleated pitifully when their lambs no longer needed them. Despite the ewes' obvious discomfort, nothing could be done but wait until their milk was gone.

Watching one ewe nudging her lamb, encouraging it to nurse, Jamie felt his throat tighten. A forgotten image returned to haunt him: Leana nursing Ian in the garden, bent over their son, weeping. Jamie closed his eyes, praying he might dislodge the painful recollection. Instead, it grew more vivid. Her hair, the color of ripened wheat, falling in soft waves round her shoulders. Her voice strained to the breaking point as she sang a lullaby, bidding their son farewell.

With a groan, he jammed his mud-covered boot into the soft ground, his frustration mounting anew. Could he not have done *something*? He found it nigh to impossible to forgive the elders of the kirk for their heartless decision. Asking a woman to give up her child was unconscionable. Asking Leana, the kindest woman he had ever known, to wean her son and place him in the arms of her sister, who…

"Och!" Jamie stamped across the waterlogged pasture, the ewes darting out of his way, taking their lambs with them. The scene before him was no longer green hills and blackface sheep but firelight throwing shadows against the walls of the Newabbey manse as Leana slipped off her wedding ring and placed it before Rose. Had he ever known a more terrible hour in his life? He'd begged the elders for mercy, but instead they demanded justice.

Justice was theirs. And Rose was his. A lovely lass, aye, and charming. But not the dear woman who'd run away from him, leaving behind a single request: *Love my sister.*

He did care for Rose; in truth, he had doted on her once, as any lad with eyes in his head might have done. Her dark eyes and hair, her creamy skin, and her sweet mouth had stolen his senses from the hour they met. Now that she was his lawful wife and the mother of his unborn child, duty prevailed. He would treat her fairly, provide for her needs, and fill her arms with the children she seemed anxious to have. But could he do as Leana asked? Could he truly love Rose? And tell her so?

"Jamieee!"

Startled, he spun about, nearly losing his footing in the wet grass. His wife's voice carried through the damp air like a high, clear bell. The heartbreaking images faded away as the grassy hillocks came into focus once more. Rose appeared a moment later at the top of the rise, bouncing Ian on her hip. As if chased away by the boy's cheerful babbling, the soft rain ceased, and the gray skies seemed to lighten.

"There's your father," she sang out, pointing in Jamie's direction. "See how he's painting the lambs?" She slowly worked her way toward Jamie, her skirts dragging in the mud since she could not spare a hand to lift them. "Someday, lad, you'll have your own flocks to tend. Won't that be grand?"

At eight months, Ian was already an armful. With long limbs and a wavy mass of dark hair, he no longer bore the look of a babe but a man-child. He'd already begun trying to crawl, rocking back and forth on his knees. Forward motion would not be long in coming. Ian had also learned to point, which he was proving admirably just now, his arm outstretched. Rose held Ian tightly against her and bent her head to press her cheek against his. "Who is that, Ian? Is that your father?"

When the child waved his arms about, showing off his new front teeth with an exuberant smile, Jamie's heart swelled. "There's my good lad." He grasped one of Ian's tiny fists in his, making the child squeal with joy. "Your stepmother will not be pleased if I cover you with paint, will she?" Jamie gazed into the boy's blue gray eyes, so like Leana's, and was astounded to find his mood quite improved. How could a small child make so great a difference?

Leana's words stirred inside him. *Ian needs you, Jamie. Even more than I do.* Only now was he beginning to understand how much he needed Ian.

Rose shifted the lad to her other hip, sweeping her braid out of Ian's reach. "Aren't you going to ask why I've come looking for you?" Before Jamie could respond, she spilled out her news like oats from a pail. "We've company arriving for dinner within the hour. Widow Douglas of Edingham Farm and her three *braw* sons. Father insists you dress properly for table."

Jamie rolled his eyes. "I suppose he's chosen my waistcoat for me as well as the words I should speak."

"Certainly not!" She laughed, turning toward the mains and inclining her head in invitation. "Away to the house, sir. I'm eager to meet the woman who has captured my father's eye."

"Instead, I fear his eye has captured her thrifite." Jamie plucked Ian from her grasp and started east with the child tucked in the crook of his arm, enjoying the warmth of the small body pressed against his drugget coat. The child's brown hair matched his own perfectly, as if a weaver with a practiced eye had chosen the strands. Jamie addressed Rose over Ian's bobbing head. "As to the widow's sons, they are neither handsome nor canny. Your *flindrikin* ways will be wasted on them."

"Jamie," she scolded, though her tone was playful, "I'm a married woman, not a flirt." She lifted her skirts clear of the wet grass and lengthened her stride to keep up with him. "You'll wear your embroidered blue waistcoat, won't you? And be civil to them?"

Jamie held his tongue but could not quell his thoughts. *Her father's daughter: 'My will be done.'* Leana's temperament was quite the opposite; she'd neither prodded nor pulled, yet Jamie had delighted in doing her bidding.

As he tramped across the rough pastureland holding their son, he imagined Leana standing on the threshold of her aunt's house, looking wistfully toward Auchengray, her arms empty. "Rose, I've been meaning to ask: Have you written Leana? Told her we are expecting a child? And that we're staying here through Lammas?"

She colored slightly, turning her face to the side. "I've started a letter to my sister. Many letters, really. I cannot seem to find the words. I fear the truth may break her heart." Rose glanced up at him as though test-ing the waters. "Perhaps it would be better to wait. At least 'til I'm three months—"

"Nae." He stopped at the edge of the farm steading, one forearm blocking Ian's flailing arms before they connected with his chin. "You cannot wait until July. What if Leana should come home to attend Lachlan's wedding and find you blooming with child?" Seeing her expression, Jamie softened his tone but not his words. " 'Tis unkind to keep this from her. Leana deserves to know."

"*You* write her, then." Rose turned away, her shoulders sagging.

Hadn't he written Leana dozens of times, if only in his mind? Yet he dared not put his thoughts to paper, let alone post them. When he was certain his voice would not give him away, he admitted, " 'Twould be cruel for me to write your sister, and you ken it well. She has suffered enough."

"I, too, have suffered. For I, too, love Leana." Rose slowly turned round. Tears shone in her eyes. "When I can find the strength to write her, I will do so. I promise."

Chastened, Jamie lightly touched her cheek. "I believe you, lass."

Six

Unbidden guests
Are often welcomest when they are gone.
WILLIAM SHAKESPEARE

Come, Rose." Jamie nodded toward the mains. "We must darken the door before our guests do."

He led her round the U-shaped farm steading, watching where his boots landed. Though it had stopped raining altogether, a gray mist still hovered near the ground. Sounds came at them from every direction. Doves cooed in the *doocot,* clucking arose from the henhouse, and the lowing of cows rumbled in the *byre.* Ian crowed along with the farmyard chorus, turning this way and that to get a glimpse of his noisy surroundings.

"Easy, lad, or you'll land in the midden." Jamie tightened his grip and swung away from the odoriferous dunghill in the center of the steading. "Though it might be worth a soiled shirt just to agitate your stepmother, aye?" Jamie hoped Rose was listening, for he meant to lift her spirits. Instead she walked on without comment.

He should not have been so insistent about her writing Leana. The envious Rose he'd once known would have written her sister at once, boasting of her good fortune. The pensive Rose now beside him was not the same girl he'd met two years past. Had a woman's tender heart bloomed inside her while he was busy tending his lambs?

Eliza stood on the broad stone step outside the back door, motioning them toward her. "Mr. McBride is pacin' aboot the hoose, waitin' for ye tae join him. Says the Douglases are expected *onie* minute."

Jamie held out his son. "See that Ian is scrubbed clean and dressed. Are Hugh and Annabel in our room?"

Eliza deftly lifted Ian from Jamie's arms, her white cap bobbing up and down. "They're awaitin' yer arrival, sir, wi' hot water and the like."

Jamie deposited his muddy boots inside the door, while Rose lifted her skirts to spare the freshly scrubbed floors and hurried up the stair. He followed close on her heels, observing the busy kitchen staff in passing. Dinner smelled promising. Horseradish tinged the air, mingled with milder scents. Leeks. Cloves. And the unmistakable aroma of bacon frying. Neda could be counted on to serve her best fare—fish, flesh, fowl, and a fine pudding—to impress their guests and appease her master.

Jamie had no doubt Neda Hastings would do Auchengray proud. Now it was his turn to do the same. Four months ago the sons of Morna Douglas had escorted him round Edingham with blatant conceit. Once he'd shown them the pastures and gardens of Auchengray, the healthy flocks and neatly planted fields, their arrogance might come down a peg or two.

The gray-haired valet Jamie shared with Lachlan stood at the ready in his bedroom. Hugh shaved Jamie's chin, then dressed him in a neatly ironed shirt and clean breeches. At university, Jamie had worn the powdered periwig of a gentleman. Among the *kintra* folk of Galloway, such pretensions were unnecessary. Hugh smoothed Jamie's hair into a sleek tail and tied it snugly at the nape of his neck. "Guid as new, Mr. McKie." He brushed the sleeves of Jamie's jacket once more for good measure. "Ye're both wanted in the parlor."

Jamie and Rose hastened down the stair, headed for the front room of the house. Square in design, the parlor faced west, inviting the afternoon light through its two tall windows. The room contained a half-tester bedstead, a sideboard, and a mismatched assortment of basket chairs and small tables—a cluttered place for entertaining their infrequent guests. Jamie and Rose arrived with no time to spare and were greeted by a grim-faced Lachlan and the sound of carriage wheels rolling up the drive.

Lachlan glowered at them. "Finally." He was well turned out for the occasion; his silvery gray coat and scarlet waistcoat were the best in his clothes press. "Jamie, I'll count on you to make her sons feel at home. Rose, a reminder that you serve as mistress of Auchengray now."

Her posture stiffened. "What would you have me do, Father?"

"Listen at all times, speak only when necessary, and see that the servants keep our plates filled with food. Your husband and I will manage the dinner conversation." His gruff instructions delivered, Lachlan marched from the room as though headed for battle, head thrown back, chin leading the way.

Jamie resisted the urge to salute his departing back and instead offered Rose his arm and escorted her to a spot by the hearth where they might stand together and welcome their guests. They did not wait long. Lachlan returned shortly with Morna Douglas in tow and steered her in their direction. Jamie had met her twice before at Edingham and so greeted her as warmly as he could. She was perhaps forty, a good deal shorter than Lachlan, and a good bit rounder. Her face was the color of *hindberries*, as if she remained perpetually embarrassed, and her movements hinted at a fidgety discomfort.

"Good to see you again, James." Her voice was high, birdlike. Morna fawned over Rose, pronouncing her "fair as any flower in the garden." At last the widow allowed Lachlan to guide her to a nearby chair before he turned to introduce her sons, who hovered just inside the door.

Lachlan cupped Rose's elbow, sweeping his free hand in the direction of the newcomers. "Mistress McKie, kindly meet your future stepbrothers: Malcolm Douglas, Gavin Douglas, and Ronald Douglas."

Three strapping lads—nigh identical in appearance and close in age—bowed as one while Rose offered them a low curtsy. Their muscular backs were hidden beneath English broadcloth coats; their hands, no doubt roughened from working their late father's land, remained clasped behind their backs. Clay-colored hair had been combed back, revealing ruddy complexions freckled by the sun and only the faintest of beards. To a man, their appreciative gazes were focused on the bonny lass before them.

"Mistress?" Gavin, the middle son, breathed the word on a tenor note. "Since you are to be our sister, might we call you Rose?"

Jamie noted the smile that played about her mouth and the way her lashes fluttered across her faintly pink cheeks. "When I am truly your sister, you may call me whatever you please."

"See if I don't." Gavin elbowed his older brother, grinning outright. Jamie bristled at the lad's impertinence. Or was it Rose's familiar tone, sweet as treacle, that disturbed him? The Douglas brothers were young—none more than twenty—and green when it came to matters of the world. A slight breach in manners could be overlooked. And there *were* three of them; he would not soon forget that.

"Gentlemen." Lachlan's voice was as smooth as linseed oil. "You'll remember Jamie, my nephew and son-in-law. Heir to Glentrool."

Malcolm Douglas jutted out his chin. "And heir to Auchengray as well?"

Jamie bit back a response. The subject of heirship had not been broached since that fateful March night with the kirk session. Would Auchengray be his someday through his marriage to Rose? Or might Lachlan's forthcoming wedding change all that?

Before Lachlan could respond, Neda appeared in the doorway, bobbing her coppery head with its starched cap. "Mr. McBride, we're prepared tae serve dinner at yer biddin'."

His uncle offered a brief nod to Malcolm. "We'll discuss such details another time, lad. For now, our meat beckons." Not one to keep hot food waiting, Lachlan swiftly led the way across the entrance hall and into the dining room, then seated them round the cloth-draped table. The polished silver gleamed in the candlelight. A vase filled with lilies of the valley scented the air. Morna Douglas, Rose, and Jamie sat on his left and the brothers on his right, oldest to youngest. Satisfied with the arrangement, Lachlan took his seat at the head of his table, and the meal service commenced.

Lachlan steered the conversation along a predictable route: the upcoming Keltonhill Fair, which interested the Douglas lads greatly. The largest fair of any in the South West, the one-day event drew horse dealers and buyers, chapmen and hawkers, Gypsies and tinklers, gentry and peasantry alike. After a bit, their conversation moved further afield to the opening of the Forth and Clyde canal that would connect Glasgow and Edinburgh.

"The canal opening is scheduled for late June, though I'll not be traveling to Bowling Bay for the festivities," Lachlan said with a nod toward his intended bride. "I've more important matters to attend to closer to home."

Jamie could not help noticing Morna Douglas's heightened color. "Tell me, Uncle, have you chosen a date?"

"I have." Lachlan cleared his throat with some ceremony. "The sixteenth of July. 'Tis a Friday, which bodes well, the moon will be waxing, and 'tis my sixtieth birthday."

Wanting to include Morna, Jamie asked the widow, "Will your vows be exchanged at our kirk in Newabbey or in Urr parish?"

Lachlan answered for her. "Reverend Muirhead will marry us at the Urr kirk. My family has given the parishioners of Newabbey enough to blether about of late." His pointed gaze, aimed at Jamie, drew every eye round the table.

"A fine plan," Jamie said smoothly, ignoring their curious stares. "I am certain you have many acquaintants in Dalbeaty and its environs who'll be glad to be in attendance."

From the periphery of the room several maidservants stepped forward to remove the dinner plates in anticipation of the final course. "I hope you and your pretty wife will come," the widow said, offering them a tremulous smile. "And your cousin…ah, Leana, isn't it? She will join us as well?"

Beneath the table Rose touched his hand, whether approving or opposing her sister's inclusion, Jamie could not decide. "What say you, Uncle?" he asked. "Shall we write Leana in Twyneholm and encourage her attendance?"

Lachlan glowered at him but did not have time to answer before the door leading to the kitchen creaked on its hinges and Neda entered bearing his favorite pudding. The man's sour mood seemed to sweeten when she placed the dish before him. "A fine meal, Neda. We'll have tea in the spence after a bit. In the meantime, serve my guests your good pudding."

The notion of Leana's attending the wedding was not mentioned again that afternoon. Not at table nor later in the spence. Both families gathered in the cramped study, holding their teacups, while Lachlan expounded on the virtues of Auchengray. His money box was prominently displayed on his desk, though the lid remained locked. Leather-bound ledgers stood guard, their worn spines a testimony to how often their greedy owner's hands had caressed them.

Jamie did what he could to engage Malcolm in conversation. As the oldest of the three brothers, Malcolm must have considered how his mother's impending marriage would affect both properties. If he had an opinion, Malcolm did not offer it. Instead he listened, nodded, and said little. Judging by the hard look in his brown eyes, the prospect did not please him.

When the mantel clock chimed thrice, the men put aside their saucers and ventured out of doors for a tour of the farm, leaving the widow and Rose behind to fend for themselves. Lachlan led the party, gathering his future stepsons round him while Jamie followed a step behind. It proved an enlightening vantage point as he heard Lachlan take sole credit for Auchengray's vast flocks and congratulate himself for everything his nephew had accomplished.

Jamie listened in disgust. Only a week ago Lachlan had insisted the Lord had blessed his flocks because of his hardworking son-in-law. Now Jamie's contribution remained unmentioned as his uncle stood at the top of Auchengray Hill, waving his arm in a slow arc to indicate all the lands and flocks that belonged to him.

Heir to Auchengray as well? Malcolm's question still taunted Jamie, a charge for which he had no good answer. He would inquire the same of Lachlan as soon as the sons of Edingham Farm found their way back home.

"Jamie?" Lachlan turned round and folded his arms across his chest, clearly put out with him. "You have not said two words since we left the mains."

"But, Uncle—"

"I presume you'd rather be marking lambs than listening to me."

"That's not—"

"Off with you, then." Lachlan jerked his head toward the hills, making his intentions clear. "Do not fear. I'll see our guests well provided for."

Jamie felt at loose ends, being so abruptly dismissed. He took a few steps, then turned back. "Will the three of you be heading to Urr parish this evening?"

Malcolm started to respond, but Lachlan was too quick for him.

"Their mother will return home in the morn. As to her sons, they'll stay for supper, then be bound for Edingham before nightfall since they've livestock of their own that require attention." He rested his hands on two broad shoulders, giving Gavin and Ronald each a firm shake. "Best see to your lambs, Jamie, or 'twill be difficult to tell which are yours and which are mine."

Seven

Wickedness is always easier than virtue;
for it takes the short cut to every thing.

SAMUEL JOHNSON

Lachlan McBride pinned a hard gaze to the lad's chest, daring him to stay. Did he enjoy being humiliated, this nephew of his?

"As it happens, Uncle, my lambs are all marked." Jamie's jaw clenched as he spoke.

Ah, but his *fists* were not clenched, Lachlan noted. Jamie lacked the *smeddum* for fighting. Lachlan released his grip on the two brothers, ne'er taking his eyes off his nephew. "How many sheep are yours? Or have you not counted?"

"I have." Jamie's tone had a sharp edge. "Twenty score lambs bear my keel mark."

"Four hundred, eh?" Lachlan took care not to smile as he pointed to a nearby pasture. "The ones that look like their necks are bleeding?"

"You ken the paint will wash out with hot water and lye soap." Jamie jerked his chin at him. "I've chosen the smaller of each twin, as I promised."

He acknowledged Jamie's words without agreeing to them, lest his future stepsons leap to the wrong conclusion. Lachlan fished his watch out of his waistcoat pocket and flipped open the gold case. *Nearly five. Enough dallying.* "With Duncan away to Kingsgrange, there must be tasks in the steading that require your attention."

His nephew glared at him. "There's always work to be done at Auchengray." Jamie spun on his heel—though none too effectively on the soggy ground—and headed downhill toward the farmyard, his polished boots covered with mud.

Lachlan watched the departure without comment. Let him muck

out the stables if his muscles needed flexing. Jamie McKie, born to a wealthy laird, had yet to learn the meaning of hard labor. Did the gentry ever grasp those truths? They did not. Not like a man who'd worked all his life.

A yellowhammer flitted past, catching his eye for a moment with its bright coloring and musical call. He scanned the brightening skies, inhaling the rain-freshened air. "Our afternoon will be more pleasant without my nephew's sullen countenance, wouldn't you say?"

The Douglases laughed—uneasily, he thought—then quickly fell silent. After a lengthy pause, punctuated only by the bleating of sheep, one of them spoke up.

"Mr. McBride, my brothers and I have been wondering…" Ronald shifted his weight, exchanging glances with his older siblings. "Will Edingham Farm be sold, sir? When you've married our mother, that is?"

A bold question for a lad who'd seen only seventeen summers. Lachlan gave Ronald his full attention. "Have you an interested buyer?"

"Nae!" Gavin blurted out. "But if it were sold, would the proceeds be split evenly among us?"

"Or will I inherit the whole," Malcolm countered, "as the eldest son?"

Lachlan locked gazes with each of them in turn. Malcolm was the oldest and the strongest. Only a daft man would challenge him to a fight. Gavin, the middle son, often seemed rash and impulsive. Harmless, though quick to speak. Ronald, the youngest, was also the canniest, Morna had warned him. Tenacious. Hard to fool. Of the three, Ronald would bear the most watching.

"Your father was a generous man," Lachlan admitted, "bequeathing Edingham solely to your mother. Verra unusual in Scotland for a woman to own property. Perhaps she might answer your question about who will inherit Edingham." Certainly *he* would do no such thing. Lachlan smiled, hoping to put them at ease. "Rest assured, nothing will happen in haste. You will remain comfortably at home at least until Lammas, when there will be more…ah, more room available at Auchengray, should lodging be required."

Malcolm grimaced. "With due respect, sir, Edingham may not be as vast a property as yours, but…to be frank, our farm is better tended."

"If we lived here," Gavin said, "there's no telling how much work 'twould take to make this place presentable. The steading alone—"

"My brother means no offense," Ronald interjected smoothly, touching Gavin's sleeve to silence him.

"Nor am I offended," Lachlan said just as smoothly. "There is much room for improvement here. Jamie has done what he could, but..." Lachlan shrugged, letting them fill in the rest. "Perhaps the greater question is, what will become of Auchengray when the time comes? For this corruptible body must put on incorruption, aye? And this mortal must put on immortality. My holdings will no longer matter to me then, but they might matter verra much to you."

Ronald's brown eyes glowed like a candlelit turnip on Hallowmas Eve. "Have you no proper heir, sir? None who might rightfully claim Auchengray upon your death?"

Lachlan left the question unanswered for the moment, directing their attention to the westward pastures with a proffered hand. "Come, enough of this morbid subject. We've barely started our tour." He sighed expansively, striking out across the rise. "I wish the weather were more congenial, but 'tis a farmer's lot to accept what the heavens send."

His words, it seemed, struck the proper chord. All four of them, he and the Douglases, were the same, were they not? Honest men braving the elements, eking out a living from fields and pastures, ever at the mercy of rain, seed, and stock. As a bonnet laird, naturally he'd moved beyond daily duties in the steading. The filthy byre, the stinking midden were no longer his domain. All the more reason to gather round him young men such as these—not one of them a laird's heir who fancied himself a master breeder, but strong, capable lads unafraid of hard work.

Genuine farmers. Laborers. *Sons.*

Glancing over his shoulder at the three of them discussing the merits of Auchengray, Lachlan smiled to himself. *Aye, Ronald. Edingham will be sold.* Thomas Henderson of Dalbeaty stood ready to buy Edingham Farm—the house, the steading, the fields, the cattle, the lot of it. Lachlan pictured his thrifite, already packed with silver coins, soon overflowing with gold ones. As gold as the knotted cord that lay hidden among his shillings. A gift from Lillias Brown, the local wise woman, meant to bring riches to his doorstep. *'Tis working, Widow Brown.*

Lachlan stepped closer to the lads, pointing them toward Dumfries. "To the north you'll find untamed moorland with stands of oak and ash and the royal burgh beyond it. My neighbors are the Newalls of Troston Hill Farm and the Drummonds of Glensone. Fine families, however modest their holdings." He swerved about with a broad sweep of his arm. "My tups come from Tannocks Farm east of here. And, as you ken, there's naught to the south but Criffell and the Solway."

The young men craned their necks to take it all in, turning at last to admire the heather-covered slopes of Criffell. The summit, draped in mist, stretched nearly two thousand feet above the shoreline of the Solway Firth, the western waters of which mingled with the Irish Sea. The brothers seemed impressed. Perhaps the time had come to answer Ronald's question about heirship.

Lachlan touched the lad's elbow to catch his attention. "A moment ago you asked who might rightfully claim this land." Ronald's brothers swiveled in his direction, the view forgotten. "The truth is I have no sons or male relatives whom I wish to see inherit Auchengray." He lifted his shoulders slightly as if to shrug off the sympathy he saw in their eyes. "Of my two daughters, the older one has produced a son. A *bystart.*"

He let the word hang in the air like a disagreeable smell. It produced the reaction he expected. Shock. And, judging by the look on Malcolm's face, aversion. The Douglases were a respected family, proud of their standing in society and unacquainted with scandal.

"Due to the shameful circumstances of his birth, I refuse to claim Ian McKie as a grandson. He will depart with his father at Lammas, and any ties to Auchengray will be severed." The relief on their faces was obvious.

"As to the child's mother, Leana," he continued, "no honest man would have her for a wife. The woman spent three weeks on the stool of repentance for the sin of...*hochmagandy.* Pardon me if the term offends you, lads, but that's the sorry truth of it."

Gavin's eyes widened. "Will she...that is..."

"Have nae fear," Lachlan assured them, bending to pluck a sprig of yellow broom. "Leana will not be welcomed back to Auchengray. As to

my younger daughter, you've already seen the sort of man she married."
He glanced down the hill toward the mains, letting his contempt show.
"My nephew is weak, easily manipulated by the women in his life, start-
ing with his mother."

A momentary light flickered in Malcolm's eyes, though nothing
was said.

"When he landed on my doorstep, looking like a *gaberlunzie* without penny or purse, I took him in, dressed him hat to boots, and gave
him a home." Lachlan exhaled with a weary sigh. "You can judge for
yourself the respect it has earned me."

Gavin curled his lip. "We'll not be sorry to see him leave." Judging
by the disdain on their faces, all three brothers were viewing Jamie in a
new light. One that cast a murky shadow across the heir of Glentrool.

Lachlan clapped his hands together, eager to press on while the
stage was set. "I'll not bore you with the rest of it. We've more important things to discuss before our growling stomachs demand supper."
He guided them down Auchengray Hill, directing them toward a stone
bothy in the glen below. Little more than a rough shelter from wind and
rain, the small building had recently been put to rights, with the sagging
walls shored up and the dirt floor swept clean.

When they stepped inside, Lachlan took advantage of the privacy
afforded them, lowering his voice to enhance the sense of secrecy.
"Here's the worst of it, gentlemen: Jamie thinks *he* is the one responsible for the fruitfulness of my flocks." He grunted, nodding at their
astonished faces. " 'Twas my silver that bought the tups. And I believe
they did most of the work." A ripple of male laughter echoed against the
stones, just as Lachlan had hoped. Before it subsided, he held up a cautionary hand. "The next is no laughing matter: Jamie has announced his
intentions to claim half the lambs for himself and take them to Glentrool at Lammas."

"What?" Malcolm's gaze grew hard. "Who does this nephew of
yours think he is? Taking all the glory and the lambs as well?"

Lachlan nodded grimly. "That's the way of it." He fixed his eyes on
Malcolm. "What makes this especially disconcerting, lad, is that I
intended *you* to be my heir."

"Me, sir?"

"Aye." Lachlan reveled in their startled faces, now certain of how they would respond to his proposal. "If, heaven forbid, something should happen to prevent you from claiming Auchengray, your brothers would inherit in your stead."

Gavin swallowed with some effort. "Wh-what are you saying, Mr. McBride?"

"I'm saying that I've chosen you as my heirs. Though I can ne'er replace your father, I will gladly see to your well-being and protect your fortune as if 'twere my own."

Disbelief gave way to amazement. "Can you mean this?" Malcolm stared at him, then at his brothers. " 'Tis more than we could hope for, with no claim on our mother's land and no land of our own."

"It's settled then." Lachlan's chest swelled with pride at his own benevolence. "We should commit the details to paper as soon as possible. If I allow this nephew of mine to swick me out of half my lambs, he will in fact be stealing a large portion of your inheritance."

"Nae!" Three voices rang in anguished chorus, Malcolm's the loudest. "Is there nothing we can do to stop him, sir?"

"Well…" Lachlan paused, as though considering his answer. Never mind that he'd rehearsed this speech for days; he meant his plan to seem newly hatched, formed at their bidding. "There *is* one thing that might be done." When he leaned forward, the brothers followed suit, their heads drawn together like Gypsies huddled round a campfire. "Duncan Hastings, my overseer, is away this evening. The timing is…ah, providential."

Eight

Twilight and evening bell,
And after that the dark!

ALFRED, LORD TENNYSON

H as the hour grown too late for you, lass?" Though her father smiled across the supper table, his words cast no warmth in her direction.

Rose pretended to stifle a yawn. "'Tis just the warm June weather making me drowsy."

In truth, Rose had not been listening to Lachlan's blether. For the last several minutes her gaze had been fixed on Jamie's hands: stabbing at his smoked mutton, slicing the cold meat with fierce intensity, spearing a bite of strawberry with his fork. He was angry—no, *furious*—about something. Every vein in his neck stood out, as though he were daring someone to cross him. Was it the red-headed brothers carelessly wiping their mouths with the backs of their hands that heated his blood? Was it Morna Douglas's irritating voice? her father's condescending manner?

Or am I the one who has vexed him? Her skin chilled at the thought. *Please, may it not be so!*

Jamie had returned to the house before the others, stamping about in a foul mood and waking her from a sound nap. "Whatever is the matter, Jamie?" Rose had asked him when he barged into their room breathing threats. "Are you unhappy with me for not writing Leana? I will do so at once."

"Nae, lass," he'd said, his temper cooling. "This has naught to do with your sister."

Nonetheless, while Jamie shed his muddy breeches, she found her writing desk and began her letter yet again. *My dear sister, I have news that cannot keep, though it would be far better to tell you in person…*

Rose had forced herself to continue writing even when her hand shook and the ink splattered. *God has answered my prayers…* She included several stories about Ian, praying such details would comfort Leana rather than add to her sorrow. Jamie was only mentioned in passing. *We will leave for Glentrool at Lammas…*

The finished letter now rested on the narrow hall table inside the front door. Willie promised to take her letter to Milltown in the morning. From there it would disappear inside the coat pocket of a westbound coach driver and arrive in Leana's hands a few days hence. Monday at the latest.

"Rose!" Spoken like a bark. "Where have your thoughts wandered off to this time?"

"Nowhere, sir." Rose turned toward her father as she gathered her wits. "That is…" She looked round the table, aware of their curious gazes. "I'm…not quite myself of late." At least that was a half truth; she could not seem to concentrate on any one thing for long.

"Do not concern yourself, Rose." Morna Douglas offered a slight smile. "I know how tired you must be. Neda has promised to serve the pears from Edingham's orchard, and then my sons will take their leave. Despite the lingering light, the hour grows late." Batting her lashes even more than usual, she added, "Your father has kindly invited me to stay 'til the morn."

The widow twittered on while the servants placed dishes of sliced fruit at each place, the creamy flesh pale against the patterned china. Picked at the end of the season and stored in a dry, cool spot, the bergamot pears still had a pleasant flavor, despite their wrinkled flesh. No doubt the widow was emptying her store before the early summer varieties yielded their harvest.

Rose ate her dessert in silence, watching the others. Her father looked pleased with himself, gazing toward the dining room window and ignoring Morna, who rested her hand on his sleeve in a proprietary manner. He'd wooed her with a gift of five milk cows last winter, an appropriate gesture from so *glaumshach* a man, knowing the cows would be his again someday. The brothers had been quiet through dinner, exchanging covert glances but little else. Their tour of

Auchengray—most of it conducted without Jamie—had stretched nigh to the supper hour. Were they duly impressed, or was Edingham a grander property? After his first visit there, Jamie had pronounced their Urr parish farm merely "tidy." But then, Jamie had no interest in cattle. All he cared about were his lambs. And Ian. And her perhaps.

Jamie leaned back from the table without tasting his dessert, his features resolute. "I believe one member of the family has yet to be introduced to our guests."

Rose closed her mouth, lest it fall open in astonishment. Surely the man did not intend to bring his illegitimate child to table!

"Mistress McKie, if you might present my son to the Douglases."

Jamie, whatever are you thinking? There was naught to be done but obey his bidding. She curtsied to avoid meeting anyone's gaze, then quit the room and headed up the stair, her heart beating faster than her footsteps. *My son.* Did he mean to conceal the true mother's identity? Pushing open the door to the nursery, Rose forced herself to smile and was greeted with two genuine grins in return—from Ian, dressed in a fresh gown, and from Eliza, her cap knocked askew.

"Look who's awake." Rose gathered her stepson in her arms and hugged him close as his bare feet kicked about. *Sweet Ian.* One chubby fist grabbed her braid and tugged hard until she bussed his neck, causing him finally to let go. Her smile fading, she turned toward the door. "Come, Eliza. The lad is to meet the Douglases."

Agog at the prospect, the maidservant followed her like a shadow down the stair. The unlit hall, grown dim in the twilight, still bore the scents of a long day of cooking. Neda's work was far from over, now that the widow was spending the night. The bed linens and towels in the parlor had just been changed; Annabel's red hair was visible above an armload of laundry that sailed past the foot of the stair.

When Rose reached the threshold of the dining room, she came to an abrupt stop. Her father and the Douglas brothers were nowhere to be seen. The table was already cleared, the family Bible in place for their nightly hour of worship. Only Morna Douglas and Jamie remained in the room, standing by the hearth. The widow looked exceedingly uncomfortable; Jamie's face was a mottled red.

Hoping to fill the silence, Rose turned the boy so he was facing them. "Ian, can you smile for Mistress Douglas?"

The older woman stared at the child. "Whose son did you say this is?"

"My firstborn, Ian McKie." Jamie's words were even, belying the firm set of his jaw. "The future heir of Glentrool."

The woman's lips twitched as if she were silently calculating the boy's age. Morna knew the couple had wed in late March; clearly the child had been born well before their marriage. Had Lachlan told her naught regarding his ill-begotten grandson?

Diversion was their only recourse. "Where have the men disappeared to?" Rose asked brightly, looking round as if they might crawl out from under the table.

Morna merely blinked—unable, it seemed, to form a coherent response.

"The Douglases have taken their leave," Jamie explained smoothly, moving toward her. "Your father escorted them to the gate."

Rose turned toward the window, only now hearing the soft murmur of male voices on the misty lawn. "They'll have a long walk home."

"A good two hours." Jamie sounded glad to see the young men gone. "Eliza, kindly attend to Ian for us." As Rose handed the wiggling boy to the maidservant, Jamie tousled the child's hair in passing. "A good night to you, lad. Your stepmother and I will visit the nursery later."

Stepmother. At least he'd clarified that point for the widow's sake. Knowing that Leana was settled in Twyneholm, would Morna Douglas jalouse the rest of the sordid details? Or assume that Jamie had been married before and was a widower?

The front door opened, then closed with a bang, heralding her father's return. Thank the heavens above, Eliza had already started up the stair with Ian; Lachlan McBride would not want the child included in their worship. He strode into the room and took his place at table once more, bidding them sit as he opened the thick, leather-bound *Buik.* It fell open to Psalms as if it, too, jumped to do the man's bidding.

Rose pulled her chair closer to Jamie's, longing to reach for his hand under the table. Longing to capture his heart as well. Might the warmth of her touch melt his resistance? Would he clasp her fingers and gaze fondly at her from the corner of his eye? Or would he simply ignore her? The risk was too great; she folded her hands in her lap and contented herself with a last look at his masculine profile, bent for prayer, before she closed her eyes as well.

Rose tried to follow all that her father said, yet her greater concern was keeping her lowered forehead from touching the table. *I will not give sleep to mine eyes, or slumber to mine eyelids.* Of all the psalms she'd been required to memorize, that one had proved the most useful, especially of late when she could barely stay awake past supper. Tonight of all nights she wanted to remain alert well after bedtime. For Jamie's sake. *And for mine.*

The prayer concluded, Rose lifted her head in time to see Lachlan jab his finger at a spot on the page. "Two passages command our attention this evening." He droned on and on, expounding on the verses, his words as monotonous as the tick of the mantel clock above the cold hearth. Although the kitchen fire was never extinguished, even on the hottest days, the hearths throughout the rest of the house had been swept clean for the summer at her father's insistence. Peat and coal required silver he was unwilling to spend. As the gloaming lingered, Rose felt the cooler night air creeping through the house. Jamie would keep her warm in their bed. Though he had yet to give her his heart, at least he'd not withheld the rest of him.

When Lachlan closed the Buik with a bang punctuating his last word, bringing their time of worship to a long-awaited end, even Morna looked relieved. Rose was doubly so and gathered her skirts to stand. "I beg your pardon, Mistress Douglas, but I must retire or chance falling asleep in my chair. Will you excuse me?"

Though Father glared at her, Morna was quick to set her free. Perhaps the woman wanted her future husband to herself for a quiet hour. Whatever would they talk about, different as they were? Ian would be one topic of discussion, of that Rose was certain. Wouldn't she love to hear her father explain *that* situation!

"Come, dear husband," Rose beckoned him, "for I dare not risk the steps alone."

Jamie dutifully guided her toward the second floor, saying nothing as they climbed the stair. A wise precaution with Lachlan and Morna just below them walking arm in arm to the parlor. Rose paused briefly at the nursery, satisfied to find Ian fast asleep, his chest rising and falling in a steady pattern. How she wished she might sing to him now, as Leana often had. *Baloo, baloo, my wee, wee thing.* But Rose knew her voice was neither sweet nor low and might wake the child besides. "Good night, precious boy," she whispered, closing the nursery door.

Moments later when Jamie followed her into their dimly lit bedroom, Rose spun about and wrapped her arms round his neck. "At last I have you all to myself."

"You've been most patient with me this evening, Rose." She did not see a spark of passion in his eyes to match her own, but his words were sincere, even contrite. "With guests beneath our roof, I should have been especially cordial. Instead I was—"

"Churlish?" she finished for him, winking as she said it. "Rude? *Ill-fashioned*?"

"All of those things, I'm afraid. Your father's behavior has grown more *hatesome* of late. As to the Douglas lads"—his sigh was heavy with regret—"I cannot bring myself to trust them."

"Jamie McKie, you're cannier than the three of them put together." She drew him closer, inhaling the scent of him. "Do not lose a moment's peace on their account, my *cliver* husband."

Her praise had the desired effect: The crease in his brow disappeared as he circled his arms round her waist. "I'm glad you find me clever, lass. Will you forgive me then?"

"I already have." Rose leaned into his embrace, nuzzling the curve of his neck. She was grateful for Hugh's expert hand with a razor; Jamie's skin was still smooth and tasted of heather soap. When she sensed him warming to her, she slowly turned in his arms, presenting him with a row of tiny buttons. "Can you manage, or shall I summon Annabel to help me dress for bed?"

After a moment's hesitation he began unbuttoning her gown, then paused at the plaintive cry of sheep bleating in the distance. Louder than usual, Rose thought, and greater in number. Perhaps it was nothing more than the moist evening air carrying the sound across the pastures. "Good night to you as well, lassies," she called toward the casement window as Jamie unfastened the last of her buttons. "May heaven watch o'er you 'til the break of day."

Nine

The flying rumours gather'd as they roll'd,
Scarce any tale was sooner heard than told.
ALEXANDER POPE

Have you forgotten what day it is?" Aunt Meg inclined her head toward the door "You know how folk will wag their heads if we don't appear at the stroke of ten."

Leana brushed her hands over the claret gown hanging from the cottage beams, smoothing out the last of the wrinkles. The women of Twyneholm parish were gathering in the parlor of the manse, as they did on the first Wednesday of every month, to share a plate of biscuits, ply their sewing needles, and join the minister in offering prayers for the congregation. By one o' the clock they would head for home, bits of gossip tucked in their pockets like pilfered sweets.

"Almost ready." Leana eyed the embroidered silk, looking for any blemishes she might have missed. A small dot of ink marring the right sleeve had come out with a dab of lemon juice. The streak of grease on the hem had proved no match for ground sheep's hooves, Neda's oft-tested remedy. Yesterday Leana had hung the dress outside to air, then carefully pressed it with a tailor's goose—a heavy iron with a gooselike neck—borrowed from Mr. Purvis. Leana smiled, satisfied with the look of it. No gown she'd ever owned meant more to her.

Aunt Meg stilled her hand. "Enough brushing, dearie. 'Tis ready to wear the Sabbath next."

Nae, Auntie. Leana would not feel the claret gown on her shoulders again. Though she had indeed worn it every Sunday in Twyneholm and many days in Newabbey, please God, it would soon serve a different purpose.

"The hour beckons, lass." Aunt Meg yanked open the painted door, then added in a stage whisper, "You look the same as the day you arrived. None will be the wiser."

Leana followed her out of doors into a thick morning mist. "I pray you are right."

Busybodies were the same in every parish, able to spot a guilty face and invent the rest. On the Sabbath last she'd slipped inside the kirk door at the second bell, then made a hasty exit when the service ended, hoping to keep her expanding waistline to herself. That morning her aunt had laced her cotton stays with care, giving her more room to breathe, though the whalebones still pinched in tender places. Would the ladies of the parish mark her discomfort and come to the same scandalous conclusion?

Leana took a deep breath of moist air and exhaled it with a fervent prayer. *I will trust in the covert of thy wings.*

Aunt and niece made their way across the graveled roadway constructed by English soldiers decades earlier, then joined arms to navigate the slippery path leading to the front door of the manse. The nicest home in the village, the minister's house was built of dark whinstone with sandstone dressings, freshly painted white. Despite her misgivings, Leana was ready to be inside and dry again. Warm, wet air, like suspended rain, clung to her clothes. Her unbound hair had expanded to a billowy cloud round her shoulders. More time dressing her hair and less time brushing the claret gown might have been prudent.

The door swung inward at the first tap. Lydia Scott, a tall woman of sixty years with fawn-colored hair and warm brown eyes, beamed at them from her threshold. "Here they are," the minister's wife called over her shoulder, then waved them inside. "We thought we'd lost you in the mist."

Leana followed her aunt into the manse, self-consciously touching a hand to her hair. The front rooms were already filled with women— sitting on straight-backed chairs, convening by the empty hearth, balancing china teacups on saucers, nibbling crisp lemon biscuits. And talking, all of them at once, their high voices like tinkling cymbals.

Leana and Meg mingled among them, trying not to knock their

teacups onto the patterned carpet, a rare find in village houses. Each wall was covered in painted paper, an intricate pattern of flowers and fruits that matched the rich colors of the carpet, and thick curtains dressed the long windows. Lydia Scott came from a wealthy family, it was said; the evidence was all round them.

Aunt Meg greeted each woman by name. "Mistress McCulloch," she said warmly, "how is your son? And, Mistress Palmer, glad to see you've brought Ann with you." Leana pretended not to notice the dusting of sugar beneath Grace Burnie's nose as the matron reached for another biscuit. Helen McGill, who'd dressed for a different season altogether, wore a faint sheen of perspiration across her brow. As for Catherine Rain, her mouth was drawn as tight as a closed purse, and her pointed gaze—aimed straight at Leana—was sharper than the sewing needles pinned to her bodice for safekeeping.

Leana averted her eyes, then turned her body as well. Did Mistress Rain suspect something? Moving to a different corner of the room, Leana found her place among a group of more amiable souls, women she'd spoken to before and knew a little. Though Leana had attended two such prayer meetings and never missed a Sabbath at kirk, there were many women in the large, rural parish she had yet to meet. She hoped her smile would suffice for manners, wishing only to be invisible for her last few days in Twyneholm.

"Miss McBride." An older woman elbowed her way closer, her voice like the bray of a donkey. "You are the very image of your mother, God rest her soul. Whatever has brought you to Twyneholm?"

One by one, heads turned in her direction. The loud chatter diminished.

"Tell us, Miss McBride." Another stranger spoke up. "Why are you here and not with your family in Newabbey?"

"*In trowth,* do tell," Janet Guthrie echoed, her speech thick with Scots. "Mony *fowk* have *wunnered* that verra thing."

Leana clasped her hands to keep them from shaking. She'd answered similar questions during her visit but never so many at once. "I am here because…that is, my aunt…"

Meg came to her rescue. "I insisted Leana visit me this spring.

Burnside Cottage gets *lanelie* with only the dogs for company." Round the room, heads nodded and expressions softened. "Besides, my niece is a fine gardener. You're invited to stop by on your way home and see for yourself."

Leana smiled at her, grateful for the reprieve. Meg had not insisted she come to Burnside, of course; Leana had pleaded for refuge. Nor was the gregarious Meg ever lonely.

"Come, ladies." Lydia Scott stepped to the center of the room, catching everyone's attention. "We've gathered to pray. Jeanie will collect your plates and cups. Kindly find a seat while I locate my husband."

The chairs were finely crafted oak—from Glasgow, if rumors could be trusted—not *creepies* made of pine like Meg had round her hearth, low to the floor, without backs or arms. Leana chose a roomy seat, and her aunt sat next to her, inching her chair closer. "Hold your chin up, lass," Meg said in a low voice, "for some of these *glib-gabbit* women are not easily convinced. I've been looking after beehives long enough to know that bees with honey in their mouths have stings in their tails."

Before Leana could respond, the Reverend Dr. John Scott strode into the room amid a flurry of greetings. Well educated and pious, he shepherded his flock with a firm but loving hand. In the pulpit and on broadsheets he bemoaned the rise in smuggling along the Solway coast, aware that most of his parishioners were involved in "free trading" to one degree or another. Aunt Meg was not above hiding smuggled salt in her cupboard to help one of her free-trading neighbors, especially when it meant receiving a pocketful of the precious commodity for her efforts.

Reverend Scott stretched out his arms, holding them over the assembly like the branches of a stalwart oak. "O thou that hearest prayer, unto thee shall all flesh come." A long time of intercession followed, with the minister speaking and the women listening. Every parishioner's need was laid before the Almighty—every need except Leana's unspoken one.

When the minister's prayer finally ended, he disappeared up the stair with his wife not far behind, requesting a moment of his time. As the women resumed their conversations, Leana sensed more than one curious glance directed toward her. Her aunt noticed it too.

" 'Tis because you are an outsider," Meg said softly. "*Fremmit.* A stranger, still new to the parish." She patted Leana's hand. "Think no more of it. You've brought something to stitch upon, aye?"

Leana held up her sewing bag. "My cotton stockings."

Meg looked round her for a moment before her face broke into a wide smile. "Aren't I the *sully* one? I left home in such a hurry I forgot my needlework." She rose, eying the door. " 'Tis but a short walk from the manse to Burnside Cottage. I'll be back before you finish the first seam."

"Meg…" Leana curled a hand round her aunt's elbow. "Would you do me a great favor? Might you…bring my claret gown with you?" Leana had only now thought of the possibility, seeing all the women together with none of the gentlemen about. "I'll explain when you return. Can you manage it by yourself?"

"Of course." A swish of her skirts and Aunt Meg was gone.

Leana pressed a hand to her throat, feeling her pulse beating hard against her fingers. Could she do so bold a thing? Hold up her gown at a parish gathering and offer it for sale? She feared it might otherwise take days, even weeks, to find a buyer. Yet she could not remain in Twyneholm a moment longer. If her many secrets were discovered, no good woman would want her company, let alone her claret gown.

Today, then—this very morning—she would sacrifice her dearest possession and pray it might pave the way to Auchengray.

Resolved, she fished her spectacles out of the hanging pocket worn round her waist, then put them on with care lest she bend the fragile silver frames. Her weak eyesight made them a necessity for sewing, reading, or reckoning long columns of numbers. With the spectacles in place, her surroundings came into sharper focus. So did the curious gazes of the women. Did they know more than she realized? Might offering her gown for sale only confirm their suspicions? Perhaps she'd acted too rashly in asking Meg to bring the dress with her.

Chagrined, Leana looked down at her sewing bag and was comforted by the familiar sight. Made of finely woven wool plaid with handles carved from ox horn, the sturdy bag was seldom far from her side. Rose had purchased it from a traveling packman selling his wares one spring day, then presented it to Leana for her birthday.

Years ago. A lifetime ago. When Rose still loved her.

Why haven't you written me, dearie? She knew why. Jamie and Rose were busy getting settled at Glentrool with no time or interest in sending letters. Blinking hard, Leana fumbled in her sewing bag for the cotton stockings she'd started working on *yestreen*. When her fingers touched the soft fabric, she pulled it out of the plaid bag and laid it across her lap, then angled her head to brush away her tears before they fell and stained her green dress.

When she turned back to her work, Leana discovered Barbara Wilkinson, the miller's wife, eying her lapful of cotton. "What's that you're making, lass? A gown for a bairn?"

Leana stared at the fabric in shock. Instead of her stockings, she had pulled out Ian's nightgown! The little sleeves, neatly embroidered, were splayed across her skirts for all to view.

"Such fine handwork." Mistress Wilkinson claimed the nightgown and held it up so the others might see. "Aren't these thistles a clever touch?" Round the room heads lifted and eyebrows as well, as the women regarded the small gown. The miller's wife turned back to Leana, her eyes bright with expectation. "This child must be very special indeed for you to stitch such a gown for him. Whose bairn is it?"

Ten

Truth does not blush.

TERTULLIAN

Leana hesitated, desperate to think of a proper answer. She could not lie. She could *not*. Nor could she tell the truth, not completely. "'Tis my…sister's child," she confessed. "Ian McKie of Glentrool." Truth enough, before God and man.

"Your sister's boy, you say?" Catherine Rain gave her a withering look. "My relatives in Newabbey tell me otherwise."

A low murmur swept through the room like an ill wind from the north, chilling Leana's heart.

Catherine's gaze narrowed. "Mary McCheyne is my cousin. Her name is familiar, I'm sure."

Leana well recalled the sharp words Mary McCheyne had cast at her like stones one dark Sabbath morning. *Ye're a filthy* limmer! *A* hizzie *o' the worst sort, stealin' yer sister's husband.* "I know your cousin," Leana admitted, struggling to keep her voice steady. "I saw Mary every Sunday at Newabbey kirk."

"On three particular Sundays, she saw *you* as well." Mistress Rain bared her teeth. "Climbing onto the stool of repentance…"

Nae!

"…for the sin of hochmagandy."

The women of Twyneholm gasped as one.

Leana pressed the cotton nightgown to her heart. A single word and she was on the dreaded stool once more. Put on disgraceful display where all might mock her. Rough sackcloth chafing her back. Bare feet against a cold stone floor.

Yet had she not confessed her sins and been forgiven?

Catherine Rain was standing now, bearing down on her. "'Tis time you told this parish the truth, Leana McBride: The child your sister is raising is your own son. Conceived in sin, born in shame. A bystart."

"Nae." Leana stood as well, supported by a power she knew was not her own. *The LORD is on my side; I will not fear.* "Ian McKie is none of those things." Her knees stopped wobbling. So did her voice. "Though Ian is the son of my womb, he is also the rightful son and heir of James McKie. Neither sin nor dishonor clouds their names."

Her adversary was quick to retort, "What of *your* name, *Miss* McBride?"

Looking directly at Catherine Rain, Leana spoke from her heart. "My reputation is of little consequence. Only that of my family matters. Ian McKie was conceived and born within the sanctity of marriage. His father, James McKie, was my husband, by habit and repute." Whispered asides swirled round each statement as every eye remained fixed on her.

Leana paused but only for a moment. Better to confess the whole of it rather than hear false rumors flying hither and yonder. "As to the charge of hochmagandy, I willingly served as a proxy bride for my sister's wedding, then presented myself to Mr. McKie in his darkened bed-chamber." She did not flinch at their horrified faces. "I thought he loved me. And he thought I was my sister, Rose. Both of us were…mistaken."

Catherine's smug look of satisfaction implied she'd heard the story before. "Then you were never his true wife."

"For a time I thought I was. My father appeared before the kirk session to have the records amended, striking out my sister's name and replacing it with mine. Alas, the notation was not properly recorded, a sad truth which we did not learn for more than a year, months after Ian was born." There was more she could say but no point in saying it; her hearers were already dumbfounded. Hands limp, jaws slack. "James McKie is now married to my sister, Rose—as, by law, he always was—and they have custody of my dear son. I have reason to believe they've returned to his family estate in Monnigaff parish."

"Where do *you* intend to live?" Barbara Wilkinson's words were threaded with condemnation. "Not in Twyneholm…"

Leana held up her hand, deflecting the woman's scorn. "I came to your parish for a brief season. When I wrote to my aunt, explaining my unfortunate situation, she opened Burnside Cottage to me." Leana glanced at the door, relieved that Meg had not witnessed her unforeseen confession. "I pray you will not think poorly of Margaret Halliday for such hospitality."

"We will not, Miss McBride." Lydia Scott stood at the foot of the stair. "You have already *compeared* before your own parish. We've no right to punish you here in Twyneholm."

Leana lowered her gaze, unaccustomed to such mercy. "You are... most kind."

" 'Tis God who is kind to us all." The minister's wife began to circle the room, weaving effortlessly round the jumble of chairs and sewing baskets. "When Miss McBride arrived in March, my husband was shown a sealed testimonial letter from Reverend Gordon. No one is ushered across parish boundaries without such a testimonial in hand." She turned toward Leana, her voice filled with gentle authority. "That letter confirmed Miss McBride's unwed state and moral repute."

When Catherine cleared her throat in protest, Lydia pinned her with a sharp look. "If John Gordon commended her to our parish, we need no other opinion." Defeated, Catherine sank back onto her chair as the minister's wife surveyed the room. Each woman's face bore a different emotion. Pity. Dismay. Remorse. Lydia's gaze seemed to fall on them all, one by one, pausing to look at Leana in particular. Mercy shone in the woman's brown eyes. "Forgive, and ye shall be forgiven," Lydia said simply. " 'Tis more than a fine text for a sermon. 'Tis the truth."

A sharp knock sounded at the door. Heads craned as Margaret Halliday was ushered back into the fold. Her sewing pouch was tied to her waist, and her silvery hair was the color of the mist. In her arms she carried the claret gown. On her face she bore a hopeful smile, which soon faded. "Have I...missed something?"

"Indeed you have." Lydia Scott nodded toward Leana. "While you were gone, we learned a great deal more about your niece. And her child."

"You...did?" The bit of color in Meg's wrinkled face quickly drained.

"I'm afraid so, dearie." Leana collected the damp gown and draped it over the chair behind her, then turned to face the stunned assembly. "My past indiscretions have followed me to Twyneholm."

"Oh, my poor niece." Meg smoothed her hands over Leana's hair, as if to calm her, though she was the nervous one. "This child of yours—"

"'Tis her *sister's* child now," Catherine Rain corrected her with a haughty sniff.

"Indeed not." Her aunt stiffened. "'Twill be Leana's bairn to raise, not her sister's. Come winter when the child is born—"

"Meg!" Leana cried, but it was too late.

Agitated comments flew round the room like a trapped bird trying to escape. "*Another* bairn?" "It canna be." "Who's the faither?" "Mebbe she doesna ken."

When their flapping died down, the women merely gawked at her, clutching their forgotten needlework. The air grew thick with their silence.

Leana looked heavenward, summoning the courage to speak. "My aunt has told you the truth: I carry a second child by Mr. McKie. Conceived when we thought we were rightly wed." The steadiness of her voice surprised her; with the fear of discovery gone, so was her shame. "The child will be born in my own parish. I hope to leave on Friday for Newabbey."

Aunt Meg gripped her arm. "But, Leana—"

"Nae, Auntie." She wrapped her in a brief embrace. "'Tis time. The good women of Twyneholm have weathered enough this morning." Leana turned toward the minister's wife. "I beg your pardon, Mistress Scott, for disrupting what should have been a peaceful hour of sewing."

"On the contrary, Miss McBride." Her voice, her gaze, bespoke uncommon grace. "You've demonstrated remarkable courage. 'Tis a more vital lesson than improving our needlework. All of us have learned something by your honest confession. Haven't we, ladies?"

Though no one spoke, their penitent expressions said enough.

Mistress Scott glanced down at the various sewing baskets strewn round the carpet, then shifted her gaze to Leana's chair. "I see your aunt brought along your pretty gown. Had you planned to mend it?"

"Nae." Leana swallowed the last of her fears. "I planned to sell it."

"*Sell* it?" Aunt Meg gaped at her. "Your best gown? Whatever for?"

"To raise the silver required to hire a chaise." Leana gathered up her gown, fragrant with the scent of lavender, and spread it before them. "While hardly new, it is clean and pressed, without spot or wrinkle. 'Twas my bridal gown. Made by Joseph Armstrong, a tailor in New-abbey village." She paused, uncomfortable at having to mention money. "Though it cost a good bit more, I need only fifteen shillings for my journey home. Even that may be asking too much—"

"Nae!" A chorus of voices responded at once.

"I'll gladly pay fifteen shillings for it." Grace Burnie leaned forward to touch the fine embroidery. "I've admired your gown every Sabbath since you arrived. Though I'm not so slender as you, I could easily have it altered."

"You could," Leana managed to say, bewildered to find them so interested.

"But 'twould fit me just as it is." Ann Palmer, one of the younger women present, pulled the gown toward her waist to prove it. "Mother, we could offer Miss McBride sixteen shillings for her gown, could we not?"

"If you think it suits you—"

"Well, it suits *me* better," Sarah McCulloch insisted with a toss of her auburn hair. "I have coins for Friday's market in my reticule and am prepared to pay eighteen shillings. Perhaps Miss McBride could use a bit of extra silver. For the bairn."

"Ye'll none o' ye *tak* it!" Janet Guthrie cried with glee. "Me dochter needs *sae* fine a *goun*. Twenty *shullins*, Miss McBride."

Leana stood transfixed, watching as one woman, then another, tugged at her gown, arguing over who might own it and for how many shillings.

"Miss McBride?" A familiar male voice carried across the room, silencing all the others. Reverend Scott appeared at the bottom of the stair. "From here, that gown looks quite new. Does it appear so to you, Mistress Scott?"

The older woman smiled, inspecting the gown more closely. "Not a mark or a blemish. Worthy of a bride, I'd say."

"My thoughts exactly." He moved across the sea of women, who parted to make way for him. "Our granddaughter will be married in the kirk next month. 'Twould please Mistress Scott and me to see her so adorned."

Worthy of a bride. Leana held out the gown with steady hands. "'Tis yours, then, for fifteen shillings."

"I said it looked new," he reminded her, laying the gown aside. "And I believe Mistress Guthrie offered you twenty. What, pray tell, did the gown cost your father?"

Dare she confess it? "Two pounds sterling," she said at last, appalled at the exorbitant figure. Indeed, she heard more than one stifled gasp.

The minister pulled a leather purse from his waistcoat pocket and shook the contents into his wife's open palm. "Pay the young woman her due."

Leana watched in disbelief as Lydia Scott pressed a fistful of silver into her empty hands. "Sufficient to see you safely home." Lydia smiled and closed Leana's fingers round the coins.

Stunned, Leana could only look at the two of them. The gracious wife. The generous minister. "Wh-why?" she finally asked. "Why would you do so charitable a deed after all I've admitted this morning?"

Reverend Scott took his time answering. "John Gordon wrote me soon after you arrived. The details of his letter were just as you confessed them here." He gestured toward the stair. "Pardon an old minister for eavesdropping."

Leana could not hide her confusion. "If you knew…then…"

"This is what I know." His tone brooked no argument. "Only a woman whose soul has been cleansed by the Almighty could speak so boldly of her past, certain of his mercy."

The minister drew his wife to his side. "The fruit of your womb is God's blessing on your life. The silver in your hands is ours."

With trembling hands Leana clasped the coins to her middle, praying her tears conveyed her thanks. *I am coming home, Neda. Home!*

"Return to the people you love, Leana." Lydia Scott rested her head on her husband's shoulder. "And to the ones who love you."

Eleven

If thou should kiss me, love,
Wha could espy thee?
If thou would be my love,
Jamie, come try me!

ROBERT BURNS

Rose gazed across the garden from beneath the wide brim of her bonnet, wondering if Jamie had spied her tiptoeing toward him. Ian was taking his afternoon nap, giving her a peaceful hour to seek her husband's company. She'd bathed her hair in rose water and donned his favorite blue gown. Might he notice?

Jamie was sitting under the yew tree engrossed in a book, his long legs stretched before him, his broad back pressed against the purplish-brown bark. The yew, taller than the house and older by centuries, had sheltered many a soul seeking respite from the heat. After two days of incessant rain and mist, Rose rather liked the sun on her shoulders, though nothing warmed her like the sight of the man she loved.

"Jamie," she called softly, not wanting to startle him. When he looked up with a hint of a smile on his face, her throat tightened. So handsome, this husband of hers! She ducked beneath the yew's branches, glad to have Jamie to herself in a cozy bower. "Why aren't you off counting your sheep," she teased him, "instead of reading that dreary book?"

His smile broadened. "Rab, Davie, and some of the other herds will arrive Monday noon for the shearing. 'Til then my flocks have little need of me. And grim as the subject may be, I'm enjoying my book." He held up Defoe's *The Journal of the Plague Year,* borrowed from Reverend Gordon's bookshelf. "Far more insightful than the Pepys account, eyewitness or not. Did you know a comet appeared in the London sky before the plague and another before the great fire?"

"Truly?" She reached for the slim volume, curious to see for herself. "I suppose 'twas a sign from the Almighty."

"Many a Londoner thought so."

When she scanned the page, several phrases caught her eye. "Doomed to be destroyed," she read aloud, shivering at the thought. " 'A blazing star… A rushing, mighty noise, fierce and terrible.' Oh!" She quickly closed the book, lest the pages singe her fingers. "Do you believe the Almighty speaks to his people in so kenspeckle a manner?"

"He spoke to me that way," Jamie reminded her, slipping the book out of her hand and tucking it inside his vest. "You've heard me describe my vision of winged creatures and a voice that roared like the sea."

The notion of Jamie's dream frightened her still. Could it possibly be true? "I've awakened from many a strange story," she confessed, "though I never imagined God as the author."

"Nor had I, Rose. Not until that October night I slept under the stars. I heard a voice say, 'Behold, I am with you wherever you go.' " Sincerity shone on Jamie's face, nigh to convincing her. "It was no simple dream, for I sensed his presence and answered him as well."

"I believe you," she said, trying hard to do so. If Jamie truly heard his voice, perhaps it meant he was…well, devout.

He chuckled. "Are you thinking I'm a bit daft, Rose?"

"Not at all." How *did* this man read her thoughts?

"Come." Jamie circled her wrist in a firm grasp and pulled her down onto his lap. She landed with a soft gasp, her skirts dragging across a carpet of dried berries and leaves. "I'll not have my young wife fearing her husband is *brainwode*."

"Your mind is quite sound," she assured him, thrilled when he drew her close. Soiled hems could be cleaned and wrinkled gowns ironed; only winning Jamie's heart mattered. "I am glad you are mine, Mr. McKie."

He gazed into her eyes for a moment, anticipation singing in the air like birdsong. "My sweet Rose," he murmured, before fitting his mouth to hers.

She responded at once, wanting there to be no doubt of her affection. *I love you, Jamie.* What she dared not put into words, she breathed into her kisses. And what he could not bring himself to say, she pretended to hear in his low sigh. *I love you, Rose.*

It was many minutes before she noticed the sound of male voices in the steading and the dampness of the ground beginning to seep into her skirts. "Oh, me." Flustered, she pushed back an abundance of wispy tendrils. "Jamie, perhaps we might…take a walk?"

"A worthy plan, dear wife." He laughed with his eyes first and then low in his chest. "The rough bark of the yew has left an imprint on my back." Jamie stood, then helped her to her feet and brushed the debris from their clothing. "Suppose we stroll round the gardens."

He ran his hand lightly over her braid, then slipped his arm round her waist as together they emerged into the sunshine, greeted by the musical *chi-chi-chi* and bright plumage of a greenfinch on the wing. Above them shone a cloudless sky, painted a pale blue gray, like Ian's eyes. Evidence of the recent rain was everywhere: The borders were as saturated as a sponge, creating puddles for them to dodge every few steps.

Jamie frowned at the unkempt rectangles of soil. "Auchengray's gardens are not what they once were."

"Eliza is too busy elsewhere." Rose gestured at the rows of freshly turned earth still waiting for *neeps,* radishes, lettuce, and peas to be planted. "I fear we may not have many fresh vegetables this season. Meanwhile, Annabel is trying to learn how to spin wool, with limited success. Now that Leana is gone…" Rose silently chastised herself. She'd not intended to mention her sister, especially not to Jamie and especially not today. But Leana came to mind so often 'twas hard to avoid.

The entire household quietly mourned Leana's absence—in the sewing room, the kitchen, the nursery, the stillroom, and in the gardens most of all. Weeds choked the beds where her gillyflowers grew, and her physic garden sorely needed tending. Leana's chair in the dining room remained polished but seldom used. Her apron hung on a kitchen hook, gathering dust. Even Ian grew fretful at times, looking round as though he expected his mother to appear.

Last Tuesday Rose had run to the top of the stair, certain she'd heard Leana's voice in the entrance hall. She'd been greatly disappointed—aye, and a tiny bit relieved—to discover a neighbor had come to call instead.

"Will she e'er return to Auchengray, Jamie?"

He did not answer her at once, but when he did, he sounded certain. "I do not believe she will. At least not until long after we've left for Glentrool." A look of concern crossed his face. "You did write her, Rose, and tell her we would not be departing until Lammas?"

"My letter should arrive at her door by Monday."

Jamie drew her to a stop at the edge of the rose beds, each shrub encircled with smooth rocks from Glensone Burn. Leana had doted on their mother's roses—grinding bones for fertilizer, watering the roots when the rain did not, staking new plants in a well-sheltered corner where the wind could not reach them. Though Rose was named for her mother's favorite flower, she did not care for their sharp thorns. Leana, however, loved every bloom: Maiden's Blush, Rosa Mundi, and the white Musk climbing the stone wall.

And you, Rose. Aye, Leana had nurtured her most of all.

Jamie tightened his arm round her, as if he sensed her shifting mood. "Do you miss your sister?"

She ran her fingertip across a firmly wrapped rosebud. "All of Auchengray does. Especially your son." A familiar ache crept into her throat. "I know so little about children, Jamie. I fear I may never be the mother Leana was nor the mother Ian deserves."

"That's not so," he countered, sounding as though he meant it. "I saw the look of wonder on your face the night he was born. You've cherished the lad from the first." When she only nodded, he bent closer. "After Hogmanay you will have a child of your own. Two bairns who need you."

"And a husband who needs me as well?"

Jamie kissed the hollow of her neck. "You can be sure of that."

She leaned against his chest, so happy it made her lightheaded. "The sun is warm, and I'm feeling drowsy. Take me up the stair. Please?"

He escorted her withindoors, acknowledging the servants in passing. The house was quieter than usual; her father had departed for Edingham Farm after breakfast. "To inspect my future holdings," Lachlan had said with a shrewd look in his eye. Rose was simply glad to have the man gone for the day.

A moment in the nursery confirmed that Ian was still fast asleep on his side, his legs folded, his arms curled round his head. Rose smoothed her hand across the lad's round bottom. Could she possibly love any bairn more than her sweet Ian? Though he was not a child of her womb, he was surely a child of her heart.

The couple left the nursery as quietly as they had entered, stepped into the cool of the bedroom, and latched the door. "'Tis pleasant in here." Rose walked across the room, wondering if his gaze followed her. She drew the curtains closed and lit a single taper, turning day into night. "Upon a bonny day in June, when wearing through the afternoon…"

"Enough of that plowman's poetry," Jamie protested lightly. "Duncan is ever singing the man's songs." When she returned to his side, he gathered her in a loose embrace. "Though he does have one fine tune. 'She is a winsome wee thing, this sweet wee wife o' mine.'"

"If you say so, Jamie." She pulled her braid round, fiddling with the ribbon. His unexpected endearments took her aback. Might he love her after all? "I met Rabbie Burns, you know. In Dumfries."

"You were on some dubious errand with a friend."

"My dear Jane." Her good friend from school, lost to her four months ago. Rose had survived her bout with croup, but Jane Grierson of Dunscore had not. "She compelled me to accompany her to the Globe Inn."

Jamie feigned shock. "My *heidie* lass frequenting public houses."

"One brief visit is hardly 'frequent,'" Rose said, swatting his chin with the tail of her braid, "though I've been called headstrong before."

"By me," he reminded her, "on several occasions."

Rose tightened the bow on her braid, mustering the courage to ask the question that nagged at her. "Do you mind awfully much, Jamie?" She studied the half smile on his face. "I am not my meek, *bowsome* sister."

His smile held, but just. "You are not Leana. But you are my wife."

"And you have…come to…accept this?" She bit her lip, wanting to ask more, afraid she'd asked too much.

"I have learned to be content," he said simply.

Precious little comfort there. Apprehension, like a thick whorl of newly carded wool, lodged itself in her throat. " 'Tis not what I'm asking, and you know it well."

A shadow moved across his face, then was gone. "You are asking if I love you as I once loved you."

"Nae, Jamie. I am asking if you love me as you once loved Leana. With all your heart, holding nothing back."

He released her from his embrace, a faint stain on his cheeks. " 'Tis not a fair question, Rose. You and your sister are very different women."

Dejected, she turned away from him. "Not when it comes to whom we love."

Twelve

Gather the Rose of love,
whilst yet is time.

EDMUND SPENSER

O ch!" Jamie stamped about the straw-covered floor, disgusted with himself. Evening sunlight poured through the open barn doors, but his mind was elsewhere—namely, with his wife hours earlier. *I have learned to be content.* What sort of response was that? Rose—his darling, infuriating, adorable Rose—had bared her soul to him. And what had he done? "I quoted Scripture to her, Duncan. Scripture!"

The overseer nodded sagely, dragging the sharpening stone across the beveled blade of his shears in long, even strokes. "A guid source, the Buik. *Fu' o'* wisdom. Whan yer ain wirds canna say what ye mean, 'tis a fitting place tae turn."

Jamie glowered at him. "And when a man cannot say what he should, 'tis a poor place to hide."

Duncan held the shears closer to the lamplight, inspecting his work. "Aye, thar are some wha use the Buik like a *shiel.* Not tae hold back the enemy, mind ye, but tae fight the Almighty."

Jamie dropped onto a tall wooden stool and jammed his boot heel onto one of the rungs. "It's not the Lord I'm struggling against. Not this time."

"So ye say." Duncan wiped the blades clean with a rag, then hung the tool on a nearby peg, ready for Monday's shearing. "I suppose ye think 'tis young Rose ye're *warslin* then."

Jamie shrugged rather than face a question he did not want to answer.

"Or mebbe ye're warslin with Jamie McKie." He folded his polishing rag and stored it on a rough-hewn shelf, then clasped Jamie's arm, giving him a firm shake. "I've a notion ye're needin' tae fight a battle that ye can win. I ken the verra place for an evenin' skirmish: the River Nith."

In no mood for riddles, Jamie shrugged off Duncan's friendly gesture. "What does the Nith have to do with me?"

Duncan's piercing blue eyes pinned him to the spot. "Twa days o' rain means the river's in spate. Ideal for *nicht* anglin'. Sea trout from the Nith make a fine breakfast."

"Are you suggesting we go *fishing*?"

"I've an extra rod and plenty o' nets. If Rose doesna mind, ye'll not be missed." Duncan inclined his head. "Unless ye have nae skill wi' rod and tackle—"

"I can manage." Jamie was already ashamed of sparring with the man. Duncan was his ally, not his adversary. If he wanted a partner for angling, so be it. Jamie started for the mains, calling over his shoulder, "Allow me a moment with Rose…"

"Ye'll want tae change yer clothes," Duncan called after him. "Dark colors so the fish willna spy ye."

Jamie headed up the stair, certain he'd find Rose in the nursery. Their afternoon tryst had ended badly. 'Twas best set aright at once, or neither of them would sleep well. When he reached the landing, he heard her alto voice, slightly off-key, singing a cradlesong to his son.

> Hush-a-ba, birdie, croon, croon,
> Hush-a-ba, birdie, croon!
> The sheep are gane to the silver wood,
> And the coos are gane to the broom, broom.

His throat tightened at the familiar words from his Glentrool childhood, once sung by a woman with a voice much like Rose's. *Rowena McKie.* Though his mother was demanding, she loved him completely. So did Rose.

Jamie continued up the stair, joining in the next verse, hoping his wife might hear him. And forgive him.

And it's braw milkin' the kye, kye,
It's braw milkin' the kye...

His words faded when he realized she had stopped singing. Disconcerted, he tapped on the nursery door before stepping into the room, lit by a single window.

Rose was sitting in the only chair, her head bowed. Ian lay curled in her arms, nigh to asleep, a linen blanket tucked beneath his chin. One small fist clasped the neckline of her gown. Her silence, so unlike his *blithesome* wife, unnerved him. Jamie dropped to one knee beside her. "What is it, Rose?"

She looked up, her eyes bright with tears. "Oh, Jamie. I thought..." Her voice broke, and she tried again. "When I asked you...this afternoon..." She turned her head away, though not before he saw the first tear fall.

"Rose, look at me. Please." He placed one finger under her chin and gently angled it toward him, lowering his head until their eyes met. "You asked me a question no wife should have to ask her husband."

She jerked away from his touch, her braid sweeping across her back. "My question was unfair, Jamie. When you left our bedroom and then were so quiet at supper, I thought..." Rose sagged across Ian, her cheek resting on the sleeping child. "I was afraid you were...angry with me."

"I am only angry with myself," he confessed, meaning it. How could he have been so thoughtless to have punished her for speaking the truth? Jamie brushed his lips against her hair, still fragrant with rose water. *My fair Rose.* He kept his voice low, trying not to wake his child yet wanting to comfort his wife. "You have nothing to fear, Rose. Your sister is gone. And I am here."

"Promise me..." He almost didn't hear her, so soft was her voice. "Promise me you will...stay."

"Always." Jamie stilled, breathing in the heady scent of her, feeling the warmth of her beneath him, the silky softness of her hair against his mouth. *Dearest Rose.* Without plot or scheme, the charming lass had won his heart all over again.

He was not angry with her. He was in love with her.

Jamie closed his eyes, letting the truth sink in. After months of holding her at bay, surrender was sweeter than he could have imagined. A declaration of love waited on his lips. Only pride kept him from confessing it aloud.

Her head lifted ever so slightly. "Will you help me tuck Ian into bed?"

Jamie gathered the child in his arms, then stood and lowered Ian into his crib, careful not to wake him. Rose watched him from her low perch, drying her tears with her sleeve. "What a good father you are."

"Would that I were a better husband." His arms empty once more, he pulled Rose to her feet and into his embrace. "Forgive me, lass."

"Only if you will forgive me." She pressed her cheek against his chest. "For all of it."

"'Tis behind us now, Rose." He softly kissed her brow, then her cheeks, then her lips, hoping she might taste the words he could not quite say.

As they stood, wrapped in each other's arms, Jamie dearly wished he'd not made plans for the evening. Yet he could not fail Duncan after all the man had done for him. Jamie vowed to make it up to her the minute he returned. "Rose..." He leaned back, wanting to be certain she saw the apology in his expression. "Duncan has invited me to join him for a spell of night angling on the Nith. We shan't be gone but a few hours. Will you mind?"

She looked up, a ghost of a smile on her face. "My Jamie...fishing? I did not know you were a sportsman."

"I am not, which Duncan will soon discover." He rested his hand lightly on Ian, though he kept his gaze locked with hers. "I'll not be long."

"Shall I wait up for you?" The desire in her eyes was unmistakable.

"'Twill be well after midnight." He berated himself the moment the words were out of his mouth. Why didn't he say what he meant? *Yes. Wait for me.*

"If I am asleep, kindly wake me so I might..." Her cheeks grew pink. "So I might welcome you home."

Her invitation was clear. And gladly accepted. "I will indeed awaken you, Rose," he murmured, leaning over to steal a kiss. He lingered there until he was certain she heard what remained unspoken. "'Til midnight then."

Duncan met him on the lawn, two long, painted rods in hand. Neatly mended nets and a bulky angling purse hung from his lanky form. He pointed to the creel at his feet. "'Tis the younger man's duty, totin' the fish." He strapped the long wicker basket to Jamie's shoulders, then aimed him east toward the village. "Nae man can tether time or tide. Like Simon Peter, we go afishin'."

Jamie could not help smiling. "Lead the way, Duncan." Though Rose's company was sweeter by far, he would not begrudge his friend a brief outing. They had the narrow country road to themselves, the edges lined with *dry stane dykes*—stone fences fitted together without mortar—and beyond them, grazing sheep. Bits of wool caught on the lower branches of the shrubs, giving the bushes and hedgerows fleecy skirts.

By the time the sun disappeared below the horizon, they'd be in the river casting their lines a dozen *ells* across the water. And not long after, Jamie reminded himself, he'd be home again, twining himself round Rose. His first love and his last. Tonight he would tell her so and put her fears to rest.

Duncan's easy manner made the miles beneath their feet pass quickly. The seasoned angler knew the shortest route to his favored beat near Airds Point and the safest approach into the water.

"Get yer footin'," Duncan cautioned as they waded into the shallow river and planted their boots on slabs of rock rather than risk the silt deposited round them. "The tide is risin' wi' the moon." Though it was cooler by the river, the air was redolent with the earthy scents of summer. Fronds of wet bracken lined the shoreline. Muddy seaweed washed up from the Solway and clung to their boots. Above them, the clear, bubbling call of the whaups ushered in the night, while below, the trout ascended with the tide.

Duncan handed him a slender wooden rod twice his height, then gauged the water with an expert's eye. "Mend the line upstream, then sink the fly afore the current catches it. And dinna be splashin' round. Sea trout are easy tae *fleg,* mair than yer Cree salmon."

The sky was a velvety black, carpeted with stars, when Duncan pulled the first fish out of the rising waters. "You *niver* tail a sea trout," he explained, breathless with exertion, plunging his net into the water. Together they lifted the stout fish and flopped it onto the riverbank. "Nigh tae half a stane."

Determined not to be outdone, Jamie cast his line, then pulled, the fly barely skimming underneath the surface of the water. The sounds of the night settled into a low murmuring as he and Duncan exchanged shepherd lore and waited for another fish to bite. Jamie's feet were growing numb from the cold water round his boots when his line tightened with a satisfying snap.

"*Haud* yer ground!" Duncan abandoned his own line and grabbed the net.

The sea trout, well conditioned from feeding in the Solway, fought valiantly, but Jamie did not give one inch. With Duncan's help, the enormous fish was wrestled into the net, nearly dragging them both into the Nith before they pulled it free of the water and carried their prize to dry land.

Duncan slapped him on the back. "I've not seen a finer catch."

Jamie wiped his brow with his forearm, hiding his elation at catching a far bigger fish than Duncan's. He nodded at the creel, where Duncan's trout was already stored. "You did all right yourself."

The older man shrugged. "Better a *sma'* fish than an empty dish. Suppose we head hame and catch a bit o' sleep afore the cock crows."

"Sleep." Jamie grinned. "Aye, there's that." The men gathered their belongings, then headed west, with Jamie toting the creel on his shoulders. Despite the added weight, his step was light and his spirits jubilant.

When they neared the last bend in the road before Auchengray, Duncan gave him a genial shove sideways. "Ye smell like a brackish river, and that's nae mistake. Rose might serve *ye* for breakfast."

Jamie rolled his eyes in mock disdain. "I hear Neda has a pan waiting for your sorry hide as well." Once inside Auchengray's kitchen, they lit a taper at the hearth, then found the necessary tools. After filleting the fish, they washed them in cold water and doused their dark olive green skins with salt.

"Me wife will handle the rest," Duncan said, leaving his fish beside Jamie's on the kitchen dressing table, where meat was dressed for cooking. "They're none too appealin' *noo,* but come the *morn's morn,* the aroma o' trout rolled in oatmeal and fryin' in butter will call ye tae a *gustie* breakfast." He pointed in the direction of the well, less than a furlong from Auchengray's door. "Let us see tae our ablutions, Jamie. Then I'll bid ye guid nicht."

After borrowing a cake of heather soap from the stillroom, the men headed back out of doors. Stripped down to his *sark,* Jamie scrubbed hard, one thought on his mind. *Rose.* Moments later, still drying his face with the tails of his shirt, he strode through the house, propelled by desire, recalling his vows twice spoken. *I, James Lachlan McKie, do take this woman.*

When he unlatched the bedroom door, he heard a slight stirring.

"Jamie?" Rose called out softly. "Come to bed, for I've been waiting so long."

"Too long." He reached for the flickering candle on the high dresser and carried it to their bedside table. Needing to see her. Wanting her to see him. She made room for him as he climbed inside the shadowy confines of their wooden bed.

Tentative fingers touched his damp cheek as her gaze searched his. "You look like a man bursting with news. Did you catch something?"

"I did." A sense of peace washed over him, more cleansing than the well water. He kissed her soft cheek. Then the other, just as soft. "I caught a beauty. With long hair and dark, sparkling eyes."

"Jamie!" Those very eyes widened in horror. "A fish with *hair?*"

His laugh was low, his gaze focused on her mouth. " 'Tis not a fish I've caught but a *loosome* wife." He kissed her thoroughly, meaning to steal her breath, losing his own instead. "My lovely Rose," he murmured, sliding his hands down her back, inching her closer, burying his face in her unbound hair. "For an impatient woman, you've been most patient with me."

"Jamie…" He heard the smile in her voice, felt her heart beating against his. "Did you *eat* that heather soap or only bathe in it? For I fear the lye has gone to your head."

"Nae, lass." Jamie leaned back, just far enough to meet her gaze. "'Tis *you* who have gone to my head. And to my heart. I love you, Rose."

"Oh, Jamie!" Her eyes shimmered in the candlelight. "Can you possibly mean what you say?"

He kissed her tears away, tasting their salty sweetness. "I do."

"'Tis too much to hope for," she whispered before his mouth found hers.

Thirteen

Hope is a good breakfast,
but it is a bad supper.
SIR FRANCIS BACON

O ch, poor Leana!" Aunt Meg's hand gripped the wheel spokes of
the chaise. "Are you certain of this? 'Tis an *unchancie* venture.
Traveling with a stranger. Arriving where you're not expected. Telling
your father news he will not care to hear."

Leana eyed the driver, who stood some distance away bargaining
with a traveling packman. She leaned over the side of the hired chaise
and motioned her aunt closer. The pocket full of coins tied round her
waist bolstered her courage. "God has provided more than enough silver for my fare." Her thoughts settled on the treasured bairn inside her.
"And he's given me good reason to return home."

"The best of reasons." Every line in Meg's pale face was visible in
the bright morning sunlight. "Though I cannot help feeling anxious."

Leana tipped forward to plant a kiss on the woman's cheek. "Auntie,
however can I thank you?"

"The blessing was mine, lass." Meg's chin began trembling in
earnest. "Agness loved you dearly. As much as you love your Ian. She'd
be proud of the *gracie* woman you've become." Her aunt reached inside
the chaise and squeezed Leana's gloved hands. "Write me the minute
you alight at Auchengray, or I won't sleep a wink for worrying."

The driver, Mr. Belford, a stick of a man with straight legs and
crooked teeth, ambled up to the chaise, then climbed in effortlessly and
landed on their shared seat with a bounce. "Ye ready, mem?"

"Almost." Leana gazed fondly at her aunt, who'd backed a few steps
away.

"God be with you, dearie." Meg pressed a handkerchief to her nose.
Leana could only nod, so tightly closed was her throat. As the two-

wheeled chaise lurched away from Burnside Cottage, she turned to watch the silver-haired woman slowly disappear from view. "And God be with you, Auntie," she finally called out, waiting as long as she could before settling back on the thinly padded seat. The chaise had seen better days; the open vehicle's stiff bonnet was worn thin, and the springs beneath them complained when the wooden wheels hit a rut in the road. But the weather was dry, and their horse had a lively gait. And she was going home.

Mr. Belford gestured toward the appealing prospect at the high crossroads. "Have ye a leuk." Rolling green countryside unfurled in all directions beneath a gentian blue sky. " 'Tis a fine Friday we're havin'," he said as though testing her, seeing if she were the sort of passenger who'd pass the hours in spirited discourse or a quiet fare who preferred to ride in solitude.

Leana hoped she would not disappoint the man by being the latter. She had much on her mind and no energy for discourse. Nor was the hearty breakfast Meg had insisted she eat—fresh trout from the burn— sitting well on her stomach. Leana aimed her gaze at the distant hills. " 'Tis a lovely day indeed."

She'd traveled the same road the week before *Pasch*—Easter, the English called it—on a cold and rainy Sabbath eve. How different things looked riding in the opposite direction on a sunny June morning. A flock of redpolls flew overhead, too high to be seen but easily recognized by their loud, twittering song. All through the hedgerows grew red campion, its deep pink leaves showy against the green foliage. Fingers of light penetrated the chinks between the stones of the dry stane dykes that divided the pastures. And round the tree trunks climbed yellow honeysuckle. Hadn't she gone for a walk each evening to drink in the sweet scent?

The chaise continued its steady pace as the road began to undulate across the countryside. Whitewashed stone farmhouses came and went, each one a poignant reminder of home. What would be blooming at Auchengray now? Sweet cicely by the roadside perhaps, but nothing in her gardens, of that Leana was certain. She'd left the household without a bit of instruction during the most critical gardening months. Eliza had probably inherited the task. She might welcome the return of her mistress if it signaled an end to her weeding duties.

Her father's reception was the one that worried her. Lachlan McBride did not like surprises or anything that might bring reproach upon his household; before the day ended, Leana would accomplish both. Would he accept the situation? Or close the door in her face?

She had considered writing her father, alerting him of her plans. But that meant explaining on paper what compelled her to come home. *I am carrying Jamie's child.* Far better done in person. It would have taken days for the letter to arrive and another week for a response, if she'd even received one. Every hour between letters would have been agony—envisioning his face, fearing the worst. This was the best way, the only way.

She would, however, send a letter to Glentrool. Jamie must know the truth. Rose, who wanted a child so badly, would be crushed. And Jamie—*oh, dear Jamie!* Would he be angry with her? Hurt? Or might he no longer care?

Grief came over her like a fever, heating her skin, twisting her stomach. Though she was returning to Auchengray, she would not find Jamie shepherding his flocks. Or Ian waving his arms, asking to be held. *Mama-ma-ma.* It might be years before she saw her son again. Unless Jamie brought Rose home for a visit, and then it could never be long enough.

Ian, my Ian. Leana pressed a gloved hand to her mouth, holding back her tears. She never should have left him, not for any reason, however noble it might have seemed. Would he ever forgive her? Would she ever forgive herself?

She imagined the nursery at Auchengray—empty, silent—and prayed she might still find a remnant of Ian's clothing or some lingering scent in the air. Anything to remind her of the son she could no longer claim. Two bedrooms would be vacant on that floor as well. Might she be given the box bed she'd slept in as a girl? Or the bed she'd once slept in as a wife? With Jamie.

Feeling ill, she gripped the driver's arm. "Please…please, might we stop?"

He brought the Cleveland bay to an easy halt. Leana alighted from the chaise and left her breakfast in the shallow ditch by the side of the road. She knew the trout was not to blame; 'twas fear, well warranted.

Leana stood, weaving a little. At least she'd managed to spare her green gown—her only gown at the moment. Mr. Belford offered his clean handkerchief, then lifted her back into the chaise. Mortified, she looked down at her feet and prayed she would not embarrass herself again.

They were on their way a short time later, the dry road hastening their progress. "Keltonhill approaches," he said pleasantly as if nothing had happened. "Four hours to Newabbey, mem. We'll stop at Carlinwark for dinner."

Dinner? She couldn't imagine anything less appetizing. Perhaps she might remain in the chaise while he took his meal.

They soon clattered across the Brig o' Dee, aimed for the quiet village of Rhonehouse on Keltonhill. A fortnight hence the handful of inns they passed would overflow with revelers from Ireland, Cumberland, and beyond as they gathered for the annual horse fair. She'd never attended—Father would not allow it—but Duncan would no doubt spend a long Tuesday among the avenue of tents.

The terrain flattened as they neared Carlinwark, which appeased her churning stomach. It also meant they were closer to home. Mr. Belford brought the chaise to a jarring stop at the Three Thorns Inn. "*Wull* ye be havin' dinner, Miss McBride? 'Tis included in yer fare, ye ken."

"Tea would be lovely." She swallowed the sour taste in her mouth. "And toast."

Above the door swung a battered sign with three hawthorn trees carved into the wood, the paint lost to the elements. Sunlight gave way to a dim interior of scarred tables and peasant faces. Leana sat by herself while Mr. Belford, obviously a frequent patron, chatted with the scullery maids loitering near the kitchen door. The smell of bacon grease made Leana's stomach rise and fall like a jolly boat lowered into a tempestuous sea. An indifferent serving girl presented her with a dinner plate before she could refuse. Leana was grateful for the lukewarm tea but left the kale brose uneaten. She took the small portion of cheese with her, lest her appetite reappear during the second part of their journey.

They would not be stopping again; her next meal would be taken at Lachlan's table. As they climbed back into the chaise, she prayed for strength. *Thou art my father, my God, and the rock of my salvation.* No other foundation had proved so trustworthy.

Mr. Belford seemed eager to be rid of his *fauchie* passenger, urging the horse to lift his feet. Or perhaps the man had another fare waiting. They would arrive at Auchengray with many hours of daylight left. Too many. She was already weary, and the day held far greater hurdles.

With each mile, Leana's trepidation increased. She tried to order her thoughts, to plan what she might say, but her mind was unfocused and her pulse fluttery. Who might greet her at the door? Would she spill out her news at once? And what would they say? *We missed you, Leana! Why are you here, Leana? Begone with your fertile belly, Leana.*

As they descended the steep road approaching Haugh of Urr, she presented her square of hard cheese to Mr. Belford, doubting she would ever eat again.

The chaise halted at the crossroads as they waited their turn. A shepherd and his dogs were herding a flock of sheep across the road that led to the Urr parish kirk and, farther south, to Dalbeaty. Leana gazed after them, reminded of her father's winter jaunts to a widow's farm in the neighborhood, and wondered if anything had come of his visits. "What do you know of Edingham?" she asked her driver.

"Owned by a wealthy widow," Mr. Belford was quick to answer. "House sits on the spur of a hill. Nice bit o' land with cattle. Three sons, not a wife among them." His brown eyes assessed her. "Mebbe a husband at Edingham for ye, Miss McBride?"

A tightening round her heart, no more. "I…do not wish…to marry."

The truth, Leana. No gentleman would choose a wife with another man's seed growing inside her. Her only hope had been Jamie. And Jamie was gone.

She pressed her hand to her waist. Not entirely gone. Her hands would still be busy; her life would still be full. A child offered hope enough for any woman's future. The thought of bearing Jamie's son or daughter comforted her, calmed her. Reverend Gordon would baptize the bairn, then see to his or her *kirkin* on that first, important Sabbath visit to church.

But when Reverend Gordon came to mind, the dreadful words he'd spoken one dark March night came too. *The sole responsibility of caring for the boy will fall to his father, James McKie, and to his stepmother, Rose McKie.* Leana gasped aloud, forgetting where she was, seeing nothing before her but the stony faces of the kirk elders.

"Miss?" The chaise driver gripped her elbow, as if he feared she might tumble onto the gravel when they jolted forward. "Are ye feelin' poorly again?"

"I am…fine." She forced the words from her lips, reminding herself that Jamie and Rose had already left the parish. Giving them custody of *this* child would not be so easily accomplished. Nor would Leana allow it. Not for one moment.

She sat up straighter as they climbed the last hill before turning east, her hands folded in her lap—stiff, numb, determined. Newabbey parish came into view, with the austere tower of Drumcultran standing sentry. Across the valley rose Lowtis Hill. Two miles beyond it, home.

Leana clasped her hands tighter, pleading for strength. *He giveth power to the faint.* Too soon they rounded Lowtis Hill and turned onto the road that led past her gate. Maxwell Park. Lochbank Farm. Glensone. Troston Hill.

"Auchengray," Mr. Belford announced, turning up the lane leading to the mains. She held her breath as the whitewashed farmhouse rose before her. Unchanged. Unwelcoming. Even on a bright day, the dark row of windows peered at her like eyes. *Please God, let me find Neda. Or Duncan. Not Father, not first.*

The steading was deserted—unusual in the middle of the afternoon, but fortunate. She could pay the man his fare and send him on his way, then face the household without the embarrassment of an onlooker.

"You have been most kind, Mr. Belford."

" 'Tis me pleasure," he said dryly, sliding her silver inside his purse. "I'm certain yer family wull be glad tae see ye." He unloaded her small traveling case and writing desk and deposited them on the grass. With a tip of his cap, he was back in the chaise. "A guid day tae ye, mem."

She watched him ride off while she kept her back to the house, afraid to think of who might see her first.

"It canna be." An older man's voice carried across the lawn. "Is that Miss McBride?"

Leana spun round. "Willie!"

The servant tottered toward her as fast as his bent legs could carry him. "Och!" His wrinkled smile was welcome enough. "We ne'er *thocht* tae see ye again, Miss."

She held out her hands to clasp his, not minding for a moment the leathery feel of them. "I am sorry 'twas not you who brought me home, Willie."

He ducked his head. "It doesna matter how ye got here, only that ye did."

"Is Neda in the kitchen?"

"She is." When she released him, Willie shyly stepped back. "And wait 'til yer sister sees ye."

Leana's heart stopped. "My…*sister*? Surely Rose isn't here?"

"She is indeed. They're all here."

"*All?*" Her mouth fell open. "But…Glentrool…"

"Leavin' in August, they are. Guid thing ye came noo."

Leana began to walk forward. "Aye," she breathed. "It *is* good." She was already past him, her traveling case forgotten. Her gaze was trained on the front door.

If Rose was here, then Jamie was here. *Oh, my dear Jamie!* And if Rose and Jamie were still at Auchengray…

Leana was running now. Pins fell from her hair as she grabbed her skirts, desperate to make her way across the lawn. The others must wait. She had to see him, *must* see him, had to hold him in her arms.

At once. Now.

"Ian!" She cried his name on a sob, flinging open the door.

A blur of stone steps awaited her, leading to the nursery, leading to her son. She stumbled up the stair. Crying, laughing, delirious with joy. "Ian, my Ian!" She whirled about on the landing, gasping for breath, hanging on to the banister for dear life.

"Leana?"

It was Rose. Standing near the top of the stair. Guarding the nursery door.

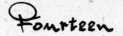

Fourteen

Do not come among women abruptly…
they do not love to be surprised.
ADAM PETRIE

Rose stared at the woman on the landing as if she were a stranger. Indeed, she *was* a stranger. The wheat-colored hair beneath her hat was in disarray, her pale face was flushed, and she was behaving rather hysterically. Like a madwoman.

"My sweet sister!" Leana flew up the stair, arms outstretched, and enveloped her in a crushing embrace. "I cannot believe it." Leana's cheek, wet with tears, pressed against her own, dry but hot. "Rose, 'tis a miracle! You're *here;* you're still here."

Leana. Come back from Twyneholm, like one come back from the dead.

"We cannot…leave for…Glentrool yet," Rose said, fighting to catch her breath. And trying to gather her wits, which had scattered like Eliza's garden seeds. "Not until…Lammas."

"That's what Willie said." Leana released her at last and took a deep enough breath for both of them, then exhaled on a lyrical sigh. "I cannot tell you how glad I am to be home. We have much to talk about, Rose. *So* much. Tonight, after supper. Oh, dear…" Leana touched her hand to her heart, a familiar gesture. "I haven't even spoken to Father yet."

Rose had never seen her sister this animated. "Leana, are you quite all right? You seem…"

"*Aflocht!*" Leana finished for her, laughing again. "Neda's word to describe *you* when you were a wee lass and got in a flutter about something." She plucked her bonnet from her head, releasing what remained of her braided coiffure, and fanned her poppy-colored face. "I could blame the heat or the long ride in the chaise or my tight stays. But it's finding you here that has me in a dither." She patted her cheeks dry. "I feared I might ne'er see you again, dearie."

"And I, you," Rose said, still reeling. Where was Jamie? Did he know she was home?

Leana tossed her hat onto the broad window sill and stepped toward the closed nursery door. "May I...may I see Ian?"

Rose stiffened. "He's sleeping."

"I'll not wake him," Leana promised, easing past her.

Rose stayed close on her heels. "I put him down for his nap before you arrived." Her tone was wary, protective. *Ian is mine now.*

"But I must see him." Leana turned and touched her hand, as if seeking her permission. "You understand, Rose. I know you do."

Fear drew a tight cord round her throat. She understood only too well: Leana would steal Ian's heart and never let go.

The nursery door creaked open. Her sister's footsteps were silent against the wooden floor, an experienced mother approaching her son's crib. Rose followed her, already feeling like an intruder. Late afternoon sunlight streamed through the window, warming the small room. The hurlie bed with its blue and white embroidered coverlet was pushed aside, no longer in use, along with the tiny cradle Ian had slept in the first few months.

Now he lay in the larger crib Willie had fashioned for him, truly asleep, his limbs splayed across the cotton sheet. His sweet mouth, shaped like Jamie's, hung slightly open. His eyes were shut tight.

Leana sighed as if she'd been holding her breath since Twyneholm. "My darling boy." She slowly knelt beside the crib, tucking her skirts beneath her like a nest. Her voice was soft as air. "Look how you've grown." She reached toward him, visibly trembling as she examined his tiny fingers, his smooth hair, his round cheek.

Ian stirred, but only a little, at his mother's touch.

Rose sank to the floor next to her sister, a dozen conflicting emotions tying her in knots. "Please don't wake him," she pleaded, then felt foolish for saying so. "If he misses his afternoon nap, he's irritable all evening."

Her sister nodded but did not take her eyes off Ian. "You were the same way, Rose. When you were Ian's age, Neda and I tiptoed through the house from three 'til five o' the clock and insisted everyone else do the same." After her exuberant arrival, Leana seemed to be winding down, easing back into motherhood. "I'll not wake the lad," she murmured, "for I know he needs his sleep."

The longer she studied her son, the quieter Leana grew. She planted a kiss on her fingertip, then barely touched it to his nose. Kissed it again, then brushed it against his lips. She traced the delicate curve of his ear and the line of his chin, caressing him with her gaze, her cheek pressed against the edge of the crib. "Ian, I've missed you so." Her voice was low, thick, as if she'd just swallowed honey. "Can you ever forgive me?"

The lad's steady breathing was the only sound in the nursery.

Tears began rolling down Leana's cheeks. Her features did not crumple, nor did she make a sound, as if she were unaware of the tears flowing beyond her chin and marking her green gown with dark circles. Then she began to sing so faintly that not all the words had notes.

> Baloo, baloo, my wee, wee thing,
> For thou art doubly dear to me.

Doubly dear. Rose looked away, undone by the tenderness in Leana's voice and the undeniable love on her face. However much she adored Ian, her sister loved him exceedingly more. How could she not? She had carried the boy beneath her heart and nourished him at her breast. Leana belonged to Ian completely, and he to her. No bond was more sacred, no love more secure.

Rose forced herself to look at them, mother and son, and thought of the child growing inside her. Could she imagine for one moment allowing another woman to raise her child as long as she still had breath? Nae, she could not.

Yet Leana had left Ian. Had left Jamie. Had left Auchengray.

For me. The realization pierced her afresh. *She left for my sake. So I might learn to love Ian. So Jamie might learn to love me.*

Rose stood, overwhelmed and more than a little frightened. She *did* love Ian. And Jamie loved her. He'd finally told her so yestreen and shown her as well. She was glad to see her sister, but Leana could not *stay.* She could not simply come home and…and…

"Rose, what is it?" Leana was standing now as well, her cheeks still moist. "You don't look well, dearie." She took Rose's hands in hers, rubbing them. "Are you eating properly? Sleeping enough? Perhaps I might I find some remedy in the stillroom. Sweet flag or chamomile?"

Rose was distressed to find her own eyes filling. "I'm…quite well." Her sister was very wise in such things. Could Leana discern just by looking at her that she was with child? 'Twas only fair that she be told. Should she reveal the truth now or wait until Jamie was with her? Oh, but the whole household knew; she dared not wait.

Rose gripped her sister's hands, her heart pounding. "Leana, I'm…I'm…"

"Och! I canna believe what I'm seein' wi' me ain eyes." Neda Hastings stood in the doorway, a look of astonishment on her face. "Willie said ye'd come hame."

Leana squeezed Rose's hands, pulling them both into the hall, then released her and fell into the housekeeper's arms with an elated cry. "Neda! How I've missed you."

Rose sank into the hall chair before her knees gave way. *Hurry, Jamie.*

Neda, meanwhile, was scolding Leana. "Ye should have warned me ye were comin'." Her frown was a pretense, hiding her smile. "I've naught planned for supper but cold *broo* and pickled mutton."

"From your kitchen, soup and meat will be a feast," Leana insisted. "Besides, I've not much appetite these days." She paused as if she meant to say something else, then smiled instead. "Won't Mr. McBride complain if there's nothing hot on his table?"

Neda's eyes twinkled. "Yer faither is in Dalbeaty, acourtin' the Widow Douglas."

"*Courting?*" Leana gaped at Neda, then at Rose. "My sister, whatever has come over Father?"

Rose stood and closed the nursery door, lest their chatter wake Ian. "'Tis true. Father has announced he will marry the Widow Douglas on the sixteenth of July."

"*Marry?* Is it as serious as that?"

"They plan to exchange their vows in Urr parish."

"Goodness! As the auld wives say, long looked for comes at last." Leana reclaimed her discarded hat from the window sill and absently held it against her middle. "Already our family is altered."

"You left more than two months ago," Rose reminded her. "Much can happen in the spring when warmer weather draws us out of doors."

"It can indeed." Neda appraised her with a wry smile. "Have ye told Leana yer ain guid news yet, Rose?"

"My...news?" Rose tried to smile and found her mouth as dry as day-old bannocks. "You mean that my husband and I are...that we are...leaving for Glentrool on my birthday?" She nearly fainted in relief at having thought of something. "Leana has already heard of our plans. Haven't you, dearie?"

Though Leana regarded her with genuine affection, Rose thought she spied a flicker of sadness in her eyes. "I have indeed heard that news, my sister. Twice."

Fifteen

Woman's grief is like a summer storm,
Short as it violent is.

JOANNA BAILLIE

S he is carrying Jamie's child.
Leana gripped the worn brim of her hat, feeling it give beneath her fingers. Why had she not noticed sooner? The bloom on her sister's fuller cheek, the light in her eyes, the snug fit of her gown. And her dissembling at the mention of "news." It seemed Rose's prayers had been answered: A babe was on the way whether the lass was prepared to confess the truth yet or not.

Neda peered out the hall window. "Willie has headed o'er the braes, seekin' oot Jamie tae tell him ye've arrived unexpectedly from Twyneholm."

"Well then." Rose looked greatly relieved. "My husband should be along soon."

Leana's heart, filled to overflowing moments earlier, began to empty. *My husband.* Rose had called him that more than once. Was she laying claim to the man or kindly sparing Leana from hearing his name? *Dearest Jamie.* She loved Jamie still, would always love him. But he had come to love her sister, just as her letter had requested; Rose's glow of contentment was proof.

"I'll be gettin' back tae me broo," Neda said, starting for the kitchen. "Yer faither returns in the morn, but the rest o' the household is eager tae see ye, Leana. I'll send Eliza tae help ye freshen up a bit."

Leana held up her crushed hat and tried to smile but could not. "I must look a fright. Hot water and a brush would be most appreciated."

Rose inclined her head down the corridor. "Suppose you see to your toilette in Jamie's old room."

" 'Twas once your room," Leana said. "Long ago."

And mine, with Jamie. Not so long ago.

How would she bear watching them together, knowing his child grew inside her? 'Twas hard enough the first twelvemonth of their marriage when she carried Ian and Jamie favored Rose. Leana never dreamed it would happen again. But it had.

And this time she had nowhere to run.

"Here we are." Rose nodded at the room, taking a lighted candlestick from the hall table. The sisters walked through the door in tandem, greeted by the musty smell of linens that needed laundering. "I'll see that Annabel cleans the room before you retire." Rose placed the candle by the washstand, then pulled open the curtains, sending dust motes flying. Sunlight made the bedroom look even more neglected. A fine layer of dust coated the furniture. The towel by the washbowl was soiled, used and discarded some time ago. "As you can see, housework has suffered of late." *Because of you.* Rose did not need to say the words for Leana to hear them.

Leana placed her hat on the bedside table and touched the box bed curtains, fond memories hidden in every fold. "It seems my departure left Auchengray short-handed." She was sorry she'd left without telling them and equally sorry she'd returned unannounced. How had it come to this?

Rose looked round the square bedroom with its large oak clothes press and carved mantelpiece. "The Widow Douglas may prefer this room once they're wed. The spence is father's domain, not at all suited for a woman."

Leana gazed toward the room where Ian slept. "I could stay in the nursery—"

"Nae!" Rose was clearly distraught. "Th-that hurlie bed is *most* uncomfortable. Please consider this your room." She moved about the room, absently touching the furnishings. "Not long after Mistress Douglas moves to Auchengray, Jamie and I will depart for Glentrool. Then she and Father may have our old room, and everyone will be happy." She turned toward Leana and held her palms up as if the matter were resolved.

Oh, Rose. Nothing was ever so easy. Leana clasped her sister's outstretched hands. "Dearie, I think you have something to tell me. Not about Father. 'Yer ain guid news,' as Neda called it. A babe perhaps?"

Rose blushed to her roots, the whites of her eyes stark against her pink skin. "Is it…that obvious?"

"Only because I know you so well, my sister. You look like you swallowed a candle."

Rose ducked her head, shy and uncertain, like the young woman of sixteen she was. "It feels more like peat burning inside me."

"So it does." Leana slowly gathered her sister in her arms, hoping it might ease the tension between them. Her own revelation would have to wait. Hadn't they competed enough? "I am happy for you, Rose. 'Twas what you wanted, a child of your own." Leana squeezed her eyes shut, willing the pain to subside.

"Oh, Leana. I wanted you to be the first to hear, not the last." Rose sniffed, hugging her tight. "I'm sorry you weren't here."

"I am too, Rose." The girl Leana remembered from childhood returned. The charming Rose. The innocent Rose. They stood in the dim and dusty room, holding each other, almost sisters again. "When do you expect your bairn to be delivered?"

Rose leaned back, drawing a handkerchief from her sleeve to dab her nose. "Early January, I think." She gave a little shrug. "Perhaps this summer you might help me prepare for…what's to come."

"I will." Leana would do what she could. For Rose's sake. And for Jamie's.

A light tap at the door announced Eliza with a steaming pitcher of water in her hands and a bright smile on her face. "Mistress, 'tis guid tae have ye hame." She hurried across the room to deposit her heavy pitcher in the washbowl, then dropped a deep curtsy.

"Bless you, Eliza." Leana touched the ruffled edge of the girl's white cap. "'Tis good to see you, too."

Eliza offered her the fresh linen towel draped across her arm. "Ye've been sairlie missed, mem." She stuck out her hands, the creases stained from gardening. "As ye can see, I've done a' I could, but yer *gairden* is mair than I can manage."

"Not to worry. I'll start with the kitchen garden in the morn's morn."

Rose stepped forward. "Eliza, the rest of the household is anxious to greet my sister. See to her grooming while I gather the staff in the parlor."

"Aye, mem." Steam swirled round the broad porcelain bowl as Eliza poured the hot water. She fished a small cake of soap from her apron pocket, bathed Leana's neck, face, and hands, then cleaned the dust from her gown. Finally Eliza offered her mistress a slender birch twig to freshen her teeth, then untangled her braids and brushed her hair until it shone.

"Like waves of spun gold," Eliza said, clearly pleased with her work. "Shall I dress it in a circle o' braids again? Though, if ye dinna mind me sayin', 'tis nice as 'tis."

"We'll leave it unbound," Leana agreed. *The way Jamie likes it.* She was ashamed of her thoughts, yet could not bring herself to coil her hair on top of her head. Just for this evening. Just for the first time he saw her.

Eliza was straightening the washstand and fretting over the sorry condition of the room when a familiar cry floated down the corridor. *Ian.*

Leana flew from the room, a cloud of hair wafting over her shoulders. "Coming, sweet boy," she called out, her heart beating wildly. Would he still know her voice? Her face? Would he welcome her or shrink away, confused? *Ian, 'tis your mother. Home to stay.*

Light steps sounded at the foot of the stair as Leana opened the nursery door. Rose must have heard him too. Compelled by instinct and an urgent need to hold her son, Leana slipped into the room and hastened to the crib.

Ian was sitting up, rubbing his eyes, not quite awake yet.

She stared at him in wonder. "My braw wee lad." The child was a miniature Jamie, from his sleek dark hair to the set of his chin. Only his eyes were like hers, blue and wide, blinking at her now.

"Will you come to me, Ian?" She reached toward him, grateful he did not whimper as if she were a stranger. Leana slid her hands under his arms and lifted the child out of the crib, surprised at the weight of him. When she held him against her, his body still warm with sleep, tears sprang to her eyes. "My dear son." Smoothing one hand over his silky hair, she kissed his brow, then his cheek. "Who would have imagined such a fine neck hiding beneath that handsome head of yours? Has Neda been feeding you her good porridge?"

"He's eating minced beef now." Rose stood in the doorway, watching them. "And *tatties* and gravy and soft cheese. Neda has cooked carrots for you tonight, Ian, and bits of the fish your father caught. Aren't you the lucky lad?" She held out her hands, and Ian dove toward her with a gleeful cry, nearly tumbling out of Leana's embrace.

"Careful!" Leana held him a moment longer before guiding him into her sister's open arms. Did he truly not recognize her? Or did he prefer Rose?

Ian patted Rose's cheeks as the two pressed their noses together, then he whirled about as if to assess this newcomer to the nursery.

"You know who this is, don't you, Ian?" Rose's voice was even. "'Tis my sister, Leana. She once took care of you and loves you dearly. Just as I do."

Leana stared at her in dismay. "Will you not tell him who I am?"

Rose averted her gaze, busying her hands straightening Ian's sleeve. "Jamie and I have not spoken of the matter. We did not expect to see you again, and so I thought…that is, I assumed Ian would think of me as…his mother."

"But I…" Leana's throat tightened. "*I* am his mother."

"You gave birth to him," Rose acknowledged, blushing as she said it. "But Ian is ours to raise now. Jamie's and mine. When we arrive in Glentrool, 'twould be so much easier—"

"Easier for *you*." Leana clutched her skirts in her hands, her grief mounting. "But not easier for me, Rose. Nor for Ian when he learns someday that you have hidden the truth from him." She reached for the sharpest arrow in her quiver. "'Tis the sort of thing Father would do, keeping secrets from his children."

Rose turned away as if she'd been slapped, then recovered just as quickly. Without a word she stepped round Leana and began changing Ian's wet nightgown as though Leana were no longer in the room. "Aren't you a fine boy," she praised him, "staying still while I dress you in your nice, clean gown?"

Before Leana spoke again, she made certain her voice was calm, and her words far kinder. "Rose, you are a wonderful stepmother. There is no shame in such a role."

Rose's hands stilled. "I am not ashamed, Leana. I am only thinking of Ian in the years to come. Even you must admit how difficult it would be for Ian, always explaining why the woman that bore him is no longer married to his father."

"Aye." Leana sank against the wall, her strength gone. The long journey by chaise, the shock of finding the McKies still here, and the babe in her womb had all taken their toll. "What you say is true, much as it grieves me to confess it."

Rose turned, Ian tucked in her arms once more. Though Leana saw compassion in her eyes, suspicion lurked there as well. "Why are you here, Leana?"

She leaned her head against the cool plaster. Bits of psalms learned long ago came to mind but brought no comfort. *I am like a broken vessel.... I am poured out like water.... I am withered like grass.*

"Leana, will you not tell me what brings you to Auchengray?"

Straightening, Leana took a deep breath as though the air alone might support her. "I came home because I could not impose on poor Aunt Meg's hospitality another hour." That was the truth; she felt no shame in saying it. "And I missed Neda. And Duncan and the others." Also a fact Rose could hardly deny. "Since I was certain you'd left for Glentrool in May, I saw no harm in returning to Auchengray."

"I see." Rose lowered Ian to the floor, letting him test his knees as he rocked back and forth. "I wish you had written first."

"So do I, for I did not mean to grieve you." At least her reasons, hastily assembled, had appeased her sister. "Why did *you* not write and tell me your news?"

"I did." Rose bent to place Ian's wooden blocks within his reach. "My letter will no doubt arrive in Twyneholm on Monday."

Monday. Leana swallowed, feeling ill. "If only I'd waited…"

"But you didn't," Rose said matter-of-factly. "And now you are here, and we will make the best of it." She gestured toward the stair. "The household is waiting to greet you. It might make things easier if Ian and I waited here."

Leana moved to the door, her legs stiff, like those of a wooden soldier being put through its paces by an impatient child.

Rose reached out a hand to steady her. "Leana, are you all right?"

"I'll be fine," she said faintly as she started down the stone steps. *'Til Jamie comes home.*

Sixteen

When things were as fine as could possibly be,
I thought 'twas the Spring; but alas! it was she.

JOHN BYROM

Jamie crossed the lawn with long, purposeful strides, Willie lagging far behind him.

"Miss McBride has come hame!" the servant had cried when he'd found Jamie in the far pasture. "Wull ye be wantin' tae *welcome* her, sir?"

Aye, he would. Very much. And then again, he would not.

Leana. Her name pounded inside his chest, louder than his heart. This would never have happened if they'd left for Glentrool in May as he'd planned. Or if Rose had written her sister sooner…or if he'd sent a letter of his own.

Why, Leana? Why now?

He could not blame her for coming home. He could only blame himself for not preventing it. Or had that been his secret hope all along? That Leana would come back to him?

Love my sister. "'Tis done," he muttered, pushing open the front door.

Jamie strode into the house, empty except for the parlor, where house servants and farmworkers alike stood in a ragged reception line. His steps slowed when he spied the graceful woman greeting each one, her hair cascading down her back, her voice low and gentle. He'd thought himself prepared to see her, but he was not. When she turned toward him, he could not move another step or take another breath, save the one that spoke her name.

"Leana."

She was more beautiful than he remembered. Her skin shone like ivory silk. Her eyes were wider, her mouth fuller. Or had her face grown thinner? Was that the difference? She looked fragile, as if her time away from home had been difficult for her. How well he understood.

The household had finished welcoming her it seemed, for the servants began filing out. A blur of browns and grays slipped past him, though Jamie paid scant attention. His eyes were on Leana, walking toward him, her hair draped round her like a silk mantle.

"Jamie." She curtsied, perhaps to hide the pink tinge in her pale cheeks. "I'm sorry to have come home without writing first." Her chin remained lowered as if she could not bring herself to look at him. "Had I known that you and Rose were still living at Auchengray, I would have waited until August."

Finally he found his voice. "This is your home, Leana. You are always welcome here."

"I am glad to hear it." Leana looked up at him at last. "I could not impose upon Aunt Margaret any further."

There was another reason, Jamie decided, barely visible in the blue depths of her eyes. Had something happened at Twyneholm?

"Jamie," she began, stepping closer. Her hair brushed against his sleeve. It felt like a caress. "Rose and I had a chance to talk. I am... happy to hear of your news."

He forced himself to meet her gaze, to witness the pain etched across her face. The slender crease between her brows. The fine lines round her eyes and mouth. Leana was anything but happy, and no wonder: She'd found her sister blooming with child, in love with the man who'd once pledged to love only her, forever.

Forgive me, Leana. He would have to say those words aloud. Not now, when Rose might appear any moment, but soon. Mere words would never be enough to assuage his guilt or ease her sorrow. Not Leana, who felt so deeply and loved so well.

Jamie mustered his courage. "May I...speak with you...later?"

"You may."

For a moment he thought he saw a glimmer of hope in her eyes, but perhaps it was only the sheen of her unshed tears. Whatever had transpired before he arrived, Leana's afternoon had been most trying. He hoped his apology would not grieve her further. But it had to be said; she must be made to understand.

"There you are, Jamie." Rose sailed into the room, Ian on her hip, a too-cheery smile on her face. "I see you've made your cousin welcome. And here's your son, awake from his nap."

"Ian, my lad." Jamie ruffled the boy's hair, grateful for something to occupy his hands. There was no such recourse for his thoughts, which whirled through his head like dervishes. Nor could he find a place for his gaze to land; left or right, he found a woman who'd given him her heart.

"I've told Leana our news," Rose said. "She has promised to…help me. To…that is…"

"I have already wished your husband much joy." Leana bowed her head. "I will gladly provide whatever guidance you might need, Rose."

"'Tis…good of you." Jamie was determined to say something, if only to keep his wits about him. Leana was standing too near. The curve of her long neck distracted him; the warmth of her body unsettled him. He stepped slightly to the left but could not escape her fragrance and the disturbing memories it evoked.

Rose shifted Ian to her other arm. The lad was growing impatient for his supper. "You once insisted, Leana, that we all speak the truth in love."

Looking at Rose, Leana took a steady breath. "The truth is, this is a very trying day for all of us. I am overjoyed at seeing my son, yet I fear my happiness comes at your expense." She turned to Jamie, her expression less strained than before. "Indeed, 'tis why I left in the first place: to spare you both the heartache of having to choose."

Distracted by Ian's antics, Rose repeated the word as though she'd missed something. "Choose what?"

Jamie's heart made a fist.

"Choose whom you will love," Leana said simply.

Rose shook her head. "'Tis not a matter of picking one or the other. I love Jamie. I love Ian. And I love you, Leana." She planted a noisy kiss on Ian's cheek. "Furthermore, I am quite certain that all three of you love me. So you see, there are no choices to be made. Not anymore."

Before either of them could respond, Rose swung round, holding the boy tight, and headed for the kitchen, her braid dusting the back of her gown. "My son cannot wait another minute for his carrots and trout. I will see you both at supper."

As she neared the door, Rose began to sing, her voice overly bright in the strained atmosphere.

> Dance to your daddie, my bonnie laddie,
> Dance to your daddie, my bonnie lamb.
> And ye'll get a fishie, in a little dishie,
> Ye'll get a fishie when the boat comes home.

The notes lingered in the room, like the pungent aroma of fried trout. Jamie said nothing for a moment, uncertain how to begin. If they were seated, he might manage better. If she were farther away. If the room were not so quiet.

"Jamie." Leana moistened her lips. "You read my letter. The one I sent from Twyneholm the day—"

"Aye," he said quickly, hoping to change the subject. "I read it." Dozens of times. The creases in the paper were nearly worn through.

Leana rested her hand lightly on his sleeve. " 'Tis obvious you have done as I asked."

He nodded, stalling. "You requested that I care for our son with the same tenderness you would have shown him if you'd been here. And so I have. He looks well, don't you think?"

"Very well," she said gently. "And your wife even more so."

His spirits sank. "Must we talk about Rose?"

"You know we must. Isn't that what you wanted to speak to me about…'later'?"

"It is, but…" The woman saw too much. Knew him too well.

"Oh, Jamie, please do not make this harder." Leana's voice softened to a whisper. "You love Rose, do you not?"

Jamie closed his eyes. He could not bear to see her face when he spoke the truth. "I do."

When he opened them again, she'd moved a step back. "You have made the honorable choice, Jamie. All of society stands with you. The kirk, the law, the parish, my father—"

"Lachlan McBride only stands where he will benefit," he protested, seizing the chance to pin blame elsewhere for something, anything.

Leana did not contest his claim. "My father's greed knows no bounds, I'll not deny the truth of that."

Truth. He seized on the word and let it fuel his courage. "And I cannot deny the vow I made to you on the day you left." Jamie wrapped his hands round her arms, her soft flesh giving way beneath his grasp. "Listen to me, Leana. Those were not idle words intended only to comfort you. I meant what I said: I will ne'er repent of loving you."

She lowered her eyes, glassy with tears. "But you *have* repented. You have wisely chosen to love Rose instead."

"You are wrong. I did not choose." His grip on her arms tightened, lest he shake her. Lest he pull her into his embrace. "Don't you see? The choice was made for me."

"By Rose, you mean?"

"Nae, Leana. By you."

Seventeen

Mercy stood in the cloud, with eye that wept
Essential love.
ROBERT POLLOK

The heat of Jamie's words and the warmth of his presence were more than Leana could bear. When her knees began to fold, Jamie caught her in his arms.

"Och, lass!" He carried her to the guest bed and lowered her onto the worsted wool coverlet. Before she could protest, he slipped off her shoes, then sat on the edge of the half-tester bed, taking care not to crush her gown. " 'Tis my fault." He swept her hair away from her face, not quite meeting her gaze. "I should not have spoken so…"

"So…honestly?" Leana finished for him. The room came into focus as her dizziness started to fade.

He was more handsome than she remembered. The strong cut of his jaw. The fullness of his mouth. The moss green eyes that haunted her dreams. The man she had no right to love.

"Jamie, 'tis just as you said: I ran from Auchengray without giving you any choice in the matter."

"That morning…when I realized you were gone…" He hung his head. " 'Twas a terrible morning."

"For me as well," she said gently. She longed to smooth back the stubborn lock of hair that fell across his brow but dared not risk even so innocent a gesture. "I asked you to love my sister. All but insisted upon it. You did not choose that either."

Jamie lifted his head. "I chose to act on it, though. Because I had to, Leana. Because she is my wife." He exhaled slightly. "And because I do love her." He fell silent, studying her at length. When at last he spoke, his voice was threaded with remorse. "Why, Leana? Why did you leave me?"

Oh, Jamie. The hardest question of all.

" 'Twas not because I wanted to." Her throat closed round the words. "I left Auchengray for your sake and for Rose's." She averted her eyes, disconcerted at having him so near. "But I did so for my own sake as well, knowing the limits of my heart."

"Your heart has no limits." He wrapped his fingers round her wrist, as though measuring the rhythm of it pulsing against his thumb. "You love completely, Leana, holding nothing in reserve. Even those who are not worthy of your love are blessed with it in full measure." After a moment he stood, carefully releasing his hold on her. "I ken the source of that love, for you have told me often enough."

"God has been most gracious to me, Jamie." She slowly sat up, then eased her legs over the edge of the bed and slipped on her shoes. "His loving-kindness is far greater than anything I might offer."

"So the Buik says." He laced her shoes, then helped her stand, making certain she was steady on her feet before letting go. " 'Tis not the first time you've fainted in my arms. I remember one Sabbath in particular."

"When you carried me from the kirk to the manse? Not an easy journey. I was very much with child." *As I am now.* Her breath caught as she realized how close she'd come to spilling out her news. Even now the words waited on her lips, ready to be spoken. Needing to be spoken. *'Tis why I've come home, Jamie.* He deserved to know, didn't he?

Aye, but not yet. The next few weeks would be worrisome enough. Leana smoothed her skirts, noting the shape of her waist. Only a slight rounding there. Surely she could keep her secret until Lammas. If she altered her gowns and minded her fork, she might reach the end of her fifth month before burdening anyone with such news.

There *was* a child they needed to discuss, however.

"Jamie, I have something to ask of you." When he turned his full gaze on her, she almost lost her nerve, so intense was his look. "Rose informed me that once you settle in Glentrool, she plans to claim Ian as her true son, born of her womb." Seeing his brow darken, she bit her lip. "Perhaps that is what you intend as well."

"Rose had no business suggesting such a thing," he said evenly. "Ian will always be your son. Nothing can change that, certainly not a whim of your sister's. I will speak with her tonight."

Heat climbed up her neck, as she imagined the conversation. "Jamie, I should not have said—"

"Nae, 'tis right that you did." He glanced down at his collarless shirt and worn breeches. "Pardon me while I dress for supper. Even without your father at table, I cannot appear in shepherd's garb."

Leana touched the neckline of her plain green gown. "Until my old gowns are aired and pressed, I fear the dress I've arrived in will have to do for dinner."

His gaze traveled the length of her. "You look bonny, Leana. As always."

Flustered, she sank into a curtsy, thinking to put their relationship on the proper footing. "I will make myself useful in the kitchen then, dear cousin."

Jamie placed his hand under her chin, slowly lifting her face until they were poised a handbreadth apart. *"Cousin?"* he said, his voice rough with emotion. "Nae, lass. It can never be that way with us."

By sheer will she stepped away from him. "Nor can it be any other way but this." She curtsied again, her legs trembling, then grabbed her skirts and fled the room.

Moments later Leana burst into the kitchen. "Neda!" she cried, then fell back a step, trying to regain her composure. Though how could she with Jamie so near? She gestured toward the dressing table with a limp hand. "Is there…some task I might do…before supper?"

Neda greeted her warmly, as if her face were not flushed nor her breathing uneven. "I've nae need o' yer labor, lass, but I'd welcome yer company."

Only then did Leana see Rose seated in the corner spooning Ian's fish supper into his eager mouth. In her haste she had forgotten that her sister would be in the kitchen as well. Rose, with her back toward Leana, did not look in her direction, nor did Ian's expression change when he caught sight of his mother.

Feeling faint, Leana started toward the door. "Perhaps later…"

"You'll join us at table, won't you?" Rose lifted her voice to be heard above the kitchen din, inclining her head only slightly.

"Aye," was all she managed before quitting the room.

Leana wandered down the back hall, feeling like a stranger in her own home. Should she simply wait in the dining room for the McKies to join her? She had never supped with them as husband and wife. Now she would share their table thrice daily. *How, Lord? How will I bear it?*

When Leana found herself in the dining room, she sank into her old chair and imagined Jamie and Rose seated across from her. Whatever would they discuss over supper? Not Ian. Not Glentrool. Too many words had been exchanged that afternoon, words that could not easily be put aside for a plate of soup.

Why are you here, Leana? She had arrived with a ready answer; now she had none.

You love completely, Leana. Indeed, she loved them both and Ian even more.

Wait upon the Lord, Leana. Her own words, whispered in her heart. In so desperate a situation, he was her only hope.

She was still deep in thought when Rose appeared in the doorway, her features arranged as carefully as flowers in a vase. "Ian is off exploring the garden with Eliza. Suppose we get on with supper. With Father gone, we've no need to make a long evening of it." Though Rose did not look at her as she took her seat, the lass could not hide the blush on her cheeks. Perhaps Rose was not as unruffled as she'd appeared. "I've instructed Neda to serve our three courses in quick succession. That is…if you do not object."

"Whatever you wish." Leana clutched the table linen in her lap, silently pleading for the courage to speak her heart. "Rose…I know this is… You did not expect…"

Jamie strode into the room sporting clean attire and a smooth chin. "Sorry to keep you waiting, ladies."

Rose smiled up at him and patted the arm of his chair. "Please join us." After Jamie spoke a blessing on the meal, Annabel brought in their barley broth one plate at a time while Rose inched her chair closer to his. "What say you, Jamie? After all these months, we have my sister back at our table."

"Aye, we do." Jamie nodded toward Leana but did not look at her nor say another word.

Rose tried again to engage him in conversation, to no avail. By the time pickled mutton was served, the tension in the room was thick enough to carve and serve for meat. Their father's presence at table was surprisingly missed. At least Lachlan, with his sharp tongue, would have given them a common adversary.

Neda delivered the last course herself, a china bowl in each hand. Judging by the broad smile on her face, she was determined to improve matters. "Is thar a certain lass wha likes her sweets ready for me apple puddin'?"

Rose brightened. "Aye."

Leana knew she could not last through another course. "The scent of cinnamon is most tempting, Neda, yet I fear a good night's sleep is more so. Will you excuse me, Rose? Jamie?" She did not wait for a response nor study their faces, knowing they felt as she did: awkward and uncomfortable. Sorry to find themselves in so impossible a situation. Dreading the months ahead.

I should never have come home.

The sad refrain had echoed through her heart all evening. Even now, as she lay in her box bed, Leana's conscience prodded her. Why had she not written first? Why had Rose not written sooner? She tossed beneath the sheets, knowing sleep would not come easily, not after so harrowing a day.

At least young Annabel had performed her duties well; Leana's bedroom smelled as sweet as any pudding. The maidservant had polished the furniture, scrubbed the floor, and changed the bedding, throwing open the window to let the cooler night air freshen the room. Leana had discovered her few treasured books stored in the cupboard and spent the balance of the evening with Richardson's *Pamela,* the lively tale of a serving maid and a young man of means. Lost in the twists and turns of their affairs, she'd managed to forget the knotty nature of her own life for a bit until exhaustion tugged at her eyelids, beckoning her to bed.

But sleep would not come.

Down the stair, the mantel clock chimed the late hour as she thought of Ian alone in the nursery. Leana would have the lad to herself for as long as she might keep her eyes open.

Moments later she stood in the darkened corridor outside the nursery door. Touching her hand to her heart, as if to calm its rapid beating, she slipped into his room, letting her eyes adjust before she latched the door behind her. Unlike the other bedrooms, no candle remained lit here. Jamie and Rose slept in the next room; they would hear Ian if he cried out. *As they might hear you, Leana.*

Undaunted, she moved toward the crib, her bare feet soundless against the wooden floor, her white linen nightgown catching a strand of moonlight shining through the window. Ian's face shone as well, turned to one side. He looked even younger in his sleep, like the child she'd said farewell to months ago.

She knelt next to his crib, longing to hold him. Might she touch his brow without waking him? She did so, holding her breath, marveling at the softness of his skin. When he did not move or make a sound, Leana continued to stroke his head, faintly skimming over his hair. She noticed his hand lay curled beside him, slightly open. If she gently slid her finger inside his curled hand, would he stir? He did not wake when her skin touched his; instead, his hand closed round her finger by instinct, holding her tight.

"Oh, Ian," she said aloud, not meaning to. Her voice did not wake him, nor would Ian let go, no matter how hard she tugged her fingers. She smiled, even as tears pooled in her eyes. "You have caught me."

"Aye," a male voice on the other side of the door answered, "so I have."

Leana tried again to pull free of Ian's grasp as the door opened and Jamie's shadow fell across the room. She could not see his face, only his outline lit by the hall candle.

"I heard you slip past our bedroom." His low voice bore no note of censure. "'Twas easy to guess where you were headed." Leaving the door ajar, he entered the room and knelt beside her, gazing at the sleeping child with obvious affection. Jamie's smooth hair hung loose, brushing against his nightshirt as he bent over the crib. After a quiet moment he confessed, "You have given me a fine son, Leana."

"He is God's gift. To both of us." She heard the slight tremor in her voice. Jamie was too close, the warmth of him too apparent. Yet if she moved, she risked waking Ian. Rubbing her thumb across the back of his tiny hand, she hoped Ian might relax his grip. But he did not. "It seems I am here to stay."

"So you are." Jamie must have sensed her discomfort, for he stood and backed away from her. "Sleep well, Leana." And he was gone.

As if on cue, Ian opened his hand in his sleep, setting her free. She rose at once, shaking from head to toe. From relief, from desire, from a sinking realization of what the next two months would require of her. *You look bonny, Leana.* She could not dwell on such thoughts.

Back in her box bed once more, Leana smoothed her hand across the sheets, back and forth, as if the motion itself might lull her to sleep. But there was no hope of that. She had sewn these sheets herself and tucked them inside Rose's cherished dresser drawer—the one every bride filled with new linens before her wedding day—never imagining the sheets would cover her own bridal bed instead.

Leana closed her eyes, unable to hold the memories at bay any longer. That December wedding night long ago had been cold, bitterly so. Cozy behind the curtains of this very box bed, the bride and groom had not even noticed the temperature: Jamie warmed by whisky, Leana warmed by Jamie. Vivid recollections sprang to life, heating her skin, robbing her of any chance of sleep.

Jamie, my sweet Jamie. She gripped the bedsheets. *I love you still.*

She sat up, sick with longing for a man she could not have. "Beloved one," she cried softly, her voice hollow in the empty box bed, "my heart does have limits."

In Twyneholm she'd had the freedom to love Jamie from afar. But here beneath her father's roof, that freedom was gone. She could not— *must* not—love Jamie as she once did. Not as a woman loved a man. Somehow she would learn to care for him as one did a cousin, a brother-in-law, a close friend.

Jamie's voice taunted her. *It can never be that way with us.*

"It must be, my love." She fell back on the heather mattress, fresh tears filling her eyes. "It must be."

Eighteen

Yet, taught by time, my heart has learned to glow
For other's good, and melt at other's woe.

HOMER

"Tell me true, Leana." Neda set a bowl of porridge at her place. A generous dollop of butter melted on top of the oats, and fresh cream circled the edges of the pottery bowl. "Does the place leuk different tae ye since ye've been gone a spell?"

"Aye, it does." Leana ran her thumb along the rose pattern on her spoon, wishing she'd slept better. Father was expected home soon; she would need all her strength to face him. "'Tis as though I'm visiting a neighbor's house. Familiar, yet changed. Not quite home anymore."

"But you *will* remain here." Rose sat across the way, her breakfast untouched. The two sisters had the table to themselves that morning; Jamie was already on the hills, fending off the pouring rain. Without him there, the tension in the air had almost dissipated. For the moment at least. "Auchengray will be your home now," Rose said firmly. "For good."

If Father allows me to stay.

Leana slipped a spoonful of steaming oats into her mouth and nearly burned her tongue. Eyes watering, she swallowed with some difficulty. "Aunt Meg likes her porridge lukewarm," she explained, putting down her spoon. "Perhaps I'll wait a bit." She eyed Rose's plate. "What of your breakfast, dearie?"

Rose wrinkled her nose. "Not today. Probably not tomorrow morning either."

Though she could not quite reach her, Leana stretched her hand across the table in sympathy. "'Twill not always be thus. As the Buik says, 'For surely there is an end.'"

"When?" Rose pushed her bowl away with a weary sigh. Apparently even the aroma was more than she could stand. "Come dinnertime I always feel better. Then it seems I cannot stop eating." She pinched her cheek, her expression glum. "Look how I've filled out. 'Tis most unbecoming."

Jamie does not think so. Leana held her tongue, but her thoughts were not so easily restrained. *He loves you, Rose. Be grateful.*

"And *you* have lost weight," Rose said petulantly. "Eat my dishful as well, for I've ne'er seen your cheeks so gaunt."

Leana answered with a slight shrug, tasting her porridge again. "Perhaps you've forgotten the shape of my face."

"Wheesht!" Rose nearly spilled her tea. "Forget my own sister? In two months' time? You can't mean that." Her gaze was clear, any wariness gone. "I have seen your face everywhere I looked, Leana. In the gardens and at your spinning wheel. By the hearth with your needle. Here at table with your fine manners." She dipped her chin. "I've missed you, Leana."

"Oh, my sister." Dropping her porridge spoon, Leana stood and hastened to her side, then wrapped her arms round her shoulders. "And I have missed you. Have I not told you so?"

Rose shook her head, cutting Leana to the quick.

"I *have* missed you, dearie," Leana assured her, kissing the back of Rose's neck as she held her close. "Forgive me for not saying so yestreen." After a long moment, Leana straightened, her hand still touching her sister's shoulder. "I am sorry I left. And I'm sorrier still that I've come home at the wrong time and ruined your summer."

"Nae." Rose looked up, her dark eyes swimming. "I am glad to have you home."

Leana felt something shift inside her, in that deep place where vows are made and kept. With God's help, she would learn to be happy—genuinely happy—for her sister and for Jamie. It was the only remedy for her wounds, the only balm for a love that could not be expressed or requited. Hour by hour, day by day, she would teach her heart a new song. *Rejoice with them that do rejoice.* Aye, just that.

"Suppose I stay busy in the garden," Leana offered, brushing her cheeks dry. "And if you'll let me, I would like to help with Ian. Oh, Rose, I was a fool to think I could live without my son."

The sincerity in Rose's face did not fade. "I understand. I do." She stood, leaving her napkin beside her cold porridge. "I will be glad for your help, and so will Ian. I think you caught him off guard yestreen, just waking from his nap. See if he doesn't recognize you today."

Rose pressed her lips together as though she meant to say something else and then changed her mind. "Jamie…" She paused, then started again. "Jamie spoke with me about…about Glentrool. And… Ian." Her cheeks matched her name. "Jamie is right, of course. And so are you. Ian will always be your son. Always."

Leana released a breath she hadn't realized she'd been holding. "You only meant to protect Ian."

"I'll not have you thinking me generous." Her blush deepened. " 'Twas my reputation I was protecting."

Touched by her honesty, Leana cupped her sister's cheek. "But I *do* think you're generous. More than you know." She nodded toward the window. "With this heavy downpour, I'll not be doing any gardening this morn. May I bathe Ian instead?"

"You may," Rose said emphatically. " 'Tis my least favorite task, for the child makes certain I am wetter than he is before we're done."

Leana smiled, picturing it. "I'll wear an apron and be prepared to find one of my old gowns when I'm finished."

"We stored them on the third floor." Rose slipped her hand in the crook of Leana's arm and led her toward the stair. "I'll have Eliza bring them to your room for an airing. You can see which ones still suit you."

"They'll all have to suit me, for I cannot afford another." Leana thought of the silver in her purse, then discarded any notion of spending it on something so frivolous as a new gown. Who knew when those coins might be needed? "I suspect my old dresses will require altering. A woman's body ne'er quite recovers from giving birth."

When Rose paused to look her up and down with a critical eye, Leana wished she'd not spoken so carelessly. Rose arched her brows. "Your waist looks ever so trim to me, Leana. And will look more so as each week passes, compared to mine."

Not true, dear sister. Leana quickly changed the subject. "I am off to find Ian, then, and receive a good soaking." They parted company when they reached the stair—Rose to the kitchen to plan their meals for the Sabbath, Leana to the nursery, eager to hold her son again.

"Father should be home by noon," Rose reminded her. "Won't he be surprised?"

"*Crabbit* is the more likely word. His temper alone will dry his wet clothes when he arrives and finds me here." Leana looked down at her from the landing. "Kindly see that I'm informed the minute Father rides up the drive. 'Tis best if he hears the news from my own lips."

"*Oo aye!*" Rose rolled her eyes. "Aren't you the brave one to face him?"

"Not brave, my sister. Desperate. I have nowhere else to call home but Auchengray." Leana turned and hurried up the steep stair.

Annabel was in the second-floor hall, standing guard over Ian, who was doing his best to pull a chair down on his round head. Leana smiled at the red-headed maid, a twelvemonth younger than Rose and Eliza. "My sister says I may bathe you, Ian, and to arm myself accordingly."

Annabel patted the cloth folded over her arm. "I've a clean apron for ye, mem."

While Leana held Ian in her outstretched arms, the maidservant slipped the linen apron over her mistress's head and tied it round her waist. "Not too tight," Leana cautioned her. At least it tied in the back and not the front. Perhaps an apron would be a wise addition to her wardrobe— not just when needed but worn throughout the day, as Neda did. Unless guests came to call, there was no shame in wearing one at home.

Ian wiggled and flapped, wanting to be held, wanting to be put down, wanting something different than being airborne. Leana laughed, pulling him close, then planted kisses all over his face, much to his delight.

A grin appeared on Annabel's freckled face. "Yer son does remember ye."

Leana cradled him close and aimed for the nursery. "Now we'll see if I remember how to bathe him."

A shallow wooden tub waited in the center of the nursery floor. " 'Twas steamin' a bit ago," Annabel said, "sae the water should be *richt* by noo. Thar's naught mair *slitterie* than a soapy bairn."

Leana pulled off his clothing, which Ian was happy to be rid of, then eased him into the water, kneeling beside the tub as she did. He welcomed her with a great splash, nearly soaking the front of her apron through. "Well!" Leana said with a laugh, realizing just how much Ian had grown. He was stronger, more vocal, and far more energetic. Even with Annabel's help, both their aprons were dripping wet when they finished, and the floor was covered with water as well.

"There's hardly a drop left in the tub," Leana teased him, lifting him onto the dry towel on her lap and rubbing his pink skin. She was still attending to his sleek cap of hair when Rose appeared at the door, breathless, her eyes like black saucers.

" 'Tis Father, home from Dalbeaty!"

Leana hastily kissed Ian's brow. "I must go, dear boy." She handed him to Annabel with instructions to finish drying and dressing him, then untied her apron strings with trembling fingers. "If only I had time to change. Look at me."

Rose tossed aside Leana's wet apron and assessed her green gown and unkempt hair. "I see bath time was worse than usual." She tickled Ian's pink foot, making him giggle. "You were in a *heartsome* mood, weren't you, lad? Doused your mother thoroughly and pulled her braids loose."

Your mother. Leana almost hugged her for saying it.

"Never mind your wet gown, for we've not a minute to spare," Rose insisted, pulling her down the stair. "He's chatting with Duncan in the steading but will head for the house next. Neda laid out refreshments in the spence, and Hugh has fresh attire waiting for him. Greet Father, let him change, then join him for fresh gingerbread and a saucer of tea."

"Rose McKie!" Leana stopped at the foot of the stair, staring at her in amazement. "While I've been gone, you've turned into the mistress of Auchengray."

Her sister ducked her head. " 'Tis a role you are more than welcome to reclaim, Leana."

"Not for a minute. I am perfectly content to serve as head gardener and nurserymaid." She glanced at the door, hearing footsteps approaching. "*If* Father will let me stay, that is."

"You're his daughter, Leana. How can he refuse you?"

"He is the laird of Auchengray," Leana reminded her, "and may do as he pleases." She clasped her hands and faced the door.

Nineteen

If Heaven had looked upon riches to be a valuable thing,
it would not have given them to such a scoundrel.

JONATHAN SWIFT

Lachlan McBride was thoroughly drenched, bonnet to boots. His mood was fouler than the weather. "Neda!" he bellowed down the hall, slamming the front door.

But it was not the housekeeper who stepped forward to greet him. It was the *braisant* daughter he'd hoped was gone for good.

"Welcome home, Father." Leana curtsied, keeping her skirts in hand as if prepared to run. "Please forgive me for arriving unexpectedly."

Heat rose inside him like a Lammas bonfire. "I've yet to forgive you for leaving."

She lowered her gaze. "I shall explain everything—"

"You shall indeed." He bit off the words, chewing on each one. "See me in the spence in half an hour." Only then did he notice Rose glaring at him from behind Leana's shoulder. When had these daughters of his become so unmanageable? "Do not keep me waiting, Leana." He marched down the hall, water sluicing off his boots onto the uneven stone floor, then abruptly stopped and turned round. "And do something about your appearance. Unless your lady's maid is also unhappy that you're home."

Rose stepped in front of Leana and met his gaze with a hard look of her own. "Eliza will gladly attend to her."

A heidie lass, that one. Like his sister, Rowena. "Verra well. Half an hour."

Aiming for his private corner of the house, Lachlan turned neither to the right hand nor to the left in pursuit of dry clothing and a dram of whisky, both of which would improve this miserable day considerably. The last thing he'd expected—or wanted—was Leana to return to

Auchengray. Could she not have waited until after the wedding at least? Or after Lammas, when the McKies were gone, and good riddance to them both?

Och! Grown children were harder to control than bairns and far more expensive.

When Lachlan reached the spence, Hugh was prepared with clean towels, hot water, a bit of soap, and a sharpened razor. Thirty minutes later—Lachlan checked his watch to be certain—he heard a soft tapping on the door. "Let her in," he growled at Hugh, settling into his favorite upholstered chair, "then be gone with you." His valet did as he was told without comment, ushering Leana into the room before he shut the door soundlessly behind him.

Leana looked somewhat better than she had when she greeted him. Her hair was neatly combed and braided on top of her head. But she wore the same dull green gown badly stained with water. Perhaps she'd arrived from Twyneholm with the morning rain.

"Father." She curtsied again—did the woman mean to garner sympathy with all this floor scraping?—then rose and stood before him, hands folded. "I am sorry my homecoming has upset you. I should not have left—"

"Nae, you should not have." He gestured toward the empty chair opposite his, a good deal smaller and less comfortable. "The household has been obliged to do their own work and yours as well. Eliza in particular."

Leana perched on the chair, not quite sitting. "I will do my best to make amends." She glanced about the small room, then turned her earnest gaze on him. "You see, I departed Auchengray because—"

"Any fool kens the reason you left. Your sister married your lover and claimed your son, all with the kirk's blissin. Few women could abide that situation."

She shook her head so slightly it might have been nerves. "I left for Jamie's sake. And for Rose. And Ian."

"A noble sacrifice, was it?" He snorted. "Could it be you were sparing yourself the shame of returning to Newabbey after your compearance on the *cutty stool*? Forcing the household to make excuses for you?"

Her pale features showed a bit of color. "It grieves me to think I might be—"

"So human? So fallible?"

"Nae, Father. So selfish."

"Ochhh," he muttered, drawing out the sound to his satisfaction. "The whole world and everyone in it is selfish, Leana. A sad truth you'd be wise to learn."

She sighed a little. "Be ye therefore wise as serpents—"

"You see?" He thumped the arm of his chair with approval. "Even the Buik says so."

"And harmless as doves," she finished quietly.

"Doves." He waved his hand in the direction of the steading. "I've a doocot full of them. Good for baking in pies and naught else."

When Leana fell silent, fiddling with a loose thread on her sleeve, he eyed her more closely. She'd lost weight in Twyneholm. Could be Meg's larder was poorly stocked. At least Leana had not stolen any silver from his money box before she left. He patted the key hanging round his neck, comforted by the cool feel of it against his skin. She'd also not written him begging for her inheritance like a prodigal child. It seemed his older daughter had more smeddum than he'd given her credit for.

Still, she'd departed without asking his permission and returned without doing so again. Such behavior could not go unpunished. "You disappoint me, lass; I'll not deny it."

Her eyes entreated him even more than her words. "How may I make it up to you? Tend the gardens, work in the stillroom, spin the wool?"

"You'll do that and more." He tented his fingers, considering the possibilities. "But first you must account for all the labor lost in your absence."

She spread out her hands, as empty as her pockets. "I will do all I can, Father. My only wish is to remain at Auchengray and call it home."

"Call it whatever you like." At least she had not asked him to find her a husband or a cottage of her own. As to the suitable penalty for her desertion, he would think of one soon enough. She'd not be permitted to darken the Urr parish kirk door on his wedding day, but that was hardly punitive. For the present, hard labor would suffice.

Scowling, he shook his finger at her. "See that I do not find you idle when you should be working. This is not Maxwell Park with a bevy of servants to keep up appearances. We've not a soul here who does not earn the right to sit at my table."

She stood, off balance for a moment, then bobbed her head. "I understand."

He waved her off with a grunt, eager to get to his ledgers. Before the spence door closed, he'd already pulled up a chair to his desk and lit another candle. The rainy weather made the house as gloomy as November.

He opened to the page marked *Edingham Farm,* then unfolded the damp sheet of paper rescued from his waistcoat pocket and scrawled the various numbers in their proper columns. The Dalbeaty property was shaping up nicely; the three lads, even more so.

Lachlan smiled, picturing Morna Douglas. However unattractive, she was the ideal wife. Docile. Compliant. Willing to believe whatever he told her. He intended to give her only enough information to complete the necessary papers and put in motion the final steps of his scheme.

His bookkeeping finished, Lachlan closed the heavy ledger with a satisfying thud. Snuffing out the candles rather than waste the beeswax, he quit the spence and followed the aroma of dinner into the dining room. He took his seat at the head of the table, straightening his waistcoat and yanking on his sleeves as the housekeeper swept through the door.

"Thar ye are, sir." Although she was but a few years younger than he, Neda still had a lively step. Her copper hair seldom stayed beneath her white cap, nor did her sly grin remain hidden for long. He put up with both annoyances since her cooking more than made up for her kintra ways.

"We've a special dinner planned for Leana's homecoming," she informed him. "'Twas Rose's idea and a guid *ane.* Fresh cod wi' an egg sauce and horseradish—*cabbieclaw,* ye ken—followed by sheep's head brawn boiled wi' bacon and weel roasted moorfowl seasoned wi' a blade o' mace."

Lachlan frowned at the description. Never mind that they were some of his favorite dishes. "What about *my* homecoming? Can a laird not be greeted with the best from his stores for his own sake?"

"Oo, aye." That peasant's grin. "The best bits will go tae ye, Mr. McBride."

She left as the clock chimed one. Lachlan seized his handbell and rang it with authority, calling the household to dinner. He would not let such a feast remain in the kitchen getting cold.

Rose entered first, fresh scrubbed as ever and a bit softer round the edges. Whatever flesh Leana had lost, Rose had found. It suited her. Wouldn't his sister, Rowena, laugh to see her niece? A twin of her *sonsie* self at that age, though at sixteen Rowena had yet to meet her husband, and Rose was already married and breeding.

Jamie was not far behind Rose; he never was. The lad was besotted, just as he'd been when he first arrived at Auchengray. At least his blue coat was well brushed; Hugh had been busy this forenoon. Leana trailed after him, sitting alone on her side of the table. After months of having the chair empty, it was strange to find it occupied again.

Something about the familiar way Leana folded her hands in her lap arrested his attention. Her features, her coloring, the tilt of her head, the clarity of her eyes. All at once he caught a glimpse of his wife. *Agness.* The only woman he'd ever loved. Lachlan looked away but not soon enough; regret, like a sharpened sword, thrust into his gut. The blade withdrew just as quickly, but the wound remained. It made him bleed; nae, it made him angry.

"Leana!" He barked the word as if it might chase away the painful image. "Could you not have worn something else for dinner? Or is that damp green gown the only one that fits you?"

Rose, ever the *cantie* one, arched her brows. "Oh, Father, how you do go on. There simply wasn't time for her to change. Suppose Eliza presses her claret gown for this evening's supper. Would that please you?"

Twenty

Then come the wild weather, come sleet or come snow,
We will stand by each other, however it blow.

SIMON DACH

Rose watched every drop of color drain from her sister's face. Had she spoken amiss?

Leana moistened her lips, a nervous habit of hers. "Eliza has several gowns hanging in my room. I'm certain I can alter one by this evening."

"But your claret gown," Rose persisted, "is by far your prettiest frock. You wore it the day you left for Twyneholm, aye? And brought it home, I'm sure."

When Leana did not respond immediately, Rose fell silent. Something was very wrong.

"I did not bring it home," Leana finally confessed, looking directly at their father. "The claret gown remains in Twyneholm. I sold it."

Rose gasped. "*Sold* it? But that gown meant…"

"More than I can say." Leana's gaze did not drop, but her voice did. "As I had no silver and nothing else of value, 'twas my only means of hiring a chaise to carry me home."

Lachlan McBride had yet to respond. His gray eyes, always cold, narrowed into slits. "Leana, are we speaking of the claret gown you wore for Rose's wedding?"

"Aye—"

"The gown I had Armstrong, the tailor, make for you?"

"Father, I—"

"The gown for which I paid a *fortune*?" He hit the table with his fist, making the pewter plates jump. "*That* claret gown?"

Rose glanced at Jamie, not surprised to find a storm brewing in his eyes. He'd felt the heat of Lachlan's temper before and knew how deadly the man's tongue could be. *Please, Jamie. Help my sister.*

He took her cue. "Uncle, it appears your daughter was sparing you the burden of sending Willie in your chaise to collect her." Jamie did not look at Leana when he spoke nor she at him. " 'Twas a thoughtful gesture on her part. And a sacrificial one."

"Och! It cost her nothing, for it was my silver that first purchased the gown."

Rose heard a faint shuffling behind the door leading to the kitchen. No doubt the entire staff had their ears pressed to the cracks, wondering when it would be safe to serve the meal.

"Now, Father…" Rose made certain her words were as sweet as Naples biscuits. "That was my sister's favorite gown. Naturally it was a hardship for her to part with it."

"Who would pay good silver for oft-worn clothing?" Lachlan demanded. When Leana explained that the Reverend and Mistress Scott had purchased it for their granddaughter, his gaze flickered with interest. "Mistress Scott, you say? She comes from a wealthy family, I'm told."

Leana's eyes widened. "Are you…acquainted with them?"

"My knowledge of Galloway is hardly limited to my own parish. Tell me, what was the cost to hire your chaise?" When she told him, he pressed further. "Is that how much the Scotts paid for the gown?"

"Nae." Leana reached beneath the table—to open the purse tied at her waist, Rose realized—and produced a generous handful of shillings. Even on a gray and rainy afternoon, the coins shone in the candlelight. "They paid me the full price, as if the gown were new. Two pounds sterling."

Lachlan held out his hand, like a child wanting sweets. "Give me the coins, Leana. My money bought the gown; the balance should be mine."

Watching her sister closely, Rose saw the glint of tears. Rarely did a woman have money of her own. For a stayed lass like Leana, a purse full of silver represented a sense of freedom, however fleeting.

Rose could not contain herself. "Father, do you not see your own daughter's eyes? They shine far more than the coins you are demanding of her." Inside her slippers, Rose's toes were curled tight, but she refused to let her nervousness show. "Can Leana not keep what is hers?"

"This is none of your concern, Rose." Lachlan did not withdraw his empty hand but shook it at her sister as though reminding Leana to do her duty. When Jamie started to speak, Lachlan's head jerked in his direction. "Not a word, Nephew. Leana kens the debt owed for her months away from home."

The coins spilled into his waiting hand.

"What need have you for silver?" Lachlan said smoothly, wrapping the money with his handkerchief. When he stuffed it in his waistcoat pocket, the coins formed an unsightly bulge over his heart. "Do tradesmen present you with bills expecting their due? Does Colin Elliot greet you with a tally of purchases when you appear at the grocer's door? On Whitsunday past did an endless parade of servants, herds, and *hinds* stick out their grimy hands, waiting to be paid for the term? You are home now, Leana, and have no use for silver. Wealth is for men to earn, manage, and disburse as they see fit."

Rose could not stomach another word. She stood, pushing her chair back hard enough to scrape the floor. "I have lost my appetite. Should anyone require me, I shall be in my room." Grabbing her skirts, she swung toward the door just in time to see Leana stand as well.

Her sister lifted her chin, her eyes still moist, but her gaze clear. "I shall be in my room also, altering one of my gowns so I might wear something more appropriate for supper."

The sisters exited the room without waiting for a response. Leana led the way, with Rose so close behind that she nearly trampled Leana's hem. Lachlan shouted both of their names, but neither woman turned back. Instead, they hurried through the entrance hall and up the stair as three servants came round the corner from the kitchen, mouths agape.

Rose didn't dare speak, fearing she might laugh or cry or both at once. They had turned their backs on Lachlan McBride! She was almost ashamed of how wonderful it felt. "Leana," she whispered when they reached the corridor outside their bedrooms, "will you truly sew this afternoon? My hands are shaking so, I would stab myself ten times just threading the needle—"

"Oh, Rose." Leana suddenly turned and pulled her into a fierce embrace. "You were so brave standing up to Father like that."

"Me?" Her voice, pinched by tears, was reduced to a squeak. "You were the *campie* one. 'I sold it,' she said. Just like that."

"Having you in the room helped." Leana patted Rose's braid, still holding her close. "My brave sister."

Rose gave a noisy sniff. "Perhaps 'tis the babe inside me making me strong."

Leana was quiet for a moment. "'Tis Jamie's love for you and yours for him that make you fearless. Father cannot hurt you now."

"But what about *you?*" Rose leaned back, her jubilant mood fading. "This is your home. Father could make the years ahead quite miserable indeed."

"Except I, too, am loved," Leana reminded her.

A bubble of fear rose in her throat. *Not Jamie.*

"Behold, what manner of love the Father hath bestowed upon us." Leana hugged her once more before letting go. "Not our earthly father, Rose. Our heavenly one. I am well loved, and so are you."

Rose pressed her handkerchief to her mouth, too full of emotion to speak. She *was* loved. Not by her father, perhaps, but by everyone important to her. Jamie especially. And Leana always. She peered down the corridor toward the stair. "I'm afraid we've left my poor husband to face Father alone."

"I do not envy Jamie the next hour," Leana agreed. "We'd best be to our rooms. Unless I am mistaken, Neda will bring us each a tray when Father is not looking."

"Good." Rose patted her stomach. "My appetite is *not* lost; it is very much found."

"Take my tray, then." Leana leaned forward and briefly pressed her cheek to Rose's, a tender gesture from their childhood. "Eat well, young Rose. Grow a healthy son or daughter for your Jamie."

Your Jamie. Rose wondered what those words cost her sister, fearing the price.

Forgive me, Leana.

Nae, it was time to stop thinking it and start saying it. *Forgive me, Leana.* The words lodged in her throat. *Say it, Rose.*

"Leana, I am…so sorry." Flooded with guilt, Rose could not look at her sister. She grasped her hands instead. "About Jamie. About Ian. About…oh, *everything*. It must be so…difficult for you. My loving Jamie…my caring for Ian…"

"Rose, 'tis not hard for—"

"But it *is* hard." She looked up, determined to be heard. "I see it in your eyes. I hear it in your voice. I've broken your heart, Leana, time and again. I have, I *have*. And you keep forgiving me, when I do not deserve it."

"Dearie." Leana shook her head, squeezing her hands tight. "Mercy is a gift, freely given, freely received."

"Are you…certain?" Rose searched her face. "Have you truly forgiven me?"

Leana's smile was grace itself. "How could I not, when I love you? Don't you see? You are my only sister and my dearest friend."

"And you…are mine." She began crying again, harder than before. "Please forgive me. Please…please."

Chin trembling, Leana kissed her brow. " 'Tis already done, Rose. Long ago."

Twenty-One

And is there any moral shut
Within the bosom of the rose?

ALFRED, LORD TENNYSON

Such a long face," Jamie chided her. "Will you not tell me what troubles you, Rose?"

She strolled beside him down the lane, her skirt hems brushing the wet gravel. After an endless day of rain, the skies had cleared during supper and bathed the countryside with sunlight, making the wet hedgerows glisten. Jamie had suggested Rose join him for an evening walk, allowing Leana to enjoy a quiet hour with Ian. Both sisters had jumped at the chance. Would that he could always make them both happy.

Rose slowed to admire a cluster of wild thyme with its rosy purple heads and long oval leaves. "The next two months will put a dreadful strain on Leana—watching the two of us together, spending hours with Ian, dreading the day she must bid him farewell." Rose leaned over to pluck a sprig of thyme from the soggy ground, then crushed the leaves and inhaled the aromatic scent. "'Tis more than any woman should bear."

They had talked of little else since Leana's arrival yestreen. He inclined his head toward the road, hoping to guide Rose's thoughts in a different direction. "Come, let me show you what I found in one of Glensone's fields."

Rose brushed the fragrant wildflowers from her hands as they approached a meadow enclosed by a dry stane dyke. "Jamie, it looks like every other field in Scot—oh!"

Baby rabbits were everywhere, hopping after their mothers, scurrying along the dyke, disappearing down holes no bigger than their tiny bodies. There were dozens of them, their velvety brown ears and white tails flicking through the wet grass, greener than ever after the rain. Rose clasped her hands with delight. "Aren't they dear? And so many."

Jamie grinned at her. "Just the remedy for my *unheartsome* wife."

She sighed with contentment, her gaze following one rabbit, then another. "We must bring Ian here."

"Morning or evening—that's when rabbits are likely to show." Jamie slipped his arm round her waist. "Though I fear you may have to bring the lad yourself if you're wanting to come soon. Tomorrow's the Sabbath, and Monday noon the herds come for the shearing."

"You'll be in the sheepfolds most of the week, won't you?" He heard the plaintive note in her voice. "From daybreak 'til the gloaming, aye?" Whenever he spent a long day on the hills, Rose often waited at the door come nightfall, watching for him with an anxious look on her face. Perhaps because Leana was older, she'd not needed his constant attention quite the same way Rose did. Like the flower she was named for, young Rose seemed to wilt without careful tending.

"Only a few days," he promised, "and then we'll have hundreds of fleeces to show for our labors."

"Hundreds?" She made a face at him. "All of them will need cleaning and carding, I suppose."

"They will indeed. A summer's work for you and the lasses. At least Leana can help with the spinning."

There. He'd said her name with a fair amount of ease that time. Not hesitating, not stumbling over it. While Leana was in Twyneholm, he'd seldom had that problem. But now that she was home again, her name had flesh to it. Lavender was no longer an herb in the garden; it was the scent of Leana's gown passing him on the stair.

Rose gazed up the road that led to Troston Hill Farm and the wild moorland beyond. "I've not seen Lillias Brown lurking about the parish. Have you?"

"Nae, lass, I have not." Rose had told him about her eerie conversations with the auld witch last spring and how much they'd frightened her. Jamie felt certain his wife would not knock on the door of Nethermuir again.

"One of her predictions did come true," Rose said. "Lillias told me, 'There is ane man for ye, lassie. And ye ken his name well.'" She reached up to brush the stray hair off his brow. "I do know his name. In fact, I share it."

"So you do." He clasped her hand and kissed the narrow silver band he'd placed there. "Mistress McKie."

Rose smiled once more at the tiny rabbits, as though they might twitch their noses at her in response, then the couple turned toward home. The evening sun threw long shadows across the road in front of them while they walked. "My sister has yet to touch her wheel, but her needle was busy today. She's altering one of her older gowns. I don't have the heart to tell her how plain it makes her look. She will ne'er catch a gentleman's eye wearing such dreary attire."

"What gentleman?" Jamie asked a bit too sharply.

"Any proper suitor who might wish to court her." Rose slipped her hand round his arm and gave him an affectionate squeeze. "Now that things are settled among the three of us, my sister is free to marry again."

Jamie looked down at her, his steps slowing. "Is that her…desire? To marry?"

"She's not spoken of it, but 'tis every woman's desire to marry. And to have children."

He stared at the rolling pastureland to the south, not really seeing the hillocks and craggy rocks, too stunned by Rose's offhand suggestion. Would Leana marry again? *Could* she marry after all that had happened? And bear another man's children?

"He'd have to be very wealthy indeed," Rose said, "to earn Father's approval."

"And be willing to…to accept…" Jamie didn't let himself finish. Not when his thoughts were unkind and fueled by the worst possible motive. Did he imagine because he could not have Leana, neither should anyone else?

"Be willing to accept what?" Rose teased him. "Leana's shocking behavior at dinner today? Leaving the table without Father's permission?"

Grateful for the diversion, Jamie pretended to look stern. "But who bolted to her feet *first*?"

"*I* did," Rose said, proud of herself.

And rightly so. Jamie had all but applauded when the McBride sisters stood up to their father, even if it meant enduring an icy meal across a noticeably empty dining table. Lachlan had choked down his food in a fit of choler and left the table. Jamie had enjoyed a second helping of everything Neda's kitchen had to offer, soup to pudding.

Rose stopped to shake a pebble from her shoe and held on to Jamie as she wriggled the leather slipper back on her foot. "I'd say Leana's remark this evening required more pluck than my earlier one."

Jamie could not remember a shorter hour of family worship. After they'd recited a few brief psalms, Lachlan announced his text for the evening: a single verse chosen with intent. "Children, obey your parents in all things." He'd read slowly, serving up each word on a plate garnished with bitterness. "For this is well pleasing unto the Lord."

When Lachlan finished, his blunt finger still stabbing at the verse on the page, Leana had said in her calmest voice, "Will you not read the next verse, sir?" He'd glowered at her while Leana had repeated it from memory: "Fathers, provoke not your children to anger, lest they be discouraged."

"Can you believe she said such a *bauld* thing?" Rose nearly skipped, so lively were her steps as they approached the mains. "My sister knows her Buik, she does."

" 'Twas courageous," Jamie agreed. Such boldness would serve Leana well when she faced the man alone come Lammas.

His gaze landed on the sheep pastured nearest the house, a healthy flock of ewes and lambs, the latter's necks still red and easily identified. Only the older sheep would be sheared beginning Monday. The lambs would remain unshorn until next summer, making it easy to count them again next week and be certain of the tally.

Twenty score. *All mine.*

"What are you smiling about, Jamie McKie?"

He laughed, pulling her into his embrace, not caring who might see them. "I'm thinking about a certain lamb."

"Are you now?" Her blush was bonnier than any sunset and quite as pink. "A lamb yet to be born, perhaps?"

"Nae." He kissed each heated cheek. "A frisky lamb that gamboled into my life on this very road one October day."

Her breath tickled his ear. "You were dripping wet. Rising out of Lochend like a *kelpie* seeking to lure me to a watery grave."

"Kelpies haunt rivers and fords, not lochs," he reminded her. "And you were dressed in peasant garb, bleating about your thirsty sheep and your overturned watering trough."

"Which you managed to turn upright, like some kind of *etin*."

"Make up your mind, lass." His scowl was playful. "Am I a water demon or a giant?"

Rose wrapped her arms round his neck. "You're the heir of Glentrool and the man I love." With that, she kissed the smile off his face and every lucid thought from his head.

Twenty-Two

Of this alone even God is deprived,
the power of making things that are past never to have been.

ARISTOTLE

I niver thought to see that *tairt* in our parish again."
Leana flinched at Lydia Taggart's harsh words, spoken loudly enough to echo down one empty pew and up the next. On such a fine Sabbath morning many villagers were still out of doors, waiting until the bell was rung before finding their seats. Instead of joining them, Leana had entered the kirk early, hoping to take her place without being noticed. To no avail, it seemed.

Rose reached over and tapped her hand. "Don't fret," she said softly. "No one heeds a glib-gabbit woman like Lydia."

Who would have imagined her sister would be the one offering support at this unsettled hour? Leana knew the parish would grow accustomed to her presence in time, but this first Sunday might be very trying indeed.

Her father had taken his usual seat farther down the pew, looking as grim as his surroundings. Though sunlight poured through the broad windows on either side of the pulpit, it only served to illuminate the austerity of the preaching house. Enclosed wooden pews faced the pulpit on three sides, as plain and straight as the parishioners who sat in them. No ornamentation courted the eye; no celestial design pointed to the heavens.

Even so, the Almighty could be found there by all who sought him. Leana gazed at the high-ceilinged room in which she'd spent so many hours, grateful for two things in particular: The stool of repentance was not on display this Sabbath day, and neither was she.

Voices floated in the door, mingled with birdsong though not with laughter—not on the Sabbath. Leana was certain she heard Ian's blithe crowing above the chatter. Jamie would bring him in at the last and hold

Ian in his lap throughout both services. The three of them had discussed the subject on the hourlong walk to the kirk and had agreed that if Jamie tended Ian, no one would blether about which mother was caring for the child.

At the muted clang of the bell, Leana glanced over her shoulder. The kirk would begin to fill now. There was Isabella Callender with her gray hair gathered in a tidy bun and her soft pillow of a nose. On the first morning Leana had compeared on the stool, it was Isabella who'd clasped her hand at the kirk door. *Whate'er betides ye, may this day be the worst.* That Sabbath had not been the worst day of her life; leaving Ian was the worst. However painful the summer might prove to be, the joy of seeing her son again far outweighed the sorrow.

"Look who's come home." A young woman with marmalade hair and eyes the color of Scottish bluebells sailed into the pew in front of them, children in tow.

"Jessie!" Leana cried softly, leaping to her feet. Jessie and Alan Newall of Troston Hill Farm were her nearest neighbors and dearest friends in the parish. Crushing her gown against the hard back of the pew, Leana hugged Jessie tight, then leaned back to admire her family. "Look how Rabbie has grown. Come, let me see your bairn."

She held out her arms for Jessie's new son, not four months old, while the rest of them found their places. His skin was pale, like Ian's, but his downy red hair marked him as a Newall, with freckles in his future. "What a fine lad you are," Leana crooned. She took one last look before handing him back to his mother, then turned to his older sister. "Annie, my *posy,* 'tis grand to see you, too."

Almost three, Annie was a smaller version of her mother in every detail, from the ringlets in her hair to her thin-lipped smile. Eyes fixed on Leana, the girl sounded out her name—"Le-a-na"—then clapped, clearly proud of herself for remembering.

"Good for you, lass." Leana longed to gather the child in her arms. But the beadle was aimed toward the door, indicating the start of the morning service, and Jamie would be along any moment with Ian. "We'll talk after the service," she promised, cupping the girl's soft cheek. "Will you sit in my lap while we eat our cold dinner?"

Annie nodded, sending her red curls dancing, then turned round at her mother's urging.

"Later," Jessie said with a wink, then faced the pulpit just as Jamie appeared in the aisle with Ian. The boy's face broke into a cherub's smile when he saw his mother.

Leana slipped out of the pew, squeezing Ian's bare foot in passing, while Jamie took his rightful place next to Rose—on the far side of her sister. *Wise, Jamie.* Distressing for her not to be seated next to Ian, but prudent not to be next to Jamie. Leana knew she could hold Ian all she liked at Auchengray. Here, with the whole parish watching, it was best that mother and son not be seen side by side.

Before discouragement sank in, Leana remembered the son or daughter she had yet to bear and was comforted. *I am still a mother.* As long as no one else knew, that fact would bring joy to her heart and grief to no one else's. Surely that was best.

Unbidden, a verse learned long ago flitted through her mind. *A faithful witness will not lie.* Despite the warm air round her, Leana's hands grew cool. Was it a sin to keep her condition to herself? Or was it mercy, sparing those she loved? The psalmist of old offered words she did not want to hear: *Mercy and truth are met together.* But what of Rose's newfound trust in her and Jamie's commitment to Rose? Would they not both be shattered if she confessed the truth?

As the second bell sounded, the precentor rose to lead the assembled in a gathering psalm. Those who were already seated remained so; those who were not, hastened to their pews, singing the words after the precentor sang them first, in *run-line* fashion. "My voice shalt thou hear in the morning, O LORD."

Please do hear me, Lord. Leana closed her eyes, not caring what others might think. *And please answer. Shall I confess the truth?*

The singing droned on, slow and unmusical, though the ancient words alone were enough to stir souls to worship. For Leana, each one mirrored the desire of her heart. *Make thy way straight before my face.* The Almighty would show her what was to be done. If she was meant to keep her own counsel, she would do so with confidence. If telling her family the unwanted news was necessary, she would seek his strength to do so. *Let all those that put their trust in thee rejoice.* Leana felt the tension inside her begin to unwind. Aye, she would trust.

At the third bell, the kirk door banged shut, and Reverend Gordon appeared. He climbed the turnpike stair into the raised pulpit, where he looked down on his parishioners with a sobering countenance. The minister offered a slight nod to the resident landowners—Lachlan McBride among them—pausing only briefly when Leana's eye caught his. She hoped they might speak between the morning and afternoon services. The two had parted amiably, but she wanted to be very certain she was welcome in her own parish. Now that Father had appropriated her remaining silver, leaving Newabbey was out of the question.

All stood for the minister's prayer, the men slipping off their bonnets, the women pulling their children against them, an unspoken warning to remain still. Leana could hear Jamie hushing Ian, his voice low and tender. His fatherly concern for their son was almost too sacred to behold. *Oh, Jamie.* What woman could not love a man for that alone?

Resuming her seat after Reverend Gordon's final "so be it," Leana aimed her thoughts heavenward, paying close attention to all that followed: a lecture on a brief section from the book of Romans, a prayer of illumination, and then an hourlong sermon on a single verse from Proverbs. Though most ministers delivered their prepared messages without notes, Reverend Gordon oft consulted his papers, adjusting his spectacles to do so.

At one o' the clock the congregants stood again for prayer, a subdued lot after the lengthy morning service. Their faces were long and their stomachs growling. On cold, wintry Sabbaths, people remained in their pews between services to eat the meals they'd brought, but whenever the weather allowed, all found a spot outside for the dinner hour.

Leana turned to ask Rose, "What has Neda packed for us today?"

Her sister made a horrid face. Pickled herring, then.

Reverend Gordon's voice carried across the emptying kirk. "Whatever would compel a young lass to look so *ugsome*?"

While Rose ducked her head, embarrassed, Leana curtsied and extended her hand. "Reverend, how good to see you again. I can only pray you feel the same way about seeing me."

"Naturally I do," he answered warmly, capturing her hand. Rose and the others made their way out of doors while Leana was trapped in his strong grip. "Reverend Scott did not inform me that you would be returning, Miss McBride. I trust your months in Twyneholm were fruitful?"

"Very fruitful," she responded, wanting to be polite even as her heart pounded against her throat, remembering the distant minister's parting words. *The fruit of your womb is God's blessing on your life.* "I am grateful for the letter you sent to Reverend Scott." She slipped her hand free. "He was most...understanding."

"Ah." Reverend Gordon raised his bushy eyebrows. "Glad to hear it. Though I must confess, I am surprised to find you home so soon. Tell me what brings you back to Newabbey."

"I was certain...that is, I expected the McKies to have left for Monnigaff parish some time ago. Instead they will depart at Lammas."

He said nothing for a moment, nodding at others in passing, his hands clasped behind his back. "A long two months for you, lass."

"And for them." She glanced toward the door, wondering which direction they might have gone. "Sir, if you might pardon—"

A woman's voice interrupted them. "Reverend Gordon!"

Leana recognized the coarse accent at once. *Mary McCheyne.*

"Is that Leana McBride ye're talkin' tae?" The slovenly woman advanced on them with a troop of small children hanging from her arms. "I thocht ye were gane tae Twyneholm for guid. Least that's what I told me cousin, Catherine."

Catherine Rain. Leana barely nodded. "I remember meeting her."

Mary's eyes had a cruel glint. "I thocht ye might. Been a month or mair *syne* she came tae visit. We had a guid chat back then, we did."

"When..." Leana wet her lips. "When might you be seeing your cousin again?"

Mary shrugged, yanking her children about as she did. "Sometime this *simmer.* Have ye a message ye need me tae *gie* her?"

"N-nae...nae message." Leana curtsied to them both. "If you'll excuse me, my family will be wondering what's happened to me."

"Dinna worry," Mary said with the slightest chuckle. "We all ken what's happened tae ye."

Twenty-Three

But see, the shepherds shun the noonday heat,
The lowing herds to murmuring brooks retreat,
To closer shades the panting flocks remove;
Ye gods! and is there no relief for love?

ALEXANDER POPE

I dinna ken what's happened, Jamie." Duncan lifted his bonnet off his head long enough to scratch at his thinning hair, then slapped it back on, his gaze scanning the horizon. The sun had shone across Galloway for hours, heating the still air, sending both cattle and sheep searching for water. " 'Tis past noon, and nae sign o' them. Have ye leuked in the far pasture?"

"Aye." Jamie knocked loose a stubborn clod of dirt stuck to his boot heel. Like most herds, Rab Murray and Davie Tait had their own notion of time. "The lads will be along."

Jamie and Duncan had spent the morning gathering the first flocks of ewes into the sheepfolds, letting the animals settle down in preparation for the shearing. The weather, if a bit warm, was ideal for the task, for the fleeces were good and dry. Damp wool could mildew and be worthless at market. Now the shears were sharpened, the sheep's stomachs were empty, and the skies were favorable. All they needed were the seasoned herds to appear, and the yearly ritual could commence.

They heard them first, singing as they walked up the drive toward the steading, their voices joined in a ragged chorus of "My Love, She's But a Lassie Yet." A moment later four ruddy-faced lads ambled into view, with the slipshod strides of young men who spent their days on the hills. "Sorry we're late, Mr. McKie." Rab Murray doffed his cap, revealing a thicket of red hair. "Had some ewes left tae shear at Jock Bell's place, we did. But we're a' weel rested and ready tae start." He nodded at the others. "Davie Tait ye ken. This here is Will Broadfoot, and the *quate* ane wi' his bonnet in his hands is Geordie Currie."

Jamie bid the lads welcome, then led them toward the cleared area near the sheepfolds, toting his own pair of shears. Though he was not so skilled as the men they'd fee'd for three days, Jamie had been taught a few things by Stew at Glentrool and had learned even more from Duncan.

Sandy-haired Davie Tait was the first to start, straddling a plump ewe with ease, then taking his shears to her brisket. "The trick is tae keep yer shears movin' and not tae make a second cut." The other herds began as well, keeping their voices low, even as they goaded one another about who would shear the greatest number that day.

Duncan brought him a mottled-faced ewe. "Yer first o' the simmer, Jamie. Gie her a go."

Aware of Duncan's observing him, Jamie gamely slipped his left thumb into the sheep's mouth and swung her toward him, lowered her to the ground, then pressed his knee against her back. "Lie still, lass. I'll not hurt you." He gripped the shears firmly lest they spring out of his hand and slowly worked his way round her fleece—chest, shoulder, head, neck, side, belly, flank, backbone. "Well done," he praised her, straightening for a moment. Then he bent to start down the other side, taking care not to pull on her ear too tightly when he sheared her neck.

"Ye'll do," Duncan said lightly, but Jamie heard the pride in his voice.

He finished quickly, then shook out the fleece, held together only by the natural interweaving of the fibers. After clipping off the dung tags and picking out the worst of the grass and debris, Jamie turned in the sides, rolled up the fleece, then pulled and twisted the neck wool to form a rope, tying the whole of it together. The other lads had finished two in the time he'd taken to do one, but his fleece was just as neatly bundled.

Rab eyed his work. "Mebbe ye'd care tae make the rounds wi' us, Mr. McKie. We could use anither guid hand at shearin' time."

Jamie laughed, knowing it was naught but jest, yet glad for the compliment. "You ken I'm not fast enough."

Rab shrugged. "Ye're the fastest *gentrice* I've e'er seen wi' a pair o' shears."

"Aye," the other lads chimed in as Duncan gave him a broad wink.

Smiling to himself, Jamie had begun sweeping clean his corner of the work area before tackling a second sheep when a woman's voice carried across the steading. "Jamieee!"

He looked up, putting his broom aside, as Rose and Leana advanced toward him, clearly on some mission with Ian. Their cotton gowns swayed as they walked across the gravel-strewn grass, both women smiling at him from beneath their broad straw hats.

"Mistress McKie." Rab grinned at his old friend, then bowed his head. "And Miss McBride, guid tae see ye hame at Auchengray." The other herds, their hands full of fleece, could neither bow nor tip their caps but offered their greetings as politely as they could.

"We've brought Ian to watch his father shear," Rose explained, holding the boy up. She nodded at Leana's linen-covered basket. "And meat pies so you won't refuse us."

Jamie was none too pleased at the thought of the two women gauging his skills. "You'll watch me once, and then you'll go. The pies can stay."

Rose propped Ian on top of a dry stane dyke worn smooth from years of rain, then folded her arms round him with a happy sigh, waiting for the performance to commence. Leana stood next to them, her hand resting on Rose's shoulder, her smile enigmatic.

"I'm hardly an old hand at this," Jamie grumbled, motioning to Duncan to bring him another ewe. When the lads all stood back to watch, he jutted his chin out at them. "There's naught to see but a grown man wrestling a frightened sheep."

"That sounds most entertaining," Rose teased him, and the others laughed, vexing Jamie even more.

"If I nick this ewe, you'll have yourselves to blame." When Duncan released the animal and stepped back, Jamie exhaled slowly, then smoothed his hand over the sheep's thick fleece, hoping to calm them both. "Steady now." As with the first one, he brought her carefully to the ground, straddled her middle, then started in with his shears, ignoring all but the task before him.

When Duncan spoke, though, he heard him clearly. "Ye're a guid shepherd, Jamie. Yer sheep ken yer voice."

Jamie felt his shoulders relax and the shears move more surely through the fleece. He had no need to impress anyone. Only the work mattered and the careful tending of his flock.

"Not mony lairds will try their hand at shearin'," Davie said by way of encouragement. "Though King David was a herd, was he not?"

"He was." Jamie shifted his position, halfway done. "But he didn't have to raise Scottish blackface." The men laughed in agreement. Blackface were a hardy breed but curious and not easily intimidated. Jamie looked up long enough to catch Rab's eye. "I'll be glad to have your help come Lammas. Yours and Davie's."

Both young men nodded. "Mr. Hastings has arranged it," Rab assured him. "We'll be blithe tae see ye hame wi' yer lambs."

"How mony will ye be takin'?" Davie asked, eying the lambs that dotted the hills.

"Twenty score. We'll be tallying them again this week, just to be certain." Jamie stood, releasing the newly shorn sheep. The ewe bleated, shook herself, then found her way to a grassy spot that hadn't been grazed since last week's rain. Jamie took a small bow. "There you are, Ian, my good lad. A shorn sheep."

The women clapped, and so did Ian. "Well done, master shepherd," Rose called out, obviously pleased with him. She looked ripe as a peach, round-cheeked and sweet. Leana's face was not so round, but he could not deny she looked bonny as well with her fair hair loosely gathered at the nape of her neck.

Duncan returned and poked his shepherd's crook in Jamie's side. "As our Laird himself said, 'How much then is a man better than a sheep?'"

"Much better." Rose lifted Ian from his stony seat.

"Far better," Leana agreed, extending her basket along with a diffident smile. "And you'll not have to nibble on grass for your dinner, Jamie. Neda has sent her best pies."

Jamie's chest tightened. *Is that why you've come, lass? To see me fed?* He nodded at the stone dyke, then pressed his forearm to his damp brow, avoiding her gaze. "Kindly leave them there." *Please, Leana.* He did not know what he wanted her to do or say. He only knew that seeing her again affected him in ways he could not fathom.

"Until this evening, Jamie," Leana murmured, moving away from him.

When he looked up, he saw that both sisters had turned toward home, swinging Ian between them, making the boy deliriously happy. Jamie turned away, vowing to think of something other than the McBride sisters. "Come, lads. Shearing awaits." He gestured to the herds. "Three score, and then dinner."

Spurred on by the promise of Neda's good food, the men worked steadily, some moving sheep, others shearing them and stacking the fleeces in neat rows as they went. The sun had hardly moved from its perch high above the horizon when they stopped to enjoy their well-earned dinner in a cool spot against the side of the barn.

While they ate, Duncan dug out a worn piece of paper and a stub of coal from his pocket. "I've been tallyin' yer spotted lambs as we go, Jamie. The count seems a bit low."

Jamie swallowed his last bite of pigeon pie with difficulty. "How low?"

Duncan grimaced. " 'Til we've gathered up a' the sheep, I canna be certain, but I've counted less than ten score. O' yers, that is. Yer uncle's lambs *wi'oot* the spots number nigh to fifteen score sae far."

Jamie brushed the crumbs from his hands harder than necessary. "We'll see how the count looks in the morn. For now, we've sheep to shear and no time to waste worrying."

But he *was* worried. All afternoon in the sheepfolds and that evening at supper and later with Rose and over breakfast with Duncan, Jamie reviewed the various flocks in his mind. Two score in this pasture. Thirty on that hill. Another score in the glen. Though sheep were rotated from one pasture to the next, it had only been a week since he'd marked them. And while full-grown sheep were known to clamber over dykes looking for greener pastures, lambs usually stayed with the flock.

Tuesday's numbers were even more alarming. Duncan showed Jamie his scribbled notes. "Eleven score o' yer lambs, Jamie. Three *hunder* and fifty o' yer uncle's. And twa dogs are missin' as weel."

By the end of the count on Wednesday, the verdict was clear: One hundred lambs—five score—were gone, all of them spotted. All of them Jamie's.

There was no explanation but the obvious one: His lambs had been stolen.

Rab Murray frowned as he ran his hands through his hair, shaking out bits of wool. "Sheep stealing is an *ill-kindit* business, Mr. McKie. I dinna ken wha would do sic a thing. 'Tis a sad day at Auchengray, tae be sure, when *reivers* come tae call."

Jamie paced back and forth, absently jabbing a rag between his fingers to get rid of the wool grease. "But why *my* lambs and not my uncle's?"

"Yers were the closest tae the road." Duncan poked the tally into his pocket. "And if ye're stealin' a man's sheep, ye'd want them a' marked alike."

"Folk will think 'tis the blackguard's own flock," Davie added, plainly disgusted. "A Sassenach, I'll warrant ye, up from Carlisle or there aboot." Grunts of agreement were exchanged. The English had a well-deserved reputation for crossing the border and running off with sheep, cattle, and, not so long ago, brides.

"They come at daybreak or at the gloamin'," Rab said, "whan the herds are off the hills and the roads are lanelie. It doesna take but twa men wi' dogs tae gather five score and spirit them *awa*."

"Och!" Jamie threw his rag to the ground. "Can nothing be done?"

"Ye'll want tae report it, o' course." Rab glanced at the others. "We can see wird gets tae the other farms. Might spare anither shepherd yer sorrow." He spread out his hands. "I wish I could do mair for ye, Mr. McKie."

"You've done a fine job shearing, which is more than enough." Jamie extended his hand to each man, noting the sympathy in their eyes. "'Til Lammas, then." The lads were paid and sent on to Troston Hill Farm, where Alan Newall was expecting them.

Duncan stood beside him, watching them climb over the braes. "After dinner we'll move yer lambs closer tae the mains. Awa from the pastures by the road and weel up onto the hills." He threw his arm round Jamie's shoulders. "Fifteen score is still a fine flock."

Jamie's head slumped forward. "'Tis my fault." They were his lambs, his responsibility. How could he have been so careless? "I fear I've been…distracted of late. Too much on my mind."

"Too mony lasses, ye mean." Duncan released his hold on him with a slight shake. "'Tis hard havin' yer old *luve* and yer new wife under the same roof."

The last thing he wanted to discuss was Leana. Not when he couldn't sort out his feelings enough to name them. Turning on his heel, he started toward the house. "We'd best tell my uncle. You ken he'll not be pleased."

Duncan caught up with him, matching his lanky stride to Jamie's. "'Tis not yer fault. Dinna let the man tell ye *itherwise.*"

They found Lachlan in the spence reading Bunyan's *Holy War.* He put aside his book and waved them toward the chairs. "You've finished with the shearing, then?"

"We have." Jamie was too agitated to sit and grasped the high back of a chair instead. "We also did a count of my lambs. Five score are missing, Uncle. Stolen."

Lachlan reached for his dram of whisky. "Are you certain of this? 'Tis a serious charge."

"Thar's nae *dout,* sir." Duncan shifted his stance. "Five score and twa o' the dogs."

Lachlan said nothing for a moment, his mouth hidden behind the small glass as he emptied its contents. "I've been to Arbigland this week for a meeting of the society. Considering what's happened here, you might jalouse one of the topics of conversation."

Duncan's shoulders slumped. "Reivers."

"Aye, just that." Like other improvement-minded landowners in the parish, Lachlan had joined the Society for the Encouragement of Agriculture, which met at William Craik's vast estate on the Solway. "There's been talk of men with sheepdogs roaming the countryside in the gloaming, gathering a small flock here, a few strays there. How many of my own lambs are gone?"

"A' o' yer lambs are accounted for," Duncan told him. "Only Jamie's were taken."

Lachlan looked genuinely distressed at the news. "Then 'tis only right you claim some of mine, Jamie. Fifty lambs, to even our flocks."

"Nae, 'twould not be fair," Jamie said quickly. Too quickly. His uncle seldom made so generous an offer. "This is not your doing. 'The LORD gave, and the LORD hath taken away.'"

"'Blessed be the name of the LORD,' aye?" Lachlan nodded. "Wise is the man who kens such a truth."

Jamie stepped back from the chair, only now noticing his greasy clothes reeking of sheep. Since little else could be done, he would wash the filth off his body and the stench of deceit from his nostrils. Whoever had managed this dark deed would not come through the parish again. His lambs were already butchered and the tender meat sold to English cooks.

Discouraged, Jamie started for the door. "I shall see you at dinner, Uncle. Though I'll not have much appetite."

"Pity." Lachlan reached for his decanter of whisky. "Neda has prepared one of your favorite dishes. Roast lamb."

Twenty-Four

Auspicious Hope! in thy sweet garden grow
Wreaths for each toil, a charm for every woe.

THOMAS CAMPBELL

Leana knelt at the foot of the kitchen garden, her knees sinking into the ground wet with morning dew. After a week at Auchengray she still was not sleeping well. The moment the first light of day illuminated the edges of her curtains, Leana sat up on her heather mattress, any hope of sleep vanished. Whether the babe inside was the reason or the approach of Midsummer Eve lengthening the days, she could not say. Perhaps 'twas the emptiness of her box bed. And the nearness of Jamie.

"Nae," she cried softly, plunging her garden spade into the earth. She would *not* think of Jamie.

Better to think of the potatoes she'd diligently planted in March. Leana dug out one after another, brushed off the dirt, and dropped them into the wicker basket beside her. Some of them were enormous, twice the size of her fist, others badly misshapen. By the time Neda boiled and mashed them for potato scones, it hardly mattered.

A wispy mist clung to the earth, muting the sounds from the steading and curling Leana's hair round her face. From the bramble bushes came the sweet, flowing song of a shy garden warbler, a plain bird that spent the summer at Auchengray before disappearing on September's first chilly morning. A tiny brown wood mouse scurried across the upturned soil, bound for some sleeping spot for the day. Their quiet company soothed her as she worked, reminding her of the One who made them all.

When her basket was filled with tatties, Leana stood, being careful not to lose her balance. Like potatoes hiding in the ground, her unborn child continued to expand. She'd slipped into Rose's bedroom one morning when all were out of doors and looked at her profile in the looking glass over the dressing table, dismayed at the image she saw. A thickening in her waist, a rounding of her belly, a slight widening of her hips. She used the warm weather as an excuse to wear her stays more loosely—not uncommon in the country—but surely Eliza would notice soon. Could she trust her maid to keep so great a secret?

She'd written Aunt Meg a letter last Monday describing her home-coming, pleading with Meg to make no mention of the child in her letters to Auchengray. Would that she might make a similar request of all the women in Twyneholm. 'Twas too late for that. The two dozen miles separating them would be her only protection.

In truth, Leana longed to tell the world her good news. No matter the situation, a bairn was always a blessing from God. She gazed up at the rows of casement windows that looked down on her like unseeing eyes. The window in Ian's room was slightly open. He would not awake for another two hours or more. She found every possible excuse to be with him. Bathing, playing, feeding, dressing, reading. Rose did not seem to mind in the least. For that kindness alone Leana would ever be in her sister's debt.

"To work, to work," she reminded herself, turning back to the task at hand. She pulled a paring knife from her apron pocket and headed for the asparagus patch—"sparrowgrass" her mother had called it—growing in a well-shaded corner of the garden. Another week and asparagus season would end. She cut each stem, none thicker than her ring finger, at a sharp diagonal and placed the stems with care in a smaller basket. Neda would blanch them and serve them in a few hours. Tatties would keep in the cellar; asparagus was meant to be eaten the day it was harvested.

Leana carried both baskets into the kitchen and left them on the pine dressing table. Scrubbed clean a dozen times a day, the wood still bore faint red stains from Tuesday's fresh-picked strawberries. She paused, not-ing the sounds of life coming from the third floor. The servants, whose beds were tucked beneath the eaves, would slip down the back stairwell before Lachlan, Rose, or Jamie pushed back their bed curtains. Leana intended to remain in the garden emptying her seed packets until late forenoon, when the sun grew too bright for her sensitive eyes and skin.

Returning out of doors, she surveyed the kitchen garden. At least

Eliza had found time to prepare the soil, hoeing it thoroughly. Leana's pockets were brimming with seeds wrapped in paper squares, purchased from a packman who came round each April. Neda had remembered to buy all her favorites: French beans and colewort, radishes and celery, spinach and cauliflower, and the crinkle-leaved cabbages known as savoys. Poking the tiny seeds in the dirt the proper distance apart was a slow process and hard on her back. By the Lammas harvest, the McKies would be gone and her condition common knowledge. Surely the household would help her then. For now, she dared not complain of her back hurting.

Leana eyed the weeds that had sprouted overnight, flourishing in the well-fertilized beds of her physic garden. She'd pull what she could and snip a few culinary herbs for Neda in passing. Bright green sprigs of coriander leaves might be tasty in a salad. So would purslane—Neda called it *purpie*—with its darker green leaves and purplish stems. At the far end stood tall stems of valerian, with pale pink flowers and potent roots often used to heal a barren woman. Rose's words from late March came to mind. *Will you prepare the valerian for me?* Leana had done so, but it was God who had blessed Rose's womb, not the garden plant.

The last of the early mist disappeared as Leana finished a long row of weeding. She rose as the back door swung open and Eliza emerged, her arms full of Ian, who was sporting her frilly white cap. "My, don't you make a charming serving lass?" Leana called out. Never mind the demands of soil and seed: A child's needs came first. She wiped her hands clean on her apron, then held them out, wiggling her fingers in anticipation. "Have you had your breakfast yet, Ian?"

"Not yet." Eliza handed him over, then stole back her cap and put it on her head backward so the strings hung over her face. Ian whooped with laughter and tugged it off again. "That's enough, laddie," Eliza cautioned him. "You'll drop me bonnet in the dirt." With her cap back in its proper place, the sandy-haired maid grinned broadly and produced two floury baps from her apron pocket. She handed one roll to Ian, who immediately stuffed it in his mouth. "Warm from the oven, they are."

"Ah," Leana breathed, plucking the other one out of Eliza's hand and inhaling the yeasty scent. "Shall we have our breakfast in the garden, Ian?" She eased him down onto the grass, then joined him there, sitting across from him and folding her skirts about her.

"I'll collect him for his bath in a bit, mem." Eliza bobbed her head and hastened back to the kitchen.

Ian, meanwhile, had covered himself in flour from forehead to chin. "I see you are enjoying your bap," Leana teased him, then took a bite of her own and sent a spray of flour across her green gown. She'd worn the old dress on purpose, knowing it would absorb the grass stains from her gardening. But the flour showed up perfectly against the dark fabric, like a dusting of snow on the lawn. "Doesn't Mother look a sight?"

A few minutes later, their breakfast rolls eaten, Leana pulled Ian onto her lap, being careful to point his energetic legs away from her stomach. "And speaking of food, have you learned this song yet? Your stepmother loved it when she was a girl." Holding out his arms as if together they might reach the sky, Leana tipped her head back and sang with abandon, louder than the birds in the yew tree.

> Cats like milk and dogs like broo
> Lads like lasses and lasses lads, too!

Ian's squeals were sweeter than music, his sticky hands more precious to the touch than silk. She kissed his hair, then bent round to press their cheeks together. "Eliza will be along any minute to claim you. Suppose you and I take a walk to Lochend this afternoon. Before your nap, aye? A loch is like your tub but a great deal larger. The water is cool, with moorhens gliding across the surface and pike swimming below. But they'll not bother us, I promise." Leana pretended Ian's vigorous repertoire of sounds meant "aye" and that his flapping arms meant he could hardly wait. "We'll leave at two o' the clock, then."

The back door banged open, and Eliza hurried toward them. "Bath time," the maid sang out. She scooped up Ian and was gone in an instant, leaving Leana's arms empty and her heart nearly so as she imagined the day when he would be stolen from her embrace forever.

Too weary to stand again, she turned onto her knees to study her ornamental garden. At least the perennials had bloomed without assistance. The scarlet Flower of Bristol, old as the Crusades, stood proudly on thick stems, clusters of bright red flowerets held high. Absorbed in her flowers, Leana did not notice she had company in the garden until a faint shadow fell across the ground before her.

"Good morning, Leana." Jamie's voice was still rough, as though he'd only just awakened.

"Good morning," she murmured, still facing her flower beds. Perhaps if she did not look at him, he would not stay. Though she wanted him to very much.

After a moment's silence, he said, "I recall another morning when I came looking for you in the garden."

She nodded slowly, remembering. Praying he would not speak aloud the words he'd said to her the day she left Auchengray. The day of his wedding to Rose. *I will always love you. God forgive me for speaking the truth.* It was the truth then. It was not the truth now.

His hand touched her shoulder. "Leana, will you not look at me?"

I cannot. She pressed her lips together, fighting back tears.

Jamie crouched beside her, elbows on his thighs, his fingers laced together. Though he did not brush against her, she felt the heat of him, warmer than any peat fire. Her body responded instinctively, turning toward him.

"Leana." A note of persuasion in his voice. "Please do not be afraid."

She looked up and met his gaze. "I am…not afraid." But there was no use pretending. She was very much afraid.

His beard stubble was dark, drawing a bold line across his cheek. The skin beneath his eyes looked bruised. Had he not slept well either? His mouth was set in a firm line, as though he had much he wanted to say. Jamie had not chanced upon her in the garden, then; he'd come looking for her.

"Leana, we must speak." Taking her hands in his, he slowly stood, pulling her up with him. Though he released her the moment she was steady, he did not step back.

She folded her hands in front of her, concealing the child he did not know existed. "Jamie, I am sorry that I came home—"

"I am not." He said it so quickly, it surprised them both. "I am not sorry," he said again, more deliberately. "There was too much left unspoken between us. After you departed for Twyneholm…" He looked away, rubbing a hand across his face. When he turned toward her again, the sheen in his eyes was unmistakable. "We did not have a chance to… We could not *finish,* Leana. I was not ready to…let go of you."

"But you're ready to do so now?" she asked softly. "To…let go?"

Though he did not answer, she saw the truth in his eyes. *Aye.* Resignation and relief flooded her soul, mingled with a deep sadness. "I understand. I do."

Still he did not speak. "Jamie, what is it?"

"I need…" He looked away. "I need to know I'm…forgiven." His ragged voice tore at her heart "For loving your sister. For loving Rose."

Oh, Jamie. " 'Tis exactly what I would have you do," she assured him, needing to hear the words as well. "There is nothing to forgive. Not for doing what is right and good."

"But I made a vow…"

"A vow to God. Just as I have." She longed to touch his cheek, if only to comfort him, but she kept her hands clasped tight. "I know that you loved me once, Jamie." He lifted his head, an acknowledgment. "Just as I know that you love Rose now."

"I do," he admitted, "very much." His face, his eyes shone with sincerity. "Yet when I see you, Leana…"

She fell back a step. "Then do not see me. Not…like that." She begged the Almighty for a strength she did not possess and sensed it filling her like wind fills a sail. "I am your cousin. Rose's sister. And Ian's mother. 'Tis enough for me."

His gaze probed hers. "You are certain?"

"Aye," she whispered, praying he would believe her.

After a moment he bowed and clasped her hand, fervently kissing the back of it. "I truly am glad you came home, Leana."

I should never have come home. But she had.

And because of Ian, because of her dear son, she could say with a clear conscience, "I am happy to be here as well, Jamie."

When he released her, when the warm touch of his lips on her skin cooled, she did not watch him leave but stood her ground in her beloved garden and turned to the One who remained.

Twenty-Five

The blooming daughter throws her needle by.

Charles Sprague

R ose had no patience for embroidery.
The afternoon light in the front parlor was more than sufficient to guide her stitches, yet they strayed across the fabric as if in search of a pattern. She'd sharpened her needle on a whetstone, but that was no help at all, for when she pricked her finger, it bled all the more profusely on the linen. Her mother's silver thimble was too big for her thumb and fell off several times, finally rolling under her chair just out of reach.

" 'Tis hopeless!" Rose cried, throwing her embroidery hoop across the room, the fabric trailing after it like the tail of a kite. The hoop landed safely on the half-tester bed, just missing Annabel as she entered the room balancing a cup on a tray.

The maidservant did not even glance at the banished embroidery. "Might a *tassie* o' punch be a welcome treat for ye, mistress?"

Embarrassed, Rose snatched her silk fan off the table and fluttered it in front of her heated cheeks. "Indeed it would on a Thursday as warm as this one."

Annabel set the tassie and a plate of honey cakes on a table within easy reach, curtsied, and quietly left the room. Ever since Jamie had informed the maidservant she would be coming with them to Glentrool, Annabel had gone out of her way to please her.

Rose sipped the cold concoction, licking her lips at the tart, sugary taste. The punch was one of Neda's specialties, made with imported lemons, freshly drawn well water, sugar from the loaf in the pantry, and mint leaves from Leana's garden. All was stirred in a great bowl and served in a cup with a slice of lime rubbed round the edge, then floated on top.

"Heaven," Rose said on a sigh, her embroidery forgotten. She would start anew some other day when her patience wasn't worn thin by the heat. Her bairn would not arrive for many months; the little nightgown could wait. In any case, it was Leana's fault: Yestreen she'd presented Ian with the most darling cotton nightgown trimmed in purple and green thistles. Rose could not stand the thought of her own son or daughter sleeping in plain white cotton when something finer could be had if she simply plied her needle.

With Leana's help, she'd cut the fabric and stitched the seams. But the tiny black-and-white magpies she'd chosen to embroider for the hem had proven beyond her limited skills. Rose looked down and spread her fingers across her child's hiding place. "I'll try again, wee one. But not today."

"Mistress?" Annabel at the parlor door again. "A visitor tae see Mr. McKie or Mr. McBride. *Naither* o' them is hame at present. Will ye kindly come and greet him?"

"Of course." Rose was on her feet at once, touching a hand to her hair. Rather than braiding it that morning, Annabel had swept Rose's dark locks on top of her head, leaving several plump curls dangling in the back, tickling her neck. Jamie had complimented her at breakfast. Did it indeed make her look more sophisticated? As there was no looking glass in the parlor, she could only hope her coiffure was still in place as she hastened to greet their guest.

A well-dressed young man stood in the entrance hall examining the pewter bowl on the hall table. "Peter Drummond!" Rose stretched out both hands to welcome their neighbor from Glensone Farm, then, remembering her manners, grasped her gown and curtsied instead. "What a pleasant surprise."

He bowed, his face more ruddy than usual. "Good…good to see you as well, Rose…eh, Mistress McKie."

Poor Peter. He was even more flustered than she. Not many months ago he'd inquired about courting her and was firmly turned away. Her affections lay elsewhere then as now. Still, he was an amiable fellow and a good friend of the family. She would do all she could to make amends.

"Won't you join me in the parlor? Annabel, do bring Mr. Drummond a tassie of punch." Rose slid her hand inside the crook of his elbow, barely touching his sleeve as she guided him into the parlor, artfully blocking his view of her abandoned embroidery.

They sat on either side of a small mahogany table—Rose first, with a toss of her curls, then Peter, flipping his coattails aside. How odd to play mistress of the house with a friend she'd known since they both were bairns.

"We haven't had many visitors of late," she confessed, then wished she had not. One hardly needed to mention the scandal that darkened the sky over Auchengray like carrion crows, visible for miles. An irregular marriage? A sister on the cutty stool? No wonder the McBrides and McKies had not been invited to any social gatherings that spring. The last invitation was in February when Jamie and Leana had attended a dinner party at Glensone. As husband and wife.

Hoping to improve their social prospects, Rose offered her brightest smile. "What brings you to Auchengray, Mr. Drummond?"

"Peter," he corrected her, smiling as he said it. His curly hair, thick as a hedgerow, was a rather ordinary light brown. It did match his eyes, though, which regarded her with a certain earnestness. "I've been away to Glasgow for a fortnight and only today learned of your father's distressing loss. The…eh, hundred lambs?"

"My husband's lambs, you mean. Aye, very bad news, that." She paused as Annabel served more lemon punch, then continued. "I am sure my father would be willing to discuss the particulars with you. At present he is in Dalbeaty on family business, and Mr. McKie has gone to the village." Jamie was arranging the necessary provisions for their journey to Glentrool and being fitted for a new riding habit, putting his mother's guineas to good use. Never a patient man, he seemed especially anxious for them to be on their way.

Peter bit his lip. "Perhaps I might call another time—"

"Oh, do stay!" Judging by his look of alarm, she'd spoken too forcefully. "That is, I do hope you've not had a similar tragedy at Glensone with your own lambs."

"Nae. But I have some information that may be useful either to your father or to your…your husband." Now he *was* blushing and shifting in his seat as well.

"I expect Mr. McKie at any moment. Please enjoy your punch while we wait for him." Rose cast about, hoping to find some clever topic of discussion, and was relieved when her sister appeared and solved everything.

"Mr. Drummond." Leana glided into the room, curtsied with the grace of a courtier, then folded her hands at her waist. "How nice to find you in our parlor." Her sister was eating better, Rose decided, for Leana's too-slender form was beginning to fill out.

Peter was on his feet and bowing even before Leana spoke. At age twenty-one he was a twelvemonth younger than Leana and quite the same height, which was to say not very tall for a gentleman. Unlike Jamie, whose chin easily rested on top of Rose's head.

"Miss…McBride," Peter said haltingly, resuming his chair after she sat. "Mother said she…saw you at kirk the last two Sabbaths but regretted that you…that the two of you did not have a chance to…chat."

"I am happy to be home." Leana smiled as though there were nothing unusual about her hasty departure or her return to the parish. "And even happier to have *you* here. Now then, how are your parents?"

Put at ease by Leana's gentle manner, Peter shared the latest news from Glensone. His father had organized a day of salmon fishing on the Urr. His mother had finished a patchwork quilt. The sheep at Glensone were duly sheared. Mundane matters, yet Rose was eager to hear any report of her neighbors' lives.

Peter was pleasant company and a true gentleman. As the Drummond heir, he would inherit the whole of Glensone someday. No wonder her father had been furious when she refused his suit. Jamie had a great deal more to offer, of course, but Peter would make some Galloway lass a fine match. Leana, for example, seemed quite comfortable with him, and he with her. Peter was attentive, well mannered, and generous with his praise. He admired the flavor of the punch, the furnishings in the room, even the lacework on Leana's pink gown—one of Mother's castoffs rescued from a dusty trunk.

It was only when Annabel brought a fresh glass of punch for Leana that a brilliant notion came to mind. Might Peter Drummond make a fitting husband for her sister? He was younger, aye, and shorter than one might hope. But wasn't his smile engaging with those fine, straight teeth? And though his eyebrows reminded her of a brown hare hopping up and down as he spoke, at least his expressions were lively and his discourse amusing. With her past indiscretions, Leana could not afford to be choosy, yet their neighbor from Glensone would be a very *good* choice, wouldn't he?

Observing them together, Rose hid behind her fan more than once, grinning at the possibilities.

"Rose?" Jamie called from the entrance hall and strode into the parlor a moment later. "Here you are. And with a welcome guest. Good to see you, sir."

Peter stood and the two men bowed, then clasped hands in a more familiar manner. "Mr. McKie, I have been duly entertained by your fair cousins. But it is you I have come to see. Shall we speak here? Or might there be…"

Rose exchanged glances with Leana, and they both were on their feet in an instant. "Feel free to discuss your business here in the parlor, gentlemen." Rose took Leana's arm. "My sister and I will tend to Ian." The women headed directly for the second floor, only to find the lad still sleeping.

"Suppose we wait in your room," Rose said softly, closing the nursery door. "Show me the gowns you're altering. The one you're wearing today is quite becoming." The color suited her sister's complexion, though the style was woefully dated.

Leana's bedroom looked like a dressmaker's shop, with gowns of every hue hanging from hooks and draped over chairs. Some gowns were satin and brocade; others were simple linen or printed cotton. Not one of them was fashionable. The sack dresses featured entirely too much fabric, and a polonese was not to be found anywhere. Since Father had confiscated her sister's silver, Rose dared not suggest a new gown. Whatever was to be done? She turned in a slow circle, taking them all in, making certain her disappointment did not show. "Which one are you working on now?"

Leana gathered up a blue satin closed gown. "I think this one has promise if I add some lace to the sleeves since they end above the elbows. And a bit of lace is needed at the neckline as well."

"It would help," Rose agreed. She'd never seen a plainer gown. "Does it fit? Try it on for me. I'll be your lady's maid."

"Nae!"

Her sister's response was so swift, Rose thought she misunderstood. "You don't wish me to help you?"

"I don't wish to try on any gowns just now." Leana sat down on the bed—or rather, dropped onto it as if in a faint.

Rose hastened to her side. "Are you ill, Leana?"

Her sister's face flooded with color. "I fear the tart punch did not agree with my stomach. Might I…lie here for a few moments? Until Ian awakens?"

"Wheesht," Rose said softly. "You let me care for Ian." She ran about the room yanking the curtains closed, darkening the room. The air felt cooler at once.

When she returned to slip off Leana's leather shoes, Rose was taken aback. "I've ne'er seen your feet so swollen." Leana really did not look well. Was it merely the punch? "Rest, dearie. Do join us later for supper if you feel you can manage. If not, I'll have Neda send up a tray."

Rose pressed a kiss to her forehead, relieved to find no fever, then tiptoed out the door and down the hall. Leana had been home for two long weeks; this was not some malady contracted in Twyneholm. Whatever ailed her, Rose intended to pay close attention to her sister through supper and make certain the lass retired early.

It seemed her clever plan involving Peter might have to wait until a more opportune time—though waiting had never been one of her virtues. "Leana Drummond," Rose said under her breath, enjoying the sound of it. Perhaps Jamie might be of some assistance with Peter. Surely her husband would be glad to see his cousin happily wed.

Rose ducked inside her room to consult the looking glass. Aye, her hair was still in place and her dress not too wrinkled for supper. If her sister did not come to table, she would have Jamie's undivided attention. Rose smiled in the glass, imagining the look on his face when she told him what she had in mind for their neighbor.

Twenty-Six

But patience, cousin, and shuffle the cards!

SIR WALTER SCOTT

Jamie's eyes widened. "Do I understand you correctly?"

"You do, sir." Peter Drummond, several years his junior, was a bright young man and trustworthy as they came. If he appeared nervous at the moment, it was not because he was hiding something. "I believe they were your lambs, Mr. McKie, though I did not realize it at the time."

"Tell me everything," Jamie urged, leaning forward in his chair. "From the beginning."

" 'Twas late in the evening a fortnight ago." Peter's animated face also conveyed his story, as did his many hand gestures. "I was walking the dogs on the hills round Glensone and saw a flock of lambs being herded past our property, headed west."

Jamie's indignation climbed another notch. "How many lambs?"

"Hard to say, sir. Several dozen. The gloaming had almost faded into night, so I could not spot any keel marks on the fleece, nor did I recognize the men. Three or four at most. Might they've been the new herds you fee'd on Whitsun Monday?"

When Jamie described the men they'd hired for the term, Peter shook his head. "I don't remember a black-haired man among them nor a fair-headed one. The collies looked familiar, though."

Jamie groaned. "We lost two of our best dogs."

"And here I thought they were simply moving the flock to another of your pastures." Peter dragged his hand over his chin, his expression troubled. "Mr. McKie, I owe you a sincere apology. I should have hailed the men, taken a closer look at the lambs, asked round the neighboring farms, done *something*. Instead, I left the next morning in such haste that I did not think of it 'til I returned home. When I heard the sad news…and then realized…"

Jamie held up his hand, stemming his apology. " 'Tis not your fault, Peter. I am grateful for the information. At least I ken the direction those blackguards were headed. And the hour."

"And the day," Peter reminded him. "The first of June."

Too long ago to matter now.

A light knock, then Neda curtsied at the doorway. "Mr. McKie, supper is ready *whenever* ye wish it tae be served."

His mood shifted a bit. The lambs could not be saved, but the evening could. "My uncle is away, which means we may eat at once if we like." Jamie stood, extending his hand. "Come, neighbor. 'Tis only the three of us at table tonight. Tarry and make it four."

Peter, well versed in the rules of Lowland hospitality, hesitated. "I fear 'twould be an imposition." Jamie pressed him to stay, as every good host was expected to do, and Peter accepted, as any wise visitor would.

They'd no sooner entered the hall than Rose swept down the stair, the heathery scent of her gown arriving one step ahead of her. "Peter, I am delighted to find you still here. Won't you stay for supper?"

"He has already accepted my invitation," Jamie told her. "Might you see if Leana is ready?"

Before Rose could respond, her sister's voice floated down from the top of the stair. "I am here." And a moment later she was, wearing a deep pink gown trimmed in ivory, the very color of her skin. If he'd seen the dress before today, Jamie did not recall it.

"A new gown?" he asked politely.

"A very old one," Leana said just as politely.

Since the day they'd spoken in the garden, all their exchanges had been thus. Formal. Cautious. And brief. The strain was taking its toll on both of them. Leana could never be simply his cousin, though she played the part well. For his part, he could not look at her without remembering all she'd meant to him.

Rose smiled warmly at her sister. "Leana, I am so pleased to see you feeling better. Peter will enjoy your company, I am sure." She took Jamie's arm. "Come, gentlemen. Baked salmon and a pottage of chopped herbs await."

They were soon seated in the dining room—Rose next to him on one side of the table, Leana and Peter across from them. Jamie held up his glass of claret in the direction of Lachlan's vacant chair. "Here's to you, sir, as we partake of your meat."

Without Lachlan's unsmiling presence, the conversation at Auchengray's table grew livelier with each course. Peter's fortnight in Glasgow, relayed in enthusiastic detail, made a fine accompaniment to Neda's thick soup. Over salmon Jamie shared several anecdotes from his days at university in Edinburgh. Rose, free from her father's censure, told a delightful tale from their childhood when Peter was but eight. And Leana offered a colorful description of Twyneholm while carrot pudding was served.

"I cannot recall a more entertaining meal," Peter declared after tipping his head back to drain the last of his wine. "Had I known Neda Hastings was such a fine cook, we would have claimed her for our kitchen at Glensone years ago."

"That would ne'er do," Rose said solemnly, "for we all know how Neda adores working for Father." Once their laughter subsided, she clapped her hands together as though inspired. "What say you to a game of whist? Oh, let's do!"

Peter's eyebrows arched. "Does Mr. McBride approve of card playing?"

"As long as we keep our silver in our purses and only tally points, he will have no cause for complaint." Rose looked round the room, then lowered her voice to a stage whisper. "But you won't mention our playing to him, will you?"

Peter chuckled. "No, Mistress McKie. 'Twill be our secret."

Rose cast her smile, bright as starlight, on Leana. "Dearie, you must play. We need four."

Jamie saw her hesitate before answering, "Whatever you say, Rose."

He followed the others into the parlor, where Hugh had already set up a square table with four hard-backed chairs. Not a spontaneous notion, then; Rose had something up her sleeve, and it was not a playing card. She seemed intent on presenting Peter Drummond—eligible bachelor that he was—in the most flattering light. For whose benefit? Surely not Leana's.

"Round games are better suited for parties," Rose declared, locating the cards in the sideboard, "but whist is the perfect game for partners. Shall we find our seats?" She took her place facing the door, as any hostess would, then nodded at the seat opposite her. "Would you be good enough to sit there, Mr. McKie? I believe Mr. Drummond and my sister make a fine pair, don't you?"

Peter coughed. "I beg your pardon, but…" He fiddled with his cravat, as if his neckcloth had grown too tight since supper. "Husbands and wives are not usually permitted to partner for whist. 'Tis considered an unfair advantage. At least, those are the rules at Glensone."

"Are they really?" Rose looked crestfallen. "Would that mean you are…*my* partner?"

"Aye." Peter sat down across from her, his discomfort obvious. "And your husband…eh, Mr. McKie must partner with…Miss McBride."

Leana took her seat, the rustle of her silk gown the only sound in the room. Jamie pulled out his chair as quietly as he could and sat facing her, gazing at her bowed head across the felt-topped table. Whatever foolishness Rose planned was not working.

True to form, his wife's zeal did not flag. "Jamie, you shall be our first dealer."

He shuffled the cards. Anything to move the evening forward and bring it to a swift end, if only for Leana's sake. Rose cut the deck, as was customary, then he distributed all the cards evenly, turning over the last one from his own hand to show the others the trump card. *Hearts.*

While Jamie eyed her over his handful of spades and clubs, Leana rearranged the thirteen cards in her keeping, her slender fingers moving them from here to there with studious intent. The others did the same, then Peter began the first trick of the game.

"I'll not be much help to us," he alerted Rose, playing a four of diamonds.

"And I have nothing but honors," Rose replied airily, laying down the queen of hearts when it was her turn, taking the trick for them. Cards landed on the felt, circling the table like a clock. Peter. Leana. Rose. Jamie. Suits were matched, trump cards were played, worthless cards discarded, and still little was said beyond the occasional, "Oh."

When all thirteen tricks were played, Rose reached for her scoring sheet. "So…shall we play short or long whist?"

Three voices answered in unison, "Short."

Jamie stretched out in the box bed with a weary groan. "Whatever were you thinking, Rose?"

She rolled onto her side to face him, her unbound hair falling round her shoulders. "Peter Drummond needs a wife," she said firmly, "and Leana needs a husband."

"And you need to leave such decisions to your father."

"My *father*?" Rose sat up, tossing aside the sheet, clearly unhappy with him. "Do you think Lachlan McBride cares one whit about my sister's happiness?"

"Nae," he admitted. "But he does care what his neighbors think of him." Through the open window the churr of a nightjar rose and fell, filling the weighty silence. "Mr. Drummond of Glensone is not about to marry his only son and heir to…a woman like Leana."

Even in the darkness of their bedroom, he saw the spark of anger in her eyes. "To what sort of woman are you referring?"

He sat up as well, hoping to make amends. "Rose, you ken what I mean—"

"You mean a woman who loved God enough to sacrifice *every-thing*." He heard her tears and sensed her temper rising. "A woman who spoke the truth. A woman who gave up her son. A woman whose only sin was *loving you*."

"Rose!" He grabbed her wrists and gently shook her. "Beloved, keep your voice down. Your sister is in the next room."

"So she is." Rose sniffed, wiping her nose with her nightgown sleeve. "Alone. While I am here with you."

He lifted her hand and kissed her palm. "Does that distress you… being here with me?"

"You know better." Her head drooped. "But it grieves me to think of Leana. When she was not here at Auchengray, when I did not have to see her suffer daily, I could convince myself she was happy in Twyneholm. Now I know the truth." She looked up, beseeching him with her dark eyes. "Why can't my sister marry Peter Drummond?"

"Because, much as you might wish it so, Peter will not court her." Jamie kissed her brow, smoothing back her hair. "His father would ne'er allow it. If and when Lachlan seeks a husband for Leana, 'twill be a second or third son with no claim on his sire's estate. Someone from another parish, not privy to Newabbey gossip."

"A…stranger." Her voice broke on the word.

"I'm afraid so. Were Leana still a maid, gentlemen would vie for her hand and pay handsomely for the privilege of claiming it. Instead, your father is the one who must do the wooing, offering potential suitors a sizable dowry for taking Leana off his hands." Jamie shuddered, imagining the riffraff Lachlan might court on his daughter's behalf. Older men with little money and limited prospects. And few moral scruples.

Rose sank against him, drying her wet cheeks on his nightshirt. "Poor Leana."

Aye. Jamie shut his eyes, but the truth remained. He could not love her. He could not help her. And he could not look at her without regret.

Twenty-Seven

Tell her, if you will, that sorrow
Need not come in vain;
Tell her that the lesson taught her
Far outweighs the pain.

ADELAIDE ANNE PROCTER

Huddled in her box bed, Leana tried not to listen. But words and phrases penetrated the walls of her room, seeking a willing ear.

"…gave up her son." Rose's voice, heated with ire. Was the lass angry with Jamie? Or disgusted with *her*? Ashamed of herself, Leana inched closer to the wall that joined their two bedrooms.

"…loving you." Leana heard that phrase distinctly, and her heart sank. It seemed her efforts to conceal her feelings for Jamie had failed.

"Rose!" Jamie's voice. Sharp, a warning. And then he spoke again. Not so sharply. "Beloved…" Leana pressed her hand to her mouth. Jamie had once honored her with that endearment in the same tender voice. *Beloved.* Though he still spoke kindly to her, there was no longer any mention of love.

Leana sat up, her nightgown twisted round her legs, and prayed she'd not hear another word. But a snippet of conversation still found her. "…marry Peter Drummond?"

Oh, Rose. Her sister's naiveté was showing. Jamie would set her straight. There would be no suitors knocking on Auchengray's door, least of all Peter Drummond. Persuaded to stay for supper and then for a game of whist, all because Rose thought he might make a suitable husband for her wayward sister. A woman no longer welcome in polite society. A woman only God could love.

Leana's breath caught. Was that true?

She gathered the sheets round her, staring into the darkness. Jamie, the only man she'd ever loved, no longer loved her. There was no one else, could never be anyone else. No one except the Almighty.

Could he fill all the empty places where Jamie's love once lived? Would he mend her heart, shattered when Ian was taken from her arms? Was the love of One she could not see or hear or touch…was it enough?

"Nae!" she whispered into the hollowness of her box bed, tears pooling in her eyes. She touched her lips with trembling fingers, remembering the feel of Jamie's mouth on hers. Was he kissing Rose now, as he'd once kissed her? How unfair, how cruel to have come home to this! Could the Lord not have intervened, not have spared her? She had given up Jamie, would give up Ian a second time. Had she not sacrificed enough? Would her pain never end?

"*Why,* Lord?" The words were squeezed from her heart. "Why must I be alone?"

No answer came.

Even the nightjar ceased its churring.

Leana sank onto her pillow, ashamed of her questions. How dare she speak of sacrifice to One who had sacrificed his life? Or complain of suffering to One who had suffered on her behalf? *Forgive me, Lord.*

Seeking comfort where she might find it, Leana rested her hands over the roundness of her belly. In a few weeks she would feel the first flutter of movement. A tangible reminder that God's blessing on her life remained. She was far from alone.

"This child will always be mine, Lord." Leana gazed at the moonlit window. "And always be yours."

"Leana, I don't know when I've seen you look so…" Jessie Newall narrowed her bright blue eyes, assessing her across the kitchen parlor table. "So *bien,* my mother would say. Comfortable. As if you'd just finished eating a dish of fresh strawberries and cream."

"That's odd." Leana looked down at her empty plate, the food reduced to crumbs. "I thought it was shortbread."

Jessie laughed and ran a hand through her marmalade-colored curls.

"You've not lost your sense of humor, I see." She draped her son over her shoulder, rubbing his back to help his milk settle. "Is there some blithe news you'd care to report, lass? A suitor in Twyneholm, perhaps…"

Leana ducked her head, feeling her cheeks warm. "You know there isn't a suitor in Twyneholm or anywhere else." Jessie Newall was as plain speaking as any woman in the parish. And the most perceptive. Care needed to be taken, or Jessie would winkle out the truth.

Leana had taken advantage of the fine weather that Saturday morning, bringing Ian along for a neighborly visit. With Midsummer approaching, warmer days were ahead, but this one was breezy and pleasant, perfect for a stroll up Troston Hill. The sky was washed in blue, the sparse clouds the color of newly shorn fleece. Atop the hill sat a one-story farmhouse surrounded by a tidy steading and a small flock of blackface sheep.

Jessie had greeted her with a broad smile and shortbread fresh from the oven. In her kitchen parlor, a small nook separate from the cooking area, the two of them had swapped stories from the last several months, stitching together their friendship with tautly woven threads. When the time came to share her secret, Jessie Newall would be one of the first to hear it. But not today.

Leana stood, Ian still wrapped round her. "Shall we take the children out of doors?"

"First we'll have to talk my daughter out of her game." The redheaded child sat nearby on the floor, surrounded by several horn cups that were easily stacked, then knocked over, making a cheerful clatter. "Annie, if you'll put them on the table, you can play with them again later."

Leana admired the kind, straightforward manner in which Jessie handled her children, neither berating nor spoiling them. Now that Ian was crawling, he could get into a great deal more trouble. Any advice Jessie might offer her about handling older bairns would be welcome, not only for Ian's sake, but for the child to come.

Jessie led the way, a child on each hip, as they strolled into her garden. A profusion of vegetables awaited them with a few poppies for color. "Colin Elliot takes some of my fancier cabbages to market for me in Dumfries," Jessie explained when Leana complimented her abundant crops. "The Dutch red, the sugarloaf, the yellow savoy. Those are the ones folk in the royal burgh seem to favor. Come sit beneath the rowan tree where the sun won't burn us."

A few white petals remained scattered beneath the branches full of berries, which would ripen to a bright red come August. They settled on the dry ground, spreading their skirts round them. Ian was content to sit by Leana's side and play with the string of colored beads she'd brought for him, while Annie went off to investigate the kitchen garden, poking a stick in the soil round each plant. " 'Tis good for drainage," Jessie noted with a wry grin. She settled Rabbie on her lap, a thin blanket across him. "He'll be asleep before Annie finds her first worm."

Leana smiled at the boy, remembering when Ian was that small. "How are you faring with two bairns?" she asked, being careful not to seem too curious. Though Ian would depart well before her new child arrived, she would always be the mother of two.

"They're a handful." Jessie adjusted her son's blanket. "Each one verra different. With Rabbie I felt as if I started all over again as a mother, *spleet-new.* Was it like that for you with Ian after a few months away?"

Leana confessed the truth. "I did not realize until I arrived that Ian was still at Auchengray." As Leana described her homecoming and its many entanglements, Jessie listened without comment, her eyes filled with sympathy.

"I am glad Rose is so generous," Jessie finally said, "allowing you to spend time with your son."

Knowing Jessie would speak honestly, Leana voiced a question that weighed on her. "Have you seen Rose…with Ian? Does she…manage well?"

Jessie did not respond at once, pursing her lips as she gazed up into the rowan tree's sturdy branches. "I have only seen your sister with Ian at kirk or in the village. Alan and I…" A faint blush stole across her face. "We've not called at Auchengray in some time."

"Hardly anyone has," Leana was quick to say. " 'Tis…difficult for people. Though Peter Drummond came Thursday and stayed for supper and whist."

"Did he?" Jessie gazed toward the lane that led downhill to Glensone. "Fine neighbors, the Drummonds."

"You've not answered my question," Leana reminded her. "About Rose. And Ian."

Amid the freckles dotting her face, wisdom shone in Jessie's blue eyes. "Rose is not you," she said simply. "Your sister handles Ian with a certain confidence now, and 'tis obvious she cherishes the boy. Still…she is not his mother, however fondly she may dote on him. But when *you* are with him, Leana…" Jessie's eyes grew moist. "I have ne'er seen a mother love a child the way you love Ian McKie."

Neither spoke for a bit. A small heath butterfly, its orange wings decorated with two dark brown dots, flitted nearby.

"I *do* love Ian to distraction," Leana said at last, combing her fingers through his hair. "A blessing since I cannot love his father."

"I ken 'tis true, Leana." Jessie's voice was low, comforting. "Yet it grieves me to hear you say it."

Leana gathered Ian onto her lap, kissing his cheek in passing. "'Tis harder than I e'er dreamed it might be. To see Jamie with Rose. To realize the love we once had is no more. I truly would despair if not for the certainty of God's love and his blessing on my womb."

Jessie gave her a baffled look. "What blessing might that be?"

Leana froze. "Th-this one." She held on to Ian, her heart racing. "My son, Ian."

"Oh!" Jessie laid her hand over her heart. "I thought you meant you were expecting another bairn. Wouldn't that be something? You and your sister both carrying children sired by the same man."

"It would be…something," Leana agreed, pressing her warm cheek to Ian's head, praying Jessie didn't notice. Perhaps if she changed the subject at once, her face might cool, and Jessie would be none the wiser. "Is Alan bound for Keltonhill Fair on Tuesday?"

"He is." Jessie flicked a rowan leaf off her sleeve. "Most of the parish men will be there and some of the women as well."

Not this one. Leana could not imagine a less comfortable place for an expectant mother or a less hospitable one for a gentlewoman.

She considered getting up from the ground, for her legs were beginning to ache, then thought better of it. Jessie would surely notice her protruding stomach as she stood and jalouse the rest. Instead, she shifted her weight and eased Ian back onto the grass. "Jamie and Duncan are riding to Keltonhill together, intent on purchasing a horse."

" 'Tis the largest horse fair in the south of Scotland. If e'er a man wanted to buy a mount, he'd find one at Keltonhill." Jessie winked. "That is, if his silver isn't stolen."

Twenty-Eight

Tig! for the morn's the Fair Day.

TRADITIONAL SCOTTISH RHYME

K eep yer purse oot o' sight," Duncan warned as he and Jamie neared yet another boisterous company of travelers, "and gather yer wits aboot ye."

Jamie adjusted his seat, his backside sore from riding. At least the skies were clear and the roads dry. The freshening air from the Solway bore no hint of rain as it ruffled the yellow blooms of St. John's wort growing by the hedgerows. Jamie tipped his head toward the wildflowers. "Shall I pick one and hide it under my vest?"

Duncan made a face. "An auld wives' tale. *Oniewise*, ye're tae pick it on St. John's Eve if ye mean tae ward awa evil."

" 'Tis not what the plant keeps away but what it draws near that interests me: peace in the house and prosperity in the sheepfolds." Jamie eyed the tall stems in passing, remembering what his mother had taught him. *I will pluck thee with my right hand, I will preserve thee with my left hand.* "Suppose I choose a bloom on the way home to wear beneath my arm. Naught but one day early. St. John will not object."

"Suit yerself," Duncan said, "though 'twill be late."

"Aye, but still light." Tradition dictated that Keltonhill Fair fell on the first Tuesday after the seventeenth of June, coinciding with Midsummer, the longest day of the year. In Galloway the sun rose not long after four o' the clock on the solstice, lighting the sky until nearly ten the same night—ideal for a one-day fair, though it made for a lengthy outing.

After a hasty breakfast at dawn, the two men had departed Auchengray. Leana watched from the garden, lifting her hand in farewell. Astride Walloch, Jamie had waved in return, gazing at her longer than propriety allowed. She seemed more peaceful of late. Less wary in his presence. He was grateful, since it eased the tension between them. Yet he could not deny the pain that gripped him each time he thought of taking her son and bidding her farewell. There was nothing to be done, no other option afforded him, but his chest ached nonetheless. He could never beg Leana's forgiveness enough.

Duncan, riding close beside him, caught his eye. "Rather than wearin' St. John's wort tae scare awa the *dei'l*, ye'd be better off lettin' Leana make ye an infusion." He paused, as if letting Jamie figure it out for himself. "Tae cure yer melancholy."

"When I have my own mount, you'll see my spirits lift."

"Och, is that what's been eatin' at ye a' month? Not havin' yer ain horse?"

Jamie shrugged, knowing Duncan saw through his ruse. "Lachlan made it clear I would not be taking Walloch with me to Glentrool. Though we'll not find his equal today, there'll be horseflesh enough to choose from." He touched a hand to the purse concealed inside his vest. "We'll need coins for food and ale. The rest will buy my mount."

Duncan guided his horse round a deep gouge in the gravel. "Hard-earned silver it is."

Jamie's jaw tightened, but he said nothing, still angered by Lachlan's stiff-necked response to his request for a loan. "If it's silver you're need-ing, Jamie, sell a few lambs. There's a flesher in Dumfries who'll be happy to fill your purse if you'll fill his meat hooks." When Jamie had protested, having already lost five score to the reivers, Lachlan showed no mercy. "You were the one who chose sheep over silver, lad. If you want money for a horse, turn to your lambs, not to me." And so Jamie had herded a small flock to Dumfries yestermorn, much as it grieved him. The cold silver in his palm felt like a betrayal. His lambs were meant to graze the hills of Glentrool, not feed hungry stomachs in Dumfriesshire.

Jamie scanned the crowded highway for familiar faces. Folk from his home parish of Monnigaff flocked to Keltonhill along with the Irish, the English, and every Lowlander in between, it seemed. Elegant car-riages vied with peasants on foot for a share of the road. Families in wheeled carts, gentlemen on horseback, barefoot servants, Gypsies in colorful clothes and tattered caravans—all were headed one direction: southwest to Keltonhill. As the morning warmed, the smell of unwashed bodies and fermenting fruit in saddlebags mingled with the more pleasant scents of freshly cut grass and heath, creating an aromatic cloud that traveled with them.

He'd come to the fair once with Evan the summer of their fifteenth year. While he entertained himself eying the lasses, his twin brother had visited the tippling houses, sampling the whisky and getting into fist-fights with the local lads. At sunset Jamie had thrown his inebriated brother across his horse and led him home to Glentrool, promising his mother they'd never visit Keltonhill again.

A decade later here he was. Might his brother make an appearance at the fair as well? They'd hardly parted on speaking terms, with Evan threatening to kill him and Jamie fleeing for his life. *A brother is born for adversity.* Aye, that was Evan. On Jamie's first Martinmas in Dumfries, he'd mistaken another man on the High Street for Evan and nearly seized the red-headed stranger before the man turned round and Jamie realized he was not his brother. He'd not make a similar blunder this day, though Jamie still intended to keep an eye out for broad-backed men with red hair and a staggering walk.

They emerged from Carlinwark with a short distance to go and a long line of carts and carriages ahead of them. Duncan gestured toward the temporary stables by the roadside. "If ye dinna mind the walk, we can leave our horses." They chose the most reputable looking of the stablers and made arrangements for their horses to be well fed and well guarded. Walloch had already been stolen from Jamie once, only to be recovered with Lachlan's silver; he would not lose the gelding again.

Without their mounts, the men were able to wend their way through the crowd and head for the high ground. Duncan pointed out a large Gypsy encampment in passing. "Billy Marshall's folk."

The Marshalls were one of many Gypsy families in Galloway. Jamie counted two dozen or more wagons, each with a pair of shelties standing nearby, nibbling on the grass. Mean tents, made of rough canvas and held up with sticks, were stationed round steaming kettles. While the women tended the cooking fires, their men sat on blankets, mending pots and carving spoons from ox horns.

"We also have Marshalls in my parish." Jamie's hand went to his purse, making certain it was well concealed. "One of them was standing o'er me the Sabbath morning I woke from my *unco* dream."

"The same Gypsy who *staw* yer boots?"

"The very one." As they walked past, Jamie looked for the elderly Marshall with his thick arms and short-legged strut, his dark eyes glowing, his breath reeking of onions. A man doesn't get tricked out of his boots and not remember the clever Gypsy who managed it.

Duncan nudged him. "Did ye spy the Marshall mark in his hand?" He held out his weathered palm and drew an *X* between the thumb and forefinger. "The lines in me ain hand go their separate ways." He picked up Jamie's hand long enough to glance at it. "Yers do as weel. But folk say true kin o' Billy Marshall, chief o' the Gypsies, have a mark on their palms, like I showed ye. The sign o' the cross."

Jamie nodded as they neared Rhonehouse, only half believing the tale. "I'll be sure to check the man's hand if I see him. Though 'tis not likely in this crowd."

The riotous sound greeted them first, then the inescapable smells, and finally the astounding sight of a sleepy village transformed. Two long lines of colorful tents created an avenue of grass along which bright flags waved in the passing breeze. Down the makeshift street hundreds of folk bustled and jostled, quarreled and caroused, the whole human mass in constant motion—farmers, tinklers, drovers, fishers, smugglers, thieves.

"This way." Duncan guided Jamie to the right, one hand gripping his elbow lest the two men become separated by the crush of people. Raised voices with foreign accents clamored to be heard. The hawkers pitched their calls above the din, promoting their wares as they held them aloft.

Duncan nigh to shouted in his ear, "I come *ilka* year, and 'tis the busiest I've seen it. *Maun* be the guid weather." He tugged Jamie toward a blanket covered with leather goods, dressed and colored by the currier who sat proudly beside them. "What say ye tae a new pair o' boots?"

"The pair I have will do," Jamie said absently, moving on to the hosier's bounty of silk, wool, and cotton stockings, some with ornamental clocks, a decoration on the side of the stocking meant to hide the seams. He soon found *fairings* for Ian—a spinning top and a wooden soldier—and at the glovers he fingered a pair of kid gloves, thinking of Rose.

The men spent several hours working their way round the tents, taking it all in, keeping watch for cutpurses and pickpockets. One merchant, a chandler, caught Jamie's eye when he spotted cakes of heather soap among the candles. "Two," Jamie told the bearded man, fishing out a coin, then slid the small cakes inside his vest as he winked at Duncan. "At least they smell better than St. John's wort."

Despite the pungent aroma of cattle and horses that permeated the air, Jamie's nose led him to a tent where *sweetie-wives* held court, their trays of sweetmeats on tempting display. His eyes were soon as glazed as the confections spread before him: candied fruit, sugar-covered nuts, butterscotch, vanilla *tablet,* barley sugar, treacle candy, sticks of *glessie,* bars of rich comfits stuffed with bits of fruit, and a charming young sweet seller prepared to take his pennies.

"What'll it be, sir? Toffee?" She held out a bite of glessie for him to sample, and he was quickly sold, buying a handful of the buttery sugar candy.

Duncan returned from the pie sellers tent with potato fritters and mutton pies for their dinner. Since there was nowhere proper to sit, they simply stood in a tent corner, enjoying their humble meal and watching the gentry and peasantry of Galloway rub shoulders for one Midsummer Day.

"Time for some entertainment, and then we've a horse to buy." Duncan led him past several low platforms on which mountebanks extolled the virtues of various medicines by way of storytelling and chicanery. They steered clear of the noisy cockfighting pit, where oiled gamecocks fitted with spurs sent feathers and pennies flying. Farther along, a tenor balladeer, his voice already hoarse, sang a tragic tale of love won then lost, while printed broadsheet ballads were offered for sale. A juggler deftly tossed wooden balls in the air as fruit sellers with

trays of apples hung round their necks made their way through the jubilant crowd, holding up their ripened goods.

Each time the two men stopped, Jamie searched the crowd for one
face in particular.

"If ye're leukin' for that Gypsy, ye're wastin' yer time."

"I'm looking for my brother," Jamie admitted, "though I've yet to
see any man with hair the shade of his. If Evan's here, I do believe I'll
spot—"

"McKie!" A familiar voice rang above the throng, stopping Jamie
cold.

Twenty-Nine

We met—'twas in a crowd.
THOMAS HAYNES BAYLY

S everal heads turned when Jamie's did. It wasn't his brother bellow-
ing across the fairgrounds, but it was a voice he knew—a voice from
home—and a braw face he remembered well. "John! John McMillan!"
Jamie hollered back, not caring who heard. He motioned the giant of a
man in their direction, even as he grabbed Duncan's arm. "Come meet
an old friend of mine from the glen."

Duncan's eyes widened. "Glad tae hear he's a *freen,* for he'd be a
meikle enemy."

The crowd parted, making room for a black-haired man who stood
a full head taller than anyone near him. He walked with a loose-limbed
swagger, tipping his cap at every lass who caught his eye, a considerable
number. "Look who's come to Keltonhill Fair," John said as he reached
them, clapping one of his meaty hands on Jamie's shoulder. "I ne'er
thought to see you again, old friend."

"Nor I you, McMillan." Jamie laughed, even as his throat tightened. Five years his senior, John McMillan was his closest neighbor
in the remote fastness of the glen of Loch Trool. As lads, John, Evan,
and Jamie had been inseparable, clambering over the hills together,
fishing in the loch, and tracking roe deer in the Wood of Cree. A loyal
friend, John, and honest. If there was news of Evan, he'd not keep it to
himself.

Jamie nodded at both men. "John McMillan of Glenhead, meet
Duncan Hastings, overseer of Auchengray in Newabbey."

"Your uncle's property, aye?" The two men exchanged greetings,
John's hand swallowing Duncan's whole. "Have you settled there for
good, Jamie, or will we see you in the glen soon?"

"At Lammas," he answered with a measure of pride, knowing the months of squirming beneath Lachlan's thumb would end. " 'Twill be good to see everyone again."

John folded his arms across his massive chest and cocked an eyebrow. "Including your brother?"

Heat crept round Jamie's shirt collar. "I believe Evan will be…ah, gone…by then."

John nodded but did not comment, his gaze drawn to a chapman with a tray of ribbons and lace. He called out to the stoop-shouldered man, immediately garnering his attention, then pilfered a handful of silk ribbons from the tray and tossed the man a coin. "For the lasses," John said with an indifferent shrug, stuffing the ribbons in his vest pocket. "As to Evan…" He eyed Duncan for a moment. "May I speak freely?"

"You may." Jamie looked at Duncan. "Like most herds on the hills, we've no secrets between us."

John directed them toward a narrow stretch of grass separating two busy tents, then planted himself between them like an oak, shading them from folk who might hear their conversation. "Here's the truth, lad: When you left Glentrool, Evan spread the sorry news of your…er…"

"My deceit," Jamie finished for him. "There is no other word for what I did to my father and brother. Will any in the parish receive me?"

John regarded him with an even gaze. "Your father does not speak ill of you. Nor your mother, of course. Only Evan. I've ne'er seen a man so fixed on vengeance. Mind you, I've not spoken to your brother in many weeks. He's been venturing south a good bit, attending to business in Wigtownshire."

" 'Tis my understanding he plans to settle there. Have you heard when Evan and Judith will leave Glentrool for good?"

John dragged his hand across his chin stubble, the sound like emery paper against dried pine. "That I cannot say. In the glen truth does not travel as swiftly as *clack*." He lowered his voice, his gaze growing more intent. "You'd best be sharpening your sword before you start west, Jamie. Evan will stop at nothing to protect his son."

Jamie's heart stopped. "His…*son*?"

"You mean to say…" John's face was awash in disbelief. "Your mother didn't *tell* you? Jamie, I'm…" He wagged his head, then started again. "I'm verra sorry you're hearing this from me: Judith was delivered of a son. Last October."

Jamie sensed the ground shifting beneath him. *October.* The same month as Ian. As things stood, Jamie would inherit Glentrool and Ian after him. But if Evan succeeded in killing him, and if Evan's son was older than Ian…

"When in October?" Jamie asked, dreading the answer.

John stared at the tent pegs near their feet, as though the date might be carved into the rough wood. " 'Twas at the start of the month," he said at last. "On a Saturday, for I recall Evan fretting o'er the auld rhyme."

Duncan supplied it, though they well knew the words. "Saturday's child works hard for a living."

"So does Evan McKie now that I've robbed him of what was rightly his." Jamie jammed his boot heel into the soft ground, angry only with himself. "Was it the first Saturday, then?" The day before Ian was born.

"Aye. The third of October, I remember it now. Judith and her babe had their kirkin at Monnigaff on Lukemas Day, the eighteenth." John McMillan's crooked smile, as broad as the rest of him, spread across his face. "The *kimmer*—Sally Crawford, you'll remember her from Carseminnoch, a sonsie lass with the greenest eyes in Galloway—handed the child to his father for the minister's blissin. A fine lad is wee Archie."

"Archibald, is it?" Their grandfather's name. Evan had bested him twice. "I've a fine lad of my own," Jamie declared, not caring if he sounded boastful. "Ian James McKie. Born October the fourth."

"Have you now?" John had no sooner congratulated him than his countenance fell. "A day apart? I fear 'twill be the older and the younger all o'er again. And here I'd hoped to see you two joined as brothers. Like the days of auld *lang* syne at Buchan Burn."

"A time best forgotten," Jamie said, though his memories held fast: he and Evan dunking each other under the Buchan's cool linns, tumbling down the slopes of the glen together, trading punches on the winding paths along the loch, and laughing all the while. Aye, they had been brothers once. But too many years and too many sorrows had come between them.

Watch your back, man. Evan's last words to him, spoken in anger.

" 'Twas good of you to tell me." Jamie clasped McMillan's arm with gruff affection. "I'll be better prepared come Lammas."

"Have your dirk where you can reach it, for Ian's too young to lose his father." John's gaze lifted, aimed over Jamie's shoulder. His smile returned in force, a glint of gold in his eyetooth. "If it's not the verra lass I'd hoped to see. The one I mentioned by name, Sally Crawford." He gave Jamie a conspirator's wink. "Must have called her to me, aye?"

Jamie chuckled, stepping aside, their conversation ended. "Our paths will cross again, John McMillan." His friend raised his hand, already past him as he navigated the wide expanse between the two lines of tents, headed straight for a buxom lass with golden hair and a blush on her round cheeks.

Duncan snorted. "We'll not see him again this day, I'll wager."

Jamie watched in amusement as John presented Sally with a bright blue ribbon from his pocket. "I'm sorry to see the man go. We've a long history together, John and I."

" 'Tis guid tae be thinkin' o' hame, Jamie." Duncan steered him toward the far end of the tents, where the sale horses were gathered. Their progress was slow, for no one was in a hurry to be anywhere but the place they were standing. "Guid tae be thinkin' aboot how ye'll mend things wi' yer *brither*."

"Mend?" Jamie stopped in his tracks. "Duncan, we're not talking about some boyhood argument, easily put to rights."

"What are we talkin' aboot then, lad? For ye've niver told me—"

"You've never asked," Jamie shot back, regretting it immediately. "I'm sorry, Duncan." He groaned, releasing some of his frustration. "If you're willing to listen—for 'tis not a pleasant story—I'll tell you the whole of it." Jamie aimed for the village street, suddenly thirsty.

If a man fancied a drink, he did not have far to walk. Rhonehouse's four inns, including the Boar's Head and the Crown, overflowed with patrons tossing back ales to slake their thirst. Every house in the village had flung open its doors, pouring libations and serving cold victuals. Evan McKie might be found in any one of them, Jamie realized. Or none of them.

"We'll not be drinkin' awa our silver," Duncan declared, pointing him toward a booth selling lemon punch. "Buy us twa cups, and we'll find a place tae rest." Procuring the punch was simple; locating somewhere to sit was not. They'd started well down the other side of Keltonhill before they stumbled on a patch of grass not yet trodden to mud, offering a fine view of pastoral hills rimmed with woods and dotted with farmhouses.

Once they were seated and their punch cups put aside, Jamie wiped his lips dry, wishing he could dispatch his past as easily. On the night of Ian's birth, when Duncan had seen him through the agony of Leana's travail, the subject of what had happened at Glentrool had been broached. Duncan had spared Jamie from sharing any details. *I ken all aboot that. There's none at Auchengray who don't.* The time had come for his friend to learn the things that no one knew.

"You've heard the gist of it," Jamie began, the punch already souring his stomach "If I say 'twas my mother's idea, I will sound like the coward I am."

"Ye're nae coward, lad." Duncan's voice was kind, utterly without judgment. "Ane Sabbath I watched ye stand tae yer feet in the kirk and defend yer wife whan she sat on the stool o' repentance."

"Leana, you mean." Jamie rubbed at his mouth, stemming his nausea. "'Tis another subject, one I cannot face this day."

"Anither day," Duncan agreed. "Tell me aboot yer mither. Is she at a' like her brither, Lachlan McBride?"

"She is. My mother is clever with words and not above using trickery to get what she wants." Much as Jamie hated confessing it, the similarities could not be discounted. Nor the differences. "Rowena McKie is more charming than my uncle, though, and more caring. I've ne'er doubted her love for me. But therein lies the *tickler,* Duncan." He stretched out his legs, crossing his boots at the ankle. "My mother favored me, and my father favored Evan. They compared us like sheep at market. 'This one has a sound mouth.' 'Aye, but this one has an even coat.'"

"Och." Duncan spat his last taste of punch onto the grass. "'Tis a daft parent wha pits ane bairn against anither. I've warned me dochters o' that verra danger."

"Would that you'd been round when we were born. Twins, but not identical. A minute apart, yet on two different days, for our births strad-dled the clock at midnight."

A look of awe came across Duncan's face. "Ye were birthed at sic a canny hour? Folk say—"

"So they do." The mention of the old belief made Jamie's hands grow cold. To think of having the ability to see the Spirit of God abroad in the land simply because he was born just after midnight.

At Duncan's prompting, Jamie continued. "While Evan and I were still in her womb, my mother sought the advice of a pious midwife. The woman declared that, by and by, the older would serve the younger. She assured our mother 'twas a word from the Almighty. My mother deter-mined it would be so."

A bevy of lasses strolled by, trying to catch Jamie's eye, but he paid them no mind.

Duncan nudged him. "What did yer mither have ye do, Jamie?"

The words seeped out like blood from a wound. "My father announced he was ready to bestow his blessing on his heir, an irrevoca-ble act. He sent Evan to hunt a roe deer for the celebration. While he was gone, Mother prepared goat meat seasoned like venison. She dressed me in my brother's plaid and covered my hands in goatskin, for Evan is birsie."

"Ye dinna mean ye pretended tae be yer brither?"

"I did." Jamie hung his head, ashamed all over again.

Duncan's brow wrinkled in confusion. "Surely yer faither could tell the difference atween ye?"

"Alec McKie has lived more than eighty summers, and his eyesight is failing." Jamie stared at his hands, remembering his father's trembling fingers unwrapping the bread. Reaching for a glass of claret. Touching his son's head. "He believed I was Evan." Jamie swallowed, the words sticking in his throat. "But 'twas not my father's eyes that deceived him."

The pain on Duncan's face mirrored his own. "Jamie, ye didna lie tae yer ain faither?"

"I...did. Repeatedly." He ground his teeth hard, wanting it to hurt. "After he...blessed me, I apologized for leaving so soon. But I did not truly ask his forgiveness."

"Have ye niver done it?" Duncan's disappointment was carefully checked, but Jamie saw it in his eyes. "Did ye not make amends afore ye left or write the man syne?"

"My mother smoothed things over before I left that night, but since then I've done…nothing." He pulled his knees toward his chest, slumping over them, hiding his shame. "Nothing except beg for the Lord's mercy seventy times seven."

"Och." Duncan chuckled softly. "That's how many times ye're tae forgive ithers, Jamie. Not how many times ye ask God tae forgive ye. Once will do on that score." Duncan hung his arm round Jamie's shoulders, a father's embrace. "Ye've some work tae do whan we get hame, aye? Some letters tae write?"

Jamie straightened, rubbing his eyes with the palms of his hands. "Aye." His burden of guilt had not lifted, but it had lightened.

"Yer raik tae Glentrool will be easier if 'tis paved wi' guid wirds, not guid intentions." Duncan slapped his back once, then scrambled to his feet. "And if ye have a fine horse tae get ye there, that'll help as weel. 'Tis what we came for, lad. Time we got on wi' it." He led the way toward the paddocks. "The sale's aboot tae start, for the bell's rung."

With Jamie's eye for horseflesh and Duncan's skill at bargaining, they were not long in finding a mount. Horse dealers from Ireland and England trotted out roan-colored horses, chestnuts, bays, and dappled gray thoroughbreds. Jamie knew what he wanted—Walloch's twin—and was pleased to find a black gelding from nearby Buittle that came close to the mark. Another piece of silver went to a blacksmith to shoe the horse, then Jamie led his new mount downhill toward the stables, his eye fixed on the road bound northeast.

"Weel, laddie, ye didna spot yer Gypsy nor yer brither." Duncan slapped his back good-naturedly. "But ye've a fine horse tae carry ye hame at Lammas. Have ye thocht what ye'll call the beast?"

Jamie stopped long enough to be certain the overseer was listening. "His name will be Hastings. To remind me of a good friend I'll miss when I leave Auchengray."

The slight sheen in Duncan's eyes caught the sunlight. "I'll miss ye as weel, Jamie. Aye, I'll miss ye sairlie."

Thirty

For, dark and despairing, my sight I may seal
But man cannot cover what God would reveal.

Standing by the dining room window to make the most of the forenoon light, Leana adjusted her spectacles until the small print of the almanac came into focus. She'd waited for her father to take his morning walk before ducking into the spence and borrowing the volume from his shelf: *Season on the Seasons.* He'd not mind her reading it but might inquire what prompted her interest in days and dates. That was a risk she dared not take.

Leana ran a finger down the calendar pages, tallying the weeks since her last night with Jamie. Four months ago to the day. If indeed that was the hour the Lord had blessed her womb, she would soon sense the child's presence. A slight movement, a gentle nudging. She was unprepared when Ian had first made himself known to her. But with this child, she was ready for the quickening. *More than ready, little one.*

She gazed out the window, picturing Jamie hard at work on the hills. Not an hour passed without her thinking of him. Missing him. Letting him go all over again. Rose was away from the house too, on an outing to the village. Leana prayed they would both find shelter if the rain arrived sooner than expected. After a sunny Sabbath, Monday had dawned on a grayer note, thick clouds promising a thorough soaking before day's end. Indeed, the almanac predicted a wetter than usual summer.

Henry Season's guide specialized in heavenly bodies with headings on eclipses and the moon's southing. Answers were included for enigmas posed in the previous year's edition, and new riddles were offered for the year at hand. One rebus caught her gardener's eye: "My daughter's two names will connected explore, an evergreen plant that grows just at my door." She would have to wait another six months to discover whether the child's names might include Laurel, Holly, or Privet. A clever ploy to assure sales of Henry Seasons's 1791 almanac, Leana decided, closing the book.

Henry was indeed a fine name, though she'd already chosen two for her child: *David,* if a son, to honor the devout king, and *Davina,* the feminine form, if the Almighty blessed her with a daughter. Scottish mothers usually named their children after parents or grandparents. Under the circumstances, a different name seemed prudent. But would it be David McBride? Or David McKie? Only the child's father could decide. *Please, Jamie.*

Leana slipped off her spectacles and tucked them inside her apron pocket, then adjusted the folds in the fabric. She'd loosened the seams of her yellow cotton gown again that morning, and still it felt snug. Could she keep her news to herself another month? Numerous times a day some remark about her babe rose to her lips and was quickly stifled. She would not diminish Rose's joy and add to Jamie's troubles. She would *not.*

Anxious to return the almanac before her father appeared, Leana hurried into the spence. The only window faced north, toward the gardens and Auchengray Hill, leaving the room in shadows on such an overcast day. She was squinting at the bookshelf, looking for the spot where the book belonged, when she heard her father's voice across the dim room.

"What, pray tell, would compel a lady to read an almanac?" Lachlan stood in the doorway, his face still ruddy from his walk.

Leana slid the book back into place, taking care not to lift her arms too high lest he see what must not be seen. "I was consulting Mr. Season's advice on the weather." A thread of truth, however slender. "How did you find the morning air, Father? Will we have rain by supper?"

"We will," he said bluntly, entering the room. "But first, we will be seated and take a bit of refreshment, you and I. Then we shall discuss your future."

"My…future." She did not pose it as a question, though indeed it was. "Certainly, Father. Shall I ask Neda to serve us?"

"Already done, mistress," the housekeeper answered, crossing the threshold with her tray as the two settled into the upholstered chairs by the hearth. Neda poured tea for Leana and a dram for her father, then arranged the plate of almond biscuits and a small pitcher of milk within Leana's reach.

Lachlan waved Neda out the door. "See that we're not disturbed."

Leana chose a sweet biscuit and managed one bite before putting it on her saucer. *Your future.* Whatever did he mean?

Ignoring her for the moment, her father sipped his dram, his gaze fixed on some distant spot beyond the window. "Leana, since your return to Auchengray, one question has remained unanswered."

She dabbed the crumbs from her mouth with a linen napkin, praying the tremor in her hand did not show. "What question is that, Father?"

"A simple one: *why?*" His gray eyes studied her more closely than she wished. "Why did you leave Twyneholm so abruptly?"

"It was not a…sudden decision." She rested her hands in her lap, the napkin still bunched in her fingers. "I'd always planned to come home in the summer but was not certain when or by what means. Once my gown was sold, those questions were answered."

"To your satisfaction perhaps. But not to mine." He drained his glass, then put it down with a bang. "I've heard the servants blether. You were shocked to find your sister and her husband still here, isn't that so?"

Leana lowered her gaze. "Aye."

"Then why did you not write and see if the couple remained at Auchengray before leaving your aunt's cottage?"

A fair question. She kept her head down and her hands busy fiddling with her napkin while she searched for an honest answer. "I was certain Jamie and Rose had already departed for Glentrool. Jamie had once assured me that we…that *he* would leave Auchengray come May. So when June arrived, I—"

Lachlan cut her off with a brutish grunt. "Stop dissembling, Leana." He leaned across the table and lifted her chin none too gently. "Did you run from some scandal in Twyneholm? Is that what brought you to my door?"

"Nae!"

"Stand up."

"Father, I—"

"Stand." He leaned back in his chair as if to give her room. "Come, Leana. Is that so difficult a request to honor? To your feet, if you please. And take off your apron."

As if in a trance, Leana stood and slowly untied her apron strings. She slipped the fabric over her head, then dropped it onto the chair, abandoning her hopes with it. *He will see. He will know.* She faced him, her hands clasped before her. Covering. Protecting. *Please, God. Hide me under the shadow of thy wings.*

"Not like that." Lachlan shook his head, eyes cold as pewter. "Fold your hands behind you."

Nae. Please. Leana laced her fingers together and pressed them against the base of her spine.

"Shoulders back, lass. That's better."

She sensed her belly growing beneath his gaze.

"Now turn toward the hearth."

Numb, Leana did as she was told, afraid she might faint or worse. *Help me, help me!* Standing in profile, she felt utterly exposed, like a woman carved on the prow of a ship. Her altered gown could no longer alter the truth. *He sees. He knows.*

The tick of the mantel clock grew louder, counting each second. Lachlan finally spoke. "It appears I have been asking the wrong question." His voice was flat and sharp-edged, like a knife. "Who is the father of this child?"

She released her hands and turned toward him. "Jamie McKie."

"Are you certain, lass? You were in Twyneholm a good while."

However cruel his accusation, she would not let it wound her. Not when she knew the truth. "There has never been anyone else."

His gaze narrowed. "Will you swear to me that is so?"

"Father, I will not swear at all. Neither by heaven, for it is God's throne, nor by the earth, for it is his footstool."

"Hiding behind the Buik, are we?" His brow darkened, like the

threatening clouds framed in the window. "Then let your communica-
tion be aye or nae, Leana. You are certain Jamie is the father?"

She took a full breath, letting her body expand as it pleased. "He is."

"Good." He threw down his napkin. "Then let him support his
bystart, for I'll not do so."

"Father, Jamie's child is—"

"An *ill-gotten* babe!" he growled, leaning toward her.

"That's not true, for we did not sin." She spread her hands before
him, a gesture of innocence. "'Twas February, when we thought we
were husband and wife."

"You *thought*? Och!" He vaulted from his chair and began pacing
the floor. "You never thought at all, Leana. 'Tis your heart that's led you
astray, not your head. I can guess what the kirk session will have to say
about *this* sorry turn of events." He spun toward her, pinning her with
his gaze. "Do not fool yourself. The kirk will find sin enough to put you
back on the cutty stool."

"My transgressions have already been atoned for, Father." She rested
her hands on her unborn babe without apology. "This child was conceived within the bonds of a marriage established by habit and repute,
as the kirk session will surely concede."

"I cannot say what the elders will do," Lachlan muttered, "only
what I must do." He moved toward her, his stance belligerent. "I insist
my nephew pay for this…this…"

"I am certain he will, Father," Leana hastened to assure him. "When
the time comes."

Lachlan regarded her with suspicion. "You have his word on this?"
Forgive me, Jamie. "I have not…told him…yet."

"*What?*" His face turned an ugly purple. "You've kept this not only
from me but from Jamie as well?"

"I have and for good reason." She stepped closer, needing him to
hear her, needing him to see her resolve. "I will not destroy my sister's
happiness. This news of mine can wait. Let them leave for Glentrool
content in their joy. I will write them once they are settled—"

"What a coward you are, Leana." The contempt on his face was apparent, the sarcasm in his voice unmistakable. "You would write a letter rather than tell the man to his face. And I ken why: Jamie does not love you. 'Tis likely he never did."

Leana knew better. "That is not true. It is also not relevant. Jamie's love for Rose and the child they are expecting is all that matters now." Strengthened by her conviction, Leana realized her legs no longer trembled, and her hands were warm. "Do what you will with me, Father, but spare my sister this news."

He curled his lip. "Do you never tire of being a martyr?"

She met his gaze without flinching. "And do you never tire of being a bully?"

Lachlan stared at her, his face livid but his mouth silent. And in that quiet moment, in that hidden place inside her, Jamie's child moved.

Her breathing stilled as Leana rested her hand where she felt a distinct flutter. *Again.* Faint, yet real. Not imagined. *My child.* Moving, kicking, alive. *Thanks be to God!* Of all the times and places he might have chosen, she could not be more grateful it was this time. And this place.

Leana exhaled, releasing the last of her fears. "Now that you know the truth, Father, and have seen proof with your own eyes, what will you do?"

He squared his shoulders as though trying to match her strength. "I will keep your secret, Leana, but only as long as it suits me."

"Until Lammas. That is all I ask." Leana retrieved her apron. "In another month I shall tell Reverend Gordon and the elders myself. And write Jamie and Rose. But for now, please tell no one."

"And if I agree, what benefit may I expect?" His words were stern, demanding as ever. "Will I be shown the respect a father is due? Will I receive the gratitude such generosity warrants?"

"The Lord rewards us according to our righteousness." Leana tied her apron round her waist, her calm gaze fixed on his indignant one. "I am certain you will receive exactly what you deserve."

Thirty-One

Ay, these young things lie safe in our hearts just so long.

EDWARD ROBERT BULWER, LORD LYTTON

Leana, whatever would I do without you?" Rose held up the tiny nightgown, admiring the neatly embroidered magpies round the sleeves and hem. "My birds looked more like badgers. Black and white, aye, but no wings and no slender tails." Leana's eye for detail and her smooth, even stitches put her own efforts to shame. Rose laid the finished gown across her middle, uneasy at the thought of the child inside her growing to such a size. "How much longer 'til the quickening?"

"Hard to say, lass." Leana lowered her embroidery hoop, then slipped off her glasses and rubbed her eyes. She'd been plying her needle since well before noon, after coming in from the garden to escape the blinding sunlight of early July. The dog days were upon them and would not let up until the eleventh of August, or so the stars said. After the midday meal the sisters had settled in the parlor—the coolest room in the house—while Ian napped in the nursery. Except for an occasional breeze wafting past the curtains, the air was still and the temperature uncomfortably warm.

Leana had opened her gown a bit and draped a damp cloth round her bared neck, trying to cool herself. "Now, about the quickening," she said. "You might notice a flutter or two at the end of your fourth month. When might that be, dearie?"

Rose counted on her fingers, then groaned. "Not 'til after Lammas. Which means you won't be with me when it happens. Not unless the quickening comes early."

"Which it might." Leana's gaze shifted to Rose's lap. "Your bairn seems intent on growing."

Chagrined, Rose tried to pull in her stomach, to no avail. "I'm not at all certain this isn't just *me* growing. I cannot go a day without eating two buttermilk scones with gooseberry jam."

"Neda is only too happy to bake them for you." Leana smiled a little as she said it, then put her glasses back in place and resumed her stitching. "Every woman is different, Rose. And they say each confinement varies too."

Rose stuck out her lower lip, not caring if she looked twelve again. "You won't be with me for that either."

"Nae, I shall be here." A tinge of sadness permeated her words. "You must write me, Rose." Leana's needle stilled. "For I will surely write you."

"As many letters as we can," Rose promised, thinking of how lonely she would be in the glen, at least until her bairn arrived. She would have Jamie, of course, but he would be busy with the autumn breeding. Heaven only knew what Aunt Rowena might be like—*speeritie*, to hear Jamie tell it. "Full of life, like you," he'd said, patting her cheek. Her Uncle Alec, on the other hand, was full of years—hard of hearing and losing his eyesight, the poor man. According to Jamie, Evan and Judith would be moving to Wigtownshire, and none of the neighbors' houses could be seen from Glentrool's doorstep.

Aye, she would miss her sister's company. Dreadfully so.

The sound of Ian whimpering floated down the stair. "Awake from his nap already," Rose said with a weary sigh. "There's no need for you to come."

Leana was already on her feet. " 'Tis my last month with Ian. As long as you do not object…"

"You know I don't. Let us see what our laddie needs."

Ian was standing in his crib, clearly proud of pulling himself to his feet. At the sight of Leana and Rose, he waved his arms in the air and promptly landed on his bottom, making Rose laugh. "Neda says in another month, when he has his balance, Ian will get about by holding on to chairs and such."

Leana lifted him out of the crib, then settled him on her hip. "Is that what you'll be doing, dear boy? Shuffling your way round your new house?"

" 'Tis a very *old* house," Rose explained, gathering the soiled linens from his crib. "With a round turret, tall chimneys, a spiral staircase, and enormous rooms." The minute the words were out of her mouth, Rose wished she could take them back. "I'm sorry, Leana." She bent over the laundry basket, hiding her shame. "'Twas…thoughtless of me."

"Thoughtless to be excited about your future home?" Leana gently laid a hand on Rose's back. "I am happy for Ian to be raised at Glentrool. 'Tis where he was meant to live."

So were you. Rose straightened, avoiding her sister's gaze. Oddly, the more understanding Leana was, the worse Rose felt about it all. "If you'll change his clothes, I'll see to fresh bedding. We'll have a bit of time to play before his supper."

Both women went about their work and soon had the nursery set to rights, except for the toys strewn across the floor on purpose. Rose was only too happy to sit among them, leaving the chair for her sister, who seemed older than usual today. Would *she* look the same five years from now, overheated in the summer months, with swollen ankles and parched lips?

Rose sat Ian across from her and rolled his doeskin ball toward him, pleased to see him push it back. "Showing off for your mother, are you?" After a few exchanges he tired of the game and reached for his wooden blocks.

"Bless Duncan for carving those," Leana murmured, stretching out her legs.

One foot touched the edge of Ian's old cradle, which he'd outgrown in the spring. A family heirloom, the oak cradle lined with linen had rocked their mother, then Leana, then Rose, and then Ian. Rose gazed at it wistfully. Might she take it with her to Glentrool for her newborn's arrival? 'Twas certain Leana would have no use for it.

When Leana's foot absently began rocking the cradle, Rose giggled. "Be careful," she teased her sister. "You know what it signifies when a young mother rocks an empty cradle, don't you? It means she is expecting again."

Leana stopped at once. "Indeed it does." She tucked her feet beneath her chair, then turned over the cloth draped round her neck. "Might you ask Eliza to bring us something cool to drink?"

Anxious to ease her sister's obvious discomfort, Rose hurried to do her bidding. Eliza followed her back up the stair with a tray of horn cups filled with water still cold from the well, flavored with lime and sweetened with sugar. "The lad's is half-fu'," Eliza warned, "and still he'll likely spill it. 'Tis why I brought a towel."

Leana downed her cupful in a single long drink and pressed the cup to her cheek when she finished. Ian drank some, spilled some, and wore some, while Rose sat on the floor and dabbed him with the towel as needed, taking sips between accidents. The simple cups, made from ox horn, were hardly suitable for company but ideal with a child in the room.

"Leana…" Rose looked up at her sister, putting her cup aside. "Father's banns will be read again at Urr parish in the morn's morn." The crying of the marriage banns three Sabbaths in a row was required before a wedding could be performed. "We've only a short time left to secure a present. Since it's Father's sixtieth birthday *and* his wedding day, is there something you and I could give him?"

The two sisters discussed the possibilities—a clock, a pair of pewter plates, a china punch bowl—all of them far too expensive. They were lamenting Rose's meager savings and Leana's empty purse when Jamie appeared in the doorway.

"Here's a cozy tableau," he said amiably, smiling at Ian in particular. "I've come to dress for supper. Eliza says my son has a dish of minced lamb waiting for him in the kitchen." When Jamie stepped aside, Eliza swung through, scooped up Ian, and disappeared just as quickly. There was nowhere for Jamie to sit, so he propped his shoulder against the doorpost, wiping his damp brow with his sleeve. Even fresh from the pastures, he was a braw sight. "Did I hear wedding gifts being considered?"

Rose groaned. "We really must give Father something, but…"

"We have no money," Leana confessed. "Though I do know what he might like: an engraved sterling *quaich*. For sharing a dram."

Rose agreed at once. The shallow silver bowl, the size of a cupped palm, had a carved handle on either side. An ideal gift, though not inexpensive.

Jamie nodded slowly. " 'Tis just the thing. And I ken a worthy silversmith in Dumfries who sells them. The letter *M* could be engraved in the center. Well done, Leana."

"But not well paid for," Rose reminded him. "I will gladly contribute all the coins in my glove drawer, but 'twill not be enough."

Jamie touched his hand to his purse. "I've a bit left from my day at Keltonhill Fair."

"I suppose I could sell something." Leana's gaze was unfocused, as if her thoughts were elsewhere. "Though I own so little of value. Only my writing desk." Her voice dropped. "And I cannot part with that."

The nursery suddenly grew quiet. Jamie touched Rose's hair, as if sensing her discomfort. "You need not sell your desk, Leana. Let me sell some of my lambs—"

"Nae." Leana rose, steadying herself with the edge of the crib. "You have sacrificed enough. I'm going to ask Father for the small sum Mother bequeathed to me. I should have received it more than a year ago."

"But you might need that money for…" Rose wet her lips, still tart with lime. "For something…more important. Must you spend it on him?"

"He *is* my father." Though Leana's blue eyes were clear and her expression earnest, the corners of her mouth curved down. "I will speak to him and see what arrangement might be made. Father is seldom willing to part with his silver."

"Aye," Rose agreed with a petulant sigh. "Nor anything else."

Thirty-Two

Truth, when not sought after,
sometimes comes to light.
MENANDER

The last of the pudding dishes were cleared away when Lachlan folded his hands on the table as though he were about to preside over a meeting. Steam from the kitchen made the dining room even more humid. Jamie slid a finger beneath his neckcloth for a moment's relief, noting that Leana, seated across the table from him, was faring no better. Her cheeks were pink, her forehead glistened, and her water glass remained close at hand. The first week of July was ending on the same note on which it had begun: exceedingly warm.

He'd left for Dumfries in the relative cool of the morning astride Hastings—a fine mount, he was pleased to discover. The silversmith had a sterling quaich among his wares, just as Jamie had hoped, and engraved it while Jamie busied himself elsewhere in the burgh purchasing a dirk, sword, and pistol for his journey home. He had surrendered the remaining coins in his purse to pay for the small quaich, and still the silversmith had been forced to reduce his price or lose a sale.

The drinking cup lay hidden in Rose's glove drawer, waiting to be presented to Lachlan and Morna at the dinner celebrating their marriage nine days hence. Though it was the proper thing to do, Jamie loathed the idea of giving so liberal a gift to one so miserly. His own silver was no loss, nor were Rose's few coins, but it grieved him to spend even a portion of Leana's paltry inheritance. According to Rose, she'd had to practically beg for it, and even then Lachlan had paid her in pennies and shillings, rather than pounds. The image of Leana groveling for her own money disgusted Jamie. And to think she'd turned round and spent it on the same hatesome man!

Jamie glowered at him across the table. Lachlan's daughters were far more generous than their father deserved. The man had yet to inform the family of his proposed living arrangements after the ceremony—would Morna come to Auchengray alone or would her sons move in as well? Once Lammas arrived, space would not be an issue, but at the moment, four more people at Auchengray would make things difficult for all of them. Except for Lachlan McBride.

"'Tis time we discussed my wedding plans for Saturday next." Lachlan regarded them as one might subjects, his brows raised with an air of disdain. "The forenoon ceremony at the Urr kirk will be brief, followed by a bridal dinner at the manse at Mistress Muirhead's invitation. Four members of this household are to attend the festivities. Jamie and Rose to represent the family. And Neda and Duncan on behalf of the staff."

Leana hid behind her water glass but could not mask the hurt in her eyes. Rose sat in stunned silence.

Jamie's neck, already warm, heated further. "Do you mean to exclude Leana, your own daughter, from your wedding?"

Lachlan unfolded his hands, laying them palms up, as if helpless to change the situation. "Morna…ah, Mistress Douglas has asked that Leana not be present. Nor Ian, of course."

Jamie pushed back his chair, prepared to throttle the man if necessary. "I suppose all three of her sons will attend."

"Naturally."

"Then both your daughters should be welcome."

"But they are not."

When Lachlan stood, Jamie did as well, his fists clenched by his side. "I cannot allow such—"

"*Allow?*" Lachlan stepped round the table, within striking distance. "The only allowances in this household are mine to make. Not yours."

"Father—"

"Silence, Rose." He did not look at her as he spoke. "Take your sister and leave my table. 'Twould seem your husband is determined to infuriate me."

Jamie heard Rose and Leana quit the room in a huff, but he did not take his eyes off his adversary. "What of the *blessing* I supposedly brought to Auchengray? What of that, Uncle?"

Lachlan's shrug was exaggerated to the point of insult. "You spoke the words yourself, young James. 'The LORD gave, and the LORD hath taken away.'"

"We are not speaking of my flocks now." Jamie dared to step closer. "We are speaking of your daughter. Just as my lambs were stolen from me, so has Leana's dignity been stolen from her. At the hands of a thief. *You*, Uncle."

Lachlan's color returned, and his eyes took on a steely glint. "Why would you concern yourself with a woman who is no longer your wife?"

"Because she is the mother of my son." His voice was even. His temper was not. "Because I still care about her…well-being."

Lachlan's laugh was low, vulgar. "Because you still desire her?"

"*Nae!*" Jamie grabbed the man's neckcloth and pushed him against the wall. "Do not say such things." Jamie ground out the words, twisting the cloth tighter as he bore down on him, nigh to choking him. "She is your daughter, sir. *She is your daughter!*"

Lachlan struggled beneath him and finally managed to wrest himself free, but only because, out of shame, Jamie had loosened his grip. His uncle staggered sideways, beyond Jamie's reach, loosening his neckcloth and gasping for air. Though he produced no weapon, his gray eyes turned to daggers, and his words, when they came, were sharper still. "How dare you treat me so ill, Nephew." Lachlan straightened, yanking his coat in place. "I ken verra well that Leana is my daughter. I ken more than that but am bound to silence."

Caught off guard, Jamie fell back a step. Whatever knowledge Lachlan held in confidence seemed to imbue him with a sense of power. Did she intend to leave Auchengray again? Had her father found some ne'er-do-well to marry her? Whatever the situation, Jamie would not embarrass Leana by asking her.

Nor would he apologize to Lachlan. "I spent the morning on an errand and so must see to my neglected duties in the steading." Jamie turned and marched out of the room without giving his uncle a chance to respond. Rose would have to present her father with the heavy sterling cup; left to his own devices, Jamie would crown the man with it.

As he expected, Rose was anxiously waiting in their room. "My sister is resting in the nursery," she informed him, keeping her voice down. "We hated to abandon you, Jamie, but—"

"'Tis good that you left." Now that his temper had begun to cool, Jamie felt nothing but guilt. What nephew attacked his own uncle, however much the man deserved it? In less than a month they would leave Auchengray for good. Surely he could put up with Lachlan's despicable ways a bit longer.

"How is your sister?" Jamie glanced toward the nursery, imagining her stretched across the hurlie bed. Weeping, if he knew Leana. And he knew her very well. *Too well.*

"She was quite upset." Rose sniffed, pulling her handkerchief from her sleeve. "I don't think she minds missing the wedding. But father was so…heartless."

Jamie grunted. "You're being charitable. He was an ogre."

"Did the two of you…fight?" She looked up at him, her sweet face lined with worry. "I heard…shouting. And scuffling…"

"I'm afraid so." He hung his head, truly repentant. "'Twas my fault entirely. He said things about Leana that were…improper."

"Oh, dear Jamie." She cupped his cheek, her damp handkerchief threaded between her fingers. "You defended her, didn't you? My brave husband."

"A brave man would have challenged him to a proper duel. Instead, I nearly choked him."

"Now I *am* sorry I left. I suppose we shan't have our usual hour of family worship this evening."

"I think not." He shrugged off his coat, eying his discarded work shirt. "I've tasks to do in the steading and two more hours of daylight. Will you mind?"

"Nae, for I have tomorrow's meals to plan with Neda. Do stop in the nursery and assure Leana that you are all right. She was quite worried." Rose kissed his cheek. "We both were."

She hastened down the stair while Jamie changed into clothes better suited for the byre. His muscles were still tense, his nerves on edge. The last time he'd felt his blood pounding in his head like this was when Evan and he had fought in Glentrool's kitchen on the dark night of his deception. Evan, broader and stronger than he, would have pummeled him senseless if their father had not intervened.

You have brought shame to Glentrool this day, James McKie.

Jamie swallowed hard, remembering his father's painful words. He could only pray that his own words, sent by letter Tuesday last, would begin repairing the rift between them. Just as Duncan advised him, Jamie held nothing back, confessing his many transgressions without stooping so low as to mention his mother's involvement. When the time had come to pretend he was Evan, *he* had spun the web of deception, not his mother. The lies were his alone.

He'd also sent a separate letter to Evan, hoping it might do some good, though it seemed an impossibility. What brother could forgive such treachery? Even Duncan had conceded, "A brother offended is harder tae be won than a strong city." After congratulating Evan on the birth of his son, Jamie had forced his pen to write the words that weighed on his soul.

> I am sorry, Evan. For everything. For claiming the inherit-
> ance meant to be yours. For deceiving and dishonoring our
> father in the process. For a lifetime of battling you with
> words and weapons instead of being the brother you
> deserved.

Seeing the truth on paper had shaken him to the core. *Deceiving. Dishonoring.* It was one thing to confess such sins; writing them out was quite another.

> If a seed of forgiveness may be found in your heart, Evan, I
> pray God will water it daily until the hour I see your face.
> My family and I plan to arrive in Glentrool soon after Lam-
> mas. I hope our paths might cross in peace.
>
> Your brother always,
> Jamie

He'd never in his life written such letters. It had taken him another day to work up the nerve to send them. Now they were in the hands of a courier. He could only wait for his father and brother to respond and pray they might be merciful.

For the moment there was work to finish in the steading and a wife's request to honor. He finished dressing, then stepped into the corridor and lightly knocked on the nursery door. When there was no answer, he opened it with care, lest he wake their sleeping son.

His eyes quickly adjusted to the dim light. Ian lay in his usual pose, arms and legs spread out, staking his claim on the crib. Leana lay on her side on the small trundle bed, her eyes closed, her breathing even. Asleep as well, it seemed. She had discarded her apron and modestly unbuttoned her gown to allow a bit of air round her neck. Her hands, usually tucked beneath the pillow, rested in front of her, crossed at the wrists.

He closed the door, lest the sounds of the household disturb them. Stepping closer, then closer still, he finally knelt beside her, resisting the urge to speak her name.

She sighed but did not wake. Turning ever so slightly onto her back, she lifted her arms above her head in sleepy repose, revealing the graceful lines of her neck. Memories, unbidden, washed over him, drowning him. He ignored his guilty conscience and let his gaze follow the curves of her body.

His heart thudded to a stop.

She is with child.

Jamie sat back on his heels, dumbfounded. How could he not have noticed before?

She looked so vulnerable lying there, so defenseless, her belly round just like last summer when she carried Ian. Jamie laced his hands together, resisting the strong urge to touch her, to protect her.

No wonder you came home, lass. An unmarried woman with a bairn would not be welcome in Twyneholm parish or any other. Though she'd kept her secret well hidden beneath her apron, it appeared she'd been carrying the child for several months.

One thing was certain: The child was his.

He bent forward, pressing a fist against his mouth, lest he groan aloud. *Oh, Leana.* A moment of anger quickly passed. She'd not meant to deceive him; she'd meant to spare him. *I ken more than that but am bound to silence.* Lachlan knew, it seemed. Yet she'd clearly begged her father to keep her secret.

The woman he'd once loved with all his heart would never lie. If he asked her, Leana would confess the truth at once. But Jamie trusted her instincts; she was concealing her child for some very good reason. *Rose.* There could be no other explanation. Leana meant to keep this news to herself rather than wound her sister. Rather than devastate him.

"Och, lass," he murmured, leaning closer. "Whatever am I to do with you?"

Her scent rose to greet him. Lavender and soap and Leana. Overcome, he leaned back, catching his breath. Should he leave? Should he stay and voice his suspicions? He watched her turn onto her side again, wondering if she'd heard him.

"Did my father win the skirmish?" she asked softly, opening her eyes. "Or did you?"

There was no leaving now. He met her gaze, still clouded with sleep. "No one did, I'm afraid."

"But you tried, Jamie. You spoke on my behalf, and I'm grateful." She drew up her knees, pulling her gown round her, covering what she could. "Have you been here…long?"

"Not long." *Long enough.* "Rose asked that I put your mind at ease about…what happened in the dining room."

"Did Father…say anything…in particular?"

Jamie hesitated, longing to expose her secret, wanting to hear her confession: *I am carrying your child.* But that was unfair and unkind. When she was ready to tell him, she would. "Lachlan and I exchanged very few words," he finally admitted. "We talked about my stolen lambs." Well, they had, hadn't they?

"Your precious flocks." She lifted her hand as though she might brush his cheek, then laid it across her bodice instead. "'Twas unthinkable what those men did."

"Whoever they were." When Ian stirred in his crib, Jamie realized his visit to the nursery was nearing an end. He stood, looking down at her all the while. "I am verra sorry about your father's decision. About the wedding."

"It matters not, Jamie." Her words sounded genuine. Leana had yet to meet Morna or her sons. Perhaps she truly did not want to go. "With the house to ourselves, Ian and I will have a fine day."

"But our gift…"

She lifted her hand, gently stopping his words. "I'll not begrudge my father a wedding present simply because I won't be there to hear the marriage vows." Her gaze shifted away from his. "I have heard them spoken before."

"So have I." *And have said them. Twice.* "I'll leave you to Ian, then."

Jamie bowed, then quit the room and bounded down the stair more quickly than was prudent. Running from the house. Running from the truth.

Thirty-Three

The miserable have no other medicine
But only hope.
WILLIAM SHAKESPEARE

Three weeks to Lammas.

Leana could think of little else this Sabbath day, even while the notes of the closing psalm rang round her head and the words of Reverend Gordon's sermon beat upon the doors of her heart. "Behold, thou desirest truth in the inward parts." That was precisely where the truth could be found. Yet all she could offer was a timorous smile while her mind turned the pages of a calendar.

The first of August would find her in this very pew with only Neda and Duncan to keep her company. A day she both longed for and dreaded. Though her hidden child could at last be revealed, Ian would be taken from her arms. Though her heart could begin to mend, the loss of Jamie's company would render it irreparable.

Three weeks to Lammas.

"Dearie," Rose whispered in her ear, "the benediction is finished."

Leana lifted her head like one grateful to be awakened from a sad dream. Some parishioners stood among the pews, others milled in the aisles, loath to face the downpour that waited for them beyond the kirk doors. All through both services the rain had pounded on the slate roof and drummed against the windowpanes.

"Miss McBride." Reverend Gordon greeted her at the end of the pew. "Might I speak with you for a moment?"

Leana turned aside as the rest of the household squeezed past her. The air smelled of mildew and damp linen, and the gray light cast a pallor on every face. Rose gave her a furtive glance, and Jamie eyed her with genuine concern. Her father, who held the truth in his hand like a trump card, looked the other way as his coattails brushed her skirt.

Giving the minister her full attention, Leana did what she could to appear calm. Reminding herself to breathe. Offering a silent prayer. *Thou art my hiding place.* She intended to tell Reverend Gordon her news but not yet. And not here.

"A certain matter has come to my attention." His solemn features gave away nothing. "'Twould best be discussed…elsewhere. What day this week might I call at Auchengray?"

A certain matter. She squeezed the cotton gloves in her hands until her fingers ached. "You are welcome any day, of course." Ministers were free to knock on parishioner doors whenever they pleased. How else might a shepherd discern the goats among his sheep? "Perhaps Friday would be best. Some of the household will be away at Father's wedding in Urr parish."

Reverend Gordon's thick gray eyebrows arched. "And will you not be in attendance?"

"I am not invited."

His look of surprise gave way to irritation as the minister stared at her father's departing back. "I'm sorry to hear it. Expect me for tea at ten." After a moment his features softened. "I'll hope for better weather by week's end."

"As shall I, sir." She curtsied, then hastened to catch up with her family. *A certain matter.* What could it be but her bairn? Pausing in the doorway to pull on her gloves with trembling hands, she spied the chaise parked near the kirk gate. Rose was already seated, clutching Ian, while Jamie stood waiting in the deluge, holding out his hand toward her.

Leana hurried across the muddy kirkyard. Holding her hands over her head made little difference; she was soaked through within seconds. "Sorry to have kept you," she shouted above the din, breathless from running. "Has Father gone ahead?"

"Aye, astride Walloch." Jamie practically lifted her into the two-wheeled vehicle, then helped her get settled. "'Tis good we brought the chaise. No woman should be forced to walk in a *plumpshower* like this. Especially one who bears a babe."

Jamie looked at Rose when he said it, but Leana thought he'd glanced at *her* in passing. Might he suspect something? Or was he merely being polite, including her? On several occasions of late, she'd caught Jamie studying her, a pensive look on his face. She ate as little as she could to keep her figure in check, but her babe was not so easily contained. Perhaps she was fooling herself to think the child well hidden. Or had her father disclosed her secret for some ill-kindit reason?

She gripped the soggy leather reins while Jamie made his way to the other side and climbed onto the seat beside Rose. The chaise, one of the few wheeled conveyances in the parish, was meant for two. Three adults and a child in arms taxed the narrow, padded seat to its limits.

"On with you, Bess." Jamie took the reins, and the chaise lurched forward. The auld mare knew the way, leading them safely through the village, then across the arched stone bridge and westward. The movable bonnet above them provided minimal protection from the elements, and the open sides, none at all. Huddled together, their hats dripping, the sisters did what they could to comfort Ian, whose plaintive cries were muffled by the rain. At least the temperature was warm. They would arrive home drenched but not shivering.

Though Leana kept a wary eye on the flooded ditches, Reverend Gordon's visit was foremost in her mind. That morning the precentor had announced the kirk session would meet on the second of August. Please God, that Monday evening would not find her in the dining room of the manse before a formidable assembly of men demanding to know the particulars of her condition. Insisting the child should be raised by his father and stepmother. *Nae.* She was innocent before God and would not let the elders decide otherwise. *Let thy mercy be upon me.*

Once they arrived at the mains, getting Ian dry and fed was Leana's primary mission. Exhausted and irritable, he refused to cooperate, swatting his food away. "All right then, laddie. We'll see to a nap." Leana walked with him in the second-floor hall as she had when he was a newborn, holding him close, hoping the rhythm of her steps and the warmth of her body would help him drift off to sleep. "Baloo, baloo, my wee, wee thing," she sang softly, watching his eyelids droop. "How I wish I'd not weaned you, little one," she murmured. "A few minutes at my breast and you'd be fast asleep."

Ian finally drifted off, drooling across the bodice of Leana's gown.

She smiled as she tucked him in his crib, then released him very slowly lest she jostle him awake. She eased out of the nursery and tiptoed down the corridor toward her bedroom. Sunday supper would be light—day-old bannocks, Dunlop cheese from Ayrshire, cherries and summer pears from the orchard—but until then, her time was her own. She'd change her gown and see if she might find a book to read, something worthy of the Sabbath.

Leana stepped into her room and lit a few candles to dispel the gloom before she began unlacing her gown. She'd stitched it soon after Ian was born, practically living in the dress those first few months. Since it laced up the front, rather than in the back, it made nursing her son much more manageable. Now she was grateful to wear it because she could dress herself without calling Eliza to help her. Regrettably, none of her other altered gowns were so designed.

After slipping off her soiled dress and loosely laced corset, Leana pulled a linen wrapper from her closet. 'Twould do for a quiet afternoon in her room. She tied it round her waist, dismayed to watch the belt inch up. Was there no hope of hiding this dear child?

"We will read," she said aloud as though her bairn might behave himself, then dug through her small cupboard full of books. She chose *Sutton's Meditation on the Sacrament*—a sober book for a sober day—then settled into the upholstered chair and drew the candle closer. Freed of her restrictive clothes, she read in blessed comfort. When occasional flutters distracted her, she pressed her hand over the spot as if to comfort David. *Or Davina.* The thought brought a smile to her lips.

The supper hour was drawing near when a soft knock at the door announced Eliza. "May I come in, mem?"

Leana was on her feet at once, her book forgotten. Since lady's maids were accustomed to seeing their mistresses in every state of undress, Eliza might think it odd if she asked her to wait. But wait she must. "A moment, please." Leana tossed aside her wrap and grabbed her corset, the lacing still threaded but quite loose. She wriggled into it headfirst and pulled it in place just as Eliza slipped through door.

"D'ye not want me help wi' that, mem?" The maidservant wrinkled her brow at the sight of her, then hurried to be of assistance. Her experienced hands made short work of the laces, drawing the edges of the corset closer. " 'Tis not sae *het* today. Shall I *pu'* them tighter?"

Leana exhaled, making as much room as she could. "Only a little." When Eliza yanked the laces, Leana gasped, her vision clouding for a moment. "Too…much."

Eliza quickly loosened them with profuse apologies.

" 'Tis not your fault, lass." Leana took the deepest breath she could, grateful Eliza was standing behind her, where she could not see her expanding stomach. "I've been eating too well, I fear."

Eliza finished her task without comment, then helped her into a clean gown for supper. It was only when the last button was finished that Eliza stepped in front of her. "Beg pardon, mem, but ye hardly eat *oniething*." Though she was five years younger than Leana, the maidservant's eyes shone with understanding. "Perhaps ye're growin' for anither reason."

Tears welled in Leana's eyes. Any pretense was over. "Does the whole staff know as well?"

"Nae." Eliza offered Leana a fresh handkerchief from the dresser. "They'd have come tae me or tae Neda, and none have."

"Oh, Eliza." Leana dabbed at her nose, gazing at the maidservant all the while. "Can you possibly keep my secret? 'Tis not a matter of shame. I will gladly confess it after Lammas. But I fear it would…complicate things for Mr. and Mistress McKie."

Eliza was quick to agree.

Leana grasped the girl's chapped hands and squeezed them. "Will you promise to tell no one? And help me conceal the…evidence?"

"Ye can be sure I will, on *baith* counts." Eliza stepped back to appraise her. "We'll trim ane o' yer corsets and tie yer apron higher. I'll dress yer hair sae folk willna bother tae leuk below yer bonny face. As tae yer gouns, lighter colors are best. Might ye let oot yer seams a bit mair?"

"After supper," Leana promised. "Eliza, I realize the burden this puts on you, keeping my secret."

" 'Tis nae burden, mem." She blushed and curtsied. "I'm blithe tae ken ye'll be a mither again." Eliza turned and hastened out of the room, leaving the door open for Leana to follow, for the supper bell was already ringing.

Leana started down the stair, steadying herself on the handrail, her heart lodged in her throat. First Father, now Eliza. Who else in the household had jaloused her secret? Neda seldom missed such things. Nor Annabel. But it wasn't the servants knowing that made her knees weak and her steps unsure. It was Jamie. And Rose. *Three weeks to Lammas.*

Thirty-Four

Skilled in every trick, a worthy heir of his paternal craft,
he would make black look white, and white look black.

OVID

"I f you plan to storm the Bastille, you're a twelvemonth late."
Jamie looked up to find Lachlan looming over him, his expression
arrogant, his frame outlined by the slanted afternoon light that filled the
entrance to the barn.

Keeping his gaze as even as his blade, Jamie drew the whetstone the
length of his sword and imagined thrusting the weapon into the man's
gullet. Every hour he lived under Lachlan McBride's roof was more
intolerable than the last. The uncle who'd once credited him with blessing his flocks seemed bent on destroying whatever kinship they might
have known.

Lachlan picked up the dirk, examining the broad blade. "'Tis badly
nicked."

"That only means the dagger served its former owner well." Jamie
sheathed the sword within its worn scabbard, pleased with the heft of it
in his hand. "As long as the point is sharp, 'twill do its duty."

Lachlan snorted. "Surely you don't envision needing to defend
yourself?"

"'Tis a long journey home to Glentrool. With a wife and child to
protect and my flocks to watch o'er, I'd rather be armed than foolish."
Jamie reclaimed his dirk from his uncle's grasp and began to polish the
gemstone-studded grip. Though the hilt was ornamental, the lethal
blade was anything but decorative. The dagger would remain hidden in
his boot until needed. Silent. Ready. A man could not be certain who
his enemies might be—a thief, a Gypsy, a scoundrel. Or a brother.

Have your dirk where you can reach it. John McMillan's words, well
marked.

Except Jamie could never kill his own brother. He would defend himself if necessary, but he would not strike the first blow. A fortnight had passed since he had written Evan. Jamie wondered if his letter had softened his brother's heart…or hardened it.

Lachlan eyed the all-metal pistol on the bench. "That flintlock must be twenty years old."

" 'Twas made by Murdoch of Doune." His *pensie* uncle could not help being impressed by the celebrated pistol maker. When the man offered no further comment, Jamie realized he'd at least won on that score. Lachlan did not need to know that the mainspring was deemed defective by the Dumfries merchant who'd sold it for a price well below its value. Jamie did not intend to fire the single-shot pistol; simply wielding such a weapon would subdue most blackguards.

He slipped the polished dirk into his boot, then began cleaning the pistol, a more tedious task than mere sharpening or polishing. His efforts were eased with a timely reminder: Lachlan's wedding was two days hence. The man would disappear for a sennight with his bride, and peace would reign at Auchengray. "What time will we be leaving on Friday for Edingham?"

"*Edingham?*" Lachlan's voice raised a notch. "You're to go straight to the Urr kirk, where the Douglases will meet us. *Not* to Edingham."

Odd, his brusque response. Jamie had already visited the farm several times that spring. Was he no longer welcome? In truth, Jamie had no desire to see Edingham again and would gladly take the chaise directly to Urr. "What time shall we arrive at the kirk, then?"

"No later than half past eleven." Lachlan tapped the watch in his pocket for emphasis. "My bride insists the ceremony begin at the stroke of noon, whether any witnesses are present or not."

Jamie could not help but feel sorry for Morna Douglas, a woman destined to live in misery. Her sons, on the other hand, merited no pity whatsoever. They were cut from the same flawed bolt of broadcloth as his uncle, worshiping property over charity and silver above all else.

"I assume you came out here for a reason, Uncle," Jamie muttered, intent on using the clever tool built into the butt of the pistol to clear the fouling encrusted in the vent. When there was no response, he looked up. "Some…favor perhaps?"

Lachlan's expression darkened. He did not like being seen through. "I need you to ride Walloch home from the kirk Friday. Morna and I shall press on to Moffat in the Douglas carriage. The Hastingses will escort Rose home in the chaise."

"Fine," Jamie said, already dreading the affair. Perhaps Leana was the fortunate one, spending a quiet morning alone with Ian.

Lachlan took a turn round the barn interior, inspecting his holdings. "Where is Duncan? I've not seen the man all day."

"Visiting his daughter at Kingsgrange. He went by way of Dalbeaty."

"Really?" Lachlan abruptly stopped, and a faint shadow moved across his features. "When is he expected home?"

Jamie peered out of doors, judging the hour to be no later than six. "I'd look for him by the gloaming." Feeling a need to defend his friend, Jamie added, "This *is* his monthly Wednesday off."

"Do you think I'm not aware of that?" Lachlan abruptly turned and marched toward the house while Jamie considered aiming his pistol at the man's back. No gentleman pointed a gun at someone in jest, not even an unloaded one. But Jamie was tempted; aye, he was that.

He returned to his task as his thoughts drifted back to Leana. Now that he'd grown accustomed to the idea of her carrying his child, he took pleasure in it. What man would not welcome another son or daughter? Yet it grieved him too, for he would leave behind not only Leana but also his child.

Rose's response was unpredictable. Would she be happy for her sister? Indeed, it might ease her guilt about departing with Ian. Or would his wife feel threatened by the news? Rose might fear he'd decide to remain at Auchengray, though Jamie could never do so. Leana understood that better than anyone.

When she told him—and it would be soon, for Leana could not hide her secret behind her apron much longer—he would assure her the child's needs would be well met. *And yours, dear woman.* He would not abandon Leana or his child to Lachlan's dubious provision.

A half hour passed while he cleaned his firearm. A futile effort, really, since he didn't intend to load it. Who would risk firing a defective weapon? The pistol was simply for show. He'd seek out a gunsmith in Monnigaff and have it repaired. In the meantime, his dirk would suffice for any minor threats and his sword for more serious ones. Evan was far superior with a bow and quicker with a dirk, but Jamie had honed his swordplay skills in Edinburgh. If his brother truly intended to kill him, he'd have to get past the point of his blade first.

Jamie unsheathed his sword with a ringing *swish,* reveling in the solid feel of it in his hand. He moved away from the bench to claim an unoccupied corner of the barn, then positioned his feet for a proper salute, saying aloud the commands his fencing instructor had drilled into his head. "Stand on your guard in tierce. Make three beats of the foot." As he went through the familiar steps of the five positions, he couldn't help smiling, even though Monsieur Fréron would not have approved. "Extend your right arm in a line with your eye, James," he said, mimicking the sword master's affected speech, "and fix the point of your sword in a line with your adversary. *Oui.*"

"Bien." Rose stepped into the barn, laughing as she did, her sweet face aligned with the tip of his sword. "Well done, Monsieur McKie."

He lowered his weapon at once, still maintaining form. "Begging your pardon, madame."

She remained a safe distance away, but he could still see the twinkle in her eye. "Show me what you were doing."

Jamie dispensed with his smile at once and moved through the salute with more care, keeping in mind his master's requirements: a genteel deportment and a graceful air. When he finished, Rose showed her delight, clapping as if she were at an entertainment. He swept an imaginary hat off his head and bowed low before her. "James Lachlan McKie of Glentrool at your service, madame."

Rose held out her hand, beckoning him forward. "Kindly sheath your weapon, sir, and come dress for supper." She offered him a coy wink. "That smile of yours is dangerous enough."

Lachlan McBride was a trickster and a knave, but he had fathered the most charming daughters.

The last hour before darkness was Jamie's favorite, particularly in the summer. He stood on the lawn, watching the sunset paint the sky in colors only the Almighty could name. After singing all evening, the birds had grown quieter, making way for the tawny owls to take their turn.

Rose had retired early, complaining of stomach pains yet assuring him it was nothing a good night's sleep could not cure. He'd tried to read, but the fine weather beckoned, and so he'd closed his book and ventured out to the edge of the lawn.

"May we join you?" Leana glided toward him with Ian in her arms, a tentative expression on her face.

Her hair was styled in a most becoming way—Eliza's handiwork, he supposed—and she'd added a lacy ruffle to the neckline of one of her old gowns to good effect. Despite such efforts, her condition was poorly masked; her radiant skin alone gave her away.

She reached his side slightly out of breath. "'Tis such a lovely evening."

"So it is." He watched her shift the child in her arms, trying to conceal the one not yet born. *Come, lass. Why not tell me?*

"Look, sweet boy." She swept one arm across the sky. "Have you e'er seen such a brilliant shade of orange?"

Ian wiggled and bucked, apparently more interested in the bright green grass below. Leana kissed his cheek, then lowered him to the lawn. "Eliza will be fash when I bring you back to the nursery with green knees," she cautioned him, smiling as she said it.

The lad crawled a short distance, then stopped to yank out a blade of grass, then turned round to wave it at them, then took off again on a meandering route without straying too far from his mother's skirts.

Jamie transferred his gaze from the child to Leana. Perhaps he might find some way to help her confess her secret. "Children grow so quickly, don't they?"

"They do," she said, folding her hands in front of her. "Overnight, it seems."

Oh, Leana. Do you think I cannot tell? He glanced at Ian to be certain the boy was safe, then tried a different approach. "I wish…I wish there was a way we might leave Ian in your care, but the kirk will not allow it. You are such a fine mother, Leana."

After a long pause, she turned toward him, her mouth slightly open.

He implored her with his eyes, giving her permission to speak. *I am listening, Leana.*

"Jamie, I…"

"Och, lad!" Duncan shouted across the lawn, running toward them. His worn clothes and lanky form gave him the appearance of a *scaurcraw* escaped from the fields. "I maun speak tae ye at once." He gathered up Ian, who squealed in protest, and delivered him into Leana's arms. "Pardon me, baith o' ye, for I've just returned from Kingsgrange." He was clearly agitated, with his cap askew and his blue eyes a bit wild looking. "Leana, will ye mind if…that is, I need tae…"

"Of course. 'Tis just as well, for Ian's bedtime draws near." She nodded at them both, then headed toward the house.

Jamie watched her leave with a sense of sadness. She seemed so close to telling him about their child. He turned back to Duncan, who also had news it seemed. "What is it, my friend? What has you so vexed?"

Duncan pulled off his bonnet, then wiped his arm across his brow. "I canna be certain, yet I canna keep it tae meself." He fanned himself with his cap, his expression more troubled than Jamie had ever seen it. "Comin' hame by way o' Dalbeaty I passed Edingham Farm. Sittin' up on a spur like it does, 'tis hard tae miss the place."

"Go on."

"In the field tae the west o' the mains—a field that used tae lie fallow, mind ye—I spied…" His shoulders sagged. "I spied a flock o' lambs."

"*Lambs?*" Jamie's heart thudded in his chest. It wasn't possible. "Surely not…*my* lambs?"

Duncan spread his hands, clearly at a loss. "I canna say, lad, for I couldna get close enough tae be certain. They didna bear yer keel mark, but they *were* blackface. Aboot five score."

Jamie stared at the overseer, his mind reeling. "Are you suggesting the *Douglases* stole my lambs? Duncan, that makes no sense. Our families are about to be joined—"

"Wait, lad." Duncan held up his hand, a cautionary gesture. "I'm not suggestin' oniething. They may not be yer lambs at a'. Mebbe they purchased a flock o' their ain."

Jamie yanked at his neckcloth, suddenly feeling as if someone were choking him. Duncan was not the only one who'd seen a flock of lambs where they did not belong. Peter Drummond had told him a tale as well. *Several dozen. Headed west.* The road that led to Dalbeaty. *'Twas late in the evening. The first of June.*

Jamie gripped the man's shoulders. "When did you last visit Mary at Kingsgrange? On the night you were gone, the Douglases were here for supper and then walked home." *Late. In the evening.*

" 'Twas not me usual day off," Duncan said. "A Tuesday, not a Wednesday…" After a moment a light came into his eyes, and his features relaxed. "Now I remember. 'Twas the start o' the month. The first o' June. Richt pleasant weather."

"A verra pleasant night. For stealing sheep." Jamie's head swiveled toward the barn, where he'd stored his weapons. "Lachlan McBride will not get away with this."

"Wait, lad." Duncan grabbed his arm, squeezing hard. "Dinna blame yer uncle 'til ye see the lambs yerself." Duncan's hold on him eased but not his fervor. "On Friday, while the Douglases are at the Urr manse for the *waddin,* find a reason tae leave early and come hame by way o' Edingham. Then ye'll ken the truth."

"Friday?" Jamie fumed.

" 'Tis not but twa days hence, Jamie. 'Twould be a sin tae accuse yer uncle or his new family unfairly, aye?"

Duncan was right, and Jamie knew it. But he did not relish the thought of sleeping under the same roof with a man who might have stolen his lambs. On their own, the Douglas brothers lacked the nerve for such swickerie; Lachlan was brazen enough for all three of them.

"After the wedding, then." Jamie would put a muzzle on his temper until Friday. But not one day longer.

Thirty-Five

Slow buds the pink dawn like a rose
From out night's gray and cloudy sheath.
SUSAN COOLIDGE

When dawn broke on the morn of the wedding, the skies were clear but not bright, as if a thin layer of muslin were stretched above Galloway. Anything might happen on such a day. Brilliant sunshine could appear by noon, only to disappear behind heavy clouds come three o' the clock, followed by a downpour at supper.

"Unchancie weather for a waddin," Neda observed, lighting another candle at the breakfast table. "Shall I bring ye some tea, lass?"

"Please." Leana was the only one present; the others were busy elsewhere, dressing for the eventful day ahead. Tightly laced into her old nursing gown, she had room for only one cup of tea and a slice of plum. Perhaps she might manage a second cup when Reverend Gordon came knocking. Unless he brought bad news, in which case she would have no appetite at all.

Her father, dressed in his best gray coat and scarlet waistcoat, had already galloped off astride Walloch. Duncan and Neda would depart on foot shortly. Jamie and Rose planned to leave by chaise well before ten. They knew nothing of the reverend's intended visit, for how would she have explained it? If the couple left on schedule, all would be well. If they were running late or if the reverend arrived early, it would make for an awkward parting. Please God, his mercy would prevail even in such trifling details.

Neda sailed back into the room, the pleasant aroma of black tea filling the air. She served Leana, then pointed to the flickering candle by her plate. "D'ye see that speck in the flame? Folk say it means a letter will be comin'." When Neda picked up the candlestick and lightly tapped it on the table, the speck fell away. "Thar now. 'Tis already on its way."

Leana smiled at the old custom, aware of how hard Neda was trying to lift her spirits. Jamie was the one waiting for a letter. He'd shared very few details with her. Only that he'd written his father and brother and prayed they might respond soon. So far, no letter had arrived from Glentrool. "I'm not expecting a post," Leana told her, "but I *am* looking for Reverend Gordon at ten."

Neda's face, as open as any book, had worry written on every line. "What's the purpose o' his visit, lass?"

"He said that a certain matter had come to his attention."

Neda eyed the closed doors to the dining room, then said in a low voice, "I'm wonderin' if 'tis the same matter that has come tae me ain attention." The lines in her face softened. "I believe a wee bairn's on the way."

Leana's shoulders slumped. "Did Eliza say something?"

"Eliza?" Neda chuckled. "Lass, I kenned ye were carryin' anither babe from the day ye came hame. When ye hugged me at the top o' the stair, that babe ye're hidin' met me first."

Leana spread her linen napkin across her lap as if another layer might mask the obvious truth. "I am sorry, Neda. I should have told you of all people."

"Ye have yer reasons for keepin' it a saicret." If Neda was hurt, her words did not show it; Leana heard only compassion. "Twa o' yer reasons will suin appear at table wantin' their breakfast."

Leana tried to sip her tea, but she could not steady the cup, her hands were shaking so badly. From relief at Neda's knowing. From shame at Jamie's and Rose's not knowing. Had she erred in trying to spare them? "Neda, I'd hoped to wait until Lammas…"

"O' course ye did. For guid reason. Tae make life easier for them ye luve."

"That's what I thought at first." Leana stared out the window at the apple orchards east of the house, her eye drawn to the bright red skins of summer permains. "Now I fear I'm only delaying news that will distress them even more once they reach Glentrool and learn the truth. Especially Rose, who will imagine the worst—that Jamie might send for me or return to Auchengray."

Neda touched her arm. "Is that what *ye* hope will happen, lass?"

"My only hope is that Jamie will give our child his name." She took a sip of tea, her mouth suddenly parched. "As to what Reverend Gordon will say this morn…"

"He canna threaten ye wi' the cutty stool, for ye've done nae wrong." Neda stood behind her, resting her hands on her shoulders. "By the leuk o' ye, the babe was *clecked* many months syne, whan the fields were still frozen. Whan ye were Mistress McKie, richt and true."

Leana turned and clasped Neda's hands. "You'll be well on your way to the Urr kirk when Reverend Gordon arrives here. Will you pray for me?"

"Ye ken I will," Neda promised, squeezing back. "Ilka hour we're gone."

Neda no sooner headed for the kitchen than the door to the entrance hall swung open.

Rose entered the dining room, dressed in her best rose damask gown. Jamie, close behind her, was equally turned out. His new brown riding coat, tailored to fit, followed the broad line of his shoulders past his tapered waist, ending at his knees. The buff-colored waistcoat and light buckskin breeches offered a striking contrast beneath the dark coat. Just above the cuff of his polished boot shone the glint of a jewel-topped dirk.

"How fine you both look," Leana said as they took their seats. Rose was trying to conceal her pleasure at being off on an outing. Jamie's mood was subdued, as if he had much on his mind.

Neda reappeared, bearing two more cups of tea. After serving the couple, she stepped behind Lachlan's empty chair, her gaze pointed at the mantel clock. "'Tis time Duncan and I were bound for the kirk. Ye'll find mair bannocks on the sideboard. Hard cheese. Sliced plums. Boiled eggs. Help yerselves as ye like." Breakfast was the one meal that even in the great houses of Scotland was often not served by the staff so the gentry might rise at their leisure and find food waiting.

When she turned to Leana, Neda's face shone with benevolence. "I'll be prayin' yer day at hame brings ye naught but peace, mistress." With that Neda left the room, the door swinging closed behind her.

Rose's bright expression dimmed. "Leana, how can we leave without you?"

"I am quite content to stay home with Ian," Leana said. "Eliza will look after him until eleven, and then he is all mine for the balance of the day. 'Tis a blessing, not a burden, to stay home." She looked at Jamie, not quite meeting his gaze. "You'll not forget to take Father's gift?"

"Already in the chaise." Jamie's frown was fearsome. "Pray I simply hand it to the man rather than giving in to my baser nature and bashing him on the head."

"*Jamie!*" Rose's mouth fell open. "Today of all days see that you do not quarrel with Father."

Jamie started to say something, then stuffed a bannock in his mouth instead. It was hard to tell whether he was chewing the food or gnashing his teeth.

Without preamble Willie stood in the doorway, where he waited for Leana to motion him across the threshold. "Beggin' yer pardon, but I didna want tae miss ye, what wi' the waddin and a'." He patted the pocket of his vest as he hobbled toward them. "I've a letter tae deliver."

Jamie nearly choked on his bannock before reaching for his tea and downing the cupful without a pause.

Seeing his distress, Leana asked, "To whom is it addressed, Willie?"

"Tae be honest, mem, I didna ask. The grocer just said tae carry it hame." Colin Elliot's shop in the village served as a posting stop, one of the many places Willie visited on his daily round of errands. He slid one, then two crooked fingers inside his pocket in a vain effort to fish out the letter.

Above Jamie's neckcloth a faint line of color began to show. "Surely you haven't been to the grocer's and back this morn?"

Now it was Willie's turn to redden. "Nae, sir. I'm sorry tae say I carried the letter hame yestreen and…forgot." After finally pulling it free, bringing a flurry of lint with it, Willie presented Jamie with the square post sealed with a dollop of wax.

The hope on Jamie's face dwindled as he read the inscription. "For Leana. From your Aunt Margaret in Twyneholm."

"Oh." Seeing his disappointment, Leana bridled her enthusiasm.

"Thank you, Willie. I'm sure one more day did not matter for this post. But if a letter comes for Mr. McKie, you'll bring it at once, won't you?"

"Aye, m-mem, I w-wull." He bowed again before making a hasty exit.

Leana slipped the letter in her apron pocket, surprised at the thickness of it. Keen as she was to break the seal and read its contents, the post would have to wait. Reverend Gordon would arrive before hour's end, and she needed to make certain Jamie and Rose were on their way. Standing with care, lest she wobble while she found her balance, Leana nodded at the sideboard. "What may I bring you? Fruit? Eggs perhaps?"

Rose gave her pretty curls a shake. "*You* must promise to eat something too. I refuse to gain weight unless you do the same."

"I feel certain I will," Leana murmured, gazing toward the window. *Two weeks to Lammas.*

Thirty-Six

Friends, if we be honest with ourselves,
we shall be honest with each other.

GEORGE MACDONALD

One prayer had already been answered: Jamie and Rose were away to the wedding, and the mantel clock had yet to strike ten. "Godspeed," Leana called out as she waved farewell from the lawn.

Reverend Gordon would not be long in coming. She hastened inside the house, aware of her babe moving inside her. No sooner had she washed her hands and face and the servants scraped up the last of the breakfast crumbs, than a knock at the front door announced the minister.

She waited for him in the spence, having instructed Annabel to escort him there. Standing beside her father's desk, willing her knees to remain steady, Leana reminded herself of all she'd endured for honesty's sake. *In God I have put my trust; I will not fear.*

Strong words, confident words. Did she believe them? Could she live them?

The minister's shoes scuffed against the stone floors as he turned toward the spence. Leana forced a smile to her lips and readied her speech.

"Reverend Gordon," she greeted him as he strolled through the door, his black coattails flapping. "Welcome to Auchengray." His bow was cordial, her curtsy polite. Leana directed him to her father's chair, which the tall minister more than filled. She sat opposite him in the smaller one. "I am grateful this day suited you, for as you can see, the house is...quiet."

"Indeed." He looked about the spence, his curiosity evident as he scanned the titles on the library shelf book by book. His gaze roamed over the locked money box, the thick ledgers, and the whisky decanter. "All the things your father values are in this room, I see."

Annabel entered bearing a tea tray, scarlet tendrils poking from beneath her white cap. She tended to their repast with calm efficiency. When she paused at the door and asked, "Will thar be oniething else, mem?" Leana shook her head slightly even as her heart said, *Aye. Pray.*

Once the door was closed and they had the room to themselves, the minister did not waste another moment. "Leana, I received a letter Friday last. 'Tis why I approached you on the Sabbath, requesting we meet."

"A…letter?" She touched the one in her apron pocket, suddenly wishing she'd read it. Perhaps the two were connected in some way. "From whom was your post, sir?"

"John Scott in Twyneholm." He withdrew the folded paper from his coat pocket as he spoke. "A good minister to his flock, as I'm sure you discovered in your time there."

"A kind soul," she agreed, even as her hands grew clammy. Reverend Scott knew too much about her. He knew everything.

Reverend Gordon unfolded the letter, then tipped his chin down, reading over the top of his spectacles. "He writes that his granddaughter was recently married wearing your claret gown."

Leana briefly explained the necessity of selling her gown in order to hire a chaise. He listened, nodding thoughtfully, but did not comment until she finished.

"Reverend Scott described the very same scenario here, Miss McBride." He held up the paper with its fine, even script. "However, he goes into greater detail about your…your confession. At the manse."

Leana saw it in his eyes. *He knows.* And with that realization came a sense of peace far greater than her fears. When she spoke, her voice was calm and her words sure. *For my mouth shall speak truth.*

"Reverend, as you might imagine, the news of my compearance on the stool at Newabbey kirk reached Twyneholm not long after I did. When the subject was…introduced at our gathering at the manse, I thought it best to speak the truth. All of it."

Reverend Gordon slowly folded the letter. "'Tis said the one that speaketh truth showeth forth righteousness. Once again, Leana, you honor your mother's good example." He lifted his teacup but did not drink from it. "Your…ah, present condition is another matter."

"It is not a 'matter,' sir." Her voice was gentle but firm. "It is a child."

He drank his tea in silence, acknowledging her words with the slightest of nods.

Leana folded her hands across her lap in such a way that, rather than concealing the evidence of her motherhood, she accentuated it. "You know, of course, that this is Jamie McKie's son or daughter. Conceived while the kirk session and all of Newabbey considered us properly married." How good it felt to confess that aloud. Was there any freedom greater than the truth?

"Your honesty on many other occasions merits my trust on this one." The reverend studied her over his spectacles. "Though I'm surprised you did not come to me with this news when you first arrived home."

"I should have done just that," she agreed. "But when I found the McKies still here and Rose expecting...I thought it best to...wait."

He said nothing for a moment, pursing his lips. "You know, of course, that I must consult with the elders."

She held her breath, waiting for the rest of it.

"I believe they will come to the same conclusion I have." He put his empty teacup aside. "Though the situation is unfortunate because of your current marital state, the child's conception was quite...ah, legitimate."

Relief, fresh as a Solway breeze, rushed through her, nearly lifting her from her seat. "Then...I'll not be forced to...compear..."

"Was *that* what you expected?" Reverend Gordon waved his hand dismissively. "The kirk is strict, as we must be, but we are not without mercy."

She pressed her hand to her heart, overwhelmed. "But the elders... but Ian..."

"'Twas another situation entirely." His brown eyes bore no condemnation. "If I may say so, this child will be born to a different mother. One whose sins have been washed clean."

"Aye," she breathed.

"Indeed, I believe you have been punished enough, Miss McBride. Don't you agree?"

She gaped at him, too overwhelmed to speak. Could this possibly be the same man who had leaned over his pulpit and charged her with hochmagandy? Clearly Reverend Gordon had changed as well.

He tented his fingers, propping his elbows on the padded arms of his chair. "Now then, Miss McBride, tell me your plans for the future."

"I will…remain at Auchengray. And raise my child." *Please God, it would be as simple as that.* "In due time I will ask Mr. McKie to give the child his name."

Reverend Gordon's brows rose. "When will you make that request? Soon, I hope."

"Quite soon." *How soon, Leana? In a fortnight? In a month?* "I thought it best to wait until I was certain that all was…well."

"Ah." Reverend Gordon stood, tugging on the hem of his too-short waistcoat. "Then I'll leave you to tell him and trust it will not be long. Every father deserves to know such things." He frowned as he added, "Mr. McKie must be very daft indeed not to have seen the truth with his own eyes."

"Not daft. Just…preoccupied." She escorted the minister to the hall, offering a parting curtsy before Annabel presented him with his hat and saw him out the door.

The minute the latch fell in place Annabel turned round, her blue eyes filled with concern. "Mistress, is somethin' wrong?"

Leana grasped the newel post at the bottom of the stair, feeling a bit dizzy. "Nothing is the matter. Nothing…at all." She straightened, not letting go until she was sure her legs would support her. "I'll be in the garden, should anyone have need of me. Tell Eliza to bring Ian to me no later than eleven, aye?"

Gathering her scattered wits about her, Leana walked through the half-empty house and out the back door, aiming for the cool shade of the yew. She sank onto the ground beneath the tree, padded with decades of needlelike leaves, and leaned back against the peeling bark. Closing her eyes, Leana took her first deep breath of the morning. *He hath delivered my soul in peace.*

Those whom she'd feared most—her father, Reverend Gordon—

knew the truth. Those whom she trusted most—Neda, Eliza—knew as well. Only the child's father and aunt remained to be told. *Soon, Jamie.* She opened her eyes to gaze at the canopy of branches above her. *Soon, Rose.* She would write the letter before they left and post it immediately so it would be waiting for them when they arrived at Glentrool. Aye, that was best.

Resting her hands on her apron, Leana felt the bulky letter from Meg waiting in her pocket since breakfast. When she broke open the wax seal, out fell another letter, addressed in a familiar hand: her sister's. The post that had arrived in Twyneholm too late.

Leana held one in each hand, debating which to read first. Rose's tardy letter would reveal nothing new, so perhaps Meg's first.

> To Leana McBride
> Thursday, 8 July 1790
>
> My dearest niece,
>
> Pardon me for being so long in forwarding this letter from your sister. I used it to mark my place in a book and forgot it was there until I opened to that page again this morning. Many apologies. Though I am sure you know by now all that her letter contains, it is only right that you should have this post in your possession.

Leana fingered Rose's letter, smiling at the thought of her aunt being so absent-minded. *Dear Meg. How I miss you.* She would write her tomorrow with news of Lachlan's wedding.

> I have read your last letter many times and still cannot fathom what it must be like for you there with Jamie and Rose. My poor niece! I pray that Ian's presence eases the heartache of watching your beloved cousin with your sister. How difficult it will be to bid your son farewell a second time.

More than difficult, Auntie. The words swam on the page. *Unimaginable.*

> Do promise you will visit me next spring with your new
> friend. My neighbors have an extra bed for Willie, so you
> need not hire a chaise.

New friend. A guarded description of Leana's unborn child. One never knew where a letter might land or who might read it. Meg's cautious wording was prudent.

Leana folded the letter and rubbed her thumb over the seal. According to the almanac calendar, she was past the midpoint of her pregnancy. *Halfgone,* Neda called it. Past the worrisome months when the fear of miscarriage pressed on a woman's heart like a stone. Past the exhaustion and the sickness upon waking. The halcyon months, before the weariness returned and the child took control of a mother's body, not relenting until delivery day.

Her sister would soon be halfgone as well. Leana opened Rose's letter with a bittersweet sense of regret. Had she received this letter in Twyneholm, she would have arrived at Auchengray after Lammas, sparing everyone much heartache, including herself.

But she was here. And so was Rose.

> To Leana McBride
> Tuesday, 1 June 1790
>
> My dear sister,
>
> I have news that cannot keep, though it would be far better
> to tell you in person. God has answered my prayers…

Guilt swelled inside her. *Far better in person.* If her sister could be so honest, why could not she? Had she been sparing Rose all this time— or protecting herself?

Leana stared at the letter, distressed by what she saw. Instead of Rose's customary graceful hand, the lines were shaky and splattered with ink. *Oh, sweet Rose. Were you crying as you wrote this?* Leana wiped away her own tears, careful not to smudge the ink, as she read the stories Rose thoughtfully included about Ian. Anecdotes about new sounds, new teeth, new foods. About how he was starting to sit and learning to point.

Leana pressed her apron to her eyes. *You will be a good mother, Rose. You have loved my Ian well.*

> My child is due in January. Not the best of months for a
> midwife to travel. I only wish you could be here.

Leana gripped the paper, nigh to crushing it. *How I wish I could, Rose!* But she could not journey to Glentrool for Rose's confinement, so close on the heels of her own. With a heavy sigh, she folded the letter, vowing to read it again when she felt stronger. She'd risen early and eaten little; Leana was not even certain she could stand.

Or perhaps it was her tears that made her feel weak. Or her too-snug laces. Or the realization of what she must do next: not write to Jamie and Rose in a fortnight but tell them. Now.

What a coward you are, Leana. Her father was right. A coward wrote letters. A brave woman spoke the truth in person. *I have chosen the way of truth.*

Leana sat up, infused with a sense of purpose. Aye, she would *do* it. She would tell them—all of them—before day's end. Jamie and Rose first, the moment they returned home from the wedding, and then the rest of the household after supper. It was time. Past time. Now that Reverend Gordon knew, the whole parish would follow. However much the news might crush Rose, would it not be worse for her to hear it as gossip in the kirkyard?

She would tell her sister today. In person.

On her feet before she realized it, Leana untied her apron with a decisive yank, pulling it over her head like one set free from a yoke of shame. She loosened the front laces of her gown, setting her child free as well, then walked into the sunlight, leaving the shade of the yew behind. Feeling stronger with each step, she lengthened her stride, her skirts brushing along the borders of her garden, her unborn child leading the way.

"Leuk wha has come tae see ye, Ian." Eliza sallied forth from the kitchen, her charge held high. "'Tis yer mither, wha luves ye. Isn't that richt, mem?"

Leana wrapped Ian in her arms, nestling his warm body against hers. "That is the truth and nothing less."

Thirty-Seven

And half in shade and half in sun;
The Rose sat in her bower.

BAYARD TAYLOR

Rose groaned as they bounced along on the chaise's tired springs. "When we leave for Glentrool, were you thinking I would ride Hastings?"

Jamie looked at her askance. "In your condition? Certainly not. Jock Bell has agreed to loan me a wagon and two horses, which Rab and Davie will return to him. Not as comfortable as the chaise, but 'twill hold more—you and Ian, above all, but our trunks and provisions, too. And Annabel."

Wincing as they jolted over a small rock, Rose tightened her grip on his arm. She tried to imagine what it would be like with two women in a *dashelt,* auld wagon, one lass holding Ian while the other held the reins. Though she could not wait to reside at Glentrool, the journey there held less appeal with each turn of the wheels.

Rose shaded her eyes, surveying the extensive valley to their left with its cultivated fields of oats, barley, and potatoes. Passing two parish farms close to the road, she noted large herds of black cattle but no sheep.

"Where are the lambs? Do the farmers not keep many sheep in this parish?"

"Nae." His mood darkened. "They do not."

He'd been peevish for two days, ever since Duncan returned from Kingsgrange. Whenever she'd asked him what was wrong, Jamie had insisted he had nothing to tell her. "Not until Friday."

Well, then. She drew closer, hoping he might catch a whiff of the rose water she'd bathed with that morning. " 'Tis Friday, Jamie, and you know what they say."

"Friday flit, short time sit."

Och. Not at all what she was after. "True, Friday is not a favorable day for moving nor for fishing, but it *is* a canny day for marrying. More people in Scotland wed on Friday than all the rest of the days put together." No sooner had she spoken than their own wedding days came to mind. *Wednesday. Saturday.* Neither of them considered lucky.

He cocked one eyebrow. "My grandfather Archibald insisted Friday was an ill choice for a wedding because that was the day Eve tempted Adam to eat the forbidden fruit."

"Jamie! Where in the Buik does it say that happened on a *Friday?*"

"It doesn't." Almost a smile. "Though you might check your father's almanac when we get home."

They crossed a shallow burn, the valley to the east having given way to a sweep of verdant hills. Though the day was warm, and the sun had brightened since morn, the scent of rain still hung in the moist air. As they climbed along a sparsely wooded stretch, a figure emerged from the trees and started toward them. An older woman dressed in garish, mismatched clothing, carrying a wicker basket in her hands. Familiar, but not welcome.

Lillias Brown. The wutch of Nethermuir.

Everything inside Rose stopped. Her breath, her heart, even her thoughts. When she jerked to life again—her breath ragged, her heart beating too fast—one thought overshadowed all others. *Flee.*

"Don't slow down," she pleaded, looking only at Jamie and not at the *wickit* woman drawing closer to the chaise. *Keep away from me. And from my family.* The last words she'd spoken to Lillias on a Sabbath morning in March. Rose had not seen her since that day. She did not want to see her now.

"Whoa, Bess." Jamie reined in the mare. Lillias had walked into the chaise's path, giving him no choice.

Rose squeezed her eyes shut, refusing to look at Lillias. But she could not stop her ears from hearing the witch's words.

"I see ye, Rose McKie. Hidin' yer face from yer auld freen."

"You flatter yourself, woman." Jamie's voice was sharper than the dirk in his boot. "My wife is not your friend, nor are you hers."

Bess shook her mane, as if anxious to move on. "Please, Jamie." Rose tucked her face behind his shoulder. "Let us away."

"Sic a fine goun ye're wearin'." Lillias stepped closer, her hand on Bess's jingling harness, preventing their escape. "If a rose from yer sister's gairden shed blood, 'twould be that verra color."

Lillias was beside her now. Rose smelled the herbs on her clothes.

Jamie stretched his arm across her like a shield. "No closer, Widow Brown."

"I see ye ken me name." Her high-pitched laugh bore no humor. "Did me *cantrips* and herbs *wark*? Did they gie yer bride the waddin *praisent* she wanted?" After a brief pause, Lillias clapped her hands once, making Rose jump. "Och! I see they did."

"'Twas the Almighty who blessed her," Jamie said firmly. "Not you."

"Rose McKie is not the only woman ye ken wi' a *wame* that's fu'. Isn't that richt, Mr. McKie?"

He stiffened. "Let go of the harness. Now."

Rose sensed her stepping away but dared not look to be certain. Whatever was the witch blethering about? Of course there were other expectant mothers in Galloway! Hanging on to Jamie's arm, Rose felt his muscles tense as he called out to Bess. The chaise was slow starting, for they were on an incline, but soon the wheels were turning round again.

When Rose opened her eyes, they were riding on a high ridge with a splendid view of rolling hills and the village not far below. Her breathing grew more even. "Jamie, I am...so sorry."

"Dinna fash yerself." She heard Duncan's accent and Jamie's kindness. "You are not to blame for that witch blocking our path."

"But I am very much to blame for her *crossing* our path." Rose exhaled, trying to rid herself of the woman's scent, to forget the sound of her voice, to block out any memory of once visiting her eerie cottage, Nethermuir. The teas, the herbs, the amulets, the spells. What a naive fool she'd been to seek out a witch! "God forgive me the sins of my youth."

Jamie glanced at her, slowing the chaise as they started downhill again, bound for the crossroads. "Are you saying you are auld now? My wife, whose seventeenth birthday has yet to dawn?"

"I will be ancient come Lammas Sunday," she assured him, feeling her spirits begin to lighten.

"Rose…" Jamie glanced her way for a moment, then faced the road again. "You ken that your father has asked me to ride Walloch home."

She'd forgotten and did not care to be reminded. "I'll miss your company in the chaise."

"With Neda and Duncan sharing this seat, you'll not lack for companionship." His gaze scanned the distant horizon. "After our meal, I will leave for home…early. Ahead of the others."

"Is there some pressing matter at Auchengray that bids you home?" A fleeting thought of Leana crossed her mind, then was gone.

"Nae, lass. I cannot say more until I have the evidence I need."

Evidence? She did not like the sound of that. "You will tell me later, then?"

"Later," was all he said. The rest of her questions, it seemed, would have to wait.

Half a mile past Hardgate they came upon Haugh of Urr, a village settled along the banks of the Urr, midway between Dumfries and Kirkcudbright. Bess turned left at Jamie's command and headed straight for the kirk. Whether Bess spied Walloch tied to the hitching post or envisioned cool water and fresh oats waiting for her, the mare was on a full trot when they reached the grassy glebe. The Douglas carriage with its two horses waited near the kirk door along with several other fine mounts. Had the family already assembled?

Duncan was apparently watching for them and came bounding out the kirk door. "*Whaur* ye been, lad? 'Tis half past the hour, and Mistress Douglas is—"

"Aye, aye." Jamie brought the chaise to an abrupt stop, jumped down, then came round to lift Rose to the ground. "Tend to Bess, will you, Duncan? I'll see Rose in."

She shook out her skirts, then turned in a circle. "Is my gown badly wrinkled?"

"You look fine, lass. Come." He sounded irritated, so she did not ask him if her bow was crushed or her hair still in place. She wasn't the bride, after all.

As Jamie escorted her to the door, Rose eyed the nearby kirkyard and was relieved to find no open graves among the headstones. Very unlucky for a wedding, that. The stone kirk, twice as long as it was wide, was noticeably cooler inside, if a bit dank. The pulpit stood halfway down the long south wall, a small loft for the heritors perched across from it. Like the Newabbey kirk, this house of worship was somber and unadorned, with clear glass panes in the long windows. The enclosed wooden pews were painted a dull green, and as usual, there were never enough candles.

A knot of people stood before the pulpit, most of whom Rose knew. Morna Douglas wore a simple blue gown, appropriate for a widow about to remarry, with a matching hat that made her look taller. Her sons were dressed in the same English broadcloth they'd worn when they visited Auchengray several weeks ago, a bit worse for wear. When Duncan joined Neda, they stood apart from the others, aware of their station, yet by far the most amiable souls in the assembly.

It was Lachlan McBride, however, who demanded Rose's attention, motioning her forward. The scowl on his face did not bode well. "At last my family has arrived."

Brief courtesies were offered in hushed tones, in deference to their surroundings. Morna smiled a little, though it seemed an effort. She *did* compliment Rose's gown, but Gavin's frank appraisal was less welcome. Rose clasped her hands round Jamie's arm, hoping the gesture might cool the young man's gaze. Morna's other sons were surly, even rude. Clearly Malcolm and Jamie had no use for each other. They only lacked pistols to be engaged in a duel, so murderous were the looks they exchanged.

"And this is Reverend James Muirhead," Morna said in a *timorsome* voice, her hands fluttering round her face. "Our fine minister."

A robust man of fifty-odd years stepped forward, his commanding physique better suited to the army than the pulpit. The man's round face was framed by a silvery white periwig, which starkly contrasted with his black brows. Though he appeared as dour as any minister in Scotland, his high brow and luminous eyes hinted at a keen intelligence.

Reverend Muirhead tipped his head toward her father. "Shall we go over the particulars of the ceremony once more, or—"

"Nae," Lachlan said bluntly. "Our guests will arrive momentarily. Morna and I have both spoken vows before. This wedding will nae doubt unfold like all the others you have performed these twenty years in Urr."

"Perhaps." The minister's gaze traveled from Jamie to Malcolm. "Though one can ne'er be certain what will happen at a wedding."

Thirty-Eight

Let fortune empty her whole quiver on me.

JOHN DRYDEN

Lachlan held out his hand, confident Morna would fill it. In a matter of minutes, he would be the wealthiest bonnet laird in Newabbey, if not the ten parishes. Rich with land, rich with flocks, rich with sons. Aye, and rich with silver, locked away where thieves could not break through nor steal. A grand way to celebrate his sixtieth year.

Morna pulled off her lace gloves, then slipped her hand in his. For such a hot day, her touch was like ice. Would she be cold in other respects, this nervous bride of his? Not that it mattered. Young men married for lust; his intentions were of a higher nature.

"We are gathered here on this most solemn occasion to join Lachlan McBride of Auchengray and Morna Douglas of Edingham in holy matrimony." Reverend Muirhead's voice carried through the kirk, though it only needed to reach the first few pews. Not many neighbors bothered to attend a wedding where the bridal dinner was limited to family members. Lachlan, however, refused to feed the parish simply to draw a crowd.

When the minister lifted his hand, he was greeted with the rustling of skirts and scraping of heels. "All stand for a reading from the Book of Common Order."

The words of John Knox rang through the stony sanctuary. Lachlan was too busy reviewing a detailed list in his mind to pay much attention to the fiery reformer's rhetoric. The Douglas carriage—about to become the McBride carriage—was cleaned and polished and waiting at the door. Driver and footman were seated in the back of the kirk, prepared to depart for Dumfriesshire immediately after the meal. Morna's bridal week in Moffat included lodging at the Black Bull Hotel, fine meals with many courses, and frequent visits to the Moffat

Well—an extravagance that would not be repeated in their lifetime. But, of course, Morna could not know that. Nor did he plan to mention it.

The minister closed the Book of Common Order and fixed his gaze on the couple. "Is there any impediment to this marriage? Any reason why the two of you should not be joined together as husband and wife?"

"Nae reason whatsoever," Lachlan said, his conscience clear.

"None, sir," Morna chirped. Since he could not alter the irritating pitch of her voice, he would have to insist on silence at table or risk losing his appetite altogether.

Reverend Muirhead moved to the side and posed the same question to the mostly empty pews. "Is there any reason why these two should not be joined in holy matrimony? If so, please present your evidence."

Lachlan could not resist peering over his shoulder. Heads were bent together, and he detected whispering, but none present lifted a hand to declare the marriage invalid. His nephew was the only one who looked as though he'd thought of something.

"If there are no objections, we will proceed." The minister nodded at Lachlan as he turned forward once more. "Mr. McBride, the ring, if you please."

Morna had insisted on a very slender silver band, confessing she was ashamed of her short, plump hands. Too narrow for the jeweler to engrave, almost too thin to handle without dropping it, Lachlan offered her the ring from his palm. She slipped it on her finger, just to the knuckle, then he held it in place. Her hands were frozen now and trembling, his own warm and steady.

Reverend Muirhead made short work of the vows, then went on at length, quoting various passages by memory, adding lines from Psalms and snippets of Scottish poetry by Ramsay and Thomson. The man was educated, that was certain. He was also long winded. At last the minister brought his discourse to a close, and Lachlan pushed the ring firmly in place. *Done.* All that once belonged to the Douglases now belonged to him.

While the parishioners collected their walking sticks and gloves, Morna squeezed Lachlan's hand, her eyes bright with tears. He briefly squeezed back, then turned away. "Come, Wife. Our dinner awaits."

The minister led the wedding party through the kirk and out of doors into the bright sunlight of midday. Lachlan conducted the final bit of business—silvering the man's hand—before the reverend dutifully kissed the bride, his last official act.

Morna turned, face uplifted, prepared to receive her first kiss from her bridegroom. Lachlan obliged her, though her lips were dry and uninviting. A smattering of polite applause followed, provided by acquaintances of Morna's who'd known her late husband. If they disapproved of her choice, their faces did not show it. Nor did it matter. Morna would be living in Newabbey parish by Lammas.

Lachlan patted her hand solicitously. "As the Scots of auld say, 'Fortune gains the bride.'"

Jamie's gaze was even. "Instead, you have gained the bride's fortune."

"Nephew—"

"Look!" Rose yanked on her husband's arm, pulling him forward. "Mistress Muirhead is waving at us from the manse door. It appears your bridal dinner is ready, Father."

Morna's neighbors headed off in various directions on foot or on horseback, while both families walked the few steps to the manse. A simple, two-story building with little adornment other than its shuttered windows, the minister's house was even plainer withindoors. And, with only two rooms on the ground floor, entirely too small.

Counting the Douglas brothers, all of a fair size, the stout reverend, tall Jamie, Duncan, and himself—never mind the four women—the room suddenly felt overcrowded. Jamie and Malcolm were sniffing round each other like dogs working up to a *collieshangle*.

Mistress Muirhead, an affable woman with fair hair and colorless features, invited her guests to the dining table. Perhaps sensing the tension between the families, she seated the Auchengray household on one side, the Edingham contingent on the other. "A most unusual manse, this," she explained as they took their seats. "We have two stairs but only one door. If dinner catches on fire, kindly run out the way you came in."

Her lighthearted comment was well timed, Lachlan decided. A few smiles were exchanged as chairs were pulled to the table. Although Jamie and Malcolm remained sullen, they had not come to blows. Not for the moment anyway. Lachlan knew once he made his announcement, it would take more than a genial remark to keep his nephew's temper in check; it would take three braw young men.

Lachlan unfolded his table linen, the scent of roasted moorhen tickling his nostrils. At least Jamie hadn't discovered the truth about his missing lambs. Their daft neighbor Peter Drummond had nearly ruined everything. Fortunately Jamie was too distracted with his wives and his bairns to sort out what had happened that June night.

As Reverend Muirhead stood to bless their meal, Lachlan bowed his head, a different prayer in mind. He needed to keep the stolen lambs a secret until Lammas, a fortnight away. The lad would leave with his remaining flocks and think no more of those that were lost. Wouldn't they fatten nicely in Edingham's rich pastureland? Duncan would be angry with him, of course. But the overseer was not a fool; he knew which side of his bannock was buttered and who held the knife.

Heads lifted, and the light dinner commenced. Fowl only—no fish, no flesh—a summer salad, cold vegetables. A meal as plain as the house. Their final course would be the bride's pie, prepared by her parish friends and baked in the manse oven. Already the sweet aroma of cinnamon, apples, and currants had set his mouth to watering.

Morna stood for the informal ceremony. "For you, Reverend Muirhead, a small token of appreciation." She blushed like a woman half her age. "From the bride."

The minister unwrapped his gift—a pair of gloves—offered his thanks, then stood to cut the bride's pie. At her request, he cut a diminutive piece for her and then a much larger slice for Lachlan. "Will you serve your laird and master?" Reverend Muirhead asked in mock sternness, handing her the sweet on a small china plate.

"I w-will s-serve my husband," she promised, hands shaking as she took the plate and turned toward Lachlan. All at once it slipped from her grasp. The moist pie landed on his lap, soiling his best gray trousers. But the china plate reached the uncarpeted stone floor, where it shattered into a dozen jagged pieces.

The assembly gasped as one before the room fell silent. Even the least superstitious among them could not deny what they had seen and heard: a bride breaking a dish on her wedding day. A very ill omen indeed.

Mistress Muirhead was the first to speak, directing one of her servants to fetch a damp cloth for Lachlan's trousers, while another swept up the remains of the plate. "Now, Morna," the minister's wife said, "do not fret. Only auld wives worry o'er such things, and you're a *new* wife, are you not? Come, let my husband finish serving your pie, and we'll think no more about it. We have many more plates, I assure you."

Lachlan dabbed at the stain, trying to contain his displeasure, reminding himself it was an accident. Morna would never wish him ill; she was a nervous sort, prone to dropping things.

After the last of the pie was served, Rose stood, garnering everyone's attention. "Father, we have a gift for you. To commemorate your wedding and the anniversary of your birth." She walked round the table and presented him with a box. " 'Tis from Jamie and me. And Leana."

He'd hoped the whole day might pass without a mention of his other daughter. But Rose being Rose had ruined that plan. Lachlan opened the box and smiled before he caught himself. "A quaich." He turned it over for the smith's mark. "Sterling, I see. And engraved." It truly *was* a fine gift. Wherever did the three of them find sufficient coins for such a purchase?

Lachlan held it up for all to admire, then tucked it back in the box. "Please be seated, Rose, for I, too, have a gift to bestow. An announcement, really." He stood, smoothing his waistcoat over his full stomach. " 'Twill not be news to those of us on this side of the table. As for the rest of you, I hope you will celebrate my…ah, good fortune."

Thirty-Nine

Think'st thou there are no serpents in the world
But those who slide along the grassy sod,
And sting the luckless foot that presses them?

JOANNA BAILLIE

When Rose sank into the chair beside him, Jamie took her hand, disturbed by the gleam in Lachlan's eye and the glibness of his tongue. Bad enough that Rose had endured the evil mutterings of a witch that morning; Jamie would not allow her father to fill her ears with more venom.

Lachlan clasped his hands behind his back, thrusting his chest forward. "When I began to court my new bride, I could not imagine the opportunity that awaited me. Not only to claim the hand of this good woman…" He nodded to his right without looking at her. "But also to welcome Malcolm, Gavin, and Ronald into my family as my own sons."

"Stepsons," Jamie corrected him, feeling Rose bristle.

"You are wrong, Nephew." Lachlan's smile was ugly. "Not stepsons. True sons by law. Adopted into my family."

Rose gasped. "*Adopted?* You mean—"

"These are your brothers now." Pride rang through every syllable of Lachlan's words. "Malcolm McBride. Gavin McBride. Ronald McBride. Heirs to my fortune."

Jamie shot to his feet. *"Heirs?"*

"But, Father…what of Jamie?" She pressed her hand to her throat. "What of our children?"

Reverend Muirhead cleared his throat rather loudly. "Perhaps my wife and I might step into the next room—"

"That will not be necessary, sir." Jamie shoved back his chair, fighting the urge to dash it against the floor or heave it across the table at his uncle. "'Tis clear whom Mr. McBride has chosen to bless. And whom he has not."

Lachlan glared at him. "Sit down, Nephew."

Morna's frightened gaze darted from one face to the other. "Please do."

Instead, Jamie bowed to each end of the long table. "Reverend. Mistress Muirhead. Please excuse me for disrupting your fine meal." He rested his hand on Rose's shoulder. Much as he hated leaving her, he had to ride to Edingham now. Had to know if Lachlan had robbed him not only of his inheritance but also of his lambs.

Jamie refused to look at his uncle. "As it appears I am no longer worthy of this family, I will take my leave. Duncan?"

"Aye, lad." The overseer was already on his feet. "What may I do for ye?"

"You will do nothing for him," Lachlan protested, "for you are in my employ, not his."

Duncan and Jamie both ignored him. "See that my wife has an uneventful journey home. This day has been most difficult for her." Jamie felt Rose tremble beneath his touch. Was she weeping as well? God help him, he would kill the man! He bent and clasped her hand, kissing the back of it firmly enough so she might be certain of his love and assured of his protection. "Duncan and Neda will take good care of you, lass. I fear I must away."

"Jamie…" Her voice broke.

"Forgive me, love. I will not be long." He kissed her hand again, then quit the room. He did not look back as he marched through the single door of the manse or bother to latch it behind him. The others would follow sooner than he wished.

Four horses remained tied to the hitching post outside the kirk: three chestnut French Trotters belonging to the brothers and Walloch. Jamie mounted the black gelding with a speed fueled by rage, then pointed his mount toward Edingham and hung on. "Like the wind, Walloch. We've no time to waste."

He'd needed an excuse to leave early. Lachlan had given him one. *The churl.*

Signs for the Redcastle estate came and went as Jamie bent closer to his mount. He was soon riding parallel with the river, barely glancing at the flat-topped *mote* standing guard over the Urr from its west bank. Hills and rolling farmlands went by in a green blur. Northbound travelers were shown naught but a brief touch to the brim of his hat and a cloud of dust kicked up by Walloch's hooves.

No horse, no chaise, no carriage could hope to overtake him now.

Jamie was a quarter of an hour from the kirk when he turned north toward Dumfries, his gaze fixed on the farms to his left. The Douglas property was by far the largest; he would not miss it, not even coming from a different direction.

There. A carved wooden sign by the gate. *Edingham.* The ruins of the old castle stood not far to the east. But it was the lambs he wanted to find. *In the field tae the west o' the mains.* Jamie brought Walloch to a stop at the gate, shading his eyes as he stared at the gable-roofed house on the spur of the hill. He could not count the sheep from here, nor identify them, but he could see them: blackface lambs.

His chest tightened. Were they his? The lambs he thought had fallen beneath the flesher's blade weeks ago? Jamie aimed Walloch through the open gate, moving at an easier pace. He did not want to upset the black cattle that grazed in the nearby pastures or draw too much attention to himself. Reaching the western fields would mean passing farm laborers and house servants alike. Surely someone would stop him and demand to know his business.

Jamie sat up straighter, buttoning his coat and knocking the dust off his new hat. He was dressed like a gentleman, was he not? Some at Edingham might even recognize him from previous visits as the laird's nephew. He would approach the mains as though he were here on behalf of his uncle, sent to inspect the lambs. Nae, on behalf of his *cousin;* he'd come at Malcolm's bidding. Let them dispute that.

He nodded at the few hinds who doffed their caps at him from a distance and returned a greeting to one laborer close enough to hear him. The tidy steading, with its cobblestone yard, doocot and granary, barns and byres, was situated to the east of the house; most of the workers would be there. When no one appeared at the corniced entrance door inquiring after him, he headed straight for the lambs.

As he neared the pasture, he noted the mottled markings on their faces and legs, the familiar sound of their bleating. Yet didn't all lambs bleat so? He dismounted by a watering trough near the pasture, allowing Walloch a much-deserved drink. Only a dry stane dyke stood between him and Edingham's flock.

Jamie easily climbed over the wall, frightening a few lambs when he landed. He stood still so they might accept his presence among them. A quick tally answered his first question. *Nigh to a hundred.* They were the right size and age to be his. All that remained was to find some remnant of his keel mark. He crouched beside one of the calmer lambs, keeping his voice even. "That's a good lass. Let me have a look at your neck."

He ran his hand over the wool, turning the animal toward the light to be sure, to be very sure. At the base of the fibers, against the pale skin, a faint red stain remained.

Tears stung his eyes. *My lambs.*

He had only to study those nearest him to be certain. There was the one with the hock-kneed legs. And that smaller one, with the swayed back. He'd seen them all being born. Held them in his arms while he cut their cords. Docked their tails when they were but days old. Watched them being tenderly nursed by their mothers.

His lambs.

Not Lachlan's. And not Malcolm's.

"How dare you." He spat out each word, as if the men were there to hear them. *Let all mine enemies be ashamed.* Jamie stood, his righteous anger hardening into resolve. He would steal them back.

Taking a long, slow breath to steady his pounding heart, Jamie looked at his flock. "I have not forgotten you, little ones." He moved slowly among them, his voice low. "You belong to me. And you belong at Glentrool." The lambs drew closer, gathering about his legs, bleating as if they understood him.

Duncan's words echoed inside him. *Ye're a guid shepherd, Jamie. Yer sheep ken yer voice.*

Pierced to the core, Jamie bent to reach as many lambs as he could, rubbing their heads and fondling their soft ears, letting them sniff his hands and touch him with their noses. All the while, his mind was spinning. If he left Edingham without his flock, the Douglas brothers might move them. Sell them at market. Butcher them. Yet he could hardly gather up five score lambs and herd them through the farm gates without being stopped by every hind and servant of Edingham.

He'd have to come back. With Duncan.

But first he would confront Lachlan. The man who'd put this vicious plan in motion.

Jamie eased toward the dyke, taking a last look at his flock before turning his gaze on the gelding waiting for him. "We're away, Walloch," he called out. The horse whinnied at him, striking the ground with his foot. Jamie had no sooner mounted than another welcome sound met his ears. Two dogs. Barking.

When Jamie called their names, the collies from Auchengray came dashing round the corner of the house and tore across the lawn, their barking exuberant. Jamie praised them, leaning down to scratch their heads. "Come, lads, for we've five miles to cover and little time." He could not take the lambs just yet, but he could take the dogs. As surety. As proof.

Jamie gave Walloch the signal and the horse took off for the front gate, the dogs in keen pursuit. A handful of men in the fields started running toward him, their faces full of alarm. Jamie lifted his hand in passing, then tore through the gates, bound for Haugh of Urr. The pounding of Walloch's hooves and the barking of the dogs ruled out any practicing of speeches. Just as well; he would know what to say when he saw his uncle.

"Liar!" Jamie shouted the word into the wind, reveling at the sound of it. "Thief!"

The mote of Urr was coming into view when he spied a small party galloping toward him at a fair pace. Three men on chestnut horses. His gut twisted into a knot. The Douglas brothers were not simply heading for home. They were heading for him.

His sword was at Auchengray, his pistol useless. But he had his dirk, and the blade was well sharpened. Jamie stopped, waiting for them, squaring his shoulders. "Down," he commanded the dogs. They ceased their barking at once.

"McKie." Malcolm reached him first, pulling his horse round as he eyed the collies. "I see you've been to Edingham." Gavin and Ronald closed ranks on either side of him, blocking Jamie's path.

Jamie pinned his gaze on the oldest brother. "I have indeed been to Edingham. To inspect my lambs and reclaim my dogs."

"Your lambs? Your dogs?" Malcolm scoffed. "Both are Auchengray property. Which means, until noon today they belonged solely to your uncle. Now those animals also belong to me. His heir."

Jamie gripped the reins with his left hand, his right hand resting on his knee, inches from the dirk planted in his boot. "My uncle and I had an agreement. The lambs were to be mine." He glanced toward the road to the kirk. "If you will permit me to pass, I shall speak with him at once and see this situation rectified."

Malcolm did not move. Nor did his brothers. "Your uncle and our mother departed for Moffat in the carriage some time ago."

"Then Duncan—"

"Is gone as well," Malcolm said, "with your wife and housekeeper."

Duncan. Gone. Jamie tried to swallow and realized he had no moisture left in his mouth, only dust from the road. And the faint taste of fear.

Ronald, the youngest, jabbed at him with sharp words. "You are the reason they left in haste. You ruined our mother's bridal dinner."

Jamie rallied at the charge. "And you, gentlemen, stole my lambs."

"We did not steal them," Gavin argued. "We moved them. At your uncle's request."

Jamie snorted. "If 'twas so noble a deed, why did you spirit them away like thieves in the night?"

"Thieves, you say?" Malcolm's gaze was even. " 'Tis a subject you ken a great deal about. Did you not steal your own brother's inheritance? With a property like Glentrool, you hardly need Auchengray."

Malcolm pretended to look behind Jamie. "I notice Evan is not here to stand with you. Only one McKie." He exchanged glances with his brothers. "And three McBrides."

One McKie. Jamie had never felt so alone, so outnumbered, in all his life. Though his dirk was near, he could never hope to wound the three of them and simply ride away. Nor would his wife and children be kept warm and fed if he died defending his honor.

Honor? He had none. He was a liar and thief. Like his uncle.

Defeated without a fight, Jamie moved both hands to his reins, looking to the road. "We will settle this another time, gentlemen."

"Indeed we shall." When Malcolm laughed, so did his brothers. "Suppose you head for home in our direction. Past Edingham. I'll not have you chasing after our mother's carriage, lest you ruin her bridal week as well."

Gavin eased back, giving Jamie room to aim Walloch south. "We'll be right behind you, Cousin. If you need anything."

Their derisive laughter hounded Jamie as he started back downhill. He would have to wait a full week to confront Lachlan. *A week!* Even with Duncan's help, he could not hope to spirit away the lambs in the night as the Douglases had done. At Auchengray, the lambs had grazed in a pasture near the road, far from the mains; at Edingham, they were near the mains and far from the road. And he had nothing in writing, nothing to prove the lambs were his.

God help me, what is to be done?

Loosening his grip on the reins, Jamie gave Walloch his head, throwing dust in the Douglases' faces as he rode hard toward home.

Forty

The face is the mirror of the mind,
and eyes without speaking confess the secrets of the heart.

SAINT JEROME

Leana heard Jamie before she saw him.

Pounding up the drive leading to Auchengray's door, he shouted the orraman's name so loudly that the sound penetrated the walls of the house. "Willie! *Willie!*"

The urgency in Jamie's voice made her heart skip. Had something happened at the wedding? Might Rose have taken ill? Leana had planned to tell Jamie and Rose about her child the moment they returned home. But if tragedy had befallen them...

Please God, not Rose. Abandoning her needlework, Leana ran through the entrance hall and out the front door, then lifted her skirts as she hurried across the lawn. Willie was already leading Walloch toward the stables, two collies at his heels, their tongues lolling. The gelding's black coat shone with sweat. Jamie, headed in her direction, was breathing as hard as his horse.

"Whatever is the matter?" Out of habit, Leana stretched out her hand to clasp his, then withdrew it just as quickly. "Where is Rose? Is she still with the Hastingses?"

"The three of them are coming home by way of Milltown." He opened the front door, then followed her into the house, close enough for her to feel the heat radiating from his body. "I took the Dalbeaty road."

Dalbeaty? Something *was* wrong for Jamie to have chosen a different route home. She guided him into the parlor, sending Annabel after a pitcher of cool water. "I assume Father and Morna have left—"

"Aye." He yanked off his hat. "Gone for a sennight."

It was not like Jamie to be rude. Leana relieved him of his new hat lest he crush it in his hands. She placed it on the bed with the brim up so it might dry properly and not stain the coverlet, then drew him toward a grouping of chairs. "Come, Jamie. Sit for a moment and catch your breath." She nodded at Annabel, who delivered the water, then curtsied and left.

Still standing, Jamie downed a glassful, then wiped his forehead with his sleeve and threw himself onto the nearest chair, having yet to meet her gaze or offer a word of explanation.

She poured him a fresh drink, then sat within reach of him yet not too close. " 'Tis clear something is wrong. Will you not share it with me?"

Jamie still did not look at her, his gaze aimed at the floor. "Your father…" His words faded into a groan. "The man is deceitful beyond belief."

Guilt stirred inside her. She, too, had been hiding something. For weeks. Was she her father's daughter after all? "Tell me what he's done, Jamie, for I can see how it grieves you."

Though handsome as ever, Jamie looked tired; the skin below his eyes looked bruised, the creases at the corners of his mouth more deeply drawn. He drank the water slowly this time. Stalling perhaps. When he finished, he balanced the glass on its heel, twisting it back and forth in his hand. "You ken me too well, lass."

She offered him a slight smile. " 'Tis not difficult to guess what a tired, thirsty man might want on a sweltering day."

He looked up, and the glass stilled. "I am not speaking of the water."

Oh.

Jamie stood, perhaps needing to walk out the stiffness in his legs after the long ride, just as Walloch did. "Two days ago Duncan spied a small flock of lambs on Edingham property."

"Not *your* lambs?"

"I could not be certain. Until today." He told her the whole sorry tale as he paced before the hearth, absently smoothing his palm across his hair. "I can only hope they will not dispose of my flock while Lachlan is gone."

"They would ne'er do so without Father's approval," Leana assured him.

"I fear they might." Jamie stopped in front of her. "Lachlan has adopted the three Douglas brothers as his lawful sons. Malcolm, Gavin, and Ronald McBride are now your brothers."

Leana's mouth fell open. "My…brothers?" She had yet to even meet them.

"Worse than that, Leana, they are to be his heirs. Not you, nor Rose. Not Ian, nor any child either of you might bear. Not I, as his son-in-law, nor Evan, as his older nephew." Jamie's voice was kind, but the truth still struck a painful blow. "Your new brother Malcolm stands to inherit all of Auchengray someday."

"Then there will be…nothing…for me." *Nor for you, little one.* She folded her hands across her waist, shielding her child from the dire news. "Pardon my selfishness, Jamie. I am sorry for you and for Rose as well."

"Nae need to worry on our behalf. We have Glentrool and its resources." He sat down across from her with his elbows propped on his knees, his eyes filled with compassion. "You are right to be anxious about your own needs, Leana. I do not trust your father in that regard and Malcolm even less. Clearly you will need someone to provide for you."

For a moment Jamie's gaze dropped to her waist.

Not long, but long enough.

He knows. Without her apron, her loosened gown left little doubt of her condition. She could not delay her announcement until Rose returned. The subject would have to be broached at once. "Jamie, I have… We must…speak."

"Indeed we must." He drew his chair closer, then captured both of her hands in his, lifting them away from her gown, further exposing the truth. "Leana, it is obvious why you came home."

Her head fell forward. *Jamie, please.* She could bear anything but his pity.

"You've no need to be ashamed, lass."

The tears pooling in her eyes dropped onto her skirt. No words would come except the ones that needed to be spoken. "Forgive me."

Jamie massaged her hands in his. "What's to forgive? 'Tis the Lord's blessing, this bairn." He spoke in his shepherd's voice: low, warm, comforting. " 'Twould seem it gives the Almighty pleasure to see you with child."

She summoned her courage and lifted her gaze to meet his. "Does it give...*you* pleasure?"

An invisible mask fell away. Suddenly he was Jamie again. Her Jamie. The man who had once defended her, cherished her, desired her. *My husband. My love.*

"Leana, it gives me great joy to think of you bearing my child."

Her heart was so full, she dared not speak.

He brushed away the tears from her cheeks. Though his touch was light, she felt the roughness of his thumbs against her skin. "My son or daughter will ne'er need a penny from Lachlan McBride," he promised. "And the child will bear my name. That is, unless..."

"Aye." She offered him a quavering smile. "McKie." His hands, wet with her tears, held hers once more. "Jamie, you do not seem...surprised by my news."

A look of chagrin stole across his face. "That day we spoke in the nursery, when I found you on the hurlie bed..." He shrugged. "I was daft not to have noticed sooner."

"Not at all," she hurried to say, "for I did my best to keep the child hidden."

He chuckled, eying the evidence. "Really?"

Now it was her turn to blush. "Not...today, for I meant to tell you and Rose this afternoon. In truth, I meant to tell you the hour I arrived at Auchengray, but..."

"But you could not," he said, "because of Rose."

"Aye." Leana straightened, feeling a reassuring movement inside her. "This child is a blessing for me, yet I fear 'twill not be so for my sister."

When he did not respond, Leana knew he shared her apprehension: Rose would be distraught. Fearful of what it might mean for their future. "I must tell her the moment she arrives, Jamie."

He nodded, releasing her hands as he did. "Do you want me in the room?"

Already she missed his touch. "Let me tell her alone. Rose will no doubt come to you straightaway. I trust you will console her in...some manner."

He leaned back in his chair and glanced toward the window as if anticipating his wife's arrival. "You can be sure of that."

Leana looked away rather than watch Jamie change back into her cousin. Keeping his distance. Avoiding her gaze. Their exchanges would fade into polite discourse, and he would become that other Jamie. The one married to her sister.

At the sound of Bess's harness jingling, Leana turned toward the window. "Here is Rose now." She stood, wishing she might don her apron long enough to greet them. Or had her sister already seen through her subterfuge, as Jamie had? Perhaps not; Rose could be quite single-minded, content to think only of herself and her bairn. Within the hour her sister would learn that another babe grew beneath Auchengray's roof.

The mantel clock in the dining room was chiming the hour of four when the entrance hall filled with women's voices. Rose and Neda appeared at the parlor door, their arms loaded with parcels. "We took our time comin' hame," Neda explained, "thinkin' Jamie might catch up wi' us. Whan we saw the *mercat* in Milltown, we couldna resist stoppin'."

Neda held up her bounty—a basket of fresh rhubarb and another filled with ripe berries. "*Aften* a bargain or twa can be found at the end o' the day. Duncan will be along shortly. Says he needs tae speak wi' ye, Mr. McKie. I'd best be tae the kitchen and see aboot yer supper." She angled toward the hall, then grinned at Leana over her shoulder. "A fu' week o' cookin' for naught but the three o' ye. Won't that be a blissin?"

With Neda bound for the kitchen, Rose hurried to Jamie's side, her brow knitted with concern. "You left in such haste, Jamie, and then did not return—"

"Forgive me, lass." He turned to Leana as if seeking her counsel. "I've much to tell you, but…"

"Take however long you need." Leana paused at the threshold of the door and glanced back at her sister. "When you and Jamie have finished, might you stop by my room?"

Rose agreed without hesitation. "Have you another altered gown to show me?"

"Nae." Leana swallowed; the lump in her throat would not be moved. "But I do need to speak with you, dearie. Come as soon as you can."

Forty-One

That crimson rose how sweet and fair!
But love is far a sweeter flower
Amid life's thorny path o' care.
ROBERT BURNS

When Rose knocked on Leana's door, it opened at once as if her sister had been poised with her hand on the latch.

Leana's blue eyes had a wary look about them. "Come sit with me, won't you?"

Rose followed her toward the corner opposite the sunny window, the coolest spot in the room, where two chairs were placed close together. She sank into one of them, hoping she might find a comfortable position. "Did your back ache when you carried Ian?" She shifted in her seat. "Nae doubt 'twas our long ride in the chaise."

"Perhaps." Leana reached for the round pillow on her chair. "Lean forward for me." She slipped the pillow behind Rose, fitting it snugly against the curve of her back. "Better?"

Rose noticed her sister's cheeks were rosier than usual, and her brow bore a fine sheen. "I believe *you* are the fauchie one."

"Only warm." A light breeze ruffled the curtains as Leana took her seat. "Though it has been an…eventful day."

"Oo aye! Did Jamie tell you we saw Lillias Brown on the way to Urr kirk?" Rose described the witch's unexpected appearance. "Jamie was furious. Sent the woman back into the woods whence she came." She shifted in her seat, wishing the dull ache in her back might cease. "I wonder how she knew we'd be on that road at that hour?"

"Many in the parish were aware of our father's wedding plans," Leana reminded her. "I imagine Lillias bided there all morning, certain you would come riding by."

"You should have heard the daft comment she made." Rose laughed, remembering. "She told Jamie that I was not the only woman he knew with a child in her womb."

Leana's eyes widened. "Lillias said that?" She wet her lips—even Rose could see how parched they were—and reached for her fan. Unfurling it with a graceful flick of her wrist, Leana batted it round her neck, though it did not keep her face from coloring further. "There are several women in our parish carrying bairns through the hot summer."

Rose had noticed them too. "Elizabeth Pickens of Drumburn, for one. And Jenny Briggs at Hillhead."

Leana's fan fluttered to a stop. "I can think of one other." She leaned forward and grasped Rose's hand, a plaintive expression on her face. "Can you, dear sister?"

"Nae, I…cannot." Confused, Rose slipped her hand free. "Whatever is the matter? You do not seem at all yourself."

"I am…ah, more than myself." Leana slowly closed her fan.

Rose shrugged, her attention drawn to a vase of fragrant roses displayed on the small table beside them. The pink petals stood out against the fine-toothed green leaves, and the yellow stamens were brighter still. "What do you call this one?" She drew the flowers closer to inhale their sweet scent, pricking her finger in the process.

"The Apothecary's Rose. Grown by the French since the Middle Ages. A tincture made from the petals is good for digestion, and an infusion cures a sore throat." Leana pressed one of the petals against Rose's damask sleeve. " 'Tis the very color of your gown."

Rose recalled the witch's strange comment. "Lillias Brown said if a rose from your garden bled, it would be the color of my dress."

"But roses do not bleed."

"This Rose does." She held out her fingertip. Stark against her pale skin bloomed a dark red dot of blood. "Now you know why I never cared for my namesake flower." She touched her finger to her tongue. "I adore the blossoms but loathe the thorns."

"With a rose," Leana murmured, "one must accept both beauty and pain."

Their eyes met. "Are you speaking of your flowers…or of me?"

"Rose, I…" Leana looked away, fingering the silky petals. "I am sorry to have spoken so…"

"Honestly?" Rose stilled her hand. "Leana, I have caused you pain more times than either of us could tally."

"Not…on purpose."

"Nae. There were times I hurt you quite…deliberately."

Leana looked up, clearly touched by her confession. "If you did so, 'twas only because *you* were in pain. I ne'er doubted your love for me, Rose. Just as I pray you will not doubt mine when I…share my news."

News? A sense of foreboding swept over her, cooling her skin. Was Leana ill? Was she leaving Auchengray? Rose forced herself to ask, "What news, dear sister?"

"I am…carrying Jamie's child."

"His…*child*?" Rose blinked in confusion. " 'Tis not possible."

Tears spilled from Leana's eyes. "I'm sorry, Rose. So very sorry."

Rose tried to breathe, but could not. Tried to reason, but her thoughts were too scattered. *Jamie. Leana.* It was happening all over again. "But…but *I* am the one Jamie loves."

"You are right, lass." Leana drew her chair closer. "He *does* love you. Very much."

Rose was no longer listening, her attention riveted on Leana's waist. "It cannot be true." But it *was* true. Plainly so. "It cannot…be… Jamie's…"

"It can only be Jamie's," Leana said gently. "But do not think ill of your husband. The child was conceived in late February, a full month before your wedding."

February. Disoriented, Rose tried in vain to count the months. "Wh-when…when…"

"Early December, long after you are happily settled at Glentrool."

Glentrool. Aye, Jamie would be there with her. Not here with Leana. Unless…unless he…

"You never need to see the child." Leana knelt beside her chair, spreading her skirts across the wooden floor. "I will raise Jamie's son or daughter here at Auchengray."

Rose stared at her hands, struggling to make sense of it all. Leana was meant to be a mother. Would it be so terrible for her to have this little one to care for after they were gone? Oh, but Jamie… He would not walk away so easily. From his child. From the woman he once loved.

"Will I…" Her throat ached. "Will I ne'er have Jamie…to myself?"

"You do have him, Rose." Leana bent forward to brush back a stray wisp of her hair. "He is your husband."

Rose looked into her sister's face and saw the truth. *She loves him still.* "Why?" Her voice was faint, each word pinched with pain. "Why did you…wait so long…to tell me?"

"I meant to confess it the moment I returned. When I discovered that you were…well, I could not ruin your joy."

"But you *have* ruined it." Rose turned away, ashamed of herself. "You've ruined everything. Just like before."

"Please, Rose." Leana's warm hands clasped her cool ones. "Things are different this time."

"Are they?" She swiveled back toward her sister. Wanting to wound her, wanting to forgive her, weary of the battle. "Last summer I loved Jamie, and Jamie loved me. Yet you were the one carrying his bairn." Rose sniffed, in desperate need of a handkerchief. " 'Tis just the same this summer."

"Not quite. He is your husband now, not mine. And you, too, bear his seed." Her eyes shone with sincerity. "Jamie loves you dearly, Rose. He told me so the day I arrived. You have nothing to fear."

Rose slipped her hands free, then fumbled for the handkerchief tucked inside her sleeve. "I have much to fear, for now I must tell Jamie this…this *news* of yours."

Leana drew back. "Dearie, I…"

A light tapping sounded at the door. "Ladies?" Jamie's voice, muffled by the wood. "Neda has informed me our supper is ready. Will you join me at table?"

Leana was on her feet in an instant. "Jamie, wait." She touched Rose's shoulder, then hurried across the room to open the door to him. "Please come in. 'Twould be best if we spoke here first."

Rose looked up in time to see him enter, still dressed in his riding habit, a wary look on his face. She rose rather unsteadily and turned toward her husband, relieved to have him standing there, strong and capable. Jamie would know what to say, what to do, to banish her fears.

When she reached toward him, he strode across the room and clasped her hands in his. She managed a weak smile. "I must look a fright."

"Not at all." The warmth of his kiss comforted her. "Though I am sorry this…situation has brought you to tears."

Rose gaped at him. "Then you…" The words turned to dust in her mouth. "How…long?"

"I've known for more than a week." His voice was tender, apologetic. "Leana and I first spoke of it this afternoon, but I'd already learned the truth simply by—"

"By looking at her," Rose finished for him. Her sister was clearly months along. How had she missed anything so obvious? Rose turned, meeting both their gazes. "What else have I not been told? Are there more secrets between you?"

"Nae!" They responded in unison, looking not at each other but at her.

Jamie tightened his grip on her hands. " 'Tis no secret that I love you, Rose. And that I would never hurt you." He glanced at her sister for only a moment. "Nor would I harm anyone dear to you. I have promised to support Leana's child as my legitimate offspring with my name and with sufficient silver. 'Tis only proper."

His name. His silver.

But not his heart. That was hers alone.

If Leana were here and the child as well… If she had Jamie to herself at Glentrool…

"Aye," Rose agreed at last. No man worth having would do any less. "I will not see my sister forsaken nor her child begging for bread."

With a soft cry, Leana pressed a handkerchief to her nose, fresh tears filling her eyes. "Bless you, dearie."

Jamie smiled down at her. "My charitable wife."

Embarrassed, Rose brushed off their praise. What other choice did she have, when she loved her sister? Jamie had not been unfaithful to her. That was all that mattered. "Tell me who else knows."

Rose was not surprised to learn that Neda and Eliza had jaloused the truth. Reverend Gordon's visit, however, took her aback. "He came here? This morning?"

Leana briefly explained about Reverend Scott's letter. "And Father knows, though he promised to say nothing until Lammas."

"Lachlan McBride keep a secret?" A sense of uneasiness crawled up Rose's spine. "Only if it will benefit him. Who knows what Father has planned?"

"He returns in a sennight." Jamie aimed them toward the door and supper. "Until then, I am making plans of my own."

Forty-Two

Vengeance to God alone belongs;
But, when I think of all my wrongs,
My blood is liquid flame!
SIR WALTER SCOTT

The lambs are mine." Jamie said it aloud in a threatening tone, rehearsing for the moment when Lachlan McBride marched through the front door of Auchengray with his bride.

From the heath-covered summit of Auchengray Hill Jamie could watch for the couple's approach and have time to reach the mains before their carriage did. He had no intention of changing into more gentlemanly attire. Better to greet them dressed in soiled work clothes, a reminder of his endless labors on Lachlan's behalf.

One of his spotted lambs toddled up to him, bleating for attention. Jamie crouched down, examining the hooves for stray stones and the fleece for ticks. He would dip the lambs in a watery mixture of tobacco and soap on Saturday next before they left for Glentrool, and again when they arrived, to keep from infecting his father's flocks.

Jamie gripped the wool beneath his fingers. *If Father will have me. If I am still welcome.* Two years past his father had sent him on his way with a blessing, even after learning he'd been deceived. And his mother's letter in May had made it clear they were expected. Then why had Alec McKie not written back?

Yestreen at supper, Rose had raised the question that troubled Jamie by the hour. "If you do not hear from your father or brother, will we still leave?"

He'd assured her that, letters in hand or not, they would leave Auchengray on Sunday the first. The Almighty alone knew what reception might await them, yet he could not tolerate living beneath Lachlan's roof a moment longer.

Jamie released the lamb, then stood, checking the road again. Dry as the weather had been all week, the carriage horses would kick up a great cloud of dust in their wake. While scanning the steading below, he spied Duncan emerging from the byre. The brim of his plaid bonnet lifted toward the hills, then he waved at Jamie and started in his direction.

Duncan climbed the hill with the ease of a goat and arrived by Jamie's side moments later, not in the least winded. Shading his eyes, he cast his gaze across the pastures and fields. "Ye're keepin' watch for the McBrides? Due at noon, Neda says." When Jamie grunted in acknowledgment, Duncan turned to peer at him. "I've given this sad business atween ye and yer uncle a guid deal o' thocht, Jamie. Mind what ye say tae the man. And remember wha owns the lambs."

"I own them."

"Nae, ye do not. Nor does Lachlan McBride." Duncan swept his arm in a broad arc. "For ilka beast o' the forest is God's, and the cattle upon a thousand hills. They're not yer lambs. They belong tae God."

"Did he not place them under my care?" Jamie protested. "Without a shepherd, lambs are as good as lost."

"And ye need a Shepherd tae leuk after ye as weel, Jamie. Ye'd best seek his counsel afore ye face yer uncle." Duncan studied him, a look of fatherly concern on his face. "'Twill not do tae claim yer lambs and lose yer blissin."

"I thought the lambs were my blessing."

"Ye've been given mair than that." Duncan rubbed a hand across his chin. "Bairns are also a blissin. Ye've three o' those that'll bear yer name. And the Buik says a prudent wife is a blissin."

Jamie snorted. "Rose McKie is many things, but *prudent* is not one of them."

Duncan only smiled. "The Almighty's favor is a meikle blissin." He clamped down on Jamie's shoulder, emphasizing his words with a firm squeeze. "He has his hand on ye, nae mistake. I kenned it from the first. Yer uncle's *ill-deedie* ways willna go unpunished." Duncan released his grip. "The candle o' the wickit shall be put oot. But not by ye, Jamie. Wait on the Lord, and keep his way."

Jamie stared at him. *Wait on the Lord?* Hadn't he waited long enough? He glanced over Duncan's shoulder in time to see dust rising along the road from Lochend. "They're here."

"I'll be prayin' for ye, lad," Duncan called after him as Jamie started down the hill, nearly losing his footing in his haste.

He tried to pray, though his thoughts were disjointed and his motives at odds. *Keep me from the hands of the wicked.* Did he simply want free of the man? Or did he want revenge? *Let not mine enemy triumph over me.* Was it his lambs that mattered most? Or his wounded pride? *Lead me in a plain path.* The one prayer, the true prayer, that counted.

His heart banged in his chest like a drum as he lengthened his stride across the garden, bound for the back door. The jingle of the harnesses drew closer, and the driver called out, bidding the horses stop, as Jamie crossed the threshold. He found Leana and Rose waiting in the entrance hall, neatly dressed in their printed cotton gowns, a look of resolve on both their faces.

"Jamie." Rose held out her hand and drew him to her side. "We should stand together. As a family. But Leana must speak first, for her…situation is more…pressing."

Leana's chin was steady, he noticed, and her gaze clear. The hands clasped above the fullness of their unborn child did not tremble. This gracie woman would not cower beneath Lachlan's harsh demeanor nor bend at his bidding. Whatever Leana intended to say, their bairn would boldly go before her. *Our son. Our daughter.* Jamie nodded toward her once in silent affirmation. *The Lord be with thee, lass.*

All three of them turned at the sound of approaching footsteps. The clock on the dining room mantel struck the first of twelve chimes when the front door swung open and Lachlan guided Morna into the hall. Dust from the road clung to their hats, and their clothes were wrinkled from traveling. Morna's weary smile looked pasted in place.

"Just as I expected, Mistress McBride." Lachlan's expression was grim. "Your new family is here to greet you."

"Welcome home, Father." Leana offered the couple a deep curtsy.

When she straightened, utterly revealing her condition, Lachlan's face reddened, while Morna's paled to ash.

"*Leana!*" Her father closed in on her. "What have you *done*?"

"I have told the truth. Everyone in the household knows I am carrying Jamie McKie's child. Reverend Gordon knows as well." Leana gave a graceful shrug. "Father, I'm afraid our secret is out."

"*Our* secret?" Morna's words were faint, as if whispered through linen. "And this is…*your* child, James?"

"It is, Mistress McBride." Jamie gave her a slight bow. "Or am I to call you Aunt Morna?"

"You are not to call her…*anything*!" Lachlan sputtered. "James, I would speak with you at once. In private. Morna, make yourself at home in the parlor. Neda?" He found her standing dutifully by the stair. "Fetch my wife something cool to drink." Lachlan turned and glowered at Jamie. "Now, Nephew. In the spence."

Summoning his courage, Jamie followed Lachlan through the house, aware of Rose and Leana close behind. When the men reached the spence, Lachlan turned to shut the door in his daughters' faces.

"Nae, Father." Rose grasped the latch, her elbow pressed against the door. "I have an important matter to discuss with you. As it involves my sister, she, too, belongs in the room." Without waiting for his permission, Rose swept into the small spence with Leana.

"Fine." Lachlan slammed the door behind them, rattling the pewter cups on his desk. "Sit," he ordered, though they remained standing. His face a mottled red, he yanked the lid off the whisky decanter and poured himself a dram.

"I won't be having any," Jamie said evenly.

Lachlan downed the pewter cupful in a single gulp. "And I won't be offering you any." He wiped his mouth with the back of his hand, his manners reduced to those of a brute. "What is it *you* want, Rose?"

Despite the quaver in her voice, she answered him at once. "I want to know why the children my sister and I bear will not be counted among your heirs."

Lachlan took his time pouring a second dram. He sipped the fiery liquid, licking his lips as he eyed the family Bible on his desk. "Because 'I will have mercy on whom I will have mercy.'" Taking another sip, he pointed his sharp gaze toward Jamie. "And whom I will, I harden." His words dropped like rocks clattering against the walls of the too-quiet room.

Jamie finally spoke. "You have indeed hardened me, Uncle. And turned me to stone." He longed for his dirk. Wished for his sword. "A stone on which you've sharpened the blade of your tongue long enough." When Lachlan started to speak, Jamie cut him off. "You may keep your precious land and your thrifite full of silver. Auchengray and its riches mean nothing to me."

"Really?" Lachlan stared at him, his eyes bright from the whisky. "Is there nothing of mine you want then?"

"Nothing of yours. I want only my own lambs. All of them. Including the ones at Edingham."

"'Tis only fair," Rose was quick to add. "They *are* Jamie's."

"Your lambs, Nephew?" Lachlan banged his dram on the desk, splashing whisky on the polished wood, where it beaded up and glistened in the candlelight. "How can those sheep possibly be yours when they are grazing on my property? Do you have any proof of this ownership? A contract of some sort? A letter prepared by a solicitor? Nae, for they are in fact *not* your lambs at all. They are mine—"

"They are *mine.*"

"—just as Auchengray is mine, and that woman sitting in the parlor is mine, and Edingham is mine."

Jamie could barely see straight, could barely think straight. "Two months ago we sat at your table—"

"*Wheesht!*" The word hissed through the air like a blade. Glaring at him, Lachlan yanked a silver key out from its hiding place beneath his shirt. He bent forward long enough to jam the key in the lock of his money box, then threw back the lid, sending it crashing against the desk top. "All of this is mine as well, Nephew. A goodly sum, wouldn't you say?"

When both sisters gasped, Jamie forced himself to look at the open thrifite. Instead of silver shillings, the box now overflowed with gold sovereigns. The knotted gold cord tucked among the coins was barely visible, so brightly did the sovereigns gleam.

Lachlan's gray eyes took on a silvery sheen of their own. "Mistress McKie agreed her inheritance was far safer with me."

"Safer? With *you*?" Jamie felt sorry for the woman. Heaven help her if she ever wanted any of her fortune back, for it surely belonged to Lachlan McBride now.

"Edingham is to be sold on Wednesday," Lachlan said bluntly, eying the wooden chest. "My, my. What's to be done with all that Douglas gold? For 'twill ne'er fit in this small chest." He shrugged. "I suppose I must chop my money box into firewood and build a larger one."

Jamie said nothing for a moment, sickened by the man's avarice.

"Father?" Leana's gentle voice. "If Edingham is sold, where will your...sons live?"

"They'll be welcomed here, of course. For they are far kinder to me than my own blood."

Jamie bit back an oath. "Why should we be kind to a man who is unkind and unfair? You promised me those lambs in payment for my labors. I will not let you swick me—"

"*Swick* you?" Lachlan's gaze narrowed. "You're a fine one to speak of deceit."

"You will not grind the axe of my sin against me any longer." Jamie threw back his shoulders. "I have sought the forgiveness of my father, my brother, and my God. I have little need of your mercy, Uncle, for I have not sinned against you. Yet you have greatly wronged me. And hurt both your daughters."

Lachlan closed his money box as vehemently as he'd opened it, his hands shaking with rage. "This family has vexed me past bearing. All the lambs are mine, do you hear? You forfeited your rights to them months ago when you planted this untimely bairn in Leana's wame. Furthermore, you will not be leaving for Glentrool as planned."

"*What?*" The room began to tilt. "You cannot stop—"

"I most certainly can. You have robbed me of a marriageable daughter, a crime in any corner of Scotland." He nodded at Leana, as though she'd been privy to his scheme all along. "No man in the ten parishes will have her. I've made inquiries since the hour I learned this unwelcome news of hers, to no avail."

Bewildered, Jamie turned round. "Is this true, Leana? Did you…wish to marry?" Her stunned expression provided his answer. When he faced Lachlan again, Jamie's ire was rekindled. " 'Twould appear your daughter was not apprised of any efforts to procure a husband."

"Do you think I seek my daughter's blessing on all that I do?"

"Blessing?" Jamie nearly spat at the man. "You do not ken the meaning of the word."

Lachlan ignored his charge, draining what remained of his whisky. "Since I cannot find another man to take Leana off my hands, then you must remain in my employ to support your bystart." Lachlan put aside his empty cup. "My sons and I will see that you do."

"You cannot threaten me on that score, Uncle." Jamie drew Leana forward. "I have already told Leana that I will send sufficient silver for the child. And for her." His gaze searched hers. *Is it enough, Leana? Will you be safe here?*

"I shall be well provided for." She directed her words toward her father, though Jamie knew they were for his benefit as well. "I have no desire to marry and want only to raise my child at Auchengray."

"There you have it." Jamie jutted out his chin, his confidence renewed. "This charge of yours has no basis, Lachlan, for her needs will be well met. Rose and I depart on the first, as planned."

"You would leave your child without a father? With naught but silver to keep him warm?" Lachlan's voice rose with indignation. "And abandon his mother to fend for herself, bearing the sole burden of raising this child?" He shook his head. "Your callousness toward Leana surprises me, Nephew. Did you not once proclaim your undying love for my older daughter before God and all this parish on the first Sunday she warmed the cutty stool?"

Jamie could not deny the truth. "I did." *Gladly.*

"Well, then. There must be some remnant of affection in that deceitful heart of yours. Enough to see that all of Leana's needs are met." Lachlan picked up one of the thick ledgers that lined his desk, then opened the leather volume to a column of numbers and studied them intently. "For I do not intend to provide for the woman nor her child in any manner. Neither bed nor board. Neither shelter nor clothing." He lifted his gaze. "Do I make myself clear?"

"Father!" Leana fell back a step.

Jamie held out his arm to steady her. "Sir, whatever are you suggesting?"

"Not suggesting, Nephew. Insisting. If you do not remain and support Leana and her child in every regard, I will cast them out of this house without a shilling."

"But…" Rose gripped Leana's arm. "How will my sister manage?"

"Someone will take pity on her, I suppose. 'Tis the kirk's business to provide for those without means. No doubt Reverend Gordon has a few spare pennies in the collection box."

"You cannot do this!" Jamie knocked the heavy ledger from Lachlan's hands, sending it tumbling to the floor. "What father would turn his back on his own child?"

Lachlan feigned surprise. "But isn't that what you're doing? Turning your back on your child and the woman you once loved?" He retrieved his ledger, frowning at the broken binding before he put the book aside. "Once again, Jamie, I fear you've brought this on yourself. As your uncle, 'tis my charge to see that you behave like a Christian and a gentleman."

Undone by the sound of Leana's soft weeping, Jamie used the only weapon in his possession. "A Christian? A gentleman? You, sir, are neither."

"And you, sir, have a choice." Lachlan folded his arms across his chest like a shield. "Stay and do your duty by Leana. Or leave Auchengray and condemn her to the life of an outcast."

Forty-Three

Life often presents us with a choice of evils,
rather than of goods.

CHARLES CALEB COLTON

Leana looked at the man she loved through tear-washed eyes. "You cannot stay, Jamie."

"And I cannot go." He clasped her hands in his, as if no one else were in the room. As if her father were not standing there gloating over their misery. As if Rose's hand did not linger on her sleeve to console her. "Leana, I cannot abandon you to this…monster."

"Monster?" Lachlan scoffed, unfolding his arms as if preparing for a fight. "I am only a bonnet laird guarding his interests."

Jamie made no comment, giving Leana his undivided attention.

When he looked at her that way—his green eyes intent, his mouth set in a firm line—she believed he could and would do anything to protect her. *Oh, dear Jamie.* Though he held her hands, he could not hold the shattered pieces of her heart.

Would Father truly see her name added to the poor roll? And a beggar's badge pinned to her gown when her time of confinement came and she could no longer work for her bread? Did he mean to send her knocking on doors, seeking lodging? Perhaps he believed his newfound riches would cushion him from his neighbors' scorn. Or perhaps Lachlan McBride simply did not care.

Whatever his intentions, he was not her true Father. *I will receive you, and will be a Father unto you.* The reminder was like an iron brace, strengthening her back, shoring up her courage. *Thou art my strong refuge.*

As she blinked away her tears, the planes and shadows of Jamie's face came into focus. She drew in a steadying breath and said what she must. "Do not change your plans on my behalf—"

"Leana." His grip tightened. "How can—"

"I am not afraid, Jamie." She had to convince him before he did something rash. "The Lord will shelter me, and so will the kirk. Our child will have a roof over his head." She lowered her gaze. His touch was too warm. His eyes said too much.

"There, you see." Lachlan clapped his hands together, abruptly drawing the meeting to a close. "Your cousin has released you, Nephew. Glentrool awaits." He gestured toward the door. "You will leave Auchengray, empty-handed of course. No lambs. No silver. But you will have my daughter Rose. Most men would consider that a sufficient reward for their labors."

"I am *not* a reward!" Rose stamped her foot when she said it. Not like a spoiled child demanding her own way; rather, like an angry woman who refused to be discounted. "And my sister will not be driven from her own home."

Lachlan turned his back on them, shuffling the papers on his desk. "That will be Jamie's decision."

Leana would not allow such a burden to fall on Jamie's shoulders, however broad they might be. "Let us away, Rose." She slipped her hands from Jamie's fervent grasp and took her sister's arm. "Your husband may prefer to finish this discussion without us."

" 'Tis finished. For now." Jamie strode past the sisters and yanked open the door, then held it for them as they exited, his gaze fixed on Lachlan. "As to the dubious choices offered me, I refuse to honor either one."

"Honor was never your forte, James."

"Nor yours." The sharp bang of the door was fitting punctuation.

Up and down the back corridor, servants scurried like mice seeking their nest holes. The threesome stood for a moment, as if regaining their balance. Despite the tension, Rose managed a weak smile. "Secret matters seldom remain so at Auchengray."

Jamie guided them toward the front door, a hand on each of their elbows. "The orchard should afford us more privacy. We've much to discuss."

Averting her gaze from the too-bright sky above, Leana hurried to keep up with Jamie as they made their way toward the orchards east of the house. The trio found a secluded spot in which to stand among the fruit-laden apple trees, though Leana feared her legs might not hold her. Her father's words prodded at her, bruised her. *Condemn her to the life of an outcast.*

"Can he mean what he says?" Rose twisted the ribbon dangling from her gown round her fingers, her back propped against a tree that would drop russet apples come October. "Whatever are we to do?"

Dappled light fell across Jamie's muslin work shirt and traced his furrowed brow. "Your father must have had this…this *choice* in mind for some time, Leana. When did he learn you were with child?"

"A month ago. I was returning an almanac to his bookshelf when he found me. When he…saw me." She still tasted the fear he'd stirred inside her that gray Monday. *Take off your apron. Turn toward the hearth.*

Rose shuddered. "I can only imagine how he treated you. Och, what a hatesome man!"

Jamie picked one of the unripe apples from the branches bending near his shoulder, then absently rolled the small hard fruit back and forth between his palms. "No doubt he was seeking some excuse to break his promise to me and reclaim my lambs. Our child provided that."

When her shoulders slumped, he was quick to console her. "This bairn is a blessing from God, no matter how your father might twist things."

Leana sensed the child moving inside her, as though vying to be included. "Aye, little one." She touched the tender spot where she'd felt an elbow or foot jab her. "You are the one we're discussing."

Jamie's gaze followed her hand, then lifted to her face, his features softening. "What names do you favor?" When she told him, his smile was genuine. "Well done, lass. We've not had a David born to the McKies in many a generation. Nor any lass named Davina."

Leana dared not confess the truth: *Davina* always came to mind when she prayed for their child, not *David.* Would Jamie welcome a daughter? And be a good father to her, even from a distance?

"Well, if it's a wee lass, she'll have a much better father than ours,"

Rose said, as if reading her thoughts. "For now, what's to be done about Lachlan McBride?"

Jamie's mood darkened. "Curse him. And quit Auchengray for good."

"But what of Leana?" Rose clasped her hand in support. "We cannot leave her."

"Please, you *must* go." Leana hid her sorrow, even as she hastened to affirm his decision. "Your life together will be ruined if you remain. I will…leave as well."

Jamie looked surprised. "And go where?"

Flustered, she offered the first place that came to mind. "To Aunt Meg's. To Burnside Cottage. 'Twill take three days on foot, but the weather is fine and the summer days are long…" Her voice faded at the sight of her sister's gaping mouth.

"On *foot*? Leana, you must be daft! You are halfgone, and yet you'd consider walking two dozen miles?"

"Perhaps it is a bit far," Leana murmured, feeling foolish. But if the McKies departed for Glentrool, the doors to Auchengray would close behind her as well.

"Father's money box is positively bulging with coins," Rose fumed, her color high. "Can he not spare a *bittie* for you? Enough to see you safely transported to Twyneholm or settled in a cottage of your own?"

Jamie threw down the green apple. "He can, and he will." He started to say more, but the faint ringing of a handbell announced the dinner hour. "Och! I've no appetite whatsoever. Nor any desire to sit at that wretched man's table."

Leana reminded him this was Morna's first meal at Auchengray. "Hungry or not, we should be present for her sake."

"How can you be so generous?" Jamie grumbled, though she heard the resignation in his voice. Even on the most desperate of days, manners had their place. He offered Rose his arm, though his gaze remained locked with hers. "Your father will not have the final word on this, Leana. Rest assured, I shall see to your needs."

She bowed her head, if only to hide her relief. "I know you will, Jamie."

Moments later they emerged from the sweet-scented orchard into the fullness of the sun, bound for a meal none of them wished to eat. Morna seemed grateful for their company at table. How much did the older woman know of the conversation in the spence? Lachlan behaved as if they'd never spoken, tucking away food like a man who'd not eaten for a week.

Jamie did not say a word through the entire meal, yet no one looking at him could miss the message his countenance conveyed. Anger. Impatience. And resolve. While Lachlan ate, Jamie planned. Leana could tell by the angle of his chin and the crease in his brow. A light came into his eyes when he thought of something new; then he'd shift his posture, as if testing the weight of his idea. Whatever Jamie had in mind, she did not envy Lachlan McBride. Nor did she pity him.

After the plates were lifted, her father ended the meal with a lengthy prayer, asking for the Almighty's blessing on his marriage. When Lachlan finished, Jamie bolted from the table, Rose close on his heels. Leana retreated to the second floor. Holding Ian in her arms was the only remedy for her sorrow.

She found the lad crawling about the nursery, exploring each surface with fingers and mouth while Eliza kept a watchful eye on him. "Have you had your bath and your *noony*?" Leana knew the answer; Eliza's apron was covered with wet spots and remnants of Ian's midday meal. "Well then, sweet boy, come play with Mother."

Leana held Ian tight against her bodice, fighting a fresh spate of tears. Where could she possibly live? And with her child, come December? Not at Auchengray. Lachlan had already made that clear. *Neither bed nor board.* Yet Jamie had made a promise as well. *I shall see to your needs.* Of the two men in her life, she trusted the father of her children far more than her own father.

"Let us away to the garden, Ian." She dried her cheeks, determined to be cheerful for Ian's sake. "We've carrots and radishes to harvest. Wait 'til you see how colorful they are." Ian gave a happy cry as she bounced him in her arms. When Leana reached the foot of the stair, she found Morna waiting for her, one foot on the bottom step.

The older woman offered a tentative smile. "Will you mind if I...have a look at your room?"

"Not at all." Leana nodded politely, then hastened past, hiding her dismay behind her son's dark head. Already changes were afoot. She went out by way of the kitchen, lifting her broad-brimmed garden hat from its hook near the door.

"Let me tie that round yer chin, mem," Annabel offered, drying her hands on her apron. "Itherwise, yer lad will pu' yer bonnet off yer head and toss it tae the *grunties* for dinner."

Touched by her thoughtfulness, Leana obliged her, lifting her chin. "We'll not go near the steading," she assured the freckled lass, "just in case Ian sees any hungry pigs. Do follow me out with a basket. We've gardening to do, don't we, Ian?" Annabel helped the two of them settle beside the carrot patch, then hurried back to her chores.

Leana paused, breathing in the earthy scents of foliage and soil, feeling the sun warm the straw crown of her bonnet. On a day filled with heartache, her garden was a balm to her soul. "Now, lad. Can you sit still while I wrestle these vegetables out of the soil?"

It seemed he could not. Ian took off crawling across the garden, squashing feathery carrot tops beneath his pudgy knees. Leana stood, then lifted him from the ground before he stuffed a fistful of dirt in his mouth. "Our gardening days are behind us, I fear." She brushed off his hands, then headed for the cool shade of the yew. When he was older, he could be taught to pull out carrots. But for now Ian wanted only to play. The harvest would have to wait.

Beneath the yew Ian found much to interest him—twigs and leaves and dried berries—all of which she had to rescue before he put them into his mouth. "Not to taste, just to touch," she said over and over, following him round the tree trunk. She taught him the names of things, knowing full well he could neither understand nor repeat the words. "Someday you will," she told him, "when you're older. When you live at Glentrool." *When I am not there to teach you.*

She pressed a palm to her rounded waist, a tangible comfort. The babe inside her indeed offered tender solace and hope for the days ahead. She would welcome another little one's arrival with utter joy. Yet the child at her feet was just as dear to her. How could she live with one and not the other?

Leana dropped to her knees beside Ian, drawing him to her, holding him close even as he wriggled to be free. "My sweet son, I'll not let you go. Not until I must." Even then she would not truly let go. He would take her heart with her, clutched in his small hands. "Please, Ian…" She moaned the words. "Stay with me."

But he could not stay. Not unless his father did.

Her arms tightened round her son, who'd ceased fighting her and nestled into her embrace. "My precious boy." She buried a kiss in Ian's dark hair and closed her eyes against the sad fact: The McKies would be gone by Lammas.

Please, Jamie. Take me with you.

Shame heated her cheeks. Jamie could do no such thing, of course. It would be improper—scandalous, in fact—and utterly unfair to Rose. Her sister had endured enough. One did not travel across the countryside with an old wife and a new one, let alone set up housekeeping with both women.

A selfish notion, nothing more. "Forgive me, Jamie."

"Forgive you for what, lass?"

Leana looked up, shocked to find him standing beneath the yew's branches, as if beckoned by her thoughts. "Jamie, I…"

"Confess your sin, Leana." He drew closer. "So I ken what it is I'm forgiving."

Forty-Four

Men must decide on what they will not do,
and then they are able to act with vigor
in what they ought to do.

MENCIUS

Jamie watched Leana's pale cheek turn as pink as the blooms in her rose beds.

He should not have startled her. Nor should he have eavesdropped. But when he happened by the yew tree en route to the steading and heard Leana speak his name and saw her arms wrapped round their son…truly, how could he not pause, knowing he might never behold such a tender scene again?

Crouching beside her, he offered his handkerchief, wishing it were not so damp. "Rose has been crying the last hour as well." As she dabbed at her nose, he gently asked, "Leana, will you not tell me what you've done that requires my forgiveness?"

She practically hid behind his handkerchief. "I had a…shameful thought."

"Oh, Leana. If I were forced to confess all my improper thoughts, the Lord would quickly tire of hearing my voice." He said it gently, hoping to ease her embarrassment. "I have a confession as well: I fear I can never please both the McBride sisters. Rose insists we remain at Auchengray for your sake. And you insist Rose and I leave for her sake."

"Poor Jamie, having to wrestle with such decisions." She returned his handkerchief, damper than before. "I pray you'll do what is best for my sister and quit this unholy place."

In the silence, a wren began to sing, filling the air with its musical trill. When Leana kissed Ian's forehead, Jamie imagined the warmth of her lips on his own brow. Disconcerted, he sat on the ground, putting some distance between them.

"What will you do?" she asked him after a bit, her gaze still trained on their son, whose sleepy eyes were at half-mast.

"I am only certain of what I will *not* do, and that is bow to your father's demands." Saying the words aloud, Jamie's strength returned. "Nor will his greed determine the course of my life any longer. 'Tis the will of the Almighty I seek."

Leana's smile lit her countenance. "I cannot tell you how pleased I am to hear you say so."

"I'm…glad." When he'd confessed to Rose his dependence on God, she had merely nodded in agreement. Leana's encouragement ran deeper, like ground water nourishing a well. "Duncan has advised me to wait for the Lord's clear direction."

"'Tis best to wait." Leana rested her cheek on Ian's head. "Too many lives depend upon you."

"Three young lives in particular."

He leaned forward and gently laid his hand across their son's back as the child drifted off to sleep in the afternoon heat, his head against his mother's breast, his legs splayed across the brother or sister not yet born. *David. Davina.* Their bairn would arrive in early December. If only he might be there. To see his son at the hour of his birth. To hear his daughter's first cry. But he could not leave Rose's side to attend to her sister. Much as he might wish to do so, it would not be fitting.

Watching her now, Jamie said what he could to comfort her. "You are a wonderful mother, Leana."

"And you are a wonderful father." She placed her hand on top of his. The faintest joining. There for an instant, then gone.

When she lifted her gaze, he was struck afresh by the soft light in her eyes and the radiance of her skin. Could he truly bid her farewell?

Come with us to Glentrool.

The words waited on his tongue, ready to be spoken. It would be the wisest and easiest solution, would it not? Leana would be safe from Lachlan, and all her needs would be met.

Aye, but…

With Leana at Glentrool, Rose might grow fearful again. Of sharing Ian. Of sharing him.

"Jamie," Leana said softly, "we should not be here. Alone."

"I know." He stood, brushing a few stray leaves from his shirt to hide his disappointment. "Rose will be glad for your company. The household is in a quandary with Morna inspecting her new surroundings."

"I shall go to my sister, then." Leana nodded toward their sleeping son. "Might you take Ian? I cannot rise very gracefully holding so dear an armful."

Jamie did so, then helped Leana to her feet and followed her toward the front door of the house, forcing himself to look at anything but the sway of her skirts.

Once they reached the hall, she turned, inclining her head toward the stair. "Would you kindly carry him to the nursery?"

Jamie started up the stone steps, his hand cupped round his son's head to hold him steady. Responsibility like a leather horse collar settled onto Jamie's shoulders. He not only had this lad to protect but both of his unborn children as well. And their mothers. What man could carry such a burden without stumbling?

"Watch your step," Rose cautioned from the top of the stair, "for 'tis easy to trip when your arms are full." She guided him toward the nursery, where Annabel waited to tuck in Ian for his nap. Jamie deposited the boy onto the mattress, then eased out of the room. Rose stood in the hall wringing her hands, as though some new worry troubled her.

He angled her away from the door, keeping his voice down. "What is it, Rose?"

"Two maidservants just arrived from Edingham. Neda is having fits trying to squeeze in another bed on the servants' floor. And Annabel is miserable, for the blether round the back stairs is that we won't be leaving for Glentrool after all." Rose paused as if waiting for him to confirm or deny his plans.

"I see." He hated to dodge her question, but he had no answers. Not yet.

"And then there's Morna." She glanced toward the bedroom door at the end of the hall. "When she told Father how much she liked Leana's room, he had Morna's trunks delivered up here instead of the spence. I have heard of husbands and wives having separate rooms but not on separate floors. She's already making herself at home," Rose added with a frown, "arranging her dressing table."

Indignation shot through him, sharp and hot. "And Leana?"

"Exiled to the nursery."

"What?" He bit back an oath. "Your father cannot expect your sister to sleep on that hurlie bed in her condition."

"I will manage." Leana appeared near his elbow, having slipped up the stair so quietly he'd not heard her. For a woman who'd just been ousted from her room, she was surprisingly calm. "Aunt Meg's hurlie bed was no wider nor softer. Yet I slept well each night, dreaming of Ian."

He studied her features. "You are certain the change in rooms will not be a hardship?"

"Quite certain." If Leana was upset, she concealed it well. "As Lammas draws near, I am grateful for every hour I spend with Ian."

Rose took Leana's arm. "And *I* am grateful for every moment with my sister."

"In that case, I leave you in each other's care." With a slight bow, Jamie headed for the door and the hills beyond, determined to work until his muscles ached and his frustration turned to sweat. No matter which direction he turned, his hopes were thwarted. If he remained at Auchengray, his family's future would be ruined. If he left for Glentrool, Leana and his child would have no future at all. If he took Leana with them, Rose would be miserable. If he stole back his lambs from Edingham, where would he pasture them? And what of his other lambs Lachlan insisted on claiming?

Och! Jamie marched up the side of Auchengray Hill, crushing the blooming heather beneath his boot heels as he climbed. Hard labor was his only refuge. He would forgo supper and toil through the gloaming until naught shone above him but the waxing moon.

Jamie worked his way across each pasture—mending the dry stane dykes, hauling water from the well, examining the lambs and ewes for illness or injury. With no other shepherd in sight, he aired his grievances aloud, leaning back to challenge the evening sky.

"Did you not promise you would always be with me?" Silence. No response echoed from the heavens; no voice whispered in his heart.

"Where are you, Lord?" His throat tightened. "Why have you hidden your face from me?"

The last rays of the sun painted the clouds in vibrant colors, yet he could not find the light of truth written across them. Compelling him to stay. Or commanding him to go.

Duncan's reminder nudged his conscience. *Wait on the Lord and keep his way.*

"I *have* waited." Jamie wiped his sleeve across his brow, drenched with the evidence of his hours in the fields. When he could no longer see to work, Jamie returned to a darkened house and a sleeping wife. Though his body ached from his labors, his anxiety had not eased. Though he'd shouted his questions into the starry night, he'd heard no reply.

Wait on the Lord. "I am weary of waiting, Duncan." He pulled off his boots and dropped them to the floor. "Does the Almighty not ken the date? 'Tis only one week 'til Lammas."

Forty-Five

Hope starves without a crumb.

LEWIS J. BATES

The LORD knoweth the days of the upright." Reverend Gordon stretched his hands over the assembled congregation. "And their inheritance shall be for ever."

Jamie bowed his head for the benediction, even as his hopes rose. Was *this* the answer he'd been longing to hear? His inheritance did indeed await him at Glentrool. But *upright*? He was hardly that. Not with the schemes he'd concocted over the years. Not with the dilemma facing him now.

The beadle swung open the kirk doors, ushering in a freshening wind that toyed with the ribbons on Rose's gown. McKies and McBrides moved toward the aisle. The second service had been shorter than the first, but it was still a lengthy Sabbath for Ian, who'd fussed and wriggled through most of it. Leana had reached for the child more than once during services, then quickly withdrew her hands, remembering her place. The sadness in her eyes grieved Jamie deeply.

What can I do, Leana? How shall I help you?

The parish gossips had been busy. All of Newabbey knew of Leana's condition. When the time came, would they support her? chastise her? shun her? If he could not take Leana with him to Glentrool, then he would at least see she was in good hands, settled beneath a solid roof, and warmed by a friendly hearth. The minister oversaw such matters. Might he put his mind at ease?

As they neared the door, Jamie caught the man's eye. "Reverend Gordon, may I speak with you on an important matter?"

The minister waved Jamie toward him, the draped sleeve of his black robe enlarging the motion. "Shall we meet in the kirkyard? Or at the manse?"

"The manse." He would not have their conversation overheard by itching ears. Lachlan and Morna had visited Urr that morning for a proper kirkin, the bride's first appearance at her parish church after the wedding. Jamie knew he would have no better opportunity to speak with Newabbey's minister than this one. He sent Rose and the others on their way, promising to catch up with them. Leana's plaintive expression and murmured thanks fueled his resolve; he would not fail her.

Swinging open the low gate to the manse, Reverend Gordon bade Jamie follow him withindoors. A maidservant brought them tea in the spence, poured two cupfuls, then disappeared with a curtsy. The minister regarded him solemnly across his steaming teacup. "This concerns Leana, I presume? And your child?"

"And my uncle."

"I see." As Jamie described Lachlan's cruel plans for Leana, Reverend Gordon's bushy eyebrows signaled his displeasure. When Jamie finished, the minister put his teacup down with a decisive clink. "The Buik tells us that if any man does not provide for his own, and in particular for those of his own house, he has denied the faith and is worse than an infidel."

Infidel. The harsh term suited Lachlan McBride. "Can anything be done, sir?"

Reverend Gordon shifted in his chair. Lachlan McBride's tithe was no doubt a generous one; landowners were handled with care, however ill-kindit their ways. "Unfortunately, your uncle is a man who maintains the letter of the law but not the spirit. He breaks none of the Ten Commandments openly, even as he confounds those who live beneath his roof."

The minister knew him well. Jamie had watched Lachlan choose his words with care—not to avoid wounding someone, but so the wounds would not show—all the while protecting his reputation as a righteous man. "Is there nothing he might be charged with? No sin of which he is guilty?"

"We are all sinners, Jamie." Reverend Gordon fell silent, pursing his lips. "Alas, the kirk session would be hard pressed to charge him with anything. You see, as laird of his household, Lachlan may discipline his family however he chooses."

"Discipline?" Jamie ground out, incensed at the notion. "Leana has done nothing wrong—"

"Enough, lad." Reverend Gordon held up his hand, stemming the flow of words. "I ken her situation. Your child was legitimately conceived yet will be born to an unmarried woman who has reached her majority. As such, the law does not require your father to provide lodging for her nor for her bairn."

Jamie thrust out his chin. "The love of God requires it."

"Indeed it does."

"Which is why I will send sufficient silver for her care and for the child's. But 'tis a home she needs. A place of refuge far from Lachlan's… influence."

"Indeed." With a heavy sigh, the reverend stood, ending their meeting. "I will look into the matter and see what might be done for her. As to your uncle, I cannot promise you the justice you seek. That rests in God's hands alone." He steered Jamie toward the door. "You can be certain the parish will look after Leana. Some good soul will take her in. Isabella Callender or Janet Sloan, I imagine. What are Leana's particular skills?"

"Sewing. Gardening. Spinning." *Loving me. Mothering our children. Honoring God.* Jamie sank beneath the weight of her gifts. He could not tally half so many for himself. "She writes with a fine hand, and her baking rivals that of any French chef. None of the womanly arts are beyond her abilities, Reverend."

"Then Leana will surely find enough work to keep her hands busy and her roof secure."

Jamie pressed him. "You are certain of this?" The minister made it sound as though her father's disownment were a problem easily solved. Could that be true? Might he leave for Glentrool without being hounded by guilt?

Reverend Gordon's hand rested on the latch. "After the child is born and some time has passed, a man in the parish may notice what a competent woman Leana is and make her an offer of marriage."

Jamie stared at him. "Is that…likely?"

The minister shrugged. "One can hope for such an outcome. For her sake."

Jamie's gaze fell to the door latch. Why did his stomach clench whenever someone mentioned Leana marrying? She deserved to be happy. To be provided for, to be loved.

"We will care for her as best we can, Jamie. I cannot pretend her station will not be reduced, for our collection box depends upon the generosity of our neighbors. Any silver you send will be put to good use."

"I will send all I can, sir."

Reverend Gordon eased open the door, the savory aroma from the dining room across the hall clearly beckoning him. "These...ah, changes will be quite difficult for Leana after all she's been through. Not having a home of her own or a family to support her."

Jamie studied a slender crack in the wooden door. Leave for Glentrool without guilt? Impossible.

"Will you join us at table?" Reverend Gordon gestured across the hall. "We've more than enough food to bid you welcome."

"I'm afraid my family expects me." Though the minister asked again, Jamie resisted.

"Away with you, then." The older man waved him toward the door. "You've much on your mind and many decisions to make. Trust in the Almighty. He will not forsake you, lad."

I will not fail thee, nor forsake thee. Jamie knew the words were true. He had read them, spoken them, prayed them, and at last believed them. Now he longed for something more: proof.

Forty-Six

Is this a dream? O, if it be a dream,
Let me sleep on, and do not wake me yet!
HENRY WADSWORTH LONGFELLOW

Jamie?" Rose's voice. Floating above him in the dim recesses of their box bed.

"Here," he answered, slowly opening his eyes. "Here I am."

Rose leaned over him, her white teeth gleaming in the candlelight. "I know where you *are,* dear man. But where have you *been?* Sleeping or dreaming?"

"Both." He raised himself onto his elbows, squinting at his surroundings. Aye, there were the familiar wooden walls and linen sheets. The heather mattress, freshly stuffed, smelled as fragrant as Auchengray Hill on a summer night. Yet it was the hills of home that had filled his dreams—Mulldonach, Buchan, Eschoncan—steeply sloped, covered with purple heath, and etched with frothy linns tumbling into the heart of the glen.

Loch Trool. *Home.*

He dragged his hand across his rough beard. "Why did you stir me, lass?"

"You were moaning." She leaned back, giving him room to breathe. "I feared you were in pain or lost in a nightmare."

He sank onto the mattress, not truly awake. The threads of his dream tugged at him, wooing him back to sleep. His eyelids drifted shut. "The Sabbath day was long, and the hour is late, Rose. Will you mind if I…"

"Sleep, Jamie." She leaned across him and extinguished the candle by their bedside. "Pleasant dreams."

Darkness enveloped him.

His body drifted into a blessed numbness.

When Jamie opened his eyes—or so it seemed, though he knew it was a dream—the sky was lit by the morning sun, the air cooled by a mountain breeze. His bed had turned into a familiar slab of rock, holding him high above the ground.

His name poured forth from the heavens.

"Here I am," Jamie called, not caring if he sounded foolish.

The voice in his dream rang out. "I am the God of the place where you slept and woke and made your vow."

Turning round, Jamie discovered the loose rock that had served as his pillow one night long ago when another dream had unfolded much like this one. *May this stone be my witness.* He knelt before it, remembering his promise. *A portion of all that I have will belong to you.* Had the time come to make good on his vow? He had nothing to offer, not even a lamb.

"Arise."

Jamie scrambled to his feet, fear jolting through him. His hands, his purse, were empty. *Forgive me.* He could not bring himself to say the words aloud, dreading to think what his admission might cost him. *Forgive me, Lord.*

"Return."

One word, and all doubt vanished. *Return.* Even with his hands empty, he could go home. Must go home.

"Return with your children to the land of your father."

Aye, he would return to Glentrool. And not with empty hands at all but with full ones. With his children. All of them.

The Almighty had proved himself faithful.

Jamie knew he must do the same.

He opened his eyes slowly, waking to a new day not yet dawned.

A slumbering Rose lay next to him. Her dark lashes fanned across her cheeks. Her thick braid, pulled loose while she'd tossed and turned in the night, lay curled round her neck like a napping cat. And tucked beneath her head, her small hands were pressed together as if she'd fallen asleep in supplication.

"If you prayed for me last night, Rose, I am grateful." He lightly brushed her cheek, then ran his thumb round her sweet mouth, longing to kiss her, yet not wanting to wake her. She stirred, though only a little. "I ken what is to be done." His dream, still vivid in his mind, had provided the answer he needed.

He would tell Rose as soon as she awakened: They would return to Glentrool. With Leana.

The decision made, doubt crept in, like the tendrils of light starting to curl round the curtains. Would Rose accept his decision? Or question his motives? Even if she agreed now, she might grow resentful once they settled in the glen. Her fears and insecurities, which had eased over the summer, could rise to a fever pitch.

And what of Leana? Would she welcome such a life? If he insisted Leana accompany them, if he exerted his will over both sisters without regard for their feelings, he would be no better than Lachlan McBride.

Jamie rose from his bed, more determined than ever. *I am not my uncle.* He splashed water on his face, then pulled on his clothes, the hours ahead clear in his mind. He would meet with Leana and Rose together, well away from the house. Describe his dream. Let them hear the truth for themselves. And let them make their own decisions.

God had revealed his will to him. Could he not also reveal it to them?

Jamie slipped from the room and down the stair, stepping lightly as he went, not wanting to wake the household. When he reached the hall, he heard amiable voices coming from the kitchen. *Duncan. Neda.* Jamie called ahead to them, lest his unexpected entrance scare them senseless.

"Guid day tae ye, Mr. McKie." Neda's hands were covered with oatmeal, though she still dropped a slight curtsy. "What brings ye tae me kitchen door sae early in the morn?"

"I can answer that," Duncan boasted. "The smell o' oatcakes bakin' on the girdle."

"Aye." It was as fine a reason as any, Jamie decided, and far easier to explain than his dream. While he waited for Leana and Rose to begin their day, perhaps he should broach the subject with the Hastingses. *Return.* The Almighty had clearly spoken; surely his friends would concur.

Duncan claimed a toasted cake while his wife was busy rolling out the next one. He finished his prize in a few bites, then winked at Jamie. "Did ye sleep weel, lad?"

"More than that, I dreamed well." Jamie straddled a tall stool. "If you can listen while you bake, Neda, I'll tell you both a story you've not likely heard."

A cock crowed twice before Jamie finished relating his dream and the message it conveyed. "It seems I am to leave Auchengray whether my uncle approves or not."

Neda's voice was thin. "And take Leana wi' ye."

The sorrow in her eyes was almost more than Jamie could bear. "We cannot leave Leana in her father's hands."

"Nae, ye canna do that." Neda wiped her hands on her apron, then dabbed her eyes with a dry corner of the fabric. "Leana is like me ain dochter. Rose as weel."

"I've not spoken with either of them yet," he cautioned her. "I trust you'll keep my plans to yourself."

"Not a wird, lad."

Duncan folded his arms across his chest, his bright blue eyes assessing Jamie. "Ye'll take the sisters and yer bairns, aye. But will ye take yer lambs?"

"I'll not play the part of a reiver, if that's what you mean, and steal another man's sheep."

" 'Tis not stealin' whan they're yer ain flocks." Duncan's voice was full of mettle. "I heard Lachlan McBride call them yers mony a time. They say a man's wird is his bond." The overseer yanked on his bonnet with a sharp nod. "Ye have a richt tae claim yer lambs. And I'll be glad tae help ye."

"Duncan, you cannot involve yourself—"

"Wheesht!" A wry grin spread across his face. "I'll not have a green herd like yerself tellin' me what I can and canna do. Let me think aboot how tae arrange sic a thing."

"*Think* about it?" Jamie threw his hands in the air. "Neda, can you talk some sense into this auld man?"

She chuckled softly, sliding her hand in the crook of her husband's elbow. "We're a pair, the twa o' us. If Duncan says he'll help ye, then I will too."

"But Lachlan—"

"Doesna ken what I'm aboot tae tell ye." Duncan motioned him closer until the three of them formed a loose knot in the center of the kitchen. "At Kingsgrange, the farm whaur our dochter Mary is in service, the laird has offered tae fee me as o'erseer and Neda as hoosekeeper. I've yet to gie the man an answer, but I will if ye say the wird."

"You would…leave Auchengray?" Jamie's mind reeled at the thought of all of them departing in quick succession. "Lachlan cannot handle this place on his own. The flocks…the steading…"

Duncan shrugged, clearly unconcerned. "His new sons arrive in a day or twa. 'Twill take all three o' them tae fill our shoes, aye?"

Jamie sat back, stunned at the possibility. His family. And his lambs. Was it too much to hope for?

"Nae matter what happens, ye maun go tae Glentrool," Duncan said firmly. "I'll see what can be done aboot takin' yer flocks wi' ye."

Jamie stood and clasped Duncan's hand. "You're a better friend than I deserve."

"Do as ye'd be done tae, me faither told me."

Jamie laughed, releasing his grip. "A good rule, that." He turned to Neda, hoping she sensed his gratitude as well. "When Rose and Leana appear for breakfast, kindly send them out to the far pasture to meet me. After they've eaten, mind you, for I'll not see my bairns go hungry."

Neda's smile was kindness itself. "Ye're a guid faither, Mr. McKie."

Forty-Seven

Things of today?
Deeds which are harvest for Eternity!

EBENEZER ELLIOTT

Monday's child is fair of face. Rose smiled to herself, spreading a thick layer of strawberry jam across her toasted oatcake. It *was* a Monday, and she'd tried to look her bonniest. She'd not meant to sleep quite so late, however. Leana was probably knee-deep in her garden by now and Jamie lost among his sheep. She would find them both and tell them her plan.

When Neda appeared with a fresh rasher of bacon, Rose scolded her. "You've no need to serve me, Neda. I am capable of putting my own food on a plate."

"Noo, lass." She placed the meat on the table. "Ye maun let me make a fuss o'er ye while I can. Afore ye leave for Glentrool and forget yer auld Neda."

"Leave?" Rose paused, her oatcake halfway to her mouth. "Do you know something that I do not?"

Neda's ruddy cheeks turned scarlet. "Pardon me, mistress. I spoke oot o' turn. Whan ye finish yer breakfast, ye'll be wantin' tae join Mr. McKie in the far pasture. Yer husband wishes tae speak wi' ye and yer sister."

Rose stood in haste, her meal forgotten. "Why did you not tell me at once?"

"He wanted ye tae eat first. For the sake o' yer babe." Neda eased her back into the chair. "Have a bite o' yer guid bacon. Mr. McKie can wait anither minute or twa. If ye've not eaten, it's me head he'll be askin' for on a plate."

Rose bolted down her food, barely tasting it. Had Jamie come to some resolution? She had yet to approach him with her own audacious notion. Could she tell Jamie and Leana together? Aye, and pray Jamie would not be livid with her when he heard what his heidie wife had in mind.

She left the table moments later, her discarded linen fluttering to the floor as she hurried out the back door in search of Leana. Just as she'd envisioned, her sister was kneeling in her garden, poking seeds into the tilled soil.

"There you are." Rose hovered over her, reluctant to sit on the grass lest she soil her gown. Instead she clasped her hands and tried to curb her anxious thoughts. "Have you seen Jamie?"

Leana straightened, brushing the dirt from her hands. "You and I are to meet him in the far pasture. If you don't mind, I'd like to finish here first. It won't take a minute."

Rose waited—quite patiently, she thought—standing on the spongy grass while her sister emptied the seed packet into the palm of her hand.

"These are the last I'll sow this season." Leana pushed each one firmly in place. "I've been waiting for tonight's full moon. It pulls the water in the ground toward the surface so the seeds sprout more quickly. And at night the moonlight helps the leaves grow. Auld gardeners say that, after Lammas, corn ripens as much by night as by day."

Rose watched the plain, dun-colored seeds disappear into the ground. If Neda's slip of the tongue proved true, and she and Jamie were indeed headed for Glentrool, she would not see this crop harvested. As for her sister, Rose knew what must be done; now she needed the courage to do it.

"Come, Leana." The sooner they found Jamie, the sooner all could be resolved.

Leana stood without mishap, then slipped off her dirt-covered apron. "Father has yet to put me out of the house, and I already look like a poor gaberlunzie begging for bread."

"Nonsense." Rose took her apron and tossed it aside, then pointed them toward the fields. "You look like my sister."

"A gardener perhaps."

"And a mother. Of two."

Leana laughed softly. "Three children, counting you."

Rose fell silent, remembering the times she had railed at her in anger, "You are *not* my mother!" She tightened her hold on her now, more than willing to claim Leana. As her mother. As her sister. As her friend.

Walking over the uneven ground, the two steadied each other. Rocky protrusions and rabbit holes were obstacles to be navigated with prudence. Though neither woman had become ungainly, their full skirts and round bellies conspired against them, slowing their progress as they climbed up and down the gentle braes. Their presence upset the skittish ewes, sending the sheep darting off as the sisters crossed each pasture.

"I wonder if they miss their lambs," Leana said, brushing the fleece of a tamer ewe.

Rose heard the hint of sorrow in her voice. "Jamie says that once they're weaned, the lambs and their mothers no longer recognize one another. It makes the separation easier."

"Oh," Leana sighed. "How sad."

They walked side by side, breathing more, speaking less. Rose shaded her eyes, staring off in the distance. "'Tis farther than I remembered. If it was privacy Jamie wanted, we shall certainly have it."

Finally they spotted him standing among his flocks, watching for them. The lambs, crowding round his legs, moved like a sea of white wool, hindering his stride until he finally reached them. "Here you are at last." Jamie brushed the loose wool from his calfskin breeches, eying both women. "I was beginning to worry about you."

"As well you should have," Rose said lightly, then perched on a sturdy dyke. "Whatever were you thinking, asking two expectant mothers to walk so far? I pray you have a good reason for summoning us here."

"An excellent reason." Jamie stood before them, the morning sun shining round his head like a golden crown. "First, let me greet you properly." With a courtly bow, he bent and kissed Rose's hand, then Leana's, bringing a blush to their cheeks. "May I offer you something to drink?"

"Jamie, you..." Rose's protest faded as he produced a silver flask from the goatskin pouch hanging round his waist and uncorked it.

"Fresh from the well this morning, I promise you."

Rose was too thirsty to complain, taking a long drink before sharing the cool water with Leana. "Your hospitality is admirable, Jamie. But why are we here?"

He stretched out his arms, as though embracing the mist-laden hills and muted green glens. "In days of auld, clans would meet on a hilltop and plan how to vanquish their enemies."

"Our only enemy is Father."

"Exactly so, Rose." He reclaimed his flask, then tucked it back inside the pouch. "I hope you will agree I have served your father well these many months, even though he has done everything in his power to make my life miserable."

"Agreed." Rose exchanged glances with Leana. "On both counts." Jamie's speech was rather formal, as if he'd prepared what he was going to say. Did her sister know where this was leading? Did *she*?

Jamie did not pace back and forth, as he often did, but stood his ground, his voice as firm as his stance. "Despite my efforts, Lachlan McBride has done nothing but deceive me, swicking me out of my wages."

"And your lambs," Rose prompted him, though the bleating flocks behind him were reminder enough.

Jamie acknowledged her with a nod. "Ever since Lachlan returned from Moffat threatening to disown Leana unless I remained at Auchengray, I have begged God for an answer. Last night I heard from him. In a dream."

Her mouth fell open. "When I woke you…"

"That was the start of it." Jamie eyed them both before he continued. "Then I heard my name. Whether 'twas an angel or the Almighty, I cannot say. He told me, as clearly as I am speaking to you, that I am to leave Auchengray and return to my father's land. With my family."

"Jamie, that is wonderful news!" Rose threw herself into his arms, nearly knocking him over in her exuberance. "I shall finally see Glentrool!"

She pressed a kiss to his neck, stemming her tears. Did he realize what must be done, as she did? Would he understand, or would his anger burn against her? Rose stepped out of his embrace to grasp her sister's hand, pulling Leana to her feet. There would be no better time than this to present her case.

"I have not heard the voice of an angel, but I know in my heart what is right." Rose looked at each of them, more certain than ever of her decision. "We cannot go without my sister. She bears your child, as I do, and needs a proper roof over her head. Leana must come with us to Glentrool."

"Rose!" They said her name as one, disbelief on both their faces.

"I cannot bear to see you humiliated by our father, Leana. Not for one more hour, let alone for all your days." She turned to her husband, desperately hoping he would not be angry with her. "I believe 'tis the fair and right thing to do, Jamie. I pray I have not overstepped my bounds."

He surprised her with a broad smile. "Indeed you have not."

Forty-Eight

These are weighty secrets,
and we must whisper them.

SUSAN COOLIDGE

Overwhelmed, Leana stepped backward, nearly tumbling over the stone fence behind her. "Rose, you have...saved my life." She sank onto the dyke, covering her face with her hands. "I was afraid that I...that my child...that we would live...and that Ian..." She rocked back and forth, trying to swallow, trying to speak.

Rose was beside her in an instant, her arms circled round her shoulders. "After all you did for me, Leana...all you sacrificed...how could I leave without you?"

They held each other tight, cheeks pressed together, until Leana could finally take a full breath. Jamie produced a handkerchief, then offered fresh sips of water. Leana clasped the silver flask, gazing up at Jamie as she drank. Was he in agreement or simply humoring his headstrong wife? She was certain of Rose's sentiments. Might he truly feel the same?

"Jamie..." Leana handed back the empty flask, not letting go until she had his complete attention. "If you would rather I stayed..."

"Nae, lass. I would rather you came." The sincerity of his words, the honesty in his gaze, dispelled any doubt. "My generous wife speaks for us both."

"Come, come. I am as selfish as ever." Rose winked and pulled her closer. "Now I shan't have to suffer through my confinement alone. You will be there to care for me."

Leana smiled through her tears. *Always, Rose.*

"It is settled, then." Rose stood, stretching as if she'd been hunched over carding wool all morning. "And we must take Eliza, for she is the only dowry Father provided for Leana when...ah, when she married."

Leana watched for a change in his expression. "Jamie, I do not mean to burden you further." Was it too much to ask to bring her lady's maid? "I must confess, Eliza is very dear to me."

"Then the lass will join us. She can keep Annabel company and help care for Ian."

"Bless you." Leana lowered her gaze, not letting herself look at Jamie any longer than necessary. She knew what this decision would cost him. And what it would require of her. *My beloved Jamie.* They must never be together, just the two of them. Never speak of the past, never touch in any way, never let their gazes linger.

Her sister had given her everything her heart desired: freedom from their father, the chance to be with Ian, a future and a hope. Leana vowed she would not demean that priceless gift for one moment nor dishonor the One whose grace made it possible.

Rose released an airy sigh. "When do we tell Father?"

"Never." Jamie surprised them both. "We will tell no one. Not the other servants nor our neighbors. No one must ken."

A look of concern crossed Rose's features. "Is there something we've not been told?"

" 'Tis best if you do not ken the whole of it." He shifted his gaze from one sister to the other as if gauging their response. "Duncan has some…arrangements to make on my behalf. Even I am not aware of the final details." His earnest expression made it clear he was not being deceptive, merely cautious. "Your father will stop at nothing to prevent our departure. Our free labor suits his purse. And he delights in making us dance to his tune."

Rose plucked a sprig of purple heather from the ground, twirling it between her fingers. "Father gave you two choices, did he not? Stay with Leana or leave with me." The corners of her mouth twitched. "Leaving with Leana *and* with me was not one of them."

"Indeed it was not." He rested his hands on his hips, nodding to himself, as though making some further decision. "You must pack your clothes and goods when no one is looking. Do not take a single thing that is not rightfully yours, lest Lachlan devise some charge to bring against us."

"I will take only my gowns and hair ribbons," Rose promised.

Jamie's gaze shifted from one sister to the other. "You'll not regret leaving without your father's blessing, knowing we can never return?"

Leana turned slowly about, drinking in the pastoral view for the last time. "There is nothing left for us here, Jamie. Neither the land nor the flocks nor the gold in my father's thrifite belongs to us." She gazed in the direction of Dalbeaty, miles beyond Lowtis Hill. "The sons of Edingham are Lachlan McBride's heirs now. Rose and I are little more than strangers."

"Never mind Father's blessing." Rose shook her braid off her shoulder, a defiant spark in her eye. "Whatever God told you in your dream, Jamie, do it with *our* blessing."

"Let us away to the mains, then. I've moved some of the lambs, according to your father's wishes. Now I shall attend to my own business. *Our* business." Jamie offered them each an arm as they started back.

Rose slipped her hand round the crook of his elbow.

Leana did not, praying he might understand.

They struck out across the pastures, Jamie's lengthy stride leading them home more quickly than they'd come. When Leana stumbled over an uneven patch of ground, he reached out to steady her, apologizing for his haste.

"Now I'll confess why we met on a distant hilltop and not in the garden." Jamie tried not to look guilty and failed. "I had to ken whether or not the McBride sisters could handle a good bit of walking."

"Jamie!" Rose swatted him with her braid. "You might have simply asked us."

"Nae, I had to see for myself." His stern expression confirmed his words. "The Galloway roads are badly rutted from wheeled traffic. Even with a horse-drawn wagon, you'll prefer to walk now and again rather than be jostled about." He paused, studying each of them closely. "If you could not manage a trip to the far pasture and back again, you'd not have lasted long on our journey west."

Rose struck a haughty pose. "As you can see, we are both in good health and could walk every mile to Glentrool if necessary."

"Every mile, eh?" Jamie snorted. "I have made that trek, lass, and you've no idea what hardships I encountered. I slept on the floors of bothies and barns, trudged through peat bogs—"

"So we've heard." She started off without him. "But did you face a *bogle* in the woodlands or fight off a kelpie while crossing the Dee?"

"I did not." Jamie caught up with her in two strides. "The only *frichtsome* apparition we need to worry about is the minister of Monnigaff." He angled his head. "Leana, do you still have your testimonial letter from Reverend Gordon?"

"I do." She pictured it folded and hidden in her trunk, stored in a corner of the nursery. The minister's kind words had opened the door to Twyneholm parish. Might they do so again for Monnigaff? "The letter lacks only a seal, which I'll attend to the moment we arrive home."

"See that you do. As heir to Glentrool, I'll be received in my home parish without dispute. But your reception is less certain, Leana. Since you are unmarried yet clearly with child, Reverend Erskine will insist upon reading your testimonial. Even so, tongues will wag." He looked at her as they walked, compassion mirrored in his eyes. "I fear you'll find more gossip than gospel in Monnigaff."

"I am…accustomed to it." She clutched her skirts, holding them free of the damp grass. Better to fill her hands with fabric than reach for the arm he kindly offered her. "What of Uncle Alec and Aunt Rowena? Will they…welcome me?"

"You are their niece and the mother of their grandchildren. They will gladly offer you a home." The words came too quickly; Jamie was as uncertain as she. A brave man, to face his parents with two wives in tow.

They reached the house at noon, both sisters somewhat breathless but no worse for wear. Rose's face was the color of wild Scottish pink, yet her grin was smug. "Have we proven ourselves worthy?"

"You'll do," Jamie said, smoothing the damp hairs off her brow. "Remember, not a word to anyone, not even to your maids. Neda will handle that for us and make certain they keep our secrets."

When they entered the house, Neda greeted them with an anxious expression. "Haste ye tae yer dressin' tables, for yer faither awaits his dinner."

The household hummed with activity as they repaired to their rooms to dress. Eliza joined Leana in the nursery, making do with a hand mirror as she dressed Leana's hair, then brushed her yellow gown clean. "Annabel has her hands fu' this day," Eliza fretted, "helpin' her mistress and carin' for Ian as weel."

"It takes both of you to keep Rose and me presentable and my son out of trouble." Leana had to bite her tongue before she gave away their secret. "Enough, Eliza. I hear my father's bell."

Leana joined the others in the dining room, the aroma of chicken and leeks rising from their soup plates like a fragrant fog. Her father's blessing on the meal was brief; he did not care for cold soup. They ate in silence at his request, which well suited their secrecy. The threesome exchanged furtive glances but nothing else.

His pudding finished, Lachlan folded his hands and turned to Jamie. "Surely by now you've made a decision, Nephew. Will you leave at Lammas with Rose? Or remain and do your duty by Leana?"

Jamie did not look at either sister. Nor did Leana dare catch Rose's eye, remembering Jamie's warning: *No one must ken.*

"As usual, you are right, Uncle," he finally said. "After seeking God's will, I have made my decision." Jamie's voice and gaze remained even, revealing nothing. "I will not leave Leana behind."

Oh, Jamie. Did he mean to confess their plan?

"Not leave Leana, you say?" Lachlan's brows lifted in obvious surprise. "You have chosen to stay then."

Jamie said nothing, neither confirming nor correcting her father's statement.

Leana lowered her head to hide her relief. *Jamie, you clever lad.* His conscience would be clear. He had not lied to their father.

Lachlan motioned the servants to clear the table, signaling the end of dinner. "'Twill soon be a busy place, Auchengray. Malcolm and his brothers will arrive here Wednesday after the sale of Edingham is complete. Since you and Rose are well settled in your room, the front parlor will become the lads' bedroom." He shrugged. "'Tis large enough to accommodate them, and we rarely have company."

Morna tugged at a loose curl near her face, repeatedly wrapping it round her finger. "What of all the furniture in my parlor?" she asked, in a voice as timid as it was high. "I thought 'twould suit—"

"Nae, 'twould not. Your husband's feeble attempts at carpentry will keep our kitchen hearth burning this winter." He patted her hand, barely looking at her when he spoke. "We've no need of more tables and chests here. Two beds from Edingham will suffice."

With that, Lachlan bowed his head, offering a final blessing on their dinner, oblivious to his wife's misery. Leana detected a teary sniff from Morna beside her and prayed the woman might find some happiness in having her sons near. It seemed Lachlan McBride was determined to break Morna's heart now that it was his.

Leana could not leave her father's house soon enough.

Five days remained. They would pack in haste, whisper behind closed doors, and pray Lachlan did not uncover their secret.

Forty-Nine

Of a rich man who was mean and niggardly, he said,
"That man does not possess his estate,
but his estate possesses him."

DIOGENES LAERTIUS

R ose, whatever are you doing in here?" Jamie stood in the doorway
to the spence, puzzled to find his wife inspecting Lachlan's bookshelf. Her father did not welcome visitors to his study unattended.

She looked over her shoulder, the picture of innocence. "'Tis a long
journey. I thought I might take something to read."

"Read?" He crossed the room and gently pulled her away from the
shelf, glancing round to be certain no one was lurking in the corridor.
"This is not some holiday we're planning."

"I realize that, Jamie." She turned beneath his hands until she was
facing him, clutching a small volume to her breast. "But you did say
we would be traveling for more than a week, and a book can be fine
company."

"Your sister is company enough." He ran his finger round her chin,
tracing the delicate lines of her face. "'Twas more than generous of you
to include her, Rose."

"And of you. To accept the idea so willingly." She sighed, a pensive
look on her face. "I would not have known a day of happiness at Glentrool if I'd left Leana in the hands of this…" Rose glanced at her father's
desk, where a new thrifite held court. "This miserly, covetous excuse for
a man!" She glared at the wooden box. "'Tis your money, Jamie. And
our children's. Not his."

"Aye, aye." He pressed a kiss to her brow, meaning to calm her.
"Enough on that subject. How is my *douce* wife today?"

"Neither sweet nor amiable." She was still pouting. "The household
has been in an uproar since Wednesday. Trunks, furniture, and every

manner of *plenishing* have been dragged across our threshold. One can barely walk through the halls, and the parlor will ne'er be the same."

"I know, lass." He tugged on her braid. "Sometimes a *stramash* can be a blessing. Amid all the clamor, we've been able to store our own trunks in the barn without anyone noticing."

"If you say so," she said, sounding unconvinced. "Auchengray hardly feels like home anymore. I thought taking a book along might boost my spirits."

"Naughty Rose." His exaggerated scowl was meant to make her smile. "Have you forgotten what I told you Monday?"

She mimicked his shepherd's stance—shoulders square, head thrown back, feet spread apart—and repeated in her deepest voice, "'Do not take a single thing that is not rightfully yours.' Aye, Jamie, I heard you." She held up the pilfered volume. "'Tis only a book—"

"That belongs to your father."

"And I mean to keep it." Lachlan swaggered into the room, then plucked his book from her grasp and slid it back onto the shelf in one effortless motion.

Jamie's mouth went dry. How much had the man heard?

"Sonnets." Lachlan studied the spine of the book she'd chosen. "'Tis not a week for reading poetry, young Rose. You should be making your brothers feel at home. Organizing the front parlor for them. Helping the maids unpack my wife's many *kists*."

"I have done those things, Father." Rose had yet to abandon her proud posture. If anything, she'd thrust out her chin farther. "And what have *you* done for my birthday? Come Lammas, you and your new sons will be halfway to Lockerbie, leaving only the three of us to celebrate my seventeenth summer."

Jamie shot her a warning glance. *Careful, Rose.* Lachlan was not a man to be baited like a sea trout. He could yank her into deeper waters before she discovered her feet had left the banks.

"As it happens, Daughter, I've arranged for a present to appear by your breakfast plate on Sunday morning." He crossed the small room, hands clasped behind his back. "Though I'll not be here, I trust your husband will see the anniversary of your birth duly celebrated."

"I shall indeed." Jamie circled his arm round Rose's waist, hoping to soften her belligerent stance. Now was not the time to provoke the man's anger. "Uncle, I see you have a new thrifite."

"A larger one with a larger key." The wooden money box, fitted with an elaborate brass lock and handles on each side, was twice the size of his old one, surpassing the dimensions of the family Bible stored in the box by the hearth. Lachlan produced a key dangling from a silken ribbon round his neck and opened the box with a flourish, inviting their appraisal.

The mound of gold and silver coins sickened Jamie. Years of avarice and selfishness had produced a fortune that would benefit no one but Lachlan McBride. Jamie stared at his uncle's treasure and realized he was looking at the man's heart.

Rose leaned forward for a closer inspection. "You have kept that knotted cord, I see."

Lachlan snapped the lid shut. "A worthless charm."

"Lillias Brown once told me you were quite pleased to have it." Though Rose's countenance was docile, her words carried a note of challenge.

"It means nothing to me." He turned the key with a sharp flick of his wrist. "Nor do I care what the auld wutch believes. She gave me that gold cord unbidden sometime ago. What of it?"

"As you say, Father." Rose ended their parry, her voice as smooth as a tempered blade. " 'Tis worthless."

"Indeed." The ruddiness in Lachlan's face began to ease.

Jamie's pounding heart slowed as well. Rose was surely her father's daughter, taught to spar at his own knee. Jamie tightened his hold round Rose's waist, a mute signal for her to hold her peace. "Tell me, Uncle. Will you be taking the Edingham lambs to Lockerbie?"

"Nae. They're the runts, the smaller of the twins."

Jamie bristled. Though they were smaller, the lambs were no less hardy. Had he not chosen every one of them?

"Rather than drive that flock all the way north from Dalbeaty," Lachlan said, "I've decided to let them feed on Edingham's good pastureland a bit longer. Fill out their hind legs, get some meat on them. Then I'll sell them at the September market in Dumfries."

And keep the silver. Jamie gritted his teeth, forcing himself to ask what he needed to know. "Will the new owner of Edingham not object to their grazing on his property?"

"When I'm paying two months' rent for a useless parcel of land? Thomas Henderson was happy to take my silver for his troubles."

Jamie filed the information away. "And what of the lambs bound for Lockerbie? Have you a plan for them, too?"

Lachlan seldom missed an opportunity to boast. "I've fee'd a dozen herds, one for every fifty lambs. Duncan will oversee things, of course. The men have twenty miles to cover—half on Friday, the rest on Saturday."

"Ten miles each day? 'Tis not prudent to drive the lambs so hard to market."

Lachlan reared up. "Nephew, I have bred, raised, and sold sheep for more years than you have drawn breath. If I want my lambs on the road Friday at daybreak, so they shall be. If I want to leave for Lockerbie on Saturday and take my sons and wife with me so they might see for themselves my standing among Galloway's landowners, it will be done."

Jamie hung his head, if only to hide his elation. All the details he required, served to him as neatly as a leg of mutton on a platter. "When shall we expect you home, Uncle?"

"Late Tuesday afternoon," he grunted. "With my purse bulging if the buyers are generous."

When Jamie looked up, Lachlan was already at the door. "The men I've fee'd are gathering in the steading tonight, preparing to leave at first light." He waved his hand as if he were brushing off a swarm of midges. "Feel free to make their acquaintance, Jamie. They're penniless shepherds. Like you."

Fifty

For friendship, of itself a holy tie,
Is made more sacred by adversity.

JOHN DRYDEN

I am not ashamed of being a shepherd, Duncan." Jamie shoved his
dirk inside the cuff of his boot with a fleeting thought of plunging
the sharpened blade into Lachlan's black heart instead. "But I'll not be
called poor."

The evening sun hung low on the horizon, gilding the steading in
a bronzed glow. Inside the barn, Jamie and Duncan were gathering the
last of their belongings before they met with the drovers.

"Thar's nae shame in poverty. Only in pride and greed." Duncan
tightened the rope round the bundle he'd packed, then threw it over his
shoulder as if testing the weight of it. "Yer uncle is a wickit man," he
said plainly, laying his bundle by the door. "He doesna seek after God.
Which is why I'll not mourn whan I leave this place. For I dinna mean
tae come back."

Seeing the telltale sheen in Duncan's eyes, Jamie blinked hard,
bridling his emotions. "Will we not see you again after the morn?"

Duncan wagged his head, his features grim. "Whan the lambs are
sold in Lockerbie, I'll head south for Kingsgrange and start wark there
on Wednesday next." He glanced toward the open barn door and the
world beyond it. " 'Twill be strange not turnin' toward Auchengray as I
pass by the road."

Jamie sank onto a wooden stool, the weight of his decision growing
heavier by the hour. "This is my fault. All of it."

"Nae, 'tis yer uncle's doin'. From the day ye arrived, he had his mind
set on swickin' ye."

"And so he has." *Many times.* Jamie had lost count of the promises
made and broken by Lachlan. But was it right, what they were plan-

ning? Was it justice…or revenge? "The Almighty has told me to return home, Duncan, and to take my family. He did not mention my lambs."

"But yer uncle did." Duncan's tone brooked no argument. "He said they were a blissin o' God and called them yers. Ye've earned these lambs by the sweat o' yer brow. We'll take back what Lachlan McBride pledged tae gie ye—nae mair, nae less—and send ye hame tae Glentrool wi' yer flocks. Ye've nae reason tae fear. The Lord is wi' ye."

Jamie stood and grasped his friend's arm, determined to know the truth. "You are certain this is God's will? For me to claim these lambs? And for you to risk helping me?"

"I am," Duncan answered at once. " 'Tis the Lord's wark I'm doin'. Not for yer sake, Jamie. For the sake o' his *halie* name. The Buik doesna lie: Many sorrows shall be tae the wickit. But he that trusteth in the LORD, mercy shall compass him aboot."

Jamie chewed on the man's words like meat. Like bread. He *did* trust the Almighty. And had been wrapped in his mercy from the hour he had left Glentrool. "But what of Neda?" Another worry. "Asking her to move, uprooting her from her home—"

"Och! Hame is whaur the woman hangs her apron. *Forby*, she'll be wi' our dochter Mary from dawn 'til dusk." Duncan pulled off his cap to dust the plaid wool across his breeches, watching Jamie all the while. "I canna call meself yer freen and not help ye, lad."

"You are…" Jamie looked away. He could barely speak for the tightness in his chest. "A…good friend."

No one had ever been kinder to him than Duncan Hastings.

They stood in silence for a moment, face to face, the air filled with evening birdsong and the muted sound of men's voices in the bothies next door. Jamie tried to ignore the heartache inside him, but it would not cease. "I will miss you, Duncan."

"And I ye, lad. Mair than I can say." Duncan wiped his nose with the back of his hand. "Weel I recall the day ye came here. Green as spring grass and fu' o' oats. But ye warked hard and were willin' tae learn."

Jamie snorted, his spirits lifting. "With you as my teacher, I had no choice."

Duncan grinned, though his eyes were moist. "I'm a' for a guid day's wark. But we've also caught a fish or twa. Swapped herd lore standin' on the braes. Rode tae Keltonhill Fair *thegither*. Bought ye a horse—"

"And named it after you," Jamie reminded him, glad to see the man's face redden if it meant he was pleased. "My gelding will ne'er be the friend you've been, Duncan. But I'll be proud to tell folk why my mount bears the name Hastings. That I will."

Duncan merely nodded, clearing his throat, then started toward the bothies at the end of the steading—small, dirt-floored cottages, sparsely furnished, reeking of the nearby midden. "Time tae meet anither freen or twa wha'll do richt by ye come the morn's morn."

They knocked on the thick-paned window to announce themselves, then were welcomed inside by a motley assembly of men of all ages. Jamie greeted the ones he recognized, including the few shepherds he knew by name: Rab Murray, Davie Tait, Geordie Currie. To a man they'd been roughened from years spent on the hills, their faces etched by wind and rain. Though their teeth were stained, their smiles were honest, and the grip of their hands sure. These were men Jamie could trust; he would need their trust as well.

"Lads," Duncan began, raising his hands to quiet them, "ye're a' from the neighborhood, so ye ken the *ill-scrapit* nature of Lachlan McBride." A low murmur circled the crowded bothy. Aye, they knew. "Twa months ago he promised Jamie McKie twenty score lambs for his labors. Ye'll believe me whan I say he's earned them. Last week Mr. McBride changed his mind for nae guid reason but greed. I canna stand by and see a man swicked oot o' twa years' wages."

As the murmuring grew louder in Jamie's favor, Duncan pressed on. "Whan we leave here in the morn's morn, the unmarked lambs will be driven north, as planned. I'll take seven o' ye wi' me tae Lockerbie for the Lammas Fair. The spotted lambs will be driven tae the glen o' Loch Trool by the northern route. I'll need five o' ye for that lang raik. Ye'll be in guid hands wi' Auld Nick as yer *topsman*."

A graying man of some years stepped forward, offering his hand. "Mr. McKie? Nicholas Donaldson of Balmaclellan." Whatever his age, his back was straight and his grip was solid, like clasping an iron handle.

"Dinna let me name worry ye, sir. I may be Auld Nick, but I'm not the de'il himself."

The herds chuckled, but Jamie noticed none of them slapped the man on the back. Donaldson was well liked but also respected. As topsman, he would ride ahead, arranging for grazing and lodging, seeing to the needs of the drovers and their beasts. An important role, not lightly assigned.

Jamie nodded at him. "I trust you'll see my lambs home. You and the other herds will be well paid when you reach Glentrool."

"Mr. McKie's a man o' his word," Duncan said. "Rab and Davie, ye'll be travelin' wi' him. As for the herds comin' wi' me, I'll see ye're paid whan we arrive in Lockerbie, then send ye tae the hills." Duncan smiled, but Jamie saw the tremor in his chin. "Whan Lachlan McBride jalouses half his lambs are missin', I'm the ane wha needs tae face him. Alone."

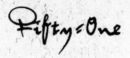

Fifty-One

Haste thee, haste thee, to be gone!
Earth flits fast and time draws on.
SIR WALTER SCOTT

A re they truly gone?" Rose leaned out the second-floor window, watching the ebony carriage disappear down the drive. A pewter sky loomed over the landscape, and the air was pregnant with rain. Minutes earlier the McBrides and McKies had exchanged farewells on the lawn. A cluster of relatives with little to say. No tears, no tender embraces. Perfunctory well wishes. Morna nervously fiddling with her sleeve. Jamie sullen.

Lachlan's final words had been as callous as ever. "Without Duncan here, the management of Auchengray rests on your shoulders, Nephew. I do not imagine much will be accomplished between now and Tuesday."

"On the contrary," Jamie had said, his tone as sharp as his gaze, "while you are gone, I will spend every hour taking care of your property."

Rose smiled now, remembering. *My canny husband.*

As she turned away from the window, Jamie came up behind her, his arms full of bedding. "Lass, come tell me what you need from the nursery." Since they finally had the house to themselves, the traveling party could finish packing their belongings without subterfuge. Willie and the others would be apprised of their plans shortly, then pressed into service loading Jock Bell's borrowed wagon. Rose spied it clattering up the drive at that very moment, Rab Murray at the reins, two barking collies by his side.

She followed Jamie into the nursery, grateful Leana had spirited away Ian to feed him a stout breakfast. The lad might have to live on cold porridge for a week. Would he behave himself in the wagon? And how would they keep him dry when it rained? Her long list of worries expanded by the hour. So did a seething resentment toward the father whose greed forced them to flee like vagabonds.

Lachlan McBride had promised to leave a small present for her.

She had a parting gift for him as well.

"Decide, Rose." Jamie did not bother to mask his impatience, though she would excuse him anything on so tapsalteerie a day. "What's to be taken, lass?"

She scoured the nursery, considering each item. "Ian's crib, which Willie made for him. And the oak cradle that belonged to my mother."

" 'Tis fair." Jamie had insisted on approving every item, determined not to be branded a thief. He dropped his armload of tattered bedding—rescued from the rag pile—into the empty crib, then wrestled it into the hall, calling for Hugh to help him carry it down the stair. All at Auchengray would turn into beasts of burden before the morning ended.

Rose waited until she heard Jamie's voice fade out the front door, then collected the old kitchen apron she'd hidden in the bottom of their clothes press and slipped down the stair, hoping to reach the spence unseen. On Thursday last, when Jamie had found her studying her father's bookshelf, the volume of poetry in her hands had been a ploy. Her true reason for visiting her father's private abode was about to bear fruit.

The apron tied round her waist swung to and fro as she walked, weighed down by the strange collection of items hidden deep inside its pockets. Rose clutched them against her, lest someone come round a corner and ask too many questions. Once inside the spence, she swiftly latched the door.

The room was bathed in shadows. Without a candle, her progress to the fireplace was slow and cautious, though her eyes soon adjusted to the meager light from the window. She knelt before the hearth and emptied her pockets with care. Though she'd heard of stone fires, she'd never had cause to assemble one. If a person left his farm because of some grievance, building a stone fire brought ill luck to the homeowner when he returned and crossed his threshold. Rose had never imagined a day when such a custom would be useful. That day was here.

She laid twigs of green hawthorn, freshly cut, on the hearth, then carefully deposited bits of glass from a broken bottle discarded behind the byre. Atop the glass she put handfuls of small, sharp stones gathered from the drive. Finally she placed several flat stones on top, covering the whole of it.

Rose sat back on her haunches, admiring her work. If there was some cantrip required, she did not know it. Instead she remembered the words Jamie had once shared with her, spoken by his father the night Jamie left Glentrool. *Cursed be anyone who curses you.* "Aye," she said softly, holding her hands over the stones as if she were warming herself at a fire. "Curse you." She could not bring herself to say her father's name; 'twas bad enough to *think* it.

Rose was on her feet at once, anxious to get away from whatever she'd wrought. She opened the casement window, easing the panels of glass out as far as they would go. Aye, the width was sufficient, and the ground rose to meet her just below the window, offering a safe landing. That would come later, when she turned her back on Auchengray forever. If she departed by the window now, any innocent soul who came through the front door would be cursed.

As she turned away from the yawning opening and the menacing clouds it framed, her gaze fell on her father's thrifite. Boldly displayed on his desk. A silent dare. *Unlock me.* Lachlan had the only key, far beyond reach by now. She could not resist touching the wood. Sliding her hand across the old pine, sanded and polished by a carpenter from the village, Rose pictured the coins and bank notes heaped inside the wooden box.

Her father's most valued possession.

Instead of me.

Grief tightened its fingers round her throat. "*This* is what you treasure." Rose slapped the money box hard, not caring that she bruised her finger on the brass lock. "You will not miss your daughters, but you would surely miss your precious thrifite."

Suddenly her mouth fell open, the pain in her hand forgotten.

Of course. She would take her father's money box.

Her own inheritance. Her sister's inheritance. Their children's inheritance. And Jamie's hard-earned silver. *That's* what the box contained. And a witch's knotted cord, which Rose would see destroyed.

Dared she risk such a braisant act?

For her children's sake, for Jamie's sake, she would.

Resolved, she pulled the box toward her, only to be dismayed by its weight. *Och!* She could hardly tuck such a thing beneath her arm and saunter out the door. What to carry it in, then? She left the money box where it was, eying it over her shoulder as she ventured into the back corridor, where a pile of goods waited to be stored in the wagon.

Among them sat the empty cradle. The perfect size for hiding a thrifite.

Wary, Rose lifted her head, listening. Not a voice could be heard in the house. The servants were out of doors readying the wagon, all talking at once from the sound of it. Please God, Jamie was with them. She needed only another minute.

Heart pounding, Rose dragged the old cradle into the spence with some difficulty. Would her father notice the gouges in the floor? Not likely. He would be too busy bemoaning the loss of his gold. She positioned the cradle beside the desk, intending to lower the money box inside. But she grunted when she tried to lift it, then was frightened by a sharp pain that gripped her back.

Might she simply push it in? Would it make a fearsome noise when it landed? Another brief visit to the hall produced the very thing she needed: linen towels to cushion the fall. Rose hurriedly padded the sloped interior of the cradle, wrapped the money box as best she could, and shoved it over the edge of the desk.

The box fell like a boulder, the corner of the brittle pine meeting the solid oak with a deafening crash, splintering the wood and breaking open the lock. Coins flew everywhere. Sovereigns, pennies, shillings. On the floor, on her shoes, and all over the bottom of the cradle.

"Help!" she cried without thinking.

Mortified, she slapped her hand over her mouth. Too late to ask for help. However could she explain herself? Nothing to be done but finish what she'd started. Rose gathered the scattered coins with trembling hands. Might someone come running, alerted by the noise?

If she could find all the coins, then cover the shattered thrifite with a blanket…*och!* Did she think she could tuck it into bed like a bairn? *Help me. Please help me!*

Tears stung her eyes as she dropped the stray coins into the cradle, then poked one linen towel after another round the misshapen box. It took all her strength to move it out into the hall. The coins shifted as the cradle tipped back and forth on its rockers, the cool, metallic sound divulging their presence. That would never do. There were no more towels. However would she muffle the sound?

When she came across a worn blanket, her heart leaped with joy. *Thanks be to God!* Nae, she dared not thank the Almighty. He could neither be blamed nor invoked for such sin. *Thou shalt not steal. Honour thy father.* Two commandments broken. *Two, Rose!*

She stood looking down at the cradle, now neatly filled with cloth goods. Hidden beneath them rested her father's treasure.

How many commandments had *he* broken? *Thou shalt have no other gods before me.* His thrifite was his altar. *Thou shalt not bear false witness.* He lied whenever it suited him. *Thou shalt not covet thy neighbour's house.* Had he not coveted Edingham? *Thou shalt not take the name of the LORD thy God in vain.* Every night when he opened the Buik and read words that he neither honored nor obeyed, Lachlan McBride did just that: He took God's name in vain.

Standing in the dim corridor, Rose patted her cheeks to be certain they were dry, her conviction renewed. Such a man deserved any punishment he received.

A tuneless whistle warned her of Willie's approach. "Thar ye are, Mistress McKie."

She swallowed her guilt, seeing his familiar grin. *Dear auld Willie.*

"Ye'll be leavin' us after a', mistress? And weel ye should. On Lammas, just as ye planned." The elderly servant pointed to the cradle at her feet. "Is that tae go in the wagon?"

"Oh, Willie…" She clasped her hands to hold them steady. " 'Tis too heavy for you."

"I've mair strength than ye think, mem. Watch and see if yer auld Willie canna handle a cradle fu' o blankets—"

"And books," Rose said quickly. "Large ones."

Willie grabbed the cradle, groaning as he lifted it. "Feels mair like bricks." He stumbled forward but did not lose his grip, pointing her cradle toward the front door.

Rose followed close behind, hoping to distract him. Perhaps he wouldn't notice the faint clink of coins striking wood. "'Tis ill luck, I'm told, to flit with an empty cradle."

"Verra unchancie, that." Willie grunted, shifting his load. If he heard the telltale jingle, he did not comment on it. The man *was* losing his hearing.

Rose walked between him and the other servants, who were gathered some distance across the lawn. The gray skies had darkened substantially, and the air smelled like damp linens. "Willie," she began, leaning close to his ear to be sure he heard her, "I've a favor to ask. For Mr. McBride's sake. Once we depart this morning, might you lock the front door behind us? And leave it locked? No one should open it but my father when he arrives home on Tuesday. For luck, you know."

"Aye, mem." Willie hefted the cradle into the wagon. "Ye can be sure yer faither wull be the first ane through that door."

Fifty-Two

And hearts resolved and hands prepared
The blessings they enjoy to guard.

TOBIAS GEORGE SMOLLETT

Aren't you a lucky lad, enjoying your dinner beneath the yew tree?"
Leana dabbed the last of the minced lamb from Ian's chin. With
all the commotion in the house, she'd chosen a quiet spot out of doors
to feed her son. "Your last meal at Auchengray," she told him wistfully,
heading toward the front of the house.

Eliza saw her coming and stepped forward to claim Ian. "I'll hold
the boy. I'm sure ye've meikle tae do afore we leave."

House servants and day laborers alike were gathered on Auchengray's lawn, stacking goods yet to be loaded. Leana could only imagine
what the two maidservants newly fee'd from Edingham must think of
the family's hasty departure.

Near the house stood the rustic conveyance that would transport
them to Glentrool. Despite its unpainted wooden sides and rough
appearance, it was larger than Leana had expected. Not a two-wheeled
cart drawn by oxen, but a four-wheeled wagon pulled by a pair of Mr.
Bell's light draft horses. As she drew near, Willie pushed the family
cradle farther into the wagon, his face as red as a fresh-picked radish.
Rose hovered beside him. Her cheeks were flushed too.

Leana greeted them with an apology. "Pardon me for shirking my
duties."

Rose wet her lips. "We've managed, haven't we, Willie?"

" 'Tis guid I've not anither cradle tae lift." Amid his wrinkles, a
smile appeared. "Have ye somethin' *licht* for me tae carry, mem?"

"A cool cup of water," Leana told him. As Willie ambled off, she
touched Rose's forehead, anxious to see if she was as overheated as she
appeared. "Are you well, my sister? For I confess, you do not look it."

Rose shrugged, not meeting her gaze. "'Tis a warm day, and I've… moved more items than I should have."

"Then you've moved your last." Leana circled an arm round her shoulders and escorted her toward the others. "Jamie can tell us when we're planning to leave."

Dressed in his dark brown riding habit, he cut an impressive figure. It seemed Hugh wanted to send him on his way looking the part of a prosperous laird, and so Jamie did, from his sturdy boots, newly polished, to the sleek knot in his hair. Hastings stood nearby, whinnying as though impatient to be gone. His master held the same opinion, it appeared, consulting the skies, then scowling at the two trunks yet to be loaded.

The servants stepped back as Leana delivered Rose to Jamie's side. "Will it be much longer? Our Rose is wilting, I'm afraid."

As he looked down at his wife, his features softened. "The wagon will be ready any moment. Neda is finishing up in the kitchen."

"We'll not perish for lack of food," Leana assured him. She'd seen Neda at work earlier, filling large wicker baskets with smoked herring, pickled beef, mutton ham, and hard cheese. The rich treacle scones would be enjoyed long before they grew stale, and the gingersnaps would keep Ian and his father happy.

Neda soon appeared, baskets in hand, with Willie not far behind her, bearing two cups of water. Rose gulped them both down without ceremony, then leaned forward to whisper something in Willie's ear.

"Aye, Mistress McKie. I'll not fail ye."

"Good." Looking more refreshed, Rose lifted her skirts, her eye on the front door. "I'll only be a moment, Jamie, and then, please God, we may take our leave." She hastened toward the house, her braid swinging behind her, Willie close on her heels.

If Jamie found their behavior curious, he did not say so.

Instead, he strode toward the wagon to oversee the last of the packing, motioning for the rest of them to follow. With Lachlan and Duncan gone, Jamie wore the mantle of leadership with ease, issuing orders without barking them and directing the servants with a sure hand. A small trunk was fitted into each corner of the wagon for balance, and folded blankets served to pad the wagon bed. Strapped to the back was Ian's crib, ready to be put into service each night.

Eliza strolled up with the child in her arms. "Ye're the only traveler wha'll be sleepin' in his ain bed," she told him. When Leana held out her hands, Ian reached for her at once, his face bright as a candle.

Rose came round the side of the house, grinning to herself and patting her pocket. Annabel joined them, her red hair neatly tamed beneath her cap, her eyes wide with anticipation. "Will we be startin' suin, mem? 'Tis a *weatherful* sky."

Jamie chuckled. "Your bonnets should spare you the worst of the rain." He held out his hand. "Maidservants first. Your carriage awaits."

Even with the *lowpin-on stane* and Davie Tait's assistance, climbing into the wagon proved a most ungraceful affair. Annabel's shoe slipped off the mounting stone, then Eliza misjudged the height of the side and caught her skirt, landing in a heap. Neda, who'd watched the proceedings with a furrowed brow, climbed in with great care, guided by both shepherds.

"I'm goin' wi' ye as far as Kingsgrange," she explained. "I ken ye'll help me not arrive wi' onie broken bones."

Watching the kind woman take her place in the wagon, Leana breathed a prayer of thanks that their parting would be delayed a bit longer. Of all the farewells this day, her final moments with Neda would be the most difficult.

Seventeen years ago when Agness McBride had slipped from this world to the next, it was Neda Hastings who'd held Leana's hand through the long and terrible ordeal of losing her mother. Neda's hands had also prepared her meals and pressed her gowns and combed her hair and taught her to cook and sew and spin. Less than a year ago when Ian McKie was born, it was Neda's hand that had clasped hers once again, providing strength and courage through a long day of labor.

Dear Neda. Leana might not miss her father. But she would greatly miss Neda Hastings.

Only the two sisters had yet to board the wagon. Jamie slipped his arm round Rose's waist. "If you lads won't mind, I'll see my wife safely boarded." With that he swept Rose off her feet and handed her over to the astonished maids, who reached up to steady their mistress.

She blushed to her roots. "Goodness, Jamie!" The others laughed, for Rose was clearly pleased by her husband's attention.

Then Jamie turned toward Leana and slowly extended his hands. Leana held her breath. *Nae, Jamie.*

He smiled and said, "Ian next."

"Oh." Her heart started beating again. After bussing the boy's cheek, Leana handed him over to his father. "Who is going to his new home? Might it be you, Ian McKie?" She watched as Jamie leaned over the wagon side and delivered Ian into Rose's waiting lap.

"And now you, Leana," Jamie said, lifting her off the ground before she had time to protest and depositing her into the wagon with ease. "We'll not have expectant mothers risking their bairns' lives on this expedition." He looked round. "Anyone else, or are five women and a young lad quite enough?"

Rose bent forward, inclining her ear to Ian's babbling. "Your son says, 'Nae mair lassies.'" She looked like a child herself, delighted to be embarking on an adventure.

Not all were blithe to see them leave. Willie, Hugh, and the remaining servants stood in a ragged line, bonnets in hand. Their faces were long, and the sadness in their eyes unmistakable. "God be wi' ye," Willie called out, his voice weak.

Leana reached out to shake their hands one by one as the wagon lurched forward. "The LORD bless thee, and keep thee." She did not try to hide her tears.

"Farewell!" Rose waved Ian's little fingers with her own.

With Jamie leading on his mount, and Rab and Davie handling the wagon reins, they started down the drive at last, bound for the winding road west.

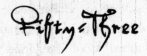

Fifty-Three

Roads are wet where'er one wendeth,
And with rain the thistle bendeth,
And the brook cries like a child!

MARY HOWITT

Rainfall greeted them not half a mile from Auchengray's drive. Big, warm drops splattered against the wood of the wagon as Rab called out to the horses, urging them toward the line of trees that banked the road.

Leana huddled beneath a blanket with her back to the driver's seat, watching Auchengray disappear behind a gray veil of water. The rain muffled the bleating of the ewes. Odd to see the lambs gone and only their mothers remaining.

"Glensone," Rose called out, waving as though Peter Drummond were standing at the window waiting for them to roll past.

Leana lifted her hand toward Troston Hill Farm, her heart aching. *Jessie.* So many farewells never spoken. She would write to their parish friends—few in number but loyal—and offer her apologies for their unexpected departure.

By the time the wagon reached the sheltering canopy of trees, Ian was miserable and whining loudly. Rose lifted him up. "Will you take him, Leana?"

"Gladly." Ian crawled into her lap with a weary sigh, seeking the comfort of his thumb and his mother. "Not to worry, lad. The rain will leave us alone for a bit." Leana took advantage of their leafy covering and removed her straw hat, shaking it over the side of the wagon.

Lochend soon came into view. Reeds poked above the rippling surface, and trees bowed over the shoreline, paying homage. On the western shore stood Maxwell Park, the finest manor house in the parish. In years past Lord and Lady Maxwell had singled out Rose, offering to introduce her to society at their Hogmanay Ball. Invitations to Maxwell Park had ceased when Auchengray's marriage scandal unfolded. Society closed its doors, and neighbors became strangers.

There were some things about Newabbey parish Leana would not miss.

When their wagon emerged from the trees, the downpour had already eased considerably. "Better," Neda declared. The dark clouds were moving east at a good clip, taking the rain with them.

Jamie appeared moments later astride Hastings, water sluicing off his tricornered hat. He surveyed the group like an army officer assessing damage. "It appears you've weathered our first bout of rain. Maintain a smart pace, lads."

The narrow track of road pointed southwest to Dalbeaty. Leana propped Ian up on his bare feet, holding him tight. "You've not viewed Lowtis Hill from this side. Look how big it is." Ian tipped back his head, eyes widening, as if he understood her perfectly. "See the black cattle on those far hills?"

Annabel and Eliza joined in, finding new things for the boy to see, while Neda busied herself rearranging the stores in her baskets. After complaining earlier, Rose now sat quietly, mile after undulating mile, hands folded across her rounded waist.

The rain had all but stopped, and the sky had lightened in the west when the granite ruins of Edingham Castle commanded their attention. "Look, Ian." Leana gestured at the decrepit tower house overgrown with ivy. "See that turnpike stair? Now it leads only to the sky."

Jamie rode up, bearing a look of resolve. "Edingham Farm is across the way. As the lads and I have business here, Neda will take the wagon reins. I trust you ken the way to Kingsgrange?"

"I do." Neda stood with the grace of a woman half her age. "Duncan and I have visited thar mony a time." Rab and Davie climbed down to make room for her, taking their collies with them, as Neda settled onto the driver's seat. "Yer ladies will be weel leuked after, I promise ye that."

"I've nae doubt." Jamie's obvious fondness for Neda warmed his words. "Kingsgrange is fortunate to have chosen you as their new housekeeper. I've never known anyone more capable."

"Weel…" Neda sniffed, lifting her apron to her nose. "I pray Duncan and I will find a guid hame wi' the laird and his folk. Ye'll not forget us, Mr. McKie?"

He reached for her hand. "Not in a lifetime."

Bless you, Jamie. Leana looked away, giving them a moment to bid each other farewell.

"We will meet at Buittle kirk in a few hours." Jamie swung his mount toward the farm gate. "Rab kens a farm near the kirk where we can spend the night. I'll ride ahead and make the arrangements once we've taken…ah, herded the lambs from Edingham." He turned to face Leana, studying her so closely she felt her cheeks warming. "Are you strong enough to handle the horses? In your…condition?"

"I cannot ride in a saddle, but I can perch on a wooden seat and hold the reins." She leaned forward to have another look at the draft horses. "Those are seasoned mares and none too lively."

Jamie grunted, as if not quite agreeing with her. "Neda, see that she does not climb down from this wagon, for I'll not be there to assist her."

Neda pretended to scowl. "She'll not move from her perch. Ye have me wird."

"Rose, you're to remain in the wagon as well." Jamie nodded at each woman in turn before tugging on the reins. "Until Buittle kirk, then."

The herds stood back as Neda called to the horses, sending the wagon forward. She seemed comfortable with her duties, and the horses responded to her lead as they made their way through the small village of Dalbeaty. The sway of the wagon and the steady clack of the wheels soon lulled Ian to sleep. Leana tucked a dry blanket round him and eased him onto the wagon bed next to her, then discovered her legs had fallen asleep beneath his weight. Feeling came back in her thighs with a painful tingling, even as the babe inside her stirred, jabbing her hard.

Her sister looked uncomfortable as well. "You've been quiet, Rose. Is something wrong?"

She rolled her eyes. "Other than leaving the only home I've ever known? And facing day after day of traveling like this?"

"Aye." Leana smiled at little. "Other than those two things, are you well?"

"Well enough." Rose looked the other way, ending their conversation.

Leana guessed the problem: Her sister's birthday was in the morn. She would make certain the occasion was duly celebrated.

Once past Dalbeaty proper the wagon eased onto a northbound road and began climbing. Leana turned round to kneel behind the driver's seat, her elbows resting beside Neda, her knees padded by a blanket. One nagging question would not be silenced. "Neda, are they expecting you at Kingsgrange?"

The older woman's ever-present smile faded. "Nae. They're leukin' for us baith on Wednesday. But Duncan…" Her grip on the reins tightened. "Duncan bade me leave afore him. Said he didna want me at Auchengray whan…whan yer faither came through the door."

Oh, Neda. Leana touched her arm. "Duncan is a very wise man."

"I canna help but worry what will happen tae that guid husband o' mine whan yer faither kens the truth. Duncan says…" She cleared her throat. "He says, the wickit shall fall by his ain wickedness."

"Duncan is right." Leana offered Neda her handkerchief. "My father has brought this on himself. Jamie is not at fault for claiming his lambs, nor is Duncan to blame for helping him." Saying the words, Leana realized she believed them. If righting such wrongs required diverting lambs to their proper owner or slipping away without Lachlan's consent, so be it.

"The way o' the wickit niver pleases the Almighty," Neda murmured behind her handkerchief. "But I believe Duncan pleases the Laird. 'Tis a' the man thinks aboot."

Wanting to comfort her, Leana rubbed her hand across Neda's back, grateful for well-trained horses that clopped along, needing little guidance. "Even if they are not expecting you at Kingsgrange, I know they will make you welcome."

Neda's smile returned. "Mary will pave the way for her auld mither. I'll start by cookin' a tasty puddin'."

Leana laughed softly. "That will do the trick."

Much as she longed to continue their conversation, her knees and back ached, forcing her to resume her seat on the wagon bed. She gazed across the river as they passed the mote, an earthen mound that reminded her of molded pudding on a plate. Annabel and Eliza sat with their heads tipped together, speaking in hushed voices, while Rose had dropped off to sleep, napping along with Ian. Left to her own thoughts, Leana closed her eyes and prayed for Duncan in Lockerbie and Jamie at Edingham: two courageous men doing what they could to honor God and see justice done.

After a gradual uphill climb, the wagon reached the crossroads at Haugh of Urr, then continued on past Spottes Hall, surrounded with woods. The road wound through another two miles of rolling farmland before Neda eased the wagon to a stop at the entrance to Kingsgrange. " 'Tis a fine property with a fine laird," she said, nodding at the impressive gate. "He suffered badly whan the Ayr Bank failed in '73, owin' tae a' the stock he held. But he recovered weel, as ye can see."

Enclosed by a stone wall as tall as Jamie, Kingsgrange was far grander than Auchengray. The thought comforted Leana, knowing Neda and Duncan would live in such a place.

Neda rose halfway, then turned, helping Leana to her feet. "Sit here, lass."

As Leana eased onto the well-warmed driver's seat and grasped the reins, Neda nimbly climbed down, then gave her careful directions to the Buittle kirk—the landmarks to watch for, the signposts that pointed the way. "Ye'll *foord* the river just past Redcastle. And go at an easy pace, aye?"

"I shall," Leana promised, her vision blurring. *Dear Neda.* Was it really good-bye?

Neda had a kind word for each of the maidservants, leaving them sniffling, then pressed a kiss to Rose's brow and laid her hand on Ian's sleeping form. With Eliza's help, Neda unloaded her trunk and a small valise, parking both at the gate. "I'll send ane o' the lads oot tae fetch them," she said, returning to Leana's side. "Dinna fret aboot me, lass. I'll be fine."

Leana looked into Neda's face, her tears flowing in earnest now. "When we parted in March, I knew I'd see you again. But this…this time…"

"Och, dearie!" Neda hung her head. "Please dinna say the wirds, for I canna bear it."

Undone, Leana leaned over and pressed a kiss to the ruffled white cap that still smelled of starch. "'Tis like leaving behind my own mother."

"Nae, nae." Neda waved her handkerchief in protest. "Yer ain mither was an angel from *heiven*. I'm a puir hoosekeeper wha's been honored tae care for ye."

"You did more than care." Leana gently lifted her chin. "You loved me when no one else did."

Neda tried to dry her cheeks, but her hands shook, and the linen was already wet. "Niver did a woman have an easier task than luvin' Leana McBride."

They tarried a moment longer by the well-shaded gate—hands clasped tight, hearts in tune, a thousand thoughts unspoken yet shared. When Ian began to stir behind her, Leana was reminded of her duties. And of Jamie, who would be expecting them.

She gazed down at Neda for the last time, memorizing her kind face as she whispered, "Godspeed."

Neda touched her cheek, then took a step back. "The Lord preserveth a' them that luve him. And weel ye do, Leana. Weel ye do."

Fifty-Four

While shepherds drive the fainting flock
To the cool stream, or shelt'ring rock.
HENRY SEASON

E dingham Farm was a mile behind them, yet Jamie's heart still
pounded in his chest.

Thomas Henderson, the new proprietor of Edingham, could not
have been more accommodating. "You are here to claim your lambs,
you say?" He'd run a meaty hand over his beard while considering the
notion. "Since Mr. McBride has already paid a generous rent for the
grazing land, I can hardly protest your taking them sooner than
expected." He'd eyed Rab and Davie standing some distance off, collies
by their sides. "Looks like you have two able lads to handle things for
you." Then he'd stuck out his hand. "Godspeed, Mr. McKie. And do
give your uncle my regards."

A brief discussion, a matter of minutes, and the lambs were his.
Clearly the man did not know Lachlan McBride very well. It did not
seem the time or place to educate him.

Jamie and his shepherds wasted little time gathering the sheep and
herding them south. They did not take the road to Dalbeaty but skirted
round it, driving the flock onto softer ground. Gravel hurt their unshod
feet, and passersby made them skittish. Cattle drovers often covered ten
or twelve miles a day; Jamie hoped to manage six to eight, a less gruel-
ing pace. They were livestock, aye, but dependent on their shepherd's
good care.

He rode well to the rear, while Rab and Davie worked as a team,
walking behind the lambs to drive them forward. Their collies trotted
along either side of the flock, careful to maintain the proper distance—
close enough to establish control, far enough not to frighten the lambs.

"Mr. McKie, we're comin' up on the Urr Water." Rab Murray had fallen back to consult with him, his brow damp from the afternoon's efforts. "I'm aimin' for Buittle Castle. Lady Devorgilla's place, ye ken."

Jamie glanced across the river at the ruinous remains of a courtyard. "I don't believe the woman will be having us in for tea."

Rab grinned. "She's been gone five hunder years, nigh tae the day. Mither tae a king, she was. Dochter tae the laird o' Galloway."

"And put to rest at Sweetheart Abbey." A slight tug at his conscience, a fleeting memory, no more. Newabbey parish was part of his past now. "Make certain the lambs don't reach the Urr before we do, for they'll not care for the look of that water."

Rab stared down at the river. "I don't care for it meself. That plump-shower made the river rise, just as ye said it might."

Jamie dismounted and loosely tied the reins to a stout clump of broom, letting Hastings feed on the moist grass. As he surveyed the river and the small, flat-bottomed skiff the lads were carrying down to the waterside, Jamie formulated a plan for getting his lambs across the Urr without getting them wet.

Moments later he was seated in the borrowed boat, oars in hand. "Climb aboard, Davie." He ferried the herd and his collie across to the west bank, rowing upstream against the current. To spare his riding coat and hat, he left them draped across a blackthorn bush, then rowed back to the east bank, where Rab was rounding up a few lambs at a time.

Seated at the square end of the boat, Jamie stretched his legs apart in order to hold the skiff steady and guard the lambs as they were lifted aboard. They bleated pitifully, shaking all over, from their mottled black noses to the stubs of their docked tails. Though the river was not especially wide or fast moving, more than one terrified lamb tried to leap from the boat, nearly capsizing the craft. Jamie rowed as fast and hard as he could, back and forth across the Urr—a dozen times, two dozen times—until his shoulders ached and his shirt was drenched with sweat.

" 'Tis the last o' them," Rab said, relief apparent on his face. His collie paced along the riverbank while the final lamb was loaded into the skiff. "Ane mair trip back tae get the twa o' us, if ye won't mind, sir. I'll be glad tae handle the rowin'."

Jamie merely nodded, conserving his energy as he started across.

Earlier he'd ruled out driving the lambs several miles north to cross the old Urr Bridge; now he wondered if it might have been the better choice. At least when they traversed the River Dee at Tongland, they'd be herding the lambs over a sturdy bridge, all in a flock.

Lachlan's warning from months past chided him. *Sheep will not ford moving water.* "Aye, aye," Jamie grumbled, his gaze fixed on a lamb at the far end of the boat. Its eyes were rolling in its head as a thin yellow stream ran down its leg. "Steady now, lassie." He kept his voice even. "Don't be looking at that water."

As the skiff reached midriver, the lamb suddenly bolted, leaping over the side and landing with a sickening splash. *"Rab!"* Jamie shouted. The shepherd was already wading into the chest-deep water. Both collies started barking, signaling their distress.

Jamie rowed harder than ever. "Can you swim to him, Rab? Can you reach him?" But the lad was better suited to land than to water; his flailing arms did not carry him any faster than the current.

The instant the skiff reached the bank, Jamie vaulted to the grass, ordering Davie to unload the lambs as he shucked his boots. Wading into the Urr, he dove forward, plowing his arms through the water. He finally spotted the lamb just below the surface and grabbed for its leg. Slick from the water and the wool's natural grease, it slipped from his grasp. When he lunged for it a second time, Jamie got a firmer grip and pulled the lamb to him, struggling to lift it above the water so it could breathe, all the while trying to find a toehold on the uneven river bottom. The water nearly covered his chest, but at least he could breathe, and the lamb was out of danger.

Jamie headed for the east bank of the river, fighting the current and his own exhaustion until he reached the grassy edge. He deposited the weary lamb there first, then dragged himself out of the river, shaking the water from his sleeves and slicking back his hair. Cradling the lamb round his shoulders, he climbed the embankment, grabbing handfuls of weeds and brush to pull himself up, then walked upstream. He found his horse precisely where he'd left him, patiently grazing, oblivious to the drama in the river below. Gripping the lamb's hind legs to keep it from sliding off his shoulders, Jamie eased onto his mount.

Just as Jamie suspected, the long-legged gelding forded the river without difficulty, his sleek, black head well above water. Hastings charged up the other side, whinnying when they reached level ground. Jamie dismounted, then dropped to his knees and bent forward, lowering the lamb to the ground.

Something was wrong. Its eyes were shut tight and its limbs unresponsive. With a growing uneasiness, Jamie pressed his hand over its chest, feeling for a heartbeat or an intake of breath.

Rab knelt beside him and ran his skilled hands over the animal. "Mr. McKie, I...I fear you've lost yer lamb. 'Tis me ain fault. I wasna fast enough—"

"Nae," Jamie said at once, ashamed of the tightness in his throat. "Do not blame yourself." He reclaimed his riding coat and hat from the blackthorn's prickly grasp, pulled on his discarded boots, then gathered the lifeless animal in his arms and hung it round his shoulders. "We've ninety-nine other lambs that need our attention, lad. I ken you'll take good care of them while I'll ride ahead to Little Knox Farm and make arrangements for the night. This farmer..."

"Mr. Alexander Cameron, by name. Ye'll find him most agreeable."

"If he's a friend of yours, I'm sure I will." Jamie rode on, aiming toward Buittle kirk, his thoughts scattered all over Galloway—his father in Glentrool, his brother in Wigtownshire, Duncan in Lockerbie, and Leana making her way south. Would the women be waiting at the kirk? Had Ian behaved himself in that open wagon? Jamie touched the hind legs of his lamb, reminded again of how fragile life was and how easily it could end with a single foolish leap.

Jamie caught a glimpse of a stone belfry on the next rise, and his heart quickened its pace. Was the wagon there? Could at least one burden be lifted from his shoulders? He galloped up to the kirk, relieved to find the wagon parked beneath the shade of an oak tree, all four women still aboard. Ian was propped up on Eliza's lap. Clapping.

"Well done!" Jamie could not hide his pleasure as he rode up, beaming at all of them.

Rose, however, wore a plaintive expression. "Is your lamb hurt, Jamie?"

Och, the lamb. He touched the animal's drooping head. "Nae, Rose. I'm…" He looked at Ian, glad his son was too young to understand. "I'm afraid this lamb drowned in the Urr. I thought I might offer it to our host this evening."

"A good end to a sad beginning, the auld wives say." Leana still held the reins in her hand. "You're off to meet with this farmer now?"

Jamie nodded. "Unlike in the Highlands, Galloway farmers charge for the privilege of grazing on their lands and sleeping on their plaids. Whatever hospitality Mr. Cameron offers for my paltry silver will have to suffice. As for the lads and me, we'll spend the first few nights on the braes, for the sheep are apt to stray in search of home." He looked fondly at Rose. "What of you, dear wife? Will you be wandering off in the night, trying to return whence you came?"

"Nae," she said, still eying the lost lamb. "I'll not walk through Auchengray's door again."

Fifty-Five

Gold is a living god, and rules in scorn
All earthly things but virtue.
PERCY BYSSHE SHELLEY

The gold haunted Rose in the night, then woke her before dawn, parting the curtain of her dreams with the painful light of truth. *What have you done, Rose?* There was no hope of sleep, not when guilt and remorse weighed on her conscience as heavy as the thrifite itself. She dressed in the dark, braided her hair, then tiptoed across the one-room cottage, bound for the cradle full of coins stored in the wagon, determined to think of a solution.

She could not keep the gold. And she could not give it back.

Either possibility required an explanation. She had none.

Because he is a hatesome father. Because he deserved it. Because I could.

Rose unlatched the door, wincing when the sound of scraping metal echoed off the stone walls. Leana did not stir from her sleep, nor did Ian, curled up in the crib at her feet. Annabel's light snoring went on unabated, and Eliza slept with her face beneath the sheet. None of them would notice her absence.

She stepped into the murk of a Sabbath morn, struck by the chilliness of the air after the cozy warmth of the cottage. Though the women slept two to a mattress, at least they were on beds and not on the hard, earthen floor. Breakfast would surely be porridge and a rasher of bacon, since Little Knox Farm had a sizable number of pigs. Rose heard them grunting not far off and wrinkled her nose at their pungent smell.

Somewhere to the east lay her sleeping husband and two shepherds. She'd missed Jamie's company last night, the solid warmth of him slumbering beside her. Would they ever have a quiet moment together before reaching Glentrool?

She stared across the steading at the farmhouse window where a candle flickered. Once she reached the cradle, light would not be necessary; simply touching the gold would be a sufficient reminder that she'd truly done this foolish thing and had yet to be found out.

But when Father returned on Tuesday…

Rose shuddered, thinking of the stone fire, remembering too late the words that were meant to be spoken. *Cursed shalt thou be when thou comest in, and cursed shalt thou be when thou goest out.* Her father would indeed consider himself cursed when he discovered his money box missing.

The wagon was parked at the far end of the steading, from which a row of flagstones led to the cottage. If she could find the first stone with her foot, following the rest might keep her skirts out of the muck. She did not intend to begin her seventeenth year sitting in the parish kirk reeking of the midden.

There. The first stone. A rough-cut square. Then the next. Soon she was able to anticipate each one, arriving at her destination without mishap. Using the sides of the wagon as her guide, Rose made her way round it until she reached the cradle, which Willie had fitted snugly between two baskets of linens. *Poor Willie.* The thought of involving so loyal a servant made her stomach clench. Willie was utterly innocent. And she was utterly at fault.

Heartsick, Rose reached over the side and plunged her hand inside the cradle, groping beneath the blankets until she struck gold. Grabbing a fistful of coins, she lifted them out, even as she used her left hand to smooth the blanket back in place. When she clutched the money to her chest, the coldness of the metal quickly penetrated her thin cotton gown, making her shiver.

A male voice floated across the dark lawn. "I have a pistol and no qualms about using it."

She froze. "Jamie?"

"Rose?" Footfalls muted by the damp grass. "Heavens, lass! Whatever are you doing out of doors at this hour?"

In a panic, she leaned forward and slid the icy coins inside her corset, praying they would move no farther than the cleft between her breasts. Turning round ever so slowly, she watched Jamie emerge from the mist with his pistol at his side, his clothes loosened from sleeping on the braes, his unbound hair brushing his shoulders. He had never looked more handsome. Nor more dangerous.

She glanced at his weapon and tried to sound nonchalant. "I thought you weren't going to shoot that."

"I'm not." He gave her a sleepy grin, shoving the barrel into the waist of his breeches. "Nor is it loaded. But a common thief wouldn't ken that, aye?"

"Is that what I am?" She jerked her chin at him to mask her nervousness. "A common thief?"

His grin broadened as he drew closer. "Oh, there's nothing common about you, Rose McKie."

The coins had settled at the swell of her child. Yet if Jamie touched her waist, he would feel them. He would know. *Forgive me, Jamie.* She lifted his rough hands to her cheeks, then feared he'd feel the heat of her shame. "Might I have a birthday kiss?"

Jamie responded at once. Tears stung her eyes as his mouth moved over hers, his hands cradling her face. When he leaned closer, the butt of his pistol pressed the stolen coins against her skin.

Jamie, Jamie. Could he not taste the guilt in her kiss?

A sudden realization of the truth made her clasp his shirt lest she faint: Lachlan would accuse him of thievery! The very thing Jamie had vowed would not happen. Would her father summon the sheriff? Send a party of blackguards to hunt him down?

"Nae!" Rose pulled away from his embrace. "Jamie, I…"

"Pardon me, lass." He quickly stepped back, a guilty look about him. "'Tis neither the time nor place—"

"Wheesht!" she cried softly, touching her fingers to his lips. "Do not apologize. 'Tis *your* forgiveness I need." Could she tell him? Simply confess it? Oh, but Jamie would be furious with her. What if he insisted on taking the broken thrifite back? And facing her father? *Nae, nae.* She could not bear it.

He pressed a tender kiss to her palm. "Tell me what's bothering you, Rose."

"I did not...sleep well," she told him truthfully. "If my head nods during the morning service, will you nudge me awake?"

"If you will do the same for me." He stretched, rolling his shoulders as he looked toward the eastern horizon, tinged with gold.

Buittle kirk, built of rubble in varying shades of gray, sat in the midst of the kirkyard, surrounded by headstones. The broad door hung open, daring Rose to proceed. She clutched her flowered reticule with the handful of silver and gold coins hidden inside, wrapped in a plain linen handkerchief. Her plan was simple: Deposit the morning's stolen bounty in the collection box at the door when no one was paying attention, Jamie in particular. However grateful the parish poor might be to receive her anonymous offering, Rose would be happier still to leave behind a portion of her guilt in Buittle.

She and the others from Newabbey approached the kirk, as tidy in their appearance as the farm cottage washstand allowed. Their unfamiliar faces drew curious stares from the parish folk. Jamie led the way, head held high, every inch the heir of Glentrool. His surroundings were suitably regal; Buittle kirk had welcomed ancient princes and kings. *And now, James McKie.* Emboldened by his strength, Rose lifted her chin. Aye, she could do this.

They all paused at the door to admire the single-light windows in the chancel. "Look, Ian," Leana whispered. "See how tall they are? And they face east, which means the morning sun chases away the darkness inside." Ian stretched his arms, as if he might reach the top of the arched windows, drawing everyone's attention upward, including Jamie's.

Rose saw her chance and ducked through the door unnoticed. Spying the wooden collection box attended by an elder, she nodded politely at him even as she slipped one hand inside her reticule. If he might look away just for a moment...

The bundle of coins landed in the box, barely making a sound. She spun round in time to capture Jamie's arm, pulling him forward as if she were eager for worship to begin. Instead, her trembling knees were about to give way. Though her purse was lighter by a few sovereigns, her heart was not. So much gold remained. None of it hers.

When the service ended at one, the travelers found a shady spot on the edge of the kirkyard, intending to dine before resuming their journey. No sooner were they settled onto the worn plaid, surrounded by baskets of food, than Leana produced two gifts, one folded inside a sheet of paper, the other wrapped with fabric and a pink silk ribbon. "Many happy returns of the day, dearie."

Rose reached for the plain one first.

"From Father," Leana said. "He left your present with me a few days ago."

A single gold sovereign caught the sunlight, winking up at Rose.

Jamie grimaced. "*Now* the man is generous."

" 'Tis yours." Rose pressed the coin into Jamie's hands, feeling ill. "For our lodging."

She slipped off the pink ribbon and opened Leana's gift: a much-loved pair of silk gloves. Agness McBride had worn them on her wedding day. So had Leana. Delicately stitched in pure white, the gloves were presented to Leana as the oldest daughter. Except for very special occasions, they remained wrapped in linen and tucked away for safekeeping. Until now.

"Leana, I cannot…" Rose barely touched the gloves, as if they held some unseen magic. "These were…Mother's."

Leana leaned forward to lay her hand on top of Rose's, like one conferring a blessing. "On the anniversary of our mother's death and your joyous birth, I cannot think of anyone who deserves this gift more than you do."

Rose pinched her lips shut, and still they trembled. "I deserve… nothing. Yet you are…" She looked up, praying the gratitude showed in her eyes. "You are always so good to me, Leana. So…kind."

Leana touched her cheek. "I am more penniless than kind. Since I have no silver of my own, I chose something of great value to me, hoping it might please you."

"*Please* me?" Rose sniffed. " 'Tis the dearest gift you could have given me." She carefully pulled on the gloves and held them up for all to see, smiling at Leana through a sheen of tears. In years past she'd borrowed them from her sister's glove drawer. Now they were hers to wear forever.

Jamie laid a small woolen pouch in her hands. "I fear my present cannot possibly measure up to Leana's, but 'tis given with an equal portion of love."

After removing her gloves so she could open the slender drawstring, Rose shook out the contents and gasped with delight. Cupped in her bare palm, a sterling brooch featuring a pair of ravens gleamed in the midday light. "The McKie crest! Wherever did you…"

"Dumfries. From the same silversmith who made your father's wedding quaich." Jamie tugged at her braid. "Like your sister, my resources were limited. I wish it were made of gold, Rose."

"I'm not particularly…fond of gold." She pricked her finger pinning the brooch to her gown. "I much prefer silver."

"And I meikle prefer food," Rab Murray announced, laughing as he opened Neda's well-stocked basket of provisions.

Rose was glad for the distraction, however temporary. The problem of her father's gold would not vanish on its own. And Tuesday grew closer by the hour.

When their stomachs were satisfied and the crumbs brushed away, the men doffed their coats and helped the women load the wagon in preparation for the day's journey. "Just five miles or so," Jamie said, "since we're getting a late start. We'll stop at Rhonehouse for the night. Our lasses will be lodging at the Crown. The lads and I will be sleeping on Keltonhill, watching the Lammas bonfire."

Rose stared at him, an idea taking shape in her mind. *Keltonhill. Kelton parish.* "Will we be riding past…Kelton kirk?"

"I imagine you will." Curiosity lit his eyes. "Did you want to see the place, Rose?"

"Aye," she breathed. Kelton kirk would have a collection box by the door, and so would every parish kirk they passed. She'd dispose of all the stolen gold before they reached Glentrool! And could not the shattered thrifite be fed into the Lammas bonfire a piece at a time? Without any evidence, Jamie could hardly be arrested for theft.

Rose put on her brightest birthday smile. "Jamie, how many parishes will we travel through?"

He splayed both hands, counting. "Buittle, Kelton, Tongland, Twyneholm, Girthon, Anwoth, Kirkmabreck, Monnigaff. Eight in all," he finished. "Ten, if you count Newabbey and Urr."

Nae, I'll not count those. That night while the others slept she would tear up one of her cotton shifts to make pouches, divide the coins evenly, and be prepared to bless the poor in every parish between here and her new home. 'Twas her only hope, the only possible solution: Give the gold to the Almighty and let him do with it as he pleased.

Then forgive me, Lord. Please, forgive me.

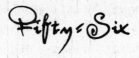

Fifty-Six

Being myself no stranger to suffering,
I have learned to relieve the sufferings of others.
VIRGIL

Her sister was in pain. Leana saw it on her face and in her posture, in the way her hands shook for no reason and her eyes shimmered with tears while she stared at the passing countryside.

Nor was she eating well. Sunday evening at the Crown their supper had been potted *hough* shaped in a fancy mold. Rose had only poked at the well-seasoned meat and barely touched her apple tart.

An hour later at sunset, when the Lammas bonfire was lit—an enormous mound of dried bracken and heather, broken furniture and fallen timber—Rose had insisted on helping the neighborhood shepherds add more kindling, an anxious look about her as she tossed splintery fragments of pine onto the roaring fire.

Most telling of all, en route to Rhonehouse, Rose had begged the others to let her visit the parish kirk in Kelton.

"But no one is here, dearie," Leana had told her, drawing the horses to a stop as she'd eyed the empty kirk and its sagging collection of headstones. "The afternoon service must have ended hours ago."

"'Tis…better that way," Rose had said, disembarking from the wagon, a plaid draped round her shoulders even though the weather was quite warm. "I'll not be a minute."

Leana had bent down to catch her hand. "Did you mean to pray, Rose?"

"Oo aye." Her sister's sober expression had brightened a little. "Indeed I shall."

Rose had ducked in the kirk door and stayed less than a minute before she came bounding out, her step lighter and her mood improved, however briefly. Jamie would not be pleased to hear she'd climbed in and out of the wagon without his aid. But he'd been a half mile west tending his lambs. And Rose had seemed adamant about her mission.

Leana could hardly have refused her so minor a request. Stop and pray? Aye, they could do that. Especially if it might ease her sister's mind or heal her body. She would also give Rose a few drops of tincture of St. John's wort before bed and add some damask rose oil to her washbowl in the morning to calm her nerves.

After yestreen's winding route through Kelton parish, this day found them heading southwest, following the path of the Dee through hilly farmlands. Hedgerows, rather than dry stane dykes, lined the roads and divided the dairy farms. Though the women could not see the river, the lambs and lads remained well in sight beneath a hopeful sky of blue gray clouds with a shimmering edge of yellow.

Leana invited Rose to sit beside her so they might keep each other company while the maids cared for Ian in the wagon bed. Eliza entertained the child with endless games and rhymes. Neiveie-Nick-Nack was his favorite, with Eliza hiding a button in one hand and chanting, "Neiveie Neiveie nick nack, what one will ye tak?" Annabel practiced reading from a volume of poetry Rose had produced from her pocket that morning. Stolen from their father's library, Leana feared. Would Lachlan write them at Glentrool, demanding the book be sent back?

They maintained a slow but steady pace until early afternoon when the party stopped for dinner. Gathered round the wagon, they shared a cold meal prepared by the Crown's able cook and swapped opinions of the countryside, edged with hills that framed the rugged, uncultivated ground.

"Our view niver changes," Rab confessed. "Davie and I have been leukin' at lambs' tails since Dalbeaty."

Jamie grinned. "The view from astride my horse is markedly better. I can see their heads *and* their tails."

"Ah," Rose said, rising to their challenge, "but *we* see their woolly legs."

"And ours as well?" Rab teased her, making all the women turn pink. While Jamie was dressed as a gentleman, the lads were barelegged with shepherds' plaids kilted round them. Jamie scolded Rab for his impropriety, but Leana was grateful to see some color in Rose's cheek for any reason.

At meal's end Jamie mounted Hastings, nodding at the lads as they headed toward his flocks and the collies tending them. "We'll do a bit of salmon fishing in the Dee before we cross the bridge at Tongland—"

"Tongland?" Rose pounced on the word as if it were a wood mouse and she a hungry cat. "Might we stop at the kirk while you fish?"

"I suspect Leana will be eager to carry on to Twyneholm and your Aunt Meg's, but of course, you may visit the kirk." Jamie barely hid his amusement. "If you have any secrets, be warned: They say tongues wag in Tongland."

Rose gaped at him in astonishment. "Is *that* where the name comes from?"

"Do not let your husband tease you so." Leana admonished Jamie with her eyes. "The parish is shaped like one. Hence, the name."

Rose responded by sticking out her tongue.

Jamie trotted off, laughing. "Get thee to a kirk, lassie, and mend your ill-mannered ways."

"Haud yer wheesht!" Rose called after him, though her laugh equaled his.

"Sleep well, fair wife." He lifted his hand in parting. "We'll see you in the morn at your aunt's cottage."

Leana signaled the horses, sending the wagon forward. Such lively banter! Notably different than her own conversations with Jamie. With her, he was more serious. Thoughtful. Vulnerable. With Rose, Jamie matched his clever wit against her spirited nature. No wonder Jamie had chosen her sister from the first. Now that they were free to love each other without impediment, it was obvious that they did. Very much.

"Stop, Leana!"

Startled, she jerked the reins, bringing the horses to a ragged halt.

"There it is!" Rose pointed toward a cluster of buildings on the far side of the river. "Tongland kirk."

They continued past the signpost for Culdoach Farm, then turned sharply and began their steep descent to the river. Leana paused short of the bridge, listening to see if they had the old stone bridge to themselves, for the arch did not allow her to see the road beyond it. Gamely urging the horses across, she drove them into Tongland parish, then followed the road to a wooded glade, where the preaching house stood above the rushing waters of the Dee.

Rose climbed down before Leana could insist she wait for one of the maids to help her, then she yanked the tattered plaid round her shoulders.

Leana moved toward the edge of the driver's seat. "Would you like me to pray with you?"

"Nae!" Her sister's face went white. "You may pray *here,* of course." She hastened toward the old kirk. "I shan't be long."

Leana watched her sister tug open the wooden door. *Poor Rose.* Expectant mothers did many a strange thing to ensure a safe delivery. Leana dutifully bowed her head and prayed for her sister's health.

When Rose did not return at once, Leana bided her time studying the older building with its rectangular windows in the gable, topped with a birdcage belfry. The wall facing her was surrounded by well-worn rubble, as though it had been there much longer than the rest. Not uncommon in Galloway, where new kirks were built from the remains of previous ones—sometimes in the very same spot, sometimes a stone's throw away. The ruins were left standing before God and man, roofless and abandoned, surrounded by gravestones long worn smooth by the elements.

The door swung open, and Rose appeared, led from the kirk by a crooked-back man full of years. The beadle, Leana guessed. He was chattering away like a magpie, while Rose slowed her steps to match his. Leana could see her sister was agitated, with her hands clutching her plaid and her eyes wide.

Leana tipped back her hat in greeting. "Who's this you've found?"

"This is Mr. Lang!" Rose blurted out. "He can tell you all about the kirk. I…I've left something behind." She turned and practically ran across the kirkyard, the door not closing behind her before she was out of doors again, looking greatly relieved.

Mr. Lang assisted Rose into the wagon and did indeed tell all four women more than they cared to know about the history of the parish kirk and the ancient thorns that marked the glebe boundary. When he started describing the bridge over the Tarff Water leading to Twyneholm, Leana saw her chance.

"That is precisely where we're bound, sir. You have our thanks for sharing your…store of knowledge. God be with you." The horses moved at her command, and Mr. Lang's gray head faded from view.

Rose sat wrapped in a silence thicker than her plaid. Leana slipped an arm round her sister and planted a light kiss on her forehead, then gently released her and guided the wagon onto the road bound west for Burnside Cottage.

"If there is something specific I might pray for, Rose. Something I might do…"

"Nae." Her voice was small. "'Twill be over soon."

"Our journey, you mean?"

Rose nodded but said nothing more.

The sharp tang of salt filled the moist air as they crossed a bridge no wider than their wagon and entered Twyneholm parish. Two more miles, most of it uphill, and they would reach the village. How good it would be to see Aunt Meg! She was not expecting them; there'd been no way to let her know they were coming. But she seldom vacated her cottage for long. Leana was certain that when they knocked on Burnside's door, Meg would be there to welcome them.

Indeed she was.

"Leana? Och, *Rose!* Can it really be you?" Aunt Meg swept them through the door like pennies spilled from her purse, not wanting to miss a single one. "This must be Ian. What a braw wee lad! And who are these bright-eyed lassies? Such lovely red hair you have, dearie."

Burnside Cottage was suddenly bursting with women. At Meg's insistence, they each found a creepie or a stool or a chair. She, however, claimed Ian, who stared at the older woman with a look of confusion.

"Do you ken what you're staring at, laddie? I'm your mother in forty years." Aunt Meg winked at Leana. "She'll be holding your sons and your grandsons the same way I'm holding you. With this silver hair and these blue gray eyes."

Leana blinked away tears, amazed at the thought of holding her son's children someday. Aye, even his *granbairns,* if she lived to see such a blessing. When Ian began to fuss, Meg handed him over, then loosely embraced mother and child. "You look wonderful, Leana. How I've missed you."

"And I you, Auntie." Leana drank in her familiar scents: honey from her hives and coal from her cooking hearth and yeast from her baking. "We'd hoped to stay 'til the morn's morn. Might we bide for one night?"

"Will you not stay two?" Meg looked them over, counting heads. "I've kept your hurlie bed made up just in case you hastened back to me, so we'll put Rose in that. You can share my bed, Leana, and I've blankets and heather ticks for your maids. We'll set up Ian's crib in this corner, away from the window."

The sleeping arrangements for her tiny cottage sorted out, Meg next saw to supper. Sharp cheese and oatcakes baked fresh that morning were served on her good silver plate, taken down from its place of honor over the hearth. Her table was so small that two women at a time took their turns eating supper. Rose excused herself to take a short walk—"for a bit of fresh air," she said—and soon returned, flushed but smiling.

"Now that I've fed you properly," Meg said, "and promised you a place to lay your head, I expect to be paid in full." She held out her hand as if waiting for their coins. After an awkward moment, Meg cackled the way a woman of sixty years might. "Not in silver, mind you. In stories."

Leana sagged to a chair in relief. "We have plenty of those. Why don't you start, Rose? I'll warrant you've an interesting tale to share. Has anything happened to you since we left Newabbey?"

"Someone else go first." Rose's smile faded. "I'm not…feeling well."

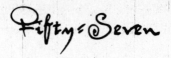

Fifty-Seven

Fear is an ague, that forsakes
And haunts, by fits, those whom it takes.
SAMUEL BUTLER

Drink this, dearie."

Rose stared at the steaming cup of tea, wrinkling her nose at the bittersweet scent. "Betony, you say?"

"From the old Celtic words meaning 'good for the head.'" Leana pushed the cup closer. "'Tis said to calm the nerves and chase away fear. I've only given you a bittie of it in your tea, Rose. When it comes time to deliver your babe, we'll see you have plenty."

They sat across from each other at Aunt Meg's table, the first light of morning filtering through the curtains. Round the cottage the others were still fast asleep, burying their heads beneath their plaids to escape the dawn. Leana often awakened early; Rose seldom did. Fear, like a rooster's crow, had stirred her from bed.

It was Tuesday.

Half the gold was blessedly gone. Four heavy bundles, each the size of a man's fist, remained hidden in the wooden cradle with the dreaded gold cord. Yestreen's furtive visit to Twyneholm kirk had unfolded more smoothly than the earlier one to Tongland. Och, that Mr. Lang! When his gray head had popped up from behind the pews he'd been cleaning, Rose had almost swooned. Did he discover the coins soon after they'd departed? Might he try to learn who'd left such a fortune for the poor of Tongland? Please God, he would *not*.

The same errand in Twyneholm had been easier to manage. Having worshiped in the parish before, she remembered precisely where the collection box rested. She'd climbed the hill from her aunt's cottage, then crept inside the empty kirk, deposited the coins, and returned to

Burnside Cottage before anyone missed her. Though it would be easier to leave all the gold in one place, such a sum might also catch a sheriff's attention.

It was Morna Douglas's treasure too, she reminded herself. On that count, Rose felt very guilty indeed. She consoled herself with the thought that, in her father's keeping, the money would have been as far beyond the woman's reach as it was in the Twyneholm parish poor box.

Rose hid behind her teacup, certain no one suspected a thing. Not even her sister.

"When Father finds out…" Leana began, sending Rose's heart into her throat. "When he realizes we've all left Auchengray, which do you suppose will vex him more: Jamie taking the lambs that were rightfully his or Duncan making that possible?"

Rose waited for her wildly beating heart to ease. *Neither one, my sister.* She knew what would vex Father most.

"Dearie?" Leana reached across the table to brush back a tendril of her hair. "Please tell me what's wrong. You've not been yourself since we left Auchengray. Deliriously happy one moment, *dowly* the next. Are you…in pain, Rose?"

Aye. She hung her head. *More than you know.*

Leana said nothing for a moment, though Rose still felt the light touch of her hand against her hair, comforting her. "I am concerned for your health and that of your bairn. Though Twyneholm village has no physician, Aunt Meg tells me a midwife resides not three doors down. Would you mind if we asked her to examine you? Just to be certain?"

All at once Rose felt lightheaded and queasy. When Dr. Gilchrist had examined her throat, she'd nearly fainted from the pain. "Will she…will it…hurt?"

"You'll find no gentler hands than a midwife's," Leana assured her. "Once the others are busy nibbling on bannocks to break their fast, we'll pay a visit to Aggie McNeil's cottage. Trust your older sister in this: You've nothing to fear."

Rose slowly lifted her head. *I have everything to fear.*

"Aggie has delivered many a bairn." Aunt Meg beamed at the neighbor not much younger than she. "Folk say she's the finest *howdie* in three parishes."

Rose sat in the woman's cottage, her knees pressed together to keep them from shaking. Her apprehension was somewhat eased the longer she regarded Aggie McNeil. On the brief walk from Burnside, Rose had pictured a wizened auld woman like Lillias Brown living in an eerie bothy full of *eldritch* herbs. Instead Aggie was clean scrubbed and tidy. So was her one-room cottage. Perhaps the midwife might be trusted.

"Come, Mistress McKie." Aggie smiled, her face as round as her body, her cheeks firm and smooth, like a well-fed bairn. "This will not take long." She motioned Rose toward a hard-backed chair. "Sit here, if you please."

Rose did as she was told, grateful when Leana stood beside her clasping one hand and Aunt Meg the other. Aggie pulled up a chair and sat across from her, then lightly placed her hands on Rose's belly, bending her pepper-colored hair closer. For a moment naught was heard in the room but the stiff fabric of Rose's gown being massaged by the woman's hands as she followed the contours of her womb.

" 'Tis your fourth month?"

Rose exhaled with a smile. "Aye." It seemed Aggie knew her craft well. "Though I've not felt any movement yet."

" 'Twill not be much longer." Aggie's face grew still. She leaned forward as though listening for something.

Rose regarded her with awe. "Can you…hear my babe?"

The midwife laughed softly. " 'Tis not your child I'm listening for. 'Tis the Lord. Sometimes he gives me a…sense of things." She shrugged, making light of her gift, but Rose knew better. Aggie had a goodness about her. Like Neda. Like Leana. A measure of grace not meted out to many.

Meg prompted her. "What sort of things, Aggie?"

"When the bairn might be born. Whether 'tis a lad or a lass."

Rose exchanged glances with Leana, then confessed, "My sister is certain she bears a girl. And I believe I'm carrying a boy."

"A mother who kens such things is usually right." Aggie pressed

Rose's middle again, more firmly this time. Her features, drawn into a knot, suddenly gave way to a smile. "Tell me, Mistress McKie: Would you mind two sons?"

"Twins?" Rose could barely say the word. "Are you…certain?"

"Think of it, Rose!" Leana squeezed her hand. "We'd each have two children."

Aunt Meg's grin was so broad it threatened to reach her ears. "Do you remember coming to Burnside Cottage one December week and drinking water from the kirk burn?"

"Aye," Rose breathed, not remembering it at all. Could the midwife be right? *Oh, Jamie. Twin sons!*

"As I told you then, Twyneholm parish had five pairs of twins in two years. You have the burn water to thank, lass."

Aggie laughed. " 'Tis her husband, not the water, she ought to thank."

Leana reminded them, "Jamie is a twin."

"Well, there you are." Aggie leaned back, a look of satisfaction on her face.

"And all his ewes bore twins this spring," Rose said, "though I don't suppose that matters."

The other women laughed as Aggie patted Rose's cheek. "It mattered to the ewes that gave birth to them. I do wish I could attend you when your time comes. Your husband's family will ken a fine howdie in Monnigaff."

When your time comes. The words sank into Rose's heart like a stone. Frightening enough to think of giving birth to one child. But *two*?

Like smoke from a smoldering fire, another woman's prediction circled back to haunt her. *Ye must have twa sons tae win Jamie's heart.* Lillias Brown's words, spoken on a Sabbath morn, offered with a green knotted cord. *'Twill save ye from barrenness and bring ye twa bairns.*

But Rose did not take the cord. The twins she bore were not a gift from a witch but a gift from God. *Bethankit!* Rose looked at Leana and Meg. "Promise me you will not speak a word of this to anyone. Not our maids, nor the herds, and definitely not Jamie."

"A wise decision," Aggie agreed. "Such news is better heard from the birthing bed rather than from a howdie months in advance, only to be proven wrong."

Rose had yet another reason: She'd done enough to threaten Jamie's future. If she dared not tell him dreadful news, then blithe news was best kept a secret as well. At least until the gold was gone and Jamie was safe.

"Rose…" A cloud seemed to cross Leana's face. "What of the pain you've been having?"

The midwife eyed her. "In your lower back, I'll warrant. 'Tis not unusual with twins. Your body is making room for two. Fear not."

Almost giddy with relief, the three women started back to Burnside, heads together, whispering about the glad tidings, when Aunt Meg chanced to look up. "Who is that standing at my cottage door? He is your Ian from head to toe."

"So he is." Rose sighed as Jamie turned toward her. "But bigger."

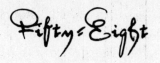

Fifty-Eight

Life is arched with changing skies:
Rarely are they what they seem.
WILLIAM WINTER

From the moment he met Rose, Jamie had realized whom she might favor in her later years: her Aunt Rowena. Dark hair streaked with silver. Sparkling eyes, deep as onyx. A clever tongue, barely tamed. Now he had a fine notion of whom Leana might resemble: her Aunt Meg. Silvery hair like a halo. Pale gray eyes, glowing like beacons. A kind face, full of wisdom.

"James Lachlan McKie, at your service." He bowed to the three women approaching him.

"And I am Margaret Halliday." The older woman curtsied, then cocked her head. "Aunt Meg to you, lad." She slipped her hand round his offered arm and directed him across the threshold of Burnside Cottage with a sweep of her plain cotton gown. "The lasses tidied up the place, I see. Will you be needing some breakfast?"

He ducked beneath the doorframe and entered her two-room home. "The herds and I have eaten, though we'll not refuse a bannock for our pockets." Jamie eyed the cramped cottage with its flagstone floor and rough beams. He imagined Leana seeking refuge within these humble walls, sleeping in the small hurlie bed. If not for the bairn she carried, might she still be here?

As if drawn by his musings, Leana hurried through the door, eyes shining, arms outstretched. "Here's the lad I've longed to see." When she breezed past him, headed for Ian, Jamie nearly bit his tongue. *What did you expect, McKie?*

Rose came in next, reaching toward him for certain. "My husband." She slid her arms round him and rested her head on his chest with a blithe sigh. "And the father of my children." She hesitated for a moment, then simply added, "I've missed you."

"And I, you," he said, pulling her closer still. Sleeping beneath the stars with his flock had little to offer except peace of mind. Perhaps different arrangements might be made for this evening. They only had a few miles to cover, and the destination had promise: a comfortable coaching inn surrounded by a vast estate.

Since Rab and Davie had already started west with the lambs, farewells were brief, with Jamie promising to bring the sisters back to Burnside for an extended visit.

"Not until their bairns are well delivered," Aunt Meg insisted, helping them pack the wagon. Curious neighbors leaned against their opened doors to watch. Twyneholm was a quiet village; a wagon full of visitors sufficed for entertainment.

The maids found their places and kept Ian out of trouble while Jamie strapped the crib to the back with a stout rope, then lifted Leana into the driver's seat. Rose sat next to a cradle full of blankets, draping her arm across it perhaps to keep it from rocking.

"Here, lass." Jamie climbed in next to her. "Let me move that cradle for you."

"Nae!" She quickly pushed a basket of linens against the rockers. "'Tis fine where it is."

"What a *kittlie* wife I have," he teased her. Rose smiled up at him, though her eyes conveyed something else. Surely not fear?

"Pardon me, Jamie. I confess, I'm tired of traveling."

He did not tell her they had nearly forty miles of hills and moors yet to cover. "I'll see that you sleep in a comfortable bed tonight." *And join you, if I can.* He bent down to kiss her brow, then vaulted over the wagon side, anxious to be off. 'Twas Tuesday. The farther away from Auchengray, the easier he would breathe.

Jamie mounted his horse and led them out of the village, casting a troubled glance at the changing skies above them. An hour ago thin clouds had stretched across a watery blue horizon, boding a hazy but dry day ahead. Now thicker clouds were moving in from the west at a steady clip, piling up like waves approaching the shoreline. Someone on horseback or on foot had little to fear from a rainstorm, but wagons were a different story.

As they climbed toward the crossroads, Jamie watched Leana out of the corner of his eye, relieved to note her confidence with the reins and her quiet strength. If a hard rain turned the roads to mud, Leana would know to seek stony ground and wait out the storm.

She caught him looking at her. "Something concerns you, Jamie."

He lowered his voice, lest he frighten the others, Rose in particular. " 'Tis only the skies that worry me. Stay to the graveled military road, and maintain a brisk pace. You'll find a shelter of trees at Littleton Farm, should you need to take cover." Judging by her calm expression, none of his words alarmed her.

Leana tugged on her kid gloves, gazing at the road ahead. "Kindly tell me where I am bound."

"Follow the signposts for Gatehouse of Fleet, then watch for the Murray Arms. 'Tis the only inn the village boasts, built round the old gatehouse of Cally Park. I'll ride ahead and arrange lodging, then see to the lambs."

Leana's smile was like sunlight on a gray day. "You make a fine topsman, Mr. McKie."

He tipped his hat, pleased by her words. "And you, Leana, a fine wagon master."

Bidding her Godspeed, Jamie galloped ahead, his scabbard slapping against his thigh. He had yet to reach for his sword. Or his dirk. The only time he'd brandished his useless pistol was the dark morning he'd found Rose leaning over the wagon. What *had* the lass been doing? She'd never bothered to explain.

The road from Twyneholm followed the swift-flowing burn for a mile or so. Low hills rose and fell on both sides, covered with heather in muted shades of purple and brown, framed against the darkening sky. At the spot where the stream meandered north he found Rab and Davie waiting for him.

"We've stopped tae water the flocks," Rab told him. "Though by the leuk o' things, they'll be wet suin enough."

Jamie watched the lambs for a moment. Instead of calmly drinking at the burn, they were leaping about, butting one another with their woolly heads—a certain sign of a change in the weather. His mount was unsettled as well, pawing the ground. Growing along the roadside was the poor man's weatherglass, scarlet pimpernel, with its red petals closed tight. Aye, rain was on the way.

"Drive the lambs straight on from here without stopping," Jamie directed, "then let them graze on Mr. Murray's pastureland this side of the Fleet. The old Castle of Cardoness looks down on the vale below. 'Tis a meikle landmark you'll have no trouble spotting. I'll meet you there later, aye?"

Water of Fleet, yet another river to be crossed, would wait until tomorrow. They would use the bridge in the village; Jamie refused to have another lamb lost in a swollen stream. Gazing north toward faraway New Galloway, he wondered how the bulk of his flock was faring under the guidance of Nicholas Donaldson. He'd provided the topsman a letter of introduction and detailed instructions for his father to accept the lambs as his, pay the men accordingly, and send them on their way.

If all went according to Duncan's plan, the shepherds and flocks taking the northern route would arrive at Glentrool on Saturday. Jamie envied them that. He would not see home until the Sabbath. *Aye, but you will see home.* Would he be welcome, though? Would he find his brother there? And would Lachlan McBride offer any protest across the miles? Those were the unanswered questions looming over him like the thickening clouds above.

Leaving Rab and Davie in charge of gathering the sheep, Jamie charged ahead, tossing up bits of gravel as he rode. If thunder rumbled overhead, he did not hear it for the pounding of Hastings's hooves against the hard-packed military road, steadily climbing, mile after mile. The air was thick with moisture but not yet with rain as he crossed the burn at Littleton Farm, the ground rising beneath him, the mountains ahead stirring a longing for Glentrool.

A massive stretch of woodlands, still dressed in the many greens of summer, forced the road to veer north. It could only be Cally Park, a thousand acres of gardens and orchards surrounding Cally House, home to the man who owned Girthon parish and all it contained: James

Murray of Broughton, a member of Parliament. Years ago Jamie had met the gentleman on a visit with his father to Cally House; if time allowed, he would bring Murray greetings from Alec McKie. For the moment, more pressing matters required attention.

Skirting the northern border of the park, he passed the entrance drive to the Grecian-styled house—not as old as Glentrool but more palatial in scale—and rode up to the inn, horse and rider both breathing hard. The clouds hung low to the ground, like pewter buckets preparing to tip. He said a prayer for the lasses and lambs both trailing far behind him as he found a stable lad to care for Hastings. Brushing the dust from his riding coat, he strode across the street and into the Murray Arms.

Cobbled together from an old gatehouse and a newer addition, the two-story inn of whitewashed stone seemed well plenished and the proprietor accommodating. Aye, they had two rooms available. "For two nights?" Jamie asked, a sudden inspiration. Why not stay and catch their breaths? The lambs already looked thinner; a day of grazing would do them good. And Gatehouse of Fleet was a thriving village, many times the size of sleepy Newabbey. Annabel and Eliza would be pleased to wander up and down the town's three streets, while their mistresses enjoyed hot baths and soft beds.

"Two nights it is, sir," the proprietor said, then directed him to the estate office where Jamie arranged for grazing land.

In less than an hour Jamie was astride Hastings once more, retracing his route. A strong wind with the scent of rain threatened to steal his hat. The rain would not be long in coming. When he spied the wagon at the eastern edge of Cally Park, he rode harder, elated to find them so near their destination.

"You made excellent time," he told Leana, bending down to clasp Rose's hand and ruffle Ian's hair. "Come, before the skies split open." He escorted the wagon round the park boundary and into the village, then carried whatever they might need for two days up the steep stair to their rooms. Leana lay down for a nap at once, while the maidservants took Ian with them on a brief tour of the village, prepared to dash back to the inn at the first drop of rain.

Rose, the happiest he'd seen her in days, twirled round the spacious room with its painted walls, sturdy furniture, and two broad windows facing the street. Jamie caught her in midspin and wrapped her in his embrace. "After several nights of shared beds and rustic cottages, I thought a quiet room to ourselves would be…"

"Wonderful," she finished for him, welcoming his kiss.

Several kisses later—and with much regret—Jamie reminded her that Rab and Davie were awaiting him with the lambs. "I'm sorry, lass. Duty calls."

"Suppose I walk out with you and explore the village." Rose preceded him into the corridor and down the stair, talking over her shoulder. "Jamie, where might the Girthon parish kirk be?"

"A good bit south of here. On the far side of Bar Hill, well beyond Cally Park."

"Will we not…pass it?" She sounded genuinely dismayed.

"Nae, we'll be heading west from here, I'm afraid."

When they reached the street, Rose clung to his arm as thunder rolled through the valley. "To think we've come all this way only to be trapped inside by the rain."

"Better to be here than at Auchengray." He could not keep the grim note out of his voice. "Your father should be arriving home shortly. When he discovers Leana gone as well as you…"

"And Neda gone as well as Duncan." Rose looked up at him, more wistful than he'd ever seen her. "At least Father will have his new wife and sons to keep him company."

"*And* his thrifite full of gold," Jamie reminded her, then felt Rose shiver beneath her plaid.

Fifty-Nine

Senseless, and deformed,
Convulsive anger storms at large; or pale,
And silent, settles into fell revenge.

JAMES THOMSON

Walloch was foaming at the mouth, sweat pouring down his flanks. Lachlan drove him still harder, using his riding crop as a weapon, his spurs as punishment. "Worthless beast," he grumbled as the horse pounded down the road south of Dumfries. Ominous clouds, thick with rain, hung overhead as a blur of familiar properties swept past him.

The farm names barely registered. *Cargen. Gillfoot. Whinny Hill.* None of them mattered. Auchengray was all he needed to see. His land, his sheep, his servants, his daughters. The property of Lachlan McBride. *That* was all that mattered.

Never in his sixty years had he been so humiliated. By his own overseer—his own man—standing up for a *scoonrel* like Jamie McKie within earshot of his new wife and sons. The shame of it was not to be borne. Lachlan shouted an oath to the dark heavens, his words swallowed up by the wind.

The family carriage was far behind him by now. He would not torture himself imagining their conversation. The five of them had arrived in Lockerbie on Sunday and gone straight to their lodgings at the Kings Arms. He'd not bothered to see after his lambs, pastured a mile from the bustling town. Among twenty thousand sheep, how could he have located a few hundred? It had been Duncan's job to see the lambs readied for the English dealers come Monday's sale.

"And my job to bring home the silver." Lachlan gripped the heavy purse beneath his shirt, his rage easing only slightly at the heft of it. The lambs had sold for a good price. But what of the rest of them, spirited off to Glentrool? "*My* lambs," he fumed, aiming his exhausted mount past Kirkconnell. "*My* silver."

It was not until Duncan delivered the bill of sale in his hands yestreen that Lachlan knew the truth. *Received for four hundred lambs…* Duncan had neither flinched nor apologized when Lachlan accused him of treachery. Half the folk in the sellers tent must have heard him threaten to withhold Duncan's pay for the term.

" 'Tis just as weel," Duncan had told him, his voice maddeningly calm. "I canna take silver from a man I canna respect."

Livid, then and now, he'd bellowed, "You'll not work for me another day!"

"I'll not wark for ye anither hour." Then Duncan had walked off. *Walked off.*

There were too many witnesses; Lachlan had no choice but to let Duncan leave the tent unchallenged. Where the man went was none of his concern. Let Duncan walk the twenty miles home. At least he'd not stolen Walloch. The horse was stabled at the Kings Arms, waiting for his master.

Duncan Hastings would show up at Auchengray soon enough, wool bonnet in hand, begging for his old position. Where else could the man go? Lachlan would see him well humbled before he'd fee him again. And make certain he suffered for his disloyalty.

Jamie would pay for his crime as well. A bill for the selling price of three hundred lambs would be sent by post to his nephew. Better still, to the lad's father. Let Alec McKie see the duplicity of his useless heir, and his sister, Rowena, the *sleekit* ways of her favored son.

Walloch straggled onto the road for Auchengray. "You'll not slow down now," Lachlan growled. " 'Tis five o' the clock, and I've had nae dinner." And what would Neda Hastings have to say about her husband's perfidy?

Thunder rolled across the skies over Auchengray as the signpost appeared. Lachlan straightened in the saddle, his pride returning. He was still a prosperous landowner, was he not? Still the laird of his keep? When his sons and wife arrived later, he would remind them of that fact. The key to the thrifite hung round *his* neck. No one else's.

Deaf as he was, Willie still heard Lachlan's approach, for he stood waiting at the end of the drive. The auld man had a nervous look about him, though he managed a shaky bow. "Walcome hame, sir."

Lachlan dismounted, ignoring the stiffness in his joints as he handed over the reins. "I've ridden him hard, make no mistake." He did not wait for a reply but marched toward the front door, relieved that Willie didn't ask where Duncan might be.

When Lachlan leaned into the front door, expecting it to swing open, his shoulder met a solid wood obstacle. *Locked?* The door was never locked, for good reason. Who would dare rob Lachlan McBride of his worldly possessions?

"I have what ye need, sir." Hugh, his valet, stood behind him on the lawn, holding out a stout iron key. " 'Tis meant for luck, walkin' across yer ain threshold whan ye return from a raik."

Lachlan rolled his eyes as he snatched the key from Hugh's hand. "Luck indeed." He unlocked the door, then flung it open and was taken aback when no one was standing there to greet him.

"Neda?" He strode down the hall, certain he would find his house-keeper hard at work in the kitchen, even though no tantalizing smells wafted his way. He had a taste for roasted goose. Surely it could be prepared on short notice.

But the kitchen was empty. Worse, the hearth was cold. He felt the chill of it climbing up his back as he stared across the abandoned room, not a bite of food in sight. "Neda?" he called again, certain of an answer. None came.

Hugh appeared behind him, quiet as a ghost. "Pardon me, sir, but Mistress Hastings has flit tae her new hame."

Lachlan turned on him. "*What* new home?"

"Kingsgrange, sir. She's tae be their hoosekeeper."

He stared at his manservant, too shocked to speak. If Neda was gone, then Duncan did not mean to come back.

Anger and fear rubbed inside him like two sticks starting a fire. "Leana!" he shouted abruptly, marching through the kitchen and out the back door. His daughter lived in her garden. She would not be hard to find.

But Leana was not in the garden or in the orchard. Neither was Eliza, her shadow.

Out of the corner of his eye, he caught a glimpse of one of the new maids brought from Edingham at Morna's request. She stood by the corner of the house like a fawn about to bolt in search of its mother. "You, lass." He motioned her toward him. "Where are my daughters? And my nephew?"

"Th-the McKies are...g-gone, sir."

"Gone?" He fell back as though the clap of thunder overhead had struck his chest. "Do you mean to say they've left for good?"

He could not tell if the maid was nodding her head on purpose or trembling so violently that it shook on its own.

Jamie and Rose were bound for Glentrool, it seemed. Chasing after the lambs and taking their bystart of a son with them. "Leana, then. Where is my older daughter?"

"Sh-she...she..."

Irritated, Lachlan prodded her. "She *what,* lass? Can you not say two words?"

"She...Miss McBride...left. Wi' the ithers."

Fat drops of rain began splattering on the toes of his dusty boots as he stared at the maid in disbelief. "I have been gone but *three days,* and already my household is dismantled?"

"Their maids left as weel, sir. Annabel. And Eliza." She lowered her head as if ashamed to share such news. "Yer daughters said the servants were the only *tocher* ye gave them."

Biting back an oath, Lachlan left her standing in the rain and marched through the vacant kitchen, ignoring his growling stomach. Morna would be home shortly and attend to supper. He found a candle and carried it into the gloomy spence, inhaling the scent of books and leather and whisky. Outside his window, the skies darkened as the rain unleashed its fury.

He moved slowly across the room, squinting in the darkness, holding his candle aloft. When the faint light fell on the hearth at his feet, he stopped, arrested by the strange fire laid before him. Stones and glass were neatly stacked, as if waiting for the touch of a flame. Except they would never burn nor keep a house warm.

A stone fire.

Lachlan's innards began to churn. An unco practice among kintra folk, meant to convey ill luck to the landowner. Who could have done it? Willie knew the auld ways but would not dare speak a curse against his master. Neda was too righteous, and Leana cared nothing for such cantrips.

He stared at the false fire with a growing sense of dread. Had Lillias Brown been inside his house? The thought made the hairs on the back of his neck rise. Nae, the witch would never be so bold.

Rose. She was the only one braisant enough.

"My own daughter." He breathed out the words, not quite believing them. Staring hard at the window, he imagined Rose climbing out, as custom dictated. She was the one who'd locked the door, then. For ill luck. *My own daughter. My unfaithful Rose.*

Kicking the stones with his boot, he knocked apart the cursed fire, attempting to destroy any power it held over him. When he bent down to claim the heaviest of the rocks, his silver tumbled out of his shirt and onto the floor. "Och!" He snatched up the doeskin purse, then balanced stone and silver in each hand, like the scales of justice. "And did you curse me, lass? Did you curse your own father?"

Fueled by rage and a pain too great to bear, he threw the rock with all his might, shattering the window glass. Shards flew across the floor as rain poured through the ragged opening.

"Lachlan!" Morna stood in the doorway, eyes and mouth agape. "Whatever is the matter? We've just walked in the door…" She stared at the rocks and glass piled at his feet, the broken glass beneath the window, then finally looked up to meet his gaze. "What—"

"My household has conspired against me." As he chronicled the list of those who'd departed Auchengray while the rest of them were at Lammas Fair, Morna's ruddy skin turned the color of bleached muslin. "So you see, my wife, we will require a new housekeeper. And Malcolm will serve as overseer."

He took a full breath, only now beginning to feel his heart beating again. Though four family members had fled from his door, four new ones had moved in. No true loss, then. As for the others, they were mere servants. Replaceable.

Lachlan gestured toward the broken glass. "Have Willie sweep this up. And board the window." While Morna hurried off to find him, Lachlan poured a dram of whisky and sank into his chair, feeling every minute that he'd spent in the saddle.

"Here's to you, Rose." He lifted his pewter cup toward the hearth, then drank it down too quickly to be prudent. Heat tore through him. With no food in his stomach since breakfast, the whisky's potency hit him full force.

"Mr. McBride...ah, Father?" Malcolm stood where his mother had a moment earlier. "Mother said I am to be...overseer?"

Lachlan fixed his gaze on him. "Do you think you can handle it, Son? 'Tis a meikle responsibility for a lad who's seen but twenty summers."

Malcolm threw back his shoulders, his bravado as thick as his neck. "I can, sir. Will I be in charge of keeping the ledgers?"

"Nae." Lachlan wagged his finger at him. "Those will be mine to tally. And the gold, mine to count."

Malcolm took another step into the hallowed room. "You'll be wanting to add the money from the lambs to your thrifite, aye?"

Lachlan pushed himself to his feet with some effort. One hand reached for his purse, the other for the key round his neck, as he turned toward the desk.

His thrifite was gone.

Gone.

Like a man who's been shot, Lachlan stood there, stunned and unmoving.

"Father...where is..."

Jamie. He cleared his throat. "Stolen. Jamie."

"Your *nephew*?" Malcolm was beside him at once. "Does he think we won't come after him? 'Tis our money as well. And Mother's."

Lachlan shook himself all over, as though waking from a drugged sleep. "We will indeed go after him." He tore into the corridor, where Gavin and Ronald stood, their faces like stone.

Willie tottered round the corner, broom in hand. "Am I tae clean up the glass, sir?"

"Not now. We need fresh mounts." Lachlan nodded at his sons. "Four of them."

Morna hovered near the front door, hands fluttering. "I trusted you with our gold, dearest…"

"I ken you did." Lachlan swallowed the bile in his throat. "By this time tomorrow, we shall have it back."

Less than an hour later the McBride men were riding hard for Haugh of Urr, already exhausted from a long day of travel and now soaked through by the relentless rain. Apparently Jamie and his women—had there ever been a man with more lasses round him?—headed for Glentrool in a wagon borrowed from Jock Bell. No narrow cart tracks for them. The military road was the obvious choice for a thief with a pot full of gold.

When they crossed the road leading to Edingham, five miles away, Malcolm shouted against the storm, "You still have a hundred lambs in our old pasture, Father. Jamie hasn't claimed those."

Lachlan's spirits were somewhat buoyed at the reminder. "Indeed, he has not," he hollered back, spurring his mount forward.

By the time they reached the Three Thorns Inn at Carlinwark, men and mounts were drenched, starving, and bone-weary. After a plate of soup, the lads fell onto their mattresses, asleep within minutes. Lachlan stared at the rough walls, the bare floors, the curtainless windows, and missed his spence with its comfortable bed and decanter of whisky.

Above all, he missed his thrifite. Wanted it. Needed it. His fortune—aye, his future—rested inside that pine box.

His nephew deserved nothing. Yet he had taken everything.

My daughters. My grandchildren. My gold.

Lachlan finally willed himself to sleep, thoughts of revenge fueling his dreams. The Almighty would see that justice was done. And what God would not do, Lachlan stood ready to accomplish.

"God speaketh in dreams," he mumbled to himself, reciting the ancient words. "In a dream, in a vision of the night, when deep sleep falleth upon men."

Deep sleep fell upon Lachlan McBride.

But when he woke, what he felt was deep fear. And outrage. And dread.

"We ride for Glentrool," he told his sons over a hurried breakfast. "By way of Twyneholm and Gatehouse." More than that he would not tell them. The thunderous voice he'd heard in the night, the dire warning that could not be ignored—nae, his strange and terrible dream was no one's business.

Malcolm leaned back in his chair, boasting, "We'll not be long tracking down a man with a wagon full of women."

Lachlan stood, impatient to be gone. "'Tis not the women who concern me."

Sixty

Full of a secret that thou dar'st not tell!
GEORGE MACDONALD

Rose waited on the cobblestones outside the Murray Arms, bonnet in place, prepared to embark on a morning walk with her sister. Tucked inside her reticule was a surprise for Leana. Hidden beneath her plaid was a larger one for the parish kirk. Surely by now Father knew his money box was stolen. She could not get rid of the evidence quickly enough.

The door to the inn opened, and Leana appeared. "Sorry to keep you, Rose. Have you somewhere in mind for us to visit?"

Rose took her arm, pulling her forward. "I do." Wisps of fog softened the brightly painted doors, and the smell of leather and grain permeated the village. Laboring folk hurried by, en route to the cotton works or the tannery or the brewery. "Birtwhistle Mills employs three hundred or more, and there are at least a dozen shops, the innkeeper says." Rose peered through the open doors as they walked down the street, the gravel surface still wet from yestreen's hard rain. "See, Leana? Stockings, gloves, shoes, and all sorts of cotton goods."

She steered her sister into a mercer's shop, where bolts of cotton and wool in every hue filled the wooden shelves. The dyes stung her eyes, making them water. "Might you want a length of fabric for a new gown?"

Leana looked at her askance. "Dearie, you know I haven't a penny to my name."

Rose dabbed her eyes, hiding her smile. "I have a bit of silver to spare." She loosened her purse strings and produced a handful of coins. "You are welcome to whatever this might purchase."

What it purchased was several yards of woven cotton in a muted blue. "'Tis the exact color of your eyes." Rose drew Leana closer to the shop window and held the fabric up to compare. "A perfect match."

While the clerk wrapped the cotton goods with twine, Rose paid the shopkeeper with Lachlan's silver. Sweet revenge for the gown money Father had pilfered from Leana when she returned home from Twyneholm. Rose had also deposited a few of his shillings in Meg's cupboard drawers in Twyneholm, to be found some weatherful day when her aunt might need them. What was the use of having money if one didn't give some away?

Leana admired the folded material in her arms. "However shall we explain this to Jamie?"

"I don't need to explain a thing, because 'tis not my fabric." Rose guided her into the street, the moist air awash with the pale light of forenoon. "And *you* don't need to explain a thing, because he's not your husband and dare not ask you whence the money came. See how easy it will be?"

Leana patted her cheek affectionately. "What I see is a lass who likes to keep secrets."

"But I have nothing to hide from you, my sister." Rose swept her braid over her shoulder, aiming Leana across the Fleet Bridge. "In a moment we'll be in the next parish. I hear they have a lovely old kirk nestled in the woods. 'Tis but a mile and a half."

Leana slowed her steps. "Might I leave the fabric at the shop then? I fear I'll soil it on a stroll through the countryside." When they ducked back inside, Leana tugged on Rose's plaid. "Why not leave this here as well? It's much milder now than earlier."

"Nae." Rose drew the plaid round her shoulders, covering the fist-sized bundle tied to her waist. " 'Twill be cooler in the woods."

The sisters crossed the bridge, then veered at the blacksmith's forge and followed a well-trod footpath through the hilly woodlands. Ash, birch, and oak trees crowded them on both sides. The loud piping of a wood warbler floated down through the canopy of leaves. Rose could not see the distinctive yellow stripe on the bird's head, but its song was unmistakable. She leaned back, searching the oak branches above.

"Dearie…" Leana stopped by her side, looking up as well. "Did you…take something of Father's?"

Rose kept her gaze pointed upward. "Whatever do you mean?"

"In the wagon I found…" Leana sighed. "It's nothing, really. A book of poetry. But he might well miss it."

"A *book*?" The plaid nearly slipped from Rose's shoulders. If only her theft were so trifling! "Father cares little for verse," she managed to say. "I doubt he will notice it's gone." Her cheeks sufficiently cooled, Rose turned toward her sister, the wood warbler forgotten. "Shall I send the book back to him by post?"

Leana's laugh was soft, apologetic. "I'm being silly, aren't I? Enjoy the poetry, and I shall read it as well." She slipped her hand through Rose's arm. "*Then* we'll send it back."

Rose was relieved when they came upon the Anwoth kirk at last, for her back ached and the sack of coins had grown heavy. Enclosed by a dry stane dyke and surrounded by trees, the preaching house where Samuel Rutherford had won the hearts of his parishioners was a simple rectangle of gray stone with a belfry high above the door and a steeply pitched roof. Not a soul was in sight that quiet Wednesday morning; the bleating of sheep and the cawing of crows were all that could be heard as they strolled round the kirkyard.

" 'Tis a great deal older than Newabbey kirk." Leana glanced at the date chiseled into the arched doorway—1627—before her eyes were drawn to an enormous raised tomb. "What have we here?" A closer inspection of the ornate monument revealed its contents. "It seems the laird of Cardoness had two wives." Leana ran her fingers over the bold inscription. "Margrat and Christen."

Rose peered at the years beneath their names. "How young they were when they died! Thirty-one and thirty-three." She touched the carved stone, cold beneath her fingertips. "Is this what Jamie will do someday? Build a tomb…for both of us?"

"Such a morbid thought!" Leana slipped an arm round her shoulders and turned toward the path back to the village. "No more auld kirks for you, lass."

Rose hung back, remembering her duty. "I'll join you in a moment."

Leana lowered her arm but still held her with her gaze. "May I not stay and pray with you?"

Easing away from her, Rose promised, "I'll not be long," then ducked inside the empty kirk. She squinted in the dim light. *There.* Though the wooden collection box was locked, she found a small, rectangular hole on top. With some difficulty she squeezed the sack of coins through the opening, pinched between two fingers. Finally she let go, hoping Leana would not notice as the gold and silver landed with a noisy clink.

Rose stood still and waited for her heart to slow. Three small bags and the wutch's cord were all that remained of their father's treasure. With a lighter load, the cradle in the wagon had rocked back and forth too easily, emitting the telltale sound of shifting coins. Rose had been forced to find a new hiding place. Now the gold rested at the bottom of a basketful of cotton stockings in their room at the Murray Arms, safe from view. Jamie's especially.

Forgive me, dear husband. Once the gold was gone—and it would be very soon—Rose prayed such a painful confession would not be necessary.

"I confess, dear wife. Dinner was later than I'd planned."

Rose had paid little attention to the food or the hour, so taken was she with Jamie's altered appearance. After returning grass stained and rumpled from their walk, the sisters had found Jamie disheveled as well, having spent the morning moving his lambs across the bridge and settling them in the meadow below Cardoness. He'd promptly ordered a hot bath delivered to both their rooms, intending to pay a call on Murray of Broughton after their meal. Only his best attire would do.

Jamie had worn his gold-trimmed satin coat only once before, when he'd escorted Rose to Maxwell Park for a private dinner with his lordship. She had never forgotten the richness of the fabric: dark green with claret in a subtle pattern. Without Hugh to attend him, Rose had dressed Jamie's hair for him, delighting in the silken feel of it between her fingers. Round his neck, the lacy white cravat showed off the firm line of his jaw. At his side hung his sword, the mark of a fashionable gentleman. Though Annabel had dressed her mistress in elegant damask, Rose was only too glad to let her husband carry the day for Glentrool.

The proprietor of the Murray Arms had snapped to attention when Jamie appeared duly attired, requesting dinner at two o' the clock. Seated in a private dining room just inside the entrance door, the three of them were treated royally, as the kitchen offered up salmon, venison, and grouse, liberally seasoned and swimming in buttery sauces. Though Leana would not be accompanying them to Cally House—Jamie apologized profusely—she was most understanding and had dressed in her best gown for dinner as well.

"And how did you two spend your morning?" Jamie wanted to know.

"Shopping," Rose said, winking at her sister. "And praying at kirk."

Their waiter had just finished serving the plum pudding when a disturbance arose on the cobblestones outside the inn. Raised voices, sharp with anger, traveled beneath the door to their dining room, seeking an audience.

Male voices. Lowlanders. Familiar.

Rose gasped, and her spoon clattered to the table. *"Father!"*

Jamie was on his feet at once. "Stay seated," he ordered the two of them, facing the door to the entrance hall, his hand on his sword.

The sound of boot heels striking the oak floor matched the desperate pounding of Rose's heart. "Leana, what are we to do?"

"Trust Jamie." The sisters held hands across the table, staring at the closed door, dreading the moment it would swing back on its hinges.

Instead, Jamie yanked it open. "Lachlan McBride is it?" Loud, strong, fearless.

Father stood in the doorway, his sweat-stained clothes covered with dust from the highway, his hands clenched by his side. Behind him, a wall of sons. Broad shoulders, thick necks, sullen faces.

"I'm sure you've been watching for me, Nephew." Lachlan ventured inside the high-ceilinged room, the lads close behind him. "Considering that you stole away, like a thief in the night—"

"We left in the afternoon," Jamie said evenly.

"—and robbed me of my most valuable possessions."

When Rose whimpered, Jamie looked over his shoulder at her. The message in his eyes was unmistakable. *Do not be afraid.* He turned back to their father. "What have I taken that belongs to you?"

Rose gripped Leana's hand as a dull pain inched across her womb. As if her bairns were listening and shared her terror. *You cannot know, Jamie. Must not know.*

"I'll tell you what you've taken." Lachlan's eyes narrowed. "My daughters."

Rose exchanged glances with her sister. His words were merely a ploy. Father cared nothing for their welfare.

"Oh, 'tis your *daughters* you value most?" Jamie's voice rang with contempt. "Including the woman you planned to cast out of your house without a shilling?"

Lachlan did not respond immediately, his gaze fixed on Jamie's scabbard. "Is that how you coerced Leana into coming with you? At the point of your sword?"

"Nae." Jamie touched his weapon. A warning. "Leana came willingly."

Lachlan's gray eyes measured each of them in turn. "If you agreed to depart together, why was I not told?"

"Because you might have objected," Jamie said bluntly, "and tried to stop us."

"Now, Jamie." Lachlan's conciliatory tone said more than his words. He was toying with him. Trying to gain the upper hand. "I ken you are eager to return to your father's house. Had my wife and I known you intended to take your leave, we might have celebrated with a special dinner. Invited some of our neighbors. Had an evening of entertainment."

Rose stared at her father. *Entertainment?* Had the man gone daft?

Jamie spoke for all of them. "Uncle, you have never—"

"At the very least, you might have let me kiss my daughters and grandson farewell."

"Och!" Jamie was having none of it. "Now Ian is your *grandson*, and not merely my bystart?"

"Jamie, Jamie." Lachlan produced a linen handkerchief and mopped his brow. "Such harsh words when I am being generous with you. Why, I haven't even mentioned the lambs you stole from me. Nigh to four hundred." He shoved the handkerchief into his coat pocket, his gaze hardening once more. "It was the Edingham flock that gave away your hiding place, Nephew."

"Aye." Malcolm's smirk was ugly. Condescending. "We were bound for Ferrytown of Cree until we saw the lambs in the meadow below the castle. Your uncle kenned the two shepherds with them were Newabbey lads. That's what led us back here."

Gavin inclined his head toward the front door. "That and the old wagon beside the stables. Mother's maid described it to us."

Lachlan held up his hand as if expecting Jamie to bolt for the door. "We've already searched the wagon."

Rose was in agony. *Lord, help me!* Had she missed a coin? A splinter from the thrifite?

Unaware of her fears, Jamie pressed for an answer. "You mean to say you searched our wagon for your *lambs?*"

"Nae, Jamie." Lachlan's voice was edged with steel. "We searched it for my thrifite. We searched it for the gold you stole from me."

As Rose slumped in her chair, Jamie unsheathed his sword with a ragged cry. "How dare you make such an accusation!"

Lachlan gazed at the blade, frighteningly calm. "I dare because my thrifite disappeared when you did."

Jamie stepped closer, brandishing his weapon. "While you were in Lockerbie, any number of people might have stolen your gold."

"Any of the three people before me, aye. And you, Jamie, are the most likely suspect." Lachlan looked over Jamie's shoulder, one brow cocked. "Though I suppose Leana might have absconded with it to provide for her bairn."

"Father, I would not dream—"

"Or Rose, who built me a fine stone fire. She might have taken my thrifite for spite."

Rose sat absolutely still, pinned by her father's gaze, as lethal as Jamie's sword.

Jamie moved sideways, blocking Lachlan's view of his daughters. "No one in my party stole your money box."

Lachlan shrugged. "Am I to simply take you at your word?"

"Not my word, but my blade." Jamie stepped back, holding the hilt of his weapon across his chest. "If you find even a single coin of your gold in our possession, I will run my sword through the heart of the one who stole it."

Nae, Jamie! A tear slipped down her cheek.

Lachlan stared at the three of them in turn. "You are that certain that none among you is a thief?"

"Utterly certain." Jamie sheathed his sword. "Else I would not make so brash a vow. Search our two rooms at the top of the stair, if you like. Take your sons as witnesses. If you find your gold, I'll make good my promise. But you'll not find it, Uncle."

Leana stood at once. "Search my room first. Come, I'll take you there myself." She touched Rose's shoulder, then hastened from the dining room, collecting Lachlan and the others in her wake.

Jamie leaned down and kissed away her tear, the heat of battle radiating from his skin. "I must go with them, dearest, for I do not trust these men for a moment."

"Aye...you must." Rose eyed his sword. When her husband learned the truth, he would not pierce her heart. But his honor would be sacrificed just the same. And their love left in tatters.

"Do not wait for me." She stood on legs that barely supported her. "I will be in our room...preparing for their...inspection."

"Beloved," he said softly, leading her toward the stair, "you have no need to fear. I have not stolen your father's gold. Lachlan will find nothing in our room, I promise you."

Sixty-One

Fear
Stared in her eyes, and chalk'd her face.
ALFRED, LORD TENNYSON

Oh, my Rose. What have you done?

Leana stood in the center of her lodging room, Ian in her arms, Annabel and Eliza huddled beside her. While they watched, Lachlan dragged gowns out of trunks and tossed linens out of baskets with brutish disregard. He would plunder Rose's room next. And Leana feared what he might find.

Her sister had stolen their father's gold. Leana was almost certain of it.

She could not imagine how Rose had accomplished such a reckless deed, but all the signs pointed to that disastrous possibility. A cradle full of blankets, carefully guarded. Secretive trips to the kirks. And yester-morn, a purse filled with silver.

When Jamie had made his rash promise, the fear on Rose's face had stopped Leana's heart.

Why, dearie? Why did you take it? And not tell Jamie? Such questions would have to wait. Leana's only concern now was protecting her sister. "Father, you are welcome to search our room again—"

"I do not need your permission." He emptied the contents of her reticule on the mattress and pawed through her few personal items. "You are my daughter, these are my maidservants, and my silver purchased everything in this room."

"Except Ian," she said softly, holding him close.

Her father swung round to glare at her. "You paid for him, all right. That bairn cost you everything."

She shielded Ian's ears from Lachlan's cruel words. "No price would ever be too high."

Morna's three sons—Leana could not think of them as her brothers—stood near the fireplace like sentinels, arms folded across their chests. Menacing her without words.

When Jamie appeared at the door, she saw Rose slip past him, headed to their room. Leana nodded at Jamie, praying he might stay while Rose did whatever was necessary to save herself. *Quickly, Rose.*

Just as she'd hoped, Jamie strode into the room, his fine clothes accentuating his superior rank in society. Judging by her father's curled lip, the effect was not lost on him.

"So, Uncle, it appears you've not found any stolen property."

"But I am not finished." Lachlan ordered Gavin to search beneath the bed, only to see him emerge empty-handed, covered with dust. "Och! Keep looking." Lachlan made a great show of heaving furniture about, searching in places he'd already examined, to no avail.

"We have one room left." Lachlan marched past Jamie. "Are you coming, lads?"

The moment the men reached the corridor, with Jamie close on their heels, Leana turned to the maidservants, both on the verge of collapse. "Eliza, I need you to care for Ian. I must go to my sister, and 'tis not…safe for my son there. Can you do that for me?"

Eliza bobbed her head, reaching for the child. He'd started whimpering, clearly frightened by the loud sounds and the presence of strangers.

Leana cupped Ian's cheek and assured him of her swift return, then hurried to her sister's aid. Whatever secrets Rose might be hiding, Leana would not see her threatened or harmed in any way. Though she lacked a sword, Leana did not enter the room unarmed. *Wisdom is better than weapons of war.* She would fight for her sister using any means God provided.

Leana skirted the knot of men and went directly to Rose, who was seated on a hard wooden chair, her back to the window, her face white as chalk. Leana stepped to her side and clasped her sister's icy hand in hers. *I am here, Rose.*

When Jamie moved to join his wife, Lachlan held out his arm, blocking him. "Not until we've searched round that chair." He then turned and examined every spot but where Rose was seated—the tester bed, the pine wardrobe, the dressing table, both their small trunks, her basket of stockings, her leather valise, her flowered reticule—as if to goad Jamie, to remind him who was in charge.

Sensing her sister's anguish, Leana leaned down and whispered, "Father cannot hurt you, Rose. I will not allow it, and neither will Jamie."

When Rose turned toward her, Leana saw the truth in her eyes. Rose had indeed stolen the gold. And it was here. In this room.

"Now then, Rose." Lachlan swaggered toward her. "Stand, if you please, for I'll not have you hiding my gold beneath your chair."

Jamie clamped his hand on the man's shoulder and yanked him back. "Do not be ridiculous. The chair sits far too low to conceal your entire thrifite of gold."

"But I don't need to find the whole of it." Lachlan shrugged off Jamie's hand. "You said if I located a single gold coin—just one sovereign—you would run your sword through that person's heart. 'Tis what you said, lad. One coin." As he shifted his gaze from Jamie to Rose, a fiendish smile stretched across Lachlan's face. "Will you honor your vow, Nephew? For one piece of gold?"

Nae, Jamie! Leana implored him with her eyes, pleaded with him to understand.

But Jamie did not look at her; he looked at Rose. And touched his sword as a pledge. "I will honor my vow."

"See that you do." Lachlan held out his hand to assist her. "To your feet, Rose."

She lifted her head, and a band of sunlight fell across her face. "Please do not be angry with me, Father. I fear I cannot rise."

"Cannot?" he challenged. "Or will not?"

"I cannot." Rose wet her lips, her eyes starting to glisten. "Pardon me, but I am having…that is…because I am expecting…"

Lachlan glowered at her. "I am the father of two daughters. The mysteries of the female body are not unknown to me, lass."

"Father, please!" Rose's face turned scarlet, and so did Leana's. "Not…here. Not with…" Both women looked down, mortified that such a subject would be discussed in a room full of men.

"Very well." He waved his hand, dismissing their embarrassment. "Leana, inspect the small square of space underneath your sister's chair. If you say there is no gold there, I will be satisfied. You are not brave enough to lie to me."

Jamie leaped to her defense. "Leana is very brave. Yet she would not lie for any reason. Nor will that be necessary." He inclined his head toward Rose's chair. "Leana, please look on our behalf so your father may be proven wrong."

Leana leaned down as far as she gracefully could, then swept aside the hem of Rose's gown, praying she might speak the truth before God and man. "Nothing." She could not mask her relief. "Nothing but the polished oak floor." Straightening, she released her sister's garment, then took Rose's hand once more. Already her skin felt warmer. "It seems that Jamie is right. And that you, Father, are in error."

Lachlan hesitated, but not for long. "I do not believe you are telling me the truth." He stormed forward, grabbing Leana's elbow to pull her out of the way even as he thrust his other hand toward Rose. "Suppose I look for myself—"

"*Nae!*" Jamie's sword was in his hand. *"You will not touch my wife!"*

Sixty-Two

I have no words:
My voice is in my sword.
WILLIAM SHAKESPEARE

Which wife do you mean, Nephew? Leana or Rose?"
Jamie slowly extended his blade until the point grazed Lachlan's neck. "Do not touch either one."

Straightening, Lachlan backed away as he eyed the sharp tip. "Perhaps you misunderstand me. I have no wish to harm my daughters. Only to reclaim my gold."

Jamie maneuvered his sword until the point lodged in a button-hole above Lachlan's heart. "We have not stolen your gold. And you ken it well."

Lachlan's chest swelled beneath his blade, daring him to press harder. "You have yet to convince me of that."

Jamie gripped the carved hilt. "How have I wronged you that you would pursue me like a thief?" He pinned him with his blade and hounded him with his words. "What crime have I committed? What law have I broken?" Jamie waved his left hand across the disheveled remains of their room, holding his sword steady. "You have searched everything we own, aye? Every trunk, every bit of clothing. Show me what you've found that is yours."

Jamie glanced at the three brothers, who stood against the far wall, smoldering like peat. Did they, too, see the falseness of Lachlan's charge? Or were they waiting their turn, itching to brandish the dirks sheathed in their boots? Jamie reverted his attention to Lachlan, refusing to be intimidated by their presence. "These lads are your family now. Let them judge between us who is right and who is wrong."

Even with his shoulders pressed against a corner, Lachlan would not yield. "*I* am the one wronged this day."

"This *day*? Uncle, I have been wronged for *two years*." The rage building inside Jamie would not be contained. "Two years of putting up with your swickerie. Two years of herding your flocks without pay. In the cold, in the heat, round the clock, and it was never enough for you. *Never!*"

"Please, Jamie…" Leana's soft voice behind him.

"Nae, lass." Jamie's arm began to shake and his voice as well. "I will not be merciful when no mercy has been shown me."

Malcolm stepped forward. "Cousin, I—"

Jamie silenced him with a raised hand. "My quarrel is with my uncle."

"Och." Lachlan thrust out his chin. "Your quarrel is with yourself—"

"Nae." When Jamie twisted his sword point, the button on Lachlan's coat tore loose, striking the wall. "My quarrel is with you and no one else."

With military precision, Jamie plucked off another button, then another, as if Lachlan were a general being stripped of his medals. "I worked for Rose's hand in marriage, yet you deceived all three of us." A button shot to the floor. "I chose lambs instead of silver, yet you stole them both." Another ricocheted off the wardrobe. "You are the thief, Lachlan McBride."

Lachlan's eyes narrowed. "But you robbed me in return. My daughters, my lambs, my gold—"

"I have *not* stolen your gold."

"Jamie! Please don't…"

Despite the blood pounding in his head, Rose's plaintive voice drew his eye. She was slumped in the chair, her face ravaged with tears. *Och, lass. Is my anger not justified?* He fought to steady his voice. "What is it, Rose?"

"I am…" She looked away. "He is…still…our father."

"So I am." Lachlan yanked the lapels of his coat, dislodging the slackened blade. "I would gladly cross swords with you, James, with three sons prepared to attend me. You, however, have no second."

"And you have no blade." Jamie sheathed his sword with a satisfying ring of metal. A duel was unnecessary. The victory was already won.

Stingy as ever, Lachlan retrieved his buttons without comment and dropped them into his coat pocket. When he stood before Jamie once more, his features bore a hard look of resolve. "Had we four swords among us, I still could not hold one to your throat."

Jamie barely hid his disgust. "Do not pretend that you care for me."

"'Tis not any fond regard for you that stays my hand, Nephew. I would run you through without regret. But I cannot." He abruptly dismissed his sons, ordering the threesome down the stair to search for warm ale.

The tense atmosphere in the room eased considerably with the lads' departure. Rose dried her tears, though she still did not stand, and Leana seemed to be breathing more calmly. The brothers had said little, yet their presence had served as a constant reminder of Lachlan's strength in numbers.

"I'm curious, Uncle." Jamie folded his arms across his chest. "Why did you not press your advantage with your sons on hand? Might it be because you found no evidence for your ill-scrapit charges?"

Lachlan's gray eyes clouded over for a moment, as if he were considering something. When he finally spoke, the resignation in his voice was clear. "I had no choice in the matter. Though I do not bear you any true affection, there is One who does. And he will not see you harmed."

Jamie stared at the man, confused by his words. "Have you heard from…my father?"

"Nae." Lachlan colored slightly. "'Twas the God of your father. He spoke to me yestreen. In a dream."

Leana's mouth fell open. "Truly?"

Lachlan shrugged, clearly uncomfortable with the admission. "When I awakened at the Three Thorns, the words of the Almighty were vividly etched in my mind." He averted his gaze. "I believe you've had…such dreams."

"I…have. Twice." Jamie's heart hammered against his chest. Was it possible? Had the Lord intervened on his behalf?

Leana gently urged her father, "Please tell us what you heard."

"A warning, that is what I heard." Lachlan looked up, a spark of anger in his eyes. "I was told not to harm you. Nor to impede your journey. I had intended to do both."

Jamie acknowledged him with a nod, struggling to find words for a truth that could not be denied. "God has been with me…from the beginning. Even when I was at Auchengray…even when I was suffering beneath your yoke." Jamie dropped his hands, the pain already easing. "He is with me still."

"So it would seem." Lachlan consulted his watch, his interest visibly fading. "You will not hold this charge against me?"

"I will not," Jamie assured him, surprised at how little effort it took. His days of wrestling with Lachlan McBride were over; the future was all that mattered.

His uncle was already halfway to the door. "Then we will away, my sons and I. Our business here is done."

As Lachlan's footsteps faded down the stair, Rose spoke up. "Jamie? Might you do something…for me?"

He turned to her, noting at once her pained expression. Had she truly not been able to stand? Was she ill or merely upset? Jamie closed the gap between them and knelt beside her chair. "What a trial this has been for you, lass." He kissed her soft cheek, chafing her icy hands. "Is there some medicine you require?" Glancing up at Leana, he was struck by the concern in her eyes. "Something your sister might prepare for you?"

"Not just now. But…please see that Father leaves for home…and does not follow us." She pressed a fervent kiss to his knuckles. "I cannot bear looking over our shoulders all the way to Glentrool, fearing his retribution. Might you strike some peace with them? Father said he would not harm you, but his sons made no such promise."

"Wisely said, Rose." Jamie stood, adjusting his waistcoat. "I will find them at once and put your fears to rest."

When Jamie reached the foot of the stair, Lachlan was nowhere to be seen. At a small dining table near the entrance hall sat three empty ale glasses, the sides still glistening. The lads had not gone far. Jamie hastened out of doors, determined to see the four men astride their horses and pointed east. He trusted the Almighty completely. But he did not trust his uncle or his new cousins.

Encouraged by the sight of three French Trotters near the entrance of the inn, Jamie approached the stable lad, offering him a penny before asking his question. "Have you seen their riders? Three lads with hair the color of clay?"

"I have." The stout lad grinned, pocketing his coin. "Said they were off on a walk through the village afore takin' their leave. Doon the main street they went not twa minutes syne."

"Was an older man with them?"

"Wi' a scowl on his face? Aye, they left thegither."

As Jamie strode down the busy street dressed in his lairdly attire, many villagers tipped their hats at him. His costume had served him well. Though he'd not conversed with Murray of Broughton, Jamie had indeed confronted Lachlan McBride.

The row of cottages and shops ran down to the water's edge, where he spied the three brothers leaning over the stony expanse of the Fleet Bridge, tossing rocks into the water. Lachlan stood with them, gesturing wildly as he spoke—still enraged about his missing gold. Jamie pitied the thief who'd taken it, for Lachlan would not be merciful.

"Gentlemen." Jamie approached them, his hand well away from his scabbard lest they misconstrue his actions. "I wonder if I might have a word with you before you leave."

Ronald leaned back, his elbows propped on the bridge. "Have you not spewed enough words in our faces, Cousin?"

"They were not aimed at you, lad." Jamie nodded at the rest. "Nor at your brothers." He did not look at Lachlan. "I've come to make certain that we part on…ah, good terms."

Malcolm threw a jagged rock in the water with more force than necessary. "The only terms that interest us involve the return of our gold."

"I wish I knew who took it, for I would gladly confess his name." Jamie meant it sincerely and hoped they heard it as such. "You can be sure Duncan Hastings would never stoop to such a crime."

"He had good reason to rob me," Lachlan grumbled, "for I refused to pay him for the term."

Jamie flinched at the news. *Poor Duncan.* When he arrived at Glentrool, he would send the man sufficient silver to cover his losses. "Duncan had many chances over the years to pocket your silver, and he touched nary a coin. He is not a thief, and you ken that's so."

Lachlan grunted in response.

"Willie does not have the smeddum," Jamie continued, "nor Hugh the nerve. In any case, had one of your servants done anything so foolish, he would have departed Auchengray at once. Both men were still there when you arrived, aye?"

"They were," Gavin said bluntly. "Since it appears you are not the culprit, we've little choice but to return to Newabbey and inform the sheriff of our loss."

Jamie thrust out his hand. "May the Lord watch over you on your journey home, even as he sees us safely to Monnigaff."

One by one, the brothers begrudgingly shook his hand. When Jamie turned to Lachlan, no hand was offered him. Only a scowl and a narrow gaze.

"I want your pledge that you will treat my daughters well."

"You may depend on it, Uncle." *Far better than you have treated them.*

Lachlan's brow darkened. "Nor will I allow you to put my daughter aside to marry another."

"I will have no wife but your daughter," Jamie assured him.

Lachlan smacked his fist on the stone bridge that spanned the Fleet. "When you cross this bridge heading west tomorrow, do not turn back, thinking to harm me. Nor will we cross it in pursuit of you."

Jamie almost smiled. 'Twas precisely the assurance Rose wanted. "With the God of my father as witness, we will go our separate ways in the morn's morn."

Lachlan would not shake his hand, but he did meet his gaze. Jamie saw the flicker of fear there. Whatever Lachlan had heard or seen in his dream, the Almighty had left his mark on the man's soul.

"Come," Jamie said, extending his arm toward the inn. "You've traveled all day with nothing but a glass of ale to slake your thirst. Let me arrange for a hearty dinner and suitable rooms for the night. At my expense." When Lachlan cast a suspicious eye on him, Jamie explained, "'Tis my father's silver that will pay for your repast. Not your own."

Jamie led the way toward the Murray Arms, knowing what he must do: lock his door and guard his purse until the four men disappeared from view in the morn.

Sixty-Three

The Morn! she is the source of all sighs,
The very face to make us sad.

THOMAS HOOD

When Leana heard the gentle tapping at her door, she turned the key, disregarding Jamie's last words yestreen: "Unlock your door to no one." This tentative knock could only belong to her sister. And they had much to discuss.

Rose stood in the corridor, already dressed for the day. Dark circles beneath her eyes hinted at a poor night's sleep. "Leana, might you join me for breakfast? I realize 'tis naught but six…"

Leana pressed her forefinger against her lips, eying the sleeping maids behind her and Ian dozing soundly in his crib. "Let us away, for they'll not miss me for another hour."

The kitchen staff greeted their first guests of the day with fresh scones, still warm from the inn's brick ovens, and pots of honey, creamy and thick. Leana helped herself to sliced fruit from the sideboard and served Rose as well, while steaming cups of tea were delivered by a bleary-eyed waiter.

"Leana, I've news that cannot keep." Rose leaned forward, ignoring her breakfast, her gaze darting about the empty room. "Yestreen…when I could not rise from my chair…when I…"

Leana waited for her to continue, certain of what would come next.

"I could not stand because…" Rose's eyes began to mist. "Because I was afraid that my…that something was wrong with…my bairns."

Leana blinked at her for a moment. "You mean it had nothing to do with father's gold?"

"Nae, nae!" Rose's voice was stretched taut as a fiddle string. "I was…in pain. And then when I changed my cotton chemise this morning, I found…"

"Oh, Rose!" The gold forgotten, Leana reached across the small table to catch the tear on her sister's cheek, praying her instincts were wrong. "Was it...blood?"

Rose gave a little sob, then nodded her head.

Heaven help us! Leana scooted her chair closer, then rested her hand on Rose's arm. "Listen to me, dearie. Jostling about in a wagon and climbing inn staircases are not proper activities for an expectant mother. No wonder you've had a bit of bleeding."

Rose looked up, hope dawning in her eyes. "You've had this problem too?"

Leana would do anything to comfort her sister, but she could not lie. "I did not. Yet 'tis not uncommon, Rose. And there are measures that may be taken to keep your bairns safe. Let me speak with the cook."

Moments later Leana returned to the table bearing a bitter-scented cup of tea. "Just as I'd hoped. The cook fancies herbs, as I do, and keeps dried nettle in her stillroom. 'Tis the best cure to ease a woman's bleeding."

Rose wrinkled her nose. "The same nettle they use for fishing nets and tablecloths?"

"And nettle soup. A most useful plant." Leana took her seat, trying to sound calm, while her beating heart was sounding an alarm. "Drink some, Rose. I believe it might help."

Rose downed it quickly, then requested another while Leana offered what advice she could. "Elevate your feet when you ride in the wagon. Let Jamie lift you in and out, rather than managing on your own. Place your bairns' health above all other concerns." Leana made sure Rose was listening when she asked, "Have you told Jamie?"

"Oh, I dare not." Rose pushed away her empty teacup. "He has too much on his mind already. But I will do everything you've asked me to do, Leana. And it was only a tiny bit of blood. And only once." Her voice grew softer and more persuasive. "Promise you won't tell him?"

Leana finally agreed, with serious misgivings. If it happened again, she would insist Rose tell Jamie, or she would tell him herself.

Their breakfast was nigh ended when Ian appeared, babbling like a burn in spate as he sailed through the door in his father's arms.

"What a lucky boy you are," Jamie told Ian, strolling over to their table. "You have two women who love you dearly." He claimed a seat, smiling at them both. "I promised the maids I'd have scones sent to their room if they'd let me bring my son to breakfast." He leaned round to catch Ian's eye. "Will you nibble on a scone, lad, or would you rather drag it through your hair?"

"He'd prefer to drag it through *yours*." Rose brushed back a loose strand from Jamie's brow, fond affection sketched across her face.

Leana watched her sister closely. If she was in pain, it did not show.

The sound of male voices and boot heels on the stair put an end to their lighthearted table banter. *Father. And his sons.* Jamie handed Ian to Rose without a word, then stood facing the door. Though he did not bear his sword, Jamie's daunting countenance would give them pause.

Only Lachlan made an appearance. He did not presume to take the fourth chair but simply stood beside their table—his manner subdued, his voice steady, without a hint of rancor. "I have come to bid you farewell, my daughters. For we shall not see each other again."

Dismayed to find her throat tightening, Leana looked away lest Lachlan see the moisture in her eyes and think her weak. Relieved as she was to see him go, he was still her father. She would not miss his presence. But she would mourn what might have been.

With her head turned, Leana did not realize he'd reached for her hand until Lachlan startled her with a brief kiss on her knuckles.

"Godspeed, Leana."

She looked up to find her father dry eyed, stoic as ever. Yet in those gray depths she saw a man whose heart had been broken so thoroughly that the pieces were misplaced and the pattern lost forever.

"I am sorry, Father," Leana said. And she was.

Lachlan briefly kissed Rose's hand as well, then spread his fingers across Ian's head and murmured the oft-spoken words, "The LORD bless thee." With that, Lachlan McBride turned toward the door and was gone.

Jamie sat once more, rather stiffly. Lachlan had not said a single word to him, neither greeting nor farewell. "At least I am blessed of the Almighty," Jamie said evenly. "And I do not envy my uncle the days ahead. Facing his new wife without silver or gold. Perhaps when he returns home, he'll find his thrifte buried in the lawn."

Rose kissed Ian's head. "Perhaps."

As their breakfast plates were cleared, a commotion in the entrance hall drew their attention. "'Tis the mail," Jamie informed them, nodding at the clock above the hearth. "According to the innkeeper, two coaches arrive at seven each morning. One from Carlisle, the other from Portpatrick. They'll sort out the posts, change horses, then send the coaches on their way."

Rose arched her brows, her interest obvious.

"Come, Rose." He helped her to her feet. "Half the town folk congregate outside the door."

Leana claimed Ian, sparing Rose the additional weight, then followed the couple across the hall, where a desk overflowed with cotton sacks stuffed with mail. A harried clerk squinted through his spectacles, deciphering the handwritten addresses scrawled on the sealed posts. Most letters went back inside the mailbags, destined for other parishes, but a few were put aside for local residents of Girthon and Anwoth.

Both wooden doors were propped open, allowing bystanders to watch the proceedings withindoors and out. Passengers on the mail coach stretched their legs, admiring the village beneath a clear blue sky, while fresh horses were harnessed and the carriage swept clean.

The clerk lifted his head, scanning the onlookers until his gaze lighted on Jamie. "Mr. McKie? James McKie, aye? 'Tis a fortunate thing, sir, you being here this morn." He held up a letter written on stiff cream-colored stock and sealed with scarlet wax, then peered at the address again. "'For James Lachlan McKie of Auchengray. From Glentrool.' No sense delivering it there when you're here. Might you be expecting this, sir?"

Leana's own pulse was fluttering; she could not fathom how Jamie felt making his way forward to claim the post. He paid the man his threepence, then held up his prize as he headed back in their direction, his face a jumble of emotions, all of which Leana shared. Fear. Anticipation. Dread. Hope.

Rose nearly tore the post from his hands. "*Please,* Jamie! Do not keep us in suspense."

He honored her wishes, unfolding the letter without delay and reading to them both.

> To James Lachlan McKie
> Tuesday, 3 August 1790
>
> My dearest son,
>
> May this letter find you well and your wife and child in good health. We are pleased to hear of another grandson or a granddaughter in the offing.

Leana and Rose exchanged smiles. *One granddaughter. Twin grandsons. Please God.*

> Kindly excuse this tardy response to your last letter. Since you addressed it to your father, a servant delivered the letter to him directly. I'm afraid he misplaced it for a month or more.

Jamie's exasperated groan said a great deal about life with the McKies at Glentrool.

> As to your letter for Evan, I forwarded it to Wigtownshire as soon as it arrived. He has since written me to say that he has read it and will watch for you to pass by the Cree Bridge soon after Lammas.

"*Watch* for me?" Jamie stared at the letter. "So he might welcome me…or kill me?"

"Does it not say?" Rose pulled the paper closer, her anxiety clearly mounting as Jamie continued to read.

> I cannot predict how your brother will receive you. The birth of Archibald last October tempered him a bit. Still, extending mercy to others does not come easily to Evan.

"But you stood up to Father and won," Rose reminded him, her pride showing. "Surely you can stand up to your brother."

Jamie shook his head. "Two entirely different matters, Rose. Your father was in the wrong, accusing me of theft. My brother has every right to accuse me, for I am guilty as charged."

Leana heard the years of regret threaded through his words. He would have no peace until things with Evan were resolved, for ill or for good. As Jamie finished reading the last few lines of his mother's letter, Leana heard a note of hopefulness return to his voice.

> Though I cannot speak for your brother in Wigtownshire, I can speak for myself. You are more than welcome at Glentrool, my son. I await your arrival.

Jamie folded the letter, his eye already on the door.

Sixty-Four

Happy he whose inward ear
Angel comfortings can hear.
JOHN GREENLEAF WHITTIER

Rose could not have been happier. Comfortably positioned at the far end of the wagon, she'd elevated her legs, as Leana insisted. The last three bags of her father's gold, wrapped in old plaids, formed an ideal footrest. Just as they'd made a fine seat cushion when her father searched her room at the Murray Arms.

Lachlan McBride had not discovered her secret. Neither had Leana nor Jamie. Rose intended her record to remain spotless on that score. Three more collection boxes, and she'd be set free from his gold and her guilt forever. The witch's knotted cord was not so easily discarded. Too evil to be placed inside a kirk, too hazardous to be left lying about, the gold cord needed to be buried in unhallowed ground. When the opportunity presented itself, Rose would see to it.

She was convinced that sitting on the coins, hard as they were, was not what had caused her spotty bleeding. "Not uncommon," Leana had said. Rose trusted her sister completely on such matters, opposing her on one point only: She would not tell Jamie. Not until they reached Glentrool and all his concerns about Evan were resolved. Besides, she'd not noticed a single spot of blood since early that morning and might never see another. Why trouble her husband and embarrass herself needlessly?

At peace with her decision, Rose leaned back, basking in the Galloway sunshine. The skies were utterly clear, the air freshened by the winds off Fleet Bay. Rising high above the hills, the Castle of Cardoness dominated the scenery with its stark stone walls. Brief glimpses of the water came and went as they rolled along the shore—one minute rocky, the next boggy and full of dangerous channels that changed with the tides.

Annabel kept a watchful eye on Ian, lest he crawl too near the edge of the wagon. The maids amused him with cradlesongs and hearthside tales, using hands and fingers to act out a favorite old rhyme.

> This is the lady's knife and fork,
> And this is the lady's table;
> This is the lady's looking glass,
> And this is the baby's cradle.

At the word "cradle," they pointed to Ian's old oaken bed—no longer a repository for stolen goods—and he shook his head.

Rose laughed. "That cradle is too small for you, isn't it, dear boy? Don't grow up *too* soon, or your twin brothers won't be able to keep up with you." Before Annabel or Eliza caught her slip of the tongue, Rose pointed to the bay, hoping to distract them. "Look, there are Mr. Murray's islands!" She squinted across the broad expanse of water. "They say on a clear day you can see the Isle of Man." What she really longed to see was Jamie, who was trailing far behind them, with nowhere else to drive his sheep except along the road. The wagon had not passed many vehicles that day or any herds at all. With the Lammas fairs over and the crops harvested, Galloway was at rest, enjoying the August sunshine before the days grew short and the green hills faded to brown.

Just past the ruins of Barholm Castle, Leana guided the wagon to the side of the road, then turned round to check on her passengers. "Jamie thought we'd spend the night on the high ground near Kirkdale, where the lambs might graze."

"A kirk?" Rose shifted her feet, thinking of the gold.

"We'll be sleeping beneath the stars, for there are no decent inns to be found between here and Monnigaff. And any farmhouses in this neighborhood would require more clambering over the braes than is prudent." Leana's gaze landed on Rose, her meaning clear. "Hang on to your bonnets, lasses, for the horses have a steep hill to mount on our behalf."

Rose took Leana at her word, holding her hat by the brim as the wagon tipped back to a precipitous angle. Their horses, after a two-day rest in Gatehouse, easily pulled them up the hill. Blackface sheep bleated on one side of the narrow, winding road, while far below them a burn snaked its way through the wooded glen. Rose stared in amazement at the octagonal steading in passing, but her hopes were dashed when she saw the abandoned estate kirk. She'd find no collection box within its decrepit walls.

Ferrytown of Cree would have a preaching house, though, followed by Jamie's kirk at Monnigaff. She would find a home for her last fistful of gold before the round turret of Glentrool came into view.

Leana eased the wagon to a stop on a bare, almost desolate rise surrounded by a thickly wooded glen. Behind them were two chambered cairns. A row of standing stones guarded one of the ancient tombs, the gray slabs of rock stark against the blue sky. Far below them, the early evening sun gilded the bay, transforming it into a glistening pool of silver and orange.

Since both sisters had promised Jamie they would not climb down on their own, they sat on the wagon bed and entertained Ian. Annabel and Eliza spread out a blanket on a grassy expanse not far from the wagon and unpacked their cold supper, provided by the Murray Arms.

Within the hour, bleating lambs signaled the lads' arrival. Rose stood with care, balancing herself against one of the taller trunks. "There's Rab!" she cried, waving at him. She noticed Eliza had stood as well, shading her eyes against the setting sun to watch the young shepherd approach. Might the maid have second thoughts about moving to Glentrool if it meant never seeing red-haired Rab Murray again?

Davie Tait ambled toward them as well, and Jamie brought up the rear astride Hastings. They'd traveled six miles since morning; a short distance for wagons and horses, a long one for lambs. At Jamie's command, the dogs herded the flock toward the burn and the lush grass along its banks. The men washed their hands and faces, carried Rose and Leana safely to the ground, then threw themselves on the outstretched blanket, eying the food with obvious interest.

"Beef *bridies,*" Rab said, reaching for the meat-filled pastry. "Haddock *smokies.* Och, sic a feast!"

Supper was consumed at leisure, served up with the herds' stories of their adventures thus far. Rab was gregarious and Davie shy, but both lads could tell a good tale, encouraged by the rapt attention Annabel and Eliza afforded them and the eerie setting the cairns provided. Leana, meanwhile, had her hands full with Ian, while Rose leaned against Jamie and tried not to notice the ache low in her back.

With a cloudless sky above, the gloaming seemed to last for hours, suspending time in a perpetual twilight of purplish blue. As the light finally began to fade, Davie surprised them with a ballad. They promised to sing along, but no one did, letting Davie's tenor float through the still evening air.

Rose did not remember drifting off to sleep. But she remembered waking in Jamie's arms, wrapped in a warm plaid and her warmer husband. Night had truly fallen.

He pulled her closer. "I did not mean to wake you, lass."

"I'm glad you did." When she kissed Jamie's neck, his skin felt rough against her mouth. "Is everyone else asleep?"

"Aye. Your sister and the maids are in the wagon with Ian, and the lads are over the brae." He fell silent. "I've not…slept yet."

She turned in his embrace, seeking a better look at him. " 'Tis Evan that worries you?"

His silence was answer enough.

Rose longed to comfort him as only a wife could, to wrap herself round him on their grassy bed and chase away any thoughts of his vengeful brother. But she dared not. *Place your bairns' health above all other concerns.* Leana's words of caution, well noted.

Rolling onto her back, Rose gazed up at the blackness of the night and the quarter moon beginning to rise. If she could not offer her husband solace, perhaps the One who inhabited the heavens might. "Jamie…" She rose to a sitting position, the better to collect her thoughts. "You said this morning that you are blessed of the Almighty."

He groaned. "How prideful that sounds."

"We all know 'tis true. Even Father said so." Rose smiled into the darkness. "Much as it grieved the man to admit it."

Jamie sat up beside her, his elbows resting on his bent knees. "I've done naught to deserve God's favor. Who knows when he will tire of me and lift his hand?"

Rose rested her head on the solid warmth of his shoulder. "When you dream, Jamie, when he whispers to you in the night, does the Almighty put hedgerows round his promises? 'I will do this, but only if you do that?'"

Jamie was not long in responding. "Nae. In spite of my foolishness, his mercy has never wavered."

"Then why would he forsake you when you cross paths with Evan?"

He slid his arm round her. "Perhaps you are right, dear wife. Though you ken 'tis not my own life I value but yours. And our child's. And the lives of Leana and Ian and all the others entrusted to my care." Jamie leaned forward and kissed her soundly, the strength of his conviction clear. "I do not fear death for myself, Rose. Only for those I love."

"Then have no fear," she said softly, welcoming his kiss again, opening her heart to him. *My brave Jamie. My love.*

It was only when he lifted his mouth from hers that Rose noticed the colors in the heavens above them. "Jamie, the sky!"

They were both on their feet in an instant, mouths open in awe.

"'Tis the *merry dancers.*" Jamie clasped her hand, his gaze pointed upward. "Like angels on the wing. Have you seen them before, Rose?"

"Once, as a lass. But never like this."

A display of northern lights flooded the distant horizon with flaming patches of red and gold, waxing and waning, dancing across the sky. A shimmering veil of light, moving in majestic silence. A presence bearing down on them.

Jamie swept his arm in an arc, taking in the ancient stones, black against the vivid hues. "They call this place Cairnholy. The name suits it, aye? This night especially."

Rose turned at the sound of snapping twigs. Rab and Davie drew near, rubbing their eyes in wonderment.

"Will ye leuk at that?" Davie said. "A blissin, tae see sic a thing in Gallowa'."

Rab tipped his head back. "A miracle, I'd say." As they watched the curtain of light waving over them, he confessed, "I'm glad tae see the merry dancers, Mr. McKie, but the cairns make me skin crawl. We'll sleep aside the wagon, if ye dinna mind."

"Not at all, lad." Jamie shifted his gaze to the upright stones, barely visible beneath the glowing sky. "Though I slept on a cairn once. The night I left Glentrool."

Jamie said no more, but Rose saw the memory of that night reflected in his eyes. Sleepless hours filled with remorse. And loneliness. And fear.

Sixty-Five

Like one, that on a lonesome road
Doth walk in fear and dread…
Because he knows a frightful fiend
Doth close behind him tread.

SAMUEL TAYLOR COLERIDGE

I mean to kill you, Jamie.

Jamie's gaze stretched across the sands to Wigtownshire, his brother's warning from two years past still twisting in his gut. Each hour they traveled today passed too quickly, each mile seemed too short. The heavenly visions of yestreen had faded into the grim realities of the present.

When they'd turned away from the waters of Wigtown Bay for the salt marshes and mud flats of the Cree estuary, Jamie had felt his brother drawing closer—one minute stalking him on foot on the shore road, the next charging down from the hills on horseback, then stealing across the river by boat instead of waiting for him seven miles north at Cree Bridge. Evan was equally at home on water or land and far more comfortable out of doors than within. His hunting bow was nigh attached to his shoulder, his flintlock musket an extension of his arm, and his dirk seldom far from reach.

Jamie glanced down, relieved at the sight of his own dagger lodged inside his boot. Good for hand combat, if it came to that, but useless if Evan pointed his musket at him across Cree Bridge. As a safeguard, Jamie now rode ahead of the others, with his flocks and herds behind him and his household positioned last.

He would take another precaution the moment they reached Ferry-town of Cree.

A small riverside village—bordered by Balloch Burn on the south and Moneypool Burn on the north—Ferrytown of Cree was nigh to an island. Sailors and smugglers alike moored their vessels at the tidal harbor. When Jamie had described the place to Rab and Davie that morn, he'd told them, "You can hardly enter or leave the place without crossing a bridge."

Rab had looked at him through narrowed eyes. "And thar's a brig o'er baith o' these burns, aye?"

Jamie had assured him they would not spend the day ferrying sheep. "The Balloch is shallow enough to walk across at low tide. And the Moneypool has a fine granite bridge. Nae need to worry, Rab."

Moments later Jamie found the shepherd walking up beside him, swatting at the midges with his bonnet. "Whaur shall we pasture the lambs while we wait for the tide tae drop?"

"At the Ferry Thorn, this side of the Balloch Burn." Jamie pointed ahead to the hawthorn tree, a familiar trysting place. "I'll join you after I attend to some business in town."

Jamie rode past the Ferrytown landmark, then eased down to the banks of the Balloch. Even now, at high tide, the small burn was easily forded. A sturdy row of steppingstones poked above the surface for travelers on foot. Astride Hastings, Jamie gamely entered the water, which barely reached the heels of his boots.

Horse and rider were soon on dry ground again and headed up the harbor street with its abundance of tippling houses. Choosing the busiest establishment among them, Jamie tied Hastings to a wooden post near the door, then crossed the threshold. The stench of malt, tobacco, and unwashed fishermen nearly knocked him back into the street. He forged on, his eye on the proprietor. "I need a lad with a horse," Jamie told him, fingering a shilling. "Someone I can trust to run an errand for me."

Stroking his woolly beard, the older man scanned the rough-beamed room. "See that lang strap o' lad wi' the *broon* hair? That's wha ye're leukin' for: Lewis McMinn. He'll earn onie shullin ye gie him."

Jamie caught the lad's eye and motioned him out of doors, where the air was fresher and the blether diminished. "If you've a decent mount and a few hours' time, I have a fair proposition for you."

"I'm listenin', sir."

Jamie guessed Lewis McMinn had seen twenty summers. His eye was clear and his stance straight. Aye, he'd do. "I need you to ride to Monnigaff, to the Cree Inn at the foot of the bridge. You ken the place?"

When the lad nodded, Jamie wasted no time. "You are looking for a man my age. My twin brother, though we look nothing alike. He is a bit taller than I am and stouter round his chest. With a full head of red hair, as bright as a linnet's crown in summer, and the same thick hair on his arms. He's more likely to be wearing a plaid than a coat and breeches, and you may smell whisky on his breath. Goes by the name of Evan McKie. Formerly of Glentrool, now settled in Wigtownshire. If he's not staying at the inn, someone there will point you in his direction, for I'm told he's in the vicinity of Cree Bridge."

Lewis eyed the shilling in Jamie's hand. "And after I find him?"

"Give him this message." Jamie pulled a small letter from his pocket, crudely written at dawn, roughly folded, and sealed with candle wax.

Seven words, chosen from the Buik. *May I find grace in thy sight.*

He had wronged his brother and confessed it in his last letter. Nothing remained but to plead for mercy. Jamie handed the lad the sealed note. "Be sure he reads it. Once I hear what my brother has to say, I'll ken what's to be done next."

"Judgin' by the way ye've described him, ye might want tae run the ither direction."

"I've done that long enough." Jamie dropped the silver in Lewis's outstretched hand. "I'll have another shilling for you when we meet later at the Ferry Thorn. Eight o' the clock?"

"Aye." Lewis glanced at the cloud-strewn skies. "Afore *daurk.*"

Jamie watched him trot off, then climbed astride Hastings and forded the Balloch again, waving his hat in the direction of the parked wagon. Rab and Davie were attending to the lambs while Leana and the maids chased after a crawling Ian. Rose was nowhere to be seen.

"She's off tae the parish kirk," Annabel explained. "Said she'd not be lang."

True to her word, Rose returned after a bit, gingerly stepping across the stones in the burn, then strolling up the footpath, bearing their next meal and a crafty smile. "Fresh bannocks, hard cheese, and ripe summer apples."

Jamie stared at her, incredulous. "It appears my wife has robbed the parish collection box. Wherever did you find the coins to purchase our supper?"

She struck a flindrikin pose. "I borrowed them from *you*, good husband."

Jamie did not argue with her, but he knew the contents of his purse to the last penny, and no coins were missing. While the others ate, he fixed his restless gaze on the road heading north. It would take them no time to cross the bridge at the other end of the village. Better to wait here than to risk missing Lewis McMinn.

Late afternoon faded into early evening. As the lasses watched the oyster catchers wade about the water and the curlews probe deep in the mud for food, Jamie watched the skies turn to solid pewter. *Hurry, lad.*

The tide was ebbing when Lewis came splashing across Balloch Burn.

Jamie ran ahead to meet him, lest his report alarm the others. "What news from Cree Bridge?"

Lewis dismounted, leading his horse to higher ground. "I found Evan McKie, quite as ye described him."

Jamie suddenly wished he'd eaten supper, for his mouth felt glued shut.

"I gave him yer note." Lewis inclined his head, as though unsure how to proceed. "Yer brither gie me a wird for ye as weel."

Two years of guilt closed round his throat. "And?"

"I told him ye were at the Ferry Thorn." Lewis didn't quite meet his gaze. "He said tae watch for him."

"He's headed *here*?" Jamie's hands grew clammy. Was his brother eager to resolve things? Or did he want justice served on a lonely riverside at night without witnesses? "What else, lad?"

"Mr. McKie will not be comin' alone. Yer brither had ten lads wi' him."

"*Ten?*" Jamie's knees barely held.

Lewis stuck out his palm. "I'll tak that shullin, if ye dinna mind, sir."

Jamie went through the motions of paying him, though his fingers had trouble sorting through the coins. Two shillings for the worst news of his life.

Lewis eyed the lambs. "Ye're not thinkin' o' takin' yer beasts tae Monnigaff?" When Jamie assured him he was, the young man wagged his head. "Have ye not heard? The brig o'er the Moneypool is gane."

Jamie almost laughed. "What do you mean it's *gone*?"

"Fell into the burn, it did."

"The whole *bridge*?"

Rab ran up in time to hear the sorry news. "Surely ye dinna mean it?"

Lewis took his time pushing back the brim of his cap, making the most of their undivided attention. "For years fowk said the brig was weak, that the bulwarks couldna hold. After a frichtsome storm on Tuesday last, the water came rushin' doon the hills, and…" His careless shrug said the rest. " 'Twill take thirty pounds sterling tae rebuild it and mair men than Ferrytown can muster." Lewis waved in the general direction of the village. "Go and see for yerself. Naught but meikle rocks stickin' oot o' the water."

Almost before the lad had finished, Jamie was astride Hastings, bound for the Moneypool. First his brother's impending arrival and now *this*! Anger sent him charging up the harbor street at a hard gallop, veering onto the high road at the kirk. When he reached the burn, the scene was just as Lewis had described. Large sections of rough-edged granite littered the steep banks and stream, sinking deep into the silt and sand.

" 'Tis worse than I'd imagined," Jamie admitted when he returned to the Ferry Thorn. "We'll need to carry the lambs across this wee burn while the tide is manageable, then do the same o'er the Moneypool in the morn."

Lewis looked at him askance. "Ye'll not be sleepin' aside the burn, will ye? By the leuk o' the sky, 'twill be a daurk and misty nicht. I'd hate tae find ye gane in the morn's morn, dragged tae yer grave by the kelpie o' Moneypool. 'Tis like a meikle horse that rises wi' the tide…"

Jamie only half listened to the lad's superstitious rambling. A water demon haunting the ford was the least of his worries. A collapsed bridge, deteriorating weather, and Evan McKie—armed and leading ten men— were far greater fears. By the time Jamie had sent Lewis on his way, Rab and Davie were already toting lambs across the shallow water while Annabel and Eliza herded the growing flock on the opposite bank.

Jamie carried Ian astride Hastings, then led his party through the village, his spirits as low as the tide. Instead of being safely sequestered at a local farm, his household and flocks would spend another night out of doors, exposed to the elements. And to his brother's wrath. Was there nothing that could be done?

Once they reached the banks of the Moneypool, Jamie helped them find a patch of solid ground for the wagon and sufficient grass for the lambs. Leana and Rose said little, but he sensed their apprehension as they shared the last of the apples, then spread thick plaids over the wagon bed for the night.

With each passing minute, one truth became clear: Evan had to be stopped before he reached Ferrytown of Cree.

Rab pulled Jamie aside, his freckled brow drawn into a knot, Davie close behind him. "Mr. McKie, is there oniething I can do tae help ye? For I can see ye're fash, and I jalouse yer brither's the reason."

"Aye." Jamie could withhold the facts no longer. He related Lewis's grim report, not sparing them the worst of it. Ten men. Untold weapons. "Rab, you've offered to help, and I'll not refuse it. Suppose you start for Cree Bridge—"

"Richt noo, sir?"

Jamie nodded, a drastic plan unfolding in his mind. "Take a flock of lambs with you as a peace offering for my brother. Two score, I'd say." A tithe, Jamie realized. "We're at low tide; the sooner we carry the lambs across, the better. Between here and Cree Bridge there's but one road. You are sure to meet my brother, though I cannot say the time or place." Jamie described Evan in detail, warning Rab of his strength. "Treat the man with respect. When he asks who you are and where you're headed, speak the truth. Tell him the lambs you're herding once belonged to his brother but now are his as a gift from me. And tell him I will be heading his direction. Soon."

Though Rab listened and nodded, fear hung round his slumped shoulders like a plaid woven in bold colors, easily seen even in the murk. "What if he kills yer lambs, Mr. McKie? And what if…"

"He will not harm the flock. My brother may be birsie, but he's no fool. The lambs are worth far more to him alive and breeding than slaughtered along the road." Jamie made sure their eyes met before he added, "He has no quarrel with you, Rab. Nae reason whatsoever to harm you and nae law on his side that would allow it." Jamie shifted his weight, though he could not shirk his burden. "Take the lambs, Rab. If God is merciful, my brother may look more kindly on me. As I shall look verra kindly on you for this good deed."

There was no time to lose. With Davie's help, the men gathered forty of the choicest lambs, then led them down the banks of the burn. Slippery mud, waterlogged sand, and swirling tides made for a deadly alliance; the fallen granite provided the only safe landings amid the lurking pools of silt and quicksand.

After several trips across, a lamb under each arm, Jamie realized what must be done while Rab was still with them: His household and the rest of his flock should be moved as well. They dared not wait until the morn with Evan en route. If the women remained in the wagon, they'd be forced to witness his confrontation with Evan. The very thought of it made his insides churn. And although his brother was a gentleman and would never harm woman or child, Jamie knew nothing of the ten men with him.

Better to lead his household across the burn before the water rose any higher, then guide them to their lodging and leave them in Davie's capable hands.

He alone would meet Evan.

Sixty-Six

Then, water-kelpies haunt the foord,
By your direction,
An' nighted trav'llers are allur'd
To their destruction.
ROBERT BURNS

Night was falling.

While the lads started the arduous task of fording sixty more lambs, Jamie sought out Rose and the others, who'd watched the proceedings with worried faces. He explained about Evan's approach and quickly sketched his plans, noting the quiet concern in Leana's expression, the heightened fear in Rose's.

Ian, unaware of impending calamity, was his usual blithe self. Jamie stroked the boy's head, reminded afresh of his obligations. "Tuck my son in his crib for the night while we attend to the lambs. I will do everything in my power to protect you."

Rose put on a brave face, but her lower lip trembled. "We trust you utterly, Jamie. You are the heir of Glentrool, are you not?"

He kissed Rose's hand, then gently reminded her, " 'Tis better to trust in the LORD than to put confidence in princes."

"Well said, Jamie." Leana smiled at him. "We shall trust the Almighty to guide you, then."

Jamie met her gaze. *I am glad you came, lass.* He could not tell her so; perhaps she knew. On such a night, Leana's presence strengthened him in ways he could never explain, even to himself.

"To the lambs." He eased away from the wagon. "With your prayers."

Back and forth the three men went, making the most of the hour afforded them, with the tide at its lowest ebb and the misty gloaming still lighting their way. Rab was ready to depart at last, wrapped in a dry shepherd's plaid, courage pinned to his chest like a badge.

"We'll start north in the morn's morn and meet you on the way," Jamie told him, shaking his hand with a firm grip. "The lambs and your pluck may spare us all, Rab Murray."

The shepherd bobbed his head, then started up the road with his crook, leaving both collies behind. Davie waved in farewell, then turned to Jamie, his concern apparent. "I'll mind the sheep, Mr. McKie. Ye'd best be crossin' the water for the ithers while ye still can."

The water already felt deeper, Jamie realized. Leaping from one rock to the next, the smooth soles of his leather boots a liability, he kept his eye on the far bank of Moneypool Burn and his mind on those whom he cherished, waiting for him.

Fog rising off the burn had turned the twilight into a thick gray shroud. Once he reached the other side, he climbed the steep bank and found the women waiting, their faces pale in the lantern light. "I will lead you across the burn. Quickly now, for every second counts."

"Take Rose first." Leana helped her sister to her feet. "She must not fall, Jamie."

He met her gaze and meant the words he spoke. "I promise you, she will not." He lifted Rose from the wagon and did not put her down again, holding her tight as he worked his way across while she clung to his neck and wept with fear. "You are fine, lass," he assured her when they reached the other side. "Wait here for your sister."

But Leana would not hear of it. "Ian next," she insisted, "for the water is rising."

Lighter than one of his lambs and limp with sleep, Ian was easy to carry, though Jamie's heart still pounded. "My son, my son," he whispered, holding him close until he laid him in Rose's trembling embrace.

Leana tried to send the maidservants next, but Eliza protested, and Jamie refused to listen. "Come, Leana," he said firmly, sweeping her into his arms. Their unborn child pressed against his chest as he carried her, a tacit reminder of all who were depending on him this night. *Remember me, I pray thee, and strengthen me.*

With Leana on hand to calm Rose and help with Ian, he could take a bit more time with the maids. Caution was called for: He could only see from stone to stone now, and water swirled over the rough surfaces.

Eliza stood on the bank with the lantern held high to guide him. "Bless you," he called out, following the diffused glow until he was climbing the bank once more.

Annabel squeezed her eyes shut and held on. When it was Eliza's turn, the maid abandoned the lantern and whispered a prayer before the two of them ventured across the murky stream.

When they reached the other side, Jamie respectfully ignored Leana's plea that he cross back at once. "I ken the water is rising, lass, but it will not reach high tide for many hours. The farm I have in mind is not far. Let me see you safely to your lodging first."

The ground was damp and uneven, slowing their progress through the trees and brush. At last they reached the farm property he'd remembered from his rambles as a youth. "You'll find dry beds and ample food," Jamie promised them. "The folk here know the McKies and will see you well cared for." He said his farewells, turning back toward the village with some reluctance. How much simpler it would be to stay here! To hide in the steading and pretend that Evan was not headed in his direction.

Nae. The time for hiding was over.

Jamie strode down the lane, now blanketed in fog and darkness, grateful to have solid ground and a well-marked path beneath his boots. 'Twas the same route Evan would travel on his way to Ferrytown. His brother would have to ford the burn as well, along with his ten men. At least their approach would not be silent. Or swift.

The moon had yet to appear on the horizon and would be of no use when it did. Less than a quarter remained, and even that would be obscured by clouds. Jamie was soon at Moneypool Burn, standing directly opposite the lantern, a meager light on the far shore. Not enough to illumine the rocks or to reveal the depth of the stream.

But he could hear the water swirling below him. The rising tide slowly moved up the Cree, against the current, pushing the brackish water round and round, stirring up the mud and silt and sand. Along the water's edge, underground springs made the sands quick. And treacherous. In one spot his boot might only sink in a few inches; in another, his leg could disappear up to his hip.

Jamie stared at the water below, trying to get his bearings, even as his feet began to slide along the mud, drawing him inexorably closer. Should he wait here rather than cross? Nae, for a borrowed wagon and horses, as well as his own mount and all their possessions, stood unprotected on the other side. And his weapons were stored in the wagon.

He would go. Must go. Now.

Jamie thrust his foot into the water, hoping to strike one of the larger segments of granite, and nearly shouted with relief when he did. Since the surface was slick and his balance unsure, he crouched down and crawled across the rock. The water smelled like seaweed, decaying bracken, and fish. The Cree was known for its salmon. What might the Moneypool have swimming beneath its waters?

A kelpie.

Lewis McMinn's voice taunted. *'Tis like a meikle horse that rises wi' the tide.*

"You're daft, man," Jamie muttered. Kelpies were no more real than fairies or brownies, though stories about them persisted. Tales were told of finely groomed mounts that inhabited the water, inviting lads to stroke their manes, then dragging them into the deep, never to be seen again.

Foolish legends meant to frighten children away from the water's edge.

From the far bank, Jamie heard the horses moving about. That *was* where the sound was coming from, wasn't it? He reached the edge of the rock, uncertain of his next step. Was that a large stone to the left? Or a pool of black water? Or a patch of mud, waiting to swallow his boot?

He bit back an oath, determined not to lose his nerve. The bank was not far away. Better to ease into the water and walk across than to risk stepping into a void and losing his footing on the sharp-edged rock. He unfolded the cuffs of his boots over his knees, then lowered one leg into the stream, bracing himself against the cold.

The bottom was miry, but he had no sensation of sinking into it. He plunged his other leg into the water and held out his arms to maintain balance. Reaching for the next rock, he found himself pulled along by the flowing water, dragged downstream. The faint lantern light seemed farther away instead of closer, and the mud beneath his boots was growing more tenacious.

By sheer will, Jamie lifted his left foot, then his right, moving forward before sinking into more mud. And deeper water. No matter which way he stretched his arms, there were no rocks to be found. Only a quagmire of silt and mud, which now had a firm grip on his boots. When he tried to shift his stance, he could not. Neither foot would budge. The harder he fought, the farther into the mud he sank. Water sloshed inside the cuffs of his boots.

"Help!" Ridiculous to shout when no one was there. "Help!" Louder this time. And more desperate. All he needed was something to grab on to, some means of leverage.

If he could pull one leg free… If he could hold on…

Jamie fought against the downward pull, struggled against it, railed against it. "Nae!" he cried out, throwing his weight forward, making things worse. Wet clothes bogged him down further. His boots began filling with silt. *"Nae!"* Jamie rescued his sheathed dirk, jamming it inside the waist of his breeches for safekeeping, but he could not dislodge his boots. His eyes were hot with tears, his throat so tight he could no longer say the words. *Help me! Please help me!*

Fear rose inside him, choking him. *I will not die here. I will not!*

Jamie summoned all his strength and managed to loosen one boot, but the momentum threw him tumbling into the water. His head struck an unseen rock with a sickening thud. The dark night turned black as he sank to his knees.

Save me, O God. For the waters are come in unto my soul.

Water. Cold. Pain. Nothing else.

I sink in deep mire, where there is no standing.

Not his words. He had no words. He had only his will.

I shall not die, but live.

Jamie grabbed the immovable rock, the one that had wounded him, and pulled with all his might. He tasted blood, but still he strained to extricate himself. His muscles screamed for mercy, but he would not relent. Fighting, struggling, wrestling.

In God have I put my trust. I will not be afraid.

The mud, like a hungry beast, would not let go of his boots. But Jamie would not surrender. Not to this…this *thing,* nor to a kelpie, nor to his brother. A worthy adversary, yet Jamie knew he would prevail. He would.

"Aye!" Jamie roared, yanking as hard as he could.

He pulled one leg free of the enemy's grip, leaving his boot behind. But he did not need his boot. He needed to live. He needed out of this water and onto this rock. Now.

Jamie pulled harder still, his thigh straining against the deadly drag of the mud. "Not yet," he growled. "I'll not give up yet." All at once, his other leg jerked loose from its boot. But not before he felt a fierce wrenching, and a jolt of pain shot through him.

It did not matter. He was free.

Jamie threw himself onto the rock, his body splayed across the great boulder, well above the surface of the burn. Let the tide rise all it wished; he could no longer drown in its cold waters.

He lay there for some time, catching his breath, letting his racing heart slow down and his thoughts come into focus. When he tried to sit up, the searing pain at the juncture of his thigh and hip would not let him. No matter. He would lie there until daybreak if necessary. His brother would find him. Or Davie would find him. But no man would find him dead.

Jamie managed to roll over onto his side, the one that did not hurt. His head was still bleeding where he'd struck the rock, and he could feel a lump growing beneath his fingers when he touched it. Not a fatal wound. He would recover.

Peering into the mist, Jamie tried to determine his location. Though he still heard the horses shuffling about, he could not see them. The lantern oil had run out, and the banks of the burn were dark. Where was Evan? Had his brother been delayed by the fog? Or had Lewis McMinn been confused about Evan's intentions?

Many questions, few answers. All of them would wait for the morn.

I am blessed of the Almighty. It was not prideful to confess what he knew to be true. He was not worthy of the least of God's mercies. But even so, mercy was his. The gift of gifts. *In God we boast all the day long.*

With a stone for his pillow, Jamie laid down his head and slept until the sun warmed his face and a man's voice called to him across the water.

Sixty-Seven

Earth bears no balsams for mistakes.

EDWARD ROWLAND SILL

Rose stood at the edge of the Moneypool Burn, staring in bewilderment at two men: Jamie, prostrate on a rock in the middle of the stream at low tide, his clothes unkempt and his boots missing; and a black-haired man addressing her husband from the Ferrytown side.

"Sir, if ye dinna mind me askin', whatsomever are ye doin' on that stane?"

Rose watched Jamie struggle to sit up, wincing as he did. Much as she wanted to hail him, if he moved about too quickly, he might tumble from his rocky perch. Instead she waited her turn to speak with him—an unsettling start to her bright and sunny morn. She'd left the farm early, hoping to surprise him. Instead, Jamie had very much surprised her.

"A good day to you," Jamie said, unwittingly turning his back toward her to face the older man. "I am blithe to report that I bested your kelpie yestreen. The beast will bother your village no more."

The fellow laughed, showing off a full set of teeth. "Is that sae? And what might yer name be?"

"James McKie of Glentrool."

"Weel, we'd better be changin' that. Any gentrice wha defeats the kelpie o' Moneypool is a prince *amang* men. Can we not call ye laird o' Glentrool?"

"Nae, you cannot." The playful note in Jamie's voice disappeared. "Not as long as my father lives."

"That's richt," the stranger agreed. "Might ye be needin' help tae climb doon from yer rock? For thar's a lassie waitin' for ye on the ither side."

When Jamie turned round, his smile nearly sent her splashing across the shallow burn to collect him. *My poor Jamie!*

"You're a sight for sore eyes, Rose." He slid from his perch with obvious difficulty and started limping toward her.

"I believe 'tis not your eyes but your leg that's sore." She stretched out her arms, ready to welcome him, filthy though he might be. "Whatever have you been up to, Jamie?"

Barefoot and clearly in pain, he took some time reaching her. "Did you not hear me tell that villager I wrestled with a kelpie?" When Jamie turned to acknowledge him, they realized the man had wandered off without sharing his name or bidding them farewell.

"Odd, that one." Rose offered her hand as Jamie stepped onto the bank. "I heard what you said to him. Now are you going to explain what truly happened?"

"Perhaps." He lightly kissed her mouth.

She would never tell Jamie he tasted like seaweed. Not when she was so glad to see him. But a *kelpie*? He'd have to do better than that.

"Leana and the others will be along soon." Rose leaned back, eying him more closely. "Did Evan do this to you? Injure your leg, then abandon you?"

He glanced toward the road. "I've yet to see my brother, though I feel certain we'll meet him on the way north." His answer was matter-of-fact, as if he no longer dreaded the encounter. "And on the Sabbath, the whole of my parents' household will be at the kirk in Monnigaff. With so many folk to see, 'tis well that I lived through the night, aye?"

Rose narrowed her gaze, trying to sort it all out. No boots. Clothes a slitterie mess. And a limp. "If not Evan, then *who*, Jamie? What manner of man or beast left you in such a state?" She folded her arms across her bodice, letting him know she expected an answer forthwith.

"I…fell," he began, running a hand through his unbound hair. "The current was swift, the fog was thick, and the mud was determined to pull me under. When I bashed my head on that rock, I very nearly drowned."

"Jamie! I had no idea…" Perhaps the kelpie was not so daft an explanation.

" 'Twas a fight for my life, make no mistake. When I could not drag my boots from the mud, my only choice was to leave them behind, though I twisted my leg badly in the process. By the time I pulled myself onto that rock, my strength was gone, which is why you found me still there this morning." He looked down at his right leg. "A bit worse for wear. But grateful."

"Not half so grateful as I." She kissed him again, not minding the taste of seaweed one bit if it meant her Jamie had survived such an ordeal. "My campie husband."

"I'm not certain I was brave, lass. Just determined." He turned his attention to the other side of the burn. "Our first task of the day is to get the wagon and horses across while the tide is still low."

She tugged him away from the water's edge. "And Davie Tait will be the one doing that, because Jamie McKie has a limp that will not be improved by yet another trek o'er Moneypool Burn. Once we reclaim our wagon, I'll find you some dry clothes and a piece of soap." Rose looked down at his bare feet. "Though you'll need to visit a cobbler in Monnigaff for boots."

"Bare feet are very popular among the peasantry in Galloway," he reminded her. "I certainly look the part today."

The weather, at least, was improved. Gray clouds and mist had given way to clear skies and drier air. When Davie appeared, Rose put the young shepherd to work leading the horses and wagon across a shingly stretch. Neither hooves nor wheels sank into the mud. Leana and the maids came along in time to see Hastings ford the burn without incident, and the party reassembled themselves for the last two days of their journey.

Davie scratched his head. "I'm thinkin' ye need tae sit in the wagon for a bit, Mr. McKie."

"Please do," Rose pleaded, eager to have Jamie's company for any reason. "You can ride in the wagon bed with me and stretch out your sore leg." The last two sacks of coins and the gold cord were well concealed at the bottom of a basket of dirty linens, so she had no fear her husband would unearth her secret at the last hour. Leana assured him she was prepared to drive the wagon on to Monnigaff.

"I'll ride yer mount," Davie offered. "We'll meet up wi' Rab aye?"

Jamie hesitated before answering. "I confess, I'll breathe easier when I spy the lad coming our direction."

"If ye'd like, Davie…" Annabel turned bright pink beneath her freckles. "I can…help ye wi' yer lambs."

"Are ye sure, lass?" The hopeful note in Davie's voice was hard to miss. "The collies will wark each side o' the road. If ye'll not mind walkin' behind the flock—and mind yer step whan ye do—I'll ride ahead and see aboot Rab. And then I'll…then I'll join ye, miss."

Jamie's scowl was mere pretense. "It seems my job as topsman has been usurped."

Davie pulled off his cap and hung his head. "Beggin' yer pardon, sir."

"Nae, nae." Jamie waved away his concerns. "Your plan is a fine one, lad. Carry on."

Taking his responsibilities to heart, Davie lifted both gentlewomen into the wagon. Eliza and Ian joined them as Leana took the reins, turning round in her seat to get instructions from Jamie. "Let the flocks and Annabel go ahead of you," he told Leana. "If my brother intends to meet us, it will give us time to see him coming."

Rose slipped her hand round his arm with a sigh. "Hard as it will be, I am relieved this day has finally come, Jamie. Yet I wish you were not limping. I would not have your brother think you weak."

"Jamie is not weak," Leana was quick to say, "but he is in pain, and for that I am sorry." She shifted her gaze to Jamie. "Suppose I prepare a poultice for you. Comfrey may be found in any damp woods in the Lowlands, near rivers especially. The yellow flowers are gone by now, but 'tis the long, oval leaves I need. I'll take the roots as well, since comfrey is also useful to stop bleeding."

Leana did not look at her when she said it, but Rose felt certain the offer was for her benefit. The spot of blood she'd found on her nightgown that morning was small but alarmingly dark. Traveling was surely to blame. Or the excitement of nearing Glentrool. Or the promise of twins. Jamie thought they might reach home sometime Monday. Could she not take special care for two more days?

"I'll appreciate the comfrey," Jamie responded, smiling down at Rose. "Until then, I'll try not to complain about the pain."

Rose gazed up at him. *And I will do the same, my love.*

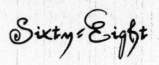

Sixty-Eight

'Tis not for mortals always to be blest.

JOHN ARMSTRONG

When Rose snuggled closer, taking care not to put any weight on Jamie's sore leg, she heard him groan. She quickly sat up, full of apologies.

"Don't be daft," he chided her. "You did not mean to hurt me." He took her hand and lightly touched the place where his thigh and hip met. "A joint of some sort pulled from its mooring. Leana's comfrey will help. So will time, the best of healers."

Rose could not keep her anxiety to herself. "But how will you fight Evan? You cannot walk without cringing, let alone unsheathe your sword…"

"I will not fight my brother."

She stared at him in confusion.

"What a *taigled* look you have, Rose! I'll also not let Evan kill me. Nor hurt one hair on your bonny head." Jamie adjusted his position on the wagon bed, favoring his leg. "'Tis his forgiveness I am after, not his neck beneath my sword. I believe my injury may well serve some good purpose. 'For when I am weak, then am I strong?'"

"Oh, Jamie!" She rolled her eyes. "Wherever do you come up with such things? It must be that nasty scrape on your brow. Leana," she called out, "have you anything in your medicine case for Jamie's head wound? For I fear it has addled his brain."

"I do," her sister said over her shoulder, a smile in her voice. "Lavender."

Jamie closed his eyes, tipping his head against the back of the wagon. "I did enough fighting yestreen to last many a season." As he described in greater detail his harrowing experience, a sense of awe permeated his words. "I might have died, Rose. But I did not."

She lightly stroked the bruise on his forehead. To think, she'd been sleeping soundly in a cozy farmhouse while he fought for his life! "We should have been there. All of us. To help you…to save you…"

"I was not alone, Rose." After a moment he opened his eyes. She had never seen Jamie look so peaceful. "When I face my brother this day, I will be stronger than ever. And when I face my father at kirk on the Sabbath, I pray I will be stronger still."

Rose believed him. How could she not when he was so confident? Yet there he sat, wounded and in pain, without boots on his feet or weapons in his hand. *Something* had happened to her husband; he was not the same man who had disappeared into the fog yestreen.

Blessed of the Almighty. Aye, he was that.

Such a man deserved a gracie wife. Not a thief.

Her gaze fell on the basket of soiled linens that hid the last of the pilfered coins, and her heart sank. While God was busy protecting Jamie, she'd foolishly put his freedom at risk. Rose turned away so he might not see her fresh tears and ask their source. He must never know of her transgression. But she had to tell *someone.* Had to unburden herself of the guilt that weighed far more than the gold. She'd thought getting rid of one would solve the other. But she was wrong.

Could she confess her crime to her heavenly Father, if not her earthly one?

All at once a terrible cramping seized her, as if an unseen hand held her in its grip.

Oh, Father. Perhaps it was too late for confessions. The damage was already done.

Rose sagged against the back of the wagon, pain radiating from a place deep inside her, moving to her limbs, flowing from her body. Aye, more blood. *Please forgive me. Please heal me.*

"Rose?" Jamie's voice. Concerned. "Beloved, is something wrong?" Louder, speaking to her sister. "Leana, might we stop? Rose is not well."

She sensed the wagon slowing to a halt and wrapped her hands round her middle, wishing she could heal her bairns with her touch. *Too late. Too late.*

Leana bent over her, helping her lie down, propping up her feet.

"Jamie, I think it best we not move her. There's a croft there behind the trees. Eliza, take Ian with you and see if the folk who live there might help us. We need cool water to drink and hot water for compresses. And clean rags."

Eliza was gone in an instant, Ian in her arms, while Jamie inched back, giving Leana room.

"My sweet Rose." Leana leaned over her and pressed their cheeks together. "Do not be afraid."

Rose struggled to focus her thoughts. "Please...do not tell..." In the morn perhaps. After Jamie faced Evan. Not now.

"Nae, Rose." Leana's voice was low but her words unbending. "Jamie is your husband. He deserves to know."

When Leana sat up, Jamie moved in beside her. His expression left no room for debate. "Tell me, Leana. For it seems my wife cannot."

Leana looked at them both. "Rose had some...bleeding."

"*Had?* Is this not the first time?"

"I'm sorry, Jamie." Rose lifted her hand, hoping his temper might soften beneath her touch. "'Tis my fault you were not told sooner. Not Leana's." She closed her eyes against the bright sun, while a thin trail of tears escaped from each eye, flowing into her hair. *'Tis all my fault.*

Leana brushed away those tears, her voice as soothing as her fingertips. "Forgive us both, Jamie. It was only a bit of spotting. And 'tis not...unusual. But now that it's happened again, I will take additional precautions and put my medicine case to good use. Rose is young and healthy. You've both nothing to fear."

Rose sighed as Jamie kissed the palm of her hand. *He loves me still.*

"I ken verra well it was Rose's idea to keep this from me." Jamie's tone was no longer quite so stern. "The lass is good at concealing secrets."

Leana looked down at her fondly. "She is that."

Eliza hurried up, bouncing Ian on her shoulder, a peasant lass by her side. "This is Mistress Hughan of Calloch Croft," the maid said, making hasty introductions. "She has a fine gairden o' herbs. Leuk what's she's brought ye, mistress."

Rose watched her sister receive the young woman's humble gifts with heartfelt joy. "Comfrey leaves! Already ground."

"Aye, mem," the crofter said. "Enough for a poultice or twa. And the ither things ye asked aboot are here as weel. I thocht some nettle tea might serve."

Leana eased Rose to a sitting position so she might drink the luke-warm tea from a horn cup. "As you can see, I have two patients, both of whom will benefit from the comfrey." She pinched a bit of the damp herb and added it to Rose's tea. "This evening we shall lodge at an inn where I might nurse you properly. Won't we, Jamie?" Leana gave him a pointed look.

Sitting up, tea in hand, Rose felt somewhat improved. Thank the heavens above, she had worn a dark gown. Perhaps the blood would not show. As she watched the tawny-haired crofter empty her apron full of herbs and pour glasses of cool water for her uninvited guests, her heart went out to the poor lass in her faded gown and tattered cap. Could they not do something for Mistress Hughan in return? Did kindness not deserve a reward?

Her spirits lifted ever so slightly. *Aye. The gold.*

'Twould do much good at Calloch Croft. But however would she place it in the young woman's hands without the rest of them knowing? The basket of linens was at her side. Dared she fish out one of the remaining sacks? And then what?

When Mistress Hughan put her empty wooden pitcher down next to Rose to entertain Ian for a moment, the rest of it came easily enough. The child's squeals of delight at the lass's heartsome antics, twirling him round, drew everyone's attention while Rose quietly transferred the gold. She added two linen handkerchiefs to muffle the sound.

"We must be on our way," Jamie announced, turning to look at her, the green of his eyes more vivid in the sunlight. "Are you feeling well enough to travel, Rose?"

"I am." She pushed the pitcher toward their hostess. "You'll not want to forget this, Mistress Hughan. I tucked a few linens inside. In gratitude for your provision." Not a lie; there *were* linens. If the wooden pitcher seemed heavier to her, the peasant lass did not comment but merely went off, swinging it by her side.

Leana, meanwhile, had pressed the poultice between her fingers into a flat compress the size of her hands. "Rose, you'll need to put this on Jamie's…that is, on whatever part of him is injured." Her pale sister had no hope of hiding a blush. "The skin is not broken, is it, Jamie? For comfrey will not do on an open wound."

He threw a plaid over his lap and grimaced as he eased down his breeches, while Leana and Eliza looked the other way. " 'Twould be easier to manage this in a kilt."

Rose dutifully pressed the poultice against the tender place he'd shown her. When he winced, she knew she'd found the spot. After arranging the plaid for modesty's sake, Rose assured the other women that they were free to ride on. "We've left Annabel tending her sheep by the roadside for a very long time."

The wagon was soon rolling along the meandering banks of the Cree. Annabel walked ahead of them, holding Davie's shepherd's crook over the lambs like a talisman.

After a mile or so Leana turned to see how her passengers were faring. "The kintra folk say comfrey bodes a safe journey."

"If ever we needed such a blessing, 'tis this day." Jamie held the poultice in place with one hand and clasped Rose's hand in the other. "We're not far from Monnigaff."

Rose saw her sister's back stiffen. "And here come Rab and Davie astride Hastings. No doubt with news. From your brother."

Sixty-Nine

I want that grace that springs from thee,
That quickens all things where it flows.

WILLIAM COWPER

Until he saw his brother face to face, Jamie would not know if his letter or his lambs had softened his brother's hard heart. But Rab Murray might know. As the lad rode up, Jamie steeled himself for the shepherd's report.

"Yer brither was waitin' at the Cree Inn after a'." Rab let Davie dismount to join Annabel, then turned Hastings round to walk alongside the slow-moving wagon. "Said that yestreen was too *dreich* for man or beast."

"So it was," Jamie agreed. Vivid memories of his night in Moneypool Burn rose before him. "What did my brother say about the lambs? Did he accept my gift, small as it was?"

"He did." Rab scratched at his shirt, as though a bath might be in order. "Ane o' his herds was plannin' to drive the lambs tae his farm in Sorbie parish."

Jamie sat up straighter in the wagon. "The men with him are *shepherds*?"

"Herds and hinds, the lot o' them. Whan I walked through the inn door, me heart thumpin' 'neath me sark, I thocht I'd be facin' ten scoonrels." Rab grinned. "Turns oot, I was leukin' at ten o' meself."

Jamie rubbed the back of his neck, all the while erasing the image he'd carried in his mind. Of Evan glowering at him from the head of a rough-hewn table, flanked by ten ruthless men. Scoundrels, just as Rab had expected. "Shepherds," Jamie repeated, still trying to grasp the truth. "And farmworkers."

"Braw lads, they were. Like most workin' men." Rab winked at Eliza, who turned the color of red campion in May.

"And plainly attired, I hope." Jamie put aside the cooled poultice and rearranged his clothing. Though his coat and breeches were clean, they had little else to recommend them. He'd hoped to meet Evan in the manner in which he'd confronted Lachlan—a well-dressed prince, not a barefoot pauper. Instead, Jamie would take a humbler approach in every respect. And pray it would not cost him his life.

"Was Evan kind to you?" Rose asked.

"Weel, he wasna cruel." The shepherd rubbed his chin, covered with red bristles. "Nor was he a man o' mony wirds."

Jamie nodded in acknowledgment. "When we were young, I was the one who used words, mostly as a weapon. My brother used his dirk."

His own dirk would be useless now, Jamie realized, since without boots, he could not carry the dagger properly. The weapon would remain in the wagon, along with his harmless pistol. Not his sword, though; he had a use for that.

They'd reached the edge of Monnigaff, an old village of one-story houses thatched with straw that clustered along a low piece of ground where the Penkill Burn spilled into the River Cree. Not nearly so wide here as at Ferrytown, the river was tamed by stony banks and spanned by a bridge built some forty years past. Monnigaff's Saturday market was under way with visitors from surrounding parishes bustling about, purchasing meal and malt.

Jamie wondered if he would even find his brother in such a crowd. "Davie, get the lambs settled north of town. And, Leana, kindly park the wagon where you can."

She continued past Cree Bridge to a shady spot along the road running parallel with the Penkill and guided the horses to a stop. "Will we...*all* be meeting Evan?"

"You will," Jamie said firmly. A public confession, with his family as witnesses, would be best. Easing onto the ground, he strapped on his scabbard and forced himself to put his full weight on his leg. He'd not waited two years to greet his brother with a limp. It was not sympathy he wanted but mercy. Forgiveness for the unforgivable. Only then could he hold up his head as laird of Glentrool. Only then would he live in freedom.

When Leana stood, he cautioned her, "Let Rab lift you down, lass. I am sorry that I cannot."

Leana leaned over the edge of the wagon so Rab might catch her. Once on her feet, she gathered a sleeping Ian in her arms, then turned toward her sister. "Jamie, I think it best that Rose not be moved."

Though Rose was sitting up, her face was chalky and her eyes wide. "Jamie, will you mind terribly if I wait here?"

"Not at all." He leaned across the wagon side to clasp her hands, which were too cool for a warm August day. "I only mind that you are not well, Rose." Was she still bleeding? Was their child in danger? *Heaven help me!* 'Twas impossible, having his heart and mind in two places. "We'll not delay after services tomorrow," he promised, "but will press on to Glentrool. Would that suit you?"

"Aye," she said on a sigh, clearly relieved. "I shall sleep in my new home tomorrow night."

"You will, Rose." He tightened his hold on her. "Your new home. On the Sabbath." *Lord, may it be so.* He was loath to leave her, yet his search for Evan could not be delayed. "I must find my brother. Pray for me, lass."

"Every moment you are gone." She lowered her head to kiss his hands. "Our children need a father, Jamie. Please come back to me."

With her words pounding inside him, Jamie lined up his party, intending to present them to Evan with all the dignity the occasion merited. Though they were a bedraggled group, worn down from days of travel, they were important to him and deserved a proper introduction. "Rab, you'll stand behind me, aye? And have Davie join you? Then Annabel and Eliza. Then Leana, with my son."

Jamie turned round to catch his wife's eye, hoping to encourage her. "This is your place, Rose. The place of honor."

Rose's smile was faint. "If you say so, Jamie."

"Mr. McKie." Rab yanked at his coat sleeve. "Thar he is."

Jamie looked up in time to see his brother emerge from the Cree Inn, not fifty ells away. Dressed in a drugget coat and unpolished boots. Bright red hair tied at the nape of his thick neck. *Evan McKie.* Bold as ever, standing on the threshold, surveying the crowd. His herds and hinds gathered round him, none taller than his shoulders.

Jamie held his ground, waiting until Evan looked his way.

Their eyes met. *At last, my brother.*

Jamie moved first, leaving his household well behind him, where they would be safe. He walked erect, without limping, ignoring the pain in his leg. Though his head and feet were bare, his sword hung at his side. *Wait for me, Evan. Let me come to you.*

The milling crowd between the two men stepped back, giving Jamie room. Or so it seemed to him, so focused were his thoughts. *For thou art my hope, O Lord.*

When Evan took the first step toward him, Jamie stopped and bowed. Low, as a servant might. His fingers brushed the ground. Dirt covered his feet.

After a moment he straightened and moved forward, the path before him widening. As he walked, Jamie put his hand to his sword, slowly pulling it free of the scabbard. Not with a mighty, metallic ringing, but with a quiet sound, a single note.

Jamie stopped again, ten ells from his brother, and laid the blade of the sword across his outstretched palms. The language of surrender. Gritting his teeth against the pain, he slowly knelt in the dusty marketplace. Head bowed, arms trembling, Jamie lifted the sword above his shoulders, above his head, reaching toward his brother until he could reach no more.

Footsteps thundered toward him. The blade was knocked from his hands. Rough hands pulled him to his feet.

"Jamie!" Evan dragged him into his embrace, his tear-stained face buried in Jamie's neck.

He collapsed in his brother's arms. Tears streamed down his face. Jamie did not care who saw him thus. He was no less a man.

"You've come home, my brother." Evan groaned the words, tightening his hold on him. "You've come home."

Jamie tried to speak, tried to say the words he had come to say. "I have sinned against heaven. And against you, Evan. I am no longer worthy to be called your brother."

"Och, Jamie." Evan released him but not before he shook him.

Hard. "You are the only brother I have." He scowled, but Jamie knew the look well. There was no malice in it. "Did you think I'd bear a grudge against you forever?"

"I did." Jamie wiped the heels of his hands across his eyes, his relief so great he almost laughed aloud. "If not forever, at least my own lifetime."

" 'Tis true, I threatened to kill you. On the night you swicked our father, I well might have." Evan clamped a meaty hand on Jamie's shoulder, emphasizing each phrase with a firm grip. "But the humble man who wrote me that letter was not the same man who ran from Glentrool two years ago. My lost brother is found. I'll not lose you again, Jamie."

Jamie swallowed. "Nor I you."

Evan dragged his sleeve across his unshaven face with a ragged snort, then pointed to the men behind him. "These are the new herds and hinds I fee'd at Lammas." He scratched his head, tangling some of his woolly red hair. "I'd introduce you to them, Jamie, but I haven't learned all their names yet."

The men smiled among themselves, clearing their throats and shuffling their feet. Whatever sort of man they thought had hired them, Jamie felt certain they'd seen a new side of Evan McKie. The market crowd began to disperse, as if they'd received what they came for that day.

Evan looked past him, his features softening. "Are those folk yours, the ones lined up by the wagon? I'd best meet them, aye?" He swept Jamie's sword from the ground and returned it, then both men walked toward the McKie household. "Mother says you've married, Jamie. Is the lad my nephew, then?"

"Indeed he is. The Lord has blessed me far more than I deserve." Jamie proudly named each member of his party. "Rab Murray you've met. And here's another shepherd from Newabbey parish, Davie Tait." It was hard to ignore their astonished expressions, their mouths hanging open like fish hoping for a fly.

Eliza and Annabel dropped deep curtsies as Jamie introduced them. "I'll be sending the lads back with the wagon, but the lasses will be coming with us to Glentrool."

"You'll not like cleaning the place," Evan warned them. "See that

Jamie calls you lady's maids from the start so Ivy Findlay won't get ideas about putting you to work with mop and broom, aye?"

"Aye!" they answered in unison, blushing at his attention.

Two more steps, and Jamie stood in front of Leana. Her moss green gown followed the contours of their growing child. She'd been crying, for her pale cheeks were still wet. He leaned forward and murmured, "Tears of joy, I hope."

Her eyes shone like stars. "I have never been more proud of you, Jamie."

He maintained control, but barely. "Evan, this is my first wife, Leana McBride. And our firstborn, Ian James McKie."

Evan bowed to Leana, appraising her with a decidedly male eye. "A lovely lass and a fine mother, I see." He stuck out a stout finger for Ian to latch on to, which he promptly did, giving it a hearty shake. "Your lad must be about my son's age."

Jamie hesitated before he answered. He would not allow their sons to drive a wedge between them or to fight with each other in years to come. "Ian was born on the fourth of October, the day after your Archie."

"Ah, so you know about Archibald." Evan grunted. "I suppose Mother told you the news."

"Nae, 'twas John McMillan of Glenhead. I saw him at Keltonhill Fair." Jamie smiled as Ian bent his uncle's finger hard enough that Evan yelped and snatched it back. "Truth is, Brother, I thought I might see *you* at Keltonhill."

Evan's red eyebrows arched. "As I recall, Mother ordered us ne'er to climb that hill on Fair day again."

"You'll not tell her, aye?" Jamie adjusted Hastings's bridle. "I bought this beast there."

"I've no interest in your horse, James, when I've another fair *flooer* to meet." Evan swung round, a broad grin on his ruddy face. "Who might this lass be?"

"A flower indeed." Ashamed of his negligence, Jamie kissed Rose's hand in apology, relieved to find it warmer than before. Her dark blue gown made her skin look like porcelain. Despite the dryness of her lips, she was smiling, and her eyes bore a bit more sparkle. "Evan, this is

Rose McKie, my second wife. She will bear me another blessing come January."

Evan lowered his head and said in a hoarse whisper, "*Two* wives? I didn't think you'd been gone that long."

Jamie shifted his stance, for his leg had begun to ache. " 'Tis a complicated story, which I'll save for somewhere other than the street."

"If you say so." Evan straightened. "Though you might want to have an answer ready when you see folk at kirk in the morn's morn." He nodded toward the old Monnigaff church across the Penkill Burn. "Two wives, both carrying your bairns…"

Evan's voice trailed off, but his meaning was clear. Leana had her letter ready for Reverend Erskine, but it would hardly be passed round the kirk. As the native parishioner, Jamie knew the answers must come from him.

" 'Twill be strange," Jamie admitted, "to see the household in the morn. And trail home behind them after services. Is Father in good health?"

"I've not seen him in a fortnight, but, aye, he was well. Mother, as always, will be glad to see her beloved son." His brother's words bore no bitterness. Jamie had been their mother's favorite, and they both knew it. Evan slung an arm round Jamie's shoulders and walked him up the road a bit. "About the forty lambs you sent me. I've pasturelands of my own down in Sorbie, with more sheep than I can count. Why not keep what's yours and take them on to Glentrool?"

Jamie knew why. "Because I gave those sheep as a tithe. Not only to you, but to the Almighty." He glanced sideways at his brother, wondering how he might react. Their father had always been the halie one at Glentrool, seeking an audience with God. Not them. "The lambs were stolen from me," Jamie confessed, "but the Lord restored them. 'Tis only right that you keep my tithe meant for him. And for you."

Evan slowed his steps, releasing his hold on Jamie's shoulder. "You've become a right gracie man, James McKie."

"I ken what the grace of God looks like." Jamie met his gaze, brother to brother. "Because today I saw it on your face."

Now it was Evan's turn to look uncomfortable. " 'Tis what the Buik says, aye? 'Grace for grace.'" Evan shrugged, though Jamie could see that his words had pleased him. "I'll keep your lambs, Jamie. Though they appear to be runts of twins. Like someone else I ken."

Jamie laughed. "They *are* runts, every one of them."

"Sometimes runts fill out." Evan eyed him from head to toe. "I believe you could take me in a fight now."

Jamie extended his hand. "A fight won't be necessary, my brother."

Evan clasped Jamie's hand in his. "Indeed it will not."

"Jamie?" Leana came hurrying up to him, anxiety etched across her brow. "I wonder if we might find our lodging. Rose would be more comfortable…if she…"

"I'll come at once, lass." He touched her arm in assurance. "Evan, I fear I must away." Jamie started for the wagon, walking backward as he called to his brother, "Bring Judith and your son to Glentrool for a visit. Or we'll head south to Sorbie in the spring, when my children are safely delivered."

Evan gestured toward the Cree Bridge. "Might you not come to Sorbie now? At least let me send a herd or two along with you to lend a hand for the morn."

Jamie slowed his steps, longing to have more time with his brother, yet feeling the pull of his own family, who needed him. "You've done more than enough."

Evan lifted his hand in farewell. "Godspeed then, for your journey's far from over."

Seventy

He travels safest in the dark night who travels lightest.
HERNANDO CORTEZ

Y ou are certain the valise is all you need?"

"Aye, Jamie." Leana motioned him inside the Cree Inn's cramped second-floor accommodations, where she was watching over a slumbering Rose. Jamie had his own lodging next door, the maids and Ian were tucked in a corner room on the first floor, and the herds were sleeping on the braes.

Leana kept her voice low, not wanting to wake her sister. "Rose and I will wear the same gowns tomorrow. The valise and my medicine box are truly all we require."

Jamie handed them both to her with a slight grimace. "I fear my leg is not improving with each climb up the stair."

He'd hidden his discomfort valiantly while in Evan's company and all through their supper hour at the inn. Now pain lined Jamie's face and clouded his eyes. Leana folded her hands, resisting the urge to touch the tender wound on his brow. "I have some remedies that might help you sleep comfortably. And speed your healing."

"After you've cared for Rose, I would welcome anything you and your medicine box might have to offer." Jamie dipped his head, a gentleman's bow, then walked past her and sat on a low wooden creepie beside one of the two narrow beds. He stretched out his legs, clad in a new pair of boots purchased in haste as the market stalls were closing. "And here is my 'fair flooer,' as my brother rightly called her."

Though her color looked better, Rose had eaten little at supper and had fallen asleep the moment her head touched the pillow. At least her bleeding had been less than they'd feared. Not enough to stain her gown, which hung on the wall for the Sabbath. Nor had the spotting continued after that morning's bout. Leana was grateful for both those things, but it did not lessen her concerns.

Jamie leaned across the bed and ran his hand over Rose's unbound hair, the dark strands fanned across the pillow. "I'll be glad when she is home, and we can feed her Aubert's rich hotchpotch."

" 'Twould be good for her," Leana agreed, making no promises; the thick soup was one of her sister's least favorite dishes. "Might you like some time alone with Rose? I can visit with Ian, if you like."

He did not say anything for a moment. When he did, his voice was strained. "You are ever thoughtful, Leana." As Jamie turned his head, she saw the mist in his eyes. "Will she... Will the child Rose carries..."

Leana sank to her knees beside him, wanting to comfort him, yet knowing she must speak the truth. "I am praying for Rose by the hour. I fear she may be growing weaker, though she'll not admit it." She bowed her head as guilt settled round her shoulders. "Please forgive me, Jamie. I should have told you about her bleeding when she first confessed it to me."

"Indeed you should have." His hand rested on her head so lightly that she could not feel the weight, only the warmth. "But then you would have broken a promise to your sister. You are a woman who honors her vows, Leana. Even if others do not." When he stood, the warmth was gone. "I leave Rose in your good care. If she awakens, come find me."

Leana took Jamie's vacated seat as he closed the door behind him. She pressed the back of her hand against Rose's brow—no fever, thanks be to God—then dipped her finger in a cup of cool water and moistened Rose's chapped lips. The stuffy room's only window had no sash, letting in light but not air. Leana did what she could, folding back the thin blanket and straightening the sheet, before going in search of her medicines.

Even in her sleep, Rose must have noticed the change in temperature or sensed someone moving about. She stirred and opened her eyes. "Leana?"

"Pardon me, dearie." Chagrined, Leana hurried back to her side. "I did not mean to disturb you."

"Truly, you did not." Rose stretched, her toes reaching past the end of the small bed. "I've only been half-asleep, drifting in and out. Dreaming of holding my twins."

"A fine dream." Leana lifted a slender brown bottle from the collection in her medicine box. "I fear I've not many remedies that are safe for you just now. Not lady's mantle, certainly. Wild sage, cowslip, and juniper are not for expectant mothers. Nor shepherd's-purse." With care she pulled the cork from the bottle in her hand. "Ah, but selfheal. This will do." She added a generous dose of the syrup to the cup of water from the washstand, then helped Rose sit up. "Drink this down, please. The kintra folk call it 'prince's feather.' Good for bleeding."

While Rose sipped her medicine, making faces as she did, Leana hunted about for a linen towel to soak up a stray drop of syrup from the washstand. A basket of soiled linens caught her eye. Had Jamie brought them up for some reason? When Leana reached in to retrieve a towel, Rose began to choke.

"Heavens, dearie!" Leana was by her side at once, whisking away the cup. "Can you breathe?"

Rose sank against the roughly plastered wall beside her. "I can breathe. What I cannot do…that is…oh, my sister." She pointed across the room, her hand shaking. "Look inside the basket. I fear it holds…all my secrets."

Leana crossed the room in a few steps, dreading what she might find hidden beneath the linens. A lumpy pouch, cool to the touch. Its heavy contents shifted in her hands as she pulled it out. She did not need to untie the ragged knot to know what the bundle contained.

"Father's gold," Rose said, sparing her the effort. "The last of it. If I am not well enough to attend services in the morn, you must put it in the offering box for me when no one is looking."

"Rose!" The bag of coins slipped from her hands and landed on the wooden floor with a thud. "Is that what you did with the rest of it? All those kirks you visited… I thought you were…praying."

Rose nodded, color returning to her cheeks in full measure. "I did pray. But I also gave a generous offering. For the poor."

"Very generous." Leana left the bag on the floor for a moment, almost afraid to touch the coins that once belonged to Lachlan McBride.

So few left there was no point in returning them. 'Twas too late. "When Father searched our rooms at the Murray Arms—"

"They were underneath my gown. I was sitting on them." A note of satisfaction rang through her words. "The thrifite is long gone. Kindling for the Lammas fire on Keltonhill. But something else remains."

The wutch's cord. Leana swallowed. "I cannot—"

"You *must* not touch it!"

"Someone must." Leana retrieved the bag of coins and placed them on the battered dresser. "Rose...we have to tell Jamie."

"Nae!" Her sister clutched the bedsheet as if prepared to hide behind it.

Leana shared her apprehension; Jamie would be furious. Still, she would not make the same mistake again, keeping something from him at Rose's bidding.

"Secrets have no place in a marriage, dearie." Leana hated the tone she heard in her voice. The scolding older sister. But Rose had endangered them all—her husband more than anyone. Had their father found the gold, he would have blamed no one else but Jamie. And seen him condemned as a thief. How could Rose have been so foolish?

Leana took a deep breath, exhaling her frustration. Rose was her only sister, and she loved her no matter what she had done or why she had done it. Yet one fact remained: "Jamie must know. We'll tell him together."

Rose huddled against the wall, her dark eyes wide with fear. "He will never forgive me."

The knock at the door was sharp, insistent. "Leana? Rose?"

It seemed the paper-thin walls of the inn had not guarded their secret.

Leana opened the door, hoping she did not look as guilty as she felt. "Do come in, Jamie. My sister and I have...something to tell you."

His coat was absent, and his shirt hung loose about his neck, as if he'd already retired for the night and been rudely awakened. When he stepped into the room and closed the door, Leana instinctively backed up. His gaze was fixed on her alone and was not cordial.

"I asked you to find me if Rose awakened."

"Jamie…" Rose spoke in a voice meant to soothe. "I've not been awake but a short time. Leana and I were…talking."

When he turned, his hard gaze raked past the sack of coins, then stopped. He lifted the bundle off the dresser, hefting it in his hand for a moment before letting it drop to the floor. "That is what I heard while lying in my bed not five minutes ago. The unmistakable sound of shillings and sovereigns." Jamie's voice was frighteningly even. "But these coins do not belong to us. Do they?"

Seventy-One

But the beating of my own heart
Was all the sound I heard.

RICHARD MONCKTON MILNES, LORD HOUGHTON

Leana held her breath. *Let him be merciful, Lord.*
Jamie looked at Rose first, as though gauging her guilt. Then he turned to Leana, his expression almost as cold as the morning he'd awakened expecting Rose in his marriage bed and had found her instead. *Did you hope I simply wouldn't notice?* She shuddered, remembering.

"Speak to me, Leana." His voice, his gaze, demanded obedience. "Though I ken you are not the one who stole your father's gold."

"I just learned the truth tonight," she began, then realized she was protecting herself. And incriminating Rose. "But I've suspected…that is, I've known…for the last few days…"

"And said nothing to me."

"Jamie, it wasn't my place."

"Your *place*?" He threw his arms in the air, clearly exasperated. "You are the mother of my son and the sister of my wife. I trust you with everything that matters to me."

Everything that matters. Leana feared she was no longer included on that list.

His low voice bore a note of anger. "If you suspected…nae, if you even *imagined* for one moment that Rose had done such a preposterous thing, you should have come to me." Jamie snatched the coins off the floor, crushing the bag in his fist. "You heard the vow I made to your father. If Lachlan had found this gold…if he had…if he…"

With an anguished cry, Jamie threw the bag of coins against the dresser, bursting the seams of the cotton. Gold and silver went everywhere.

"Jamie, please!" Leana flew to Rose's side. Her sister was weeping, her face turned to the wall. "Have you forgotten that your wife is not well? Rose did not know that Father would follow us. Or that you would make such a...rash vow."

"Rash?" Jamie groaned, lowering himself onto the edge of her bed. "But I was certain...so very certain..." His voice, taut with pain, finally broke. "*Why*, Rose?"

She struggled to lift her head from the sheet. "I wanted to...hurt my father. For what he did to you. And to me. And to my sister. I did not think...I did not...*think*." Rose collapsed into sobs, her back rising and falling beneath Leana's gentle stroking.

Leana took a breath to steady her nerves. *Please, Father. Help him see the truth.* Leaning forward, she lightly rested her hand on Jamie's shoulder, praying he would not shrug it off or reject the plea she was about to make.

"Jamie, your..." She faltered, then began again. "Your brother willingly forgave you, even though you once stole something of great value to him. Might you extend mercy to my sister...for the same sin?"

Beneath her hands, Jamie and Rose both stilled. Leana held her breath, listening for a different sound. Not the crash of coins, but the sound of grace.

Rose's voice, scant more than a whisper. "Please...forgive me."

Jamie reached toward her. "Only if you will forgive my anger. I did not mean...I did not... Oh, my love." He moaned, almost a keening.

A half turn, and Rose was in his arms.

Leana inched along the edge of the bed, giving them room, even as her heart burst its dam. Pain, relief, sorrow, joy poured through her soul like water. Drowning her. She loved them both. She did. But to see them like this...their hearts joined as one. It was too hard. It hurt too much.

"Please..." Leana stifled the word with her hands.

Neither of them looked up.

She slipped out of the room unnoticed and fled down the stair, one thought on her mind. *Ian.* The Lord had taken Jamie from her arms, but he had given her a son. And one day, a daughter. *More than enough, Lord. More than enough.*

She knocked on the maidservants' door, ashamed of her tears, mortified by her need.

Eliza opened the door and ushered her in at once. She asked no questions nor needed direction. "Ian?" The maid lifted him from his crib, which took up half the tiny room. "Leuk wha's hastened doon the stair tae see her boy. Guid ye're still awake, eh?" Eliza poured him into his mother's arms, his body warm and languid, his head nuzzling beneath her chin as Leana drew her son to her heart.

One embrace, and she was healed.

All the broken places were mended. All the empty corners were filled.

Leana offered her thanks, then stepped into the hall, so glad to have Ian she did not care if she had nowhere to go. It was a mild night. Perhaps she might step out of doors and drink in the freshening air.

She would remain near the inn rather than have the elders of the parish find her wandering the streets of the village. Monnigaff was her home parish now. It would not do to begin on the wrong foot. She had the testimonial letter from Reverend Gordon in her reticule and would take it to services in the morn, where she would meet Jamie's parents and the Glentrool household.

"I am Ian McKie's mother," she would say when asked. A sufficient depiction of her role. A worthy title. *The future heir of Glentrool.* She would not say those words, but they did comfort her. To raise so blessed a child, was that not honor enough?

Without the moon's lantern, the sky was black, awash with stars. She took a few steps away from the door, lest it fly open without warning, and simply stood there, basking in the beauty of the night and the peaceful sound of flowing water. Eliza had tucked a small blanket round Ian, though Leana prayed her body and her love were enough to keep him warm.

When the door did open, it was not with a bang but with a soft creak, followed by stealthy footsteps. "Leana?"

Startled, she spun round, guarding Ian with her arms. "Jamie?" His face was shrouded in darkness. She could see the knotted cord half-concealed beneath his shirt. "Whatever are you doing?"

"Getting rid of something."

Bethankit. "Do you need my help?"

"Only as a witness that this unco thing has been buried. I will not allow anything so…evil, so *fause* beneath our roof again." He strode forward, his hand pressed to the small of her back. "I ken the verra place to bury it."

Leana knew as well. "Beneath an oak. 'Twas the first tree God made, some say. Strong. And safe."

They did not have far to walk to reach the spreading branches of an oak, still green and thick with leaves. Jamie found a stout stick and dug as deep a grave for the cord as he could, loosening the dirt, chopping at the ground until his stick broke in two. Even in the black of night, the gold cord was visible, palpable.

Leana turned away, shielding Ian. Though he was fast asleep, she would not allow him to be sullied by its cantrip.

Jamie grasped the knotted cord with his shirttail and tossed it in the gaping hole between the roots of the oak. He filled in the dirt, scraping his new boots across the ground until the strange grave was filled, then he stamped on the loose soil, packing it down. " 'Tis done."

She could not see the relief on his face, but she heard it in his voice. "And the coins?"

"In the collection box for the poor come the morn."

Rose's wishes had prevailed. A fitting end to ill-gotten gain.

Jamie steered her back toward the inn, his eye on Ian. "Will you put him to bed now?"

"I am afraid he *was* in bed. But…" How could she explain herself? *My heart was breaking. I needed to know my son loved me. Even if you no longer do.* She could say none of those things. "I wanted to see Ian." The truth, no more.

"We've had a most trying day, Leana. No wonder you wanted the solace of holding your son." Jamie paused at the door, his gaze locked with hers. "I do understand, lass. More than you ken." He started inside, then turned, as if remembering something. "I have ordered a hot bath brought to your room and another to mine. With all that has transpired and my family meeting us at kirk tomorrow, I thought that a stab at cleanliness might be in order."

422 Liz Curtis Higgs

"A fine idea, Jamie." She could already feel the warmth of the water and smell the fragrance of her lavender soap.

He knocked the dirt from his boots against the doorjamb. "You mentioned having some remedy to help me sleep. Might that offer still hold?"

Seventy-Two

But God to man doth speak in solitude.

JOHN STUART BLACKIE

His bath was steaming, the wooden tub and pails of water having been delivered by two inn servants who grunted rather than spoke and took the pennies Jamie offered them without a word of acknowledgment.

Now that he had the room to himself, Jamie longed to do away with his clothes and climb in, letting the hot water ease the throbbing pain in his thigh. But Leana assured him she would stop by his room the moment she got Rose settled, delivering an herb for his bath and another for his head wound. His only choice was to wait and hope the water did not grow cold.

Jamie ran his fingers across his brow, feeling for the nasty abrasion and the painful lump beneath it. The swelling had gone down considerably, but the skin had been scraped open and seemed in no hurry to heal. Leana would have to look upon his ugly wound long enough to dab it with one of her concoctions.

Leana. He was glad she had come, for myriad reasons. But it seemed she was anything but happy, forced to be with him and Rose round the clock. At Glentrool, he would see that she had a corner of the house all to herself. The second floor of the turret perhaps, allowing her to come and go down the spiral stair without constantly crossing paths with him. Would such solitude make her life easier? *Or would it make yours easier, Jamie?*

He heard her gentle tap at the door. The murmured syllables of his name.

Ushering her into the small room furnished with naught but bed and tub, he apologized again for their humble lodgings. "I do not even have a chair to offer you, Leana."

"Nor do I need one." She placed a teacup, covered with a saucer, on the floor by his tub, then propped her medicine box on the low bed, avoiding his gaze, her unbound hair swinging round her like a veil. "I'll not be here a moment, for your bath awaits."

At her bidding, he sat on the edge of the bed so she might treat his wound. He recognized the scent at once. "Lavender," he said as she gingerly dabbed the open skin. "Will I smell like you, then?"

Her smile was faint. "The scent fades with time. As do most things." *Not all things, Leana.*

She pulled out one brown bottle, then put it back, still searching. "Rose is feeling much improved. Or so she assured me when I left her soaking."

He was relieved to hear it, for Rose had not looked well earlier. *And whose fault is that?* His angry outburst was the last thing Rose needed. They'd forgiven each other, but such histrionics were not good for her health. "Will Rose be able to join us at kirk in the morn? To meet my family?"

"I believe so." Leana sorted through the medicine box Duncan had fashioned for her long ago, then plucked out a small vial and held it up. "Ah." She emptied half a dozen drops in his still-steaming bathwater. "Oil of thyme. The scent alone is said to give a man courage and strength."

"I'll need both, come the morning." Jamie leaned over the water, breathing in the pleasant aroma. "It will help me sleep, you say?"

"The thyme in your bath is meant to improve your limp." She bent down to reclaim the teacup, sliding the saucer beneath it. "For sleeping, I've brewed some dried leaves in tea. Medieval apothecaries considered thyme an infallible cure for that troublesome disorder..." She paused, handing him his hot drink. "The nightmare."

He sipped it just to humor her. The taste was bitter, pungent, earthy.

"You'll drink it all, aye?" Her hand was on the door latch, her honey-colored brows arched as she waited for an answer.

"I shall." Jamie lifted his cup to her. "Sleep well, lass."

Whether because of the heat of his bathwater or the herb that scented it, Jamie had crawled into bed and fallen asleep instantly, almost free of pain. But the thyme did not hold his frightening dreams at bay. At least not the dream he vividly remembered, the one that woke him long after the break of day.

A dense fog had crept across Galloway overnight, its damp tendrils curling beneath the inn doors and through the window cracks. The air was as gray withindoors as out. Jamie sat up, heart pounding, trying to remember the words that were spoken. That was all his dream was, a voice. Unquestionably divine. Speaking directly to him.

Your name is no longer James. Laird of Glentrool shall be your name.

"Nae!" he had argued. As if one might spar with God and emerge victorious.

But Jamie knew he could not be laird of Glentrool. Not yet.

The voice identified itself, quite clearly—*I am God Almighty*—leaving no room for doubt. And then the promise came that had filled Jamie with dread and awakened him with trepidation. *The land that I once gave Archibald and Alec McKie, I give to you and to your seed.*

Glentrool could not be his. Not unless his father was dead.

"Nae, I will see him at kirk." Jamie threw aside his bedsheet, wishing he might do the same with his unsettling dream. Glentrool would be his someday. *But, please God, not this day.*

He dressed in a fresh shirt and breeches, then brushed his coat clean, shaking his head in disbelief. "James McKie, heir of Glentrool, without valet or manservant," he chided himself. "How are the mighty fallen!"

His heart stopped. *David's words at the death of Saul.*

Jamie threw his few possessions into a leather traveling bag, then limped into the corridor and rapped on the door next to his, doing a poor job of curbing his anxiety. By his reckoning 'twas well past eight. The women took their time answering the door. He'd lifted his knuckles to knock a second time when the door opened no more than a handbreadth.

Leana gazed at him through the narrow space. "Rose is...not ready."

He tried to look round her, but Leana was tall for a woman, and her hair was piled on her head beneath a feathery bonnet that matched her green gown. The color of his eyes, she'd once told him. "I see you are dressed for the day," he said.

"And so is Rose." Leana opened the door another inch. "But we are not certain… That is, it might be best…"

"Leana, for heaven's sake. Let me see my wife."

She opened the door at last, bidding him enter. Rose was indeed attired for kirk, wearing the same blue gown, the hem brushed clean, the lace collar pressed. Her hair, too, was neatly dressed—the maidservants had been busy that morning—and a small hat he'd forgotten she owned was perched atop her dark hair.

But her face was ashen. As gray as the fog that hovered outside the inn's curtainless windows.

"Rose!" He stepped closer and pulled her into his arms. She came willingly, but he felt the weakness in her body. As if she were standing by sheer will. "Tell me, beloved. Have you… Is there…" He could not even bring himself to say the word. *Blood.*

Her nod confirmed his fears.

Jamie held her tighter still, as if his love might heal her, as if his strength might seep through her gown. Words tumbled out of his mouth, words that made little sense. "Leana, what can we… Isn't there …something?"

When he saw her blue eyes pool with tears, he knew the answer.

"Rose…" He pressed his cheek to hers, praying she would understand. "Perhaps it would be best if you…waited here."

Her back stiffened. "But, Jamie—"

"After the morning service, we shall see whether you are able to travel or if it would be better to remain—"

"Nae." Rose stepped out of his embrace, her heidie nature in full force, even if her strength was not. "I want to go home, Jamie. I want to rest in our own bed until I am well." She looked up at him, the shadows beneath her eyes stark against her skin. "The moment the service ends, come for me and take me home."

"I shall." He kissed her, sealing their bargain, then helped her stretch out on the bed. After loosening her collar and unpinning her hat, he hesitated, reluctant to leave her behind. "Rose, I fear we must go. My family should be arriving shortly, and I…" Nae, he would not burden her with his fears. Not now.

"I will be fine, Jamie." She did sound better. "Rest is the best cure."

"You are certain?" He waited until her eyes convinced him. "Annabel will keep you company. Send for us at once if you feel worse."

"Go, Jamie. My sister is already halfway out the door." Rose swatted him with the edge of her sheet, though not very hard. "Off with you, and let me sleep."

Jamie left the room with misgivings, torn between wanting to stay with Rose, yet needing to see his father and mother and know that they were well. Leana descended the stair ahead of him, the feathers on her hat bobbing with each step. Her reticule disappeared in and out of the folds of her gown, the shape distorted by her father's gold. The three of them had agreed that Leana, a stranger in Monnigaff, would be the best one to slip the coins in the poor box unnoticed.

Wrapped in fog thick as broth, Jamie waited outside the inn while Leana made arrangements with the maids. Before long she appeared with Eliza, who bore a fresh-scrubbed Ian in her arms.

Jamie smiled at his son and felt the tightness in his chest ease. His father could not help but be pleased at having another grandson. Especially one so healthy and bright eyed as this one. "If we can find the kirk in this weather, we'll be there shortly." Though the fog slowed their steps, they soon crossed the arched bridge over the burn and followed the curving road uphill to their destination.

Six centuries old with a yew tree older still, the medieval kirk stood high above the watery confluence of the Cree and the Penkill, overlooking their union like a minister presiding at a wedding ceremony. The rising mist from the river and burn swirled round the headstones—the oldest in Galloway, parishioners boasted.

Though Davie had stayed with the lambs, Jamie and the others found Rab among those who'd arrived early and were milling about the kirkyard. "Leuk, Mr. McKie!" He pointed to a gravestone faintly marked with the year 1416. "Maun be a relative o' mine. 'A. Murray,' it says."

Jamie acknowledged him, even as he leaned toward Leana. "Now is the time, lass. 'Twill be empty inside." While she hastened away, bound for the kirk door, Jamie surveyed his neighbors from the hills and glens as they prepared for worship, anticipating the first bell.

Some peered at him, curious, as if they thought they knew him but were not certain. Others recognized him at once and rudely turned their backs. *Will any in the parish receive me?* John McMillan had avoided his question; now Jamie understood why. Things would not improve when the parish met his two cousins—nae, his two wives.

Evan told him to have an answer ready, and Jamie had one: the truth. "This is Leana, my first wife and the mother of my son, Ian."

A realization struck him, and on its heels a sharp stab of guilt: Not having Rose with him this first Sabbath would make things less awkward. Jamie confessed his transgression at once. *Forgive me, Rose. You will be here next Sabbath. And I will gladly introduce you.*

Leana walked toward him, her reticule swinging by her side, noticeably lighter. She did not take his arm, nor did he offer it. "All is well," she said simply, tipping back her head as the kirk bell rang in the belfry, calling all to worship.

With Jamie leading the way, the small group skirted the headstones. "Are a' these deid McKies related tae ye?" Rab asked.

"Distant relatives, aye." Jamie glanced at several graves in passing. "But my grandfather and grandmother are buried at Glentrool. We've a private mausoleum for the family, consecrated by the parish minister. I'll not be buried here at the kirk, nor will my parents." He shuddered, thinking of his waking dream.

Rab was quick to say, "May that day be a lang time comin', Mr. McKie."

A long time indeed.

The stone kirk, as plain a rubble rectangle as any they'd seen that week, seemed colorless, swallowed up by the mist. Jamie proceeded through the door, his empty stomach tied in a mangled knot. He had yet to be welcomed home, had not spied a soul from Glentrool, and Rose's well-being weighed heavily on his conscience. Had she fallen back asleep? Might the bleeding have stopped by now? Never had he felt more divided between duties.

Jamie had made one decision at least: He would send the herds on with the lambs the moment the service ended. Of all the concerns pressing down on him, that one was easily solved: The lads would be on their way by one o' the clock.

As he sat in the kirk, memories flew at him like house sparrows descending on a garden. There was the family pew where he'd sat every Sabbath of his youth. There were the families he'd known since childhood: Carmont, Galbraith, Laurie, McFadgen. Soon Reverend Erskine would appear: balding, stoop shouldered, grim faced, wearing a black robe as stiff as his demeanor.

Jamie guided his group to his father's pew, knowing it would grow crowded once the family arrived. But surely they'd be pleased to find him there waiting for them. On the Sabbath, the McKie household usually left Glentrool at seven o' the clock—the servants on foot even earlier—to make the long trek south to the kirk. They were seldom early, but they were never late; Alec McKie saw to that. "Give God the first and the last of every day," his father had always said. Never was that more true than on Sundays. Only in severe wintry weather did the household remain at Glentrool, and then the patriarch led a lengthy time of family worship.

Father, please forgive me. Jamie rehearsed the words, for they would need to be spoken. Though Alec McKie had sent him eastward with a goodly blessing, he'd done so in spite of Jamie's deceit, not because of it.

The second bell of the morning clanged above them, muted by the damp air. Jamie looked over his shoulder, expecting to see his father's bent figure toddle through the door. And his mother behind him, her raven head held high, her black eyes snapping. Envisioning her, Jamie thought of Rose. *You will like her, beloved. And she will very much like you.* They were two of a kind, his mother and his wife.

The precentor stood for the gathering psalm. Still no McKies.

When the minister climbed into the pulpit, it was not Reverend Erskine but a much younger man, no more than thirty. "Reverend Moodie," Jamie heard someone say. Disconcerting, having a stranger leading the service, today of all days.

A quarter of an hour later, when the minister stood for prayer,

Jamie's spirits had sunk to his boots. Something was very wrong. Had his father's health kept them away? Alec McKie was eighty-four years of age. Not many in Galloway lived so long. Perhaps Reverend Erskine was bound for Glentrool, summoned to his father's bedside. And what of Rose, was she improving? Should he go to her at once?

Spent with worry, Jamie bowed his head for prayer. 'Twas not the young minister's words he lifted up to heaven but the words of a king, hidden in his heart. *Be not far from me, Lord. Trouble is near, and fear is on every side.*

Seventy-Three

There's nae medicine for fear.
SCOTTISH PROVERB

Rose eyed Leana's box of herbs. "Annabel." She pointed past the maid's shoulder. "Do you know which medicine Leana would use…"

"Nae, mem." Annabel glanced at the box made of hazel, its contents a mystery to all but its mistress. "Yer sister will be back onie time noo. She'll ken what ye maun take."

Rose shifted her gaze to the door, willing it to open. *Hurry, Leana. All is not well.*

After Jamie and the others had left for kirk, Rose slipped off her gown and dozed for a bit, only to be awakened with a nagging pain. It had started in her back, then moved lower, creeping round her body as if embracing her unborn children, intent on stealing them from her.

Nae! Rose drew her knees closer to her chest. Guarding, protecting. If she lay very still, perhaps she might feel the twins move. *A flutter or two at the end of your fourth month.* Leana's description, committed to memory, anxiously anticipated.

The time was right. Could *that* be what this was all about?

There. She froze, her hand glued to the spot. Was that a flutter? If she sensed her bairns moving and knew they were alive and well, she could bear any pain, endure any bleeding. *Wait.* Was that a kick?

Hope gave way as a sharp cramp besieged her.

Annabel hovered over her, patting her face with a damp cloth. "May I bring ye a cup o' tea, mem? Or would ye rather I fetched yer sister at the kirk?"

"Tea," Rose said, wincing. "Leana will be along shortly."

Annabel flew from the room. Rose was grateful for her loyalty, but the maid was too fretful to be of much help. Leana's soothing touch was what Rose wanted. Her cool hands, her soft voice, her wise words, her healing herbs. "Hurry, my sister," she said, inhaling the dank air.

The unpainted plaster walls and scuffed pine floors looked even more depressing by day. If Jamie carried her down the stair and laid her in the wagon amid the fresh air, she would feel better at once.

Until the wheels began to move, and then she would feel worse.

Another sharp pain ground through her. Not like anything she'd felt before or had heard described. Intense. Frightening. *Help me bear it, Lord.* After an excruciating moment, the ache subsided once more. Each time she prayed 'twould be the last.

When Rose heard footsteps on the stair, she pressed the wrinkled bedsheet into the corners of her eyes, stemming her tears. How she hated to have Jamie see her this way!

Annabel tapped on the door, then opened it wide, bearing a fragrant cup of tea and the two people Rose loved most in the world.

She tried to smile and held out both hands. "You've come to rescue me."

Leana perched on the edge of the bed and Jamie on the low creepie, both of them taking her hands, just as she'd hoped.

"My poor sister." Leana leaned over her, pressing a fervent kiss to her cheek. "'Twas the longest morning of my life, worrying about you."

When Leana sat up, Jamie leaned forward to take her place. Rose closed her eyes as he kissed her, then felt her throat tighten as he whispered in her ear, "I love you, Rose. I will care for you. Fear not."

I fear only for our children, Jamie. Only for your sons. She would tell him the truth when she had him to herself. *Twins, dear husband. Yours and mine.*

Annabel lingered by the door, tea saucer still in hand, her nervous movements hard to watch.

Rose set her free. "Leave the tea, Annabel. I am certain Eliza could use your help with Ian." The maid was gone in an instant, the saucer resting on the dresser.

Leana retrieved the hot drink, then took her seat once more. "Jamie, might you help Rose sit up?"

"Gladly." His strong arms slid behind her back, lifting her as though she weighed less than the thin covering across her legs.

No matter how warm the day might become, Rose would not remove the blanket, lest Jamie see the blood. It was darker now. There was more. She sipped the bracing tea, realizing how parched her lips were.

The moment she swallowed, another pain seized her abdomen. Sharper this time. And longer. Rose hastily pushed the saucer into Leana's hands, unable to stifle a groan. "Stop," she pleaded. *"Stop!"*

"Rose, what is it?" Jamie was halfway to his feet, his arms circled round her, keeping her from collapsing. "Leana, we have to *do* something."

Rose saw the fear in her sister's eyes, mirroring her own. "Does a physician reside in the village, Jamie?"

"Nae." He groaned the word as if it were his fault such a person could not be summoned. "Only the minister, and he's not been in the parish a month."

"Have Eliza run to the manse. See if Reverend Moodie will come and bring any medical books he might have on hand." Leana discarded the teacup and quickly unpinned her hat. "If there is a midwife in Monnigaff, we'd best send for her as well."

Rose did not protest. Not if these strangers might spare her children.

She lifted her face for Jamie's hurried kiss, then watched him leave, praying he would not be gone long. She could not bear it if he were not here. If something happened.

I am with thee to deliver thee.

The words came and went like a breeze wafting across the room, though the window had no sash.

Leana brushed back her hair. A mother's touch. " 'Tis just the two of us now, Rose. Will you tell me where it hurts?"

A moment's hesitation. "Here." Rose placed a wary hand on her womb. "And here."

"Are you…still bleeding?"

She could no longer hide the truth. Not from her sister. Rose swept away her bedcovers and watched Leana's face turn to ash. Worse than she'd imagined, then. Lying on her back, Rose could not see past her rounded stomach, but she could feel the wet blotches on her cotton shift and sense her body's traitorous contractions growing stronger. "What is happening, Leana? What *is* it?"

With trembling hands, Leana examined her. "Rose, oh my Rose."

"Is it... Will I not..." Her words faded into a groan as another fierce pain racked her body. Then another, a harder one, bending her in two.

It cannot be. It cannot be. "Help me, Leana!"

But her sister could not help her. Could not stop the pain or the blood or the anguish as her babies were torn from her womb, as surely as if they were torn from her arms.

"Nae!" Rose screamed the word over and over. *"Please!"*

Leana clasped her hands, sobbing with her. "I'm here, Rose. I'm here."

Her labor was hard and swift. Struggling to breathe, Rose grasped fistfuls of Leana's gown in her hands, squeezing the fabric as waves of pain moved through her, crushing her hopes and her heart as well. *My babies!*

Tears coursed down her face. "I wanted to be...a mother. I wanted to..."

"I'm...sorry, Rose. So sorry." Leana was panting as hard as she was, straining with her. "Almost there, dear sister. 'Twill end...soon."

An urgent knock at the door. Male voices.

Leana did not let go, only held on tighter. "I am with you, Rose. This...cannot last...much longer."

But it did. It went on and on, as if she were truly giving birth to her children.

But she was not. Not truly.

"Jamie!" Rose cried, before her head slumped and the darkness came.

Seventy-Four

That it should come to this!

WILLIAM SHAKESPEARE

Jamie burst into the room at the sound of his name and was devastated by the sight that greeted him. Leana was weeping. Rose hung limp in her arms, nearly unconscious. Blood saturated the sheets.

"Rose! My sweet Rose." He fell to his knees beside the bed, gathering his wife in his arms. "I should never have left. Forgive me...forgive me."

"Let her breathe, Jamie." Leana gently eased him away from her sister, then lowered Rose back down onto the bed. "That's it, dearie. Deep breaths. 'Tis almost over now."

Jamie looked at Leana in horror. *"Over?"*

Her tear-drenched eyes met his. "Rose has... She has lost your child." Leana stood, giving him room. "I am...so very sorry, Jamie."

"Oh, my Rose." Distraught, he leaned over her. Cupping her cheek, wiping away her tears with his thumbs, whispering her name. "I am here, beloved." When her eyes fluttered open, he choked back a sob. *Thanks be to God.*

"Jamie..." Rose spoke so softly, he had to lean closer to hear her. " 'Tis my fault."

"Nae, lass. This is no one's fault." *Except mine. For bringing you here.* He dared not think of that now, or the guilt would tear him apart.

Nor could he look at the ruined sheets or the sorrow they contained. Instead he quietly tugged the blanket back in place. *My poor Rose.* Someday they would have another child. He would not remind her of that now, but he would later. When such hope would offer comfort. When such words would heal.

"Now we must get you well," he murmured, his heart aching at the sight of her. Could she be only seventeen? Far too young to have suffered so. He longed to hold her, to comfort her in his arms, but she was so weak, he feared he would hurt her. Instead he dried her cheeks and whispered every endearment he could think of. *My brave lass.*

"Jamie." Leana's hand touched his shoulder. "I must...attend to things here. If you might give me a very few minutes..."

Reluctantly he stood and backed away from the bed. Did Rose want him to stay? Or to leave?

Her head rolled to the side, tears streaming onto her pillow. "Leana will...care for me. Come back as soon as she calls you, aye?"

He had never felt more helpless in his life. "I will wait right outside the door." Both women nodded. His presence was merely delaying the inevitable.

When Jamie stepped into the corridor, he discovered the minister, whom he'd nigh forgotten, standing a few feet away from the door, perhaps allowing them some privacy. Fair-haired and ruddy-skinned, Reverend Stephen Moodie was neither tall nor muscular, but he exuded a quiet confidence Jamie desperately needed.

The young minister cleared his throat. "She has...lost the child, then?"

Jamie stared at the floor. The impact of those words was only now beginning to hit him. "She...has."

Reverend Moodie offered his condolences in a kind and sympathetic tone. His many words were no doubt sincere. But Jamie could not hear them. His mind was fixed on the bloodied sheet and the reality he'd pretended not to see. *Two bairns.* Smaller than the palms of his hands. *Twins.* His darling wife, who wanted nothing more than to be a mother, had lost two children in one day.

The door opened, and Leana stepped into the dim corridor, her arms full of stained bedding, her stance unsteady. "Jamie, she... Rose needs you. She is...still... She..."

He was already across the room, claiming the low chair, tucking the sheet round her slender neck. So fragile, so pale. "I am here, Rose."

Her face was etched with mourning. "Jamie...I had... It was..."

"I ken, lass." He leaned forward and kissed her, his lips wet with her tears. "Twins. I...saw them. And I am so very sorry. We will...try again, beloved." He had to say that much now, had to assure her.

But her tears did not stop. "'Tis my fault, Jamie. Lillias Brown gave me horrid herbs. Before we married." She turned her head, hiding her shame. "And a stone necklace that she bade me wear. And spells, cantrips... Oh, Jamie, don't you see?" Her whisper was tortured. "Our bairns died...because of *me!*"

"Nae, lass!" He pulled her into his arms more roughly than he intended, shocked by her words. "Do not say such things."

"But 'tis *true!*" she sobbed. "'Tis...*my fault.*"

"Och, Rose." He rubbed her back, wishing he might erase the wretched memories of this day and every painful one before it. "Do not punish yourself, my love." He lowered his voice, lest the minister overhear and think his next words blasphemous. "The Almighty has promised me many children. Have no fear, Rose. You will get well. Your womb will bear sons."

"But, Jamie..." When she touched the sheet to her body, the linen turned scarlet before their eyes. "Something is...not right."

He stared, refusing to believe what he was seeing. *'Tis not possible.* There had been enough blood. Too much blood. "Perhaps this is...customary...when a woman..."

Jamie sensed someone behind him and turned to find Leana bearing a pitcher of water and a haunted expression. He searched her eyes for answers. "'Tis not unusual, is it Leana? To have this... To..."

She gestured toward her medicines. "Jamie, I must do what I can to stanch the bleeding. If you might let me near her..."

"Of course." He stood so quickly that the small creepie tumbled over. "Is there anything I might do?"

She nodded toward Reverend Moodie, who'd appeared in the corner. "You can pray."

"Mr. McKie..." The minister pulled him aside, turning their backs to the women. "I fear I have no medical guides in my small library that address...this...situation. And our village howdie is in Talnotry, delivering a babe for the McCallans."

Jamie stared at the floor, unable to look at the man's apologetic face, unwilling to hear what he was saying. "'Tis not a 'situation,' sir. Rose McKie is my wife. My...*wife...*"

"Aye, aye." The man gripped his arm. "And she is being well cared for by her sister. Let us do as she suggested."

When the minister bowed his head, Jamie did the same, though his heart and mind were across the room with Rose. *Do what you must, Leana. Then let me come to her. Let me hold her.*

Though he listened to Reverend Moodie's solemn words, Jamie had his own entreaties for the Lord. *Make her well. Make her whole. Let there be other children.*

Rose moaned, louder than ever. The sound tore through his chest like a rapier. He was beside her in an instant, abandoning the minister to his prayers. "Rose, my Rose! What can I do for you, lass? How can I ease your pain?"

He was vaguely aware of Leana soaking rags in the herb-scented water and pressing them to his wife's body, but he kept his gaze on Rose's face. Her eyes were unfocused, red from weeping. Her mouth hung slack as she fought for breath. *Help me, Lord! Give me the words to say.*

Jamie leaned closer still. "You are not alone, Rose. We are all here to help you. Try to relax, my love. Your sister kens what she is doing." He could only hope that was true. Without a physician or a midwife, God's mercy and Leana's remedies were their only hope.

And why is that, Jamie? Because he had dragged his wife halfway across Galloway to spite her father. In a wagon. Sleeping on plaids, like common shepherds. If they were in Auchengray, he could ride to Dumfries and summon Dr. Gilchrist. But they were in the wilds of Monnigaff. *Because of me.*

"I should…not have brought you here, Rose." He stroked her brow, her cheeks, her neck. As if his touch might heal her. As if his words might make everything right. But they could not help. It was too late for that. "Forgive me, Rose. Please…please forgive me."

"Only if…" With some effort, she turned to face him. "Only if you will…forgive me." Her dark gaze met his. He saw no spark of hope there. "I brought this on…myself, Jamie. I cursed my father."

The young minister gasped. "I am sure you are mistaken, Mistress McKie."

"I...did. I...cursed him." Her head drooped to the side as if she'd spent all of her energy on her confession.

"Your father deserved it, Rose." Jamie gripped her shoulders, his despair mounting. "This...this bleeding has nothing to do with him. Nor anything you might have said or done."

"If I may speak with you a moment, sir." Reverend Moodie leaned forward and whispered in his ear. "Pardon me, but your wife... Well, I'm afraid the Buik clearly says, 'For every one that curseth his father or his mother shall be surely put to death.' Prepare yourself, Mr. McKie. I fear the worst is yet to come."

Seventy-Five

So fade the roses of those cheeks of thine.
SAMUEL DANIEL

Leana was grateful she'd not heard Reverend Moodie's comment; Jamie's response was frightening enough.

"*Nae!*" He spun round and grabbed the minister's coat by the lapels, his voice low but lethal. "I will not have you speak of such things!"

The man's ruddy skin turned redder still. "I can only speak the truth, Mr. McKie. 'Tis my calling and duty."

"Then your duties are finished here." Jamie abruptly released him. "Kindly see yourself out." Flustered, the young man left the room as Jamie turned back to grasp Rose's hands.

Stunned by his outburst, Leana kept her head down. Whatever the minister had said did not bear repeating, for it would only upset Rose further. *Jamie, Jamie. Now is not the time.* Yet it was unkind to judge a man who had just lost two sons and was in danger of… *Nae!* She would not even think the words.

After rinsing the linen cloth, Leana applied it once more to her sister's body, begging the Lord for mercy. A small pouch, stitched of butter muslin, sat steeping in the hot water; dried lady's mantle, picked from her physic garden in June, was tucked inside. Leana had stirred in a measure of rose water as well. And tears.

The water should have been pink. Instead it was red.

In her store of medicines, nothing was more healing than lady's mantle. She'd sent Eliza after a pot of hot water to brew a tea of the herb as well. But if the garden remedy did not work, if the bleeding did not stop…

"Leana?" Rose's voice was no stronger than a cotton thread. Thin, weak, easily broken.

"Yes, dearie. I am here." She lightly touched Rose's hip. "Are you…in pain?" A foolish question.

But Rose surprised her. "Not…like before. I feel…very little."

Jamie glanced over his shoulder, as if to gauge her reaction. Leana tried not to let her distress show, though her heart ached and her hands trembled. *No feeling. Oh, Rose.*

Mustering what strength she had left, Leana cast her gaze about the tiny room and realized what must be done. "Jamie, if you pulled this bed away from the wall, then I might sit on one side of Rose and you on the other. We'll not crowd each other then." *And I can see my sister. And I can say…*

"Of course, Leana." He was already standing, waiting for her to do the same.

Grasping her bowl of herbs, Leana stepped out of the way while he angled the narrow bed, allowing room for her to perch on the right side of the thin mattress.

A light tap at the door announced Eliza, bearing a teapot in one hand and a second footstool in the other. "I thocht 'twould spare yer back, mem, tae have yer ain creepie."

"Bless you, lass." Leana prepared the tea at once, using the last of her lady's mantle. "When this is good and strong, you'll bring me a cup for Rose, aye?"

Leana scooted her chair as close to the bed as possible, then continued her ministrations, despite the sad truth that they did not seem to be helping. Though she'd tried every possible remedy, they were not enough. Rose was not getting better. Her body no longer twisted and bucked, but the flow of blood was unceasing.

Now that she could see Rose properly, the sight was almost more than Leana could endure. The light was gone from her sister's eyes. Her smile had faded, and the paleness of her cheek held no promise of color.

The truth was undeniable. Rose was dying.

Leana's arms went limp. The wet cloth slipped into the bowl. *By sorrow of the heart the spirit is broken.* "Jamie…she…"

"Aye." His voice was ragged. "I ken."

Leana abandoned her efforts. Only the Almighty could heal her sister now. She placed the washbowl on the floor, then inched closer, fixing her gaze on Rose. Jamie released one of Rose's hands and pressed it into hers. How cold her sister's skin was. When Leana looked at him in silent thanks, she saw her own pain reflected in his green eyes.

The two of them stayed that way for many minutes. Holding Rose's hands. Murmuring encouragement because they could do nothing else. "I am glad the pain is gone, Rose." "You will feel better soon." "I love you, Rose." They both said that many times.

Leana held back a sob when Rose whispered, "And I love you." It did not matter whom she meant.

The room was so quiet that Leana jumped when Eliza touched her shoulder. "Mem, will ye be…wantin' this tea noo?"

Leana glanced at Jamie, and they both shook their heads. "Eliza, if you would not mind…"

"Not at a', mem." Eliza sniffed, holding her apron against her mouth. "I'll be doon the stair wi' Annabel and Ian. The innkeeper says we may stay as lang…as lang…"

Jamie spared her. "Aye, lass."

Eliza was gone without a sound except the door latch falling into place.

"Rose, can you hear me?" Leana leaned forward, trying to catch her sister's eye. "Is there…anything…anything we might do…" She squeezed Rose's hand until she feared she might hurt her.

"Aye." Rose's voice was startlingly clear. "Name…my children."

Leana stifled a gasp. "Oh, Rose…"

"We'll have…time…" Jamie fought for the words. "Time for that …later."

"Please, Jamie." Rose looked directly at him, her eyes focused. "William. And Alexander."

"Aye." His face crumpled.

Leana turned her head, shattered by Jamie's pain more than her own. *Comfort him on every side, Lord.*

Rose had not finished. "Bury them…in the kirkyard."

When Jamie could only groan, Leana instinctively reached for his

other hand, joining the three of them. *You will not do this alone, Jamie.*
"Aye, sweet Rose." She clasped both their hands tight. "We will take
good care of William and Alexander."

Rose sank deeper into the bed. Her hand seemed to grow smaller.
Like a child's.

Leana felt a stillness in the room. A peaceful silence, like the northern lights in the heavens. Visible, but not audible. Faraway, yet close.
She searched her heart for the words of consolation needed, placed there
long ago. "Be not afraid, Rose. Neither be thou dismayed. For the LORD
thy God is with thee whithersoever thou goest."

"He is." Rose breathed the words. She looked at each of them, as if
memorizing their faces. "I am not afraid." A smile crossed her parched
lips. "He loves me."

"I do, Rose." Jamie could barely say the words. "I do love you."

Leana watched Rose's hand in his tighten for a moment. "Never
fear. Jamie has you, lass."

"Nae." Rose slowly closed her eyes, but her faint smile remained.
"'Tis not Jamie."

Seventy-Six

In all the silent manliness of grief.

OLIVER GOLDSMITH

One hand still held his. *Leana.*

"She is gone, Jamie."

His head sank onto Rose's heart to receive the last breath. But he felt no air against his cheek. Only the still form of the woman he loved. Grief rose inside him, overwhelming him. He released Leana's hand, leaving behind her warmth and strength to embrace his wife, holding Rose against his chest, as if that might stanch his pain. *We could not stop the blood, beloved. We tried, but we could not.*

Jamie wept in silence. Tears soaked her nightgown and his shirt as well, though it did not matter. None of it mattered.

He had failed her. Nae, he had killed her.

Forgive me, forgive me. However often he might whisper those words, Rose would never hear them. However loud he might shout from the turret of Glentrool, his pleas for mercy would change nothing.

She is gone, Jamie. The irrevocable truth.

Jamie slowly pulled the pins from her hair, letting the rich mane fall round her shoulders. He buried his face in her rose-water scent. *This cannot be good-bye. It cannot.*

He held her, not speaking, not moving, for a long time. While he watched through half-closed eyes, Leana quietly attended to the necessary tasks. The room had no looking glass to cover, nor a clock with a pendulum that needed stopping. Leana opened the door, though she could not open the window. It signified nothing; Rose's spirit was already gone.

At last Leana knelt beside him, her cheeks wet with tears. "May I...hold my sister?"

She received Rose's body as a mother would a child, cradled in her arms, head tucked against her breast. "Oh, Rose, how can I… What will I do…without you?"

Knowing all they had been through, all they had meant to each other, Jamie's grief was compounded until he was numb with pain.

After a time, Leana lifted her gaze, her sorrow mirroring his. "I must wash and dress her now. Would you call Eliza for me?"

Jamie stood, his legs nigh to buckling underneath him. He could not bear to see the woman who had given him so much pleasure reduced to a…body. *God help me, to a corpse.* "I will get Eliza," he told her. The women of the household were needed now. "And then I will see Reverend Moodie. If he will even speak with me."

"Jamie." Leana laid her hand on his arm. "He will understand. You were…not yourself."

"I was entirely myself," he muttered, grief giving way to shame as he bolted down the stair, ignoring the pain in his leg. He strode down the dim corridor with an uneven gait, his steps slowing as he reached the door to the maids' room. The lasses loved Rose as well and would be undone by the news.

Eliza opened at his knock, her cheeks chapped from crying. "Oh, Mr. McKie." She sagged against the doorjamb when he told her. "I'm sae sorry. I dinna ken what else tae say."

"I'm sorry as weel, Mr. McKie." Annabel stood behind her, wringing her hands, while Ian sat at her feet. The boy clapped at the sight of him, smiling as ever.

"Here, lad." Jamie lifted the child into his arms, not caring if the maids saw fresh tears in his eyes. "Come cheer your father's heart." Rose had adored her stepson, and he had warmed to her as well. Even young as he was, Ian would miss her. "You are all the family I have now, Ian." Jamie swallowed hard. "Just the twa McKie men, aye?"

There would have been five of us. The realization struck him a crushing blow.

Rose had so longed to be a mother. She'd talked about little else last spring. Cursing her father had not shortened Rose's life, no matter what the minister might insinuate; he did not know Lachlan McBride. The very thing she'd wanted most—motherhood—had cost Rose her young life.

Not true, Jamie. The nagging voice inside him would not be silenced. *Leaving Auchengray cost Rose her life. If you had waited until the bairns were born...*

Suddenly feeling ill, he handed Ian to Annabel. "Eliza, you are needed up the stair. Will you be... That is, can you...manage?"

She straightened her white cap and wiped her cheeks with her apron. "I can, sir." Ducking round him, she hastened off to do her duty by her mistress.

"And you, Annabel." He ran his hand across his hair, trying to get his bearings. "Will you and Ian be all right?"

"We will, Mr. McKie. I'll see tae supper for us a'. Are ye bound tae visit wi' the minister noo?" When he nodded, she inclined her head toward the pitcher and basin in the room. "Though I'd make a puir valet, I'd be honored to see ye properly groomed afore ye go."

Shaved, combed, and scrubbed, Jamie left the Cree Inn a short time later, studying the sky as he walked toward the bridge, trying to determine the hour. Three o' the clock, he guessed. Though the fog had dissipated by noon, the air was still moist. Gray clouds blotted out the sun.

He crossed the Penkill, aiming for the manse beside the kirk, where he was met at the door by Mistress Moodie, a brown-haired woman with a timid smile. "Mr. McKie. We've been expecting you."

Reverend Moodie rose from his chair when Jamie entered the parlor. Both men stood for a moment, eying each other, until Jamie cleared his throat and said what he'd come to say. "I beg your pardon—"

"And I beg yours, sir." The minister crossed the room, extending his hand. "My earlier admonition was true, but harsh and poorly timed. I cannot think what I might have done had a stranger been thoughtless enough to say such a thing about my wife. Do forgive me."

Taken aback, Jamie shook the man's hand. He'd not known many ministers to be so quick to apologize.

" 'Tis clear, Mr. McKie, you've come with tragic news."

Jamie stared at the carpet, trying to keep his emotions in check as he forced out a single syllable. "Aye."

He bade Jamie sit, a cup of tea appeared, and words of sympathy were spoken. After a suitable interlude, the minister shifted their conversation to matters of necessity. "The beadle cannot work on the Sabbath, but I'll have him dig the grave at first light."

"Nae, my…family in Glentrool has a…mausoleum…" The thought of his young wife sealed in a granite tomb made Jamie's empty stomach churn.

"Glentrool is ten miles off," the minister reminded him. "Since it is improper to carry a coffin on a wheeled conveyance, you would need to find several men willing to carry her kist a great distance on their shoulders. Have you friends in the village on whom you could depend?"

Jamie knew the answer. That morn in the kirk not a soul had welcomed him home to the parish. "I'm afraid I have been gone from Monnigaff…too long."

"Then 'tis best to bury your wife here, Mr. McKie, on hallowed ground. I'll have the beadle ring the deid bell through the village this evening. Mr. Lamont will also meet you at the inn at nine in the morn for the procession, soon after the joiner comes." Reverend Moodie stood, his duties discharged. "Your family misses you, I am sure. May the Lord comfort you this night."

Jamie stumbled back to the inn, seeing nothing but the grass beneath his feet.

Rose is dead. His mind kept turning the words over, examining them, rejecting them. She was here yestreen. Alive, if not well. Had he imagined it all? Was it another of his vivid dreams? Perhaps when he climbed up the stair, when he walked into the room, he would find her recovered, sitting up. *You've come to rescue me.*

A desperate hope, a foolish wish, but it fueled his steps through the inn. He barely knocked before throwing open the door and turning toward the bed.

Rose lay in utter stillness, dressed in a rose-colored gown. Her gloved hands were crossed over her breast, pennies covered her eyes, and her skin was like wax.

He staggered backward, stunned by the truth afresh.

"Jamie." Leana stood, beckoning him closer. "I regret we could not dress her in the gown she last wore." She glanced at Eliza, sniffling in the corner. "Though such may be the custom, the blue dress was no longer…appropriate."

How like Leana to put it so delicately. "You have chosen well," he managed to say, stepping closer. The damask gown was the one Joseph Armstrong had tailored for their December wedding. "Those are…your mother's gloves." Jamie remembered Leana's giving her sister the treasured silk gloves on the Sabbath last for her seventeenth birthday.

Another layer of grief fell across his heart like a plaid: Rose had died on her birthing bed. Just as her own mother had.

Jamie looked down at her now, though it was not Rose who lay before him. Not his warm and vibrant wife, with her charming smile and her flindrikin ways. This was a shadow of that dear lass. The small dish of earth and salt resting on her breast served as a patent reminder: earth for the corruptible body, salt for the incorruptible spirit.

He would wake tomorrow, and Rose would not be there. Nor the next day. Nor all the days of his life.

Leana touched his sleeve. "Jamie, I hope you will not feel I've overstepped my bounds…"

"You could never do so."

"I found…" She lowered her head, showing him her swirl of wheat-colored braids. "A wooden box…a small box for your…for…"

My sons. He turned away, holding back the sob that welled in his chest.

She said nothing for a moment. "Jamie, there is no shame in grieving."

Her tender words, like a key, opened the pain locked inside him. A sound came forth, the low lament of a wounded animal, trapped and in agony. *My sons, my own sons.* He had never held them, had never blessed them.

When Leana presented him with the tiny coffin, he wrapped his hands round the wood. *May Almighty God bless you, my sons.* The words of his father, of Alec McKie. Spoken too late.

She said softly, "The joiner will come in the morn, aye?"

Jamie gripped the wooden box. "Early, the minister said."

"When he does, we will put this box beneath Rose's head, like a pillow. For you and I both know that children who've not been baptized are buried beneath the wall of the kirkyard."

Jamie only now remembered that unkind practice. "In the gloaming."

"Worse, they could be buried on the north side of the kirkyard. 'Amang the goats,' as Neda used to say." She let out a lengthy sigh. "Rose would ne'er want that. I thought it best if we simply buried her precious bairns with her."

"Well done, Leana." He gave her back the small coffin, afraid in his grief it might slip from his hands. "As always, you have thought of everything."

Tears welled in her eyes. "I did not think of how to save Rose."

"Och, lass." He cupped her elbows. "You did all that you could. Her death weighs on my shoulders, not on yours." When she did not protest at once, his greatest fear was confirmed. *Leana blames me as well.*

Seventy-Seven

Words that weep and tears that speak.

ABRAHAM COWLEY

Leana sat in tear-filled silence, surrounded by candlelight, wrapped in memories: Rose running across the garden, her braid dancing in her wake; Rose bravely standing up to their father, then marching up the stair and hugging her tight; Rose holding a length of cotton next to her eyes and declaring the fabric a perfect match.

Come back to me, Rose. But she could not.

The hour was late; the candles were steadily burning down to stubs. Realizing the family did not have the customary lighting—remnants of Yule candles from the year past—the innkeeper had generously donated a dozen tapers from their kitchen stock. Since midafternoon the small group had maintained a *lykewake,* a vigil meant to guard a loved one's body until it was duly buried. The maids had long since retired to their beds; only she and Jamie remained, seated on low stools a foot apart.

Her sister's face almost looked animated, a cruel trick of the flickering candlelight. Bathing her, dressing her had been unspeakably hard. Leana had wept from first to last. And yet each moment had been sacred. To think that, while she held her sister's body, her spirit was in the hands of the Almighty was more than she could comprehend or imagine. And comforting beyond measure: Her dear Rose was not alone.

The gloves were the most difficult of all. *Mother. Rose.* Running her hands over the seams, remembering the special times she had worn them, Leana offered a prayer of thanks that she had given them to her sister while she still could.

You are always so good to me.

Leana knew better. But she took solace in knowing her last gift to Rose was her best.

"Leana?"

Deep in thought, she started at the sound of her name.

Jamie's voice was low, hoarse. "Will you inform your father? Or shall I?"

"It might be best if I wrote to him." When Jamie did not respond, she added, "Unless you would rather—"

"Nae, lass." He angled toward her, candlelight gilding the planes of his face. "The news will be painful enough without also being in my hand."

"I shall put pen to paper at dawn." She'd write Neda at Kingsgrange as well, then post both letters before they left for Glentrool. As concerned as Jamie was about his parents, they'd not tarry long in the village after the morning funeral. "Might you send a messenger ahead to Glentrool?"

"'Tis not necessary. We'll be home by midafternoon. And my mother will much prefer hearing the news in person." He stood, stretching his long legs. They had spoken little since midnight. Both of them were exhausted from lack of sleep and bleary-eyed from weeping.

"Jamie, why not rest an hour or two in your room? I will be fine here alone. Rose will be in good hands."

He looked down at her. "No finer hands have cared for Rose than yours." With that, he leaned down and brushed a kiss across her fingers, a gentleman's gesture of respect.

She folded them in her lap, suddenly self-conscious. "A bit of sleep will do you good."

He stepped lightly toward the door, aware of the hour and the inn's sleeping patrons. "Only if you will promise to do the same when I awaken, for I'll not be long."

Jamie honored his promise, returning while the sky beyond the window was still the color of ink. Leana had no fear of being alone with Rose's body, but she was glad to change places with him, if only to allow him time alone with his wife.

When she stretched out on his bed, Leana found it no more generous in size than hers had been. The sheets were still warm from his body, though, and bore his scent: a stray whiff of thyme from his bath, lavender on his pillow from the wound she had dressed, some plain soap the inn had provided. Most of all, the bedding smelled like Jamie, a masculine scent she had never quite forgotten.

Leana turned her head away, taking a deep breath of unscented air, clearing her mind. She was there for one purpose—a restful hour—so she might have enough strength for the trying day ahead. Closing her eyes, her hands wrapped round her growing child, she sank into the thin mattress and sought the blessed release of sleep.

"Leana." A knock at the door startled her awake. "The joiner is here."

She was on her feet in an instant, brushing the wrinkles from her gown, touching her hair. Was it truly morning? Naught could be done but a quick splash of cool water from the washstand. She'd see to a proper toilet as time permitted.

Jamie stood in the hall, waiting to guide her back to the room she'd shared with Rose.

Leana followed him in silence, preparing herself for the shock of seeing her sister's body in the bright light of morning. So pale, so still. Leana turned away until the room stopped tilting.

"Leana, this is Mr. Gammel. He's brought…ah, what we require." Jamie stood back as the man wrestled a pine coffin through the door and placed it next to the bed where the stools had rested through the night.

Mr. Gammel eyed them both. "You ken what they say, aye? If a dead body lies unburied over a Sabbath, there'll be another death in the parish within the week." Not waiting for a reply, he leaned over the coffin lid, which was loosely attached with nails. He pried it open with his bare hands. The hammer in his belt would drive the nails home for good.

"Mind the sharp points," he warned Leana, laying the lid aside. From inside his shirt he pulled a burial shroud of Scottish linen, as the law required. "I thought you'd be needing this since you may not have one in your plenishing."

When the joiner handed the fabric to Leana, she put aside the dish of salt and earth, then enlisted Jamie's assistance in carefully wrapping her sister's body in the thin shroud. Her arms and her heart both ached by the time she finished. While Mr. Gammel was looking elsewhere, Leana positioned the precious box with her nephews' remains, then stood back as the men eased Rose's linen-swathed form into the coffin.

The joiner washed his hands at once—more from superstition than necessity—then nailed the lid in place. Every swing of his hammer made Leana cringe, every solid bang on the wood felt like a nail driven into her soul.

Two lads appeared at the door, bonnets in hand. "These are my apprentices, pressed into service as pallbearers when circumstances warrant. We'll put the *mort-cloth* on when we get down the stair. I see you've a bad leg, Mr. McKie. Can you help us or nae?"

Leana knew how he would respond: Jamie was not about to let someone else carry his wife on his behalf. They worked their way down the stair one step at a time, Jamie at the last. He led with his left leg, no doubt letting it take the brunt of the weight, but still he grimaced with each step.

Standing at the top of the stair, Leana watched as they made the sharp turn at the landing. Eliza and Annabel were waiting below with Ian, concern on their faces. When the men reached the floor with grunts of satisfaction, Leana hurried down the stair behind them, relieved they had managed thus far. She was proud of Jamie, standing upright, his shoulders square beneath the coffin's edge.

Mr. Lamont, the beadle for the parish, was waiting for them, bearing the deid bell in one hand, the mort-cloth in the other. "O' course, thar's usually a fee for usin' the mort-cloth, paid tae the kirk session," he explained, draping the black fabric over the coffin. "But seein' as ye're comin' from anither parish, the reverend thocht it only richt not tae charge ye oniething." He lowered his voice, muting the noisy bell clapper with his hand. "Forby, we found a meikle purse o' *goud* in the puir box yestermorn. Yer shullin isna needed."

Jamie and Leana glanced at each other, and for one small moment on a mournful day, they exchanged the slightest of smiles; Rose would be pleased that her gold was being put to good use.

Mr. Lamont started down the street first, taking his duties seriously, ringing the deid bell in a steady rhythm. At one time, the noise was meant to chase away evil spirits. Now the bell served as a signal to the village that a funeral was under way. Some would attend out of curiosity. Not to support, but to stare.

The four pallbearers followed the beadle, with Leana, holding Ian, and then Eliza and Annabel forming the smallest of funeral processions. Fresh tears covered their faces. Ian patted his mother's cheeks and seemed unhappy to find his hands wet.

At her mother's funeral, Leana had been but five years old, clinging to the hand of their housekeeper. *Oh, Neda. Would that you were here!* Hers would be the hardest letter of all to write. Leana had meant to do so this morning, but instead Jamie had let her sleep. *Soon, Neda, I will write and tell you the saddest of stories.*

When the funeral party reached the kirkyard, a number of village folk trailed behind, gathering in a knot near the kirk door. Reverend Moodie stood before a yawning grave, dressed in his black robe. His expression was somber, his manner reserved, yet his brown eyes shone with compassion as he welcomed the small assembly and began the brief service.

They stood quietly in the morning stillness, the clear skies brightly lit by the sun. Birdsong filled the silences, which were many; whispered conversation was frowned upon at funerals. Eliza and Annabel were together on one side of Leana, their tears in plain sight, while Jamie stood on her other side, hands folded behind him, his face a portrait of grief.

Leana pressed Ian to her heart, so full of pain she did not know where to look or what to do. *My dearest Rose, my only sister! How can you be gone forever?*

As the pine box was lowered into the grave, the minister stretched forth his hands, his words ringing with conviction, offering Leana the hope she desperately needed. "Blessed be the God and Father of our Lord Jesus Christ, which according to his abundant mercy hath begotten us again unto a lively hope by the resurrection of Jesus Christ from the dead, to an inheritance incorruptible, and undefiled, and that fadeth not away, reserved in heaven for you."

Incorruptible. Jamie's earthly inheritance, vast and prosperous as it might be, could not possibly measure up to the heavenly inheritance reserved for Rose. *And for Jamie. And for me. And for all that love Christ's appearing.* What was property in light of eternity? What was youthful charm compared to the unfading beauty of Christ?

The truth comforted Leana on that bright, sorrowful morning and slowly dried her tears. Rose had said it best. *I am not afraid.*

'Twas not the end, but the beginning.

Seventy-Eight

I am far frae my hame, an' I'm weary aften whiles,
For the longed-for hame-bringing an' my Father's welcome smiles.
ERASTUS W. ELLSWORTH

Home beckoned like a beacon. Now Jamie had to choose the best means to get there.

If he lagged behind, guiding the wagon north at its slow, rolling pace, then he'd be of no help to his family in Glentrool until later in the day. Something dire had happened to his father to keep him from kirk on the Sabbath. And Rab and Davie were surely getting anxious, unaware of the tragedy at Cree Inn.

Yet if he galloped ahead to offer his assistance and share the sad tidings about Rose, then he'd be leaving three defenseless women and his heir traveling on a lonely road through the wilds of Monnigaff parish with nothing to protect them but a useless pistol.

In the end, his injured leg made the decision for him.

Jamie had not ridden Hastings since before his misadventure at Moneypool Burn. Trying it now, he discovered the pain in his leg was torturous. Sitting astride the horse strained the very muscles he had wrenched in the stream. A swift ride to Glentrool was out of the question; he could not ride Hastings at all. With a sigh of resignation, he tied the horse to the back of the wagon and climbed onto its rough wooden seat.

"It seems I'll be driving," he told Leana, who'd moved to make room for him.

She glanced over her shoulder. "Shall I climb into the wagon bed with the maids, then?"

Please stay. That was what he wanted to say. *Do not leave me here alone.* After the most heartbreaking morning of his life, he longed for someone beside him who shared his grief. But he dared not impose upon her; perhaps she preferred to be alone with her thoughts. "Do what suits you, lass."

Leana stayed.

At his command, the horses started off, crossing the Penkill bridge before turning north at Knockman Wood, leaving Monnigaff kirk behind. After the ceremony, Jamie had received halfhearted condolences from the few villagers who'd witnessed the burial. He'd paid the minister, the beadle, and the joiner their due and ordered a headstone from the village mason. Though penned in haste, he prayed Rose's epitaph suited her. He'd not written one before and hoped he would not be pressed to do so again for a very long time.

Funerals in Galloway were usually lengthy affairs, allowing several days for the lykewake, with ongoing provisions of food and drink for every neighbor for miles. Jamie had neither the silver nor the heart for such a public display. He had lost his wife. He had lost two unborn sons. Only those who loved Rose as he did were invited to mourn with him.

It was noon before they'd quit the Cree Inn, having bathed, eaten a light meal, then packed their belongings for the last time. Leana had sent a hasty post to Neda and to her father and kindly wrote one to Evan for him as well. Lord willing, Jamie would not have another letter to write when he reached Glentrool. *Brother, I am sorry to inform you that our father, Alec McKie…*

The thought made Jamie shudder.

"Would a plaid help?" Leana started to reach behind him for a blanket. "The air has cooled since we left the village."

He stayed her hand. "'Tis because we're gradually climbing as we go." He pointed out the ruins of Castle Stewart in the lea of Penninghame Farm. They'd veered east from the Cree for a bit, but soon the road would hug the river's banks all the way to House o' the Hill Inn.

Aromatic woods gave way to waterside meadows along the ill-named Loch Cree, little more than a broadening of the river. Half a dozen shallow burns tumbled across their route; all were troublesome to ford. Jamie walked the horses and empty wagon across the rocky streams, then helped the women cross on foot and climb back in. He thought again of how swift his journey would have been on horseback—no more than two hours—and reminded himself that his first duty now was to his son and to those who cared for him.

"'Tis a fine prospect, Mr. McKie," Eliza called out.

The moorland and mountains did have a rugged, uncultivated beauty about them. Enormous gray boulders, as tall as their wagon, perched on the gorse-covered hillsides overlooking the road. Where old trees had toppled over in the boggy lowland, the exposed roots formed fantastic shapes, grotesque and marvelous at once.

As the wagon skirted the Wood of Cree, the most ancient forest in Galloway, Jamie thought of Evan and the years his brother had spent hunting for roe deer among the oak and ash and fishing for salmon in the river. Had their reunion in Monnigaff truly taken place? It seemed a distant memory now; so did everything else, good or ill, that had crossed his path on the long trip home.

Only thoughts of Rose remained. Her face, her voice, her touch were carved into his mind and heart as surely as the stonemason of Monnigaff would use chisel and hammer to cut her name into her granite headstone.

Rose McBride McKie. Beloved Wife and Mother.

Jamie's head fell forward, brushing the reins. Tears, unexpected and unwelcome, dropped onto the floorboards beneath him. When a pair of graceful hands slipped the reins from his loosened grasp, he captured them both and held on tight until the wave of grief passed.

"I'm...sorry, Leana." He lifted his head, then turned to meet her gaze. "Sorry for being..."

"Do not say 'weak,' Jamie McKie." Despite the sheen in her eyes, Leana had a confident look about her. "You are the strongest man I have ever known. You stood up to my father, yet bowed down to your brother. You buried your wife and sons this morning and must face the father you wronged this evening."

"Please God, I *will* face my father." Jamie could agree with that much. Leana had a way of phrasing things that made him sound virtuous, yet he knew he fell far from the mark. "As for my darling Rose...'tis my fault, Leana." When she started to protest, he lifted his hand. "Do not pretend otherwise. Had I not insisted we leave Auchengray..."

"Nae, Jamie. Long before we left, Rose was complaining of aches and pains. Since I have traveled with my bairn without mishap, we must assume it was something else and not this journey that…led to…that…" Leana sighed, dabbing a handkerchief to her eyes. " 'Twould break Rose's heart to think of you punishing yourself like this. Did *she* ever fault you?"

He considered that for a moment. "She did not."

"Then do not blame yourself." Leana leaned forward, catching his eye once more. "Rest assured, *I* do not."

He could see that she meant it, that she did not hold him responsible for her sister's death. But he could not begin to forgive himself. His only hope was to forge on, fulfilling his duty to those who survived her, to those who loved her. Providing for Leana. Raising his children. And mourning his wife.

Taking the reins once more, Jamie passed the property of Larg, the final landmark before the turn toward home. Had it truly been two years? Two years since he'd fled his brother's wrath, then stumbled upon him at House o' the Hill hours later. They would stop at the old inn on the way to stable the horses and store the wagon. The only way into the steep glen of Loch Trool was to walk.

"Will we spy Glentrool from the top o' the hill?" Annabel wanted to know.

"Nae, for we must wind through the glen first. 'Tis on the north side of the loch, the only laird's house for miles. You'll see the turret and chimneys when we reach the foot of the loch." Despite the heaviness in his chest, his pulse quickened as a clear picture of home took shape in his mind. Within the hour, his mother would be standing in the entrance hall, meeting her grandson. Please God, the laird of Glentrool would be by her side.

"There's the inn!" Eliza's exuberance was infectious. Ian was clapping and hollering, and Annabel burst into song in a trilling soprano.

Farewell, farewell, Eliza dear,
The maid that I adore!

Jamie did not begrudge the lasses a moment of joy. In their young lives they'd never been in service anywhere but Auchengray. Glentrool would be a marked improvement for them. Eliza would serve as Leana's lady's maid; as for Annabel, he would insist Ivy Findlay find a place for her in the household. Perhaps as a nursery maid for Ian, if Leana approved. And for their second child at year's end.

The stables of House o' the Hill came into view, situated downhill from the inn and sheltered by sycamores. Jamie brought the wagon to a halt in the shade as a young man with a crooked-toothed grin headed his direction.

"Mr. McKie, aye? The laird's son?"

Jamie narrowed his gaze, appraising the lad. He had a familiar look about him.

"Me name's George," he offered. " 'Like the king himself,' ye said tae me that nicht."

A vague memory surfaced. Of a scruffy stable lad in tattered clothes who'd cared for Walloch the night Jamie had run for his life. Realization dawned. "I owe you a penny, George."

He ducked his head, clearly pleased. "Ye said ye'd lost yer travelin' pouch. I'll wager a Gypsy staw it. The woods are aften thick wi' fowk."

"You are quite right." Jamie dropped five copper coins into his dirt-creased hand, glad to discharge a debt, however small. "The extra is for your patience." With the lad's good service assured, Jamie made arrangements for the draft horses to be fed, groomed, and stabled until the herds appeared. "Look for them in the morn's morn." Jamie paid for the horses' care, then unloaded a few light items easily carried on his shoulders. He'd send servants with handcarts for the trunks. "You'll keep an eye on my goods?"

"Ye can depend on George, sir." The lad grinned, pocketing his coins.

Jamie and the others continued on foot up a road edged with dykes until they passed the plain stone inn and reached the crest of the hill. "Welcome to the glen," Jamie said, inhaling the pine-scented air. Steep hills covered with heather unfurled before them, forming a narrow glen with Trool at its heart. Fir woods lined the shores of the long, sinuous loch. From this vantage point, the water was a shimmering thread of silver woven through the pines by a canny hand.

Jamie pointed out the massive mountains, his chest swelling with pride. "Mulldonach and Lamachan rise to the right and the Fell of Eschoncan on the left. Glentrool stands in its shadow. Three miles and we're home." He led the way down, with Leana close behind, then Eliza with Ian, and Annabel leading Hastings, carrying goods instead of a rider on his back.

The maids chattered away, their voices swallowed up by the vastness of sky and land, the sound no louder than the warbling of a redstart. Jamie gazed at the distant hills, which folded on top of one another. Though most were rounded at the top, precipitous rocks jutted out below the summits. When the track broadened, Leana moved up next to him, her skirts swinging as she walked. Eager as he was to reach their destination, Jamie slowed his gait to match hers.

"Robert the Bruce hunted deer in this glen," he told her, repeating the ancient poem, "In Glentrool awhile he lay, and went well oft to hunt and play."

"And killed a few Englishmen from the heights of Mulldonach," Leana added.

The lass knew her history. "His men rolled boulders down the mountain from the Steps of Trool, as sheer a drop as any in the glen. The Englishmen were buried at Soldier's Holm in the meadow at the head of the loch."

When Leana said no more, he chastised himself for his careless blether. Neither of them needed a reminder of deaths and burials that day.

They'd reached the foot of the hills, where the ford across the Minnoch awaited them. The water level was lower than usual; still, he was relieved when they reached the other side of the stream with naught but wet boots and dripping skirt hems. The narrow footpath, bordered by tall firs with long, drooping branches, followed the meandering contours of the Water of Trool. Any sense of openness was gone; now they were shut in a pine-laden prison. With each step, Jamie's apprehension grew—keen to be home one minute, dreading it the next. His injured leg was beginning to ache again from the walk, and his new boots had ceased to be comfortable half a mile ago.

Leana finally spoke, the tenderness in her voice penetrating his defenses. "Jamie, I know this is not the homecoming you imagined…"

He slowed his steps. "Nae, it is not." *Not without Rose.* "But it is my home, and for that I must be grateful." Jamie stopped for a moment and caught her elbow, pointing ahead. "There, Leana. Beside the loch. 'Tis Glentrool."

Leana's eyes widened. "So it is."

Two stories tall, with a third story in the square central tower, the gray granite house stood among the foothills, surrounded by Scots pines. Though it presented a broad, flat face to the loch, Glentrool boasted a round turret in the crook of its L-shaped design, with a conical roof harking back two centuries or more. As a lad, Jamie had once crawled up the steep roof to plant a triangular flag on top, like drawings he'd seen of French castles. His mother had coaxed him down before he fell and broke his neck, much to Evan's disappointment.

"'Tis a meikle hoose, Mr. McKie." Eliza held up Ian for a better view. "I had nae idea we'd be livin' in a mansion."

Annabel said nothing, only stopped where she was, clinging to Hastings's reins with both hands. "Sir, d'ye see that licht o'er the hoose?"

Jamie peered through the trees. "The sunlight, you mean, falling across the roof?"

"Nae…'tis higher than the roof. By me soul, sir…'tis the *deid licht!*"

His blood froze.

"D'ye see it, Eliza?" Annabel cried. "Or ye, Miss McBride?" Her freckled face was terror-stricken. "Naught but ane can see the deid licht. And I do, I surely do."

Jamie knew the superstition. *The deid licht.* Seen by one person at a time, never two. A foreshadowing of death.

Father.

Plunging forward without waiting to see if the others followed, Jamie strode along the widening loch, his eye on Glentrool, his thoughts running up the stair to the bedroom his parents had shared for nigh to five decades. Fearing what he would find there. A loved one. Dying. *Nae. Not again.*

Seventy-Nine

Death at one door, and heirship at the other.

SCOTTISH PROVERB

Laird of Glentrool shall be your name.
The words pounded at the door of Jamie's heart as he crashed through the pine branches barring his path to Glentrool's gate. *Father, I cannot be laird yet. I have an heir, but no wife. I have your blessing, but no respect in the parish.* It was too soon, much too soon, for the death of Alec McKie.

With each step Jamie took, the rushing waters of Buchan Burn grew louder, and the gray stone walls of Glentrool loomed larger. He was almost to the threshold when he heard Leana walking not far behind him. Guilt brought him to a halt and turned him round. "Forgive my rudeness, lass." He held out his arm, as any gentleman should. "Come, let me escort you through the door of my home."

Leana patted her brow with her handkerchief. "Jamie, you've no need to apologize for your haste."

As she caught her breath, Jamie stared at the carved oak door, as old as the house itself. Should he knock or simply barge in? It was his family home, yet he felt like a stranger here.

When the door opened, the matter was resolved.

"Mr. McKie!" The astonished face of Ivy Findlay greeted him. "Ye've heard the news then." She ushered them both inside with a brief curtsy. "We were worried… That is, yer faither…he… I am sae sorry, Mr. McKie."

A too-familiar pain sliced through him. *'Tis true, then.*

The evidence was everywhere: Glentrool was in mourning. Cloth hung over the massive looking glass in the entrance hall, and the mantel clock on the hearth in the drawing room had been stopped at the hour of eight. *Was it this morning? Yestreen?*

Jamie looked round for his mother, then realized she would be at his father's bedside. He would join her momentarily. "Ivy, my... Pardon me, this is my...cousin, Leana McBride."

Ivy curtsied again, then stepped back as Eliza and Annabel came hurrying up the front path with Ian. "And who might the lasses be, sir? And the wee lad?"

"Leana can explain..." Jamie tugged on the sleeves of his coat, as if so little an effort could improve his unkempt appearance. His mother liked him neatly dressed. Perhaps she'd make an exception, considering the circumstances. "I must see my father at once."

"Aye, aye, ye must. He's just in there."

Jamie turned to face the library door. Odd that his mother had not heard his voice and come looking for him. Though the large front room included an ornate half-tester bed among its furnishings, the bed was seldom used. But then, he could not remember there ever being a lyke-wake at Glentrool. Jamie knocked lightly on the door, then eased it open, steeling himself for the sight of Alec McKie's wizened body in a state of eternal rest.

But that was not what Jamie found.

On the bed, hands folded across her chest, was Rowena McKie.

"*Nae!*" Jamie stumbled into the candlelit room. " 'Tis not possible..."

But it was.

At her breast was the dish of earth and salt. At her feet stood his father, hunched over with grief. "Och, Jamie!" Alec held out his trembling arms. "The Lord has brought you to us, lad. We did not ken where to send a post or how to find you. Your mother, your poor mother..."

Jamie had no sense of crossing the room. He was simply there, by her side, stunned. And ashamed. Why had he not come home months ago? Why had he not written her from Gatehouse of Fleet? His mother lay in deathly stillness. Gone from his reach. Just like Rose. "What... happened, Father?"

Alec worked his jaw, his rheumy eyes more watery than ever, the tremor in his hands markedly worse. "Yestermorn we rose early for the Sabbath. Your mother mounted her horse, just as she's done for most of her sixty-four years. She'd not quite found her seat when the horse reared back—none of us kens why—and she fell to the ground, land-ing on her bonny neck."

Jamie flinched at the image of his lively mother tumbling to her death. Had she suffered? No wound scarred her thin neck. No blood marred her gown. *Not like my beautiful Rose.* How could he come to grips with the awful truth? The two women he loved most in the world had been taken from him on the same Sabbath.

Alec looked at his wife, and his shoulders sank further still. "Rowena ne'er did open her eyes. She died an hour after her fall."

Jamie remembered the empty pew at Monnigaff. "No wonder you were not at the kirk yestreen."

"None of us could leave her." His father came round the bed and touched her arm. "We heard the music, Jamie." A superstition as old as Glentrool itself: Sometimes while a person was dying, the sweetest music could be heard in the room.

Jamie gazed at his mother, her dark hair stark against the white bed covering, her chin pointed upward, a heidie woman to the end. Age had not diminished her beauty or crushed her spirit. But death had claimed her nonetheless. "I am sorry I was not here, Father."

"'Tis good you've come home, lad." Tears coursed down Alec's wrinkled face. "I'm a *shooglie* auld man who cannot walk from one room to the next without help. I cannot see well, nor hear…"

"I ken, Father…"

"Nae." Alec leaned hard on his arm, his bony hand wrapped round Jamie's wrist. "You do not ken what it is like to lose your wife."

Jamie nearly shook off his grip. "I *have* lost my wife."

Alec lifted his hoary head and turned toward the doorway, pointing a shaky finger at Leana standing in the hall. "And who might that be?"

"My cousin." Jamie kept his voice even. "Leana McBride."

She looked up at the mention of her name. Ian was now wrapped in her arms. The sorrow in her eyes was unmistakable. Leana had seen enough to assess the situation or had learned from Ivy whose funeral they'd hastened home to attend without realizing it.

"If she's not your wife," Alec demanded, "then whose child is that lass carrying?"

Jamie hesitated. *The one in her arms? Or the one in her womb?* "We…were married once, Father. The child Leana bears is…mine."

"Eh?" Alec squinted at her, as though he might sort it out if only he could see more clearly.

Jamie groaned, his soul so burdened with grief he could no longer contain it. "'Tis not the time or place to explain things, Father." Later, when his father was not so distraught, Jamie would tell him about Rose. And about Leana. About two weddings and two brides. But not this day.

"Come, young James." His father pulled him away from the bed. "I've a blissin to bestow on my son whom the Lord has favored." Alec held on to Jamie's arm with one hand and planted the other on his head. His voice shook, whether from age or emotion, Jamie could not tell. He'd heard the words once before, on a dark autumn night when his lies had purchased his blessing. Today, in a brightly lit room, his father's words, freely offered, rang with sincerity.

"May Almighty God bless you, my son. May he bless your land with rain and sun, your flocks and herds with abundant grazing. May all Glentrool look to you as their laird."

"I pray they will, Father. Someday."

"Nae." Alec said the word with such authority, Jamie straightened. "I am as good as dead now, Son, with your mother gone. You ken verra well how it was with us: Your mother did all that I could no longer do. Come December I will have lived eighty-five years. I have ruled these lands long enough. At the hour of your mother's death I made my decision. You must assume the role of laird now, Jamie, or Glentrool will suffer."

Laird of Glentrool shall be your name. His waking dream. At eight o' the clock.

Jamie felt the weight of his father's hand and the significance of his words. He'd never felt weaker than he did this day; perhaps that was by God's design.

"Aye, Father." Jamie stood as tall as he could beneath Alec's hand. "If you believe I am ready, then I am willing."

"Nae man is truly ready to be laird. But the time has come, Jamie. And so have you."

Eighty

Do not cheat thy Heart and tell her,
"Grief will pass away."
ADELAIDE ANNE PROCTER

Gray clouds hung low in the sky, and the dry air was uncommonly still as family and friends stood round the granite mausoleum for Rowena's interment.

Leana had sewn her black mourning gown along the plainest of lines, hoping she might not draw further attention to herself as the newcomer to Glentrool. This was Rowena McKie's day to be remembered and an important Saturday for Jamie and Ian as well. Annabel was caring for the lad in his new turret nursery, trying to keep him tidy until the gathering moved to the house. Uncle Alec planned to introduce his grandson, the future heir of Glentrool, to his neighbors in the glen and present his son in his new role as laird.

Jamie looked the part. Dressed in the fine clothes he'd last worn in Gatehouse—the muted green coat that matched his eyes, a ruffled white cravat, claret silk breeches and stockings, and buckled shoes polished to a luster—he managed to convey both elegance and power. The black mourning band round his arm was doubly significant, as all those present were acutely aware. News of the tragic deaths of Rose and Rowena had spread through the glen like snow on a January wind.

Jamie had not often spoken of Rose since they arrived, but when he did, his eyes grew moist, his voice broke, and his posture lost its regal air.

In those bleak moments, Jamie turned to her. "Leana, I ken you suffer as well."

Aye, Jamie. I do.

Wednesday they'd walked through the heath together, saying very little, watching the wind dance across the top of the loch. Yestreen they'd shared a seat on the stone pier at the end of the front walk, while

Jamie put words to his grief. In response, Leana had offered a comforting reminder from one of the psalms she'd learned at Neda's knee: "The LORD is nigh unto them that are of a broken heart."

"Then why was he not nigh unto Rose?" Jamie had shot back.

"The Lord *was* nigh unto Rose," Leana said as gently as possible. "He healed my sister as only he could: by drawing her unto himself."

Jamie had looked up, as if prepared to do battle, and instead found tears in her eyes.

She'd confessed to him, "The questions you've raised are the same ones I've asked."

Those questions haunted her still. *Why, when Rose was so young? Why, when she wanted only to be a mother? Why, when Jamie loved her so?*

The Almighty's unspoken yet undeniable answer remained: *Trust in me.*

Far above her the eerie cry of a peregrine falcon, echoing through the silent glen, drew Leana's eye upward. Reverend Moodie paused in his eulogy to lift his gaze as well. Those who resided in the glen barely glanced at the bird, but outsiders—Leana among them—were entranced by the natural wonders of Trool. Hardy blackface sheep nibbled on the heathery scrub. The plaintive call of a golden plover echoed among the hills. Water plunged down steep Buchan Burn, creating a constant flow of music without notes.

Aye, the glen was a *ferlie* place. But it was also remote. Lonely.

How hard it had been to bid Rab Murray and Davie Tait farewell. And to write Neda and Duncan still more sad news. Leana knew very few of the faces surrounding her, though some she recognized from the lykewake.

Evan McKie was present for his mother's funeral, of course, with Jamie standing on one side and Evan's wife on the other. Judith McKie's clipped speech marked her as English. From Cumberland, Jamie said. Their son, Archibald, was a copy of his father: sturdy limbed, boisterous, sporting a woolly cap of bright red hair. Other McKie relatives hailed from nearby Glencaird, an old estate along the Black Burn. Such a different world than Auchengray, these venerable families with vast holdings and ancient bloodlines.

Jamie had whispered names in her ear all week as visitors filled the big, square rooms of Glentrool, exchanging condolences for refreshments. *McTaggart. Galbraith. Tole. McFadgen.* Leana nodded at each one, vowing to sort them all out when she was stronger and her grief weaker.

Their closest neighbor, John McMillan of Glenhead, was too memorable to confuse with anyone else. Black haired, broad shouldered, as braw as they came, John appraised each woman who crossed his path, yet he seemed to be watching for one in particular. When a sonsie lass named Sally appeared, John's crooked grin signaled his affections. There'd be a wedding in the glen before Martinmas; Leana felt certain of it.

And a baby born at Glentrool a month after.

She discreetly folded her hands in front of her, sensing her bairn shifting about. Would Jamie still welcome this child? Or resent her ease at childbearing? And what role did she serve now, other than the obvious one of producing his children?

Leana hardly knew her place at Glentrool. The estate employed its own gardener, Robert Muir. Annabel served as Ian's nursery maid. Ivy Findlay had the house staff well in hand. And Aubert Billaud did not allow interlopers in his kitchen. Determined to be useful, Leana had helped Ian get settled in his round nursery, then in the quiet evening hours, busied herself with stitching. No household ever had enough linen towels and sheets. She'd also altered the shirts left behind in Jamie's clothes press, lengthening the sleeves and letting out the shoulders.

When neighbors had come that week to pay their respects, Jamie introduced Leana as his first wife and Ian as his heir. *"First wife?"* their eyes said. The proud angle of Jamie's head had dared anyone to offer a disparaging word. As to the child she was obviously carrying, no one spoke openly of such things in polite society, but Leana felt their stares and heard their whispers.

The dull scrape of granite dragging against granite drew her gaze where it belonged: on Aunt Rowena's resting place. Reverend Moodie stepped aside as Jamie and Evan, joined by several neighbors, carried Rowena McKie's coffin into the shadowy mausoleum. Built among a dense cluster of pines east of the house, the tomb was ornately carved, a fitting memorial to the McKies who'd gone before. But inside the tomb, Leana was reminded of a cave she'd once visited along the Solway coast—dark, dank, chilly.

Alec McKie would be buried there. And on some distant day, Jamie. And Ian.

The thought made her weak-kneed. *Let me die first, Lord. When I am old and Ian is strong. Like his father.*

She had not known her Aunt Rowena well. Letters from Glentrool were rare, and the McKies had only visited Auchengray once, when Leana was eight and Jamie and Evan both twelve. Leana recalled how dramatic her aunt was, so like Rose in appearance and temperament. No wonder Jamie had loved them both. 'Twas clear Rowena had been the light of Alec's life. Even with his walking stick, the elder McKie could barely drag himself from one place to the next, his heart as heavy as his feet.

Leana closed her eyes, seeking answers. Perhaps that was her role at Glentrool: to help two men mourn their wives. And find the strength to press on.

"We've finished, lass." Jamie caught her elbow, steering her through the pines and toward the house. Subdued chatter buzzed round them like bees.

She looked about, flustered. "Jamie, I'm sorry, I…"

"Do not apologize, Leana." He walked alongside her, matching her steps. "You barely knew my mother or any of the folk who came this week looking for a bite of gossip."

"I thought they came for biscuits and cheese," she murmured. "Or whisky and porter. I've never seen so much of either consumed."

Jamie leaned closer to explain. "Father believes a proper display of food and drink honors the memory of the deceased."

"Ah," she said. His cheek was near enough for her to smell his heather soap. "Rowena has been well honored then."

He straightened with a sudden look of concern. "Are you thinking I should have mounted such a feast for Rose?"

"Nae, Jamie. You honor my sister's memory every time you speak of her."

His features softened. "You always ken the right thing to say, lass." Jamie lengthened his stride, guiding her past a grove of bird cherry trees and along the front walk. Those ahead of them waited by the entrance to the house, perhaps in deference to the young laird. His reign had already begun.

Once withindoors, Jamie was pulled this way and that by old friends and distant relatives, leaving Leana to fend for herself. She wandered through the house, relieved to find that death no longer cast its pallor over the rooms. Candles brightened every corner, and roses fresh from the garden sweetened the air. With the curtains drawn back and the windows scrubbed clean, the richly patterned wallcoverings came to life—muted blues and moss greens, the McKie colors.

A renowned Glasgow cabinetmaker had spent a year at Glentrool, Jamie said, designing intricately carved tables and chairs, sideboards and chests, bookshelves and cabinets from oak trees felled in the glen. Leana had never seen such furniture; she touched the wood in passing, marveling at the craftsmanship. Neither Aunt Meg's two humble rooms nor Auchengray's many low-beamed ones could begin to match the refined interiors of Glentrool with its broad dimensions and high ceilings.

The library was her favorite room on the ground floor. Alec's oversize desk commanded the front of the room facing the loch, the half-tester bed stood near the hearth, and the polished hardwood floor was covered with a plush carpet. His prized fiddle and bow hung between two bookshelves; someday Ian might learn to play as well as his grandfather. Yet it was the oil painting over the mantel that beckoned Leana closer.

She'd seen Alec McKie's formal portrait in the dining room, last in a long line of ancestors. Painted twenty years ago when Alec was in the prime of his maturity, the rendering bore a fair likeness of him. But this painting featured a younger Alec, in his late thirties perhaps, standing in a less formal pose: out of doors amid the misty hills aglow with the setting sun. The collar of his brown coat was turned up on one side, like that of a man who'd dressed in haste. Over his shoulder he carried a leather traveling pouch. His waistcoat, dark greenish brown in a subtle plaid, was half unbuttoned, his ruffled white shirt hung loose about his neck, and he had a day's growth of beard, as if he'd done without his valet that morning.

Leana smiled as she stood beneath the portrait, discovering that Jamie had his father's mouth: generously formed, the top and bottom of equal fullness. Alec was not smiling on the canvas but seemed to be considering it. The slope of his nose drew a thinner line down his face than Jamie's did; it appeared the bone had broken and healed some years before the painter took brush to canvas. What delicate ears he had! Yet it was the faraway look in her uncle's eyes that intrigued her. As if he were seeing something he wanted, something for which he was willing to fight.

"Do you ken what I had in my sights?"

Startled, Leana turned to find a much older Alec McKie tottering toward her, waving a bony finger at the portrait. "Jeremiah Davison painted that at Rowena's bidding. Soon after she came to Glentrool in the summer of 1744. Said she wanted a painting of me exactly as I looked when she first clapped eyes on me." He chuckled, a wheezing sound. "In truth, she wanted to capture my expression when *I* first clapped eyes on *her.* Made me wear the same clothes, the same rough beard, and the same besotted look on my face." Alec leaned hard on his walking stick. "I loved Rowena from the moment I saw her." His unfocused eyes watered. "I love her still."

As they stood before the portrait, her uncle described that day as if it were yestreen and not half his lifetime ago. Leana could only imagine such devotion. Jamie had loved her deeply once. But not season after season. Only one season, really. *Spring.*

"There you are, Father." Jamie strolled into the room with an even gait, any evidence of his injury well hidden. "You asked me to find you when Ian was brought down the stair."

Alec turned to his son, the portrait forgotten. "You'll let me introduce him as your heir?"

"Most certainly." Jamie's gaze met hers. "Ian is my firstborn son and the future heir of Glentrool."

Leana dipped her head in silent thanks. Jamie loved her son, of that there could be no doubt.

She watched the McKie men stroll across the entrance hall and into the drawing room, uncertain if she was expected to follow or to be included in any way as Ian's mother. It seemed not: There were only men in the room. Annabel surrendered Ian into his father's arms, then flew out the door after a brief curtsy. Jamie held Ian propped up on his chest, almost shoulder high, facing the august group, while Leana watched from the hall.

"There's a braw lad." A young woman stood at her elbow, grinning. The lass surely had her eye on Jamie, though she was dressed in the plain clothes of the kintra folk. "Not quite a year auld, I'd say."

Leana laughed, feeling more than a little foolish for jumping to conclusions. "That's my son, Ian, who just celebrated his tenth month. You've a good eye."

"'Tis what I do, mem. I deliver bairns." She aimed a pointed gaze at Leana's waist. "Jeanie Wilson's me name. A howdie, like me mither afore me, and me granmither as weel." Jeanie stole another look at Ian, then leaned closer. "I heard ye're guid wi' herbs, mistress. Will ye start a physic gairden at Glentrool? For I canna find the time, wi' me ain bairns."

Leana had been considering that very thing. "If our gardener will allow me a small plot—"

"Robert Muir? Oo aye! He'll be pleased tae have a sonsie lass like ye planted in his gairden."

Leana turned her back on the festivities to give the midwife her full attention. "As you can plainly see, I'll be needing your services come December."

Jeanie wrinkled her brow. "As late as that for your wee girl?"

Surprised by her perceptiveness, Leana held a finger to her lips. "Hush, Jeanie. I've not told Mr. McKie to expect a daughter."

"The young laird is the faither of this ane, too?"

"'Tis a long tale for a winter's night." Leana regarded her closely. "Will you help me when my time comes?"

Jeanie Wilson grinned. "Send for me afore yer waters break. The glen needs a birthin'. We've had enough tears for the deid."

Eighty-One

A prince, the moment he is crown'd,
Inherits every virtue sound.

JONATHAN SWIFT

Jamie rubbed his eyes, the ledger entries blurring after several hours with quill and ink. Thomas Findlay, overseer to Glentrool, had once taught Jamie all he knew of keeping estate records. "Noo that ye're laird, sir, I'm blithe tae let ye handle the ledgers," Thomas had informed him. "Ye can see for yerself whaur yer silver is spent and decide what's best for Glentrool."

What's best for Glentrool. A refrain oft repeated since his arrival home last month. His father had confessed that Rowena had seen to the duties he could no longer manage. Now Jamie knew the truth: His mother had handled everything. Not a penny or a person had come or gone without Rowena's approval.

A tap at the open library door interrupted his musings. "Mr. McKie?" Thomas Findlay stuck his head in. "Have ye a moment, sir?"

Jamie motioned him forward, still uneasy with the formality of his new role. Thomas had called Jamie by his first name all his young life, even after he returned from university. Things were different now. He looked up from behind his father's oak desk, folding his ink-stained hands over the ledgers. "What is it, Thomas?"

"Wi' September here, sir, Henry Stewart needs yer permission tae arrange for the tups."

Further evidence of his mother's strict policies. Stew, Glentrool's head shepherd and veteran of many an October breeding season, hardly needed Jamie's sanction to perform his duties. "Of course he may arrange for them." Jamie kept his voice even so Thomas would not misconstrue his irritation. There was no point belittling his mother's methods. He would simply change the ones that needed changing.

Jamie sat back to resume his work. "Kindly give Stew my regards."

The overseer remained, wool bonnet in hand, his curly black hair on full display as he bent his head. "Mr. McKie, ye're doin' a fine job. A' the lads agree."

Jamie hid his smile, though perhaps not too well. "Good of you to say so, Thomas." How he hated such *mainnerlie* talk! Could he not simply shake the man's hand, as he had Duncan's, and thank him? 'Twas not a laird's place, it seemed. "Your servants must respect you," his father had cautioned him just that morning. "And a bit of fear never hurts."

Fear was Lachlan's stock in trade. Rowena had chosen manipulation. Jamie considered fairness the best means to an end. He would work hard, then ask the same of his people.

"Guid day tae ye, sir." Thomas swept his cap before him and departed, leaving Jamie to his ledgers. And his memories of Rose, which were legion.

Her sweet laughter wafting down Auchengray's stair. A wink when they shared a secret. The tilt of her chin when she was displeased. Her hand seeking his beneath the dining room table. The playful swat of her braid. An off-key cradlesong floating out of the nursery. Her small hands caressing his cheek. His unforgettable, irreplaceable Rose.

Jamie had found the best remedy for his grief: He diligently kept his mind and hands occupied from dawn until the gloaming. The nighttime hours were more difficult. Surrounded by darkness and a quiet household, he lay in his old room, listening to the flowing burn beyond the window and missing his sweet Rose. Though she had never been to Glentrool, never curled next to him in that bed, it was not difficult to imagine her there. He'd done so many times before they left Auchengray.

But Rose was not there. Instead, he had the large bedroom overlooking the loch all to himself. Evan's old room adjoining his now belonged to Leana. It was the one nearest the nursery, and the small turret room could only accommodate Ian's crib and Annabel's bed. In deep mourning for her sister, Leana had not decorated her new bedroom in any manner. It remained as stark and unadorned as her black gowns.

Some nights when sleep would not come, Jamie heard her quietly weeping and found his own pillow wet as well. Of all the ways in which Leana was helping him to recover from Rose's death, their shared tears in the night meant the most to him, though he'd never tell her so. She might become self-conscious, imagining him listening in the next room, or muffle her sobs, leaving him to mourn alone.

'Tis daytime now. To work, McKie.

Jamie spent another half hour balancing his ledgers before Ivy came to the door, inviting him to dinner. Had a bell been rung, as at Auchengray, he would have removed the clapper at once. At Glentrool the midday meal was lighter and the hour later, served at two o' the clock. Supper was also delayed and more formal. Aubert saved his best dishes for the evening meal, dispatching course after course beginning promptly at eight.

Jamie rose from his ledgers, more than willing to trade his dull numbers for food and company. At their first meal together, Alec had insisted Jamie take his place of honor at the head of the long table. Jamie in turn asked his father to sit at his left hand, across from Leana, seated at his right. His mother would not have approved, but Jamie preferred warm conversation at his table, not silence and distance. With his back to the hearth, in which peat burned year round, thrice daily Jamie welcomed his family's advice on the management of Glentrool.

He entered the dining room from the hall and found them standing at their chairs waiting for him. Some formalities remained. Jamie blessed the meat, then they took their seats as the kitchen staff entered from the far door of the portrait-lined room, bearing soup plates.

"So this is Aubert's famous hotchpotch." Leana lifted her eyebrows in anticipation as she tasted it. "Thick," she said after a bit. "And... flavorful."

Jamie smiled. "You have just described every one of Aubert's soups. Even his broths manage to be thick. 'Tis a mystery to us all."

His father ate slowly, leaning over his plate at such an angle Jamie feared he might dip his forehead in the soup. Of all his senses, Alec's taste for highly seasoned foods remained intact. But the hand holding the spoon trembled, and his aim was not always true, sending the spoonful of soup onto the table or, worse, his lap. Linens helped, but Alec still needed his valet, an Englishman named Gilbert, to set him to rights after each meal.

Jamie honored his father's wishes: No special provisions were made at mealtime. Accidents were ignored and swiftly amended without a fuss. Soups and sauces were a challenge, but they were also what his father most enjoyed; hence, they were served.

In Jamie's youth—which he now realized had continued well through his ordeal at Auchengray—he'd disregarded Alec McKie as weak, ineffective, useless. An embarrassment to the family. Now he knew differently. Spending time in his library, Jamie had discovered all that his father had accomplished in his earlier years. Seeing Alec separate from Rowena, standing in his own light rather than in her formidable shadow, had given Jamie a new appreciation of his father's steady temperament. And compared to Lachlan McBride, the man was a saint.

Jamie finally understood the truth: His father was the wisest man he'd ever had the privilege of knowing. And the most merciful, for he had loved his prodigal son through it all. However many months or years appointed to him, Alec McKie deserved Jamie's highest regard, and he would have it. *A wise son maketh a glad father.* Gladness was long overdue at Glentrool.

Jamie raised his voice slightly. "How have you spent the morning, Father?"

He pointed his empty soupspoon across the table. "Watching this fair lass dig her garden."

I ken the appeal, Father. Jamie turned to Leana, whose wispy hair and wind-chapped cheeks gave away her morning activities. "Plying the soil again, eh?"

"Robert and I are creating a physic garden. I hope you do not mind."

"Mind?" Alec was the one who answered. "We're fortunate to have a woman skilled in the use of herbs beneath our roof. You'll find many such plants in the Buik, you ken. Coriander and rue, anise and hyssop."

"I cannot grow those in Scotland, Mr. McKie. But I'll have agrimony and speedwell, meadowsweet and valerian. And chickweed to help you sleep."

"That'll do." Alec continued with his soup, nodding to himself.

Jamie tried to sound nonchalant. "Has Robert been…helpful to you?" *Respectful* was what he meant but did not say. Thirty and unmarried, Robert was reputed to have an eye for the lasses. *You'll not look at this one.*

"He's a gifted gardener." Leana's response was more enthusiastic than Jamie had hoped. "His handbarrow is full of interesting tools I've not used before. Caterpillar shears, straw bells, and a clever transplanter with a long handle. I've managed all these years with a spade, a trowel, a pruning knife, and a garden fork."

"And done quite well," Jamie reminded her, alerting the maids to serve the next course. It was the first of September; Jamie had instructed the gamekeeper to provide woodcock for the dinner table since the bird was now in season. "Let Robert do all the strenuous work, Leana. I'll not have you tiring yourself." *Or risking our child's life. Or yours.*

When she looked at him, it was clear she grasped his meaning. "I promise to do nothing but point. And let Robert plant."

"Well said, lass." Jamie trusted her implicitly. But he would watch Robert Muir. "Bring on the grilled woodcock, then, for my father's appetite is far from sated."

Leana was more talkative than usual through the meal. Though her dress was somber, her air was light as she shared Ian's latest accomplishment. "He distinctly said the word *shoe.*"

Jamie pretended to look shocked. "Is our son old enough to wear shoes?"

She smiled, shaking her head. "The child has only just learned to stand on his own two feet, and then not for long. He'll not need shoes until he is truly walking and doing so out of doors."

"Is that so?" For a woman who'd grown up without a mother, Leana's maternal instincts were impressive. "What a store of knowledge you have. Where did you learn such things?"

Her shrug did not hide her pleasure. "By asking Neda questions. By watching Jessie Newall with her bairns. A woman prepares all her life to be a mother."

So I see, lass.

Leana was a living portrait of motherhood, her body round with their growing child, her face lit with expectant joy. Even in her mourning gown, even in her sorrow, her delight in mothering could not be contained. Nor would he ever want it to be.

After pudding, Jamie returned to his father's desk—it would be some time before he could think of it as his—and tackled the basket of correspondence that had accumulated after his mother's death. Since his father could no longer hold a pen steady enough to write, the task fell to his heir.

Notes of sympathy were intermingled with bills that would require his immediate attention. He'd nearly sorted through the lot of them when Ian crawled through the door of the library and headed his direction, as if exploring Glentrool unaccompanied.

"Who is this coming to see his father?" Jamie abandoned his letters and leaned down, holding out his hands. "Can this fine-looking boy be mine?"

"He cannot possibly be anyone else's." Leana stood in the doorway, gazing at them both. "Look at those dark eyebrows of his, and tell me they are not your own."

Jamie held Ian up and scowled at him fiercely, which the child promptly imitated. "The lad is mine," Jamie agreed, smiling broadly so Ian would too. "I hope our second child favors you, Leana."

She started across the room. "Pale, you mean?"

"Not pale. Fair." He looked up to make certain she was listening. "Fashioned in gold and blue, the colors of the sky."

"Ah," was all she said, though her cheeks were far from wan.

The hour crept past midnight, the house fell silent, and still he could not sleep. Jamie tried various positions, always ending up on his right side, staring at the door to the adjoining bedroom where Leana lay softly weeping. However light one's spirits were by day, in the quiet darkness, grief demanded its due.

For once his eyes were dry; he did not share her tears this night. Instead, Jamie longed to go to Leana, to comfort her. To listen, as she so often had listened. To console her with tender words.

Comfort? Listen? Console? Are you certain, Jamie?

He was not at all certain.

About his work at Glentrool, aye. About his feelings toward Leana, nae.

When Rose was alive, his path had been abundantly clear: His love for Leana had been pruned to the ground and the roots left to wither, while his love for Rose had grown and blossomed. She was his wife. She was his love. She was his life.

But now his beloved Rose was gone. And though his love for her remained steadfast and his memories fresh, it was her sister who sat at his table. The mistress of his household. The mother of his children. The woman he had once promised, "I will always love you."

And so I have, Leana. And yet, have not.

With a groan, Jamie shifted to his left side, turning his back to her door and his face toward the rising quarter moon.

Eighty-Two

For God's rose-thought, that blooms in thee,
Will bloom forevermore.
GEORGE MACDONALD

Oh, Rose. You would love this." Leana held up her gift for Jamie, then buried her smile in the fabric before someone heard her and discovered her secret.

"Ian, you won't tell a soul, will you?" She leaned down to kiss his round head before he took off across the nursery floor on hands and knees.

When the laird of Glentrool turned twenty-six next Monday—the twentieth of September—his unique birthday present would be ready.

Leana was having trouble keeping her stitches small enough, now that her fingers were starting to tingle. The same numbness, followed by a burning sensation, had afflicted her when she carried Ian. She had to put aside her sewing needle more often than she liked. And at bedtime she resisted slipping her hands underneath her pillow, or the pressure made the pain worse in the morning.

At least she was finally resting at night. After weeks of crying herself to sleep, Leana had come to a place of peace. The Sovereign One held Jamie and Rose close to his heart. She could trust him and let go. *Return unto thy rest, O my soul.*

Contentment had begun to seep into her life. And with it, a desire to create a peaceful home for Ian and for the child wildly kicking inside her. A woman's seventh month was the most active one for her bairn, midwives said; the gymnastic display beneath her loose-fitting gown was proof.

Leana slowly stood, then took a turn about the nursery, following Ian's progress. She thought it the nicest corner of Glentrool, though it had no corners at all. Completely round, the first floor of the turret served as an office for Thomas and Ivy Findlay, with a door leading out to the garden. The nursery on the second floor had remained vacant since the day Evan and Jamie had outgrown their nursery maid. Not an enormous room, like the others at Glentrool, it was perfect for a little boy stretching his legs. There was one window—slender but almost as tall as the room—made of heavy glass with swirls in the center of each pane that caught the sun. As the window faced west, light poured in all afternoon, brightening the room considerably. A blue velvet drape easily dropped into place when it was time to sleep.

Rowena had done a fine job of designing a nursery. Thick carpet covered most of the floor, and the wall sconces were mounted far above the reach of little hands. A sturdy set of chairs marched round a diminutive wooden table, the edges of which were rounded and smooth. Rowena would have been a mother to be reckoned with, a woman who knew exactly what her sons required.

Behind a door neatly fitted into the curved wall, a spiral stair led down to the first floor of the turret. Dark, steep, and narrow, the steps were not meant for a child learning to walk nor for an expectant mother. Someday Leana would fly up and down them with candle in hand, but for now the door to the stair stayed closed.

She watched Ian pull himself up using the table, then release his hands for a moment. Ah, the look of achievement! He sat back down almost at once, but the freedom shining in his eyes gave her pause. Once Jamie McKie's son could walk, he would run.

Since she could no longer safely lift Ian from the floor, Leana eased down beside him and invited him into her embrace. He came willingly, though he did not stay long, his curiosity outstripping his need to be held. Colored blocks and bright cups and animals on wheels were much more interesting than Mother. When he was ready for his nap, though, he'd crawl into her lap and sigh with the satisfaction of coming home.

While she waited for her son to wind down like his toys, Leana examined her sewing project and smiled again, picturing Jamie's face Saturday next. An unusual present—he could neither open it nor use it. She still felt certain the sight of it would please him.

The idea had come to her when she'd finished altering all of Jamie's sarks and begun digging through his mother's old sewing kist, looking for remnants that might be put to good use. Beneath layers of linen, cotton, wool, and silk, she'd unearthed a treasure: an ell of heavy satin in dark green, woven with a claret design. The very same fabric used to make Jamie's best coat.

Now the future heir of Glentrool had a coat just like his father's, alike to the last detail. Making a pattern required borrowing the coat from Jamie's clothes press while he was off to the village on an important errand and shooing Annabel out of the nursery for several hours. Fitting her wriggling son had presented a much greater challenge, but Leana had made a game out of it—"What is hiding in this sleeve, Ian? Can you poke your hand inside and find out?"—and soon had the coat styled to her satisfaction.

Ian would protest when she tried to dress him in anything so stiff, and he'd outgrow her creation in a matter of months. But the effort would be worth it to see Jamie's face. Especially if it made him laugh. How she missed that sound! Rich, warm, masculine laughter, rolling from deep inside him. It made her toes curl to remember it.

Will you laugh for me, Jamie? Only then could she be certain that he, too, was starting to heal. There were hopeful signs. His appetite had returned, and he seemed happy to join his family at table or welcome visitors to their door. The family worship he led each evening after supper was well prepared and his comments sincere. He'd taken a bold step and invited the servants to join them. Not perched on rough benches along the periphery of the room, nor standing in shadowy corners, but seated at the long dining table in comfortable chairs. "We are all members of God's family and equal in his sight," Jamie had announced to their collective astonishment.

Each day he also found time to walk among the flocks, to visit with his father, to spend a playful moment with Ian. But he had yet to look completely relaxed. Instead, a stoic grief had etched new lines on Jamie's handsome face. If Leana could, she would smooth them away with one of her potions. Egg whites mixed with alum and rose water, perhaps.

She could not pretend her touch alone would banish the evidence of his pain. Or erase the memories of Rose that brought a sheen to his eyes in quiet moments.

Leana would not rush Jamie nor impinge on his mourning. The first moment each day when she thought of Rose, her heart broke afresh, realizing she would never see her dear sister again. Yet the cracks were growing smaller, and they healed a bit more quickly. Not because she did not love Rose or cherish her memory, but because she *did* love her sister and knew how she'd want to be remembered. *Weeping may endure for a night, but joy cometh in the morning.*

Voices on the spiral stair made Leana scramble to her feet, using the little table for support, just as Ian had. She would not miss feeling so ungainly come December. By the time Annabel and Eliza eased the door open, peeking round the edge to check Ian's whereabouts, Leana had stuffed Jamie's gift beneath her apron, folding her arms over the suspicious-looking lump.

" 'Tis time yer lad went doon for his nap." Annabel swept Ian off the floor and into his crib with the ease of youth and a trim waistline.

Eliza eyed her mistress's apron but said nothing. "And *ye,* mem, have a surprise waitin' for ye in the gairden. Let me walk ye doon the stair."

The door to the hall opened directly across from the bedroom that Leana shared with Eliza, as was the custom for a lady's maid. Leana had a roomy curtained bed with neatly carved posts, and Eliza slept in a box bed tucked in the wall behind a folding door. Yet the room was so large they hardly heard each other turn over on their mattresses.

"A moment while I discard my apron." Leana ducked into their bedroom to wrap the linen apron round the little coat. Moments later she emerged into the hall where sandy-haired Eliza stood, looking round as if she'd hardly noticed her mistress's strange behavior.

"You say someone has a surprise for *me?*" Leana took Eliza's arm with one hand, the railing with the other, as they walked side by side down the wide oak staircase that divided the great house down the center.

" 'Tis not sic a surprise, syne ye ken 'tis comin'—"

"My rose!" Leana released her and hurried down the last few steps.

"Aye," Eliza called after her. "Mr. Muir's waitin' for ye."

The lanky gardener was standing near her new physic garden, one elbow propped on his long-handled spade, a bare-looking shrub at his feet. "If ye'll point, Miss McBride, I'll plant."

"Well done, Robert." He'd remembered their promise to Jamie.

When the two had worked together on her herb garden, Leana had expressed her love for roses—one bright pink variety in particular. Robert in turn had boasted about the hothouse roses at Bargaly House, an estate built in the foothills of Cairnsmuir. "Bargaly's gardener is a freen o' mine. Whan next I visit the man, I'll see if he has yer favorite."

Robert Muir was a man of his word. He'd brought her an Apothecary's Rose.

"We need a spot with full sun," Leana explained, eying the rocky hills dotted with sheep. "Yet it must be protected from the wind."

"In the glen?" He shook his head. "Sunshine we have, but ye'll not easily hide from the wind. The east side o' the hoose might be best." He picked up the small shrub and followed her round the corner. "I've soaked the roots for an hour. 'Tis ready."

Leana chose a spot below the dining room window, then had Robert cut the roots short and straight. When the rose was duly planted and pruned and the soil well watered, the gardener ambled off, giving her a bit of privacy.

Leana knelt and carefully placed her hands near the plant's bare shoots, then sat for a moment. The September sun felt warm on her shoulders. Westerly winds passed her by, sheltered by the house that was meant to shelter Rose.

"My dearest sister." She smoothed her hands across the soil, her eyes wet with tears. "Welcome home."

Eighty-Three

How can I tell the signals and the signs
By which one heart another heart divines?
HENRY WADSWORTH LONGFELLOW

He could tell Leana had something on her mind. Her hands fiddled with the silverware, yet she'd not tasted her breakfast. Not even Aubert's freshly baked baps, warm from the oven and fragrant with yeast. Was she worried about not having a gift waiting for him at his plate? Birthday presents were not expected when a household was in mourning.

Before he could tell her so, Leana abandoned her place at table.

"Gentlemen, if you'll excuse me." She stood, a hint of a smile crossing her features. "I shan't be a moment." With a slight bob of her head, she disappeared into the hall. Her footsteps faded up the stair.

Alec looked up from his porridge, blinking in confusion. "Is your wife...eh, is Leana...ill?"

Your wife. Jamie forgave his father's blunder, considering how easily she had stepped into the role of Glentrool's mistress. Such confusion about Leana's role was understandable.

His own confusion was another matter.

Jamie leaned toward his father. "Leana is fine, sir. I believe she simply...forgot something."

Minutes later as he was spooning out the last of the porridge from his plate, Jamie heard laughter floating down the stair, accompanied by Ian's exuberant babbling. "It seems what she forgot was my son." Children generally did not come to table until they were...well, until they were not children. Perhaps she intended a short visit in honor of his birthday.

Someone tapped on the door panel—there were at least three amused women on the other side—and announced, "Behold, the future heir of Glentrool!" As if to heighten the drama, the door slowly creaked open, swinging toward Jamie.

The exalted future heir, enthroned in his mother's arms, was revealed at last.

Oh, my.

Leana smiled. "Jamie, aren't you going to say something?"

What could he say? It was the most outrageous thing he'd ever seen: Ian, dressed exactly like him, right down to the leather booties on his feet.

"Well, it's…" Jamie didn't mean to laugh. It just came out. "You've obviously worked…very hard." Another laugh, which he tried to turn into a cough with little success. "Ah…thank you, Leana. Is this my…present?" On the word *present*, a great roll of laughter came out, which he could no more recall than a top spun across the floor. Out of reach. Too late.

"James McKie!" His father glared at him. "Whatever is the matter with you?"

"Father…you might want to take a look." Jamie turned his head away, thinking if he didn't *see* the child, he could restrain himself. But when he turned round, the miniature Jamie was still there, beaming at him, flapping his little lacy cravat up and down. "All he needs…," Jamie managed to say, "is a sword." At which Leana turned the boy sideways and displayed the silver teaspoon attached to his waist.

There was no hope after that.

Jamie laughed until his limbs were weak and his eyes were wet with tears. Ian found his father's behavior most diverting and leaped into Jamie's open arms. Annabel and Eliza peeped round the door, as did half the household staff—'twas a good thing the dining room had several entrances. When Ian's grandfather got a good look at the boy, Alec laughed harder than all of them, dissolving into a wheezing cough that worried Jamie until he saw the joy on his father's face.

Leana was laughing as well—a bright, cheerful sound, like bells ringing. "I'm pleased you like your gift, Jamie."

"Most *shortsome,* this present of yours." He fingered the rich fabric, marveling at her skill. "I only pray you did not cut up the original coat to create this one."

"Your coat awaits you in your clothes press. I did...borrow it, though."

"Stealing, eh?" He handed Ian back to her with an exaggerated frown. "Be forewarned, Miss McBride, that your birthday is six months hence. Sufficient time to prepare my revenge."

Another birthday came much sooner, though: Ian celebrated his first year in early October. Across the glen the vibrant greens of summer faded into the muted shades of autumn—burnished red oaks, prickly brown hedgerows, golden yellow gorse, dark green pines—while Ian's sunny demeanor continued to shine, casting a warm glow across the household.

Mourning or not, there were presents waiting for Ian that Monday. Jamie gave him a wooden hobbyhorse, crafted by a carpenter from the village, and sent another like it to Evan's son in Sorbie. Leana's gift was a large cloth ball made of quilted cotton and stuffed with wool. His grandfather provided the most useful of gifts, a gold sovereign. And Aubert was coaxed into preparing the child's favorite foods: tatties and neeps, properly mashed; applesauce sweetened with sugar and cinnamon; and tender lamb roasted with rosemary and cut into tiny bites, suitable for Ian's sprouting teeth.

Jamie remained in the nursery while Leana fed Ian his birthday dinner and put him down for a nap. Her soothing voice had rather the same effect on Jamie as it did their son. Ledgers and correspondence no longer held his attention. Worries about the start of breeding season were left at the nursery door.

He was in Leana's domain now. And blithe to be there.

Jamie watched her bend over the crib. The graceful line of her neck, the narrow span of her shoulders, made him long to reach for her. But if he held her, he would press a kiss to the back of her neck, to that tender spot he remembered. His hands would find their way to the swell of her waist where their child grew...

Nae, he dared not think of embracing Leana.

Together, mother and father watched their son. The child's eyelids fluttered, his mouth drooped open, and finally he sank into the mattress with a noisy sigh. Jamie wondered aloud, "Is that what I look like when I fall asleep?"

"Aye," Leana said lightly, turning toward the stair. "You do."

Embarrassed, Jamie quickly followed her into the upper hall. "I beg your pardon…"

"Jamie, you worry too much." Leana paused at the top of the stair, her smile genuine. " 'Twas an innocent question."

Unintentional, perhaps, but not entirely innocent. He felt so comfortable with Leana he sometimes forgot they were no longer husband and wife. Even now, walking down the stair with her on his arm felt natural, felt *right*. But she was not his wife; she was his cousin. He would do well to remember that, lest he risk offense. Or was it his heart that he risked each hour, each day that Leana McBride lived beneath his roof?

That he loved her still, had always loved Leana in some way, was not the question. Could she love *him* again after he'd so thoroughly put her aside for her sister? It was a great deal to ask, even of a woman as generous as Leana.

Eighty-Four

Words, like Nature, half reveal
And half conceal the Soul within.

ALFRED, LORD TENNYSON

I have a gift for you."

Leana looked up from her reading as Jamie handed her a rough square of paper, crudely folded, covered with a fine gray dust. "A gift?" She took it with some hesitancy. "For Lukemas Day?" Other than in Rutherglen, where the old holiday was duly observed, the eighteenth of October usually came and went without ceremony.

"I was not thinking of St. Luke," he confessed. "And perhaps *gift* is not the right word."

She'd pulled her chair near the hearth. Jamie did the same, sitting rather closer than usual. Two hours before supper the gloaming had already settled across the glen. The drawing room's three long windows no longer ushered in enough natural light to read by, so the maidservants were going through the house lighting more candles. Lovely, tall bees-wax tapers, bright and fragrant. Lachlan McBride's miserly nature was nowhere to be found at Glentrool.

Leana began to unfold the stiff paper, scattering the pale dust across her black gown, until Jamie stilled her hands. She glanced up, surprised to find him looking quite serious.

"Before you open this, Leana, let me say again how sorry I am that you cannot join us at kirk each Sabbath."

Though she'd protested at first, Jamie had been adamant: No trips south to the village for her this autumn. "The risk to our child and to you is too great," he'd insisted. Even on the Sabbath last when her sister's headstone was finally set in place, Jamie would not allow Leana to travel. After a lifetime of Sunday services in Newabbey, she missed the time of worship each week and—though she would never confess it aloud—the chance to sit with Jamie by her side.

Leana nodded at the paper. "This has something to do with the kirk?"

"Not really. It has more to do with Rose." He helped her unfold it, brushing away the dust. Granite dust, she realized. "It's the stonemason's drawing," he explained, spreading it across both their laps. "When I told him how you longed to see your sister's headstone, he presented me with this. He confessed that had he known a lady would be studying it, he'd have rendered it more carefully. But it *is* a good likeness, Leana. I hope you are pleased."

She touched the paper, following the mason's lines with her fingertips. The design was graceful. And familiar. A wreath of roses, delicately carved in stone, just like the one that adorned their mother's gravestone in Newabbey. "How did you remember?"

Jamie's voice was softer still. "How could I forget?"

Leana gripped the sketch, struggling to maintain her composure. Her sister's name was etched below the wreath. *Rose McBride McKie.* Then the dates that fell much too close together. *Born 1 August 1773. Died 8 August 1790.* Finally the tragic facts. *Beloved wife of James Lachlan McKie. Mother of William and Alexander.*

"Oh, Jamie. 'Tis good that…you…"

"Aye." He brushed away the dust that obscured the epitaph at the bottom. "I chose some lines of poetry by Isaac Watts. See what you think of them."

Leana read the epitaph aloud, imagining Jamie on the worst day of his life having to think of such things.

> How fair is the Rose!
> What a beautiful flower.
> The glory of April and May!

" 'Tis perfect," she told him. And it was. *Our beautiful Rose.*

"Leana." He slowly refolded the sketch, his eyes the color of moss and mist. "I am glad…so very glad to have you here at Glentrool. With Ian. And with me."

A single knock sounded on the drawing room door. Ivy Findlay's voice slid through the cracks like emery paper. "Supper is ready whan ye are, Mr. McKie."

They both looked up with a guilty start. Jamie caught her elbow and helped her stand. "As I was saying, I am glad you are here."

Leana remembered what else he'd said a moment earlier. *With me.* Dared she ask him what he meant? *What's to become of us, Jamie?* That was the question on her heart. Could she speak it aloud? Nae, it was still too soon. Their grief was too fresh.

She would wait. *Let patience have her perfect work.*

Leana slipped out the front door at half past six to watch the day begin. Once Davina or David arrived—she had to keep an open mind in case her instincts were wrong—such early morning forays would be out of the question. But this morning, all things were possible. She followed the front path to the stone pier, neatly built with roomy seats. A small boat was lodged beneath it. Perhaps in the spring, when Jamie's days of mourning ended and her babe was safely delivered, he would take her rowing on the loch. How still the surface was this morning. Without the sun, it had no color at all.

She dared not stray far from home, for today was the start of stag season, and the hunters would soon be on the hills, bows drawn, eyes alert for red deer. The sky was a luminous dark blue with a faint pattern of clouds. As she watched, the color changed to turquoise so gradually she could not discern how or when it happened. Yet when she looked down for a moment to brush a leaf from her lap, then looked up again, the sky was lighter. And fading to gray.

Now she could see the ground, covered in dew. Or was it frost? The glistening foliage on the nearby birch and rowan trees, as well as her shivering arms, confirmed that it must be frost. Icy particles blanketed the mountains across the loch, outlining the deep ruts carved by winter torrents. She pulled her plaid tighter and moved her feet up and down to warm them.

The air was blessedly calm. Usually the winds sighed through the pines, moaning across the glen, the saddest of sounds. But not today. Instead, she was rewarded with the most stirring of sights: an eagle soaring high above the loch, headed for its cliff-side aerie near Glenhead.

Leana heard footsteps. Then Jamie's voice. "'Tis a beautiful sight first thing in the morning."

She stood and turned to greet him. "Oh, did you see it?"

Jamie closed the distance between them, taking off his greatcoat to slip it round her shoulders. The wool hem touched the ground. "See what, lass?"

"The golden eagle." She peered at him. "What were you looking at that was so beautiful?"

He smiled, and then she knew. Frosty morning or not, heat rose to her cheeks. She turned to face the loch and felt his hands rest lightly on her arms.

"Do not stay long, Leana. The hunters will be out soon."

Jamie left her to enjoy the solitude. Moments earlier she would not have welcomed someone's company. Now she missed his voice, his touch. Even wearing his coat, warmed by his body, she was chilly. And lonely, standing by herself on the pier. The loch was gray, like the sky. Like the hills, like the house. Yet with Jamie there, Glentrool was warm, full of color, brimming with life.

My Jamie.

He was the husband of her heart if not her hand. He was the father of her children and their hope for the future. She would never deny her love for him. Not even if he asked her. *Please, Jamie. Ask.*

Eighty-Five

Sorrow and the scarlet leaf,
Sad thoughts and sunny weather;
Ah me! this glory and this grief
Agree not well together!

THOMAS WILLIAM PARSONS

As the days of autumn grew shorter, the work hours grew longer. While Leana spent more time resting for her bairn's sake—a practice Jamie heartily approved of—he poured his energies into the land that was now his responsibility. Glentrool's flocks were more than ten times the size of Auchengray's, and the terrain they covered more rugged. Henry Stewart and the shepherds who labored for him remained on the braes past the gloaming, preparing the ewes for breeding.

Jamie joined Stew when he could. The man was more taciturn than Duncan and not as likely to dispense advice, but Stew had the same even temperament, the same shepherd's wisdom honed from time alone on the hills.

"How is yer faither?" Stew asked early one evening as they worked side by side with the dogs, herding the ewes into the sheepfold. It was the last Friday in October, yet there were still many sheep to be bred. "Way-to-me!" Stew called, and the collies headed round the flock *widdershins,* like a clock turning backward. Though Stew had seen fifty years come and go, his weathered face appeared older, and his agile body, younger. He was the color and texture of a walnut shell—wiry hair, rough skin, close-set eyes, wrinkled clothes—all stained a nondescript light brown, blending in with the faded heather.

"For a gentleman his age," Jamie answered, "my father is doing remarkably well."

Stew took his time before saying, " 'Tis hard on a man whan he loses his wife."

"Aye, it is." Harder than Jamie had imagined.

He could still see Rose when he closed his eyes. But he could no longer hear her voice. However much he tried to recapture the timbre, the inflection, the pitch, Rose's voice was simply *gone*. He remembered many things she'd said, but he could not hear her saying them.

When he heard a woman's voice, it was Leana's. Singing to Ian. Laughing with his father. Praising the servants. Even in the midst of their mourning, Glentrool was a place of quiet joy. Sometimes he wondered if Leana *willed* it so. His mother had exerted her influence over the household, yet it produced envy and discord. Leana's methods were entirely the opposite, and so were the results. Not a soul at Glentrool would dispute the positive difference Leana had made in three months' time.

Stew lifted his head, scanning the darkening horizon. "We're losin' our licht, Mr. McKie, and yer family will be wantin' their supper. Best be headin' hame, aye?"

Bidding Stew good night, Jamie strode down the hill, still wincing when his right leg twisted a certain way. He had but half a mile to walk. As the sunlight faded, so did the warmth in the air and the colors of the earth. The trees round Glentrool turned to black, outlined against the sunset. Orange at the treetops gave way to pinkish clouds, then a pale blue gray, growing darker as the eye moved upward.

His many thoughts of Leana made him long to get home to her. *Aye.* To her, not just to the house. Leana was the very heart of Glentrool, even if she was not his wife.

Can you not change that?

He slowed his steps, gazing at the loch below, glistening in the sunset.

They had spoken their wedding vows once before. Then lived as husband and wife, not knowing the days of their marriage were numbered.

Is there any impediment to this marriage?

There were so many impediments Jamie did not have fingers enough to tally them all. Except when he started to count them, none of them mattered. Only one thing counted. Nae, two: Leana was the mother of his children, and he loved her completely.

"Then she will be my wife." He said it aloud to the hills and the braes, to the pines and the winds. If she was reticent, he would woo her again. If her heart needed mending, he would heal it with his love. If the kirk did not allow it, he would convince them. If the parish did not approve, he would remind them he was the laird of Glentrool, whose only desire was to honor the Laird of all. *What therefore God hath joined together, let not man put asunder.*

Jamie lengthened his stride, his eye on the stone manor house that sheltered his future bride. If there was any pain in his leg, he no longer noticed it.

Marry me, Leana. The words were as sweet as an autumn apple in his mouth.

As he drew closer, he realized Leana was standing at the front door. As if she knew. Watching for him, waiting for him. He shouted her name, raising his hand to her, quickening his pace, not caring if he looked eager. Wanting her to see the truth on his face before she heard it from his lips.

She opened the door behind her, smiling as he approached. "I feared we'd lost you among the ewes."

"Nae, lass. I am not lost but found." Jamie held the door as she turned and walked back in. Moving with care, he noticed, looking sturdy and fragile at the same time. Five weeks at most, she'd said that morning. Arrangements had been made with Jeanie Wilson, the howdie of the glen.

Now he had some arrangements of his own to make.

He caught up with her and drew her hand into his as he stopped outside the library door, too impatient to find somewhere else to meet. He was laird of this house and would speak where he chose and with whom.

"Jamie, what is it?"

Where to start? At the beginning.

"Leana, there was a time…when you…" *When you loved me.* That was true, but that was not what needed to be said.

He started again. "There was a time when we loved each other. As a man loves a woman. As a husband cherishes his wife. I cannot… I dare not…"

"I understand, Jamie." Tears lined her eyes, not quite spilling over.

What did she understand? He'd not finished. Nae, he'd not truly begun. "Leana, I believe that…"

"Perhaps someday…," she said faintly.

Someday? There was no promise in that. "Listen to me, Leana…"

Without warning, the library door banged open, and Alec McKie stepped out, speaking in a voice louder than Jamie ever remembered. "Hearken unto thy father that begat thee!" Alec banged his walking stick on the floor for punctuation, then rapped twice on the open library door. "I would meet you in here at once, James. Supper can wait."

Bewildered, Jamie turned to Leana, who'd already backed away from him.

"We will speak another time," she said softly, then hastened up the stair.

"Nae, Leana," he called after her. "We will speak tonight."

Alec poked his side with his stick. "At once, lad, before I lose my temper."

Jamie did as he was told, though his own temper was brewing. He and Leana were far from finished. And what had vexed his father so? He found out before the door was slammed shut.

"Do you not know the Scriptures, James McKie?"

Now he *was* angry. "You ken well that I do, Father, because you taught them to me."

Alec had the family Bible open on his desk and pointed to it, his finger shaking, but his voice like steel. " 'Rejoice with the wife of thy youth.' That is what it says, Jamie. 'Be thou ravished always with her love.' "

"Father!" he chastened him, his eyes cutting to the door. "Keep your voice down."

"I have kept my voice down in this house long enough!" His father was coming unhinged. "You may be laird, but you are still my son."

"Aye, but—"

"And as my son, you will heed my words: Leana is the wife God has chosen for you. Be done with your mourning, and marry the woman."

Jamie's eyes widened. "Take Leana as my wife?" Had Alec read his mind? "Father, as it happens—"

"You are one of the heritors of the parish, Jamie. Surely you can persuade that young minister in Monnigaff to marry the two of you."

"Sir, I'd already intended—"

"And *I* intend to speak my piece!" Alec shook his walking stick at the ceiling. "My eyesight is failing, lad, yet I can see the woman loves you. Do you not hear it in her voice when she speaks your name?"

Aye, Father, I do. Jamie dared not smile, the man was on such a rampage. "That's precisely why—"

"Och!" His father fumed about the room, banging his stick on any obliging surface. "This child of yours that's due in December. Would you have him born outside the bonds of wedlock? Marked as a bystart by folk in the glen? Lad or lass, 'twould be a meikle burden to carry all one's life."

"It certainly would." His father had just given him the perfect argument for marrying Leana sooner rather than later. A brilliant man, Alec McKie.

"Do what you must, Jamie. Beg the woman's forgiveness, beg the kirk session's mercy, but see that my grandchild has a legitimate name." Alec suddenly collapsed forward, as if he'd spent energy he did not have.

Jamie caught his father in his arms and helped him to a chair. "Are you all right, sir?"

"I will be when you've done your duty by the lass." Alec clutched Jamie's shirt, pulling him closer, his voice reduced to a rough whisper. "You married Leana once, Son. Marry her again."

Eighty-Six

A hope beyond the shadow of a dream.
JOHN KEATS

Leana waited for Jamie in the second-floor sitting room. But she could not sit, so tightly wound were her nerves. And she could not stand, for her knees refused to hold her. And she could not gaze out the window, for nightfall had shrouded the glen in darkness. And she could not concentrate for all the voices in her head.

There was a time when we loved each other. Jamie's words in the hall, spoken with conviction. His touch on her hand. His eyes shining with intensity.

Rejoice with the wife of thy youth. Alec McKie shouting in righteous anger behind a closed library door as she fled up the stair.

Hearken, O daughter. Incline thine ear. A different voice, heard only by her heart. She would heed his words above all.

Listen to me. "I'm listening, Jamie." She leaned her forehead against the windowpane, her breath steaming the cold glass. *Hurry.*

A door opened in the entry hall one floor below her. Cordial parting words. Jamie's footsteps on the stair. She'd never mistake them for anyone else's. Leather striking wood. Resolute, steady beats, like a soldier marching toward a cause.

We will speak tonight.

Turning away from the window, Leana faced the stair. *Now, Jamie. Please.*

The moment he reached the top step Jamie started toward her, crossing the floor with measured strides. Though he was dressed like a shepherd and covered with heath, he carried himself like the laird he was. Tall and strong and full of grace. He was the same Jamie she had loved for two long years, and yet he was a great deal more.

At last he stood before her. He did not speak. Instead he took her hands in his, studying them as he did. Rubbing his thumb over the back of each hand. Caressing her fingers until she feared she might faint.

"Leana." More breath than word. He pressed a kiss inside each wrist, finding her pulse. "Marry me, my love. Say you will."

Jamie, my sweet Jamie! If he released her hands, she would sink to the floor. Instead, she said, "I will."

He looked up, his green eyes shimmering in the candlelight. "You are certain?"

'Twas the easiest question she had ever answered in her life. "I am certain that I love you, Jamie." She touched their joined hands to her waist with a shaky smile. "And I am very certain that I am meant to be the mother of your children."

Though his mouth smiled, his eyes did not. "Many heartaches lie behind us, Leana."

"And many joys lie ahead." She leaned down to kiss his hands, as he had kissed hers. Tears filled her eyes. *Dearest Jamie. The husband of my heart.*

"There are…things that must be arranged, lass. With Reverend Moodie. For we cannot wait. Our child needs a father." He kissed her bowed head. "And I need you, Leana."

Oh, my dear Jamie! Leana straightened and did not bother to brush away her tears. " 'Tis everything I could hope for, but…your father…"

"He wants us to marry. As soon as possible. Alec McKie will insist it was his idea from the start. When he overheard our conversation in the hall, he misunderstood my intentions and…ah, made his wishes known."

"And is this what *you* wish, Jamie?" She searched his eyes, longing to search his heart. To be sure, to be very sure. "Perhaps it is only our bairn that bids you hasten me to the altar?"

"I've not made myself clear, then." He kissed her brow, then each cheek. Slowly. Tenderly. "I love you, Leana. I want you for my wife."

She let the words sink into her heart. Words she had waited a lifetime to hear. "And I long for you to be my husband, but…" There was no avoiding what must be discussed. "We are both still in mourning."

"We are. And I loved Rose." His voice was heavy with regret. "I cannot pretend otherwise." He gripped her hands tighter still. "I will always mourn Rose, always miss her, as you will. I would never do anything to dishonor her memory. Yet I truly believe she would want us to marry."

"But she loved you so…"

"She loved you, too, Leana." A slight catch in his voice. "You were mother, sister, and friend to her. Rose would want you well loved and your children's needs well met."

Would her sister truly smile down on their union? *Oh, my Rose. How can I be certain?* To think that Jamie loved her! All that she'd dreamed of coming true. And yet…

Leana looked down at her black mourning gown, and another wave of doubt washed over her. "'Tis too soon, Jamie."

Despite her qualms, Jamie would not be dissuaded. "We will tell Father tonight at supper, the moment the first course is served. And then on the Sabbath, I shall speak with the kirk. We cannot wait, lass."

Saturday morning Leana knocked on the entrance to the Findlays' turret office, bearing an armful of newly stitched linens. If only tenderhearted Neda Hastings were on the other side of the housekeeper's door! Neda would help her decide what to do about marrying Jamie. And mourning Rose.

Instead, Ivy's pinched features greeted her. "More linens, mem?"

"Aye." Leana handed them over. Ivy kept a careful record of each item in her linen closet and did not allow things to be added to the shelves willy-nilly.

Her task accomplished, Leana was left standing in the entrance hall, feeling at loose ends. With Jamie on the hills for the day and Annabel entertaining Ian in the nursery and Eliza busy pressing another mourning dress for Leana's Sabbath at home, there was little to do this Saturday.

Except to make the most important decision of her life.

Did she honor Rose best by disappointing Jamie and putting off their wedding, even as she gave birth to Jamie's second child out of wedlock? Or would her love for Rose be better served by honoring Jamie's desire to protect their child by marrying him now, even though it meant enduring the scorn of their neighbors and her own doubts?

Jamie harbored no doubts whatsoever: They would marry in November.

Leana had never seen him so tenacious. When they'd told his father their wedding plans yestreen, Alec had been elated. Naturally she had joined in the celebration. How could she not? The thought of being Jamie's wife made her weak with joy. To be truly married, to speak their vows, to live as husband and wife, to grow their family together...*oh!*

But then she thought of Rose. And her joy began to fade. She felt disloyal. Selfish. Uncaring.

If she could somehow *ask* Rose, if she could have her sister's blessing, Leana would renounce her fears and gladly embrace her future with Jamie. But Rose could not be consulted. Peace could not be found there.

Jamie was most persuasive. "We both loved Rose," he'd reminded her that morning at breakfast, "and will honor her memory together."

Was it possible? Or would guilt hound her by day and shame haunt by night?

Needing to walk, to think, to *do* something, Leana found her wool cloak and draped it round her shoulders. The afternoon was chilly but dry. A stroll through the garden would not risk her child's well-being— her foremost concern the last few weeks, and Jamie's as well.

She lifted the hood of the cloak over her hair, tucking in the stray wisps, then started to circle the various garden plots on the grassy paths that separated them. Since Robert was not working today, she had the garden to herself. Except for a few blooms here and there that needed pruning, the ornamental gardens had fallen dormant. There were vegetables still to be harvested—parsnips and colewort, cabbages and leeks. How odd to have a servant whose primary duty that was.

Her own hands had already grown soft. If she was not careful, she'd be spoiled in a year and of no use to anyone. When she'd said as much to Jamie that morning, he'd replied with a grin, "I like your soft hands," and kissed them to prove it. Oh, he could be very convincing, the laird of Glentrool.

Yet even more than pleasing Jamie, even more than honoring her sister, Leana wanted to bless the One she loved most. *I delight to do thy will, O my God.*

She perched on one of the stone benches along the garden walks and gazed at the rowan tree with its scarlet leaves, the last of the berries plucked by fieldfares and blackbirds. Planted at Rowena's request, her namesake tree was the centerpiece of the garden. The rowan would bloom afresh next May, then carpet the garden with white petals after a June plumpshower. Through the summer the berries would ripen to a rich yellow red, a vivid contrast to the green leaves. Legend said the Highland tartans were inspired by the bright berries and leaves of the rowan. And then next October, the tree would look as it did now, beautiful through all four seasons.

In the sacred rowan Leana found her answer: Just as Rowena would always be remembered at Glentrool, Rose would reside in their hearts forever, whether Leana married Jamie now or a year from now. Leana smiled up at the rowan tree's graceful branches. For their child's sake— for her own sake—she would marry him as soon as the kirk allowed.

"I thought I might find you here." Jamie strode into the garden and joined her on the bench, his smile matching hers. "How happy you look, my love. Perhaps you've come to some decision about marrying me in November?" He wrapped one arm round her and pulled her close. "I warn you, I'll not take nae for an answer."

She nestled her head in the warm curve of his neck. "My heart and hand are yours, Jamie."

"Bless you, Leana." She felt him swallow, and his arm round her tightened. "And all that is mine is yours. My love, most of all."

She sank into his embrace, breathing in the warm scent of him. Might he truly be hers before St. Andrew's Day, the last of the month? The kirk might not decide as easily as she had. Nor as favorably. "What of Reverend Moodie?"

Jamie planted a kiss among her circle of braids. "If he agrees to my request to marry at once, we can be certain of the Almighty's blessing."

Leana lifted her head to seek his gaze. "And if he doesn't agree? If the minister will not allow it?"

Jamie's expression was resolute. "By this time tomorrow, lass, I'll be home. And we'll have our answer."

Eighty-Seven

But till my last moments my words are the same—
"There'll never be peace till Jamie comes hame!"
ROBERT BURNS

Leana straightened Jamie's cravat with trembling hands. The house was already empty, despite the early hour, and the entrance hall dimly lit. "You have my testimonial letter, aye?" She'd not had a chance to show it to Reverend Moodie on her first and only Sabbath at Monnigaff kirk. Reverend Gordon's words might prove useful now.

Jamie patted his waistcoat pocket. "'Tis right here, lass. I need nothing else but your prayers."

She smoothed her fingers across his close-shaven cheek. "You shall have my prayers from the moment you ride off until you are home again."

His gaze was troubled. "I do not ken what news I will bring home to you. Reverend Moodie may agree to marry us yet insist we wait six months or even a year, to allow for a proper time of mourning."

"I can wait, Jamie."

"I cannot. And neither can our bairn."

She broached the unthinkable. "He may refuse to marry us at all."

"Indeed he may." Jamie's mouth drew a firm line. "But I will not allow that to be the end of things, Leana. I have failed you too many times before." He spread his gloved hand across their bairn as a pledge. "I *will* have you for my wife, Leana. Soon."

She touched her hand to his heart, making her own vow. "And I will have you for my husband." *However long I must wait. Whatever heartache I must endure.* "Come home to me, Jamie."

"You ken I will." A tender kiss to her cheek, and he turned for the door.

From the lawn came the voices of the others gathering to leave. The servants on foot had already departed for House o' the Hill Inn, where a McKie wagon was kept for the weekly journey to kirk. There was talk of building a chapel of ease in the neighborhood, a smaller church for the folk in the northern half of the parish, but the presbytery frowned on the notion, saying it smacked of laziness.

Thomas and Ivy, Jamie and his father would ride on horseback together as far as the inn, then Mr. McKie would be transported in the family carriage from the inn to the village. In light of Rowena's fatal accident, even a few miles astride an old mare made Jamie nervous for his father. But Alec McKie would not hear of staying home from services in decent weather. And there was no way out of the glen except on foot or hoof.

Leana followed Jamie onto the lawn, rubbing her arms to keep warm. 'Twas the last day of October—Hallowmas Eve—yet the skies did not portend anything frichtsome. The air was crisp, the horizon clear. A drying day, Thomas called it. The sun had barely risen, and the high half-moon was pale white, almost transparent against the blue sky. Autumn's colors had faded on the hills. Along Loch Trool, the bright green bracken had turned to yellows and browns, and a mist rising from the water softened the dark outlines of the pines.

Jamie was mounted on Hastings now, though his eyes were on her. "I hate to leave you, lass."

"Ian and I will have our own time of worship." She smoothed a hand over the gelding's black mane. "And I will pray without ceasing. 'Tis an unchancie day on the calendar."

"Not for us, Leana." He reached down to touch her cheek, then straightened and was off with the others, his hand raised in farewell.

Hurry home, my love.

From the corner of her eye, Leana spied a tawny owl dropping silently onto its prey. A mouse, perhaps; breakfast, before the nocturnal bird flew out of sight for the day. She'd heard the owl hooting in the night, defending its territory, and thought of the old Galloway rhyme that would be spoken in eldritch circles this very night.

When the gray owlet has three times hooed,
When the grimy cat has three times mewed,
When the tod has yowled three times in the wud…

Leana had yet to notice many foxes in the wood, though she'd heard their mournful cries. Her own lad would be yowling soon, she reminded herself, hurrying back withindoors to wake Ian for his breakfast.

Aubert had left a pot of fresh porridge warming on the stove and mutton pies for their dinner. Leana did not mind a quiet day at Glentrool with Ian all to herself. She fed, bathed, and dressed the lad, then sat with him on the nursery floor, telling him stories from the Buik, praying with him nestled in her lap, reciting a psalm she would teach him someday. Only six verses to learn and well suited for a son who had James McKie for a father. *The LORD is my shepherd, I shall not want.*

As the day unfolded, Leana's thoughts kept turning to Monnigaff, counting each hour, guessing what Jamie might be doing, pleading for mercy. He would not arrive home until late in the afternoon—before dark, she prayed, for 'twas an eerie eve, Hallowmas. Though she had no fear of ghosts and witches, there would be tricksters abroad using the night as an excuse to cause trouble for their neighbors.

Leana and Ian ate their mutton pies and took an afternoon nap. Still the Sabbath travelers had not returned home. She thought of Neda's saying—"Fear has lang legs"—even as she sensed her own fear running down the road to Monnigaff. Would Jamie's plea find a sympathetic ear, or would Reverend Moodie chastise him for even considering marriage to a woman with a dubious past? And so close on the heels of his wife's death? *Rose, our dear Rose.*

By the time the household returned, the sun was lost behind a layer of thick clouds, and the air smelled like rain. At the sound of their hoofbeats, Leana hurried outside in time to watch Thomas ride up first, a grim expression on his face. Then Ivy, riding sidesaddle, with Alec McKie not far behind her on the mare, both of them looking spent.

Jamie was nowhere to be seen.

"Mem." Thomas dismounted, then bowed politely. "I've a letter for ye from Mr. McKie. Said tae gie it tae ye straight off."

Dread, like a nimble-legged spider, crawled up her spine. *Jamie, whatever has happened?*

Thomas pressed the letter in her hand. "I'm sorry, mem. He bade ye read it as suin as ye could. He was…most vexed whan he wrote it."

Leana stared at the folded paper. Sealed in haste, by the look of it, with a thumbprint in the wax. She broke the seal and unfolded the letter, recognizing Jamie's bold hand at once. Did the minister say aye or nae? Marry now or marry never?

Though Jamie had written very few words, they struck more fear in her heart than any Hallowmas Eve cantrip.

> My dearest Leana,
>
> All did not go well. I must present our case to the kirk session. Since they meet in the morn, I remain in the village. Please God, I will prevail. Then I shall ride home like the wind.
>
> Yours always,
> Jamie

Eighty-Eight

Madame, bear in mind
That princes govern all things—save the wind.
VICTOR HUGO

He had no choice but to spend the night at the Cree Inn, the only public lodging in the village. The innkeeper, meaning to be helpful, had given Jamie a room on the first floor. Not on the second, where he'd stayed in August.

But it made no difference. The rustic walls and bare floors of the cramped rooms were all the same. Painful memories of Rose assailed him from every corner. One look at the steep stair, and he felt Rose's coffin on his shoulder. The empty bowl on the washstand seemed to permeate his room with the astringent smell of lady's mantle. From down the narrow hall came Leana's whispered words over and over. *She is gone, Jamie.*

Jamie tried to sleep but could not. He prayed but found no peace. Tears did not lessen his agony. When morning dawned on Hallowmas, he settled his bill and quit the place at once. He cherished his memories of Rose...but not these. Not the final hours when he could not save her.

At half past eight he emerged from the inn and found the entire village painted in November gray. A light rain hung in the air, so fine it did not fall so much as rise, like mist. *Smirr,* Duncan called it. Overnight the temperature had dropped, leaving a numbing chill that seeped into his bones. The few villagers out of doors tipped their bonnets to Jamie as they hastened past. Being the laird of Glentrool brought him a modicum of respect. The family's vast property would carry little weight with the kirk session, however. On moral and spiritual matters, all were equally guilty in the sight of the kirk.

Hidden inside his waistcoat pocket was a hefty purse of silver. If fined for his transgressions, Jamie was prepared to add to the parish's funds for the poor. He carried a greater sacrifice in his heart: a desire to speak the truth, whatever it might cost him. In the dark hours of the night he'd written his thoughts on paper, now tucked in his pocket. Though he could not know what questions the kirk session would pose, Jamie knew what he'd come to tell them.

Headed for the manse, he passed the oak where he'd buried the gold cord from Lachlan's thrifte and the marketplace where he'd knelt in the dust and surrendered his sword to Evan. A village brimming with recollections, Monnigaff. All of them overshadowed by the one that drew him to the kirkyard along a familiar path: beyond the yew tree, not far from the red sandstone monument raised by the Chesneys, in sight of the Penkill Burn.

He knelt in the damp sod and ran his gloved hand over the carved roses, recalling Leana's fingers tracing the mason's sketch. His throat tightened anew. "We both miss you, beloved." Brushing a few stray leaves from the headstone, he read the words again. *Wife of James Lachlan McKie.* Though he could not see it, a silver wedding band circled her gloved finger and would for all eternity. *My wife.*

He gripped the granite headstone. "Rose…dear Rose, I will always love you. Nothing will ever change that." It felt good to confess the truth aloud, if only to the yew and the graves and the burn. "You ken I loved your sister once as well, and our love has been rekindled. I have asked Leana to be my wife. I pray that would please you, Rose. She loves you so."

Jamie waited in the stillness. Not for a sign nor a voice from above but simply for peace to enter his heart. *And now, Lord, what wait I for? My hope is in thee.*

"Mr. McKie?" Reverend Moodie stood not far from him, wearing a broad-brimmed hat and a somber expression. "The men are gathering round the table. If you are ready…"

"I am." Jamie rose and shook the debris from his greatcoat, then followed the minister the short distance to the manse, his resolve growing with each step. *I will go in the strength of the Lord GOD.* His own strength would not serve him here. Neither his wealth nor his sword arm would suffice. Only the truth.

Mistress Moodie relieved Jamie of his damp coat, then seated him in the parlor with a cup of tea, compassion in her brown eyes. "My husband will call you in shortly."

Jamie drank his tea without tasting it, his mind fixed on the task before him. He cared nothing about what the parish leaders thought of him, but he cared very much what they thought of the woman he loved. And intended to marry. Soon.

Reverend Moodie stepped outside the dining room and summoned Jamie with a nod. Though slight in stature, the young minister did not shrink from Jamie's superior height as he passed him entering the room. Clearly, Stephen Moodie was certain of his calling, a workman worthy of his meat.

Coal burned brightly on the grate, warming the low-ceilinged room so thoroughly that the windows were covered with steam. Chairs lined the periphery, many more than would fit around the oblong table. Jamie took the seat offered him, nodding at each of the men present. He knew them, knew their families. Samuel McTaggart was as old as Alec McKie, though spryer. His piercing gaze bore no hint of cloudiness as he assessed Jamie. Richard Galbraith, the session clerk and *dominie* of the parish school, had stick-straight hair as black as the coal in the minister's grate. Jamie thought the young man's bony features might be due to a sparse diet; schoolmasters were paid a pittance. Richard's intelligent eyes regarded Jamie closely, his pen poised over the session record book. The third elder was Duncan's age. A quiet, thoughtful man, ever smoothing his full beard and adjusting his spectacles, David McFadgen would say little, yet miss nothing.

They were all seated now, with Jamie on one side of the table, the four men on the other—more like a trial than a meeting. Let it be a trial of his faith, then. A test of his loyalty to the Almighty and to the woman he loved. Jamie withdrew his notes from his pocket and laid the paper in front of him, folding his hands over the words, as if the ink itself might bolster his courage.

Reverend Moodie had papers of his own in hand. Letters, judging by the remnants of wax seals along the edges. "Mr. McKie, we are ready to begin." The minister's smile caught Jamie off guard. Seldom was any levity involved when the kirk session met. "You represent our first order of business for this month's session meeting, which should be duly noted in the records."

Across the table, Richard Galbraith's pen scratched across the unlined page.

The minister continued. "Yestermorn you requested that the kirk witness your marriage vows, to be spoken by you and Leana McBride, formerly of Newabbey parish. And the date you intended for this wedding was…?"

Jamie cleared his throat, wishing he still had his tea. "The earliest possible date, sir."

"And what is the reason for your haste?"

He did not flinch. "Leana is expecting our second child in early December."

Samuel McTaggart's eyes bored into him. "Obviously this child was conceived outside the bonds of wedlock."

"Nae, sir. We were married at the time by habit and repute. And, by your mercy, we will be married again before the child is delivered."

Richard Galbraith did not bother to hide his consternation. "Then *who* is the young woman buried in our kirkyard with your name on her headstone?"

Speak every man truth with his neighbour. Jamie said in an even voice, "She was my wife as well."

"You had *two wives at once*?" Samuel McTaggart banged the table with his fist. "Mr. McKie, you are no gentleman but a bigamist!"

"I did not have two wives at once, Mr. McTaggart. For more than a year I believed I was married to Leana McBride. But the kirk session records stated I was married to her younger sister, Rose, and they held me to that vow."

McTaggart persisted, "But which woman did you *choose* for your wife?"

Jamie knew his answer would not please them, but it would be truthful. "I chose them both. Rose first. And now Leana."

"Are you suggesting you are without fault in this sordid situation?"

Jamie heard the incredulity in Richard Galbraith's voice and did not blame him. A stranger tale of matrimony did not exist in all Christendom.

He unfolded his hands and pulled his paper into view. The elders had given him the perfect opening; it was time to walk through it.

"Gentlemen, I am completely at fault. I have in various ways failed both the women I have loved. As to the exact details of my marriages, I would refer you to the Newabbey parish records. I am certain Reverend John Gordon would be willing to provide a copy."

The minister patted his stack of papers. "He already has. I've shared the contents with the elders. Continue, Mr. McKie."

They knew the whole of it, then.

Jamie looked down at his paper. Two lists made in the dark of the night. He began with the harder of the two.

"I have before me a brief list of my transgressions. Were I to tally them all, there would not be paper enough to hold them." Though his heart was pounding, his voice remained calm. "I deceived my father. And I robbed my brother of his inheritance." No one seemed surprised or asked for details. All of Monnigaff had heard the story. "To their eternal credit, both men have forgiven me."

McTaggart flapped his hand. "Go on, Mr. McKie."

The list did not get easier. "I shirked my responsibilities as husband to Leana by continuing to behave like a suitor with her younger sister, Rose, even though Leana was carrying my heir." They had not heard that. Shame heated his neck and crawled up his face. "When Leana was sentenced to three Sabbaths on the cutty stool for hochmagandy, I supported her, but I did not do what I should have done."

"And what was that, Mr. McKie?"

"I should have taken her place."

The room fell silent.

Looking down at his scribbling, Jamie could only see how many sins he'd omitted from his list.

"The Newabbey parish records confirm all that Mr. McKie has confessed." Reverend Moodie consulted his notes, then pushed the stack of papers aside. "I also have two letters. One from Reverend John Gordon dated the twenty-third of August, and one from Reverend Dr. John Scott of Twyneholm, dated the first of July. The second letter was actually written to John Gordon, but he forwarded it to me upon my recent inquiry concerning Miss McBride." He looked up. "When a woman arrives in my parish with child but without a husband, I have a right to ask questions. Both these letters address the moral standing of Leana McBride."

"No woman stands higher." Jamie looked the four of them in the eye. "The Buik says, 'a gracious woman retaineth honour.' These, then, are the graces of Leana McBride." He stood without thinking, the scrape of his chair echoing in the quiet room.

Jamie gripped the second list in his hand.

"She loves unconditionally." His throat began to squeeze shut. *You loved me, Leana, even when I did not love you.*

"She extends mercy." *You do, beloved. Always.* The list started to swim.

"She binds the wounds of the hurting. She comforts the afflicted." *You cared for our Rose. And for me.*

"She is the finest of mothers and the kindest of wives." *And far more than I deserve.* He folded his list with care, then placed it inside his waistcoat.

Jamie met each man's startled gaze without apology. "Kindly permit me to marry this gracie woman without delay. For I am confident that the letters you hold attest to all I have said."

Reverend Moodie smiled. More broadly this time. "You are correct, sir. Both these men, who are highly esteemed ministers of the gospel, state emphatically that Leana McBride is a woman after God's own heart. Imperfect, as we all are. Forgiven, as we all must be. We are fortunate to have her in our parish."

As abruptly as he'd stood, Jamie resumed his seat, taking his first full breath in several minutes. "Are you saying that…we may marry? Without impediment?"

David McFadgen finally spoke, addressing the other elders. "What of his hurry to wed while he is still in mourning for his first…ah, his other…wife? Should we allow it, gentlemen?"

Reverend Moodie pursed his lips for a moment. "Mr. McKie's fond regard and respect for his late wife is obvious. So are his responsibilities to Leana McBride and the impending birth of their child. 'Tis a hasty wedding, aye, and there are social implications. But nothing that falls under the authority of the kirk." The minister almost smiled. "You will be gossiped about, Mr. McKie, but I suspect you've grown accustomed to that."

Jamie restated his question, still in disbelief. "Then Leana and I will be permitted to marry at once?"

The minister nodded toward the session clerk. "Provided you have the *cryin siller* for Mr. Galbraith, required for the reading of your banns..."

Jamie was already pulling his purse from beneath his waistcoat. *Beloved, they have agreed. They have agreed!*

Richard Galbraith laid down his pen in the seam of his record book to receive Jamie's silver. "If it suits you, I will read the banns on the first three Sundays in November with the expectation that you will marry shortly thereafter." He slipped the coins in a small collection box and noted the payment in his records, watched carefully by Jamie. There would be no clerical errors made concerning *this* wedding. "You'll pardon me for saying so, Mr. McKie, but why would so virtuous a woman want you for a husband?"

Jamie laughed, blinking away the last vestige of tears. "That, sir, is a question you will have to ask her." He put away his purse. It was lighter now, his heart more so. "I do have a question for you, Reverend. If you had these letters in your possession and knew all the facts before I arrived—"

"Then why did I invite you here? I had two outcomes in mind, Mr. McKie. As a leading figure in our parish, you deserved an honest hearing. Rumors cannot put down roots where truth has first been planted." The elders grunted in agreement. "And to be quite frank"—the minister's brown eyes twinkled—"I wanted to see what kind of man you are. A test of your mettle, if you will."

Jamie, half standing, hesitated. "And?"

"You passed, sir. With rather high marks for honesty. And humility." Reverend Moodie walked round the table and offered Jamie his hand. His attentive wife stood at the door, Jamie's greatcoat in her arms. "I am certain Miss McBride is waiting to hear of our decision. Are you homeward bound?"

"Aye, sir." Jamie smiled as he reached for his coat. "Like the wind."

Eighty-Nine

Blaw yer pipes and beat yer drum,
The best o' life is yet to come.
SCOTTISH PROVERB

A capricious wind blew across the loch as Leana paced up and down the pier, her cloak wrapped snugly round her shoulders and neck, the hem brushing the damp stones at her feet. Her steps were slow and cadenced, like a woman walking a baby. Or like a bride dancing. *Please, may it be so!* If the kirk session allowed it. If the Almighty answered her prayers. *On thee do I wait all the day.*

'Twas noon. The smirr had dissipated, leaving the air chilly, breezy, and moist. Jamie would be vexed with her for waiting out of doors. But the pier was the best vantage point for watching his approach. If she waited in the drawing room, she would not know until he walked through the door what their future might hold. This way, she would know by his very riding posture what the kirk had decided and have a moment to digest the news before they stood face to face. *Hurry, my love.*

As if in answer, the distant thunder of Hastings's hooves echoed against the hills, carrying across the loch. Her heart pounded in a matching rhythm as she turned due west. Jamie was at a full gallop. Did that bode well? Or was he riding hard out of anger and frustration? Because the session had refused. Because the two of them could not marry.

She gripped the wool fabric of her cloak with her gloved hands. *Please, Lord. My child needs a father. And I need Jamie.*

He was almost in sight. The gelding's black flanks and Jamie's voluminous blue greatcoat darted among the trees, teasing her eye. She started toward the house, hurrying along the walk as quickly as her heavy cloak and heavier womb would allow.

She could see Jamie now. His head was held high. His hat was in his hand, waving. His voice carried over the wind. "Leana! Leana!"

Grasping her skirts, she began running toward him, calling his name, tears choking her voice. *Oh, my dear husband!*

Jamie dismounted before Hastings had come to a full stop and covered the distance between them. Before she could catch her breath, he stole it from her and swept her into his arms. "Leana! My love, my bride."

She clung to his neck. "Can it be true? Has the kirk session agreed?"

His words were muffled against her cloak, but she heard every one. "You are mine, Leana, and I am yours. Always."

My Jamie. Truly mine. She stanched her tears against his shoulder and waited for the earth to stop spinning. Or was that him, swinging her round in a circle?

"Jamie, please!" she managed to say, laughing. "Kindly put me down, dear man, or the child will come too soon."

He lowered her at once, stepping back with a look of concern. "Och, lass! How could I be so careless?"

Leana pressed her hand to her heart, which was beating a merry pace. "No need to apologize." She looked into his eyes, wanting to assure him. "I have never felt more cared for in all of my days."

"Ah." His worried expression vanished, and something else took its place. A certain light in his eyes, a sly curve to his generous mouth. A look she remembered well and had feared she might never see again. " 'Tis my job to care for you, lass." Jamie pulled her closer. His voice was both tender and rough. " 'Tis my privilege to provide for you, to see to your comfort. To love you as your husband."

His gaze landed on her mouth. Since proposing, Jamie had kissed her hand, her cheek, her brow. But he had not kissed her lips, not since that evening long ago in the bothy at Auchengray when they were still husband and wife.

He slowly leaned down, then paused, as if awaiting her permission.

Leana closed her eyes and lifted her mouth, granting it.

Their lips touched. Warmth seeped through her, as if she were standing before a stack of glowing peat. His mouth fitted perfectly to hers. Familiar and forgotten sensations sang through her limbs.

Yet it was the kiss of a gentleman, not a lover. Of a betrothed, not a bridegroom. She understood and was not disappointed. On the contrary, she was thrilled. To be desired and yet honored was the greatest gift of all.

When their lips parted, he smiled down at her. "Passion must wait, lass, until we are wed."

She glanced down at their bairn. "A bit longer than that, I'm afraid."

His deep laugh made her shiver beneath her warm cloak. "I can be a patient man, Leana, when 'tis required. Though consider this fair warning: Once we are wed, I will kiss you however I please."

"Aye." She hid her smile in the double collar of his greatcoat. *Please.*

Leana was waiting when Jamie returned from kirk the next Sabbath afternoon, still harboring a vague fear someone might have protested their union when the banns were read.

"The parishioners raised their collective eyebrows," Jamie reported moments after walking through Glentrool's door, "but none raised their hands. Two more Sundays, and all will be settled. Come the twenty-third of November, you will be my wife."

"Then let me practice my wifely duties." Leana led him from the entrance hall into the library, where she had a blazing fire in the hearth and a pot of hot chocolate on his desk, whisked from the kitchen the moment she heard his voice on the lawn. The day was raw with a biting wind from the north. Leana warmed his icy cheeks with her palms, taking the cold into her hands even as she delighted in the rough feel of his beard against her skin.

He smiled down at her, still wearing his greatcoat. "Two weeks and two days, my love." Jamie had chosen a Tuesday so their wedding guests would not be required to journey on the Sabbath, no doubt thinking of Evan and Judith coming from Sorbie. Since Leana could not travel to the kirk, Reverend Moodie would come to Glentrool to perform the marriage service and bring the bride stool with him.

Leana reversed her hands so the warmer backs now pressed against his face. "I have started your waddin sark." A bride's tasks included sewing her betrothed a shirt for their wedding day. She'd fashioned

Jamie's shirt from a bolt of fine cambric unearthed from his mother's sewing kist. "I've also cut out my blue gown," she told him. "Though once the child is born, I'll need to restyle it."

"Blue, is it?" Jamie's smile broadened.

They both knew the auld rhyme. *If blue, 'tis love true.* "You may recognize the fabric when you see it. Rose bought it for me in Gatehouse of Fleet." Leana paused, letting a ripple of sorrow wash over her. She could speak of Rose more easily now but never without missing her. "Later my sister confessed she'd used some of our father's silver to buy my fabric."

" 'Tis only fitting." Jamie lifted her hands from his face and kissed each one in turn. "The bride's father is responsible for providing his daughter's wedding gown. Good for Rose."

Leana did not intend to use a tailor but would sew her gown herself with loving stitches and fond memories of the day she and Rose had shopped in the village. Though blue was an especially fine color for a wedding gown, Leana had chosen it primarily to include her sister in some way. Were theirs a June wedding, she would have filled the house with roses in her sister's memory. But there were no blooms to be found in November gardens. Only holly and fir branches to brighten the rooms and add a sylvan scent.

Leana helped Jamie off with his coat and seated him at his desk. "Enjoy your chocolate while it's hot. Our cold Sabbath meal awaits us on the sideboard in the dining room whene'er you choose."

Instead, he slipped his arm round her waist and drew her beside him, resting his hand tentatively on their child, whose actions at the moment were so marked that even Jamie couldn't miss seeing them. Once such attentions would have embarrassed her beyond bearing. But this was Jamie, the husband who'd rushed into Ian's birthing room moments after their son was born and knew all there was to know about her body. If feeling his child kick against his hand gave Jamie peace of mind, even pleasure, she would not deny him.

Looking down at the wonder on his face brought a lump to her throat. Jamie was anxious to see this child safely delivered. "I am afraid one of the wedding customs will have to be put aside," she said, lightly stroking his hair. "I cannot flit for seven days before the wedding." *Like Rose did to Aunt Meg's.*

His brow darkened. "I do not intend to let you out of my sight. Your confinement has begun, lass."

"I pray I'll still be permitted to write letters," she teased him. "I've already sent posts to Neda at Kingsgrange and Aunt Meg at Burnside."

"Have you indeed?" Jamie pressed one hand into the small of her back, rubbing circles in the very spot she needed it most. "I have written a few letters myself. Including one to my Uncle Lachlan."

Her bairn kicked especially hard, as if equally surprised at the news. On Jeanie Wilson's last visit, the midwife had told Leana the child would arrive before St. Andrew's Day. *'Twill not be a December bairn, mem. I can tell ye that.* Leana felt the child turning yet again.

Unaware of her distractions, Jamie continued, "When we parted ways at Gatehouse, I made a pledge to your father: 'I will have no wife but your daughter.'"

"Oh…" Leana understood. *He meant Rose.*

"Yet I did not mention his daughter by name. The Almighty stilled my tongue." He stood and guided her toward their supper. "He kenned what the future held, Leana, even when we could not."

Before he opened the door into the hall, Jamie touched his lips to hers once more. A longer kiss, brimming with promise. "The best is yet to come, my bonny bride."

Ninety

And to his eye
There was but one beloved face on earth,
And that was shining on him.
GEORGE GORDON, LORD BYRON

Jamie was stationed on the lawn to welcome his arriving guests yet could not resist glancing up at the sitting room window. Leana was just down the hall, he knew, being dressed by Eliza. He had not spoken with her all morning. A wedding custom, strictly enforced. Ivy had stood guard at the bottom of the stair, cautioning him, "Ye canna see the bride, Mr. McKie. 'Tis not done."

There was some benefit to be found: If he could not go up the stair, Leana could not come down. When the gardener from Bargaly House arrived earlier with the roses Jamie had purchased, the flowers were arranged throughout the first floor rooms without Leana appearing and spoiling his surprise.

The expense was considerable; the look on her face would be worth every shilling.

Vases of roses in every hue—pale pink, creamy white, dusty rose, amber yellow, purplish red—filled the house with color, defying the gray November skies. Leana had mentioned in passing how she wished they might have roses for the wedding. Now they did—every stem in Bargaly's hothouse. Dozens upon dozens, with every thorn removed at his request.

"Leuk, Ian!" Annabel strolled up, his son in her capable hands. " 'Tis yer faither, all dressed for the waddin."

Jamie straightened the lad's wrinkled coat, another of Leana's creations, and smoothed back the boy's wayward hair. "I should have sent my valet to *your* room, young man." He smiled at Annabel, lest she take offense. She'd done her best; Ian was simply his father's son, easily rumpled. "Do not stray far, lass. Leana will want her son where she can see him."

"Oo aye, she said the verra same thing." Annabel stepped aside as another contingent of guests rode up, attended by two lads from the stables. Every pair of hands at Glentrool was hard at work this day.

At least the weather was cooperative. The sky was the color of a newly minted shilling, a single wash of silver high above them. Cold but dry, the air bore no threat of rain or snow, a boon for those coming some distance.

"Brother!"

Jamie looked up to find Evan dismounting, his face ruddier than ever from the long ride north. The two men clasped hands, then embraced, slapping each other's backs. Jamie still marveled at their reconciliation. *How pleasant it is for brethren to dwell together in unity.*

"Sorry to have left Judith at home, but she's not in a traveling way just now." Evan's grin was anything but subtle. "I'll be a father again come May. And *you* will have your second child…ah…"

"Any second," Jamie finished for him. Only yestreen Leana had cautioned him that the babe could come sooner than they'd expected. Not December, but late November. He did not voice his deepest fears or let her see them in his eyes. *Keep her safe, Lord.*

Jamie drew his thoughts back to the present and the blithe occasion at hand. "I'm glad you've come, Evan." He gestured toward the front door. "You'll find a seat waiting for you in the drawing room." The brothers parted with a pledge to speak at length before day's end.

Jamie scanned the road, watching for two invited guests in particular. They should have reached Monnigaff yestreen by way of mail coach on the route from Carlisle to Portpatrick. He'd sent sufficient silver for their passage, as well as a letter to their employer, requesting they be released from their duties for a week and enclosing enough silver to ease their employer's loss of their services. Now he could only wait and watch for them.

It was noon when Reverend Moodie appeared, his horse pulling a small cart with the bride stool. He pretended to scowl, with little success. "You'll be charged for this, you ken."

Jamie laughed as he reached in his purse for the necessary coins.

"To be honest, I'm ashamed to take it," the reverend admitted, even as he pocketed the silver. "We received a most generous offering in our collection box a few months ago." Reverend Moodie eyed him with amusement. "Indeed, that sack of gold showed up the very Sunday you arrived in Monnigaff, Mr. McKie."

"What a strange coincidence," Jamie murmured, directing two servants to unload the small pew used only for weddings. "You will find all in readiness for you, sir. Kindly follow the bride stool into the drawing room."

The flow of guests increased as one o' the clock drew nigh. Apparently no one in the parish intended to miss such a scandalous event, however much they might disapprove.

Finally Jamie saw them. His long-awaited guests walking toward him on the hard-packed dirt road. A lanky man and a copper-headed woman. Dressed in their best Sabbath clothes. Grinning like brownies.

"Duncan!" he called out, not caring how undignified he looked hastening across the lawn to greet a pair of servants. "Neda, welcome!" He embraced each one in turn, his throat squeezed tight as a fist.

Duncan's eyes were bright with tears as he handed his handkerchief to Neda, who dabbed at her cheeks. "Ye were kind tae send the silver, Mr. McKie. The laird was most impressed."

"It was good of the man to let you come. I ken you'll be missed at Kingsgrange." Jamie threw his arms round their shoulders and led them toward the loch. "As we've not much time, my plan is thus: Wait on the pier and watch for Leana to join me at the door. Then you shall stroll up and surprise her, aye?"

When they were settled on a stone bench, Neda's blithe expression grew more sober. "Mr. McKie, 'tis not the day for sad thochts, but I canna neglect me duties. Our hearts were *sair* at the news of Rose's passing. She was a dear lass, and we ken ye baith luved her verra much."

"Aye." Jamie's gaze met hers, grateful for her sympathy. "We will always love our Rose."

"It maun be said, what ye're doin' is richt." Duncan gripped his arm. "Dinna let some foolish soul tell ye itherwise. Leana is the wife God meant ye tae have."

Jamie laughed in spite of the tightness in his chest. "You and my father share the same opinion." He consulted his watch, then glanced over his shoulder. "When you see her, come along without delay."

Jamie left them with some reluctance, though they would have plenty of time later for visiting. All was in readiness now; he needed only a bride.

No sooner had he reached the door than the bridal party strolled round the corner of the house, their laughter preceding them. Holding up Leana's hem, the maids cleared her path of late-arriving guests and delivered her to Jamie's side.

"Leana, my love." He held out his hands to receive his bride.

Her hair was unbound, a halo of gold round her shining face, draped in a lacy *kell*. Her gown was the color of bluebells in May. *A fine choice, Rose.* And her eyes were filled with a love he would spend the rest of his life trying to deserve.

Leana smiled up at him as she took his offered hand. "Jamie, how fine you look."

"I am glad my attire pleases you, lass." He'd not given his costume a moment's consideration, though his valet had fussed over him for an hour. "The shirt you've made for me is the finest in my clothes press. However, not one pair of eyes will notice it once they see the woman on my arm." He leaned closer, inhaling her scent. "You are the most beautiful lass in all of Scotland. And I, its luckiest man."

She blushed like the bride she was, the very shade of the roses in the entrance hall.

At his request, the maids had taken her out the back door so she would not see the roses until they entered the house. Soon, but not yet. The Hastingses were his first surprise.

He spied them coming from behind her and grinned. "Leana, I've taken the liberty of spending some of the estate's good silver on bringing two guests I thought you might welcome to Glentrool."

Just before Leana turned round, Jamie watched the truth dawn in her eyes like the sun breaking over the horizon.

"*Neda!*"

Ninety-One

And when my lips meet thine
Thy very soul is wedded unto mine.

HJALMAR HJORTH BOYESEN

Leana threw herself into Neda's embrace without a thought for her carefully pressed wedding gown or her neatly pinned kell. "I cannot believe you are *here!*"

"Ye have yer guid husband tae thank." Neda hugged her for a moment, then held her at arm's length. "Come, let us see yer loosome goun."

Leana brushed away her tears, knowing it was not her gown Neda wanted to see but her bairn. "Isn't she a beauty?"

"A fair sight for sair eyes. Not lang in comin', I'd say." Neda smoothed her hands over Leana's imported lace kell, a gift from Jamie, and shook out the wrinkles in Leana's full sleeves. "Ye did leave somethin' unstitched 'til ye were dressed, did ye not?"

Leana smiled at the reminder. It was unlucky for a bride's gown to be completely finished until the day she wore it. "Fear not. I stitched on a button this morning."

"I'm afraid thar's nae hope for *ye,* lad," Duncan told Jamie. "For 'tis unchancie for a man tae marry a woman wi' a bairn." When Jamie started to protest, Duncan added, "Except whan the bairn is his, o' course."

The four of them laughed, though Leana could not imagine any heart lighter than her own. To have Jamie as her bridegroom and his child due in mere days and Neda on hand for her wedding! "Have you seen Ian?" Leana waved over Annabel, who was standing nearby as promised. "Hasn't he grown, though?"

Neda and Duncan made a proper fuss over the lad until a stern voice demanded their attention.

"Mr. McKie." Reverend Moodie stood at the door, his arms folded across his chest. "Were you planning on marrying today or not?"

"Most assuredly." Jamie sent Duncan, Neda, and Annabel in ahead of them and called the piper to his task. Since there would be no procession from house to kirk, the piper would stroll round the mains three times like a clock while Leana and Jamie made their entrance. The young piper tucked his tartan bag under his arm, filling the bag with air. After much grunting and squeaking, the chanter finally settled on a happy note, and the lad walked off in rhythm with his music, the sound carrying across the loch and echoing off Mulldonach.

"I like the tune you chose, Leana."

She sang the first line. " 'I luved ne'er a laddie but one.' You know it's true, Jamie McKie. You are the only man I have ever loved."

He looked at her for a long time. "And you, Leana McBride, are the only woman I will love for as long as God grants me life. Come, lass. Be my bride."

When the door opened, Leana saw their neighbors gathered in the entrance hall, lining the walls to make room for the blithe couple. But that was not all she saw.

Roses. Everywhere.

"Jamie…" She hung on to his arm, overwhelmed at the sight. "I *did* smell roses! I thought it was some sweet memory of my sister. How did you… Where did they… Oh, Jamie, 'tis more than…"

"Nae, 'tis not enough. Could never be enough." He kissed her brow through the thin veil of her kell. "Before this day is done, you will choose your favorite rose and scatter the petals across our marriage bed."

He remembers. She took a long, shaky breath, though her bairn gave her little room for air. Alas, they would not have a wedding night like most couples. Yet to hold Jamie in her arms and shower him with kisses…aye, there would be pleasure in that.

Jamie, dressed in his new coat and waistcoat, led her through the door. She'd chosen his dark blue fabric to complement her dress, and the tailor had done a fine job, but Jamie was right: Every eye was on her.

Yet they did not look down at her bairn, as she'd feared, nor at her new gown; they looked into her eyes. Many smiled. Some shed tears.

Leana both smiled and wept.

She, who had sat on the stool of repentance, would sit on the bride stool. Her sins, which were many, had been forgiven. And God, in his infinite mercy, had given her the desires of her heart. *Every day will I bless thee. Every day, Lord.*

Jamie escorted her into the drawing room, ablaze with candles and fragrant with roses. Round Glentrool the piper's merry tune went forth, while Leana sang the lyrics in her heart. *He is willing to make me his own, and his own I'm willing to be.*

The bride stool, nicked and scraped from many a wedding, had been placed before the hearth, where pine logs burned and crackled. Above it, the mantel was blanketed with roses in soft yellow, rich cream, and pale pink. Chairs were scattered everywhere, all of them claimed. Many guests stood, while others craned at the doorways. Annabel held up Ian so he could see both his parents; the lad clapped, generating several titters. Neda and Duncan were seated close to the stool, and Alec McKie as well. All three were beaming.

The couple barely found enough room to stand in front of the stool, where Reverend Moodie waited for them none too patiently. He leaned forward and said in a stage whisper, "I thought you two had eloped to Gretna Green."

Jamie chuckled. "Nae, sir, for I'll not risk anyone saying Leana is not my lawful bride." He nodded toward the small table at the minister's right. "I see you have the session record book."

"As you insisted, Mr. McKie. Your marriage will be properly noted." The minister straightened, assuming the dour expression of his calling, and raised his voice to the assembly. "Stand for a reading from the Book of Common Order."

Chairs scraped, gowns rustled, throats were cleared. The solemn words of John Knox rang through the room.

Leana tried to breathe but could not. Was she truly here, marrying Jamie? After all the sorrow, all the pain? When her betrothed gazed down at her, peace reigned in her heart once more. *My beloved is mine, and I am his.*

As their witnesses resumed their seats, the minister put his book aside and turned his attention to the couple. "Is there any impediment to this marriage? Any reason why the two of you should not be joined together as husband and wife?"

They smiled at each other and answered in unison. "None."

Reverend Moodie lifted his voice again to ask those crowding the room, "Is there any reason why these two should not be joined in holy matrimony?"

Leana stilled, aware of her heart quickening and her knees trembling. But there was not a sound. No reason was offered. No impediment given.

"Do you have a ring, Mr. McKie?"

Jamie produced the ring from his waistcoat pocket and slipped it onto her left hand, stopping short of her knuckle. Her new wedding ring was wider than the silver one she'd worn before, the one buried with their beloved Rose. This ring was solid gold and beautifully etched.

His gaze sought hers, seeking her approval. She made certain he saw it in her eyes. *It is perfect, Jamie.*

They both turned to the minister, preparing themselves for their vows, as the piper's last note hung in the air.

"Do you, James Lachlan McKie, take this woman, Leana McBride, to be your lawfully wedded wife?"

Jamie looked at her, not the minister, when he made his pledge. In his eyes she saw the rest of their days together beginning to unfold.

His voice was strong, his intentions clear. "Even so, I take her before God and in the presence of his congregation."

Dearest Jamie. She could not wait to make the same promise.

Reverend Moodie turned to her, though she had eyes for Jamie alone. "And do you, Leana McBride, take this man, James Lachlan McKie, to be your lawfully wedded husband?"

Her heart leaped, and her child as well. "Even so, I take him before God and in the presence of his congregation." *Always.*

"Give diligent ear then to the Gospel," Reverend Moodie commanded as Jamie pressed the ring in place. The gold, warm from Jamie's touch, gleamed in the firelight.

The minister read from the gospel of Matthew, "For this cause shall a man leave father and mother, and shall cleave to his wife: and they twain shall be one flesh."

One flesh. Soon, Jamie. Not yet, but soon.

"What therefore God hath joined together, let not man put asunder."

"So be it!" Alec McKie blurted out, and a smattering of giggles ran round the room.

Never was the traditional wedding psalm sung with more conviction, especially by Jamie. "My wife shall be a fruitful vine," he sang out, "my children like to olive plants."

Leana bowed her head to hide her smile. She could not grow olives in Scotland. But she could grow sons and daughters, with her husband's able provision. Aye, she could do that.

The moment Reverend Moodie concluded his blessing the household broke into a joyous uproar. Chairs were overturned and laughing guests shoved aside as each person tried to be the first out the door in order to carry off the blessing and the luck it conveyed.

Reverend Moodie groaned aloud. "Oft as I've watched that custom, I ne'er have understood it. Trampling your friends to steal a blessing."

Jamie looked over at Evan. "I understand it rather well, I'm afraid."

His brother's gaze was even but not unkind. "I understand it too." He extended his hand. "Best wishes on your marriage, Jamie."

Jamie clasped Evan's hand. "And on yours. And on your children."

Evan pointed to Jamie's waistcoat. "Brother, you'd better have a fistful of pennies in your purse, for the young folk are calling for them on the lawn."

Leana heard the children's voices as well, shouting, *"Ba! Ba!"*

Jamie patted his purse. "I'm ready." With Jamie in the lead, the wedding party made their way through the entrance hall and out the door, stepping round tumbled chairs and abandoned coats.

Now that the house was nigh to empty, Leana saw just how many roses decorated the rooms. "My love, you spent a small fortune."

"Aye," he admitted, squeezing her hand, "I did."

Not only were the children waiting to scramble after the coins; many of the adults seemed eager to catch them as well. Leana's eyes widened when Jamie emptied his purse into his open hand. Not pennies, but shillings.

"Ba! Ba!" the call came. Jamie tossed the coins as high as he could, showering the lawn and all who waited to catch them. Leana winced, though they didn't seem to mind having shillings land on their heads.

"Most generous, Mr. McKie." The minister stepped round them, adjusting his cape, for the afternoon had turned colder. "I am afraid I must ask you to be charitable once more and allow me to do my duty by your bride."

Jamie eased back, giving the man room, though Leana noticed his expression hardening. "Be quick about it, Reverend, for the lass belongs to me."

"I'll not overstay my welcome," the minister promised. As custom required, he kissed Leana briefly on the lips, as chaste a kiss as a father might give his daughter. "Now then, sir, 'tis your turn." He smiled and started toward the stables. "I'll not ask you to be quick, however."

As Leana waved farewell, Jamie caught her hand and wrapped it round his neck. "Our minister has obliged me to kiss you, dear wife."

She let him draw her into his warm embrace. "Is this naught but duty, then?"

"It is, lass." He tipped his head, his mouth so close to hers that she could already taste her husband's kiss. "A duty I will gladly fulfill."

Ninety-Two

Peace and rest at length have come,
All the day's long toil is past;
And each heart is whispering, "Home,
Home at last!"

THOMAS HOOD

For a moment Jamie forgot where he was. Forgot he was standing outside his home on a chilly November afternoon. Forgot that half the parish was watching him. Forgot that a fiddler, a piper, and a cook were waiting for the bridal festivities to begin.

His only thought was the woman in his arms and the kiss he had never forgotten. *Leana, my love, my wife.*

"Jamie." Her eyes were half open and her voice breathless. "Take me...up the stair. Please..."

He lifted his head, suddenly remembering where they were. And where they were not. "Leana, dearest, we have guests..."

"And I have a bairn who cannot wait." She slumped in his arms as a dark stain soaked her hem.

Stunned, Jamie shouted the first name that came to mind. "Neda!"

Duncan was there first, holding back the crowd that surged forward, a great mass of anxious voices. "She's on her way, lad. Dinna fear."

Jamie watched in horror. The stain was spreading, fluid pooling beneath Leana's feet. *Nae.* He would not allow it. It would not happen again. "Come, Leana. Let me hold you." Lifting her, he cradled her against his chest, grateful when she stirred a little.

"Jamie..." She sighed. "Help me..."

Neda was already beside him, clasping Leana's hand in hers. " 'Tis Neda, dearie. We're takin' ye in the hoose."

Jeanie Wilson, the midwife, was right behind them. "Dinna fash yerself, Mr. McKie. Yer bairn is early, that's a'."

"That's *not* all." He pointed his gaze to her drenched gown. "She is…"

"She's fine, Mr. McKie," Neda said in a low voice. " 'Tis her waters. Naught tae worry aboot."

"So…she's…" Jamie tried to sort it all out as the women ushered him withindoors and down the hall. "Leana is…"

"Havin' yer bairn is what she's doin'," Jeanie said matter-of-factly. "Can ye carry yer wife up the stair, sir, or would ye rather she labored in here?" She pointed to the library with its large bed, where his mother's body had lain for her lykewake.

"Nae." He marched past the library and started up the stair, certain of his course. "She will have our bairn in our bed."

Leana was not heavy, but their child made it hard for him to hold her as close as he liked. Her arms barely circled his neck. "Hang on to me, lass. I'll not let you fall."

"Jamie…" She said his name over and over, groaning as she did.

"Yes, my love. Almost there." With their child squeezed tightly between them, Jamie suddenly felt a contraction seize Leana's body. He stopped and leaned against the wall, in awe of the power he felt pressing against his chest.

She grabbed handfuls of his coat. "Hurry, Jamie."

He climbed the last steps and strode down the hall to the laird's bedroom his father had vacated for them only that morning. "You're home now, beloved." He eased Leana onto their marriage bed. The room had been thoroughly cleaned, new sheets put on the mattress, and candles scattered all over the room. He'd wanted everything just right for her, never knowing…never imagining…. "Leana, what can I do for you?"

"Roses." A husky whisper. "Pink…roses."

Jamie stood, missing the warmth of her against him. "Then roses you shall have."

Neda and Jeanie were already at work, tying back the bed curtains, loosening Leana's gown. Maids hurried into the room with fresh towels and pitchers of hot water. "Go, Mr. McKie," Neda said kindly. "Get the lass her flooers. We have a' else we need."

He rested his hand on the carved post nearest her head. "My mother gave birth to me in this bed."

"And me granmither, Jean Wilson, was the howdie that delivered ye." Jeanie mentioned it almost every time she saw him. "Leave her wi' us. We ken what's tae be done."

Duncan was waiting for him in the hall. "Gie me a task, Mr. McKie. I'm here tae serve ye."

"Help me bring the flowers." Jamie started down the stair, his mind spinning. Not until he saw the crowd in the entrance hall did he remember that he had a houseful of wedding guests expecting a bridal celebration that would last well into the night. His guests had not traveled all this way to hear the marriage vows spoken; they had come for the whisky and the ale, the bridal supper and the dancing, in that order.

"Mr. McKie!" a voice shouted up to him. "Is yer wife all richt? Is it yer bairn, sir?"

"Aye, 'tis my bairn." But was Leana all right? Neda would tell him, wouldn't she? *Lord, help me!*

Determined to solve one problem at least, he paused halfway down the stair and pointed to the young fiddler, who struck his bow across his strings long enough to garner the crowd's attention as Jamie held up his hands. "Ladies and gentlemen, my servants will see you well sated with food and drink. The musicians will be in the drawing room, and I...well, I will be delivering flowers to my laboring wife."

The wedding guests broke into applause as Jamie bolted down the last few steps, then headed toward the first pink roses he saw. Did she mean light pink or dark pink? Those tall blooms in the porcelain urn— were they pink or rosy red? *Och!* With Duncan's assistance, he claimed every vase of flowers that seemed remotely the right color. They made several trips up the stair and deposited the roses on the floor outside the bedroom.

Each time he neared the door, Jamie strained to hear Leana. Was that a sob? Did she call his name? Was that...*nae*. Not the baby, not so quickly. He heard Neda's soothing voice and Jeanie's younger one, but he could not hear Leana. *Please, Lord. I cannot lose her.*

When they'd brought up the last of the roses, Duncan stood about the second-floor hall, clearly wanting to be useful.

"I ken you just met my father," Jamie said, "but you would be doing me a great service if you looked after him. He doesn't hear or see well, and crowds are a bit of a tickler for him."

"Done, Mr. McKie." Duncan's wry smile was a welcome sight on such a day. "Whan a' this stramash is behind us, I'll be eager tae hear aboot yer raik west. And we've meikle tae tell ye aboot Kingsgrange as weel."

"In the morn, Duncan, we will do just that." The men clasped hands, then Duncan headed for the stair. Jamie faced the bedroom door, working up the courage to knock. Though if the women did not let him in, he would tear the door off its hinges.

"Come in, Mr. McKie." Neda, sounding calm.

He entered the room with a vase in each arm and closed the door with his foot. Neda and Jeanie were conferring on the other side of the room. Was Leana not faring well? He went to her side at once, the flowers quickly placed on the dresser and forgotten.

His bride of less than an hour lay beneath a sheet blessedly free of blood, her eyes closed, but her color promising. He knelt by the bed and leaned over her, brushing her cheek, then smoothing back her hair. "Leana?"

Her eyes fluttered open. "Oh, Jamie...you're here." A smile stretched across her face as she lifted her hand toward him.

Clasping it at once, he was grateful to find it warm and not icy. "The bridal festivities have commenced without the bride." He pressed a fervent kiss to her fingers. "Do you mind all the noise? I'll send the lot of them home at once if you do."

"Nae." She winced as another contraction started. "I can cry out all I wish and not worry someone will hear it."

"Shout all you like, lass." He gripped her hand as she curled forward.

Neda moved beside her, taking her other hand. "That's it, Leana. Steady as she goes."

Jamie looked across the bed at the woman who'd seen Leana through so many difficult days. "'Tis good to have you here, Neda."

Neda pushed back an errant curl with the heel of her hand. "The Laird kenned I'd be needed."

He gazed down at Leana. "How long until…"

" 'Tis hard tae say, Mr. McKie. Not sae lang wi' a second bairn."

"But she's…all right."

"Och! Leana was made tae be a mither. Isna yer Ian proof o' that?" Neda's smile reassured him as much as her words did. "A' she needs is time. And privacy. If ye'll keep folk awa from her door…"

Including me? He did not need to ask. Resigned, he kissed his wife's hand once more. "It seems the women want you all to themselves, Leana."

"Nae." Her gaze locked with his. "I want you, Jamie. With me."

"You are certain?" The clear light in her eyes answered his question. "Are you…afraid, Leana?"

"Only of losing sight of you." She turned to Neda. "Will you mind if he stays?"

Neda rolled her eyes. " 'Tis not done, lass. Menfolk dinna ken…"

"But Jamie does. We were together…with Rose…"

When Leana looked at him, he understood. She was doing this for him. So he would not wait in fear. "Leana, if you truly want me…I would be honored."

She smiled. "Find my husband a chair."

Jamie was soon settled by her side, his coat and waistcoat thrown over the dresser, the sleeves of his wedding shirt rolled up past his elbows. Whatever was required of him, he would do. For Leana. For their child.

Neda and Jeanie brought in the rest of the pink roses and arranged them round her bed. The sweet fragrance was heady, almost overpowering.

"How beautiful." Leana closed her eyes as another contraction made her draw her knees toward her chest.

Jamie did not know what to expect—what gentleman would?—but he did not turn away when her pains increased. Instead he gripped her hand and pressed a cool cloth to her brow. He spoke words of encouragement, taking his cue from Neda and Jeanie, who hovered nearby.

"Good, Leana. Keep breathing. I am so proud of you, beloved. Our child will be here soon."

Afternoon faded into the gloaming, and still she labored. Down the stair, the music grew louder, the laughter more boisterous. But in the laird's bedroom, a quiet miracle was unfolding. The woman he loved was laboring to bring forth their child, and he was doing his best to labor with her as night fell across the glen. Damp hair clung to her face, and tears coursed down her cheeks, yet her mouth was dry and cracked. Neda cautioned him that he could not give her water, only wet her lips with his fingertip, which he did repeatedly.

"Be thou my strong rock," Leana pleaded between efforts. "Be thou my helper."

At first Jamie leaned forward, thinking she was speaking to him. Then he realized the truth: She was speaking to the Almighty.

"My times are in thy hand." Leana's words dissolved into a groan. "Deliver me. Please...deliver me!"

Jamie could see that she was suffering, felt the tension in her body, saw the pain on her features. "What can I do, Leana?"

She gripped his hand harder. "Pray."

His head fell forward, tears dropping onto the crumpled sheets. *This is the woman I love, Lord. This is the woman you gave to me. Have mercy on her. Strengthen her. Protect her. Please, Lord. Please deliver this child.*

Neda touched his shoulder. "Mr. McKie, I'd best take that seat unless ye want tae handle things yerself."

He was on his feet before he remembered standing.

Leana did not let go of his hand. "Here. With me." She pulled him next to her at the head of the bed while Neda folded back the sheets, giving instructions.

Jamie knelt by her side, vowing he would not make a fool of himself and faint. If his wife could bear it, he would bear it with her. "I am here, Leana. I am with you."

"Jamie!" She cried out his name as her face contorted.

Neda's voice. Decisive. "Push noo, lass. Ye're almost thar."

Then she *was* there. And the babe was there. Pink, wet, beautiful.

Neda's voice again. Exultant. "A daughter for ye, Mr. McKie!"

Leana was weeping with relief. Jamie was simply weeping. *Thanks be to God!* He wiped his face on a corner of the sheet, then kissed his bride. The mother of his son. And of his daughter, whose vigorous cry was even louder than the piper down the stair.

"Davina." Leana almost sang the child's name.

"A wonderful choice." Jamie moistened her lips with his tears as he kissed her, while Neda tucked a clean sheet round her for modesty's sake.

Moments later the midwife came forward with their child wrapped in fresh linen. "Here's yer lass, Mistress McKie."

Leana smiled. "How I do love the sound of that name." She nodded toward Jamie. "Let my husband hold her first."

Jamie's arms shook as the midwife laid his newborn daughter in the crook of his arm. "Davina," he whispered, sniffing hard. She was tiny. Delicate. Perfect in every way. "I am...your father." He swallowed, though it did not help. "And this is your dear mother." He carefully transferred the warm bundle into Leana's waiting arms.

She touched her nose, her cheek, her tiny chin. "My precious girl."

A knock at the door and a squeal of joy announced another arrival. Jeanie cracked open the door and waved the maidservant inside. Eliza barely stepped inside the room before she paused and curtsied, her eyes wide. "Mr. McKie, pardon me, but 'tis Ian. He heard the bairn. And...I did...too."

"Come, my dear boy!" Leana motioned with her free hand. "Your sister is here."

Eliza approached the bed with obvious misgivings, but Ian had none, waving his arms, reaching for his mother.

Jamie intervened, capturing his son and holding him firmly against his chest. "Your mother's arms are full just now. What do you think of Davina? Isn't she a bonny wee lass?" Ian stared at the bundle and blinked.

"Did you notice her hair?" Leana pulled back the linen round their tiny daughter's head. "Not dark brown like yours or gold like mine."

Jamie peered at her in disbelief. *"Red?"*

Leana laughed. "Another red-headed McKie, like your brother."

"Mistress," Neda said softly, "d'ye ken the day? 'Tis a Tuesday."

Leana's smile was like candlelight, brightening the room. "Ian, *you* were born on the Sabbath day, which means you are 'blithe and bonny and good and gay.' But Tuesday's child is full of grace."

Jamie gazed down at his wife. *Like you, dear woman.*

When Ian began to wiggle, Jamie handed him back to Eliza rather than risk the child accidentally kicking Leana's tender body. "There's a good lad. You can still see your sister." He caught Neda's eye. "Kindly find your husband and have him bring my father up the stair."

Leana laughed. "You'll have the entire household in our room before we're through."

"Indeed I will not. They can gather in the sitting room. For 'tis our wedding night and time I had you to myself." He turned round. "Eliza? Jeanie, might you…"

Both women were already halfway out of the room. They curtsied before they closed the door behind them. Down the stair the fiddler still fiddled and the piper still piped, yet in the laird's bedroom, silence was music enough.

Jamie leaned down and cupped Davina's head, surprised at how warm it was. And how small. "You have given me a fine daughter, Leana."

His wife's sweet breath was warm on his ear. "And you have given me a fine home."

"Glentrool, you mean?" When she didn't answer, he turned his head, dismayed to find tears in her eyes. "What is it, lass?"

Leana touched his heart. "This is where I'd always hoped to live."

"Ah." Jamie pulled her close for a tender kiss. "Then come home, my love."

Author Notes

Land o' birk and rowan tree,
Land o' fell and forest free,
Land that's aye sae dear to me—
Bonnie Gallowa'.
GEORGE G. B. SPROAT

From my first visit, the quiet corner of South West Scotland known as Galloway felt like home. The rolling farmlands resembled my native Pennsylvania, and the dry stane dykes brought to mind the stone fences of the Bluegrass State. But there all comparisons end, for Galloway is like nowhere else on earth. The red sandstone ruins of thirteenth-century Sweetheart Abbey still rise from the heart of New Abbey (aye, two words now). Cardoness Castle has stood like a silent sentinel overlooking the River Fleet since the late fifteenth century. Dotting the countryside are sleepy villages, many no wider than one street with a row of stone cottages on each side. Sheep wander across single-track roads, and belted Galloway cattle—"belties," with black bodies and wide white stripes around their middles—nibble contentedly in grassy pastures.

Some Scottish writers, like S. R. Crockett, favor the name "Grey Galloway." One wintry visit, after endless days of gray skies, gray hills, and gray lochs, I quite agreed! But in spring when the word *green* is not sufficient to describe the verdant landscape, and in summer when the deep pink flowers of Rosebay Willowherb bloom along the roadside, and in early autumn when purple heather covers the hills—then Galloway is anything but gray and gloomy. Though I must confess, I *like* dreich weather. Thick fog and drizzling rain turn my cozy study into a writer's paradise. On such days, I roam across Galloway in my heart and on the page, endeavoring to take my readers with me.

In Jamie McKie's time we would have traversed the old military road, which carved a hundred-mile swath from the Bridge of Sark to Portpatrick. Along its route sprouted villages like Twyneholm, though the parish kirk stood its ground long before Major Rickson and his men appeared in the mid-1700s with their sledgehammers and gunpowder. Young soldiers constructed a blacksmith forge every ten miles, working their way across Galloway, building a road that provided English troops a faster means of quelling any troubles in Ireland. A modern Ordnance Survey map shows sections of the old military road still in use—from Haugh of Urr to Castle Douglas (Carlinwark in 1790) and from Twynholm (no *e* now) to Gatehouse of Fleet. How fortunate that the shore road between Gatehouse and Ferrytown was completed by 1790, just in time for mail coach service on that route to begin—and for our story to unfold.

When Leana pulled the almanac from her father's bookshelf—*Season on the Seasons*—I was holding such a book in my hands, though it was the following year's edition, dated 1791. The volume was bound in gilded red leather with seven other almanacs of the same year—*The Gentleman's Diary, The Ladies' Diary, Old Poor Robin's Almanack* among them—all published in London. The rebus about the daughter with two evergreen names must remain unsolved, I'm afraid, unless you happen across Henry Season's almanac for 1792.

Alastair Penman's book *Some Customs, Folklore and Superstitions of Galloway* proved particularly helpful in describing the stone fire and local funeral customs. Mr. Penman's booklet *Rhonehouse or Keltonhill: Its History, Its Fair and Some of Its Surroundings* and Malcolm Harper's *Rambles in Galloway* (1896) were invaluable resources for recreating a Keltonhill Fair of long ago.

As to how Keltonhill Fair got its start, Duncan Hastings is eager to relate the story: "Ane fine simmer day a packman—or chapman or peddler or whatsomever ye like—from Glesca decided his goods needed an airin'. He spread them across a thicket o' gorse on the side o' the hill near the auld Kelton kirk. Curious folk came along, buyin' this and that, and afore the day was o'er, he'd sold nearly a' he had. He vowed tae return tae the same place twelvemonth hence, and so he did, bringin' ither packmen wi' him. Then came the horse dealers and the hawkers and afore lang..." Aye, Duncan. We've been to Keltonhill Fair.

As the epigraph here suggests, birch and rowan abound in Galloway, even as ancient trees dot the pages of *Whence Came a Prince*. In Creetown (Ferrytown of Cree's "new" name after it became a Burgh of Barony in 1792), I took photos of the Ferry Thorn, where a small flock of sheep—surely they were Jamie's—tarried beside the burn. I also carried home an acorn plucked from Buittle kirkyard, where Leana brought Jock Bell's wagon to a stop beneath a stand of oaks, and later the same week I gazed up at the centuries-old yew tree in the kirkyard at Monigaff (one *n* was lost along the way) and searched about for a certain headstone bearing a carved floral wreath.

On my second visit to the Murray Arms in Gatehouse of Fleet, I slept in the room at the top of the stair where Rose bravely hid her father's gold beneath her skirts. Then I spent a meaningful hour in the room where Jamie and Lachlan had their initial confrontation. Three years later, as it were, Robert Burns penned his famous ode to Bannockburn, "Scots, Wha Hae," in that very room. Thomas Newbigging, in his charming book *A Nook in Galloway* (1911), described the fateful night. On August 1, 1793, after a visit to Kenmure Castle, Burns and his companion "encountered a terrific storm of wind, lightning, and rain, whilst riding across the moors." When they arrived at the Murray Arms, "the poet entered the room mentioned, sat down at the table, and wrote out the ode which he had composed on the way." Though said table is long gone, I touched the present one and thought of our travelers in August 1790.

At the Burns Museum in Alloway I smiled when I read a snippet of the writer's correspondence with his editor: "Your proposed alterations would, in my opinion, make it tame. So, if you please, will you let the line stand as it is." I am blessed to work with a wonderful team of editors whose "proposed alterations" invariably improve my efforts. To these dear encouragers who examined every word of *Prince* and offered priceless advice go my deepest thanks: Sara Fortenberry, Dudley Delffs, Carol Bartley, Danelle McCafferty, and Paul Hawley. I'm also grateful for proofreaders like Leesa Gagel and Nancy Norris—not to mention my own sweet husband, Bill—who take turns catching stray typos before they end up in print.

The evocative image of Cairnholy on the back cover was captured by Allen Wright, a gifted photographer whose Galloway calendars decorate my writing study. You'll find more of his work at www.Lyrical Scotland.co.uk.

I wouldn't dream of writing a Scottish novel without the help of Benny Gillies—bookseller, cartographer, proofreader, and friend—who, along with his wonderful wife, Lyn, welcomed me into his Kirkpatrick-Durham home and shop, fed me magnificently, and sent me home with my suitcase packed with books. Visit his bookshop online at www.bennygillies.co.uk. Benny informed me that in all his years in Galloway he had never seen the northern lights. But since Jacob of old saw angels in the heavens, I thought Jamie miraculously seeing the merry dancers in Galloway was only fitting. Then, just weeks before this novel went to print, Benny had his first sighting!

For my sheepish scenes, I am indebted to Tony Dempster of Castle-hill Farm near Lockerbie and Barbara Wiedenbeck of Sonsie Farm, who, along with Benny Gillies, made certain my lambs were properly cared for. Ian Niall's *The Galloway Shepherd* (1970) was also a fine resource. Since I'm no more adept at fishing than I am at herding sheep, I'm thankful to have found a recent reprint of Izaak Walton's *The Compleat Angler* (1653) and am especially glad to count fisherman Stephen Tweed among my helpful friends. Ginia Hairston kindly offered her horse sense, for which Walloch and Hastings neigh their appreciation. Bill Holland, the minister for New Abbey parish, and his dear wife, Helen, made me feel at home in the manse parlor not once but *three* times over the years, offering valuable historic information with a plateful of fine Galloway cheeses and crisp oatcakes.

Tromping about the old kirk at Anwoth, I met Carrie Peto, who owns both the newer church next door—built in 1826 and only recently vacated—and the former manse. Not only did this generous woman give me a tour of the sanctuary, but she also put me in touch with Mrs. Katharine McCulloch, who lives in "the Big House," as they say in the UK. Her famous family's ties to Anwoth parish go back at least six centuries. A timeless treasure, Mrs. McCulloch.

More helpful information awaited me when I reached the old Ferry-town of Cree. Heartfelt thanks go to Rosemarie Stephenson at the Gem

Rock Museum and my trio of experts at the Creetown Heritage Museum and Exhibition Centre—Andrew Macdonald, Val Johnson, and John Cutland, local historian and author of *The Story of Ferrytown of Cree and Kirkmabreck Parish*. These folk are the true gems of Creetown. I pray they will forgive me for having the bridge over the Moneypool Burn collapse twenty years after the fact—1790, rather than 1770—though I'm told it was 1809 before the span was fully restored.

Why not join me on a virtual tour of the Scottish countryside featured in *Whence Came a Prince,* including all the kirks where Rose deposits her pilfered coins, by visiting my Web site: www.LizCurtis Higgs.com. You'll also find a free Bible study guide examining the source material on which this novel was based—Genesis 31–33, 35— as well as a listing of my Scottish resource books, additional historical notes, readers' comments, links to my favorite Scottish Web sites, a discography of Celtic music and soundtracks that inspire me as I write, and some delicious Scottish recipes.

Few things delight me more than staying in touch with readers. If you would enjoy receiving my free newsletter, *The Graceful Heart,* printed and mailed just once a year, or would like a free bookplate for this novel, please contact me by post:

Liz Curtis Higgs

P.O. Box 43577

Louisville, KY 40253-0577

Or visit my Web site:

www.LizCurtisHiggs.com

Thanks to your support, many more Scottish historical novels are in progress. Do join me on the misty isle of Arran for Davina's story in *Grace in Thine Eyes,* coming to stores in spring 2006. Until then, dear reader, you are a blissin!

Whence Came a Prince

READER'S GUIDE

Books should to one of these four ends conduce,
For wisdom, piety, delight, or use.
SIR JOHN DENHAM

1. Though Jamie McKie appears on the cover, Leana McBride begins our story. What are your hopes for Leana by the end of the first chapter of *Whence Came a Prince*? And by the end of the tenth chapter? How might this story have unfolded if Leana had remained at Auchengray all along, rather than fleeing to Twyneholm? What if she'd stayed at Burnside Cottage instead of going home?

2. Though Jamie McKie's affections are captured first by one sister, then by the other, he takes his time shifting allegiances. Do you sympathize with his struggles or find him fickle? Does Leana's written entreaty—"Love my sister"—justify his actions? How would you explain Jamie's turning his heart toward Rose once more?

3. Though wee Ian can only babble and wave his arms about, he is integral to this family's story. How would you describe Leana's relationship with her son? What of Rose's bond with Ian? And Jamie's, father to son? Did you find yourself wanting to care for Ian—or perhaps for your own child—while reading *Whence Came a Prince*? At what points in the story did your mothering urges surface?

4. How do marriage and impending motherhood help Rose mature? Leana tells her, " 'Tis Jamie's love for you and yours for him that make you fearless." Do you agree? What else might make Rose fearless? If you've read *Fair Is the Rose*, how have your feelings toward her changed after reading this novel? From your viewpoint does Rose become a true heroine at the last?

5. In what way is Rose like her father, and how is she different? If Rose were *your* daughter, how might you have counseled her at the pivotal moment she is alone in the spence with Lachlan's money box? What do you think of Rose's solution for distributing the stolen gold? What would you have done with it? How might things have been different if Rose had told Jamie from the beginning?

6. The epigraphs that begin each chapter are meant to link the previous scene with the current one or to hint at what's to come. In what ways do Sir Walter Scott's words at the start of chapter 42 epitomize Jamie's dilemma? Choose an epigraph that you especially like. How does that quote foreshadow the scene it introduces?

7. True to this period in Scottish history, religion plays a major role in the day-to-day lives of these Lowlanders. How would you define Leana's relationship with God? What of Jamie's faith? and Rose's? Which one of the three most closely parallels your own spiritual journey? God promises, "I will not fail thee, nor forsake thee." What evidence do you find of his steadfastness in this story?

8. Throughout much of the novel Leana finds herself in a very difficult situation, offering her sister loving support even as she, too, carries Jamie's child. How would you characterize Leana—a role model? a martyr? a righteous woman? a fool? Do you empathize with her plight? What other options appropriate to the late eighteenth century might Leana have explored?

9. Scottish folklore is replete with kelpies—water spirits that assume the form of a horse. John Mactaggart, in his *Scottish Gallovidian Encyclopedia* (1824), calls them "evil-disposed beings of the supernatural stamp." On that fateful night in Moneypool Burn, was Jamie indeed wrestling with a kelpie? with mud and sand? with God? with his brother? with himself? How did the experience change him, and why?

10. Were you prepared for the story to take a tragic turn in Monnigaff? What feelings did those scenes with Rose evoke? Was anyone truly

at fault for what happened? Did the emotional aftermath ring true to your own life experiences?

11. How would you define Jamie's character at the start of this novel? Through his trials and tests in Gatehouse of Fleet, Ferrytown of Cree, and Monnigaff? And at the end of the story in Glentrool? Jamie sees in his wife's eyes "a love he would spend the rest of his life trying to deserve." Does Jamie in fact deserve her love? When all is said and done, has Jamie McKie earned the title of "prince," of hero?

12. This reader's guide opens with a quote from Sir John Denham, an Irish poet of the seventeenth century. Do you agree that books should lead to one of four ends: wisdom, piety, delight, or use? In reading *Whence Came a Prince,* what wisdom did you glean? Was there anything of spiritual significance for you? What engaged you most in the story? And how might you apply the lessons you've learned? If you were describing this series of three novels to a friend who enjoys fiction, what would you tell her?

Scots Glossary

a'—all

aboot—about

aflocht—in a flutter, agitated

aften—often

ain—own

amang—among

ane—one

anither—another

auld—old

awa—away, distant

ba—handful of coins tossed after wedding

bairn—child

baith—both

baloo—used to hush a child to sleep

bauld—bold

bethankit!—God be thanked!

bien—good, pleasant, comfortable

birk—birch

birsie—hairy, hot-tempered

bittie—small piece

blaw—blow

blether—jabber, gossip

blissin—blessing

blithesome—cheerful

bogle—ghost, specter

bothy—small cottage

bowsome—compliant, obedient

brae—hill, slope

brainwode—mad, insane

braisant—shameless

braw—fine, handsome

bridie—pasties made with meat

brig—bridge

brither—brother

broo—broth, soup

broon—brown

Buik—the Bible

burn—brook, stream

byre—cowshed

bystart—bastard

cabbieclaw—a dish of salt cod

campie—bold, brave

cantie—lively, cheerful, pleasant

cantrip—charm, magic, trick

clack—gossip, idle chatter

cleck—conceive

cliver—clever, quick

collieshangle—disturbance, dogfight

compear—appear before congregation for rebuke

coo—cow

crabbit—in a bad temper, cross

creepie—low chair, footstool

cryin siller—coins required for the marriage banns to be read

cutty stool—stool of repentance

dashelt—battered

daurk—dark

deid—dead

deid licht—strange light that foretells death

de'il—devil

dochter—daughter

dominie—schoolmaster, teacher

doocot—dovecote

doon—down

douce—amiable, sweet

dout—doubt

dowly—sad, doleful

dreich—bleak, dismal

dry stane dyke—stone fence without mortar

dwiny—wasting away, failing in health

eldritch—mysterious, unearthly

ell—a linear measure, just over a yard

Embrough—Edinburgh

etin—a giant

fairing—a present from a fair

faither—father

farle—segment of baked goods

fash—worry, trouble, vex

fauchie—sickly-looking

fause—counterfeit, false

fee—engage, hire

ferlie—superb, wonderful

fleg—frighten, scare

flindrikin—flirtatious

flit—move one's household

flooer—flower

foord—ford, as a river

forby—besides, furthermore

fowk—folk

frae—from

freen—friend

fremmit—an outsider, a stranger

freshening—cool, refreshing, healthy

frichtsome—frightening

fu'—full

gaberlunzie—beggar

gairden—garden

gane—gone

gentrice—gentry

gie—give

girdle—griddle for cooking

glaumshach—greedy, grasping

glessie—toffee

glib-gabbit—gossipy

goud—gold

goun—gown

gracie—devout, virtuous

granbairn—grandchild

granmither—grandmother

green—young, youthful

gruntie—pig

guid—good

gustie—savory, tasty

halfgone—the middle period of pregnancy

halie—holy

hame—home

hatesome—hateful

haud—hold, keep

haud yer wheesht—hold your tongue

heartsome—merry

heidie—headstrong, impetuous

heirship—inheritance

heiven—heaven

herd—shepherd

het—hot

hind—farmworker

hindberry—raspberry

hizzie—hussy

hochmagandy—fornication

hoose—house

hough—hock; hind-leg joint of meat

howdie—midwife

hunder—hundred

hurlie—trundle, move about on wheels

ilka—each, every

ill-deedie—mischievous, wicked

ill-fashioned—ill mannered

ill-faured—ugly, unattractive

ill-gotten—illegitimate

ill-kindit—cruel, inhuman

ill-scrapit—rude, bitter

in trowth—indeed! upon my word!

ither—other

itherwise—otherwise

jalouse—imagine, presume, deduce

keel—means of marking sheep for identification

kell—headdress worn by a young, unmarried woman

kelpie—a water demon

ken—to know, recognize

kenspeckle—conspicuous, familiar

kimmer—godmother

kintra—of the country, rustic

kirkin—first appearance at kirk

kist—chest, coffin

kittlie—itchy, sensitive

kye—cow(s)

lanelie—lonely

lang—long

leuk—look

licht—light

limmer—prostitute

loosome—lovely

lowpin-on stane—leaping-on stone, used to mount a horse or a carriage

luve—love

lykewake—vigil kept over corpse

mainnerlie—mannerly

mair—more

maun—must

mebbe—maybe, perhaps

meikle—great, much

mem—madam

mercat—market

merry dancers—northern lights

mither—mother

mony—many

morn's morn—tomorrow morning

mort-cloth—a pall covering a coffin

mote—a mound, an embankment

naither—neither

neep—turnip

nicht—night

niver—never

noo—now

noony—late morning meal

och!—oh!

onie—any

oniething—anything

oniewise—anyway, anywhere

oo aye!—yes! (from the French *oui*)

oot—out

orraman—odd-jobs man

Pasch—Easter

pensie—pompous, self-important

plenishing—goods, provisions

plumpshower—heavy downpour of rain

posy—term of endearment for a child

praisent—present, gift

pu'—pull

puir—poor

purpie—purslane, an herb

quaich—shallow drinking cup with handles

quate—quiet

raik—a journey, a trip

reiver—robber, thief

richt—right, authentic

run-line—psalm sung one line at a time

sae—so

saicret—secret

sair—sore

sairlie—sorely

sark—shirt

scaur-craw—scarecrow

scoonrel—scoundrel

shiel—shield

shooglie—shaky, wobbly

shortsome—amusing, enjoyable

shullin—shilling

sic—such

simmer—summer

sleekit—smooth-tongued, deceitful

slitterie—messy, sloppy

sma'—small

smeddum—courage, drive, energy

smirr—a fine, misty rain

smokies—smoked haddock

sonsie—substantial, appealing

speeritie—energetic, spirited, vivacious

spleet-new—brand-new

spurtle—porridge stick

stane—stone; also a measure of weight

staw—stole

stayed lass—an old maid

stramash—clamor, disturbance, uproar

suin—soon

sully—silly

sweetie-wife—female seller of sweets

swick—to cheat, swindle, deceive

swickerie—trickery, deception

syne—ago, thereafter, since

tablet—a sweet made of butter and sugar

tae—to

taigled—confused, hampered

tairt—tart, a promiscuous woman

tak—take

tapsalteerie—topsy-turvy, upside down

tassie—cup

tattie—potato

thar—there

thegither—together, concerted

thocht—thought, believed

thrifite—money box

tickler—problem, puzzle

tig—to tap the hand, as in playing tag

timorsome—timid, fearful, nervous

tocher—dowry

tod—fox

topsman—lead drover

tup—a ram

twa—two

ugsome—gruesome, horrible

unchancie—unlucky, dangerous, risky

unco—strange, eccentric, odd

unheartsome—sad, melancholy

unweel—unwell, sickly

verra—very

waddin—wedding

walcome—welcome

wame—womb

wark—work

warse—worse

warslin—wrestling

waukens—awakens

weatherful—stormy

weel—well

wha—who

whan—when

whanever—whenever

whatsomever—whatever

whaur—where

wheesht!—hush!

wi'—with

wickit—wicked

widdershins—counterclockwise

wi'oot—without

wird—word

wud—wood

wull—will

wunner—wonder

wutch—witch

wyne—wind, turn

yestermorn—yesterday morning

yestreen—yesterday, last night

On the Isle of Arran in 1808

a desperate
young woman seeks...

Grace in Thine Eyes

Spring 2006

WATERBROOK
PRESS